WHODUNIT?
A Who's Who in Crime & Mystery Writing

WHODUNIT?

A Who's Who
in
Crime &
Mystery Writing

Rosemary Herbert

OXFORD
UNIVERSITY PRESS

2003

OXFORD
UNIVERSITY PRESS

Oxford   New York
Auckland Bangkok Buenos Aires Cape Town Chennai
Dar es Salaam Delhi Hong Kong Istanbul Karachi Kolkata
Kuala Lumpur Madrid Melbourne Mexico City Mumbai
Nairobi São Paulo Shanghai Taipei Tokyo Toronto

Copyright © 2003 by Oxford University Press, Inc.

Published by Oxford University Press, Inc.
198 Madison Avenue, New York, New York 10016

www.oup.com

Oxford is a registered trademark of Oxford University Press

Library of Congress Cataloging-in-Publication Data

Whodunit : a who's who in crime & mystery writing / edited by Rosemary
Herbert.
   p. cm.
Includes index.
   ISBN 0-19-515763-3 (alk. paper) — 0-19-515761-3 (pbk. : alk.
paper)
   1. Detective and mystery stories—Encyclopedias.   2. Crime in
literature—Encyclopedias.   I. Title: Who's who in crime and mystery
writing.   II. Herbert, Rosemary.
   PN3448.D4 H37 2003
   809.3'872'03—dc21

                                                        2002029791
                                                        Rev.

9 8 7 6 5 4 3 2 1
Printed in the United States of America
on acid-free paper

Acknowledgments

As editor, I would like to thank Dennis Lehane for his Preface, and the following people for their advice and support: Kate Mattes, Elaine M. Ober, Chris Rippen, Linda Robbins, Mr. and Mrs. Roberto Nardone and the reference librarians at Harvard University's Harry Elkins Widener Memorial Library. Gratitude also goes to the many contributors to *The Oxford Companion to Crime & Mystery Writing*, some of whose work is included here. For unfailing encouragement, I wish to thank my mother, Barbara Herbert, and Jean Behnke, Margaret Byer, Diana O'Neill, Clara Silverstein and Bill Wyman. Finally, for computer problem-solving and dance lesson breaks from my writing, I tap out a big "thank you" to my daughter, Juliet Gazelle Herbert Partington.

Acknowledgment

To
Juliet
With love

Contents

Preface

Crime fiction is the drunken cousin who crashes your daughter's wedding and accosts you for not inviting him. It's the naked angry guy in the park who shouts soliloquies that don't make sense until you're through the office door and the memos have piled up on your desk. It's the librarian down the street, content with a cup of cocoa and two cats until a dead body drops into her midst and she suddenly shows mettle and acumen that no one ever suspected before. It's the woman in the bus station who asks you for a dollar and whom, you realize (only afterward, unfortunately), really needed it. Crime fiction is the voice that says, "Everything is not all right."

Crime fiction, in recent decades, could be likened to the ghetto undergoing gentrification. It's the neighborhood you used to drive through with a shudder but where you now wish you'd bought real estate just before the dot-commers discovered it. For a few years now it's even been fashionable to use the term "renaissance" when discussing the state of it. I'd argue a better term is urban renewal, because much like urban renewal what often gets lost in the giddy "discovery" of a place that was always there are the names of those in the community who kept it alive for all those years while others drove through it. Quickly. Accompanied by those shudders.

This is not to say the genre has entirely lost its identity as a literary ghetto—it's crime fiction, after all, and it probably needs the ghetto more than the ghetto needs it (or, put another way, dress up a mechanic in a tuxedo and he still retains his identity as long as his fingernails show traces of grease)— only that the literary landscape has continued to grow and expand to the point where what once lay at its farthest reaches, unknown to most, unkempt to all, and almost lunar in its loneliness, has now been incorporated into the fold if by nothing other than the necessities of urban sprawl.

And who goes there?

Characters. And when I say characters I don't mean Metaphors Named Steve. I mean people. People who seem akin to those we've come across in the human race as opposed to those we've come across only in books.

Within the pages of this marvelous reference tome, you will have a chance to meet the writers, the characters, the motifs and archetypes that make crime fiction the vivid, even vivacious, art form that it has become. There has long been a dearth in reference material on crime novels, a dearth that turned the process of discovering the writers you might like into a search fraught with red herrings, wrong turns, and a multitude of, well, mysterious entanglements.

No longer. Rosemary Herbert has gone to great pains to compile a compendium of not only the elder statesmen and stateswomen who make up the mental Rushmore of crime fiction history, but also the new blood—the people who are writing now and writing well and, one hopes, will stand the test of time. So you will meet, of course, Dame Agatha Christie with her corkscrew plots and mammoth cast of characters, her sterling silver tea sets and antique daggers. And you may find yourself introduced to the icy Patricia Highsmith with her graveyard wit and her strangely enchanting misanthropy. And you could be forgiven, and quite possibly commended, for seeing how favorably their company could be shared with the classy, sumptuous plots of Elizabeth George, Anne Perry, Elizabeth Peters or Minette Walters, or the chillier, more mordant genius of Val McDermid or Patricia Cornwell. You'll find Lew Archer ambling along the darkened streets for a chance meeting with compatriot, Philip Marlowe, and see how similar streets have been visited in more recent days by the slightly more tortured brilliance of Harry Bosch.

In fact, the more I looked through these entries, the more I was taken by the sense that this genre may not simply be in a state of renewal, so much as exploding. And exploding straight across the globe. How did we ever live, it seems now, without the Edinburgh of Inspector Rebus and his creator, Ian Rankin? Isn't the world so much fuller now that the Italy of Michael Dibdin or the Amsterdam of Janwillem Van De Wetering have been placed on the cultural map? And as much as it's hard to imagine a Los Angeles without Chandler, could you ever consider it again without seeing it to some degree through the hardened-to-pewter eyes and bile-ravaged hearts of James Ellroy's lost-soul policemen? And, please forgive me, but I barely knew where Montana *was* until James Crumley carved it straight through the heart of our country in my personal all-time favorite crime novel, *The Last Good Kiss*. Would Washington, D.C. really exist without George Pelecanos? Sure, but it would be the lesser for it. The same goes for San Francisco without Hammett, Boston without Linda Barnes or Robert B. Parker, Paris without Georges Simenon, Detroit without Loren Estleman, or Chicago without Sara Paretsky. I'm enthralled by the New Jersey of Janet Evanovich, and usually "enthralled" and "New Jersey" are not words I'd ever use together. The Tennessee mountains of Sharyn McCrumb form a strange kinship in my mind with the Louisiana bayous of James Lee Burke because both are rendered so artfully as to become as much a character in the novels as are the people who inhabit them. And then there is the South Florida pack. If the father is John D. MacDonald and the prodigal uncle is Elmore Leonard (late of Detroit and arrived under suspicious circumstances just in time to make everyone a little nervous), then the nutjob of a middle child is Carl Hiassen, who trains his skewed vision on Miami and lets rip with such a colorful burst of humor, rage, gunfire, and hideous anatomical calamity that seems to know no bounds, which is perfectly fitting for a city that doesn't know any either.

And if we'd be nowhere without these novels's sense of place, then we'd be even further lost without their sense of character. How do you remove Stephanie Plum or Spenser or Lew Archer from the rolls without the whole façade crumbling? The answer is: "You can't." The names of crime fiction's great characters are the championship banners hanging from the rafters of the stadium. They remind you that greatness can be achieved, even if you have to ride out some rebuilding years. And so you could no more have a world without oxygen than you'd choose to live in one without Miss Marple, Easy Rawlins, Ellery Queen, Aurelio Zen, Phillip Marlowe, Kinsey Millhone, Nero Wolfe, Travis & Meyer, Nick & Nora, the cops in the 87th Precinct, Kay Scarpetta, Jules Maigret, Rabbi Small, Sherlock Holmes, or the brutal, brilliant master thief known only as Parker from the brutal, brilliant pulp novels of Richard Stark (aka Donald Westlake).

Crime fiction, some have noted, has taken the place of the social novel, and it's no surprise as to the reason. By being so firmly rooted in a sense of place and a sense of character, all coaxed into being by writers who tell a damn good story first and foremost (if you can't keep 'em awake at the campfire, after all, they're probably going to doze right off into it), the works easily lend themselves to a moral fury that is, at times, easily detectable and worn on the sleeve but just as often floats below the margins of the story itself.

And so we're back to margins. Above them is the world you see. Below them is where our stories live. And within the margins of this book is where you'll find all you need to know to draw your own map and use it to travel the world and meet the people who live the lives your mother wouldn't tell you about. Lives not unlike your own, only slightly edgier, a lot more violent in some cases, often sexy or funny or ribald, lives where injustice and justice wage their battles on fields both small and large, where the sun so often hides behind a cloud, and just when it comes out, that's when a strange figure walks up to you. He may look like that drunken cousin who ruined your wedding. Or he may appear as harmless and forgettable as Tom Ripley. In either case, he doesn't stop for long. He barely stops at all. But he whispers as he passes. He whispers five simple words:

Everything is not all right.

Dennis Lehane
Brighton, Massachusetts
July 2, 2002

Introduction

Who goes there?

That's the question Dennis Lehane asks in his preface to this book.

Who populates the pages of crime and mystery writing?

Who are the characters we willingly follow into the uneasy imaginative territory Lehane so vividly describes? What is it about their personalities, courage—even their human flaws—that makes us want to keep company with them? And who created those characters in the first place? What life experience and expertise informs their work? What are the sources of their themes, regional accents, and even the axes that some grind? Why do some wish to give us a good laugh, while others seem hell-bent on making us shudder?

Dennis and I want to know. And we're sure you do, too.

That's why I put together this volume. In three hundred and eighty essays, it lets readers know whodunit, identifying fictional people who perpetrate and solve crimes in this exciting genre. It answers the question "Who's done it?" too, helping readers get to know the writers, too.

Think of this editor as a host who opens the door to a crowded room. You may recognize some of the company gathered here, but you need a nudge to remind you where you last met a few of them, a quick whisper of what that grande dame in the armchair has been up to lately, an elbow in the ribs telling you to take note of that tough guy lurking in the shadows. Even more urgently, perhaps, you crave an introduction to that sassy newcomer who's lighting up the room.

A good host works hard before the party, mulling over which guests will make the most stimulating mix. Memorability is a must. Many here are already well known, even famous. Others have been on the scene more briefly, but seem unforgettable nonetheless. It's a good crowd, but some guests are not at the soirée. Don't worry. They're not forgotten. They turn up in the context of conversations.

I invite you to get up close and personal with hundreds of characters and authors. More than three hundred are found in entries devoted to individuals (and some pairs) listed under their names in the main body of this volume. Hundreds more (whose names are listed in the index) are mentioned in seventy-two entries on types of characters and authors. Some—such as the Academic Sleuth, Judge, or Great Detective—are admirable figures. We also consort here with those we love to hate—including the Con Artist, Master Criminal, and Femme Fatale. Even pet characters hiss or frolic in our entry on Animals.

Anyone who joins us here knows no single volume can accommodate the population explosion of new talent in the crime and mystery writing genre. Especially during the last two decades of the twentieth century and in the years following the turn of the twenty-first, great numbers of gifted new authors have demonstrated their powers. I have added one hundred and one new entries to represent them here. Some serve up culinary mysteries that are as light and lively as gourmet soufflées while others turn out dark depictions of twisted criminal minds—and there is a wide range of work in between those extremes. Because I've culled from that crowd characters and authors who are all masters of what they do, you might say the mix is exclusive in the best sense of the word.

But what makes a master?

The quality of long-lasting appeal, even of greatness, may seem nebulous—but you know it when you see it. Looking back as a scholar, critic, book review editor and lifelong reader of the genre, I carefully scrutinized those who have already stood the test of time. I found that they vary in many particulars, but they all have one quality in common. Classic or contemporary, their work shines with highly individual personality that arises from—and transcends—their life experience, attitudes, and voices. I sought to include such luminaries here.

Of course there are cases where many must be represented by a few. An editor is haunted by the spectre Dennis describes—"the drunken cousin who crashes your daughter's wedding and accosts you for not inviting him." Enraged cousins or not, there have to be criteria for inclusion. One is obvious: If several authors or characters are high achievers in a similar area, groundbreakers get their own entries. A good example is Lillian Jackson Braun who here represents represent a legion of writers who make cats major characters in their books. Braun, who is known as the author of "The Cat Who . . ." series is not only one of the earlier authors to use cats as crime solving sidekicks, but she makes actual feline behavior—such as some Siamese cats' taste for eating wool—essential to her work. Marian Babson, is included in this context, too, but not only because her groundbreaking 1992 novel, *Nine Lives to Murder,* remarkably succeeds at making readers believe a human and a cat can trade points of view. Another important factor in including Babson is her production of other series. Carole Nelson Douglas, who writes a series featuring a cat called Midnight Louie is also covered here, thanks to her entire output, not just her cat-related capers. Additional creators of feline characters receive mention in our article on Animals, allowing us to maintain space to represent other major types of characters and authors rather than to profile every cat-loving author individually.

Similarly, to solve a case of too many cooks—and caterers, bakers, candy-makers and others who combine culinary expertise with detective work—I created a new group entry on the Culinary Sleuth. This essay gives attention to a representative group of authors and characters who have come to the fore in the last two decades. The writers and characters included in this and other group entries are also listed in the index under individual names.

Inevitably, some will stew over the selection here. But it must be remembered this is a representative mix. May anyone who feels excluded howl at our door. There's always the promise of a new edition. For now, this is the company. Dennis noted many of them in his preface. I'll point out some more.

Here's Barbara Neely, who staked out new turf by making her African American sleuth, Blanche White, a domestic worker. Using lively dialogue and cutting internal monologues, Neely endows White with an ironic moniker and an unforgettable attitude—about her employers, racism in America, parenting, sex and more. And then there's Sarah Caudwell, an English barrister whose years working as a tax lawyer in a bank robbed the London courtrooms of one of the world's masters of understatement. She managed to write three novels that raise questions about gender without ever mentioning it directly. Readers never discover if Caudwell's major character, Hilary Tamar, is a man or a woman. There's no doubt about the gender—and sexual preference—of Kate Brannigan, the lesbian lawyer-sleuth created by Val McDermid.

In fact, the characters in this group make marvelous fodder for gossip. Take Stephanie Plum. The New Jersey bounty hunter may get her man if he's a miscreant she's hauling to a court appearance—but she's not so successful when it comes to nabbing a mate. Linda Barnes's Carlotta Carlyle hob-nobs with a certain male cop, but shares her digs with a female punk. George Pelecanos's Demitri Karras can't quite kick his drug habit.

Some of the authors here collar readers for causes. Nevada Barr stumps for environmental issues. James Lee Burke opines on recovery from alcoholism. John Mortimer prods readers to ponder freedom of speech and more. Some just enjoy waxing eloquent, as Jane Langton does when her professor sleuth Homer Kelly delights in quoting Henry David Thoreau. And some guys grab your ear with wisecracks: Raymond Chandler, Dashiell Hammett, and Spenser come to mind.

Here you will meet authors who bring unusual expertise to their writing. Hammett's lonely hours working for the Pinkerton Detective Agency undoubtedly add depth to his portrayals of the Continental Op and Sam Spade, two characters who typify the sleuth as loner. Peter Lovesey brings a love of sports history to his early work including *Wobble to Death* (1970), about a quirky Victorian walking marathon. Patricia Cornwell's saw blood and gore in the Richmond, Virginia, medical examiner's office, and used it in her books about the fictional M.E., Kay Scarpetta.

This book reveals, too, that some writers eschew life experience and rely instead on flights of imagination. H.R.F. Keating and Colin Dexter are two. Keating wrote several books about the beleaguered Indian policeman Inspector Ganesh Ghote without having visited any part of India. Dexter certainly knows his Oxford milieu well enough, but he counts it a point of pride that he created Chief Inspector Endeavor Morse while knowing absolutely nothing about police work.

Finally, the mix includes a good group of local yokels—authors and characters who seem intimately and very memorably linked to their environs. There's John Harvey, whose mean streets of Nottingham are so well-described that the reader almost feels grit on the hands while turning the pages, and Joan Hess, whose denizens of Maggody, Arkansas make this hillbilly haven one of the quirkiest on the map. Here's Carl Hiaasen, whose Miami is as attention-getting as a neon sign; and Dennis Lehane, whose Irish Catholic, working class Boston neighborhood becomes a kind of group character in his latest work. Another writer who is inseparable from her scene is Patricia Carlon, who uses her intimate knowledge of the remote Australian Outback to make her novels remarkable. Newcomer Alexander McCall Smith places his private eye, Mma Precious Ramotswe, in the brand new No. 1 Ladies Detective Agency at the foot of a hill in Botswana. Smith is the man to meet if you want to get acquainted with a classic author in the making. Literally last, but certainly not least, there's Aurelio Zen, a character who does an imperfect job of solving crimes in Italian venues that are ultimately controlled by the Mafia.

In the end, this representative *Who's Who* celebrates the multi-faceted personality of the genre as a whole. Taken individually, or as a crowd, may the company here, like a room full of people in real life, surprise, puzzle, frighten and delight you—while providing a lifetime of reading enjoyment.

—Rosemary Herbert
Newtonville, Massachusetts
July 4, 2002

USE OF THIS VOLUME

This volume is organized alphabetically. Extensive cross-references guide the reader to related articles; these cross-references are of three types:

1) Within an entry, the first occurrence of a name, word or phrase that has its own entry is marked with an asterisk (*).
2) When a topic is treated in another entry or a related topic is discussed elsewhere in the volume, the italicized words "see," or "see also," direct the reader to the appropriate entry term(s).
3) "Blind entries," or entry terms that have no accompanying text but are terms that readers might expect to find discussed, appear alphabetically in the volume and refer to the entries where the topics are actually treated. Thus the blind entry "Criminal Mastermind" refers readers to "Master Criminal."

Cross-references, including terms that are marked with asterisks and those used in blind entries, match the entry terms, with the exceptions of plurals and possessives. Therefore the asterisked terms "*sleuth" and "*sleuths" will lead the reader to the entry "Sleuth."

Real people and characters are alphabetized by last name, the former in bold capitals and the latter in ordinary bold type (e.g., Edgar Allan Poe under **POE, EDGAR ALLAN,** and the Chevalier C. Auguste Dupin under **Dupin, The Chevalier C. Auguste**). Each author is listed by the name under which he or she is best known in the crime and mystery field. Thus **"RHODE, JOHN"** is the entry title for the article about Major Cecil John Charles Street, who produced much of his detective fiction under the Rhode pseudonym. Throughout the volume, any author who is not the primary subject of an entry is also referred to by the name he or she most commonly uses on works in this genre. In the cases of authors who write mysteries under more than one name, the editor has chosen the name she believes is most likely to come to mind for most readers. In the case of Street/Rhode, his second pseudonym, Miles Burton, is mentioned in the context of the Rhode entry. In the case of Frances Fyfield, who first made her name in crime writing under that psuedonym and then wrote additional mysteries under her real name, Frances Hegarty, a blind entry serves to direct readers to the main entry, **"FYFIELD, FRANCES."**

Authors and characters who are known by last names and nicknames are generally given entry titles under their full names. Thus Oxford chief inspector known throughout most of the books as just "Morse," is listed under **"Morse, Chief Inspector Endeavor"** since, late in the series, the character was finally endowed by his author with a first name. In the case of the author who is sometimes known as Sapper, blind entries lead from this nickname to the entry for **McNEILE, H(ERMAN) C(YRIL).** It is important for readers to remember that the index will point them to favorite authors and characters whose names may not appear as entry titles or as blind entries but who are discussed in the context of other entries.

Every published work cited in this volume is followed by the date of its first publication, placed in parentheses. When the same work was published in two countries during the same year but under different titles, the first title given here is the one published in the author's country of origin. When there are additional variant titles, up to three are placed in parentheses following the first edition's publication year. When a book was originally published in a language other than English, the title of the first edition is listed first, followed (in parentheses) by the publication date and the title(s) of any English edition(s). When it is known how a title may be translated, but no translated edition has been published, this is noted in the body of the entry, not in parentheses.

Abbreviations used in this volume include acronyms for organizations or police and intelligence agencies, as well as for magazines that are frequently cited in these pages. A list of abbreviations follows:

AHMM   *Alfred Hitchcock's Mystery Magazine*

IAEP   Asociacion Internacionale de Escritores Policianos (International Association of Crime Writers)

CADS   *Crime and Detective Stories*

CIA   Central Intelligence Agency

CID   Criminal Investigation Department

CWA   Crime Writers Association

EQMM   *Ellery Queen's Mystery Magazine*

FBI   Federal Bureau of Investigation

MWA   Mystery Writers of America

All entries in this volume are signed by their authors.

WHODUNIT?
A Who's Who in Crime & Mystery Writing

A

Abner, Uncle. One of six detectives created by Melville Davisson *Post, Uncle Abner is a squire in the western counties of Virginia in the time of Thomas Jefferson. A self-appointed protector and avenger, Uncle Abner harks back to a time when crime was not a social issue but rather a matter of violation of God's order. Nevertheless, he employs the ratiocinative techniques of a nineteenth-century detective in stories that Post crafted to exhibit the criminal mystery as the basis of plot and narrative development. The career of Uncle Abner is related exclusively in short stories that enjoyed success in popular magazines and are collected in *Uncle Abner, Master of Mysteries* (1918). Three additional stories appear in *The Methods of Uncle Abner* (1974). All extant stories were reissued in 1977 in *The Complete Uncle Abner*.

—Donald Yates

ACADEMIC SLEUTH. Working in the academic milieu, the academic *sleuth is a prevalent character type in crime and mystery fiction. By far the greatest number of academic sleuths has come from the ranks of higher education, but they can also be schoolteachers, college librarians, administrators, or students. When engaged in detective work, academic sleuths employ the sharp analytic skills they have developed through their scholarly pursuits, and their efforts are not always confined to on-campus crimes. As Robin Winks points out (introduction, *The Historian as Detective: Essays on Evidence,* 1968), the reasoning processes that facilitate productive academic research closely parallel the reasoning processes necessary for successful detection.

Academic sleuths are most commonly experts in English literature, but nearly all academic disciplines have their representatives. Among the more esoteric fields represented are Sanskrit (Anthony *Boucher's Professor John Ashwin) and agronomy (Charlotte *MacLeod's Peter Shandy). Whatever his or her field of expertise, the academic sleuth has a body of information to draw upon to enliven discussion, confound suspects, and guide the investigation. For example, those who are professors of literature employ their esoteric knowledge and familiarity with literary allusions to interpret clues the police find impenetrable.

The first professorial sleuth to achieve widespread popularity was Professor Augustus S. F. X. *Van Dusen. Created by Jacques *Futrelle, Van Dusen is a master of all known sciences; his brain is so large that he wears size-eight hat. Thanks to his prodigious powers of deduction, Van Dusen is known as the Thinking Machine. A sometime member of the faculty at the fictional Hale University in New England, Van Dusen makes his debut in *The Chase of the Golden Plate* (1906).

Craig Kennedy was Van Dusen's immediate successor as the preeminent professor-detective. The creation of Arthur B. *Reeve, Kennedy is a professor of chemistry at a university in New York City that resembles Columbia University. Although proficient in logical deduction, Kennedy triumphs over evildoers largely by his talent for inventing scientific crime-fighting instruments such as a lie detector. Kennedy begins his literary life in *The Poisoned Pen* (1911), and his subsequent detection career focuses exclusively on off-campus crimes.

Of all professor-detectives, Dr. Lancelot *Priestley holds the distinction of bringing the largest number of criminals to justice. Created by John *Rhode, Priestley investigates crime off campus beginning with *The Paddington Mystery* (1925). Priestley, a mathematician, is less concerned with the human aspects of crimes than with the puzzles they present. Depending principally on Scotland Yard detectives to provide him with information, Priestley seldom leaves his London home in the course of his ratiocination. Like Van Dusen, he does not suffer fools gladly; a man of independent means, he takes up detection after leaving a major British university following a succession of bitter quarrels with the administration.

Van Dusen, Kennedy, and Priestley are all *Great Detectives, and all three stand apart from the stream of ordinary life. Egocentric as well as intellectually arrogant, the academic sleuth became an appealing target for satire. Among the most popular of the academic sleuths constructed as a satirical commentary on real-life professors was Gervase *Fen, an eccentric whose detection is often erratic and inefficient; his efforts are fueled more by his own high opinion of his sleuthing abilities than by any innate brilliance. The creation of Edmund *Crispin, Fen—a professor of English language and literature at the fictional St. Christopher's College, Oxford—is introduced in *The Case of the Gilded Fly* (1944; *Obsequies at Oxford*). A lean man of about forty, his hair plastered down with water, he owns a red sports car, which he drives badly, wears bizarre clothing, and offers pompous opinions on all forms and genres of literature, whether or not he has any significant familiarity with them. His brilliant mind and elite education are regularly contrasted with the matter-of-fact attitudes of people in nonacademic life. Although he is sometimes shown at St. Christopher's and some of his faculty colleagues appear in his stories, all of the tales are essentially off-campus mysteries.

In recent decades many professor detectives, including several women sleuths, have been depicted as appealingly human, even sympathetic figures. Dr. R. V. Davie, the creation of V. C. Clinton-Baddeley, is a wry septuagenarian fellow in classics at the fictional St. Nicholas's College, Cambridge. He first appears in *Death's Bright Dart* (1967). Neither a detecting genius nor oppressively eccentric, Dr. Davie is a more congenial character than most of his colleagues: He is a man with friends who enjoys a wide range of activities and associations. In detection he is curious and astute rather than arrogant and pushy.

Women academics have played a large part in deepening and humanizing the character of the academic sleuth. Amanda *Cross's Kate *Fansler first appears in *In the Last Analysis* (1964). She is a serious-minded, thoroughly professional academician who must often juggle the demands of her teaching and research with detection. She leads the reader through the academic world as it is experienced by women: a place of discrimination, smallmindedness, and ambition. Joan Smith's Loretta Lawson is even more avowedly feminist and does not confine her detection to the campus. She works closely with a fellow professor and in *Don't Leave Me This Way* (1990) explores the life of a friend who comes to her for help and is later found murdered. With her close friendships, humane attitudes, and philosophical commitment to improving the life of women, Lawson is the diametric opposite of the earliest academic sleuths.

[*See also* Eccentrics.]

—John E. Kramer Jr.

ACCIDENTAL SLEUTH. "Accidental sleuth" is a term applied to the protagonist who is not a detective by avocation or profession, either amateur, private, or official, but who nonetheless assumes the role of *sleuth. Often a character falls into the role because of his or her proximity to the scene of the crime, whether as a guest in a country house that becomes a murder scene or as an unwilling bystander who observes a criminal act in the mean streets. Accidental sleuths are frequently related to or personally involved in the lives of other characters directly affected by crime. They may assume the role of detective contrary to personal preference, or they may find themselves in the role of accidental sleuth with a mission, as is the case when a mother's determination serves to avenge or prevent a crime against her child where police efforts are failing. Several of Mary Higgins *Clark's novels feature mothers who find themselves taking this role. There is notable tradition of accidental sleuthing in the Had-I-But-Known school of writing, which generally features female characters whose chance encounters with crime, often in isolated settings, cause them to undertake amateur sleuthing in a way that parallels the official police investigation.

Individual characters whose repeated encounters with crime fill multiple books are generally not considered accidental sleuths. Agatha *Christie's Miss Jane *Marple, for instance, is an *amateur detective: she

comes to be known for her sleuthing abilities and is often called in to help with perplexing crimes in her neighborhood. Characters whose professions regularly cause them to visit crime scenes—primarily journalists, photojournalists, doctors, and lawyers—fall into a closely related category. When these characters use their expertise to guide them in investigating crimes in tandem with, along parallel lines to, or especially in lieu of official investigators, they become *surrogate detectives.

One of the earliest recognized works in the crime and mystery genre features a character who illustrates how closely related the two categories are. In William *Godwin's novel *Things as They Are; or, The Adventures of Caleb Williams* (1794; *Caleb Williams; The Adventures of Caleb Williams*), the secretary to Ferdinando Falkland finds that his position enables him first to suspect and then to prove the identity of a murderer. A more classic example of the purely accidental sleuth is Rachel Innes in Mary Roberts *Rinehart's early novel *The Circular Staircase* (1908). When this character rents a country house for the summer, her natural curiosity draws her into investigating the mysterious occurrences that arise. The unnamed protagonist of Daphne *du Maurier's *Rebecca* (1938) is another accidental sleuth, whose love for her brooding new husband drives her to penetrate the mystery surrounding his deceased first wife.

Writers who use accidental sleuths have an advantage over those who use amateur detectives, for readers may find it easy to identify with a protagonist who is an ordinary citizen caught up in a web of intrigue. The lack of fixed expectations regarding the character's expertise, courage, and personality also allows for greater depth of characterization, more potential surprises, and sometimes a greater sense of jeopardy threatening the protagonist. For instance, in Josephine *Tey's *Miss Pym Disposes* (1946) the sleuth character develops from an observer into an active participant in the circumstances surrounding the crime. In Tey's *Brat Farrar* (1949; *Come and Kill Me*), the eponymous antihero finds himself investigating the circumstances surrounding the death of the youth he is impersonating in order to inherit the deceased's fortune, transforming him in the reader's eyes from an opportunist adventurer in to a sympathetic character who is himself in jeopardy.

—J. Randolph Cox

Adler, Irene. Although she appears in just one story in the Sherlock *Holmes Canon, Irene Adler is perhaps the most famous woman in detective fiction. The only woman to dupe Holmes, Adler is regarded by the *Great Detective as "*the* woman," who "eclipses and predominates the whole of her sex." Born in New Jersey in 1858, Adler is a contralto who has performed at La Scala and held the role of prima donna at the Imperial Opera of Warsaw. When she claims the attention of Holmes in "A Scandal in Bohemia" (*Strand*, July 1891), she has retired from the operatic stage as well as from the embrace of Wilhelm Gottstreich Sigismond von Ormstein, grand duke of Cassel-Felstein and hereditary king of Bohemia. The Bohemian king engages Holmes to secure a compromising photograph in which he is posed with Adler. Von Ormstein believes that his former paramour will use the photograph to ruin him when he marries another.

Described by Holmes as "the daintiest thing under a bonnet on this planet," she is seen by the threatened grand duke as having "the face of the most beautiful of women and the mind of the most resolute of men." Indeed, Adler impulsively disguises herself as a man and tails Holmes to his own door after he literally tries to smoke out the photograph's secret hiding place. The Great Detective's scheme involves two uninvited visits to Adler's *bijou* villa in London. He first gains entry disguised as a loafer who has been injured in a scuffle, and subsequently presents himself as "an amiable and simple-minded clergyman." But despite Holmes's cleverness, Adler uses her "woman's wit" to remain a step ahead of the sleuth, marrying Godfrey Norton and fleeing with her new spouse—and the scandalous photograph—while rising in Holmes's regard to the point that he prefers to accept her portrait rather than the Bohemian's showy jeweled ring in payment for his services.

[*See also* Femme Fatale.]

—Rosemary Herbert

AFRICAN AMERICAN SLEUTH. In the twentieth century, African Americans began the mass migration that would transform them from a rural to an urban people. Although the African American writers who chronicled this transition examined the impact of crime on the black community, they did not typically write genre mystery fiction. Among those who did was Rudolph Fisher, whose *The Conjure-Man Dies* (1932), a classic mystery novel, features Harlem detective Perry Dart and Dr. John Archer. Twenty-five years later, expatriate Chester *Himes, living in France, created Coffin Ed *Johnson and Gravedigger Jones, who in policing a ghetto that has become a slum are both more cynical and more brutal than Perry Dart.

By the 1940s, African American police officers as minor characters included Detective Zilgitt in Ellery *Queen's *Cat of Many Tails* (1949) and Officer Connolly in Bart Spicer's *Blues for the Prince* (1950). But a significant step forward occurred with the publication of "Corollary" in the July 1948 issue of *Ellery Queen's Mystery Magazine*. Written by African American writer Hughes Allison, the story features Detective Joe Hill.

During the Civil Rights era, other sleuths were created. John *Ball's *In the Heat of the Night* (1965) featured Virgil *Tibbs, a Pasadena homicide detective. In marked contrast to George *Baxt's flamboyant homosexual detective Pharoah Love (*A Queer Kind of Death*, 1966) and his successor, the hip Satan Stagg (*Topsy and Evil*, 1968), Tibbs was conservative in dress and behavior. But he brought to his work a compassion rooted in his own struggles.

However, African American sleuths were becoming more assertive in demanding respect. As hard-boiled *private eyes, they also became more violent. This was linked to the urban milieu in which private eyes such as Ernest Tidyman's John Shaft, Percy Spurlock Parker's Bull Benson, and Kenn Davis's Carver Bascombe functioned. They followed in the footsteps of private eye Toussaint Marcus Moore, created by Ed Lacy in the 1950s.

In the 1990s, a group of African American mystery writers shaped their sleuths within the context of their own culture-based awareness of the social structure. Thus Walter *Mosley's Ezekiel "Easy" *Rawlins is a migrant from the South, financially secure, but still painfully aware of the precariousness of being black in 1940s Los Angeles. And although Barbara *Neely's eponymous sleuth in *Blanche on the Lam* (1992) lives in the New South, she too experiences a sense of jeopardy. As a domestic worker, Blanche conducts a murder investigation while dealing with issues of race, class, gender, and oppression.

Perhaps the one thing that sets African American sleuths apart from their European American counterparts is what W. E. B. DuBois once referred to as a "double consciousness." When the sleuths are fully realized as three-dimensional characters, the writers who create them present them as the products of a society in which they must develop a heightened sense of awareness that sometimes amounts to "cultural paranoia." This awareness serves them well in encounters not only with criminals but also with police officers and others, who may respond to them based on racial stereotypes.

However, in the tradition of the genre, African American private eyes also have their police contacts. And the client who comes through the door is sometimes white. Sometimes, as with Virginia Kelly, the lesbian investment counselor in Nikki Baker's *The Lavender House Murder* (1992), the case is one in which the sleuth is intimately involved. But on other occasions private eyes such as Clifford Mason's Joe Cinquez and Gar Anthony Haywood's Aaron Gunner turn to their kinship and friendship networks for information and resources. The sidekicks of these sleuths are varied and eccentric. Easy Rawlins has an uneasy relationship with "Mouse," who is as lethal as he is loyal. Richard Hilary's New Jersey-based private eye, Ezell "Easy" Barnes, has a sidekick named "Angel," who is a transvestite. The plot conventions are all there. What is different is how the African American sleuth interprets them.

—Frankie Y. Bailey

AIRD, CATHERINE, pseudonym of Kinn Hamilton McIntosh (b. 1930), English author of detective novels and works of local history. Born in Huddersfield, Yorkshire, she is the daughter of Dr. R.A.C McIntosh, a physician who encouraged his daughter to develop powers of observation. Educated at Waverly School and Greenhead High School, both in Huddersfield, she dreamt of becoming a doctor, but a life-threatening illness struck her in early adulthood, confining her to bed for several years. Upon her recovery, she served as practice manager and dispenser for her father's medical practice in the village of Sturry, near Canterbury, Kent. She continued to live in the family home, caring for her parents, as they aged and became housebound through ill health. She has found an involvement in village life, including her experience on the burial committee of her parish council, for instance, to be a useful source of information and ideas for a crime novelist.

On the surface, Aird's good-humored crime writing falls into the cozy category. All but one of her novels is set in the fictional countryside of Calleshire, a typically English world where local church fetes and tours of grand country houses are *de rigeur*. In Aird's hands, however, the classic settings are updated with contemporary detail, and the author's humorous observations often illuminate dark truths about human character. Aird's knowledge of pharmacology often informs her plots; it also causes the author to take care not to write a recipe for murder in her books. In one book, *Little Knell* (2000), the plot turns on understanding of the affects of the anthrax virus.

In her long-running series, Aird pairs Inspector C.D. Sloan—who is inevitably nicknamed "Seedy"—with a "defective constable" William Crosby. The duo was introduced in the *Religious Body* (1966), a book which establishes Aird's flair for writing dialogue enlivened by puns and plays on words. Their impatient police Superintendent Leeyes and the pathologist, Dr. Dabbe, are two memorable characters in the series. Leeyes believes, usually incorrectly, his gleanings from adult education courses should illuminate questions that arise in the course of casework, while Dabbe remains unruffled by the most shocking crimes. Aird's non-series novel, *A Most Contagious Game* (1967), is sometimes likened to Josephine *Tey's *The Daughter of Time* (1952), since archival materials are essential to the solution of the crime.

Aird has also penned short stories [some are collected in *Injury Time* (1995) and in *Chapter and Hearse* (2003)], local history, *son et lumiere* productions, and articles. She is an editor of *The Oxford Companion to Crime & Mystery Writing* (1999). In addition she has engaged in much voluntary work. She was made a member of the order of the British Empire (MBE) for her work with the Guides Association. In 1990 and 1991, she served as chair of the Crime Writers Association. She received the Crime Writer's Association's Golden Handcuffs Award for lifetime achievement, and she was also presented with an honorary M.A. from the University of Kent at Canterbury.

[*See also* Police Detective.]

—Rosemary Herbert

Alleyn, Roderick. Inspector (later Superintendent) Roderick Alleyn is almost the *victim of his own elegance, entering Ngaio *Marsh's first detective novel in 1934 as tall, handsome, well dressed, and well connected:

the sort who would "do" for house parties. With his brother a baronet and his mother Lady Alleyn of Danes Lodge, Alleyn retains his aristocratic sang-froid through thirty-two novels from 1934 to 1982, traveling to France, Italy, New Zealand, and South Africa in his pursuit of criminals. In that time he acquires a wife, the famous portrait painter Agatha Troy, and a son, Ricky. Alleyn ages little, but he and his reliable helper Inspector Fox become somewhat stranded in the police methods of the 1950s.

Marsh created Alleyn very much to suit her own world, naming him after the famous Elizabethan actor Edward Alleyn, and endowing him with her own love for William *Shakespeare and the stage. His marriage to Troy opens up a number of interesting plot possibilities, and even Marsh's penultimate novel, *Photo-Finish* (1980), which is set in New Zealand, has Troy's portrait commission at its heart. Troy is infinitely understanding, but distant, and her career is never subsidiary to that of her husband.

Comparisons between Alleyn and Lord Peter *Wimsey may have been inevitable in the early novels, but Alleyn soon proves to be a very different sort of character. He is no gentleman amateur, but a serving police officer who is always seen as part of a team. Marsh describes him as "an attractive, civilized man with whom it would be pleasant to talk, but much less pleasant to fall out." Although his role as upholder of the law may sometimes create tensions with the wealthy and powerful circles which are his natural milieu, Alleyn accepts no deviation from his sense of duty, no matter how well-mannered his investigative technique may be.

[*See also* Aristocratic Sleuth; Police Detective; Sleuth.]

—Margaret Lewis

ALLINGHAM, MARGERY (LOUISE) (1904–1966), English author, considered one of the great mystery writers of the Golden Age. Allingham published her first novel in 1928 and her last, posthumously, in 1968. She came of a writing family and was a published novelist before she was twenty. When she failed to complete a mainstream novel about her own 1920s generation, she turned with relief to the mystery story, which she saw as a box with four sides: "a Killing, a Mystery, an Enquiry and a Conclusion with an Element of Satisfaction in it." She felt safe within the box, "at once a prison and a refuge," keeping her in line but allowing free play to her imagination.

The White Cottage Mystery was serialized in 1927 and appeared as a book the following year. An effective whodunit with a daring solution, it is more interesting in some ways than *The Crime at Black Dudley* (1929; *The Black Dudley Murder*), which followed in 1929 and is much better known, less for its merit than because it introduces a "dubious" character known as Albert *Campion, a typical 1920s *silly-ass sleuth. From the first his foolish appearance and manner make it almost obligatory to underestimate him, yet he proves unexpectedly resourceful and reliable when trouble starts. Over the years he matures into a figure of weight and authority.

The Crime at Black Dudley was written by what Allingham called the "plum pudding" method, whereby anything may be stirred into the mixture to enhance its richness. Three further novels were composed on the same principle, all lively and inventive, all set in rural Suffolk, all less concerned with methods of murder than with precious objects and the struggle to possess them. Mystery Mile (1930) introduces Magersfontein *Lugg, Campion's lugubrious manservant, and Sweet Danger (1933; The Fear Sign; Kingdom of Death), the Lady Amanda Fitton, who after a long and eccentric courtship eventually becomes Campion's wife. Police at the Funeral (1931) marks a new stage in Campion's career and is notably accomplished in its more formal manner. Investigating murder in a grimly repressive Cambridge household, he has perforce to behave himself, and though he lapses occasionally into calculated inanity, he never loses sight of the seriousness of his undertaking. He is, in fact, ready to grow up and take his place in the smart urban world of the 1930s.

Four novels feature aspects of contemporary culture and together form a distinctive group within the Canon. Each is set in a specific world with the mystery evolving from the particular preoccupations of those who inhabit it: art in Death of a Ghost (1934), books in Flowers for the Judge (1936; Legacy in Blood), musical theater in Dancers in Mourning (1937), and haute couture in The Fashion in Shrouds (1938). A lighter, shorter novel, The Case of the Late Pig, also appeared in 1937. Though based on an improbable premise unquestioningly accepted by all right-minded persons, it is a most engaging story, narrated by Campion himself with echoes of P. G. Wodehouse.

Campion does not appear in Black Plumes (1940), despite its wartime date set firmly in an opulent prewar world, but he makes a memorable return in Traitor's Purse (1941), contending with amnesia, an emotional crisis, and a secret vital to national security locked in his brain. Coroner's Pidgin (1945; Pearls Before Swine) shows a segment of the smart set adapting to life in a Blitz-ravaged London.

The postwar novels were less frequent, and each differs significantly from its immediate predecessor. More Work for the Undertaker (1948), fizzing with wit and fancy, introduces Charlie Luke, a young policeman with a "pile-driver personality." The Tiger in the Smoke (1952) is dark and disquieting, set in a fogbound London with a vicious killer at large. The Beckoning Lady (1955; The Estate of the Beckoning Lady) returns to rural Suffolk, enveloping even Luke in sunlit languor. Hide My Eyes (1958; Tether's End) charts the events of a memorable day in which a murderous psychopath learns that he, too, can be a *victim. The China Governess (1962) is a dense and intricate study of deception within a privileged family conditioned to denying the truth. The Mind Read-

ers (1965) combines schoolboy daring with adult deceits in an exuberant thriller about extrasensory perception. Cargo of Eagles (1968) takes Campion on a last exhilarating treasure hunt. It was completed after her death by her husband, Youngman Carter.

Allingham remains among the most beguiling of mystery writers, for her warmth and humor, her eye for character, her vivid inventive powers, and her graceful, pointed style. She also adapted to a changing world and was not afraid to test her range, refining and deepening her fictions and exploring significant themes. Above all, she created a world that is indisputably her own.

[See also Aristocratic Sleuth.]

—B. A. Pike

AMATEUR DETECTIVE. The first detective of the mystery genre was an amateur. In Edgar Allan *Poe's story "The Murders in the Rue Morgue" (1841; in Graham's Lady's and Gentleman's Magazine, Apr. 1841), the Chevalier C. Auguste *Dupin is the quintessential amateur detective: eccentric in his personal habits and brilliant in his deductions, smarter than the police and his adoring chronicler, moved to investigate by the intellectual challenge of the crime. This description remains in broad terms the definition of every amateur *sleuth that follows Dupin.

Early writers in the genre worked hard to make their series characters distinctive, and we may distribute amateur sleuths into several broad categories. After decades that saw the creation of overly cerebral and emotionally flat sleuths, E. C. *Bentley introduced Philip Trent in Trent's Last Case (1913; The Woman in Black), the first *silly-ass sleuth; his most famous successor is perhaps the early Albert *Campion, in The Crime at Black Dudley (1929; The Black Dudley Murder), by Margery *Allingham. Among the eccentrics are Agatha *Christie's Hercule *Poirot, the retired Belgian policeman with his egg-shaped head, waxed moustaches, and "little gray cells" introduced in The Mysterious Affair at Styles (1920). Philo *Vance, who first appears in The Benson Murder Case (1926) by S. S. *Van Dine, is a younger man who lectures insufferably on art and life while tailing after the police. Far more likable but just as eccentric is Gervase *Fen, Edmund *Crispin's Oxford don introduced in The Case of the Gilded Fly (1944; Obsequies at Oxford, 1945), who prefers murder to Milton and lives in a fey world.

"Little old ladies" capable of deceiving suspects by their benign aspects were popular from the early years of the genre. Christie's Miss Jane *Marple in The Murder at the Vicarage (1930) knits and twitters but always sees through people's behavior, and Gladys *Mitchell's Mrs. Adela Beatrice Lestrange *Bradley is an alienist with a sometimes caustic personality, as seen in The Saltmarsh Murders (1932). In more recent years, writers have modified the character of the elderly female sleuth and made her more realistic. Dorothy Gilman's Mrs. Emily Pollifax, well into her sixties, answers the call of the government to track down stolen plutonium in Europe in *A Palm for Mrs. Pollifax* (1973), and Stefanie Matteson's Charlotte Graham, a once-famous actress now in her early sixties, visits friends and unravels crime in *Murder at the Spa* (1990). The amateur detective may be a cleric, as is G. K. *Chesterton's Father *Brown; an aristocrat, like Dorothy L. *Sayers's Lord Peter *Wimsey; a physician, such as Josephine Bell's Dr. David Wintringham; a teacher, as is Leo *Bruce's Carolus Deene; or any other occupation and age.

Beginning with Poe's Dupin, the amateur sleuth has usually been smarter than the police and makes much of the stupidity of the officers of the law: Christie's Poirot is a fine example. It is also a convention that over time the police may come to respect the mental acuity of the amateur, as is the case with Miss Marple, and may even seek his or her advice, as they do with Crispin's Gervase *Fen. The relationship between the amateur and the police has vexed many writers who preferred to solve the problem by establishing a friendship between amateur and police, as Anthony Oliver does between Lizzie Thomas and retired police detective Inspector John Webber in *The Pew Group* (1980). Additional strategies include locating a relative among the police, like the character Ellery *Queen's father, who is a police detective, in *The Greek Coffin Mystery*, by Ellery *Queen (1932); or leading the amateur into an engagement and later marriage with an attorney, as Amanda *Cross does with Kate *Fansler and Reed Amherst in *Poetic Justice* (1970); or with a private detective as is the case with Annie Laurance and Max Darling in Carolyn G. *Hart's *Honeymoon with Murder* (1988). Other amateur detectives remain on a precarious footing with the authorities. Faith Sibley Fairchild evokes polite but firm skepticism from the French police in *The Body in the Vestibule* by Katherine Hall Page (1992); Simon *Brett's Charles Paris, an actor limping through his career, is barely tolerated by the police, whereas Brett's Mrs. Melita Pargeter, an elderly widow, has a clear view of the police from the opposite side of the line, thanks to her late husband, in *A Nice Class of Corpse* (1986). Frank Parrish's Dan Mallett, a poacher who has little good to say about the local police, groundskeepers, and anyone else in the middle class, often works against the police to clear himself of suspicion, as in *Fire in the Barley* (1977). Joyce *Porter's Honourable Constance Ethel Morrison-Burke is absolutely despised by the authorities in *A Meddler and Her Murder* (1972).

The sleuth moves among the suspects as an equal, engaging in light conversation at parties or on holiday trips, listening intently with no hint of suspicion, exploring possibilities without indicating who is the favored suspect; this ability to blend with the community under examination is in fact a considerable advantage of the amateur detective. In addition to these visits and polite queryings, detectives use a number of techniques to arrive at the correct solution. Some, like Page's Fairchild, merely follow their curiosity until the murderer reveals

himself or herself; others, like Van Dine's Vance, apply psychology and make much of their method; and still others, such as R. Austin *Freeman's Dr. John *Thorndyke, rely on rigorous logic and evidence. For the most part, however, amateur detectives arrive at their conclusions by intuition and circumstantial evidence, as does Joan *Hess's Claire Malloy. A good number arrive at erroneous conclusions; for instance, Anthony *Berkeley's Roger Sheringham raises false reasoning to an art form in *The Poisoned Chocolates Case* (1929).

It would be a mistake to assume that every amateur detective is the alter ego of his or her creator; many are as different from their creators as the writers can manage. And yet in many passages the reader senses that the sleuth speaks for the writer. Christie's Marple offers judgments on Americans, punishment for criminals, and the class system that have parallels in her autobiography and interviews; Chesterton's Father Brown expounds on faith and doubt, sin and redemption in passages that clearly reflect the developing theology of his creator. Gwen Moffat's Melinda Pink casts an acute eye on the deadly consequences of foolish behavior in a harsh environment, reflecting her own experience as a highly regarded rock climber.

[*See also* Academic Sleuth; Aristocratic Sleuth; Eccentrics; Great Detective, The.]

—Susan Oleksiw

ANIMALS. Animals have long played an important role in the mystery genre. Closely connected with the origins of the genre, animals can be killers, clues, detectives, and sidekicks; they can and in fact do take any role normally held by human beings. In the earliest mystery story, "The Murders in the Rue Morgue" (*Graham's Lady's and Gentleman's Magazine*, Apr. 1841) by Edgar Allan *Poe, the murderer is an orangutang kept as a pet. In "The Adventure of the Speckled Band" (*Strand*, Feb. 1892) by Arthur Conan *Doyle, the murderer is a swamp adder. More subtle is the use of an animal to provide a clue. Perhaps the best known example is the dog who did not bark at night in Doyle's "Silver Blaze" (*Strand*, Dec. 1892; 1894).

Some animals, such as the frequently appearing cats in mysteries, have an evidently inherent attraction for writers and readers of mysteries. The many works of Dick *Francis concerning steeple chasing have made horses strong competitors to felines and canines.

Aside from the consuming interest we take in certain animals, though, there is also to be considered the utility they have for story-telling. Animals may set the plot in motion by aiding in the discovery of a crime while they explore the natural world according to their own nature. In addition to their role as agents of death, wild animals may give a murderer the opportunity to conceal a crime, as in Freeman Wills *Crofts's *Antidote to Venom* (1938). Animals also serve as witnesses to crimes. Though rarely able to identify the criminal clearly, their presence may cause the guilty to react and reveal culpability. In those rare cases in which they identify the criminal, they still must work with humans to resolve the situation; in Frances *Fyfield's Shadows on the Mirror (1989) a dog aids a victim at a vital moment. Animals may also serve as assistants; Lillian Jackson *Braun's two Siamese cats have become crucial to their owner's sleuthing success in The Cat Who . . . series. Rita May Brown takes the notion of an animal assistant further by sharing authorship of a series initiated with Wish You Were Here (1990) with her tiger cat, Sneaky Pie Brown, a collaborator in detection but also contributor of animal conversation to the narratives. A hard-boiled variation of feline detection appears in the series by Carole Nelson *Douglas pairing a tomcat named Midnight Louie with Las Vegas publicist Temple Barr.

Animals define the character of humans as good or evil. The owner of two Alsatians uses them to abuse his neighbors and the local nature trails in Die Like a Dog by Gwen Moffat (1982). The murderer who kills an animal as a prelude to human destruction becomes a totally unsympathetic character, as in H. R. F. *Keating's Inspector Ghote Plays a Joker (1969). In The Deer Leap (1985), Martha *Grimes explores the character of one who would kill animals and one who would protect them.

Animals have also become the focus for exploring the conflict between the needs of human beings and the environment, between consumption and conservation. In such instances the theft or abduction of an animal functions as a plot development as significant as kidnapping or burglary. In Roll Over and Play Dead (1991) Joan *Hess explores the dark side of medical research that sanctions the abduction and maltreatment of family pets. Karin McQuillan raises the question of preservation of nature in her series featuring Jazz Jasper; Africa and its wildlife are vivid background in Deadly Safari (1990) and other novels. The danger of using animals in fiction is that of falling into sentimentality or cuteness. Both McQuillan and Moffat avoid this, focusing instead on the needs and manners of the animals. In Grizzly Trail (1984) Moffat depicts the very real dangers of hiking in parts of Montana, the habitat of the grizzly bear; in The Stone Hawk (1989) the harsh realities of life in a remote corner of Utah form the backdrop for the murder of a child.

The expanding role of animals in mysteries may reflect growing concern for animal welfare and animal rights as well as a deepening understanding of the very nature of animals. They may have first appeared in mysteries as criminals and clues, but they have become more than plot devices. As humans see them more clearly, animals are finding new roles.

[See also Sidekicks and Sleuthing Teams.]
—Sharon A. Russell

ANTIHERO denotes an antithetical character, often lacking in nobility, virtue, bravery, and morality, qualities generally associated with the traditional hero. There are famous examples of the antihero throughout literary history; these include Don Quixote, Tristram Shandy, and Willy Loman. However, this *archetypal character is quite prevalent in formula fiction, particularly in crime writing.

From its early days, detective fiction has drawn on the antihero archetype, embodied in characters as notable (and noble) as Sherlock *Holmes and Lord Peter *Wimsey. Both Holmes and Wimsey are, in a conventional sense, virtuous and moral figures, but they are also social misfits, psychologically damaged or lacking in some way. Holmes, a cocaine addict, is alienated from society, and relies upon his friend, Dr. John H. *Watson, for a normative grounding in the world; Wimsey struggles to come to grips with the psychological trauma he suffered during the war, and often depends upon his butler, Mervyn Bunter, to enable him to function.

As detective fiction evolves as a genre, the figure of the antihero evolves along with it. Such authors as Graham *Greene and Patricia *Highsmith have been credited with transforming the detective antihero, who, in their hands, becomes less idiosyncratic and more degenerate. In works like Stamboul Train (1932; Orient Express), It's a Battlefield (1934), and Brighton Rock (1938), Green focuses on unconventional and disillusioned social misfits, and in A Gun for Sale (1936; This Gun for Hire), his protagonist, James Raven, becomes a scapegoat for his society's sins. Because Raven's crimes result from poverty, A Gun for Sale is as much a social critique as a murder mystery. Highsmith depicts a *gentleman thief and social deviant, Tom *Ripley, who is introduced in The Talented Mr. Ripley (1955) and appears in a number of Highsmith's texts. He is involved in a number of shady activities. In Ripley's Game (1974), Ripley is responsible for arranging and conducting the murders of several mafiosi. He is not condemned for his behavior, since the narrative delineates the Mafia hoods as the "real" villains, thus justifying Ripley's elimination of them. Despite the unconventional traits of the protagonist, Highsmith's novels, like Green's, conform to a certain moral code, even if it is a code that is largely self-defined by the antihero. While both Ripley and Raven play fast and loose with certain aspects of law and order, they also uphold and abide by others.

The American hard-boiled tradition provides for more radical developments in this archetypal character. In hard-boiled fiction, the protagonist is often as unsavory as the criminals. Lacking the moral impetus of the earlier detective antiheroes, hard-boiled protagonists, even in early exemplars of the mode, are solitary figures who do not hesitate to take the law into their own hands. Same *Spade in Dashiell *Hammett's The Maltese Falcon (1930), serves as a good example of the deviant antihero, for while he has some moral scruples (he cannot be bribed by the villains, for instance), he also shows little attachment to his murdered partner, Miles Archer, with whose wife he is having an affair. Nor does he hesitate to hand over his former bed partner, Brigid

O'Shaughnessy, to the police. In Mickey *Spillane's *I, the Jury* (1947), Mike *Hammer's misogyny motivates his behavior and engenders much of the novel's gratuitous violence.

Hard-boiled authors dramatize the blight pervading the social order, as exemplified by their antiheroes and the mean streets of the major urban centers through which they walk. Some of these novels encourage readers to identify with their distasteful protagonists and then prompt readers to analyze the affinities they feel with the characters. The texts thereby move to implicate readers in their social critique and suggest that we are all criminals in one way or another. Jim *Thompson's *The Killer Inside Me* (1952), serves as a culmination of this trajectory of detective fiction, for it is narrated by a psychopathic killer. Readers are embroiled in the protagonist's murderous action because they experience it through him, and they are cast as accomplices to his crimes because the author manipulates them to identify with him and the enjoyment he finds in beating and killing women.

In the hands of contemporary authors who are consciously revising it, the representation of women in hard-boiled fiction gives rise to a new development in the antihero archetype. Writers like Sara *Paretsky, Sue *Grafton, and Liza *Cody cast their female sleuths as hard-boiled detectives. These characters are generally moral and upstanding, but they are placed in an ambivalent position in the novels as a result of their gender. The female *private eyes disrupt and subvert traditional portrayals of women as *femmes fatales or as "good" female detectives like Miss Jane *Marple and Harriet *Vane. Rejecting the loner stance of the conventional hard-boiled private eye, the female protagonists function in communities on which they draw for support. Such variants on the hard-boiled female detective as Meg O'Brien's Jessica "Jesse" James—an alcoholic investigative reporter who is romantically involved with a Mafia leader—not only subvert the established rules of the genre underpinning feminine representations, but also provide further twists to the antihero archetype.

Through the use of the antihero, who is unscrupulous, unsavory, and often amoral, the detective genre queries conventional portrayals of *victims and victimizers and of crime and punishment. By implicating the reader in the actions of the protagonist through narrative point of view, the texts suggest that the divisions between law and justice, and truth and appearance, are not as simple as they may at first appear, and cause the reader to speculate on the nature of crime and criminality. Thus, these novels not only offer "deviant" perspectives, they also provide a venue through which readers can explore crucial social constructs and interrogate simplistic moral judgments.

[*See also* Scudder, Matthew; Crumley, James; Outcasts and Outsiders.]

—Priscilla L. Walton

Archer, Lew. The featured character in most of Ross *Macdonald's detective fiction, Archer when first introduced is a rather stiff exemplar of the hard-boiled *sleuth. However, he becomes distinctive over the course of more than a dozen novels and a smattering of short stories. While Macdonald's detective fiction originated in the wake of Dashiell *Hammett and the *Black Mask* school, Archer can be seen as evolving into the prototypical figure of the Vietnam and Watergate years. He is "not the usual peeper," as one character observes in *The Far Side of the Dollar* (1965) and he becomes less so in the course of the series. He retains traits of the hardboiled detective, such as durability in a violent world, when, in *Find a Victim* (1954), someone notices he has been injured and he replies, "I don't matter at the moment. I'll survive." But his principal milieu, Santa Teresa (a thinly disguised Santa Barbara) is an elaboration of Raymond *Chandler's suburbia—one in which commercial competitiveness subsumes the most intimate social relations.

Archer's occasional observations make clear his relation to this world. Comfortable surfaces cover histories of self-deception and the plastic morality of the marketplace. The older generations have hidden their failures and buried their atrocities, but not well enough or deeply enough to evade Archer. Quarreling adults and disoriented children are the telltale symptoms of the social chaos of which Archer becomes more a quiet moral center and less the focus of action. Macdonald himself identifies *The Galton Case* (1959) as the pivotal novel in which Archer's investigation takes a more psychological turn. Although Archer does not assume the role of the psychoanalyst, the plots as well as the settings and discourses demand a detective figure who becomes less prone to physical action and more to talk. Interrogations become less matters of intimidation and more the opportunity for participants to unburden their knowledge. Archer is mediator in this process, observing in *Sleeping Beauty* (1973) that "every witness has his own way of creeping up on the truth." This innovation requires a detective who displays more human qualities than the traditional hard-boiled detective while not appearing soft. Ultimately, as in *The Ivory Grin* (1952; *Marked for Murder*), Archer is the vehicle for moral distinctions that emerge in the language of the times: "It's not just the people you've killed. It's the human idea you've been butchering and boiling down and trying to burn away. You can't stand the human idea."

[*See also* Hard-Boiled Sleuth.]

—Larry Landrum

ARISTOCRATIC SLEUTH. The aristocratic sleuth has been a mainstay of detective fiction since its inception, when Edgar Allan *Poe introduced his series character, the Chevalier C. Auguste *Dupin. Despite his poverty, Dupin comes "of an excellent family—indeed an illustrious family," but because Poe is more interested in his reasoning powers than his pedigree, we learn nothing more about Dupin's antecedents. In this Dupin contrasts with later aristocratic sleuths, whose personal lives and histories constitute part of their strong appeal.

Although drawn from a single class, the aristocratic sleuth exhibits great variety. Baroness *Orczy introduced Lady Molly Robertson-Kirk in a series of short stories collected in 1910; this character brings "feminine tact" and "intuition" to Scotland Yard, where, guarding a personal secret she heads the Female Department. Although she is a daughter of the earl of Flintshire, her title is no great factor in her success as a detective, which derives primarily from her being "ultra-feminine."

Beginning in the Golden Age, the aristocratic sleuth was typically an old and venerable family's younger son who had to find something to occupy his time, talents, and energy. As a detective, he had obvious advantages: he understood the code of the upper classes and had an entrée into high society. Such sleuths may have regarded setting off after a murderer, blackmailer, or terrorist as serious business, but personal danger could also be something of a lark. Although some writers quickly outgrew the silliness of this approach and endowed their characters with a measure of maturity and wisdom that substantiated their abilities to solve crimes, behind the success of every aristocratic detective was some measure of acknowledgment of the sheer force of class.

Perhaps the most famous aristocratic sleuths are three characters introduced during the Golden Age. Dorothy L. *Sayers endowed her character Lord Peter *Wimsey with a pedigree going back to William the Conqueror; this was examined at length by C. W. Scott-Giles in *The Wimsey Family: A Fragmentary History Compiled from Correspondence with Dorothy L. Sayers* (1977). As the younger son of a duke, Wimsey has wealth and position, which contribute immeasurably to his success in criminal investigations, especially among the upper classes. Margery *Allingham's creation Lord Rudolph K——is also a venturesome younger son freed from responsibility by a stodgy elder brother. He goes much further than Wimsey by breaking with his family, disowning his identity, and adopting various *noms de guerre*, one of which, Albert *Campion, becomes his established name. The woman he eventually marries, the Lady Amanda Fitton, is a sister of the earl of Pontisbright, whose title is in abeyance until Campion ensures its restoration. Ngaio *Marsh's Roderick *Alleyn, a professional policeman, is the younger son of a baronet in the diplomatic corps. A natural aristocrat with a high degree of finish, Alleyn is in his element in *Death in a White Tie* (1938), in which he investigates blackmail and the death of a friend after a ball. The continuing contrast with his esteemed plebeian assistant, Detective Inspector Fox, enhances Alleyn's image, showing him to be egalitarian and likable.

Many writers adopted this form of sleuth. The Honorable Richard Rollison figures in a long series of light-hearted thrillers by John *Creasey and is better known

as the Toff. He is "tall, immaculate, a perfect specimen" of the wealthy and leisured class, with a flat in Gresham Terrace and a manservant called Jolly. As both man-about-town and man of action, he is equally at home in the West End and the East End of London. More recently, Martha *Grimes has paired her police detective Inspector Richard Jury with an aristocratic friend, Melrose Plant, who has declined his title (Lord Ardry, earl of Caverness); Elizabeth *George joined her detective, Viscount Lynley, eighth earl of Asherton—known professionally as Inspector Thomas Lynley—with a working-class sergeant, Barbara Havers.

The aristocratic sleuth has not been as readily embraced in the United States; he or she may be distrusted by the authorities, face financial difficulties, or move more comfortably outside the upper class. S. S. *Van Dine's creation, Philo *Vance, is the complete "social aristocrat," both by "birth and instinct." Rich enough to indulge his passions, which briefly include the investigation of bizarre murders, he talks like a caricature of a clubman, swallowing syllables and (like Lord Peter *Wimsey) clippin' the ends of present participles. He displays his erudition plainly. Anthony Abbott follows the investigations of Police Commissioner Thatcher Colt, who though born to wealth and family position is unjustly derided by the popular press as a "flaneur" and a "dilettante in crime." More recently, Charlotte *MacLeod created Sarah Kelling (Bittersohn), who is of a financially declining family of Boston Brahmins; she escapes her slide into genteel poverty and her family by taking in paying guests, eventually marrying, and investigating crimes. Clarissa Watson's detective Persis Willum is the niece of a railroad heiress. Though the least affluent member of the Gull Harbor community, she nonetheless moves freely among the "old money, old property and upper class." A bridge between the British and American aristocratic worlds is Joyce Christmas's Lady Margaret Priam, who lives in New York and works in an antiques shop. The aristocrat who is never troubled by financial worries and changing society is a rarity in American crime fiction.

Just as the richest aristocratic sleuths are British, so too is the most biting satire of the form. Joyce *Porter's creation, the Honorable Constance Morrison-Burke, is the daughter of a viscount, wears only army surplus clothing, and is belligerent, dense, and offensive. She enters criminal investigation as an act of noblesse oblige (*Rather a Common Sort of Crime*, 1970), and detects by grilling everyone until even she can discern the truth. The police want nothing to do with her; nor does anyone else, save her near poverty-stricken companion, Miss Jones. In her stories of the Hon-Con, Porter plays on the absurdity of an idle rich playboy or matron being taken into the confidence of the police and allowed to examine evidence, interrogate suspects, and generally interfere with serious government work.

[*See also* Bluestocking Sleuth; Gentleman Sleuth.]

—Susan Oleksiw *and* Rosemary Herbert

ARMCHAIR DETECTIVE is a phrase that describes a type of fictional detective who solves crimes solely on the basis of secondhand information, rather than through personal observation of evidence. The first example of armchair detecting can be found in the work of Edgar Allan *Poe. In "The Mystery of Marie Rogèt" (*Snowden's Lady's Companion*, Nov. 1842), the Chevalier C. Auguste *Dupin, working wholly from newspaper accounts, arrives at the correct explanation for a young woman's mysterious disappearance. Arthur Conan *Doyle employs the character type in the person of Mycroft *Holmes, Sherlock *Holmes's older brother, who is even more brilliant at "observation and deduction" but is too addicted to the comforts of his club to be anything but an occasional consultant in investigations. In "The Greek Interpreter" (*Strand*, Sept. 1893), Sherlock Holmes says of his brother that, "if the art of the detective began and ended in reasoning from an armchair," Mycroft would be the greatest detective "that ever lived."

The most fully developed armchair detective is the creation of Baroness Emmuska *Orczy, in the series of stories about the *Old Man in the Corner, published between 1901 and 1925. The Old Man sits in the corner of a tea shop, tying intricate knots into a piece of string (as an "adjunct to thought") and recounts for the benefit of a young woman journalist his successes in solving famous crimes that have foiled the police. Although occasionally journeying to a crime scene or courtroom to verify a deduction, he arrives at his solution entirely on the basis of newspaper accounts of the crime. His interest lies in the intellectual challenge of the mystery and the chance to show up official detectives, with whom he scorns to share his knowledge, even when it means a criminal gets away with a crime.

Later writers who use the armchair sleuth include Agatha *Christie, and Isaac Asimov. Christie confines the inquisitive Miss Jane *Marple to dinner-table detecting in *The Thirteen Problems* (1932; *The Tuesday Club Murders; Miss Marple and the Thirteen Problems*), a series of stories in which a circle of village friends (lawyer, clergyman, former police inspector) take turns recounting some mysterious crime of which they have personal knowledge. Invariably, Marple arrives at the solution before the teller reveals it. Isaac Asimov made use of a similar device in several volumes of short stories, beginning with *Tales of the Black Widowers* (1974), in which five professionals—writer, lawyer, chemist, artist, and cryptographer—meet monthly at dinner to match wits over a difficult puzzle; the solution is regularly reached first by their waiter Henry.

As these examples suggest, inherent limitations in the armchair detection form make it more suitable to the short story than to the novel. Describing the crime indirectly, in a narration that becomes a virtual monologue of quotations within quotations, makes for a cumbersome structure, and emphasizing the ingenuity of the detective, who is usually more attracted by the intellectual game than by the pursuit of justice, diminishes the human interest. Among the few writers who have used an armchair detective in a full-length work are Anthony *Boucher, whose Dr. John Ashwin, Professor of Sanskrit, solves a series of bizarre murders at a university in *The Case of the Seven of Calvary* (1937), and John *Rhode, whose Dr. Lancelot *Priestley, a prickly scientific genius in the vein of Jacques *Futrelle's Professor S. F. X. *Van Dusen, the Thinking Machine, appears in several novels, beginning with *The Paddington Mystery* (1925). Rhode achieved some variety by having Priestley leave his study occasionally to gather evidence or, more often, delegate the legwork to others—a device adopted by most later writers of armchair detection.

An example of this device is found in the work of Ernest Bramah, who introduced the first blind detective in a volume of stories, *Max Carrados* (1914). In the initial tale, "The Coin of Dionysius," coin collector Max Corrados realizes his wish to become a detective by teaming up with Louis Carlyle, an old school friend now turned private investigator. Carrados's acute senses of touch and hearing keep him from being an armchair sleuth in the strict sense, since they let him detect subtle physical clues invisible to others; but his partnership with Carlyle, carried on through two more volumes of stories, is the prototype of the relationship in which a reclusive or disabled detective takes on a younger, active partner. The best-known such pair is Rex *Stout's Nero *Wolfe, largely housebound by his girth and taste for comfort, and Archie *Goodwin, who functions as commentator and sidekick. Their partnership begins in *Fer-de-Lance* (1934; *Meet Nero Wolfe*) and continues in a series of books written over the next three decades. By making Archie Goodwin the narrator and developing the human side of his relationship with Wolfe, Stout overcomes the structural limitations of the armchair-detective form and suggests a way to extend its application, although not without compromising the central element of information obtained only by report; evidence and witnesses are brought to Wolfe for direct examination. Other writers have a sleuth temporarily become an armchair detective when he is immobilized by accident or illness, for example, Inspector Grant in Josephine *Tey's *The Daughter of Time* (1951) and Inspector *Morse in Colin *Dexter's *The Wench Is Dead* (1990).

The phrase "armchair detective" is sometimes used now in a more general sense to refer to the reader who, at the hands of a writer abiding by rules of fair play, has all the necessary clues for solving the crime before the writer reveals the solution. A similar meaning is implied in the title of the popular journal *Armchair Detective*, which, beginning the 1960s, published articles and reviews on all types of mystery and detective fiction.

[*See also* Great Detective, The; Sidekicks and Sleuthing Teams.]

—Mary Rose Sullivan

ARMSTRONG, CHARLOTTE. (1905–1969), American author. After working as a fashion journalist, publishing some poems in magazines, and seeing two of her stage plays produced in New York, Armstrong turned to crime and mystery writing. Her first works in the genre narrated cases of a *sleuth whose name, MacDougal Duff, permitted the allusive titles *Lay on, Mac Duff!* (1942) and *The Case of the Weird Sisters* (1943). After carrying Duff into a third work, *The Innocent Flower* (1945; *Death Filled the Glass*), Armstrong abandoned the conventions of a serial detective, taking up as the focus of her next twenty-five novels the subjective experience of hazard in ordinary life. Sherry Reynard's father-in-law in *The Balloon Man* (1968) has a class-based but otherwise inexplicable dislike for her and employs an ambitious social climber to acquire evidence for use against Sherry in an impending child custody case. Once the situation is established, the novel's cadence of threat and escape intensifies until the familiar matter of domestic friction nearly reaches fatal conclusion. *Mischief* (1950), for which Armstrong wrote the screen adaptation (*Don't*

Bother to Knock, 1952), capitalizes on the ordinary anxiety of parents leaving their children in someone else's care to introduce the peril of a baby-sitter whose apparent normality belies her deranged condition. *Lemon in the Basket* (1967) invades the territory of an eminently accomplished family to portray dangers consequent to the resentment of the one underachieving sibling and his resentful spouse. Armstrong constructs plots for her novels and the stories in her two collections of genre short works to create suspense. Her characters represent the innate goodness of ordinary people in conflict with the self-serving excess that can arise in commonplace circumstances, all with the result of tapping her readers' fear that terror may invade everyday life.

—John M. Reilly

AVERAGE PERSON AS DETECTIVE. *See* Accidental Sleuth; Plainman Sleuth.

B

BAANTJER, ALBERT CORNELIS (b. 1923), Dutch crime author who writes under the single name Baantjer. With more than forty titles to his credit, Baantjer has sold more than four million copies in the Netherlands, a country of fewer than fifteen million inhabitants.

Baantjer's main character is a short, fat, irascible policeman named DeKok, who carefully spells his name to everyone he meets. DeKok's assistant is Vledder. Although Baantjer has been called "a Dutch Conan Doyle" by *Publishers Weekly*, and DeKok has been compared to Georges *Simenon's Jules *Maigret, both comparisons are off the mark. DeKok is a much more normal and less eccentric character than is Holmes, much warmer and more humanistic than Maigret.

Baantjer bases his writings on thirty-eight years' experience serving in the Amsterdam Municipal Police, with more than twenty-five of those years in the homicide division. He uses the upstairs office at 48 Warmoes Street (the real-life police station) as a setting where DeKok can look down a narrow street and see the notorious Amsterdam red-light district.

Several of Baantjer's works begin with a prostitute being fished out of one of the numerous canals in Amsterdam, the victim of a horrible murder. The author displays great sympathy for such victims, viewing them as terribly abused by their customers. DeKok enjoys the prostitutes' trust and uses them in solving the crimes against them generally perpetrated by the wealthy and powerful, against whom Baantjer has unchanging animosity. Despite a deep-seated grumpiness, Baantjer has a warmhearted respect for all downtrodden people and for the human race in general.

[*See also* Police Detective.]

—Ray B. Browne

BABSON, MARION, pseudonym for Ruth Stenstreem (b. 1929), American-born writer of comic mysteries and suspense novels, identified with her long-time place of residence, London, England. Born in Salem, Massachusetts, Babson worked briefly in the Boston Public Library before setting off, in 1960, to achieve her dream of living in England. There she held a variety of jobs, including some in public relations, before becoming a full-time writer. Her public relations background came in handy when she served for ten years as the secretary for the Crime Writers Association. In that post, she not only worked on correspondence and newsletters but she generously helped to promote the work of her colleagues in crime writing. A bibliophile with a passion for scouring bookshops and street markets for odd volumes, she delights in finding and presenting books of

interest to her friends, and her London abode is packed with her finds.

Babson is best-known for her light and lively books—many of which offer readers entrée into a variety of worlds that are drawn with humor, and several that feature inquisitive cats—but she is equally capable of writing dark suspense. Babson finds humor in character interactions and comic situations, but even in her lightest novels, some of the laughs arise from the author's penchant for social criticism. Her tone may be bubbly, but because she stands ready to burst the bubbles of the pretentious, her work is never merely frothy. In her darker books, social commentary sometimes underlies—and often drives—the suspense.

Babson's first published book, *Cover-Up Story* (1971), features public relations workers Perkins & Tate. While describing the duo's efforts to promote American hillbilly singers in England, Babson here shows her flair for playing with transatlantic elements. Perkins & Tate also deal with delicate situations *in Murder on Show* (1972; *Murder at the Cat Show*), *Tourists are for Trapping* (1989), and *In the Teeth of Adversity* (1990). Babson's second series features aging actresses Trixie Dolan and Evangeline Sinclair. Their often hilarious efforts to make a comeback are interrupted by encounters with crime, beginning in *Reel Murder* (1986).

Babson enjoys taking the reader into a variety of venues and timing the entrées to particular occasions. For instance, in *The Lord Mayor of Death* (1977), the climax is set during an annual London parade, which is threatened by a terrorist. In *Queue Here for Murder* (1981; *Line Up for Murder*), the action happens among a crowd waiting to enter a department store sale. In *Murder on Show*, cat-lovers are shocked when death enters their midst.

Babson enters several different worlds in her suspense novels, too. The social situations in those mileus can be central to the action, as is the case in the thought-provoking *So Soon Done* (1979), in which the denizens of an affluent neighborhood seek to remove squatters from their area. In *Tightrope for Three* (1978), tension is enhanced by the setting and circumstances, as an escaped murderer threatens a trio who find themselves in "The Hound of the Baskervilles" territory—fog-enshrouded Dartmoor. In another of Babson's suspense novels, the vulnerability of the mentally retarded is central to the plot as the manipulative *Pretty Lady* (1973) of the title tries to get a mentally challenged man involved in the murder of her husband.

Beginning in the 1990s, Babson brought more cats into her books. In the most daring of them, *Nine Lives to Murder* (1992), Babson has a human and a cat exchange points of view and use their new perspectives to solve a crime. Babson has another claim to fame. She won the CWA's Poisoned Chalice Award for killing off the most characters in her novel, *The Cruise of a Death-time* (1983).

[*See also* Animals.]

—Rosemary Herbert

BAILEY, H(ENRY) C(HRISTOPHER) (1878–1961), English fiction writer, who for over thirty years contributed richly to the form, producing twenty-one novels and perhaps a hundred stories, and creating two exceptional series detectives. Bailey deals in moral certainties: the protection of the innocent, the punishment of the guilty.

In the wake of the Great War he turned from the historical fiction with which he made his name to crime writing. In 1920 Reggie *Fortune appeared in *Call Mr. Fortune,* the first of the twelve collections that bear Fortune's name. Fortune is Scotland Yard's foremost pathologist, a master of forensic evidence, whom nothing escapes. He features also in nine novels, occasionally appearing with Joshua Clunk, a wily solicitor, introduced in 1930, who also appears in novels on his own. Despite considerable differences, the two characters share a singleness of purpose: Once embarked on a course of action, neither fails to complete it.

Bailey makes demands on his readers, through his oblique and subtle approach and a style that is mannered, elegant, and elliptical. His narrative achieves a smooth and decorous surface that masks all manner of threats and tensions. The lines between *victim and predator are continually smudged by ironies and ambiguities. While Bailey's writing might challenge the modern reader, once the reader is attuned to the idiom, the rest is pure pleasure. The short stories have always been admired, and their classic status is not in question. The novels have been undervalued and are now undergoing reassessment.

[*See also* Forensic Pathologist; Gentleman Sleuth.]

—B. A. Pike

BALL, JOHN (1911–1988), American author, best known as the creator of the *African American sleuth Virgil *Tibbs. Born in Schenectady, New York, John Dudley Ball Jr. served in World War II with the U.S. Army Air Corps and was later a columnist, broadcaster, and director of public relations for the Institute of Aerospace Sciences in Los Angeles.

In the Heat of the Night (1965) introduced Tibbs, an astute black *police detective from Pasadena, California, who becomes inadvertently involved with murder in a racially and socially bigoted town in South Carolina. In this award-winning novel and the 1967 film adaptation, Ball's message was "don't judge minorities until you know what you're talking about." His social consciousness is also evident in *Johnny Get Your Gun* (1969; *Death

for a Playmate), in which he addressed the implications of gun ownership.

Ball prided himself on research into such fields as jade collecting and the import-export business (*Five Pieces of Jade,* 1972) and forensic detail, which was always crucial to the solutions he presented to his crimes. His impeccably researched settings and police procedures are also evident in his books featuring Jack Tallon, beginning with *Police Chief* (1977), as well as in his non-series works.

—Melvyn Barnes

BARNARD, ROBERT, (1936), British author of *detective novels and literary criticism. An Oxford-educated academic, Barnard taught English at universities in Australia and Norway before returning to his home country in 1983. His first novel, *Death of an Old Goat* (1974) and his seventh, *Death in a Cold Climate* (1980), have Australian and Norwegian settings, respectively, while many of his other books draw on his knowledge of politics, opera, and literary history. His *A Talent to Deceive: An Appreciation of Agatha Christie* (rev. ed. 1990) includes a perceptive analysis of Christie's strategies of deception, and Barnard's depth of understanding of the genre and experience as a crossword compiler make it unsurprising that ingenious plotting is one of his hallmarks. The formal constraints of the short story suit his gifts; *Death of a Salesperson* (1989; *Death of a Salesperson and Other Untimely Exits*) is a strong collection. Barnard regards himself primarily as an entertainer, and his flair for comedy and distaste for pretension are evident in much of his work. He does not consistently employ a series detective, although Perry Trethowan and Charlie Peace are policemen who appear in several of his novels. His more darkly psychological novels, notably *Out of the Blackout* (1985), *A City of Strangers* (1990), and *A Scandal in Belgravia* (1991), are compelling and suggest that this versatile writer may yet extend his range even further. Barnard has also written historical novels under the pseudonym Bernard Bastable, including a series that features Wolfgang Amadeus Mozart as an amateur detective.

—Martin Edwards

BARNES, LINDA (JOYCE APPLEBLATT) (b. 1949), American author of a series of witty mysteries featuring the actor-sleuth Michael Spraggue, and a separate series featuring the wisecracking, cab-driving private eye Carlotta Carlyle. Barnes lives with her husband and son in Brookline, Massachusetts, near the city of Boston where most of the books in her two series are set. Born in Detroit, Michigan, Barnes studied theatre arts at Boston University and briefly worked as a high school drama teacher before writing full time. Spraggue is introduced in *Blood Will Have Blood* (1982). That book and *Dead Heat* (1994) are set in Boston. The latter centers on a murder during the running of the Boston Marathon. Wealthy, cultivated and apt to spout literary allusions (particularly to dramatic works), Spraggue is a sleuth reminiscent of the English aristocratic amateur. He goes to California wine country in *Bitter Finish* (1993) and to New Orleans in *Cities of the Dead* (1994). Carlyle is a much more American and up-to-date character who drives a cab to help support her private eye career. Her mix of Jewish and Italian heritage is emphasized in every book, and her Jewish grandmother's words of wisdom are often sources of humor and strength. Although Carlyle is unmarried, a "family" of unrelated characters surrounds her, including the policeman Mooney, her roommate Roz, and the girl she mentors in the Big Sister program, Paoletta. Social issues are at the heart of many of her cases.

[*See also* Femme Fatale.]

—Rosemary Herbert

BARR, NEVADA (b. 1952), American writer who draws upon experience as a former United States National Park Service Ranger in a series of mysteries featuring Anna Pigeon, a law enforcement ranger. Born in the state of Nevada, the author was raised in California by her parents who also ran a small airport not far from Lassen Volcanic National Park. She was educated at Cal Poly, San Luis Obispo and earned a master's degree in acting from the University of California at Irvine. She pursued her acting career in New York and Minneapolis, and has acted in commercials and industrial films. Then, after marrying a National Park Service employee, became a ranger herself. This experience and her commitment to the cause or natural resource conservation inform and drive her mysteries, which are each set in different national parks. Barr brings her acting experience into Pigeon's history, making the character the widow of an actor who worked in New York City. Barr introduced Pigeon in *Track of the Cat* (1993), a novel set in Guadalupe Mountains National Park in Texas, where Barr worked as a ranger. She takes her character back to New York in *Liberty Falling* (1999). Set on Ellis Island, this novel shows Pigeon as a lonely woman. But in other books, her solitude is interrupted by romantic outings and it is softened by a cat called Piedmont and a dog named Taco, who appear in some of the novels.

—Rosemary Herbert

BAXT, GEORGE (b. 1923), American author, creator of three popular detective series. In his first published novel, *A Queer Kind of Death* (1966), Baxt introduced Pharoah Love, an African American, irrepressibly gay New York homicide detective who follows his case through the byways of the homosexual world. This series continued with *Swing Low, Sweet Harriet* (1967) and *Topsy and Evil* (1968), which introduced still another *African American sleuth, Satan Stagg. Baxt set aside the well-received saga of Love for twenty-six years and then revived it with two additional works published in quick succession: *A Queer Kind of Love* (1994) and *A Queer Kind of Umbrella* (1995). In these later books, Love fol-

lows crime into a wider venue, but the earlier tone of irony and satire continues.

The year after he started the Pharoah Love series, Baxt began his second sequence of novels with *A Parade of Cockeyed Creatures; or, Did Someone Murder Our Wandering Boy?* (1967), featuring Sylvia Plotkin, an author, and Max Van Larsen, another improbable New York *police detective. The relationship between Sylvia and Max is one of unconsummated and unstated love, but the cachet of their series lies in the carnival atmosphere of their section of Greenwich Village, peopled by zany characters with a penchant for zingers and a gift for falling into strange plots, including the case of a thirty-six-year-old disappearance in *"I!" Said the Demon!* (1969). *Satan Is a Woman* (1987) marks another entry in this series.

In 1984 Baxt undertook his third distinctive series with *The Dorothy Parker Murder Case*, a rewrite of celebrity history. That formula continues in *The Alfred Hitchcock Murder Case* (1986) and *The Tallulah Bankhead Murder Case* (1987). Baxt has also authored nonseries novels, at least nine screenplays, and short stories usually published in *Ellery Queen's Mystery Magazine*.

—John M. Reilly

Beck, Martin. The main character of ten police procedurals written between 1965 and 1975 by Sweden's Maj *Sjöwall and Per Wahlöö, Martin Beck is a Stockholm policeman who eventually rises to become head of the National Homicide Squad. Born in 1923, Beck is portrayed as the son of a lorry driver. He becomes a patrolman in 1944, then studies crime investigation at the police academy and joins the Stockholm CID in 1951. The same year, he meets and marries Inga. They have two children, but the marriage goes downhill over the years and ends in divorce. Beck eventually meets a new woman (in every sense of the word), Rhea Nielson.

The stories about Beck and his colleagues, particularly the early ones, are fiercely realistic descriptions of crime and detection, yet Beck is also an idealized character, a model investigator, and a truly good cop. He keeps his grievances to himself and consequently suffers from a chronic bad stomach. Though loyal and strictly professional, he is increasingly aware of the deteriorating spirit inside his organization, and at a turning point of his career, almost loses his life in a Christ-like attempt to atone for his colleagues' sins.

Sjöwall and Wahlöö conceived their series as a whole, a ten-part "Novel of a Crime" of Balzacian scope, the crime in question being the betrayal of socialist ideals by the Social Democrat government. The criticism becomes more outspoken as the series progresses, but the authors' attitudes are expressed less by Beck than by his friend, the left-wing hedonist Lennart Kollberg, and by the fierce-tempered, well-dressed giant detective Gunvald Larsson.

[*See also* Police Detective.]

—Nils Nordberg

Beef, Sergeant. A series character created by Rupert Croft-Cooke writing as Leo *Bruce, the working-class Sergeant Beef is a stolid village policeman and an obvious contrast to the *aristocratic sleuths and methodical inspectors of the day. Fond of darts, beer, and plain food, he is identifiable by his untidy ginger mustache and cockney speech. In his investigations Beef relies on doggedness and skepticism, interviewing relentlessly and recording all in a large notebook. When he is not promoted to Scotland Yard after two successful cases, he resigns to become a *private detective. His cases are chronicled by the prim Lionel (sometimes Stuart) Townsend. Beef consistently reproaches Townsend for failing to make him famous, or at least as well known as other sleuths; Townsend in turn laments the poor material with which he has to work. The comic byplay between detective and chronicler that frames each case may reflect the author's disappointment with the course of his own literary career.

[*See also* Country Constable; Police Detective; Sidekicks and Sleuthing Teams.]

—Susan Oleksiw

BELLOC LOWNDES, MARIE ADELAIDE (1868–1947), British writer. Sister of the Roman Catholic historian and poet Hilaire Belloc, Marie Belloc was educated in convent school and, like her brother, lived for a time in France. She married F. S. Lowndes, a member of the staff of the London *Times*. Under the name Mrs. Belloc Lowndes, she earned a place in the literary history of the crime and mystery genre because of her imaginative analysis of the Jack the Ripper murder in her novel *The Lodger* (1912). That novel is both a skillful treatment of psychology and an early illustration of the inverted detective story in which the killer is known from the start. *The Lodger* keeps readers attending closely to the story that gives away its solution by a dramatic rendering of the subjective experience of those in the house who wonder what their lodger is up to.

Belloc Lowndes published many other books, many of which feature female protagonists, predictive dreams, elements of the occult, and incidences of poisoning, placing them in the category of sensational crime writing. Her stories about Hercules Popeau are more direct contributions to detection fiction.

—John M. Reilly

BENTLEY, E(DMUND) C(LERIHEW) (1875–1956), British journalist, biographer, and detective novelist who wrote during the heyday of the Golden Age of the detective novel. He was educated at St. Paul's School, London, and at Merton College, Oxford. Called to the bar in 1902, he later served as leader (i.e., editorial), writer (1912–34), and chief literary critic (1940–47) for the *Daily Telegraph*. Bentley is the author of two detective novels, *Trent's Last Case* (1913; *The Woman in Black*) and, with H. Warner Allen, *Trent's Own Case* (1936); a collection of stories, *Trent Intervenes* (1938); and a mild

thriller, *Elephant's Work: An Enigma* (1950; *The Chill*). Among his other works are four volumes of light verse, starting with *Biography for Beginners* (1905), written in a verse form that he invented, the clerihew.

Bentley's reputation as a detective novelist rests on *Trent's Last Case*. This book, written in his spare time as an entry for a contest, is now considered to be one of the great examples of the Golden Age form. The novel's chief innovation was the introduction of a fallible *sleuth. Bentley himself noted that he wrote the novel as a reaction against what he saw as artificial eccentricities and extreme seriousness in Arthur Conan *Doyle's Sherlock *Holmes. Bentley also was influenced by Émile *Gaboriau's *L' Affair Lerouge* (1866; *The Widow Lerouge*), a novel turning on the mistaken conclusions of a *Great Detective in which Gaboriau concludes that "one's senses proved nothing."

Bentley also collaborated with other mystery writers on a roundtable book, *The Scoop and Behind the Screen* (1983). He edited works by Damon Runyon, and an anthology, *The Second Century of Detective Stories* (1938). Other works include *A Biography of Hester Dowden; Medium and Psychic Investigator* (1951) and *Those Days: An Autobiography* (1940).

—LeRoy L. Panek

BERKELEY, ANTHONY, pseudonym of Anthony Berkeley Cox (1893–1971), British author of detective novels and psychological crime fiction who also wrote as Francis Iles and A. Monmouth Platts. Cox began his literary career as a journalist known for his humor before introducing the inquisitive *amateur detective Roger Sheringham in his first detective novel, *The Layton Court Mystery* (1925), which offered a locked room mystery. This book was at first published anonymously, as was *The Wychford Poisoning Case* (1926), a reworking of the Florence Maybrick case. Thereafter Cox made use of his forenames alone for the Sheringham novels, as well as for a number of nonseries books.

Berkeley had a flair for confounding the reader's expectations, although sometimes at the cost of anticlimax, as in *Top Storey Murder* (1931; *Top Story Murder*) and *The Silk Stocking Murders* (1928). In *Panic Party* (1934; *Mr. Pidgeon's Island*), the far from infallible Sheringham guessed correctly but did not attempt to bring the culprit to justice. "The Avenging Chance" (in *The World's Best 100 Detective Stories*, 2nd ed. Eugene Thwig, 1929) is a clever Sheringham short story which Berkeley turned, with characteristic ingenuity, into *The Poisoned Chocolate Case* (1929), in which the Crimes Circle propounded a range of solutions to a murder mystery. Sheringham's theory, correct in the short story, was this time debunked; the amateur sleuth who came up with the truth proved to be Ambrose Chitterwick, a mild little man who took a leading role in *The Piccadilly Murder* (1929). The Crimes Circle resembled in some respects the Detection Club, which Berkeley helped to found; he contributed to several of the club's publications, notably the round-robin detective novel *The Floating Admiral* (1931).

In his preface to *The Wychford Poisoning Case*, Berkeley explained that he was trying to write a "psychological detective story." His dedication to *The Second Shot* (1930) reiterated the view that in detective stories of the future the element of puzzle "will no doubt remain, but it will become a puzzle of character rather than a puzzle of time, place, motive, and opportunity."

Berkeley's experiments were not always successful, and some of them seem unsophisticated today, but he played a key part in the development of the genre. His first two novels as Iles, *Malice Aforethought* (1931) and *Before the Fact* (1932), are notable examples of the inverted detective story. Their main interest lies in the description of the murderer's behavior, rather than in his unmasking, yet they still offer plot twists as ingenious as those of any conventional whodunit. *Before the Fact* was filmed by Alfred Hitchcock as *Suspicion*, but with a very different ending. Both books had a long-term influence upon the development of crime fiction, but Iles published only one more novel, *As for the Woman* (1939). After starting to write and review as Iles, Cox soon lost interest in Sheringham, and the last three books he wrote as Berkeley were nonseries. Of these, critics agree that by far the best is *Trial and Error* (1937), again featuring Chitterwick, which in its description of Lawrence Todhunter's misadventures while trying to commit an altruistic murder displays to the full Berkeley's gifts of wit and originality.

—Martin Edwards

BIGGERS, EARL DERR (1884–1933), American author and creator of Charlie *Chan. Born in Warren, Ohio, and educated at Harvard, Biggers began his writing career as a humor columnist for the Boston *Traveler*. Promoted to drama critic, he was fired for writing excessively scathing negative notices. Turning to the stage, he wrote an unsuccessful play, *If You're Only Human* (1912), before achieving major success with his first novel, *Seven Keys to Baldpate* (1913). A farcical mystery about a writer who holes up in an allegedly haunted inn to finish a story, *Baldpate* was adapted for the stage by George M. Cohan and subsequently filmed several times. Biggers, whose fictional impulses to pen humorously observed romance and gentle satire seemed perfectly in tune with the tastes and requirements of his time, followed by other romantic mystery melodramas, *Love Insurance* (1914) and *The Agony Column* (1916), and several more plays.

Moving west to Pasadena, California, for health reasons, Biggers wrote for motion pictures. He made his major contribution to mystery fiction with the introduction of one of the great fictional detectives, Charlie Chan of the Honolulu police, a character both lovable and formidable, whose image was intended to counter the sinister Chinese villains found in the works of writers like Sax *Rohmer, creator of *Fu Manchu. Ironically, Chan has himself come to be considered an ethnic stereotype, more because of the film adaptations than Biggers's original novels. Chan's first case, *The House Without a Key* (1925), was followed by *The Chinese Parrot* (1926), *Behind That Curtain* (1928), *The Black Camel* (1929), *Charlie Chan Carries On* (1930), and *Keeper of the Keys* (1932). Though the early Chan books did not offer models of fair play, by the last book in the series Biggers had been influenced by such American Golden Age writers as S. S. *Van Dine and Ellery *Queen to place more emphasis on the generous planting of clues. As a result of the immediate success of Chan, Biggers devoted most of his subsequent literary energies to the character, producing only one more non-Chan book, the romantic novella *Fifty Candles* (1926), before his death from heart disease. The collection *Earl Derr Biggers Tells Ten Stories* (1933) was published posthumously.

[*See also* Ethnic Sleuth.]

—Jon L. Breen

BLAKE, NICHOLAS, pseudonym under which the Irish-born poet Cecil Day-Lewis (1904–72; also known as C. Day Lewis) wrote a series of detective novels. The son of a Church of Ireland clergyman, Day-Lewis was raised in England and educated at Sherborne and at Wadham College, Oxford, where he became part of the celebrated group of young poets (dubbed "MacSpaunday") whose other members were W. H. Auden, Louis MacNeice, and Stephen Spender. After graduating from Oxford, he found work as a schoolmaster, was active in left-wing politics, and published several poetry collections. Throughout the remainder of his life he pursued several careers simultaneously: poet, translator, critic, broadcaster, and crime writer. Notably, he was professor of poetry at Oxford (1951–56) and, from 1968 until his death, poet laureate.

When Day-Lewis found himself in need of £100 to repair his cottage roof, in the mid-1930s, he promptly wrote a detective novel and thereby marked out an alternative career for himself which continued right up until a year or two before his death. The opening novel of the series written under the pseudonym Nicholas Blake was *A Question of Proof* (1935), set in a boys' preparatory school, and brimful of the kind of insouciance and ingenuity associated with the first Golden Age of the detective novel. It introduces the cool-headed investigator Nigel *Strangeways, whose amiability is not as deeply ingrained as it might seem. Like all classic detectives, Strangeways's purpose is to establish the facts whatever the cost.

The early Blake novels are marked by a distinctly literary flavor and plot-making expertise, as well as being topically left-wing in approach (this is toned down later in response to changes in the world at large, and in the author's own circumstances; his membership in the Communist Party was short-lived). They are very high-spirited and agreeable in tone—apart from Blake's unaccountable tendency to go in for generalizations on the subject of women, as when he remarks that "in the last resort decisions should be made—where women are concerned at least—by the instinct." The author's mastery of the deft plot is still evident as late as 1959. *The Widow's Cruise* of that year provides a good example of his craftsmanship; though after that, a slight touch of weariness sets in: *The Morning After Death* (1966), set in America, seems insufficiently resourceful; and in the last Blake novel of all, *The Private Wound* (1968; not a Strangeways title), an unresolved ambiguity in the author's attitude deforms the narrative. Interspersed with the Strangeways investigations are a number of out-and-out thrillers, all enjoyable, indeed, but more conventional in spirit than the exercises in straightforward detection. Novels like *There's Trouble Brewing* (1937), *Minute for Murder* (1947), and *End of Chapter* (1957)—a classic example of a novel set in the publishing milieu—are among the greatest pleasures of the genre.

—Patricia Craig

BLIND DETECTIVE. *See* Disability, Sleuth with a.

BLOCK, LAWRENCE (b. 1938), versatile American novelist, short-story writer, and writing teacher. Born in Buffalo, New York, Block initially wrote paperbacks and magazine tales in the tough tradition, but most of his series characters established his reputation as a humorist. Examples of such characters include insomniac spy Evan Tanner beginning with the novel *The Spy Who Couldn't Sleep* (1966); Leo Haig, the would-be Nero *Wolfe of two parody-pastiches written under the pseudonym Chip Harrison, *Make Out with Murder* (1974; UK: *Five Little Rich Girls*, as Block, 1984) and *The Topless Tulip Caper* (1975); and professional burglar Bernie Rhodenbarr in *Burglars Can't Be Choosers* (1977) and sequels. The cases of unlicensed New York *private eye Matthew *Scudder are in a much darker vein. The first three—*In the Midst of Death* (1976), *The Sins of the Fathers* (1976), and *Time to Murder and Create* (1977)—were overlooked paperback originals, but the hardcover cases, beginning with *A Stab in the Dark* (1981) and including the Edgar-winning *A Dance at the Slaughterhouse* (1991), are among the most honored products of the private-eye renaissance, combining classical plotting and a seemingly effortless style with a rare depth of character and emotional resonance. Block's own experiences with alcohol and alcoholism inspired him to portray Scudder as a sleuth who also triumphs over the problem.

—Jon L. Breen

BLUESTOCKING SLEUTH. "Bluestocking," a term sometimes used derisively for women engaged in literary pursuits, was coined in the eighteenth century in reference to literary gatherings in London at which the guests eschewed "full dress" and men wore blue worsted stockings instead of the customary black silk. The women who organized such soirées came to be known as Blue Stockingers or Blue Stocking Ladies. As a label designating a particular type of fictional female detective, the word "bluestocking" is used when the character in question is herself in some manner "bookish," often performing her amateur sleuthing in a setting congenial to either literature or scholarship. "Bluestocking" can also imply "unworldly," and is sometimes used in tandem with "tomboy," another mildly derisive term signifying a noticeable lack of traditional femininity. A famous example of this convergence is the character Jo March in Louisa May Alcott's *Little Women* (1868–69). But, with regard to mystery fiction, the important attribute of bluestocking *sleuths is that it is, above all, their intellects that guide them. In addition like tomboys, they are stubbornly active and energetic when it comes to unraveling clues and following a case to its conclusion.

Probably the genre's best-known example of the bluestocking type is Dorothy L. *Sayers's Harriet *Vane, who makes her first appearance in *Strong Poison* (1930)—the fifth novel featuring the debonair sleuth Lord Peter *Wimsey. A detective novelist by profession and herself a murder suspect in *Strong Poison*, Vane is at center stage in a pair of books, *Have His Carcase* (1932) and *Gaudy Night* (1935). The latter novel is literally a convention of bluestockings, for it is set at Vane's old college, Shrewsbury—a lightly disguised version of Somerville College, Oxford—Sayers's own alma mater, where the annual convocation, or "gaudy," is taking place. Although Vane's investigations into a malicious letter-writing campaign and episodes of mischievous vandalism plaguing the close-knit Shrewsbury community are in the end undertaken with Wimsey acting as consultant, he is unavailable to her throughout much of the story's unfolding. No stranger herself to the volatile imbalance between emotions and intellect that lies at the heart of the college disturbances, Vane responds to the complex situation with the mix of empathy, intuition, and heartfelt concern. Vane's success proves that the bluestocking detective is very like her less erudite sleuthing sisters in all her most fundamental reactions and tactics, and that her tendency perhaps to overanalyze any given course of action can in fact be an added strength helping lead to an acceptable and humane resolution.

Another important bluestocking detective is Amanda *Cross's Professor Kate *Fansler, a member of the English faculty on a large New York City campus, whose debut case was *In the Last Analysis* (1964). The Fansler novels echo themes found in Sayers (who was, as Cross has testified, one of her major influences), for Kate Fansler, like Vane, is prideful and intellectually set apart from the average woman. Yet Fansler, too, is a woman who also readily allows herself to take risks in the name of intellectual curiosity and who often finds herself functioning as a source of steadiness in the midst of chaos when murder intrudes into her academic milieu.

Elizabeth *Peters has created her own versions of the bluestocking detective three times over. Peters's characters Vicky Bliss (*Borrower of the Night*, 1973), Jacqueline Kirby (*The Seventh Sinner*, 1972), and especially Amelia

Peabody (*Crocodile on the Sandbank*, 1975) all qualify as bluestockings because it is their confidence in their own learning that fuels their forthright independence; in turn, it is this quality which enables them to act as puzzle solvers and amateur agents of justice.

Historically, the *spinster sleuth has always been far more common than the bluestocking detective (who may or may not be unmarried). Examples of bluestocking sleuths from the past are surprisingly rare. One could try to squeeze Mignon G. *Eberhart's Susan Dare (*The Cases of Susan Dare*, 1934) into the pigeonhole, since she, like Vane, makes her living as a author of mystery fiction. But in fact, Dare is simply an example of a plucky "regular" girl whose adventures are marked by no "bookish" flavor. Lucy Pym, in Josephine *Tey's *Miss Pym Disposes* (1946), is also a writer, and her foray into detection takes place at a women's college, but there her resemblance with Vane ends, for the contagious joy Sayers takes in such things as the quote-capping duels between Vane and Wimsey, and in the scholarly sanctuary that Shrewsbury provides for its female fellows, is entirely missing.

[*See also* Academic Sleuth.]

—Michele Slung

Bonaparte, Napoleon. Detective-Inspector Napoleon "Bony" Bonaparte, the creation of expatriate English author Arthur W. *Upfield, appears in twenty-nine of Upfield's thirty-four books and in numerous short stories. Bony is based on Tracker Leon Wood, a man whom Upfield met twice in his wanderings through Australia. Half British and half Aboriginal, Bony is in his early to middle forties. Like Herman Melville's Queequeg before him, Bony benefits from his mixture of races. He is described in *Sands of Windee* (1931) as "the citadel within which warred the native Australian and the pioneering, thrusting Britisher . . . a little superior to the general run of men in that in him were combined most of the virtues of both races and extraordinarily few of the vices." Five feet ten inches tall, he is slight of frame, and "was never handsome." Bony is married to "half-caste" Marie, who appears only as a reference point, and has three sons, all college graduates and headed toward success in life.

A man of multiple capabilities, Bony can train the wildest horses, endure great physical strain and pain, and be a savage antagonist or gentle advisor; but his greatest skill lies in tracking. Among a nation of aboriginals noted for their ability to read tracks, Bony is preeminent. Though a relentless pursuer of outlaws, Bony is gentle with people, especially young women of both races. Although he is well known throughout Australia, Bony is often the victim of discrimination, especially by young women, and is often called "Nigger." By his author he is properly called "The Spirit of Australia," since he possesses great resilience and humanitarian spirit (such traits are frequently discussed in articles in the *Bony Bulletin*, edited by Philip T. Asdell and devoted exclusively to discussion of Upfield and Bony). To a world that knew little of the Australian Aborigine, Bony represents a fair and unprejudiced picture, though treated with what his author felt was the truth about his race. Bony was portrayed in a 1972 Australian television series. However, the character has been repudiated at Australia's aboriginal university, Monash University, for what is claimed to be an unsympathetic picture of the aboriginal people.

—Ray B. Browne

BOUCHER, ANTHONY, pseudonym of William Anthony Parker White (1911–1968), American mystery writer and influential critic. Although his novels were considered "modest triumphs," Boucher was best known as a critic, editor, and anthologist. From 1951 to 1968, he wrote the popular "Criminals at Large" column for the *New York Times Book Review*. At the same time, he reviewed fantasy and science fiction for the *New York Herald Tribune Book Review*.

The Case of the Seven of Calvary (1937), Boucher's first detective novel, sets the stage for the six that follow. Like them, it has fair-play puzzle plot in the tradition of the work of John Dickson *Carr and Ellery *Queen, favoring complex clues and dry humor. The protagonist is Dr. John Ashwin, Professor of Sanskrit at the University of California. Although Ashwin never appears in any of the later novels, Boucher does use Irish private detective Fergus O'Breen in four of them: *The Case of the Crumpled Knave* (1939), *The Case of the Baker Street Irregulars* (1940; *Blood on Baker Street*), *The Case of the Solid Key* (1941), and *The Case of the Seven Sneezes* (1942). Under the pseudonym Theo Durrant, Boucher, with others, published *The Marble Forest* (1951, *The Big Fear*). Under the pseudonym H. H. Holmes he published *Nine Times Nine* (1940) and *Rocket to the Morgue* (1942), both featuring series character Sister Ursula. His mystery short stories, the best of which appear in *Exeunt Murderers* (1983), are highly regarded, especially those featuring Nick Noble, a former policeman and alcoholic. He also published two other short-story collections: *Far and Away: Eleven Fantasy and Science-Fiction Stories* (1953) and *The Compleat Werewolf and Other Stories of Fantasy and Science Fiction* (1969).

Anthony Boucher was a true Renaissance man. In addition to novels, short stories, and radio plays, he edited eight anthologies of crime stories and two anthologies of science fiction. The best of his numerous reviews were published in *Multiplying Villainies: Selected Mystery Criticism, 1942–1968* (1973). He also contributed frequently to *Opera News*, founded the Golden Voices program for Pacific Radio and hosted it for twenty years, served a term as president of Mystery Writers of America, translated mysteries from French, Spanish, and Portuguese, and regularly indulged his passion for sports and poker.

Boucher was a three-time recipient of the Mystery Writers of America's Edgar Allan Poe Award for nonfiction. It is for his nonfiction that he is best remembered—those chatty, urbane, and unfailingly polite reviews in which he championed the literary merit of the mystery story. Quoting William *Shakespeare, he once referred to good detective stories as "the abstracts and brief chronicles of the time," pointing out that they are invaluable records of the times they mirror. His pioneer efforts to gain recognition for the art of mystery writing are celebrated in an annual convention of authors and fans known as the Bouchercon, at which the awards known as Anthonys are presented.

—Thomas Whissen

BRADDON, MARY ELIZABETH (1835–1915), British author, a leading writer of the lurid sensation novels that shocked Victorian moralists in the 1860s and later. Her own life caused her to question the hypocrisy of conventional morality. Her father, a solicitor, deserted the family when Braddon was four years old. In 1857, when she was twenty-two, Braddon went on the stage under an assumed name to support her mother and herself. In 1860, a wealthy admirer provided her with a means of support so that she could write, but she soon cohabited with John Maxwell, a London publisher of periodicals whose wife had been confined to a Dublin asylum. Braddon helped him to raise his five children and bore him five more, two of whom became novelists. Braddon married Maxwell in 1874, after the death of his wife.

Although Braddon also edited magazines, produced more than seventy novels, and wrote drama and poetry, her 1862 novel *Lady Audley's Secret* remains her best-known work. It concerns arson, bigamy, child desertion, disguised identity, insanity, and murder among the genteel classes. Such ingredients were the staples of a prolific output that earned her the sobriquet Queen of the Circulating Libraries.

Lady Audley's Secret was one of the earliest novels to feature an *amateur detective. Braddon's *sleuth, Robert Audley, displays persistence, close observation, and inductive reasoning to unravel tangled clues that point to his aunt's crimes. In this and other of her early novels, Braddon constructed mysteries around incident and focused on the techniques of detection. Later, she became more interested in characterization. In *The Fatal Three* (1888), regarded by her biographer Robert Lee Wolff as her best novel, the mystery is spun around the psychology of the characters.

Braddon also created a professional detective, John Faunce, who appears in *Rough Justice* (1898) and *His Darling Sin* (1899). Like other early creators of series sleuths, she endowed hers with a memorable habit—in Faunce's case, the reading of French novels. She was herself a Francophile and influenced by Balzac, Flaubert, and Zola.

—Michael Steed

Bradley, Mrs. Adela Beatrice Lestrange, a "little, thin, black-eyed, witch-like being" is the benign but alarming center of Gladys *Mitchell's detective novels written over a span of more than fifty years. Medically qualified, she serves as a psychiatric adviser to the Home Office. Her adherence to Freudian interpretations originally invoked police animosity, but her methods were justified by success. She also has an assistant who is married to a CID detective; Bradley herself is related to most of England's chief constables.

Her "saurian smile" initially alarms, but her "beautiful, low, contralto voice" seduces all save the evil. She finds astonishing empathy with the young. Perhaps her open-minded approach wins their trust: She accepts the occult, ancient Greek mysticism, and revelatory dreams, and is prepared to believe in the Loch Ness Monster.

Her three marriages have left her tolerant of men but never easily deceived. Once involved in defending her son on a murder charge, she is herself prepared to overlook murders or even commit one herself. Professionally, she encounters incest, gender-crossing, impersonation, and murders of—and by—children. None of it ever fazes her, although cruelty and malice provoke her anger. Her domestic staff, especially her chauffeur, serve her for decades, despite a daily round which might involve sheltering suspected criminals or fighting off Bradley's would-be attackers. Acknowledged by her young assistant as an Amazonian equal, she is capable herself in armed combat.

—K. D. Prince

BRAMAH, ERNEST (1868–1942), English author, the creator of Max *Carrados. Many details of his life are uncertain. Born Ernest Bramah Smith near Manchester, England, he spent time as a journalist on the magazine *Today* and as editor of the *Minister* and briefly was a farmer, a career he relates in *English Farming and Why I Turned It Up* (1894).

Bramah, who dropped the family name Smith from his author's byline, began a literary career with short stories concerning a Chinese storyteller published as *The Wallet of Kai Lung* (1900). The chinoiserie of these stories was evidently appealing enough to allow Bramah to continue the series through seven additional volumes, the last, *Kai Lung Beneath the Mulberry Tree*, appearing in 1940. Bramah's reputation in popular fiction rests, however, on the achievement of the three collections and one novel relating the cases of Carrados, who is both the genre's most compelling example of a blind *sleuth and a successful example of the *Great Detective.

—John M. Reilly

BRAND, CHRISTIANNA (1907–1988), British author, one of the last in the Golden Age tradition. She was born in the Far East, where her motherless first years were lonely and unhappy. This changed when she was sent to a convent school in England. After various short-lived and ill-paid jobs during the 1930s, she turned to writing and made a notably assured debut with *Death in High Heels* (1941), which included a fictional vengeance on one of her supervisors during her hungry years. Popular success came with *Green for Danger* (1945), which was filmed with Alistair Sim as the raffish, shabby, nicotine-stained Inspector Cockrill, her series detective based on her father-in-law.

Brand's high-spiritedness, often noted, should not be allowed to hide the craftsmanlike qualities of her books: They are meticulously planned, written with a sense of style rare in Golden Age writers, and the sympathetic characterization avoids stereotypes and caricatures. The exuberant and stylish *Tour de Force* (1955), with its corrupt and sinister island of San Juan, where the natives speak a bastard Italo-Spanish entirely of Brand's devising, represents her writing at its most sunny and energetic. *Cat and Mouse* (1950) is darker, fruitfully drawing on the traditions of the Gothic novel. In *Green for Danger* the natural liveliness flourishes in a context of war and random devastation. Her last novel, *The Rose in Darkness* (1979), underappreciated and never published in the United States, displays a brilliant circularity in its plotting and a familiar interest in the self-absorption of the attractive young.

Brand was, like Ngaio *Marsh, a lover of intricate and involved plots. Only in *Death of Jezebel* (1949) does this militate against the novel, becoming tiresome and unlikely, and destroying character interest. Elsewhere she always retains a light touch, so that her ingenuity and her exuberance go hand in hand, carrying the reader along. In all her work there is a strong element of the comedy of manners: social gestures, public words and behavior, become indices of generosity or hardness of heart. Though she always emphasized that her aim was to entertain, writing a whodunit was for her a rigorous intellectual discipline, and when other preoccupations prevented her giving her writing that kind of concentration she preferred to turn to less demanding forms. At the time of her death she was engaged on a crime novel featuring a duchess as detective and a barmaid called Topless among the cast list.

—Robert Barnard

Brandstetter, Dave, fictional insurance investigator and *private detective in Joseph *Hansen's twelve-volume series, starting with *Fadeout* (1970) and ending with *A Country of Old Men: The Last Dave Brandstetter Mystery* (1991). Not only was Brandstetter the first gay protagonist in the genre to reach a large mainstream audience, but he is one of a very few characters in detective fiction to have aged at approximately the same pace as the novels appeared. Thus, when he suffers a fatal seizure in the final novel, he is in his mid-sixties. While Brandstetter's sex life is never a focus of the series, neither is it ignored. After the death of Rod Fleming, his lover of twenty-odd years (before the time of the first novel), Brandstetter meets Cecil Harris, a young African American news reporter, in *The Man Everybody Was Afraid Of* (1978); they establish a relationship in *Gravedigger* (1982) that, though rarely described in physical detail, provides a secondary storyline throughout the remainder of the series.

Hansen insisted that he hoped to destroy stereotypes of homosexual figures in mystery fiction by creating Brandstetter as a thoroughly masculine character who happens to be unabashedly gay. Although there is some violence in nearly every book, Brandstetter is so sensitive and introspective—a lover of esoteric classical music, intellectually challenging literature, and gourmet cuisine—that he does not really fit into the hard-boiled mode. He is, therefore, a unique individual rather than a type, and has become a model for characters like Michael Nava's gay lawyer-detective, Henry Rios.

Most of Hansen's plots are structured in the pattern of the private-eye genre. In the middle and later novels, Brandstetter is involved in cases that center on socially and politically charged issues such as pornography, ultra-right-wing militias, environmental pollution, and AIDS. He is intensely aware of mortality and loss, a theme that becomes more dominant as the series draws to a close.

—Landon Burns

BRAUN, LILIAN JACKSON (b. ?), American writer of "The Cat Who . . ." series of mysteries featuring the amateur detective Jim Qwilleran and his pair of Siamese cats, KoKo and Yum Yum. Born in Boston, Massachusetts, she worked as an advertising copywriter for fifteen years and as an editor for the *Detroit Free Press* for thirty years. She began writing short fiction about cats after the death of her beloved Siamese cat. Novels soon followed, beginning with *The Cat Who Could Read Backwards* (1967). The cats in Braun's books exhibit normal feline behavior, which Qwilleran nevertheless often interprets as significant to the solution of crimes. Some of the cats' antics may be new to those who do not own Siamese cats, as is the case in *The Cat Who Ate Danish Modern* (1967), which reveals some Siamese cats' proclivity to eat wool. The book also showcases Braun's interest in interior decorating. As a newspaper features writer, Qwilleran gains entrée to many different worlds, and his assignments often lead him to meet eccentric characters in trouble.

[*See also* Animals.]

—Rosemary Herbert

BREEN, JON L(INN) (b. 1943), American librarian, bibliographer, literary critic, anthologist, and writer of mystery fiction, including parodies. Born in Montgomery, Alabama, he earned a Bachelor's degree from Pepperdine College in Los Angeles, and a Master's degree in library science from the University of Southern California in Los Angeles. He served in the U.S. Army before embarking on a career as a librarian and building a reputation as a longtime, and highly-respected, mystery reviewer *for Wilson Library Bulletin* and *Ellery Queen's Mystery Magazine*.

Combining his broad knowledge of the genre with appreciation of the needs of literature scholars, he produced two bibliographies of works about the genre: *What About Murder?* (1981) and *What About Murder*

(1981–1991)? (1993). He also put together the memorably-titled *The Girl in the Pictorial Wrapper* (1972), a bibliography of paperback originals. In addition, he is the author of feature articles (many for *The Armchair Detective*) and a book about courtroom fiction, *Novel Verdicts* (1984). He has co-edited several books including anthologies of detective fiction and of essays on the subject. Among these books are *Murder California Style* (1987), edited with John *Ball, and *Synod of Sleuths; Essays on Judeo-Christian Detective Fiction* (1990), edited with Ed *Gorman and others.

Breen's own fiction reflects the author's enthusiasm for sports, books, and some classic mystery writers. One of his series characters, umpire Ed Gordon, appears in several short stories. Another series sleuth, racetrack announcer Jerry Brogan, appears in several novels beginning with *Listen for the Click* (1983). Introduced in *The Gathering Place* (1984), Rachel Hennings is a bookstore owner who encounters crime. Breen reveals a winning sense of humor and keen eye for style in his parodies of classic mystery writing. They are collected in *Hair of the Sleuthhound* (1982) and *Drowning Ice Cube and Other Stories* (1999).

—Rosemary Herbert

BRETT, SIMON (ANTHONY LEE) (b. 1945), British author of plays, radio and television dramas, children's books, and detective fiction. Born in Surry, England, he was educated at Dulwich College in London and at Wadham College, Oxford, where he was president of the prestigious Oxford Dramatic Society. Before turning to full-time writing in 1980, he worked as a producer for BBC Radio, and for London Weekend Television. The father of three, he is married and lives in Arundel, England, on a property dominated by an Anglo-Saxon burial mound.

Brett continues to write for radio, but to readers of detective fiction, he is best known for two series of novels written in the comic, cozy tradition, and for the uncharacteristically dark but very strong novel, *A Shock to the System* (1984). Michael Caine starred in the 1990 film that was made of the latter.

Brett introduced his first series detective, Charles Paris, in *Cast in Order of Disappearance* (1975). An actor with a fondness for taking in drink and spewing out literary allusions, Paris is an actor who lives up to the title of the tenth novel of the series, *Not Dead, Only Resting* (1984). The word "resting" is here used as an actor's euphemism for "out of work" or "between roles." Paris may not always have a stage role but Brett's works do take readers behind the scenes of various acting venues, including a radio studio in *The Dead Side of the Mike* (1980).

In *A Nice Class of Corpse* (1986), Brett introduced series sleuth Mrs. Melita Pargeter, a new widow who discovers her husband's business doings were less than legitimate. Much humor derives from Mrs. Pargeter's efforts to use criminal connections to do good. With *The*

Body on the Beach (2000), Brett began a series of books set in and around the fictional village of Fethering. His short stories are collected in two volumes, *A Box of Tricks* (1985; *Tickled to Death*) and *Crime Writers and Other Animals* (1998).

[*See also* Amateur Detective.]

—Rosemary Herbert

Brown, Father, East Anglian Roman Catholic priest and *sleuth created by the British author G. K. *Chesterton and featured in fifty short stories collected in five volumes. The series began in 1911 with *The Innocence of Father Brown;* continued with *The Wisdom of Father Brown* (1914), *The Incredulity of Father Brown* (1926), *The Secret of Father Brown* (1927); and concluded in 1935 with the *Scandal of Father Brown.* The Father Brown stories tend to be conduits through which Chesterton, a Roman Catholic and a political and social traditionalist, communicated his theological and philosophical ideas. Although the plots generally emphasize symbolism rather than realism, they are made brilliant by clever characterization, lyrical writing, and constant wit.

Loosely based on a priest-friend of the author, Father John O'Connor, Father Brown is short, plump, myopic, and ostensibly absent-minded and unworldly. Yet this habitually umbrella-carrying cleric is unshocked by the most grotesque and morbid murders and other crimes. The stories often involve Chesterton's favorite literary device, the paradox, and are concerned with the perception of the extraordinary within the seemingly most ordinary. This is perhaps best illustrated by the story of "The Invisible Man" (in *The Innocence of Father Brown*), where the criminal is revealed by Brown to be someone disguised as the mailman, a person so regularly seen and so disregarded that he is able to go about his illegal business unnoticed.

Father Brown relies on intuitive detection, psychological insight, and an extraordinary knowledge of theology and moral teaching. If he shares an asset with any other fictional detective, it would be Agatha *Christie's Miss Jane *Marple. Both are at first sight no apparent threat to wrongdoers and neither has any objection to being seen as innocent or naive, since such an image aids them in their work.

Ironically, Chesterton thought the Father Brown stories his least important works, believing them to be mere slingshots compared to the great artillery of his books of Christian philosophy, such as *The Everlasting Man* (1925), or his novels, such as *The Napoleon of Notting Hill* (1904). It is the Father Brown stories, however, that remain the most popular of Chesterton's massive output.

[*See also* Clerical Sleuth.]

—Michael Coren

BROWN, FREDRIC (WILLIAM) (1906–1972), American mystery and science fiction writer. Brown began life as an office worker, but after one of his stories was accepted for publication when he was thirty, he became a proofreader and then a journalist. After a long apprenticeship writing some 300 stories for pulp magazines, his *The Fabulous Clipjoint* (1947) won the Mystery Writers of America Edgar award for best first novel. There followed twenty-two other mysteries, of which the most notable are *Night of the Jabberwock* (1951) and *Knock Three-One-Two* (1959). Brown's virtues at his best were his direct prose, his grip-of-iron storytelling, and his click-into-place plots. His unique gift was to blend convincingly the highly romantic and the sturdily everyday, as illustrated by the fantastic and ominous title *The Screaming Mimi* (1949), where a doll of that name plays a central part, eventually revealed as a storekeeper's mnemonic for catalogue item SM1.

—H. R. F. Keating

BRUCE, LEO, pseudonym of Rupert Croft-Cooke (1903–1979), English author. A prolific writer in his own name, he is now more celebrated for his pseudonymous works, all traditional detective novels written within and gleefully exploiting the whodunit conventions. Eight books published between 1936 and 1952 feature William *Beef, a plebeian provincial police sergeant who turns private investigator; a further twenty-three from 1955 to 1974 concern Carolus Deene, a wealthy history master at a minor public school. Both are outsiders: Beef because of his beery vulgarity, Deene because of a cynical detachment from life. The Beef books are less hidebound and range from a mischievous debut, in which Beef solves a mystery that has defeated Lord Simon Plimsoll, Amer Picon, and Monsignor Smith, to the somber episode that closes his career (apart from a few collected stories). The Deene series is more formulaic, with familiar rituals that lose their freshness only toward the flagging end of a long run. Bruce's level of dexterity is high: He is up to all the tricks and rings the changes on them with verve and daring. He is also consistently amusing, with a wit acknowledged by Noel Coward and a lively sense of his duty to entertain and satisfy the reader.

[*See also* Academic Sleuth; Country Constable; Private Detective.]

—B. A. Pike

BUCHANAN, EDNA (RYDZIK) (b. 1939), American journalist and crime novelist. The Paterson, New Jersey, native's climb to success required brains and determination. The daughter of an absent father, Buchanan had a difficult childhood and youth, dropping out of high school in tenth grade to work full time in a factory. She moved to Florida in 1973 and got a job as an obituary writer for the *Miami Beach Daily Sun.* Then she joined the staff of the *Miami Herald,* where she gained fame taking risks to get her stories, and writing her reports in a very original, hard-edged voice. The reporting won her the Pulitzer Prize in 1986. Her newspaper columns are collected in *The Corpse Had a Familiar Face* (1987) and *Never Let Them See You Cry* (1992).

In her first novel, *Contents Under Pressure* (1992), Buchanan introduced Britt Montero, a reporter who covers the police beat for the fictional *Miami News.* Montero often places herself in danger in order to turn in copy to the odious assistant city editor Gretchen Platt, and to solve the crimes she comes across. Additional series characters include Montero's lover, police major Kendall McDonald; her meddling mother; and news photographer Lottie Dane. Montero solves a different kind of crime in each of the novels.

In 2000, Buchanan and several other mystery writers (including Carl *Hiassen and Elmore *Leonard) co-wrote a novel, *Naked Came the Manatee,* with each contributing a chapter. It was first published in installments in the *Miami Herald's Tropic Magazine* and then in book format.

—Rosemary Herbert

BURKE, JAMES LEE (b. 1936), Texas-born crime writer known for regional mysteries featuring the Cajun detective Dave *Robicheaux and, more recently, Billy Bob Smith, a former Texas Ranger who practices law in a town called Deaf Smith, Texas. Born in Houston, Burke was raised along the Texas-Louisiana coast of the Gulf of Mexico. He attended the University of Southeastern Louisiana for two years and then earned his bachelor's and master's degrees in English from the University of Missouri. He has worked as an English professor, social worker, reporter, oil field worker, land surveyor, and member of the United States Forest Service. Married since 1960, he is the father of four. Before beginning his series of private eye novels about Robicheaux, Burke wrote five mainstream novels and a volume of short stories. His 1986 novel, *The Lost Get-Back Boogie,* was nominated for a Pulitzer Prize.

In 1987, his first crime novel, *Neon Rain,* won him immediate attention. He was not alone in placing his crime in a vividly drawn American regional setting; nor was he original in giving his detective a drinking problem. But Burke's particular settings—New Orleans and the Louisiana bayou country, Texas and Montana—are particularly rich with local customs, food, and regional speech. Burke also uses the contrast between city life in New Orleans and rural existence in the bayou to excellent effect. Robicheaux's alcoholism is set in context of a failed marriage, disturbing memories of the Vietnam War and fourteen years of work in the New Orleans Police Department. By the end of *Neon Rain,* Robicheaux leaves the police department to open a bait shop. In subsequent cases he works on his own and occasionally with the New Iberia Police department. Many of the cases put the victims and/or Robicheaux in very violent circumstances. They also highlight the author's concerns with social problems and the environment. Burke introduced his new series character, Smith, in *Cimmaron Rose* (1997), a novel in which the lawyer is called upon to defend his illegitimate son in a murder case. Not only does the sudden appearance of the son literally bring back a past mistake, but Smith still suffers from another tragic error he perpetrated—the accidental killing of his best friend.

—Rosemary Herbert

BUTLER, GWENDOLINE (WILLIAMS) (b. 1922), English historian and prolific author. Best-known for writing police procedurals under her own name and the pseudonym Jennie Melville, she also wrote romances, gothic suspense, and numerous non-series crime novels. Born in Blackheath, London, she earned a bachelor's degree in history from Lady Margaret Hall, Oxford, where she later taught medieval history. She also taught at Oxford's Somerville College and St. Anne's, and at the University of London. She married and had one child, a daughter.

Butler began her mystery writing career with *Receipt for Murder* (1956). A year later, she introduced police Inspector John Coffin in *Dead in a Row* (1957). She turned out a Coffin title every year until the 1970s, a decade when she wrote three non-series books as Butler and six more under the pseudonym Jennie Melville, three Coffin books and one book featuring her second series character Charmian Daniels. Her output during following decades is equally impressive.

Throughout the long-running Coffin series, Butler developed the character from an analytical detective with a penchant for understanding the criminals' motivation to a man whose personal life becomes important to the books. He faces marital problems, divorce and revelations about his family history as the series progresses.

Introduced in *Come Home and Be Killed* (1962), Daniels is a policewoman who strives to succeed in a male-dominated profession. Often assigned difficult cases involving women who are *victims or perpetrators of crimes, Daniels is shown as earnest about her work, which often gets in the way of her personal life.

Her 2000 novel, *The Kind Cried Murder!*, introduces Mearns and Denny, a pair of special agents in the court of England's King George III. The book reflects the author's interest in historical settings, which she also used in some of her romances, gothic thrillers and mysteries such as the CWA Silver Dagger-winning book, *A Coffin for Pandora* (1973; *Sarsen Place*), which takes place in 1880s Oxford.

[*See also* Police Detective.]

—Rosemary Herbert

C

Cadfael, Brother, figure who is central to, and whose adventures are recounted in, novels and short stories written by Edith Mary Pargeter under her well-known pseudonym, Ellis *Peters. Set in twelfth-century Britain, the series—dubbed *The Chronicles of Brother Cadfael*—is set during the time of the war between King Stephen (who reigned from 1135 to 1154) and his cousin the Empress Maud for control of the English throne. The works especially concern the effects of that conflict on the West Midlands. A native Welshman, Cadfael ap Meilyr ap Dafydd serves as Peters's *amateur detective. At age fourteen he left his home in Trefriw, Gwynedd, to serve in the household of an English wool merchant living in Shrewsbury. Years later, after participating in the successful First Crusade (1095–1099) and other adventures abroad, Cadfael returned to England and joined the Benedictine monastery at the Abbey of St. Peter and St. Paul in Shrewsbury, serving as gardener, herbalist, and, occasionally, translator. The mysteries in which he appears develop from the multiple roles served by an abbey. As land and property owner, pilgrimage site, keeper of saints' relics, hospital, and guest hostel, the abbey garners a steady flow of people and information. Cadfael's wide experiences, his keen understanding of human behavior, his unceasing curiosity, his expertise as an herbalist familiar with medicines and poisons, and his dual nature—both of the world and separate from it—allow the monk to solve the mysteries presented to him.

[*See also* Clerical Sleuth.]

—Kathryn Alexander

CAIN, JAMES M(ALLAHAN) (1892–1977), American author of hard-boiled fiction, including short stories and, several crime novels, notably the tough-guy novel *The Postman Always Rings Twice* (1934). Cain grew up in an atmosphere of culture in two small towns in Maryland. His father was a teacher at St. John's College in Annapolis and president of Washington College in Chestertown. His mother's singing talent inspired Cain to consider a career as an opera singer; his *Serenade* (1937) and *Career in C Major and Other Stories* (1938) are about opera singers, and music is a major element in many of his novels.

Having taught mathematics and journalism at Washington College and St. John's, Cain pursued a long career in journalism. He benefitted from H. L. Mencken's guidance in Baltimore and, on returning from service in World War I, worked under Walter Lippman in New York. After a stint as assistant to Harold Ross at the *New Yorker*, he wrote film scripts in Hollywood. Paradoxically, Cain's movie scripts failed, but most of his novels are inherently cinematic and have been made into movies—some more than once. Most of his works are set in California, but his favorite, and one of his finest, was *The Butterfly* (1947), a mystery of progeny, incest, and murder, set in the coal fields of West Virginia.

It was in Los Angeles that he heard the hard-boiled, first-person voice that made him famous in *The Postman Always Rings Twice*. It is not until the end of this novel that the reader discovers, as in other Cain novels, that the compelling confessional voice that seems to speak aloud is spelled out in a written account. In most of his fiction, mastery of the aggressive American vernacular is the major characteristic of Cain's style. His narrators are average educated Americans who lust for a woman who can be won only by some extraordinary act—usually an act of violence, in which the woman also plays a key role.

This pattern recurs in Cain's second-most-successful crime novel, *Double Indemnity* (1943; also published in *Three of a Kind*). Here an insurance agent helps his client's wife kill her husband so they can share the insurance and a life of passion. The theme of all Cain's novels is the wish that comes true, with catastrophic consequences. The man wishes to have the woman, the woman wishes to have the money, and the man has the means, a cunning intelligence, know-how, and violence. Forcing the wish to come true, the lovers suffer on what Cain called "the love rack." Usually, the woman betrays the man at the end, as in *Double Indemnity* and *The Magician's Wife* (1965).

The urban criminal milieu is explored in *Love's Lovely Counterfeit* (1942; also published in *Three of Hearts*), and the inside-dopester details of the white-collar crime of embezzlement is central to *The Embezzler* (1944; also published in *Three of a Kind*). The four novels of his later years, two of which were published posthumously, are interesting primarily in the different ways they employ familiar Cain elements, including religion, the lure and power of information, and—a universal interest—food.

Crime, usually murder, plays a role even in novels like *Serenade*, *The Moth* (1948), and *Galatea* (1953), all set in Cain's home state, Maryland, and in the two Civil War novels, *Past All Dishonor* (1946) and *Mignon* (1963). *Career in C Major*, a comedy that inspired three movie versions, and *Mildred Pierce* (1941), unusual in having a female protagonist and a third-person narration, lack the crime element. However, the first-person criminal confession is such a distinctive characteristic of Cain's novels that many readers mistakenly think of him as a detective novelist. His only detective narrators are the sheriff in

Sinful Woman (1948) and the insurance investigator, modeled after Keyes in *Double Indemnity*, in *Jealous Woman* (1950); these were published together in a single volume (*Jealous Woman*) in Britain in 1955.

Compared with the voices and narration of private-eye novelists with whom he was often compared, Dashiell *Hammett and Raymond *Chandler, the diction of Cain's narrators has the pure simplicity of Horace McCoy and of the more literary Hemingway; his plots were more unified and tighter. Cain agreed with the observation that his best work was "pure"—conceived and executed to produce an experience for the reader, rather than to illustrate a moral or to lay out any other thematic trappings. That purity and the stacatto, metallic style of *The Postman Always Rings Twice* so affected Albert Camus that, in a revised version, he adapted it to the first-person narration of *The Stranger* (1942).

[*See also* Antihero; Femme Fatale.]

—David Madden

Campion, Albert, *aristocratic sleuth created by Margery *Allingham, also seen as an exemplar of the *silly ass sleuth. Introduced in *The Crime at Black Dudley* (1929, *The Black Dudley Murder*), Campion is a mysterious figure himself. Although he solves the crime, Allingham notes that he has a police record. In the first several of the twenty-one novels in which he appears, much of his sleuthing success depends upon his talent to deceive. He hides his intelligence behind a vapid exterior. As the series progresses, Allingham hints at Campion's aristocratic—even royal—heritage. She also endows the character with more depth and gives him a romantic interst, Lady Amanda Fitton, who becomes his wife. While Allingham no longer mentions Campion's criminal past, she does suggest his valet, Magersfontein *Lugg, has underworld connections. Campion also appears in short stories originally published in the *Strand* and in two novels penned by Allingham's husband, Youngman Carter.

—Rosemary Herbert

CARLON, PATRICIA (b. 1927), Australian writer of psychological suspense and, under the pen name Barbara Christie and other pseudonyms, romance novels and newspaper, magazine and radio work. Born in Wagga Wagga, she was educated in New South Wales before she moved to Sydney. Like her contemporary Patricia *Highsmith, to whom she is often likened, Carlon likes to look at misfits or literally lost individuals who face physical and psychological isolation. In Carlon's case the characters' forlorn situations are underlined by depiction of atmospheric rural Australian settings. She is also inclined to write about young characters at difficult junctures in their lives. For instance, in *The Price of an Orphan* (1964), nine-year-old Johnnie, whose father is incarcerated and whose mother is dead, is fostered out to a couple who live on a remote cattle station in the Australian Outback. In *The Unquiet Night* (1965), an-

other nine-year-old, this time a girl called Ann, is the subject of a stalker after she observes a murderer while on an outing in a nature park. When a 15-month-old boy is kidnapped in *Crime of Silence* (1965), Carlon explores the guilt experienced by George Winton, who paid ransom rather than going to the authorities after his young child was abducted. By securing his child's safety in this manner, it appears he allowed the kidnapper to strike again. Kidnapping is also the crime under investigation in an earlier novel, *Who Are You, Linda Condrick?* (1962), but the plight of the outsider is truly at the heart of this mystery set on a remote sheep station.

[*See also* Outcasts and Outsiders.]

—Rosemary Herbert

CARR, JOHN DICKSON (1906–1977), American author of detective novels and historical crime fiction. He also wrote as Carter Dickson, Carr Dickson, and Roger Fairbairn.

Carr was born in Uniontown, Pennsylvania, the son of Julia and Wooda Nicholas Carr. His eclectic tastes in history and literature grew from happy boyhood hours spent in the vast library of his father, a lawyer and politician. Carr's first detective stories were written in his middle teens at the preparatory Hill School and at Haverford College.

Following the success of his first published detective novel, *It Walks By Night* (1930), which introduced French Police Magistrate Henri Bencolin, Carr moved to England, where for the next fifteen years he wrote prolifically, averaging four novels a year. His most popular detectives were Dr. Gideon *Fell, a consultant to Scotland Yard who first appeared in *Hag's Nook* (1933), Sir Henry *Merrivale, a barrister who debuted in *The Plague Court Murders* (1934), and Colonel March, chief of the Department of Queer Complaints, whose short stories were collected in 1940. The latter two detective series were written under the pen name Carter Dickson.

In his mastery of impossible crimes—he is the undisputed master of the locked room mystery—and his love of bizarre characters and highly colored atmospheres, Carr openly acknowledged the influence of his favorite writer, G. K. *Chesterton, whom he never met. Fell, like Chesterton's Father *Brown and Gabriel Gale, specialized in solving murders that seem to have been committed through witchcraft and supernatural agencies, but whose solutions were entirely rational. Fell's best adventures, including the dazzling *Three Coffins* (1935; *The Hollow Man*) and *The Crooked Hinge* (1938)—and, indeed, almost all of Carr's work—were infused with a Chestertonian love of fair play, chivalry, and respect for the past. Indeed, Fell's appearance—his wheezing, vast bulk, bandit's mustache, shovel hat and cloak—resembled the rotund and revered Chesterton himself. The Fell series holds a high position among Carr's works, claims historian S. T. Joshi, in their "atmosphere of half-controlled lunacy": "It is as if everything Fell comes into contact with is bent slightly askew; and it is only he, with his self-parodically ponderous utterances, who can set it right again."

During World War II, Carr shuttled back and forth between America and England, writing propaganda programs and a weekly mystery radio series called *Appointment with Fear*. In later years he increasingly devoted his time to historical novels with crime and detection elements. Among these are *The Bride of Newgate* (1950), set in the Napoleonic era; *The Devil in Velvet* (1951)—one of his best-selling works—set in 1675 London; *Fire, Burn!* (1957), a chronicle of the early days of Scotland Yard; and *The Hungry Goblin* (1972), in which author Wilkie *Collins solved a crime in 1869 London. Other projects included two collaborations with Adrian Conan Doyle, youngest son of Arthur Conan *Doyle: the official biography of Sir Arthur (1949) and a volume of serious Sherlockian pastiches, *The Exploits of Sherlock Holmes* (1954). In the early 1950s Doyle wrote a popular CBS radio series of exotic mysteries, *Cabin B-13* (the title story of which was filmed in 1953 under the title *Dangerous Crossing*).

Fantasy is relatively rare in Carr's oeuvre, confined mostly to some of the short stories appearing in pulp magazines like *Horror Stories, Dime Mystery,* and *Detective Tales,* and in the collections *The Department of Queer Complaints, The Third Bullet and Other Stories* (1954), and *The Men Who Explained Miracles* (1963). Among the more than seventy novels, only *The Burning Court* (1937)—arguably Carr's greatest work—has a solution involving supernatural elements, although a rational solution is also offered. Significantly, the setting, contemporary Pennsylvania, is solid and detailed. It is only in this kind of realistic setting that fantasy is allowed to intrude; by contrast, the fantastic situations and bizarre settings of the other books—haunted tower rooms, sealed chambers of all descriptions, and a gallery of witches, hangmen, waxworks, and magicians—depend on entirely rational solutions. In that sense, he is the most distinguished successor to the Gothic legacy of Ann Radcliffe.

—John C. Tibbetts

Carrados, Max. The creation of Ernest *Bramah, Max Carrados is the genre's most famous blind detective. The author explains in an introduction to the second volume of short stories featuring Carrados the principle of compensation by which a blind person develops unusual sensitivity in his remaining senses. According to the background provided earlier in "The Coin of Dionysius" (*Max Carrados,* 1914) Carrados—who lost his sight in an accident—was born Max Wynn but changed his name as a condition of receiving an independent income from a wealthy American bearing that name. "The Coin of Dionysius" also joins the career of Carrados with that of the solicitor Louis Carlyle, who, approaching Carrados for help in this first exploit, becomes his sidekick for most of the remaining criminal cases.

The first volume of short stories, *Max Carrados,* was

selected by Ellery *Queen as one of the ten best collections of mysteries. The basis of Queen's judgment, and the source of audience pleasure, lies with the characterization of Carrados as a witty, sometimes satiric man comfortably in command of circumstances, yet restrained by his author from excessive or self-pitying commentary on his disability.

After the debut volume, the blind detective appeared in two additional collections—*The Eyes of Max Carrados* (1923) and *Max Carrados Mysteries* (1927)—and a single novel, *The Bravo of London* (1934). One additional Carrados story appears in Bramah's *The Specimen Case* (1924).

[*See also* Disability, Sleuth with; Sidekicks and Sleuthing Teams.]

—John M. Reilly

Castang, Henri. This member of France's Police Judiciaire (non-uniformed detectives) is a fictional detective first presented by Nicolas *Freeling as the rescuer of a kidnapped child in *Dressing of Diamond* (1974). Then living in a canalside flat in a "good, bourgeoise, frightened" district of an obscure town in northeastern France, Castang was class-conscious because of his hard-won route up from being the orphaned ward of a dipsomaniac aunt, and nationality-conscious through his marriage to a defecting Slovak gymnast. His problems were compounded by the corruption of local politics, as seen in *Castang's City* (1980), domestic cruelty in *What Are the Bugles Blowing For?* (1975), terrorism in *Wolfnight* (1982), and, always, the temptations of his venal bourgeois surroundings.

Throughout, Castang is aware that he has neither the "temperament for excessive prudence nor discretion when in trouble." Even his promotions from his provincial northern town to Paris and to the Brussels headquarters of the European Community are merely expedient moves to get him away from where "he'd been a nuisance." Castang appreciates Humphrey Bogart's hard-boiled screen persona: He too operates in the mean streets milieu.

—K. D. Prince

CAUDWELL, SARAH, pseudonym of Sarah Cockburn (1939–2000), English author of four mysteries that draw upon the author's experience as a barrister, and feature Hilary Tamar, a character whose gender is never identified. The daughter of the writer Claud Cockburn, Caudwell was born in London. She studied classics and then law at Oxford and practiced as a barrister before working for Lloyd's Bank as an international tax law expert. When Caudwell introduced Tamar in *Thus Was Adonis Murdered* (1981), she surrounded Tamar with a cast of quirky characters including several who share legal chambers, and Julia Larwood, a tax *lawyer whose chambers are next door. By endowing her characters with strong personality traits and legal expertise, Caudwell created much opportunity for dialogue that is both witty and informative on points of law, calling to mind a similar approach utilized by John *Mortimer in *Rumpole of the Bailey* (1978) and later books. Caudwell's flair for epistolary writing is evident in all of her mysteries, which incorporate letters and other written messages, such as telexes, that convey with considerable verve their senders' personalities.

[*See also* Lawyer.]

—Rosemary Herbert

CEREBRAL SLEUTH. See Great Detective, The.

Chambrun, Pierre, the best-known of many series characters created by Hugh *Pentecost, is resident manager of New York City's fictitious Hotel Beaumont, a luxury hotel patterned after the Waldorf-Astoria. Chambrun's early appearances are in novels and short stories involving traditional detection. In his first appearance, *The Cannibal Who Overate* (1962), he even solves a potential murder *before* it takes place. In later cases, the culprits are often terrorists at his hotel, whose location near the United Nations headquarters makes it a convenient political target. Chambrun, a veteran of the French Resistance in World War II, must devise ways to free hostages without giving in to terrorist demands.

Pentecost increasingly showed his awareness of violence and terrorism in the world, patterning his work after real events such as the Kitty Genovese slaying and, in *Remember to Kill Me* (1984), rioting in midtown Manhattan following a Central Park concert.

—Marvin Lachman

Chan, Charlie, fictional Honolulu police detective who appears in a series of six novels by the American writer Earl Derr *Biggers: *The House without a Key* (1925), *The Chinese Parrot* (1926), *Behind That Curtain* (1928), *The Black Camel* (1929), *Charlie Chan Carries On* (1930; *Charlie Chan Hangs On*, 1931), and *Keeper of the Keys* (1932). All of the novels were serialized in the *Saturday Evening Post* and were translated into several foreign languages.

Although Biggers's inspiration for Charlie Chan perhaps came partly from reading a newspaper account of the exploits of Chang Apana, a real Chinese policeman in Honolulu, Biggers had formed the idea for a detective novel earlier, while visiting Hawaii: To this he added Chan as an unusual and amusing secondary character— a fat Chinese American policeman with numerous children, who speaks fractured English. It is to Biggers's credit that, within the limits of this character formula, he managed to develop a complex and enduringly popular character, full of wisdom, warmth, and *humor.

In creating Chan, Biggers gave detective fiction a corrective to the sinister Asian stereotype personified in Sax *Rohmer's Dr. *Fu Manchu. And by making his *sleuth an Americanized Chinese, Biggers established two sources of conflict that helped him to develop Charlie's character: his Eastern-Western cultural duality, and his

vulnerability to racial prejudice. We see the former in Charlie's futile attempts to instill traditional Chinese values in his thoroughly Americanized children, and the latter in his encounters with racial discrimination, which he at first quietly endures but later counters with biting humor.

Kindly, polite, protective, and sentimental, Charlie is a loyal friend, a devoted father, and an adroit matchmaker. But his most notable characteristic is his peculiar speech, in which he takes great pride. At first, Biggers has him say awkward things in tortured English for comic effect. But as the novels progress, Charlie's speech becomes increasingly flowery, aphoristic, and playful.

Charlie's detecting methods include gathering evidence from the crime scene, rummaging through old newspapers, and listing suspects, whom he carefully observes for temperament and motive. Then, out of this welter of clues, he isolates the apparently insignificant detail with which he solves the case. While he can appear as impassive as a stone Buddha, Charlie acts swiftly and fearlessly when necessary. His success in solving crimes enables him to rise in rank from detective-sergeant to inspector of detectives. Nevertheless, he remains modest throughout the novels, and in contrast to some fictional sleuths, demonstrates a growing compassion toward the culprits he discovers.

Having created a fictional detective for whom the public clamored, Biggers did not tire of him (as Arthur Conan *Doyle did of Sherlock *Holmes and Agatha *Christie of Hercule *Poirot), but had further Chan adventures planned when he died in 1933. Biggers brought to the Chan novels the skill of an accomplished humorist and storyteller, firsthand impressions of exotic locales (including California, Nevada, and Hawaii), and characters drawn from his experiences in Boston, New York, and Hollywood.

[*See also* Ethnic Sleuth.]

—Jack Crowley

CHANDLER, RAYMOND (1888–1959), American author of private eye novels, generally acknowledged as a primary influence on the development of the hardboiled fiction genre. Although educated in England, Chandler returned to the United States in 1912, engaging in a business career in California until he retired in 1933 to write full time.

Chandler's early work in the pulp magazines *Black Mask*, *Dime Detective*, and *Detective Story* shows the influence of Dashiell *Hammett, as well as the pulp writers of his era. The pulp magazines provided a literary training ground for many mystery novelists, and Chandler was no exception. In his first and best-known novel, *The Big Sleep* (1939), published when he was fifty-one, he employed a technique that he would return to throughout his career: the blending and reworking of previously published short stories into a longer work, a technique he referred to as "cannibalization." *The Big Sleep* introduces private investigator Philip *Marlowe, whose genesis was in the narrators of these early stories. Marlowe is a complex character, full of contradictions. A tough man of the streets, he is also a romantic and an idealist with a self-evolved moral code. He is, at various times, compassionate and sentimental, brutal and indifferent. He is a master of the wisecrack, and his humor often takes the form of wry self-mockery. Unlike many of his lesser imitations, Marlowe is no superhero; he freely acknowledges fallibility and fear.

Marlowe's milieu is Los Angeles and its environs, and his creator's language provides a rich, textured description of the locale and its inhabitants. Chandler's vivid use of metaphor engages the imagination, and his terse dialogue serves both to characterize and to advance the story. It has often been said that one needs only to read Chandler's works to understand what southern California was like in the 1930s and '40s. This assessment is accurate. Through his selective use of detail, Chandler brings this milieu to life with remarkable clarity.

The Big Sleep is a tale of corruption by money and power—both old and inherited and newly derived from racketeering. It is a theme that Chandler returns to in his second novel, *Farewell, My Lovely* (1940). Less convoluted in plot than *The Big Sleep*, this work represents a further refinement of the author's technique. Chandler relies on two apparently unrelated story lines that eventually dovetail, and—unlike his first novel—all loose ends are neatly tied up. Here, too, we find such Chandler hallmarks as Marlowe's uneasy, often antagonistic relationship with law enforcement personnel; the racketeer who is apparently above the law; the wayward and conniving woman; the wealthy individual threatened by blackmail and scandal. Many critics regard *Farewell, My Lovely* as its author's finest work; while this is open to debate, it definitely surpasses *The High Window* (1942), *The Little Sister* (1949; *Marlowe*), and *Playback* (1958).

In *The Lady in the Lake* (1943), Chandler again cannibalizes, using three pulp novelettes—"Bay City Blues" (*Dime Detective*, 1937), "The Lady in the Lake" (*Dime Detective*, 1938), and "No Crime in the Mountains" (*Detective Story Magazine*, 1941)—as his basis. He removes Marlowe from his customary urban setting and takes him to the mountains of San Bernardino County; his rich descriptions of this area and its people lend the novel an evocative, haunting quality.

Arguably, *The Long Goodbye* (1954) is Chandler's best work. Here Marlowe is at his most sentimental and compassionate, stepping forward time and again to rescue a dissolute and mostly undeserving friend from disaster. The plot is a natural outgrowth of the characters of Marlowe and his friend, Terry Lennox, and it is the interplay between the two men that makes the unfolding events and their shattering climax thoroughly believable. Again Chandler explores his theme of a person corrupted by money and power, and paints a memorable portrait of one man's slide into ruin. It is ironic that the character of Terry Lennox foreshadows the author's own deterioration as a result of alcoholism following the 1954 death

of his wife, (Pearl) Cecily. He would never again write such a compelling and seamless novel.

Most critics would agree that without the works of Chandler, the American school of hard-boiled detective writing would have been very different. Following in the footsteps of Hammett, Chandler removed murder from the genteel confines of the country manor and placed it where it most frequently happens—in the streets and alleys of the city. He brought a gritty realism to the mystery novel by portraying, as he states in his essay "The Simple Art of Murder" (*The Simple Art of Murder*, 1950; *Trouble Is My Business*), "a world where no man can walk down a dark street in safety because law and order are things we talk about but refrain from practicing." With the publication of *The Big Sleep*, the private eye tale became one driven by events that could very possibly happen, rather than one driven by a set of improbable circumstances designed to formulate the classic whodunit.

At the times of their publication, the response to Chandler's novels was overwhelmingly positive. With the passage of time, some critics have complained that Chandler was not adept at plotting; that he was a one-theme writer; that his characters are stock and dated. All of this may be true to some degree. However, when taken within the context of their times, the stories are remarkably fresh and powerful, the characters some of the most memorable in mystery fiction. Marlowe, in one way or another, is the prototype for every fictional private investigator—male or female—in print today.

Chandler collaborated with Billy Wilder on the screenplay of James M. *Cain's *Double Indemnity*, and wrote an original screenplay, *The Blue Dahlia*. His novels were filmed numerous times, with varying degrees of success, the best of these efforts being *The Big Sleep*, starring Lauren Bacall and Humphrey Bogart. In addition to Bogart, Dick Powell, Alan Ladd, and Robert Mitchum have portrayed Marlowe on screen.

Chandler states in his introduction to the short story collection *The Simple Art of Murder* that "a classic is a piece of writing which exhausts the possibilities of its form and can hardly be surpassed. No story or novel of mystery has done that yet.... Which is one of the principal reasons why otherwise reasonable people continue to assault the citadel." In this statement Chandler's aim in writing private eye fiction is clear: He simply wanted to write the best detective story within his capability. In the hard-boiled category, his assaults come close to capturing the citadel.

[See also Hard-boiled Sleuth.]

—Marcia Muller

Charles, Nick and Nora. Dashiell *Hammett created the sophisticated husband-and-wife sleuthing team of Nick and Nora Charles for only one novel, *The Thin Man* (1934), his last. However, they and their dog Asta have become immortalized largely as a result of six films and numerous radio adaptations. The comically offbeat pair is better known for their scintillating and teasing repartee—said to be based on Hammett's interaction with Lillian Hellman—than for their detective skills. The well-heeled pair are most memorably portrayed in film by William Powell and Myrna Loy. Nick Charles is a former operative for the Trans-American Detective Agency. His wife is a society type from California who persuades Nick to solve the crime that occurred among her social set. He serves as reluctant detective while she assists as a fond and witty sidekick.

[See also Sidekicks and Sleuthing Teams.]

—Bernard Benstock

CHARTERIS, LESLIE (1907–1993), author who created Simon Templar, the figure known to millions of readers and viewers of film and television as The *Saint. Born Leslie Charles Bowyer Yin in the British colony of Singapore, he was educated at public schools in England, and spent two years at Kings College, Cambridge. In 1926, the year before publishing his first novel X Esquire, he changed his name legally to Leslie Charteris. While working at odd jobs and journalism in Malaya and Europe, he began contributing stories about Simon Templar, whose initials provided the opportunity for the nickname The Saint, to such magazines as the Thriller. The first Saint novel was Meet the Tiger (1928), followed by The Last Hero (1930) and a group of three novellas issued as Enter the Saint (1930). In 1935 Charteris relocated to the United States, where he continued steady production of at least a book a year about his latter-day knight-adventurer. In 1946 he relinquished his British citizenship to become a naturalized American.

In exacting retribution from those whom the law is powerless to touch, the gentleman outlaw Templar bears evident resemblance to the British clubland hero Bulldog *Drummond. However, Charteris works his own variations on the thriller of the 1920s and 1930s, most notably by redrafting his protagonist as a humane outsider rather than as an agent of a xenophobic establishment and by inscribing his narratives with humor and altruism.

With The Saint in New York (1935) and such later novels as The Saint in Miami (1940) and The Saint Goes West (1942), Charteris began to employ his new homeland for Templar's adventures. Charteris returned to the magazine world when he became editor of Suspense (1946–47), before founding his own publication, The Saint Detective Magazine, later known as The Saint Mystery Magazine (1953–67). Between 1945 and 1955 he also produced a syndicated comic strip portraying The Saint.

By the 1940s the fame of The Saint allowed Charteris to use the name, in the manner of Ellery *Queen, as the aegis for a series of mystery anthologies: The Saint's Choice of Humorous Crime (1945), The Saint's Choice of Impossible Crime (1945), and The Saint's Choice of Hollywood Crime (1946). It was the name and template of The Saint, not Charteris's own screenplays, that provided the subject for the many films and the television series about Simon Templar. After 1967, additional books

about The Saint were written by other authors under the supervision of Charteris.

—Peter Ibbotson

CHASE, JAMES HADLEY, pseudonym of Rene Brabazon Raymond (1906–85). Chase entered the field of crime and mystery writing in 1939 with the stunningly successful novel No Orchids for Miss Blandish. Outside the circle of mystery readers the novel is best known for provoking a denunciation by George Orwell, who took it as representative of the worst trends in popular literature. Within the circle it is recognized as a hard-boiled detective version of William Faulkner's similarly lurid novel Sanctuary (1931). Both works exploit strains of potboiler sadism, female vulnerability, corruption, and perverse *villains and villainy. Chase adds to the mix the character of a *private eye, Dave Fenner. Violence had been a staple of crime writing, on stage and off, but Chase turned the register up several notches in his debut novel and in subsequent works, of which there are more than eighty. Dave Fenner appeared once more in a book whose original title indicates its tone—Twelve Chinks and a Woman (1940). Chase introduced a California private eye named Vic Malloy in You're Lonely When You're Dead (1949); a Lothario named Mark Girland, who takes freelance assignments for the CIA, in This Is for Real (1965); and an insurance investigator named Steve Harmas in Tell It to the Birds (1963). The character of Chase's protagonists leaves them unlikely candidates for audience heroes, but the pace of their actions firmly classes their exploits in the category of thriller. Chase sets his fiction in the United States and makes his characters American presumably because that is a conventional expectation of the hard-boiled label, even though, as an Englishman whose books were all originally published in Great Britain, his knowledge of the milieu is secondhand, making it difficult for him to achieve another convention of narrative, verisimilitude. The author also wrote as James L. Docherty, Ambrose Grant, and most extensively as Raymond Marshall, whose works feature Brick-Top Corrigan and Don Micklem.

—John M. Reilly

Chee, Jim, and **Joe Leaphorn,** members of the Navajo Tribal Police featured in the novels of Tony *Hillerman. Chee, the younger of the two, with the rank of sergeant (and later acting lieutenant) has retained a devout faith in the spiritual beliefs of the Navajo people, and returned to the reservation after college to join the police force and train to become a "singer," one who performs healing ceremonies. Leaphorn, a middle-aged married man in the earlier books and later widowed, is a lieutenant; he has been a detective for more than two decades and is something of a legend among the members of the Navajo Tribal Police, from which he has retired in late-1990s installments of the series. Like Chee, he studied cultural anthropology; unlike Chee, and despite his fierce pride in the Navajo people, he favors rationality and logic over tribal ways. In spite of a deep respect for each other's abilities, the two detectives often clash: Leaphorn sees Chee's traditionalism as individualistic and romantic; Chee finds Leaphorn's skepticism about ancient Navajo beliefs disturbing.

[*See also* Native American Sleuth.]

—Lizabeth Paravisini-Gebert

CHEFS AS DETECTIVES. *See* Culinary Sleuth.

CHESTERTON, G(ILBERT) K(EITH) (1874–1936), British author of over seventy books and collections of essays and creator of Father *Brown, the archetypal *clerical sleuth. Father Brown is a Roman Catholic priest who appears in five books containing a total of fifty short stories.

Chesterton was born in London, prided himself on his "cockney" origins and placed most of his Father Brown stories in or near the city. Educated at St. Paul's School and at the Slade School of Art, he drifted into journalism and literature but immediately attracted a following of faithful readers. His literary style is characterized by the use of paradox and by a delight in the commonplace and things taken for granted. What could be more miraculous and wonderful, Chesterton argued, than an ordinary city street at night lit by gas flames and populated by shadows? His wit, too, was dependent on his playful approach to the ordinary and predictable. "If a thing is worth doing, it is worth doing badly," he wrote.

Chesterton championed Roman Catholicism after converting to that faith in 1922. He was also in favor of traditional values of family and nation. He possessed an uncluttered wisdom and an ability to cut to the heart of a problem, but he was also led—at least for a short period of time—into a mild form of anti-Semitism by his younger brother Cecil Chesterton and by his close friend, the writer Hilaire Belloc.

Chesterton is best remembered for his Father Brown books, which began in 1911 with *The Innocence of Father Brown* and continued with *The Wisdom of Father Brown* (1914), *The Incredulity of Father Brown* (1926), and *The Secret of Father Brown* (1927) and concluded with *The Scandal of Father Brown* in 1935. Brown was based loosely on the author's friend Father John O'Connor. He stumbles his way through the books as a plump, shortsighted, untidy, and disorganized man carrying an umbrella and seemingly unaware of life around him. Of course, this is far from the truth. While discussing esoteric moral theology or worrying about where he left his prayer book, Brown can solve gruesome murders thanks to his keen sensitivity to evil. Brown's own appearance of innocence is an advantage to his investigations because it causes criminals to dismiss him as innocuous.

Father Brown debuts in "The Blue Cross" (*Storyteller*, Sept. 1910), which fixes his character and introduces the style of the later stories. In this short story he is regarded by police and criminal alike as insignificant.

As he travels along with an international thief, he manages to gain the man's trust and also to leave the police a clear trail by carrying out various absurd acts such as breaking windows or exchanging salt for pepper in a restaurant.

Chesterton's non–Father Brown stories brought him commercial and critical success. His biographies of Robert Browning (1903), Robert Louis Stevenson (1928), and various Roman Catholic saints; poetry and novels including *The Man Who Was Thursday: A Nightmare* (1908) and *The Napoleon of Notting Hill* (1904); and works of philosophy, history, and theology such as *Orthodoxy* (1908), *The Everlasting Man* (1925), and *Heretics* (1905), were also massively popular during his lifetime and are experiencing a renaissance today. He also founded and edited a small circulation magazine, known in its various stages as *Eye-Witness*, *The New Witness*, and *G. K.'s Weekly*. *The Chesterton Review* (the quarterly journal of the G. K. Chesterton Institute) is devoted to his life, work, and related subjects.

Chesterton wrote other stories featuring detective elements: *The Club of Queer Trades* (1905) is a collection of rather bizarre mystery tales, but they do not rival the undisputed genius of his Brown oeuvre.

—Michael Coren

CHRISTIE, AGATHA (Agatha Mary Clarissa Miller Christie Mallowan) (1890–1976), English author recognized around the world as one of the most important writers of detective fiction and arguably the most famous practitioner in the British Golden Age tradition. Known for her prolificity and inventiveness, Christie turned out eighty-five books that can be categorized as detective novels or collections of mystery short stories. Her series characters include the Belgian private detective Hercule *Poirot, the *spinster sleuth Miss Jane *Marple, the detecting duo Tommy and Tuppence Beresford, and Superintendent Battle. Mr. Parker Pine, investigator, and Harley Quin appear in volumes of short stories. Christie also penned original plays and adaptations, a series of psychological romances, autobiographical work, and a children's book.

Agatha Mary Clarissa Miller was born 15 September 1890 in Torquay, on the south coast of Devon, England, the third child of an American father and an English mother. A bashful and sensitive child, she was educated at home before attending finishing schools in Paris. Although she was an accomplished pianist, her extreme shyness and stage fright prevented her from pursuing a performing career. In 1914 she married Archibald Christie, an officer in the Royal Flying Corps. During World War I she served first as a volunteer nurse and then as a dispenser of drugs, gaining knowledge that would be invaluable to her career as a crime writer. She gave birth to her only child, Rosalind, in 1919.

In her posthumously published *An Autobiography* (1977), Christie revealed that she wrote her first detective novel, *The Mysterious Affair at Styles* (copyright 1920;

published in 1921) in response to a challenge from her sister Madge. She dashed off the manuscript during a scant two weeks in 1916. Published just over four years later, it was an instant success and is still regarded as among her masterpieces. The novel introduced Poirot, a prim and petite Belgian who characterizes his own immense cleverness as resulting from reliance on his "little gray cells," or brainwork. Poirot often works in tandem with Captain John Hastings, a less bright but ever-eager sidekick figure. He is also assisted by his secretary, Miss Lemon, who is not averse to performing inquiries and other tasks beyond the typewriter.

Christie's great strength as a writer of classic mysteries centered around puzzles was soon established: deliberate misdirection. A member of the elite Detection Club, a group of authors who swore to play fair with their readers, Christie was a master at manipulating the rules of the game or conventions of the genre, generally laying clues before her readers' eyes while guiding their scrutiny in the wrong direction. She was also notorious for breaking rules in her surprise ending to *The Murder of Roger Ackroyd* (1926), which proved that anyone can be a killer in a Christie novel. Many felt that the stunning solution departed from the fair-play convention of detective fiction, but they bought the book nonetheless, making this one of Christie's greatest best-sellers. *Murder on the Orient Express* (1934; *Murder in the Calais Coach*) was another rule-breaker proving that everyone can be guilty in a Christie work.

The same year that *The Murder of Roger Ackroyd* became a publishing sensation, Christie made news herself by vanishing for ten days, during which a nationwide search ensued. She was finally discovered registered at a resort hotel under the name of her husband's mistress. While Christie never explained the circumstances of the incident, many have speculated that she experienced an episode of stress-induced amnesia, inspired by the discovery of her husband's infidelity and by grief over the death of her mother that year.

Her divorce was finalized in 1928, just as the most prolific period of Christie's writing career was beginning. She introduced Miss Jane Marple in *Murder at the Vicarage* (1930). Marple succeeds as a personification of her creator's signature skill in sleight of hand. This *elderly sleuth used her older appearance as an asset, allowing suspects to fail to take her seriously while she keenly investigated their activities. While Marple used the elderly stereotype to advantage, her sharp mind and physical courage also succeeded as strong and early arguments for the reversal of stereotypes about the elderly. This was not so solidly the case, however, in some of the film versions of the Marple character.

In an effort to put her divorce behind her, Christie traveled to the Middle East in 1928, where she met Sir Max Mallowan, an accomplished archaeologist. She married Mallowan in 1930 and accompanied him on digs in Syria and Iraq, where she used her talents as a photographer to take official photographs recording his work.

During these expeditions she also explored settings that she would use in such works of detective fiction as *Murder in Mesopotamia* (1936) and *Death on the Nile* (1937). She later recounted some of her archeological adventures in *Come Tell Me How You Live* (1947), an autobiographical work.

Christie also launched her extraordinarily productive decade by publishing *Giant's Bend* in 1930. It was the first of six psychological romance novels that she penned under the pseudonym Mary Westmacott. During the 1930s she published four nonseries mystery novels, fourteen Poirot novels, two Marple novels, two Superintendent Battle books, a book of stories featuring Harley Quin and another featuring Mr. Parker Pyne, an additional Mary Westmacott book, and two original plays. She continued her prolific output, although not at the same pace, for the next three-and-a-half decades, causing readers to count on "A Christie for Christmas" until the year of her death. Her stage play *The Mousetrap* (1952) is another reliable production. Adapted from her short story "Three Blind Mice" (in *Three Blind Mice*, 1950; *The Mousetrap*), it has been playing continuously in London since its opening. The play is published in Christie's *The Mousetrap and Other Plays* (1978).

Christie is primarily associated in readers' minds with the Golden Age of crime and mystery writing, the period between the two World Wars when puzzle-centered detective fiction was built upon a conservative worldview. But during a writing career spanning the better part of six decades, Christie revealed herself as aware of changing realities of manners and mores, even if her works were often set in places where characters were comfortably situated, in terms of finances or leisure. In fact, even in the coziest of Christie's novels, where characters are enjoying relatively luxurious lifestyles, the solution to crime may reveal financial desperation as an underlying motive for murder. Coziness, like so much else in Christie's work, is often a case of deceptive appearances.

Critics agree that Christie remains unsurpassed for her ingenuity in plotting. While her contemporaries often relied upon pinning the crime on the least likely suspect, Christie dared to allow the reader's attention to focus on the murderer as prime suspect. Her forte was to then shift suspicion to an innocent character and thus cause the reader to dismiss the true murderer as a suspect.

Christie's work continues to be published in translation around the world and is said to outsell Shakespeare and the Bible. Her colleagues in crime writing voted to present her with the first Mystery Writers of America Grand Master Award in 1954. She became a Commander of the British Empire in 1956, and a Dame of the British Empire in 1971.

—Dana Bisbee *and* Rosemary Herbert

CLARK, MARY HIGGINS (b. 1928), American author of best-selling mystery and suspense novels. A New

York City native, Clark had a varied range of work and personal experience before she achieved fame and high standing as a writer. She has worked as an advertising assistant, airline flight attendant, radio scriptwriter, producer, and partner in a communications firm. In 1979 she completed a bachelor's degree at Fordham University. It is not necessary to claim autobiographical content for her writing to see that lived experience has been a source of the feeling that readers find in her work.

In place of the process of detection that contours one prominent path taken by the crime and mystery genre, Clark explores the topography originally detailed by the sensation novel. Her interest lies in the crime under way or yet to come if all goes wrong. Her narrative point of view just as often illuminates the schemes and psychology of the culprit as it does the fears of the *victim. Her plots examine familiar and, for that reason, unnerving circumstances and the material yielding the suspense, which is the chief effect of her narratives, is generally associated with the experiences and interests of women. *Where Are the Children?* (1975), Clark's first novel and the start of her string of best-sellers, places two children in danger from a kidnapper exploiting a mystery in their mother's past. *A Cry in the Night* (1982) recounts a woman's discovery that the man she thought she knew well enough to marry is in fact a stranger. Yet, while culture associates the connection of destiny and family as Clark presents it with the realm of life conventionally assigned to women, her narratives cannot be termed parochial, limited, or strictly feminine; Clark's insight is that the fears that may arise in the life of intimacy bespeak the needs at the foundation of social life for all.

With the publication of *Decked* (1992), Clark's daughter, Carol Higgins Clark, began a series that works its changes on the mystery formula by featuring a private detective named Regan Reilly who is the child of the famous crime writer Nora Regan Reilly.

[*See also* Missing Persons.]

—John M. Reilly

CLERICAL SLEUTH. The significant position of the clergy in English literature is well documented. The age-old conflict between the church and crime has yielded much detective fiction and some clerical detectives, and has also been the subject of comment in theological and other publications.

Dorothy L. *Sayers, herself a daughter of the vicarage, postulated that the first clerical detective was the prophet Daniel. She argued that in the apocryphal stories of Susanna and the Elders and Bel and the Dragon, Daniel demonstrated his investigative skills in proving the innocence of Susanna and the perfidy involved in the worshipping of a false god.

G. K. *Chesterton's celibate Roman Catholic priest Father *Brown was an early clerical investigator in the genre, first appearing in the short stories that comprise *The Innocence of Father Brown* (1911). Although a notably compassionate man with an ability to put himself in other men's shoes with all their human weaknesses, nevertheless he takes a stern theological view of righteousness, as do his fictional peers. This trained capacity for making sound moral judgements is an important feature of clerical detectives, however lovable or idiosyncratic; so too is their uniform ability to make the sound, evidence-based judgments essential in the genre.

Clerical sleuths have advantages over other investigators in that they are usually able to go everywhere, talk to everyone—no one so spans the social spectrum as the clergy—and take as much time as they need. Nor, as a rule, are they answerable to any worldly body for their actions.

Some authors in this field have themselves been clerks in holy orders and thus observant in both senses. These include Canon Victor L. Whitechurch, Dean Cyril A. Alington, Monsignor Ronald A. *Knox, and the Reverend Austin Lee who, although he wrote as both Julian Callendar and John Austwick, used his real name for *Miss Hogg and the Dead Dean* (1958). George A. Birmingham was in real life the Reverend James Owen Hannay. His *Hymn Tune Mystery* (1930) was church-based; but while an ecclesiastical setting has become less usual over the years, a more ecumenical field of professionally unshockable clerical detectives has burgeoned.

These include Methodist minister Charles Merrill Smith's Reverend C. P. "Con" Randolph; Pauline King's Wesleyan Evan Morgan (in *Snares of the Enemy*, 1985); and Margaret Scherf's Episcopalian Minister, Reverend Martin Buell. Ellis *Peters's extensive series about Brother *Cadfael, a professed monk on the Welsh Marches in the turbulent twelfth century, began with *A Morbid Taste for Bones* (1977). In Umberto *Eco's *Il Nome Della Rose* (1983; *The Name of the Rose*), set in a Franciscan Abbey in Italy in 1327, the sleuth is Brother William. A holy man is murdered in *La Puissance du Neart* (1982; *The Power of Nothingness*), by Alexandra David-Neel and Lama Youngden, in which the detection is done by a Tibetan Buddhist monk.

The cadre of heirs of Father Brown are in his tradition of the caring, endearing, shrewd but not wholly worldly; they include Andrew Greeley's fictional detective Monsignor John Blackwood Ryan, who made his debut in *Happy Are the Meek* (1985). Leonard Holton has created a series with Father Joseph Breddar as the investigator. Ralph McInery's considerable output of Father Roger Dowling stories began with *Her Death of Cold* and *The Seventh Station* (both 1977). William X. Kienzle's series hero, beginning with *The Rosary Murders* (1979), is Father Bob Koesler. Dorothy Salisbury *Davis's Father McMahon is more than usually tested in *Where the Dark Streets Go* (1969).

The higher Anglican hierarchy feature in the works of Thurman Warriner, whose hero is Archdeacon Toft, and in *Solemn High Murder* (1975) by Barbara Nirde Byfield and Frank L. Tedeschi, where the clerical sleuth is an aide to the Archbishop of Canterbury. The works of Freda Bream are set in New Zealand and cover the activities of the Reverend Jabal Jarrett, while those of John Armour are set in the outback of Australia.

In a different, older religious tradition are the works of Harry *Kemelman, whose totally logical but endearing hero is Rabbi David *Small. Joseph Telushkin, an Orthodox rabbi, is the author of *The Unorthodox Murder of Rabbi Wahl* (1986; *The Unorthodox Murder of Rabbi Moss*), in which the crime of the title is solved by his Rabbi Daniel Winter. And in *The Angel of Zin* (1984), by Clifford Irving, Rabbi Jacob Hurwicz investigates in a Nazi concentration camp.

Convents provide unlikely but effective bases for investigation, as in *Quiet as a Nun* (1977), by Antonia *Fraser. Some sequestered religious sleuths, such as Anthony *Boucher's Sister Ursula, are hampered by grille and cloister, but the scholarly Sister Mary Dempsey, created by Monica Quill, is more mobile.

The Sister Fidelma novels of Peter Tremayne—for example, *Absolution by Murder* (1994)—have a seventh-century nun-lawyer of the Celtic church as their sleuth, while the works of Henry Catalan feature French nun Soeur Angele. More lighthearted is *A Nun in the Closet* (1975; *A Nun in the Cupboard*), wherein real-life Sister Carol Anne O'Marie her detection performed by Sister Mary Helen.

A development reflecting recent ecclesiastical changes is the introduction of ordained women sleuths. The books of D. M. Greenwood feature Theodora Braithwaite, curate of London's St. Sylvester's, those of Isabelle Holland have as their sleuth the Reverend Claire Aldington, an American woman Episcopalian minister.

—Catherine Aird

CODY, LIZA (b. 1944), British author, considered a groundbreaker for her creation of the tough-gal, female *private eye, Anna Lee. She also created a second series sleuth, Eva Wylie. Born in London, Cody trained as an artist at the City and Guilds of London Art School and the Royal Academy School of Art. She also pursued art studies in Italy and she has worked as a studio technician at Madame Tussaud's in London. She married and had one daughter before making a trip to Ethiopia in 1974, where she found herself in danger during political upheaval. She chronicled that adventure in the 1988 novel, *Rift*. In the 1980 John Creasey Award-winning mystery, *Dupe*, Cody introduced Lee, one of the few female private investigators to be found in English crime fiction at the time. Lee works in the Brierly Security Agency in London, reporting to Martin Brierly, a boss who keeps insisting she prove herself in a career that is dominated by men. Often, she works to help women who have been sexually exploited or otherwise victimized by men. She is not afraid to take physical risks in order to carry out her assignments and often gets roughed up in the course of her work. Cody's second series protagonist, Wylie, makes her first appearance in *Bucket Nut* (1992). This memorable character is an aggressive, large-sized security guard whose petty illegal activities make her someone who straddles the line between the criminal and the just.

—Rosemary Herbert

COLLINS, MAX ALLAN (b. 1948), prolific American writer of comic strips and creator of several series of novels. His works include books about an aging thief called Nolan, a series about a hit man called Quarry, several books about a mystery writer named Mallory, and historical mysteries featuring Nate Heller. Born in Muscatine, Iowa, Collins attended community college there and then earned an MFA from the University of Iowa. He has worked as a songwriter, musician, college English literature instructor, newspaper reporter, and comic strip writer for Dick Tracy, Mike Mist and Ms. Tree. Collins' series about professional criminals are notable for the author's insights into what drives the men to commit crimes. Quarry, in particular, talks about his motivation and the standards he holds himself to in his grim work. In *The Baby-Blue Rip-Off* (1983), Collins introduced Mallory, a man who delivers meals on wheels to senior citizens and writes mystery novels. Critics agree, *A Shroud for Aquarius* (1985), which is strong on 1960s nostalgia, is the most noteworthy book in this series. Introduced in *True Detective* (1983), Heller is a *private eye who encounters notorious characters from history including Eliot Ness, Al Capone and others. Collins started out setting the series during the 1930s and has set books in later decades, as well. He also has written short stories about Chicago private eye Richard Stone; a graphic novel, *The Road to Perdition* (1998); film novelizations; and nonfiction about the crime and mystery genre.

—Rosemary Herbert

COLLINS, (WILLIAM) WILKIE (1824–1889), English novelist, best known for *The Woman in White* and *The Moonstone*. Collins was a Victorian success. During the 1860s, when *The Woman in White* was a popular rage, his estimated annual income was over £10,000. Despite the appearance, so dear to the optimistic age, that this monetary attainment gave of energy and labor rewarded, Collins was otherwise not a conventional Victorian. The son of the landscape painter William Collins and godson of the painter Sir David Wilkie, whose name he bore, he led a bohemian existence of long sojourns abroad with his family, experienced extreme indecision about a career, and in maturity lived serially in two common-law families. He studied painting, undertook training with a firm of tea merchants, entered Lincoln's Inn to study law in 1846, and was called to the bar in 1851. All the while, though, he was also writing, so that his eventual career came upon him more by accident than by resolute pursuit. His first publication was a short story in 1843, and in 1848 he published a biography of his father in two volumes. Literary history, with hints from Algernon Swinburne and T. S. Eliot, has tended to regard Collins as a minor figure in the shadow of Charles

*Dickens, whose close associate and friend he was. In the realm of popular fiction, however, Collins earned success by his own special talents.

Those talents included a gift for expert plotting of complex narratives that, at their best, become lucid after they have twisted their way to conclusion; precise and painterly descriptive powers; and an inventive approach to the use of narrative voice and point of view. He applied those talents to mystery first in short stories. "A Stolen Letter" (originally published as "The Fourth Poor Traveller" in *Household Words*, Christmas edition, 1854; reprinted as "The Lawyer's Story of a Stolen Letter" in *After Dark*, 1856) is, as its title suggests, reminiscent of Edgar Allan *Poe. "Anne Rodway [Taken from her Diary]" (*Household Words*, July 19 and 26, 1856; reprinted in *The Queen of Hearts*, 1859 as "Brother Owen's Story of Anne Rodway") claims interest because of its female detective and Collins's first use of a diary form, which would become one of his stocks in trade.

Through his friendship with Dickens, Collins became a regular contributor to Dickens's magazine *Household Words*. That journal's successor, *All the Year Round*, served as the outlet for the first publication of Collins's two stunning mystery novels, in serial form: *The Woman in White* was issued in installments starting in November 1859, and *The Moonstone* appeared from January 1868 on.

Apart from his work in the crime and mystery genre, Collins produced much doctrinaire fiction espousing the causes of illegitimate children and prostitutes, and attacking vivisection and the Jesuits. The bulk of this nondetective fiction belongs to the school of sensation, where the "secret" is indeed sprung upon the reader. His works that survive do so, however, because in them he exceeded the limits of both attenuated and sensational fiction.

The Moonstone, T. S. Eliot declared, is "the first, the longest, and the best of modern English detective novels." Even without the qualifications of "modern" and "English" the tribute would be just, for *The Moonstone* is incomparable. Told in a variety of voices, from the stolid but solid Gabriel Betteredge, steward in the noble household, to the religious crank Drusilla Clack, the poor relation hostile to the people Betteredge serves, the narrative is masterly in its balancing of sympathies as well as in its artful concealment and revelation of the truth. The secret—this being the essence of the difference between *sensation novel and detective novel—is gradually revealed with the collaboration of the reader. The author plays fair. He does not spring the solution on us, but instead provides a reconstruction of the crime and, in a foreshadowing of the wrap-up scenes that become de rigueur in classic crime stories, presents the answers with all suspects assembled. There are several detectives in *The Moonstone*, but the principal two between them share qualities that have become characteristic of fictional *sleuths: Sergeant *Cuff, the policeman, rational, eccentric; and Ezra Jennings, the scientific artist, intuitive, also eccentric, and a social outcast. The Bi-Part Soul, both are needed to solve the crime.

The earlier novel, *The Woman in White*, more closely resembles sensational fiction. The secret is inaccessible to the reader until the end, and the story boasts two superb villains—Sir Percival Glyde, who is one dimensional, and Count Fosco, who is anything but. Indeed, one of the great villains of Victorian fiction, Fosco could have given Dashiell *Hammett suggestions for his portrayal of Casper Gutman.

Writing of the novelist in the Victorian age, Lord David Cecil says: "He had to be Mr. Galsworthy, Mr. Huxley, Mrs. Woolf, Mrs. Christie and Mr. Wodehouse in one." This was the kind of multifaceted novelist Collins was; but his forte was to have raised the mystery novel to a level higher than that of his contemporaries, and to have virtually invented the full-length detective novel.

[*See also* Eccentrics.]

—Barrie Hayne

CON ARTIST. The con artist is a specific type of fictional character who, having raised the techniques of deception, ingratiation, and tomfoolery to the level of an art form, cultivates the confidence of others to garner profit or the favors of the opposite sex or an avenue for escape. Superior wit; skill in the use of resources, including disguise; adaptability; savoir faire; charm; and a continual desire to better his or her condition—these are some of the attributes of the con artist at work to trick, beguile, maneuver, or manipulate others. Since the confidence game is generated by and predicated upon the human foibles of the *victim, the con artist's operations serve the turn of the satirist, the moralist, the critic of society who brings into view a world of dubious and doubting humanity, one that is populated by cheats, imposters, and fools.

The range of the con artist is immense. Among the British, Randolph Mason, a skilled, unscrupulous lawyer, cons his clients in Melville Davisson *Post's *The Strange Schemes of Randolph Mason* (1896). Arthur *Morrison's less-than-honest *private detective, Horace Dorrington, is both con man and thief in *The Dorrington Deed Box* (1897). Romney Pringle, a creation of R. Austin *Freeman and John James Pitcairn writing as Clifford Ashdown, poses as a literary agent who earns a living by swindling crooks out of their ill-gotten gains in *The Adventures of Romney Pringle* (1902). Dr. James Shepard, the narrator in Agatha *Christie's *The Murder of Roger Ackroyd* (1926), is a man of many masks: a moral monster, liar, blackmailer, and greedy gambler, who manipulates characters and readers alike with great guile and without any remorse. Constantine Dix is both lay preacher and thief in Barry Pain's *The Memoirs of Constantine Dix* (1905). Milward Kennedy created Sir George Bull in *Bull's Eye* (1933; *Corpse in Cold Storage*, 1934), a con man who assumes the role of a private detective to gain entrance to a wealthy social circle.

One version of the con artist is the *gentleman thief exemplified by E. W. *Hornung's A. J. *Raffles, cricketeer, gentleman, and thief in *The Amateur Cracksman* (1899; *Raffles, The Amateur Cracksman*). Writing as Barry Perowne, Philip Atkey imitates Hornung with his own gentleman-gone-astray, Raffles, in *Raffles After Dark* (1933; *The Return of Raffles*). The American master of parody, J. Kendrick Bangs, builds several stories around the adventures of Raffles's wife transplanted to American high society. She expands her name to Henriette Van Raffles and thrives in the heyday of Newport, Rhode Island, in *Mrs. Raffles: Being the Adventures of an Amateur Crackswoman* (1905). Another American, Christopher B. Booth, created that Chicagoan "confidence man de luxe," the title character of two volumes, *Mr. Clackworthy* (1926) and *Mr. Clackworthy, Con Man* (1927).

Particularly in America, the con artist emerged as a distinct literary convention in the 1830s out of an ancestry of seducers, pranksters, devils, or rogues. So suspicious are characters of each other in the American form of the genre that we can never be sure whether some apparently decent and good-hearted person may in fact be practicing pious fraud. Frederick Anderson introduces a master thief in *Adventures of the Infallible Godahl* (1914), and Frank L. Packard's Jimmie Dale (*The Adventures of Jimmie Dale*, 1917) poses as a New York club man, a crook dubbed the Gray Seal, an *underworld figure called Larry the Bat, and an unsuccessful artist known as Smarlinghue.

Gamblers, swindlers, hypocrites, and falsifiers also appear in the hard-boiled private eye novels of Dashiell *Hammett, Raymond *Chandler, Mickey *Spillane, Ross *Macdonald, and John D. *MacDonald. In these authors' sometimes sordid and always cynical worlds, the rich make their fortunes through various scams, double crosses, and violent murders; the police, who should be able to see through these machinations, are instead incompetent and corrupt. If there is a sucker born every minute, there is also a con artist born to take advantage of human gullibility for his own selfish purposes.

—Dale Salwak

CONAN DOYLE, SIR ARTHUR. *See* Doyle, Arthur Conan.

CONNELLY, MICHAEL (b. 1957), American journalist and creator of the hard-boiled *police detective Hieronymous "Harry" Bosch. Raised in Philadelphia, Pennsylvania, Connelly is the son of a builder and housewife. He first became fascinated with the world of crime at age sixteen when he witnessed a robbery in progress and was questioned about it by the police. He started out in college majoring in building construction but earned a degree in journalism, instead, from the University of Florida. Connelly wrote for newspapers in Daytona and in Fort Lauderdale, Florida. At the *Fort Lauderdale Sun-Sentinel*, his coverage of a major 1985 plane crash led to his being nominated with others for a Pulitzer Prize. He then won a post on the *Los Angeles Times*.

Connelly portrays the journalist's life in his 1995 novel, *The Poet*, in which a reporter from Denver, Colorado, is driven to find the truth about his policeman-brother's death. The sleuth here is Jack McEvoy.

Introduced in *The Black Echo* (1992), Bosch is the orphaned son of a father who deserted him and a prostitute who named him after a modern artist and was killed while Bosch was still a boy. Bosch's experiences in foster homes and in the Vietnam War combined to form a cynical survivor who is motivated by a personal code of honor. He is also driven by a very personal need to know: In *The Last Coyote* (1995), he seeks to solve his own mother's murder, and in *The Concrete Blonde* (1994), he is determined to discover whether or not he is guilty of killing a man in error.

Similarly, in *Blood Work* (1997) another sleuth created by Connelly has a direct connection to a crime he investigates. Here Terry McCaleb, a former FBI agent, seeks to find out what happened to the woman whose heart beats in his chest. McCaleb is alive thanks to receiving her heart in a transplant operation. In contrast, in *Chasing the Dime* (2002), protagonist Henry Pierce has no connection with a woman he hopes to find and help after he receives a series of messages for her on his new telephone. His quest for a stranger leads him into the world of on-line sex and escort services.

[*See also* Hard-boiled Sleuth; Journalist Sleuth.]

—Rosemary Herbert

CONSTANTINE, K. C., pseudonym of Karl Constantine Kosak (b. 1934), American author best-known for his skills in evoking small-town life in mysteries featuring Mario Balzic, a police detective. Reticent about interviews, the author caused at least one reference book writer to raise the question of Constantine's gender. The limited information that is available mainly concerns the author's attitudes—about topics as unrelated as the Cold War and Constantine's unwillingness to participate in book signings—is offered up in "self-interviews" the author wrote about himself.

Constantine introduced his most famous series character in the *Rocksburg Railroad Murders* (1972), a novel set in the coal-mining town of Rocksburg, Pennsylvania. The overweight, hot-tempered, heavy-drinking Balzic is a police chief who tells it like it is, using coarse language when the occasion demands it. Particularly in the memorably-titled *The Man Who Liked Slow Tomatoes* (1982), Constantine excels in working the rough realities of job loss and life in and around a mine-pocked landscape into a satisfying, if not upbeat, mystery. Unlike other writers who got their starts in the same decade, Constantine is less eager to illuminate his detective's personal life, preferring to acquaint the reader with Balzic's policing skills, including the man's profound understanding of the town and the townspeople he polices. The author waits until his eighth novel, *Joey's Case* (1988), to tell readers much about Balzic's marriage.

In *Good Sons* (1996), Constantine has Detective Rugs Carlucci, take over as police chief. Fortunately, Balzic is restless in retirement and appears again as a private investigator in some of Constantine's more recent works. *Saving Room for Dessert* (2002) focuses on three more police characters while showing Constantine at his best. Here three policemen respond, at first, to three different and apparently minor incidents in the course of a working day. The personality each brings to his work sparks a much more combustible combination of factors when the three officers respond to a single situation in the evening.

[*See also*: Police Detective.]

—Rosemary Herbert

Continental Op. Dashiell *Hammett created the unnamed character known simply as the Continental Op while he served his apprenticeship as a hard-boiled detective fiction writer for *Black Mask* magazine from 1923 to 1927. Hammett wrote twenty-six short stories, a two-part novella—*$106,000 Blood Money* (1927)—and two novels—*Red Harvest* (1929) and *The Dain Curse* (1929)—featuring the Op. Hammett drew on his own experiences working for the Pinkerton Agency to give the stories authenticity.

When first introduced, the Op is thirty-five and has been an operative with the Continental Agency for fifteen years. Short and fat, he is ruthless in his work. The stories in which he appears are first-person narratives by the Op, told in a flat, matter-of-fact style enlivened by criminal slang. This straightforward style serves as a contrast to the graphic violence and mayhem to come. In "The Gutting of Couffignal" (*The Return of the Continental Op*, 1945), a woman attempts to seduce the Op. He responds by saying, "You think I'm a man and you're a woman. That's wrong. I'm a manhunter and you're something that has been running in front of me. There's nothing human about it." Later in the story, when she doesn't believe his threat to shoot her and tries to leave, the Op shoots her in the leg. "I had never shot a woman before," he remarks to the reader, "I felt queer about it."

Although the Op felt queer about shooting a woman, he did it in order to do his job, for he lives by an ethical code ruled by loyalty to his agency and fellow detectives but excluding sentiment. The most important rule is that no operative can benefit monetarily from the solution of a case. This rule puts the Op above the greed and corruption of the Prohibition society in which he works. Indeed, the Op shows no interest in money. He lives for his work.

The best-known example of his brutal work appears in *Red Harvest*, where he takes on an entire army of crooked cops and gangsters who run Personville, later Poisonville. The Op's method is to "stir things up," ma-

nipulating the crooked cops and the gangsters in ways that turn them against each other and destroy them.

—George Kelley

COOKS AS DETECTIVES. *See* Culinary Sleuth.

CORNWELL, PATRICIA D(ANIELS) (b. 1956), American writer of crime novels featuring Dr. Kay *Scarpetta, a fictional chief medical examiner for the city of Richmond, Virginia. Born Patricia Daniels in Florida, Cornwell lived in Miami until her parents broke up when she was seven years old. Then she moved with her mother and two brothers to North Carolina. When her mother was hospitalized with severe depression, she was taken care of by missionary neighbors who had recently returned from the Congo. A positive influence during those troubled years was the evangelist Billy Graham's wife, Ruth Graham, who became the subject of Cornwell's first published book, *A Time for Remembering: the Ruth Graham Story* (1982). Before that, Cornwell aspired to become a tennis pro. Although she did well in competition, she also pursued writing, turning out a novel as her thesis for graduation from Davidson College in North Carolina in 1979. She married and later divorced Charles Cornwell, a professor and then minister who was 17 years her senior.

Cornwell worked as a police reporter for *The Charlotte Observer* and then as a computer expert for the Richmond, Virginia, Office of the Medical Examiner. Both jobs provided invaluable experience that she mined in her series of books that blend expertise in forensic pathology with detection. The combination has won her great acclaim in a series of novels that pits Scarpetta's skills against the grisly work of serial killers. Cornwell's first mystery, *Postmortem*, was a sensation when it was published in 1990, and the books that followed have all been bestsellers. While Cornwell depicts the horrific work of warped minds, she never writes from the point of view of the criminal. Her commitment to writing from the side of the just may have been strengthened when, in 1991, she learned that an actual murderer, John Benson Waterman, used methods she had described in *Postmortem*.

[*See also* Coroner.]

—Rosemary Herbert

CORONER. Coroners, whose main duty is to ascertain the cause of any death that appears to be unnatural, regularly appear in mystery fiction, and the inquests they hold often play an important part in developing the story. In England and Wales coroners must have either legal or medical qualifications; in the United States they are often *forensic pathologists. In conventional mysteries, coroners are usually minor characters and the inquest is not the central event of the story, but Marc Connelly's much anthologized "Coroner's Inquest" (*Colliers*, 8, Feb. 1930) is an exception to the general rule, as is

Percival Wilde's *Inquest* (1940). In an introduction to his novel, Wilde explained that, historically, in his own domain the coroner was czar, empowered not only to conduct the inquest as he wished but also able to pad out proceedings so as to increase his claim for expenses. Such abuses led to the abolition of the office in many parts of the United States and the appointment of state medical examiners, who are public servants paid regular salaries. Yet in *Inquest* itself, the Honorable Lee Slocum proves in the end to be much more astute than he initially seems.

In England and Wales, coroners' *juries are no longer entitled to bring in a verdict of willful murder against a named individual, but in the past such accusations provided moments of drama in many novels, as is the case in Agatha *Christie's *Death in the Clouds* (1935; *Death in the Air*). The jury's verdict in *Taken at the Flood* (1948; *There Is a Tide*) seems equally to be a manifestation of local prejudice, yet with typical sleight of hand Hercule *Poirot reveals in the end that, far from being ludicrous, the verdict was correct. In Michael *Gilbert's *Roller Coaster* (1993), Patrick Petrella reflects the professional policeman's distrust of a legal proceeding such as an inquest which is "without form and void."

In general, British writers have not attempted to exploit the potential of the coroner's office for mystery series to the same extent as their American counterparts. Lawrence G. Blochman's pathologist Dr. Daniel Webster Coffee investigates in many stories as well as one novel, while the medical examiner hero of the television series "Quincy M. E." appears in two novelizations (1977) written by Thom Racina. Of all the many coroners and medical examiners to have appeared in mystery fiction, however, perhaps the most notable is Dr. Kay *Scarpetta, heroine of novels by Patricia D. *Cornwell such as *Postmortem* (1990) and *All That Remains* (1992). Scarpetta's work is an important part of her life, but the technical detail in the books does not slow down the action. On the contrary, the description of research techniques and use of DNA profiling effectively complement Cornwell's accounts of the painstaking hunt for serial killers.

—Martin Edwards

CORPSE. Golden Age writers made murder a generic requirement. "There simply must be a corpse in a detective novel," wrote S. S. *Van Dine, "and the deader the corpse the better. . . . Three hundred pages is far too much bother for a crime other than murder." The amused tone of voice in which Van Dine issues his rule, and the nineteen others he declaimed as essential to the game, signifies the peculiar place for the corpse in mannered crime stories. Because the unnatural dispatch of the *victim produces the occasion for detection, the corpse has instrumental importance—the story cannot be imagined without it—but, as the narrative of Golden Age-style detective fiction unfolds, the corpse disappears from view, except as a datum, while a plot of consequential investigation plays at the center of the narrative.

The inevitable distancing of violence when the corpse is quickly taken offstage accounts for the paradoxical effect by which some detective fiction transforms a frightful happening into the fine art that Thomas De Quincey said murder could be.

Some detective fiction does that, but not all. For hard-boiled writers, police procedural authors, and other writers whose literary leanings go in the direction of realism and naturalism rather than comedies of manners, the corpse offers an irresistible opportunity to signify inhuman conditions in a world of savagery.

Besides the telling importance obtained either because it is not seen or because its viewing is elaborated for effect, the corpse works as a prod to narrative composition. If there is to be a corpse in the story—for not all crime stories treat murder despite the demands of the Golden Age rules of the game—then the author must determine a method of murder. John Dickson *Carr reveals some of the considerations in selecting a murder technique in the famous "locked room lecture" delivered by Dr. Gideon *Fell in *The Three Coffins* (1935; *The Hollow Man*), as does Dorothy L. *Sayers in her "brief selection of handy short cuts to the grave" appearing in the introduction to *Great Short Stories of Detection, Mystery and Horror* (1928–1934; *The Omnibus of Crime*).

In real-life murder disposal of corpses seems to occupy the minds of few killers, but in fiction there is a highly developed collection of expertise on the matter. Dr. John *Thorndyke in R. Austin *Freeman's *A Silent Witness* (1914) describes cremation. In P. D. *James's *Unnatural Causes* (1967) and Tony *Hillerman's *The Dark Wind* (1982), corpses are mutilated to prevent their identification. A corpse is given a false identity in *The Conjure Man Dies* (1932) by Rudolph Fisher, and corpses are switched to confuse identity in Agatha *Christie's *The Body in the Library* (1942).

When an author does not choose to have a character dispose of the corpse, and when she or he elects to keep the corpse on view, it can become the object of forensic investigation as in the cases of Thorndyke and Patricia D. *Cornwell's Dr. Kay *Scarpetta. Lifeless the corpse may be in definition, but in the craft of crime and mystery writing it has a vital role in continuing to foster invention and variation of convention.

[*See also* Coroner; Forensic Pathologist.]

COUNTRY CONSTABLE. The country constable, found predominantly in English crime fiction, is a popular stock character in novels set in small towns or rural areas, but he is rarely presented as a main character or *sleuth. Like the New York patrolman's rank, constable is the lowest in the British police service; uniformed police constables and plainclothes detective constables are of equal rank, which is the lowest in their particular division. In fiction as in real life, the constable is answerable to a tier of supervisory officers, which severely restricts the freedom necessary for detective work. The constable is rarely able to make decisions of the kind required for a major investigation. The same applies to the patrolman, consequently these subordinate officers seldom feature as central characters in British or American crime fiction.

The stereotypical English country constable is male, middle-aged, red faced, very large, slow moving, and slow thinking; he lives in a village house, rides a bicycle, and speaks with a rustic accent. He is generally simple-minded, kindhearted, inoffensive, likeable, and malleable but often a man of deep wisdom about rural life and people. Happily married in many cases, he may or may not have children. The police station, sometimes within his house and sometimes in an annex, is usually small and contains the basics of his business: a desk, telephone, two chairs, a battered typewriter, and perhaps a notice board bearing posters of wanted criminals and warnings of animal diseases. Apprehended criminals are often confined to the cellar or a spare bedroom with a lock on the door.

Almost any British crime novel of the first half of the twentieth century, particularly those featuring country house murders, will include a country constable. He will most often be depicted carrying out simple tasks such as guarding doors or conducting house-to-house inquiries under supervision rather than initiating his own tasks. Writers often use the stereotype of the inept and slightly stupid constable for comic relief. In Dorothy L. *Sayers's *Clouds of Witness* (1926), Lord Peter *Wimsey observes that, among several footprints in the ground, one belonged to an elephant, which had trampled across the borders; Wimsey's friend, Inspector Parker, observes that the marks in fact had been made by a very large and clumsy constable. By contrast, P. D. *James gives more credit to the constable in *An Unsuitable Job for a Woman* (1972). The first policeman to arrive on the scene is young and efficient; he conducts himself in a calm, professional manner by asking eminently sensible questions.

Frank Parrish makes good use of a constable as a secondary character in the Dan Mallett novels. Police Constable Jim Gundry, the village constable of Medwell Fratorum, is forever coming up against crimes committed by Mallett, a poacher who is also the main character and sleuth. The two men have a grudging professional respect for one another's skills and serve as foils to each other. Mallett, a former bank employee who now bears little respect for the institutions of this world and who uses his quick wits to successfully defy local powers, is the opposite of Gundry, who is quick to go for help but not quite quick enough to figure out Mallett's crimes (*Fly in the Cobweb*, 1986). The stolid tortoise loses out to the flamboyant hare.

Several writers have turned the constable stereotype on its head. Leo *Bruce introduced Sergeant *Beef (*Case for Three Detectives*, 1936) to spoof the eccentric and *aristocratic sleuths popular at the time. A man who loves darts and a large pint, Beef is the tortoise beating the well-dressed hares of detection. After two successful

cases, he decides to go into business for himself as a *private detective if Scotland Yard fails to recognize his remarkable abilities (*Case Without a Corpse*, 1937). Maurice Procter, a one-time Yorkshire policeman, also featured a constable as main character: Police Constable Daniel Burns is a patrolling officer in an urban environment in *Each Man's Destiny* (1947). With his *No Proud Chivalry* (1946), Procter was the first writer of police procedural novels, predating both Hillary *Waugh's *Last Seen Wearing*—(1952) and J. J. Marric's (pseudonym of John *Creasey) *Gideon's Day* (1955; *Gideon of Scotland Yard*). In his semiautobiographical series of novels, Nicholas Rhea chronicles the work of a country constable in North Yorkshire during the 1960s, beginning with *Constable on the Hill* (1979). The stories are rich with humor and nostalgia; crime investigation is not the dominant theme, though Rhea will investigate and detect crimes, both major and minor, that occur on his wild and romantic rural beat (*Constable in Disguise*, 1989). One of the constable's main protagonists is Claude Jeremiah Greengrass, the local poacher, petty thief, and general dealer. Rhea's relationship with the public (and even with Greengrass) shows a caring and sympathetic approach, at times defying his superiors, who do not understand his gentle method of policing.

Georgette *Heyer offers a different variation on the stolid constable in *A Blunt Instrument* (1938). The charming and generous Ernest Fletcher seems an unlikely candidate for murder, and the evidence argues that the crime was impossible anyway. The solution is not obvious: The constable did the deed, one minute before he "found" the body on his nightly rounds.

[*See also* Police Detective.]

—Nicholas Rhea

COUPLES. *This entry is divided into two parts. The first surveys the roles of married and some unmarried but coupled pairs of *sleuths who are protagonists in the works in which they appear. The second section focuses on the challenges faced by the fictional sleuth, the author, and the reader when couples are used as secondary characters in a genre, that traditionally eschewed the use of elements of romance as complicating the detective's mission of discovering the truth.*

Sleuth Couples
Couples as Secondary Characters

SLEUTH COUPLES

Married couples who share in detecting emerged around the turn of the century but never came to dominate the genre, which prefers reason to romance. M. McDonnell Bodkin was among the first to portray married sleuths. The success of *Paul Beck, The Rule-of-Thumb Detective* (1898), followed by *Dora Myrl, The Lady Detective* (1900), encouraged him to bring his two detectives together in *The Capture of Paul Beck* (1909), in which Myrl and Beck compete, with the honors going to Myrl. At the end of the novel, the two sleuths decide to marry. Bodkin's series is notable for giving the woman equal importance. More typical is a series of pulp stories about the Honeymoon Detectives written by Arnold Fredericks that appeared between 1912 and 1917 and featured Richard Duvall, who relies on reason, and his wife Grace, who relies on intuition.

During the 1920s and 1930s, sleuth couples were often characterized by witty dialogue. The most famous detective couples were Tommy and Tuppence Beresford, created by Agatha *Christie, and Nick and Nora *Charles, by Dashiell *Hammett. The Beresfords first appeared as an unmarried pair in The Secret Adversary (1922) in which, despite having to be rescued, Tuppence is equal in importance to Tommy. In Partners in Crime (1928), the now-married couple opens a detective agency, and Tuppence is the brighter of the two. Nick and Nora Charles in The Thin Man (1934) are similar, although Nick had been a *private eye before marrying the socialite Nora.

It was their influence (more through the series of Thin Man movies than directly through the book) that led to a fad of married *sleuths during the late 1930s and 1940s. In 1936, Anne and Jeffrey McNeill first appeared in Theodora Dubois's Armed with a New Terror. They were followed by Craig *Rice's Jake and Helene Justus in 8 Faces at Three (1939; Death at Three) and Kelley Roos's Jeff and Haila Troy in If the Shroud Fits (1941; Dangerous Blondes). The most popular of all were Pam and Jerry *North, created by Frances and Richard Lockridge in The Norths Meet Murder (1941; Mr. and Mrs. North Meet Murder). Unlike some of the sleuthing pairs, the Norths, who appear in twenty-six novels, have no professional experience as investigators. Much of the humor of the North books revolves around Pam's portrayal as a scatterbrain.

Sleuthing couples from the 1950s to the present reflect changes in traditional relationships and the emergence of nontraditional relationships including homosexual couples. Frequently, among traditional married couples, one partner is a police officer. Emmy Tibbett assists her husband, Chief Inspector Henry Tibbett, beginning in Patricia *Moyes's Dead Men Don't Ski (1959). In many of Anne *Perry's Victorian novels, Inspector Thomas Pitt's wife, Charlotte, takes advantage of her higher birth to investigate in situations where he cannot, as in Paragon Walk (1981).

Almost as frequently unmarried lovers work together as sleuths. Private investigator Catherine Sayler, in Linda Grant's Random Access Murder (1988), works with Peter Harmon, whom she describes as her "main squeeze." Beginning with Charlotte *MacLeod's The Family Vault (1979), Sarah Kelling is first a friend, then the wife, of art investigator Max Bittersohn. Noteworthy are two other not-quite lovers, academics Penny Spring and Sir Toby Glendower, whose first case was Exit Actors Dying (1979) by Margot Arnold. In recent years, gay and lesbian partnerships have featured prominently in detective

novels. In Sandra Scoppetone's series, *private eye Lauren Laurano is assisted by her lover Kip, as in I'll Be Leaving You Always (1992). As Scoppetone's books indicate, the competitiveness and repartee of earlier sleuth couples have gradually been replaced by the authentic soundings of deeper relationships.

[See also Gay Characters and Perspectives.]

—Douglas G. Greene

COUPLES AS SECONDARY CHARACTERS

Wilkie *Collins's The Moonstone (1868) establishes the essential problem of the couple in detective fiction. While the genre depends upon the revelation of secrets, the couple, by its very existence, suggests allegiances that threaten the detective's drive toward truth. Suspecting her fiancé of the crime, Collins's heroine withholds evidence, delaying the resolution of the mystery; her loyal silence is read as evidence of guilt. The detective plot typically arrests romance: Rational exploration and private feeling cannot coexist. In Mary Roberts *Rinehart's famous example of the Had-I-But-Known school, The Circular Staircase (1908), a young couple conspires to withhold crucial knowledge that might have saved lives. Yet early authors condone couples' secrecy, acknowledging alternative standards of privacy and loyalty that counter the detective's intrusive ethic.

Proscriptions of the 1920s and '30s on the detective novel's proper elements often stipulate "no love interest," marking the genre off from romance and signaling the ascendancy of rationality. The couple automatically becomes an object of suspicion. Agatha *Christie manipulates this assumption. For example, Hercule Poirot's Christmas (1939; Murder for Christmas; A Holiday for Murder), the account of a family gathering at which the sadistic patriarch is murdered, opens with domestic scenes in which the *victim's children and their spouses reveal the interdependences that bind husband and wife. Establishing these networks, Christie puts into doubt all evidence offered by the couples and diverts attention from her murderer. While Christie uses genre expectations to assemble a challenging intellectual puzzle, for other Golden Age writers couples symbolize the disorder the detective must redress. In C. P. Snow's Death Under Sail (1932), marriage is antithetical to purity. Each couple conceals discreditable secrets, innocent parties destroying evidence of spouses' murderousness. In the work of Ngaio *Marsh, murder is often precipitated by sexual passion, whether fulfilled or frustrated. Both Marsh and Dorothy L. *Sayers portray couples as potential sites of sin. Antisocial forces are expressed as lust and adultery; in Sayers's Clouds of Witness (1926), these practices lead even Lord Peter *Wimsey's family to the brink of the gallows. The detective upholds a fragile civilization against the vast human depravity the couple often represents.

In the British novel evil is natural and individual, the couple a means of its articulation. For the American hard-boiled school, focusing on corrupt social structures, the couple is less important. In the poisoned society of Dashiell *Hammett's *Red Harvest* (1929) or Raymond *Chandler's *The Big Sleep* (1939) transient individual alliances reflect a wider malaise. However, *hard-boiled fiction often validates the romantic couple as an idyllic alternative to the detective's damaged urban world. The couple at the center of *Spenser's investigation in Robert B. *Parker's *Mortal Stakes* (1975), though guilty of various crimes, is rescued from the text's real villain, organized crime.

Couples as murderers are rare in detective fiction. But recent developments show couples sliding further into disrepute. Perhaps this reflects growing elasticity in how the term is defined: P.D. *James's *Shroud for a Nightingale* (1971) features a lesbian couple, one half of whom murders to shield the other, who responds by executing her would-be protector. While James evokes earlier authors' concern with the couple as breeding ground for individualistic passion, in recent feminist work by Sara *Paretsky, Barbara Wilson, and Katherine V. Forrest, the couple—specifically the married, heterosexual couple—embodies the evils of patriarchal society. The family becomes the place where wives collude in fathers' abuse of their female children. Forrest's *Murder at the Nightwood Bar* (1987), in which a timid housewife murders to protect her husband, only to immolate him when his incestuous past is revealed, is an extreme example of the feminist detective novel's attack on heterosexual couples and the abusive power relations they are seen to maintain.

—Anna Wilson

COXE, GEORGE HARMON (1901–1984), American author of mystery novels, short stories, screenplays, and radio scripts. Coxe pioneered the use of a newspaper photographer as protagonist-sleuth with Flashgun Casey in short stories and novels, most of them for *Black Mask* magazine. He followed the burly, tough, somewhat disheveled Casey with a series about another photographer, the sophisticated, cynical sentimentalist Kent *Murdock, in novelettes for the *American Magazine*, many of which were later expanded into novels. Jack Fenner, the private investigator in the Murdock stories, appeared on his own in a later series, set in Boston—as were the Casey and Murdock stories. Coxe used other series characters, most notably Dr. Paul Standish, medical examiner, in short stories and novelettes for the slick magazines. Almost half of his sixty-two novels, however, do not have recurring characters, but are set in the Caribbean or South America, an area he visited frequently. Born in Olean, New York, Coxe attended Purdue and Cornell Universities, and worked for several West Coast newspapers and in advertising in New England before selling his first crime fiction to the pulp magazines. His journalism background can be seen in the Casey and Murdock stories, all of which combine news reporting and crime. He was more interested in recognizable, interesting characters than clever plot twists and often set two protagonists

with differing backgrounds to solve the mystery. He never identified himself as a hard-boiled writer but wrote what the pulp market demanded.

[*See also* Journalist Sleuth.]

—J. Randolph Cox

CREASEY, JOHN (1908–1973), English author who wrote more than five hundred books under some twenty names. Born in Southfields, Surrey, the seventh child of a coachmaker, Creasey was not academically inclined. While employed in various jobs, his passion for writing gained him more than five hundred rejection slips.

His first published novel was *Seven Times Seven* (1932), and he quickly became the doyen of *industry writers. In 1937 alone, twenty-nine of his books were published, while his later output so taxed his publishers that at least twenty new titles appeared posthumously. Some pseudonyms were reserved for westerns, romantic novels, and children's books, but his fame rests on his crime fiction.

As Creasey, he created the gentleman-adventurer the Hon. Richard "The Toff" Rollison in *Introducing the Toff* (1938), Scotland Yard's Roger "Handsome" West in *Inspector West Takes Charge* (1942), and the science fiction thrillers featuring Dr. Stanislaus Alexander Palfrey in *Traitors' Doom* (1942), but his earliest series featured Department Z in counterespionage stories beginning with *The Death Miser* (1933). He also contributed to the Sexton Blake Library. His other series included tales of Patrick Dawlish and "the Crime Haters" (as Gordon Ashe), Mark Kirby (as Robert Caine Frazer), "the Liberator" and Bruce Murdoch (as Norman Deane), Superintendent Folly (as Jeremy York), and psychiatrist Dr. Emmanuel Cellini (as Michael Halliday, but as Kyle Hunt in the United States). His novels as Anthony Morton, featuring reformed jewel thief John "the Baron" Mannering, began with *Meet the Baron* (1937; *The Man in the Blue Mask*), which was written in six days.

Creasey's Toff novels were straight thrillers, although he sometimes grappled with social and political problems (*The Toff and the Fallen Angels*, 1970; *Vote for the Toff*, 1971). The West stories were often excellent in structure (*Look Three Ways at Murder*, 1964), topicality (*Strike for Death*, 1958; *The Killing Strike*), and settings (*Murder London-Miami*, 1969). The Palfrey novels were allegorical and frighteningly prophetic (*The Famine*, 1967; *The Smog*, 1970).

He also achieved greatness in the police procedural novel as J. J. Marric. *Gideon's Day* (1955) showed his Scotland Yard team pursuing six cases simultaneously, and later books developed the principal characters both personally and professionally.

—Melvyn Barnes

CRIDER, (ALLEN) BILL(Y) (b. 1941), Texas-born American literature professor and writer of crime fiction, horror/suspense books, westerns, and children's books. Born in Mexia, Texas, he was educated at the University of Texas in Austin and at North Texas State University before simultaneously pursuing careers as an academic and as a fiction writer. Presently he heads the Department of English at Alvin Community College in Texas.

Crider's gift is to make small-town or small college matters—such as the disappearance of a dentist, faculty in-fighting, and even changes in the weather—seem significant to a broad readership. He achieves this by writing locally-accented dialogue that brings characters to life, and by making his settings more than stage sets, so that they provide true contexts for the crimes. Never one to take himself too seriously, Crider is often lauded for the sense of humor that leavens his books.

With Jack Davis, Crider co-authored his first book, *The Coyote Connection* (1981), a novel in the Nick Carter series. He also collaborated with Stephen Mertz under the house name Jack Buchanan on books in the Mark Stone series. In 1986, Crider published *Too Late to Die*, his first novel under his own name. The Anthony Award-winning book introduces small-town Texas Sheriff Dan Rhodes, a widower and lawman who must run for reelection. More concerned with solving crimes than with playing politics, Rhodes's runs into campaign trouble when a murder occurs.

Too Late to Die became the first book in just one of Crider's series. In *One Dead Dean* (1988), Crider introduces series sleuth Carl Burns, an English literature professor who who solves crimes at the small Texas college where he teaches. Writing as Jack MacLane, Crider introduced a new series of horror/suspense novels with *Keepers of the Beast* (1988). During the 1990s, he launched three more series characters: Truman Smith first appears in *Dead on the Island* (1991); Sally Good is introduced in *Murder is an Art* (1999); and Stanley Waters arrives on the scene in *Murder Under Blue Skies* (1998). Crider co-authored the latter with meteorologist Willard Scott. His two non-series novels, *Blood Marks* (1991) and *The Texas Capitol Murders* (1992), concern a serial killer and political machinations respectively. Crider has also written westerns under his own name and as William Grant, short stories, and well-received children's books.

[*See also* Academic Sleuth.]

—Rosemary Herbert

CRIMINAL MASTERMIND. *See* Master Criminal.

CRISPIN, EDMUND, pseudonym of the British novelist, composer, critic, and anthologist Robert Bruce Montgomery (1921–78). Born at Chesham Bois, Buckinghamshire, he attended Merchant Taylors' School, where his lameness caused him to direct his talents toward composing and writing. While studying modern languages at St. John's College, Oxford, he spent two years as an organ scholar and choirmaster, experience he put to excellent use in his first two novels.

"Somewhat of an intellectual snob" before he encountered John Dickson Carr's *The Crooked Hinge*

(1938), Montgomery took up detective story writing in 1942 with the alacrity of his fictional hero, Gervase *Fen, an eccentric professor of English language and literature at St. Christopher's College, Oxford, and an irrepressible Renaissance man. Within the year he had chosen his pseudonym, taken from a character in Michael *Innes's *Hamlet, Revenge!* (1937), and was hard at work on his first novel.

Crispin's enduring reputation as a Golden Age detective novelist and *farceur rests on nine novels and two collections of short stories published between 1944 and 1979. *The Case of the Gilded Fly* (1944; *Obsequies at Oxford*, indulges Fen's passion for complex crime as he solves a triple murder. *Holy Disorders* (1945) calls Fen to Tolnbridge cathedral in an adventure involving drugs, ghosts, and Nazi spies. *The Moving Toyshop* (1946), perhaps his best novel, combines romance with rollicking chase scenes as Fen solves the "impossible" murder of an elderly heiress. In *Swan Song* (1947; *Dead and Dumb*), Fen solves the locked room murder of an opera company's principal bass singer. In *Love Lies Bleeding* (1948), Crispin draws on his teaching experience to craft a locked room mystery linking Shakespeare with chase scenes and heroism. *Buried for Pleasure* (1948) places Fen on the parliamentary hustings in a romp reminiscent of P. G. Wodehouse. In *Frequent Hearses* (1950; *Sudden Vengeance*) Crispin makes use of his knowledge of the British film industry to craft the story of a starlet's suicide. *The Long Divorce* (1951; *A Noose for Her Neck*) sends Fen underground to do his sleuthing incognito.

After a twenty-five-year silence following his short-story collection *Beware of the Trains* (1953), Crispin produced his final novel, *The Glimpses of the Moon* (1977), which sets an older, more conservative Fen to solve a puzzle in which dismembered *corpses compete for attention with car chases and a politicized constabulary. Another short-story collection, *Fen Country* (1979), was published posthumously.

Multitalented like his protagonist Fen, Crispin, under his real name, Montgomery, also composed choral and chamber works; wrote and conducted background scores for some forty films, including *Carry on Nurse* (1959); and edited six anthologies including *Best Detective Stories* (1959).

[*See also* Academic Sleuth; Eccentrics.]

—Jean A. Coakley

CROFTS, FREEMAN WILLS (1879–1957), British detective novelist. Born in Dublin, Ireland, Crofts was educated in Belfast and spent his working life with the Belfast and Northern Counties Railway, joining as an apprentice engineer in 1896 and rising to chief engineer before retiring in 1929. Crofts's first detective novel, *The Cask* (1920), set the pattern for his later work. With its complex plot in which an alibi dependent on railway and cross-Channel timetables is gradually broken down, it was called by Anthony *Boucher "the definitive novel" of this type, and, as one of the first examples, is considered to be a significant landmark in the history of the genre. (A subsequent edition, published in 1940, contains a preface by the author describing the novel's genesis.) *The Cask* was followed by *The Ponson Case* (1921), *The Pit-Prop Syndicate* (1922), and *The Groote Park Murder* (1923), which has a South African background. Crofts's series detective, Inspector (later Chief Superintendent) Joseph *French, first appeared in *Inspector French's Greatest Case* (1925), is featured in twenty-eight other novels, including *The Sea Mystery* (1928), *The Box Office Murders* (1929; *The Purple Sickle Murders*), *Sir John Magill's Last Journey* (1930), *Crime at Guildford* (1935; *The Crime at Nornes*), and *Death of a Train* (1946). Crofts is one of the major writers in the Golden Age tradition, and his plots—often with a railway or shipping background (as in *The Loss of the Jane Vosper*, 1936)—are put together with the care and precision of an engineer. Raymond *Chandler called him "the soundest builder of them all." His novels differ from those of most other writers of the time, however, in that French proceeds not by brilliant deduction but by the painstaking accumulation of minute detail; the reader is allowed to follow each step of the detective's ratiocination. Although French, with his bourgeois background, is more credible as a policeman than Ngaio *Marsh's aristocratic Roderick *Alleyn, Crofts knew little or nothing about the workings of the police force, and his work, unlike that of his contemporary Sir Basil Thomson (1861–1939), head of the CID at Scotland Yard, in no way adumbrates the later police procedural novel. Crofts weaknesses are a pedestrian style, a certain dullness in narration, and the complete subordination of character to plot. His attempt to achieve more depth of characterization in the late *Silence for the Murderer* (1948) is a failure, though *The 12.30 from Croydon* (1934; *Wilful and Premeditated*), modeled on R. Austin *Freeman's inverted detective story, in which the first half is narrated from the standpoint of the murderer, is not without merit. These qualities led Julian *Symons, in *Bloody Murder: From the Detective Story to the Crime Novel*, (rev. ed. 1992), to dub Crofts "a typical, but also the best, representative of what may be called the Humdrum school of detective novelists."

—T. J. Binyon

CROSS, AMANDA, pseudonym of Carolyn Gold Heilbrun (b. 1926), American author and academic. Heilbrun taught English and Women's Studies at Columbia University, where she also received her doctorate, until 1992. Her academic writing—particularly *Toward a Recognition of Androgyny* (1973), *Reinventing Womanhood* (1979), and *Writing a Woman's Life* (1988)—explores the construction of women as individuals and as literary characters. Her criticism of detective fiction, notably as represented by the novels of Dorothy L. *Sayers and the comedy of manners, demonstrates the genre's literary connections. Her fiction, originally written under a pseudonym to protect her academic career, has re-

ceived critical and popular acclaim: in addition to a scroll from the Mystery Writers of America, she received an Edgar nomination for best first novel for *In the Last Analysis* (1964) and the 1981 Nero Wolfe Award for *Death in a Tenured Position* (1981; *A Death in the Faculty*).

Cross's witty, literate detective novels are simultaneously academic mysteries, comedies of manners, and feminist fiction; their series detective, Professor Kate *Fansler, teaches English literature at a university much like Columbia. In the twenty-six years between the first novel and *The Puzzled Heart* (1998), Fansler ages little but grows both wiser and more feminist. Seeing the "ivory tower" from the inside, Fansler, Cross, and Heilbrun are increasingly discouraged by its politics, sexism, racism, and self-serving nature. Fansler detects like the literary scholar her creator is: She constructs narratives around the facts, clues, suspects, and innuendoes until one version emerges to accommodate most of what she has discovered. Beginning with the fourth novel, *The Theban Mysteries* (1971), whose setting and detection are based on Sophocles's *Antigone*, Cross addresses the feminist matters that dominate Heilbrun's academic work: The lives of women silenced, obscured, ended. Fansler detects more than murder as she reconstructs the narratives of women's experience.

[*See also* Academic Sleuth.]

—Kathleen Gregory Klein

CRUMLEY, JAMES (b. 1939), American Vietnam War veteran, former journalist, and writer of two series of crime novels. Born in three Rivers, Texas, he was educated at the Georgia Institute of Technology, Texas Arts and Industries University and the Iowa Writer's Workshop at the University of Iowa. Crumley based his first novel, *One Count to Cadence* (1969) on his Vietnam War experience. Then he introduced the first of his series detectives, Milton Chester "Milo" Milodragovitch III, in *The Wrong Case* (1975). Milodragovitch shares several characteristics with Crumley's second series character, Chauncy Wayne "C.W." Sughrue, who first appears in *The Last Good Kiss* (1978). Both are veterans, alcoholics, rednecks, and *private eyes who work out of Meriwether, Montana. While Milodragovitch served in the Korean War, Sughrue did his tour of duty in Vietnam, until he was court-marshaled for perpetrating atrocities there. Following that, the U.S. government relied on him to infiltrate the anti-war movement. The son of parents who both committed suicide, Milodragovitch is a dark enough character, but Sughrue, who seems to be in his element when violence occurs, is darker still. The two characters work together in *Bordersnakes* (1996).

[*See also* Hard-boiled Sleuth.]

—Rosemary Herbert

Cuff, Sergeant. A *sleuth in *The Moonstone* (1868) by Wilkie *Collins, Sergeant Cuff is introduced to readers as the finest detective in England. Although he does not dominate events of the narrative, his approach to the criminal problem as a puzzle to be solved piece by piece anticipates the methodical demonstration of detection technique in the tales of the archetypal *Great Detectives. According to Howard Haycraft in *Murder for Pleasure* (1941), Cuff may be recognized as a fictional rendering of the real-life Inspector Whicher who figured in the sensational Constance Kent or "Road Murder" case of 1860. In any event, Cuff's professional position links his accomplishments to those of the official police whose exploits inspired the creation of the crime and mystery genre, as well as making him a prototype of numerous successors in fiction from every period in the history of the form.

[*See also* Eccentrics; Police Detective.]

—John M. Reilly

CULINARY SLEUTHS. Throughout the history of the crime and mystery genre, descriptions of food preparation, drinking and dining have provided important sources of means to murder, clues, ambiance and characterization. Often those who prepared food, or at least were able to spike it with poison or other fatal ingredients before it was consumed, played the role of murderer. More recently, however, food professionals, including cooks, caterers, bakers, chocolatiers, gourmet chefs, restauranteurs and bed and breakfast inn owners have taken on the role of crime solver in a large number of novels produced since 1980. Acting as *surrogate sleuths, these characters are neither *private eyes nor police professionals, but they use their specialized skills to help them solve murders that they encounter in the course of their work.

Those who write about culinary sleuths work in a tradition established by earlier writers but depart from it, too. They certainly use the convention firmly established during the Golden Age of crime and mystery writing—using the delivery of food or drink at mealtimes and bedtime to establish the time a murder took place and the vehicle in which a deadly ingredient was delivered. In addition, they use knowledge of flavors to help them know how the taste of poison or of a drug overdose might be masked by strong-tasting food and drink.

Crime writers have long used the taste for gourmet food to indicate wealth, status, sophistication. They have shown that more modest food consumption can also say something about a character, while a passion for more humble fare is often used to indicate unpretentiousness. Notable gourmets from the past are Dorothy L. *Sayers's Lord Peter *Wimsey and Rex Stout's Nero *Wolfe. Somewhat more recently, E.X. *Ferrars's suggested reliability and modesty in her *elderly sleuth Andrew Basnett by making him an habitual cheese-nibbler, who always takes his small snack at the same time of day. Similarly, a taste for junk food establishes the down-to-earth character, such as Sue *Grafton's Kinsey *Millhone, Janet *Evanovich's Stephanie Plum, and Susan *Dunlap's jelly doughnut fancier, Jill Smith. A nose for

plonk—wines he characterizes as "Chateau Thames Embankment"—marks John *Mortimer's Horace *Rumpole as a man of the people. Food preparation, too, has long been used as a way to tell readers more about a character. Jessie Arnold's preparation of food for herself and her dogsled team in Sue Henry's *Murder on the Iditarod Trail* (1991) is a strong indicator of the character's resourcefulness. A flair for whipping up a meal—and serving it to a woman—helps to make Robert B. *Parker's *Spenser a tough guy with domestic skills.

Like their Golden Age predecessors, more recent creators of culinary sleuths use food to indicate character, but they are apt to take it further, to add a regional or ethnic flavor to their books that is often evident in titles (and subtitles). Examples include: Virginia Rich's *The Baked Bean Supper Murders* (1983), set in coastal Maine; Nancy Pickard's continuation of Rich's series in *The 17-Ingredient Chili Con Carni Murders* (1993), set in Arizona, and Pickard's *The Blue Corn Murders* (1998), set in Colorado; Steve Sherman's *Maple Sugar Murders* (1999), set in New Hampshire; and Tamar Myers's *No Use Dying Over Spilt Milk: A Pennsylvania Dutch Mystery with Recipes* (1996).

Myers is not the only author to attract attention by means of pun-laden titles and the inclusion of recipes. A number of authors follows this formula and adds coy sleuth monikers to the mix. Diane Mott Davidson's caterer Goldy Bear serves food and solves crimes in *Catering to Nobody* (1990), *Dying for Chocolate* (1992), *Cereal Murders* (1993) and more books. Lou Jane Temple's restauranteur Heaven Lee appears in several adventures, exemplified by *Death is Semisweet* (2002), in which she helps out a friend who is starting a Kansas City chocolate shop. Some confine their wordplay to titles and give their sleuths sensible or ethnic names to go along with their hardworking personalities. Examples include Mary Daheim's Judith McMonigle Flynn in *Creeps Suzette: A Bed & Breakfast Mystery* (2000), and other novels; and Sharon Kahn's Ruby Rothman, a Texas rabbi's wife who loves to eat and cook, in *Don't Cry for Me, Hot Pastrami* (2002) and other novels; Joanne Pence's *nosy parker sleuth and baker Angelina Amalfi in *Bell, Cook and Candle* (2002), and more. Writing as Joanna Carl, Eve K. Sandstrom created another sleuth along these lines. Divorcee Lee McKinney learns about custom chocolate making in *The Chocolate Cat Caper* (2002). The author also celebrates this candy in *The Chocolate Bear Burglary: A Chocoholic Mystery* (2002).

Michael Bond, who is probably best known for his children's books about Paddington Bear, also wrote a memorable series of culinary mysteries featuring Monsieur Pamplemousse, a French food inspector who wines and dines and detects, accompanied by his faithful bloodhound Pommes Frites, at all kinds of scenes of crimes. An example is *Monsieur Pamplemousse Afloat* (1998), in which the use of pesticides in vineyards looks likely to cut the population of snails that are used for the famous French dish, escargots. Peter King's Gourmet

Detective uses his expertise to eat well and solve crimes in a vineyard venue in *Dying on the Vine* (1999). This engaging sleuth also appears in *Death al Dente* (2000), *Roux the Day* (2002) and other books bearing the subtitle, *A Gourmet Detective Mystery*. Katherine Hall Page's Faith Fairchild is another memorable culinary sleuth. This New England minister's wife encounters crime among her husband's parishioners and in the course of her own work as a caterer. She appears in *The Body in the Basement* (1994), *The Body in the Bog* (1996) and other volumes enhanced by the inclusion of recipes. Tim Hemlin writes about a caterer, too. His Neil Marshall is a graduate student in Houston who moonlights as a caterer and becomes a murder suspect in *If Wishes Were Horses* (1995). In *People in Glass Houses* (1997), Marshall gets mixed up in murder and the world of politics when murder occurs while he caters a candidate's fundraiser.

Ellen Hart has two series sleuths. Beginning with *Hallowed Murder* (1989), her Jane Lawless looks at crime from a restauranteur's viewpoint, while Sophie Greenway, who is introduced in this *Little Piggy Went to Murder* (1994), trains a food writer's eye on suspicious dishes and those who prepare them. Former *Washington Post* food columnist Phyllis Richman also uses a food writer-sleuth in *Who's Afraid of Virginia Ham?* (2001) and other books. Additional characters in this category are: Amy Myers's gourmet chef, Auguste Didier, introduced in *Murder in Pug's Parlor* (1986); Joanne Fluke's bakery owner Hannah Swenson, introduced in *The Chocolate Chip Cookie Murder* (2000) and cookbook author and crime writer Janet Laurence's multi-talented chef, caterer and food writer Darina Lisle, who first appears in *A Deepe Coffyn* (1989).

—Rosemary Herbert

D

Dalgliesh, Adam, detective protagonist in several novels by P. D. *James who rises from the rank of chief detective inspector to commander at Scotland Yard. Dalgliesh is introduced in *Cover Her Face* (1962). A widower who lost his wife and son during childbirth when he was in his late twenties, he shows a melancholy, even saturnine, disposition. He had a lonely childhood, and he lives a solitary life as an adult. He feels some guilt about his profession; more, he has a deeply rooted passion for innocence, which he seeks to protect, in the elderly as well as the young. He also possesses a fear of emotional commitment which prevents his retaining the love of a strong-minded woman met in *A Mind to Murder* (1963) and lost in *Unnatural Causes* (1967). Some readers hope he will become romantically attached to Cordelia *Gray, introduced by James in *An Unsuitable Job for a Woman* (1972), though the two seem ill matched. Dalgliesh is quietly competent, superb at interrogation, yet not infallible. While he can use calculated charm to good effect, his coworkers find him moody and at times aloof. Dalgliesh is a published poet—James provides one example of his writing, which is not without merit—and an acute observer of character. Though he can show compassion, he is committed to justice for its own sake, and only once do we see his heart overrule his head.

Dalgliesh has been portrayed by Roy Marsden in a superior series of television films. James has said that Marsden is not at all as she imagined Dalgliesh, and one can see why, but each depiction is successful in its own right. It is appropriate that the reader view Dalgliesh in various lights—indeed, James spells his surname "Dalgleish" in her first book—for the novels in which he features change viewpoints, adding to their complexity and interest, so that at times the reader knows more than Dalgliesh does. In some of the television films, these shifts produce a choppy effect; in James's novels, the transitions are nearly seamless and almost always convincing. Thus readers do not grow tired of Dalgliesh as they might of an ever-present and hovering detective, and though they know he will produce order out of chaos in the end, they also expect that he will make human mistakes. The result is one of the most convincing detectives in modern fiction, a man who is never endearing but always intellectually compelling.

[*See also* Police Detective.]

—Robin W. Winks

DALY, CARROLL JOHN (1889–1958), American author credited with creating the prototype of the *private eye in his short story "The False Burton Combs" (*Black Mask*, Dec. 1922). The unnamed protagonist in this story is a hired impersonator who terms himself a "gentleman adventurer" and "soldier of fortune" who works on his own against crime but eschews any mission as a "knight errant." Daly's use of a tough, first-person vernacular, and of a character who is uninclined to take women seriously, anticipated the work of countless private eye writers to follow. These qualities were also shared by Daly's most famous series character, the hard-boiled private eye Race *Williams, and by two more gumshoes he created: Vee Brown, a private eye with a penchant for songwriting, and the New York cop Satan Hall. Another Daly creation, "Three-Gun" Terry Mack, appeared in the pulp magazines.

Born in Yonkers, New York, Daly graduated from the American Academy of Dramatic Arts. He began and then abandoned an acting career, and became a movie projectionist and an owner of a chain of movie theaters before he began a writing career that would win him recognition as the pioneer of the private eye story. At the height of his career, a *Black Mask* readers poll proved him to be more popular than Erle Stanley *Gardner and Dashiell *Hammett.

[*See also* Hard-Boiled Sleuth.]

—Rosemary Herbert

DALY, ELIZABETH (1878–1967), American writer of sixteen well-plotted murder mysteries featuring Henry Gamadge, a bibliophile *sleuth who solves his cases by means of logic and attention to detail. A New Yorker herself, Daly set her fictional crimes, written during the 1940s and 1950s, among a wealthy New York social set. Influenced by the novelists of the Golden Age of the detective novel, she followed in their traditions, employing traditional conventions of the genre: setting her work in a civilized milieu, emphasizing the puzzle element, and playing fair with the reader in the delivery of clues. Her sleuth, initially a bachelor, eventually takes a wife, Clara, who shares his New York brownstone complete with laboratory.

Daly came from a privileged background. Born in New York City in 1878, she attended the exclusive Miss Baldwin's School, and earned a bachelor's degree from Bryn Mawr College in 1901 and a master's degree from Columbia University in 1902. She taught at Bryn Mawr from 1902 to 1906, and for many years enjoyed producing amateur theatricals. This Edgar Award-winning author began her mystery writing career at the age of sixty-one.

—Rosemary Herbert

D'AMATO, BARBARA (b. 1938), American mystery writer best known as the creator of the *journalist sleuth,

Catherine "Cat" Marsala. Born in Grand Rapids, Michigan, she was educated at Cornell University and at Northwestern University. In addition to raising a family, she has worked as a stage carpenter, a hospital orderly, and writing instructor.

D'Amato began her mystery writing career with the locked-room mystery, *The Hands of Healing Murder* (1980), which introduces Dr. Gerritt De Graaf, a *forensic pathologist who also appears in *The Eyes on Utopia Murders* (1981). In 1989, she wrote a non-series mystery, *On My Honor*, under the penname Malacai Black. These books were well received—*On My Honor* was nominated for an Anthony Award—but D'Amato gained much more attention for her Cat Marsala series, which she launched in 1990 with *Hardball*. D'Amato apparently learned much from female mystery writers such as Sue *Grafton and Sara *Paretsky. Like them, she created an independent female sleuth who also maintains connections with a "family" of characters. However, unlike the creators of Kinsey *Millhone and V.I. *Warshawski, D'Amato knows she is not breaking new ground by writing about a strong female character: this may account for her showing rather than telling readers that detection is a very suitable job for a woman.

Marsala is memorable for taking on crimes that raise social questions. For examples, *Hard Luck* (1992) and *Hard Women* (1993) treat the machinations behind a lottery and the difficult lives of prostitutes, respectively. D'Amato's greatest achievement may be in provoking readers to think about the social ills she has revealed, even after the crimes in the novels are satisfactorily solved.

The 1990s decade was a productive period for D'Amato. In addition to writing eight Cat Marsala mysteries, she wrote *The Doctor, The Murder, The Mystery* (1992), a true account of research she did, which led to the release of Dr. John Branion, a physician who was falsely accused of murder. The book garnered both the Anthony and Agatha awards. In 1996, she launched a new series of novels centered on the activities of Chicago police personnel. The first novel in this series is *Killer.app* (1996). The start of the twenty-first century, saw D'Amato continuing both series and producing another non-series novel, *White Male Infant* (2002).

[*See also* Females and Feminists.]

—Rosemary Herbert

DAVIOT, GORDON. *See* Tey, Josephine.

DAVIS, DOROTHY SALISBURY (b. 1916), American author. Although Dorothy Salisbury Davis admits to a desire to create a series character like Georges *Simenon's Inspector *Maigret, her failure to develop a running character in her books looks like refusal of a convention. She has dedicated her work to a sympathetic investigation of characters undergoing stress, which seems to demand a variety of milieus and portrayals rather than a formula.

Born in Chicago, Davis was raised as a Roman Catholic and educated at Holy Child High School in Waukegan, Illinois. She left the church when she married. Perhaps not surprisingly, crises of faith figure prominently in her fiction, most notably in *A Gentle Murderer* (1951) and *Where the Dark Streets Go* (1969), both of which feature priests as protagonists. The Midwest—Wisconsin and Illinois, rural and urban—often serves as the setting for Davis's books; but so too does New York City in such novels as *A Death in the Life* (1976), *Scarlet Night* (1980), *Lullaby of Murder* (1984), and *The Habit of Fear* (1987). The last of these is about Julie Hayes, a young fortune-teller in a seedy district of the city, who may become at last Davis's series character.

Psychology instead of detection provides the substance of Davis's short stories, even more so than in her novels. Her collection of fifteen short stories, *Tales for a Stormy Night: The Collected Crime Stories* (1984), displays a strong sense of suspense, a skillful ability to lure the reader into mistaken assumptions, and an especially strong way of sharing with readers the minds of female characters confronting hazards and crisis.

—John M. Reilly

DAY-LEWIS, CECIL. *See* Blake, Nicholas.

DEAF DETECTIVE. *See* Disability, Sleuth with a.

DEXTER, (NORMAN) COLIN (b. 1930), British author of detective fiction. Trained at Cambridge in the classics, which he taught in various schools, Dexter published his first detective novel, *Last Bus to Woodstock*, in 1975 while employed by the Oxford Delegacy of Local Examinations. He is an avid fan of crossword puzzles, in which he has won national championships; his learning and love of puzzles inform his novels, which are formal whodunits known for their elaborate plots as well as their narrative verve and finely characterized series detective.

Through *Death Is Now My Neighbor* (1997), Dexter had published a dozen novels, all of them set in Oxford and its environs, where he lives and which he lovingly details. In *The Dead of Jericho* (1981), for example, he explores the gentrification of an old working-class neighborhood. Many of his stories revolve around colleges, schools, or related institutions; *The Silent World of Nicholas Quinn* (1977) is set at an examinations board.

Chief Inspector Endeavor Morse and Sergeant Lewis of the Thames Valley appear in every novel. Morse is a lover of Wagner, good beer, and crossword puzzles; Sergeant Lewis is the prosaic policeman, married with children. Through Morse, Dexter can display his love of words, theorizing, and general intellectual play. While Lewis slogs through the dull work of routine, Morse evolves theory after theory, sometimes wrongheaded, but always plausible and often brilliant. Dexter delights to show us the documents in the case, including epitaphs in *The Wench Is Dead* (1989) or handwritten letters in

The Jewel That Was Ours (1991). Despite its linguistic precision and much exclamatory emphasis, Dexter's narrative is relaxed and informal, scattered with asides, jokes, and wry commentary.

Like the author, Morse suffers from diabetes. The chief inspector's taste for drink and failure to take adequate care of himself is seen in the later novels, and leads to his death in *The Remorseful Day* (1999).

[*See also* Police Detective; Sidekicks and Sleuthing Teams.]

—Susan Oleksiw *and* Rosemary Herbert

DIBDIN, MICHAEL (b. 1947), English-born crime writer known for his Venetian detective Aurelio *Zen, as well as for several books that do not feature the series character. The son of parents who moved the family frequently when he was young, Dibdin spent the largest part of his boyhood in Northern Ireland. He then made many moves himself as an adult. After earning a bachelor's degree from the University of Sussex in England, he moved to Edmonton, Canada, to earn his master's degree from the University of Alberta. In Canada, he worked as a painting contractor for five years. He also spent five years teaching English in Perugia, Italy. Upon returning to England, he wrote *Ratking* (1988), a crime novel set in Italy. When he introduced Zen in this book, he had no intention of making him a series character. In fact, the book's success may rest on the fact that Dibdin was equally interested in writing about the other characters. By the time Dibdin wrote *And Then You Die* in 2002, Zen is just as much the focus of the book as are most series characters. Here he is hiding from Mafiosi who tried—and failed—to kill him in *Blood Rain* (1999). The Zen books benefit from Dibdin's penchant for playing with words and his ease in working Italian expressions into his prose. His non-series books tend to be darker and more disturbing, as is the case in *The Dying of the Light* (1993), a novel about murderous members of a religious cult, and *The Tryst* (1989), which scrutinizes the interactions of a female psychiatrist and a boy whom she is treating. Dibdin also wrote *The Last Sherlock Holmes Story* (1978) in which he imagines the *Great Detective seeking out Jack the Ripper. He has also edited detective fiction anthologies. Married three times, Dibdin now lives in Seattle, Washington, where he shares two houses with his third wife, the mystery writer K.K. Beck.

—Rosemary Herbert

DICKENS, CHARLES (1812–1870), British novelist, generally considered the greatest novelist of the Victorian age. Dickens's childhood was spent on the borderlines of poverty; central to his development was the emotionally crucial period when his father was imprisoned for debt and he, at the age of twelve, was sent to work for a pittance in a blacking warehouse. This period he kept a secret from his family and almost all his friends, but into many of the novels the words "Warren's Blacking" are inserted, as a sort of clue and reminder to himself.

It is not surprising that prisons should play such a large role in Dickens's novels. In each of the novels, crime is an important component—often the central motivator of the plot. Some of his early novels are often classed with the Newgate novels. Although Dickens does not fictionalize the lives of real criminals as do Edward Bulwer-Lytton and William Harrison Ainsworth, he takes fact as his springboard (the Gordon Riots in *Barnaby Rudge*, 1841; the fence Ikey Solomons as the model for Fagin in *Oliver Twist*, 1837–39). These early works sensationalize crime and present the criminal in a melodramatic or lurid light that almost transforms him into a hero. The treatment of Bill Sikes after the murder of Nancy is a classic example of this.

In his great mature novels crime is still central. Most significant for the whodunit is the murder of Mr. Tulkinghorn in *Bleak House* (1852–53). The treatment of Lady Dedlock's connection with the crime is one of the first uses of the red herring technique; we have a surprise solution; and the use of Inspector Bucket, and Dickens's fascination with his methods of detection, bring us close to the twentieth-century crime novel. On the other hand, the atmospheric treatment of the semi-criminal waterside areas of London in *Our Mutual Friend* (1864–65) made this novel a favorite with the Golden Age writers, who referred to it often when its reputation was not high. *The Mystery of Edwin Drood* (1870), though written at a much lower level of intensity, and perhaps in emulation of Dickens's friend Wilkie *Collins's successful fiction, bade fair to anticipate many more techniques of later crime novels, but it was only half finished at Dickens's death, and it has spawned more mysteries—and more proposed solutions—than any other of his novels.

Prison scenes, a natural corollary of Dickens's preoccupation with crime, dot the books, from Pickwick in the Fleet to the projected scene of Jasper in the condemned cell that was to conclude *Edwin Drood*. They range in tone from the grand guignol of Fagin awaiting execution to the controlled satire of Uriah Heep as a model prisoner—a critique of new penal thinking. More haunting still are the metaphorical prisons that pepper the novels, from the self-imprisonment of Miss Havisham and Mrs. Clennam, through imprisonment by political dogma in Mr. Gradgrind, to imprisonment by emotional repression in Mr. Dombey or Rosa Dartle.

Dickens's reputation dipped somewhat in his last years and in the decades immediately after his death, but in the twentieth century he has generally been regarded as Britain's greatest novelist. Central to that estimate is his handling of the themes of crime and punishment, guilt and repentance.

—Robert Barnard

DICKINSON, PETER (MALCOLM DE BRISSAC), (b. 1927), Africa-born humorist and author of children's books and crime fiction. Born in Livingstone,

Northern Rhodesia (now Zambia), he was a King's Scholar at Eton College, and earned a Bachelor's degree from King's College, Cambridge. He served in the British Army. During the 1950s and 1960s, he served as an assistant editor and reviewer for *Punch*. Twice-married, he is the father of four children.

Dickinson may be best recognized as a writer for children. Prolific and inventive, he has written picture books, books for young readers, and young adult fiction, demonstrating an ease manipulating elements of several genres, and sometimes blending them in a single volume. He seems equally adept at turning out fantasy, science fiction, and realistic, problem-centered books set in historical time periods or in the contemporary scene. He began his career as children's writer without intending to continue it, writing the first draft of *The Weathermonger* (1968) in response to a nightmare. He thought the writing of this book would loosen a writing block that had stopped progress on his first murder mystery for adults, but soon found himself drawn to writing two more books following from *The Weathermonger*.

Dickinson's foray into children's fiction did shatter his writing block, and his first mystery novel for adults, *Skin Deep* (1968; *The Glass-sided Ant's Nest*) was published in 1968. The book introduces Dickinson's series character, Superintendent James Pibble of Scotland Yard. Pibble is stolid enough, but he seems to be a magnet for strange cases, in which Dickinson blends elements of classic detective fiction with bizarre crimes. Key characters may be unusual—and they are not always human. In *Skin Deep*, tribe members from New Guinea find murder in their midst as they try to adjust to living in twentieth-century London. A pair of lions is significant in *A Pride of Heroes* (1969: *The Old English Peep Show*), an antic work in which an English country home is being operated as a theme park, complete with jungle animals. A chimpanzee witnesses the crime in *The Poison Oracle* (1974), the first of Dickinson's several non-series mysteries.

Particularly in the non-Pibble books, Dickinson is again at home in mixing genres, as when he pairs science fiction and a murder mystery in *The Green Gene* (1973). In this book a scientist is kidnapped in a near-future England that is racially divided, calling to mind the circumstances in South Africa under apartheid. In two notable books set, in part, during World War II, Dickinson delves into questions of surpressed memory. In the aptly-titled *Hindsight* (1983) a writer seeks to recall his wartime boyhood, while in *Perfect Gallows* (1988) a man who left behind his past to become an actor reluctantly recalls a murder when he returns to the place where it occurred.

Dickinson and his second wife, American fantasy author Robin McKinley, live with three whippets in Bramdean, Hampshire. Currently, the pair is collaborating on short story collections centered around the elements, beginning with *Water: Tales of the Elemental Spirits*.

[*See also* Eccentrics.]

—Rosemary Herbert

DISABILITY, SLEUTH WITH A. Relatively few writers have written crime fiction featuring a handicapped detective, probably because the limitation imposed by a disability adds another constraint to those already inherent in the form. Having deprived a detective of a sense or limb, it becomes necessary to demonstrate the lack and to bring it plausibly to bear on the development of a narrative. Ernest *Bramah's detective, Max *Carrados, was blinded by a branch while out riding. He has since refined his other senses in compensation and employs an invaluable manservant with eyes that miss nothing. Lest his powers seem excessive, his creator states clearly in a preface that his achievements, however remarkable, are founded on fact. In one story, Carrados confounds an old school friend by deducing—with expert knowledge and from handling a coin—the whole truth of a case he is investigating. In another, he turns the tables on his kidnappers by plunging them into darkness.

Thornley Colton is C. H. Stagg's detective, "totally blind since birth" but nonetheless a musician and man-about-town, with his secretary as guide. He, too, has trained his other senses and now has "wonderfully sharp ears" and "super-sensitive fingertips." In shaking hands, he rests his finger on the wrist, since a man cannot disguise his pulse rate, however impassive his face. Repeatedly, his fingers trace crucial details invisible to the eye: stitches in cushions, a tear in a lining, a scar in velvet.

Captain Duncan MacLain figures in Baynard Kendrick's novels, with two German shepherd dogs: Schnucke, his female Seeing Eye, and Dreist, his male protector. MacLain was blinded in World War I and has since worked ceaselessly "to perfect the senses of hearing, touch and smell." By counting footsteps he can estimate height and, after six years' practice, he can now "shoot at sound." Those who manipulate others by physical tricks are diminished by his presence.

Eric Ward has chronic glaucoma and suffers hideously in certain novels by Roy Lewis, with titles reflecting his condition but also commenting on the action: *A Certain Blindness* (1980); *A Limited Vision* (1983). Forced out of the police by his affliction, he becomes a solicitor, astute and observant, except when debilitated by an attack. An operation enables him, eventually, to lead a normal life. Stella Tower's *Dumb Vengeance* (1933) is a "semi-detective story" with Amelia Jenkins, a dumb woman, as its semi-detective. When her friend and host is murdered, she begins to "brood and watch and wonder," eyes and ears continually alert. Finally, aware of the truth and no longer passive, she intervenes drastically.

Drury Lane and Joe Binney are deaf, in works by Barnaby Ross and Jack Livingston, respectively. Lane has become deaf with age and lip-reading is a "latter-day accomplishment." It has "sharpened" his "powers of concentration": Once his eyes are closed, he enters a world of silence. Binney is a *private eye, whose hearing was destroyed in underwater demolition work with the navy. From lip-reading he has developed increased skill at "reading expressions" and it is "hard to hide a lie" from him.

Vicars Bell's detective, Dr. Douglas Baynes, lost a leg in World War I and still feels humiliated by his artificial limb, "wretched and somehow shameful." Despite his handicap, he drives a car and takes active part in Home Guard exercises.

Dan Fortune, in novels by Michael Collins, lacks his left arm and takes bleak comfort from the fact that he is right-handed. As a lawless seventeen-year-old he was looting a ship when he fell into a hold, smashing the arm so badly that amputation was necessary. Though always aware of his loss, he has developed "good legs and quick wits" in compensation and when matched against a single opponent can still fight and win.

Martin Cotterell is John Trench's detective, an archaeologist who lost his left hand in the desert during the Second World War. His "aluminium substitute" is attached by a harness and "covered by a glove." It allows him to drive and scale walls until it is "crushed and flattened" by a rock hurled by a murderer. Afterward, he needs help with his shoelaces. Later still, with a new "metal hook," he wards off a "swinging right" and disarms a youth with a razor.

In *Traitor's Purse* (1941) Albert *Campion suffers from amnesia and cannot recall his name, let alone the threat to national security he is working to avert. The story gains extraordinary tension from the cloud over Campion's brain: He has to rediscover not only the national secret but also himself.

—B. A. Pike

DOBYNS, STEPHEN (b. 1941), American poet, professor, and crime writer. Born in Orange, New Jersey, he was educated at Shimer College in Mt. Carroll, Illinois, at Wayne State University in Detroit, and at the University of Iowa in Iowa City, Iowa. Married and the father of three children, he has served as a writing instructor and professor at many colleges. A distinguished poet, he won the National Poetry Prize in 1984. He has written non-mystery novels that employ a kind of academic flair.

His mystery oeuvre began with the non-series novel, *Man of Little Evils* (1974). Two years later, in *Saratoga Longshot* (1976), he introduced Charlie Bradshaw, a private eye who investigates crimes in and around the horseracing milieu in Saratoga, New York. The Bradshaw books are easily recognizeable by the fact that they all have the word Saratoga in their titles. They are memorable for much more than that. The crimes can be offbeat; Bradshaw's interactions with his family and especially with his friend Victor Plotz engender offbeat humor; and the Saratoga scene—from beautiful area vistas to the mucking out of horse stalls—is lovingly described. At times, Dobyns writes in the farceur tradition of Michael *Innes and others, as when his characters get involved in antic chase scenes. In contrast with this, Dobyns' non-series novel, *The Church of Dead Girls* (1997) is a far darker examination of vigilantism that ensues

when young girls go missing in a small town. Critics agree this is the author's strongest prose work to date.

[*See also* Animals; Eccentrics; Farceurs; Poets as Crime Writers.]

—Rosemary Herbert

DOSTOYEVSKY, FYODOR MIKHAYLOVICH (1821–1881), Russian novelist and journalist. He entered the army as an engineer but resigned in 1844 to write. Sentenced to death in 1849 as one of a utopian socialist circle but reprieved immediately before execution, he was exiled to Siberia until 1859, spending 1850–54 in prison, of which *Notes from the House of the Dead* (1862; *Zapiski iz myortvogo doma*) gives a fictionalized account. Though his four great novels—*Crime and Punishment* (1866; *Prestupleniye i nakazaniye*), *The Idiot* (1868; *Idiot*), *The Possessed* (1872; *Besy*), and *The Brothers Karamazov* (1880; *Brat'ya Karamazovy*)—all deal with murder, Dostoyevsky is not primarily interested in the detection of the crime or the psychology of the criminal. He sees murder as the result of the infection of society by Western ideas encouraging the selfish assertion of the individual will. In opposition to this he puts forward a Russian ideal of self-sacrifice and, in *The Brothers Karamazov*, the doctrine that all are guilty for the sins of all, in later journalism proclaiming Russia's messianic mission to save Europe. Dostoyevsky had a profound influence on subsequent Russian literature and thought. In the West he has been in the twentieth century the most widely read and influential of all Russian authors, as can be seen in the work, for example, of Albert Camus, André Malraux, and Jean-Paul Sartre. However, despite his remark, "I am called a psychologist; it is untrue, I am merely a realist in the highest sense of the word," he has been more generally viewed as a master of psychological narrative (Freud, "Dostoyevsky and Parricide," 1928). The crime novel, from R. L. Stevenson's *Dr. Jekyll and Mr. Hyde* (1886) onward, owes much to him: Most portrayals of lonely, obsessed murderers can be traced back to that of Raskolnikov in *Crime and Punishment*.

—T. J. Binyon

DOUGLAS, CAROLE NELSON (b. 1944), American writer of genre fiction including two mystery series. Born in Everett, Washington, she is the daughter of a salmon fisherman who died when Douglas was very young, and a school teacher. Raised in St. Paul, Minnesota, Douglas studied English literature, speech and drama at The College of St. Catherine in that city. She then worked in advertising, as a features reporter and editor for the *St. Paul Dispath* and *Pioneer Press*. Meanwhile, she published first novel, *Amberleigh* in 1980, calling it a "post-feminist gothic." She followed it with several fantasy novels published during the 1980s. The 1990s saw the blossoming of mystery writing her career. At the start of that decade, she launched a series of books centered around the activities of Irene *Adler, a character originally created by Sir Arthur Conan *Doyle in "A Scandal in Bohemia" (*Strand*, July 1891). In Doyle's story, Adler celebrates her duping of the *Great Detective when she encounters him in London and remarks, "Good Night, Mr. Sherlock Holmes." Douglas shortened that remark and made it the title of her first book about Adler, *Good Night, Mr. Holmes* (1990). Douglas envisions additional adventures for the adventuress in several more historical mysteries.

At the same time, Douglas won a larger readership by creating a cat narrator, Midnight Louie, who recounts the adventures of Temple Barr, a Los Vegas, Nevada, public relations woman who encounters crime after crime in the glitzy city. Midnight Louie first appeared in *Crystal Days* (1990) and *Crystal Nights* (1990), books which had been heavily edited. Douglas later reworked them and published them as four books: *The Cat and the King of Clubs* (1999), *The Cat and the Queen of Hearts* (1999), *The Cat and the Jill of Diamonds* (2000) and *The Cat and the Jack of Spades* (2000). In addition to these books, the Midnight Louis and Barr have appeared in 13 novels through 2002, and in the anthology, *Midnight Louie's Pet Detectives* (1998). The latter volume, for which the cat receives credit as editor, includes the work of several other writers.

Douglas demonstrated her passion for drama in 1997, when she wrote and starred in *Sunset*, a one-woman show about Marilyn Monroe. Douglas also edited *Marilyn: Shades of Blonde* (1997), an anthology of fiction about the movie idol.

[*See also* Animals.]

—Rosemary Herbert

Dover, Wilfred, comic *police detective created by Joyce *Porter. Detective Inspector Wilfred Dover is the antihero of ten police procedurals, beginning with *Dover One* (1964). Rude, overweight, lazy, hypochondriacal, slovenly, selfish, mean, occasionally violent, and always incompetent, Dover has achieved promotion only through being "kicked upstairs" by colleagues who could bear him no longer. He enjoys thwarting his priggish but competent assistant, Sergeant MacGregor, who longs to be transferred away from the man.

With his cynical view of humanity and inability to comprehend the importance of facts, Dover cares little if his chosen suspect is guilty or innocent. The isolated villages in which he works are parodies of the cozy milieus of Agatha *Christie's Miss Jane *Marple, populated by men and women equally mean-spirited and narrow who hinder Dover's search for creature comforts. In the end, circumstances and the *villain's own stupidity ensure that justice, of a sort, is done.

[*See also* Country Constable.]

—Chris Gausden

DOYLE, ARTHUR CONAN (1859–1930), creator of the most famous detective in literature, Sherlock *Holmes, and his almost equally celebrated confidant,

Dr. John H. *Watson. The second child and eldest son of Charles Doyle, who added to his small salary as a civil servant in the Scottish Office of Works by book illustration and painting, Doyle was born in Edinburgh, educated at the great Catholic school Stonyhurst, and decided on a medical career. In 1876 he enrolled at Edinburgh University, and five years later took his degree as bachelor of medicine. His father had declined into alcoholism and mental illness, and most of the decade before his death in 1893 was spent in nursing and mental homes. Doyle knew he must help to support his family. In 1882 he set up practice in Southsea, a small town on the south coast of England.

Doyle was by nature a man of action. He was an excellent cricketer and boxer, and before starting his own practice had made trips as ship's doctor to West Africa and the Arctic. But he was also ambitious to be a writer, and supplemented his modest income by writing short stories. In 1885 he married Louise Hawkins, the sister of a patient, and two years later published the first Holmes story, *A Study in Scarlet*, in *Beeton's Christmas Annual*. He sold the story outright for a mere £25.

The deductive powers of Holmes were based in part on those shown by Dr. Joseph Bell, one of Doyle's Edinburgh tutors. But the creation of Holmes owed something also to Edgar Allan *Poe's detective, the Chevalier C. Auguste *Dupin, to the French writer Émile *Gaboriau, and to the combination of mystical feeling with logical power and deductive skill in Doyle himself. This first Holmes novel was not particularly popular, nor was the second, *The Sign of the Four* (1890; *The Sign of Four*). In 1891, however, the appearance of six Holmes short stories in the newly-founded *Strand* magazine made their writer almost instantly famous.

To become famous as the creator of a fictional detective was almost an embarrassment for Doyle. He valued his historical novels much more highly, and both *Micah Clarke* (1889) and *The White Company* (1891) were popular and received critical praise. When two series of Holmes short stories had appeared, Doyle sent Holmes to his death in the embrace of the arch-villain Professor James *Moriarty. He told friends of his relief at being rid of the detective who, he said, kept him from better things. But popular demand and indignation were great, and Doyle felt it impossible to deny them.

After eight years' absence Holmes returned in *The Hound of the Baskervilles* (1902), and from then until Doyle's death Holmes stories alternated with other books and short stories, including the books and articles about the Spiritualist movement that increasingly absorbed Doyle in his last years. And at times the writing of fiction was subordinated to his activities as a public figure, something acknowledged when he was knighted in 1902. He was in command of a medical unit during the Boer War, and worked as what would now be called a war correspondent and propagandist in World War I. He was also a devoted family man. His first wife died in 1906, and in the following year he married Jean Leckie. There were two children of the first marriage, three of the second.

For his early readers the very character of Holmes revolutionized the crime story. To them he appeared a kind of intellectual Nietzschean superman in his ability to make amazing deductions and to dispense justice when the law was erratic or impotent. For us it is the relationship between Holmes and Watson that comes through most clearly, and the world of gas lighting and Baker Street fogs that in the 1890s was very real now has a period charm.

The fifty-six short stories are more successful than the four novels. Their length is just right for the pyrotechnic display of Holmes's deductive skills, whereas the greater length places a strain on them. The difficulty Doyle found in maintaining the baffling phrases and ingenious deceptions called for by Holmes's presence is shown by the fact that three of the novels contain material relating to the past with which the detective had nothing to do. Even in the fourth, *The Hound of the Baskervilles*, there are several chapters in which Watson investigates and Holmes remains offstage.

There are factual flaws in the stories but they don't affect a reader's enjoyment, any more than do the inconsistencies in the depiction of Holmes that sprang in part from the need Doyle felt to make the detective less egotistic and more humanly agreeable. The stories survive triumphantly because Doyle was a greatly gifted story teller, and the best of the short stories are among his finest tales. It is not just the deductions that are gripping, nor even the relationship of Holmes and Watson, although this is one of the great partnerships in literature, along with that of Don Quixote and Sancho Panza.

The effect of these things is enhanced by that element of Celtic mysticism and sense of unease derived perhaps from Charles Doyle, whose drawings are full of fantastic figures sometimes merely whimsical but at other times frightening. There are elements in the Holmes stories that make one shiver on a second or tenth reading. They include the sound made by the snake as it comes down the bell rope in "The Adventure of The Speckled Band," the electric blue dress Miss Hunter is asked to wear in "The Adventure of the Copper Beeches," and the bloody, gory mess of Victor Hatherley's missing thumb in "The Adventure of the Engineer's Thumb," all of which are collected in *The Adventures of Sherlock Holmes* (1892). This element of something outside the stresses of everyday living pulses dangerously through many of the stories. They are a prime example of a writer working better, digging deeper, than he knew or intended. Quite casually, and without the wish to do so, Doyle created some of the finest short stories in crime or any other sort of literature.

—Julian Symons

Drood, Edwin, a character in *The Mystery of Edwin Drood*, Charles *Dickens's last, uncompleted novel, serialized in 1870. Drood was by no means central to the story—as Dickens noted, "I call my book the Mystery, not the History of Edwin Drood." The spotlight instead was to be on John Jasper, an opium addict and the guardian of Rosa Budd, to whom Drood has been betrothed. Upon Drood's disappearance from the narrative, the presumption is that he has been murdered. The point is reinforced by the characterization, of Drood, who, being neither too sympathetic nor too contemptible, possesses qualities appropriate to a *victim. In conceiving *Edwin Drood* as a mystery, Dickens is thought to have been responding to the challenge presented by his friend Wilkie *Collins in *The Moonstone* (1868); for the reader, however, it is the book's unfinished state that gives it the air of a whodunit.

—Barrie Hayne

Drummond, Bulldog, hero of a series of fast-paced thrillers written by H. C. *McNeile under the pseudonym "Sapper." Fighting evil in a number of its forms—communism in the early novels, straightforward crime as well as assorted conspiracies that threaten Britain in the later ones—Hugh "Bulldog" Drummond is a representative of a wealthy upper-middle class equated with the British nation as such. Supported by his author-creator in his contempt for the law, which is viewed as a middle-class creation, Drummond takes things into his own hands in order to save the nation from criminals who are equally insensitive to the law's majesty and to the higher natural law that Drummond intuitively obeys. Well served by his enormous physical strength, his penetrating common sense, a "gang" of old war comrades (all officers, of course), and an extensive old-boy network upon which he can draw, Drummond unfailingly corners his criminal prey. He rounds off the hunt with a bout of combat—preferably unarmed but deadly nevertheless. One suspects that his taste for adventure was his reason for getting involved in the first place.

—Hans Bertens

DU MAURIER, DAPHNE (1907–1989), British author of historical romances and mystery novels. Du Maurier was born on 13 May in London, daughter of Muriel (Beaumont) du Maurier and the actor Gerald du Maurier, and granddaughter of George du Maurier, author of *Trilby* (1894). She was educated privately and at a Parisian boarding school. In 1926, the du Mauriers bought Ferryside, a converted boathouse on the River Fowey in Cornwall. Here du Maurier began work on her first novel, a romance, *The Loving Spirit* (1931). In 1932 she married army major F. A. M. Browning; they had two daughters and a son and lived in Cornwall, in an ancient home, Menabilly, a few miles from Ferryside. Menabilly suggested the setting for her most popular work, *Rebecca* (1938), which is both a Gothic novel and a murder mystery. Isolated at a remote seacoast estate, Manderley, with her brooding husband and a hostile housekeeper, the unnamed narrator of *Rebecca* feels caught in the spell of the first Mrs. de Winter, Rebecca, and the mystery surrounding her death. The book, reminiscent of Charlotte Brontë's *Jane Eyre* (1847) in its depiction of jealousy and madness, was extraordinarily successful. Du Maurier used similar elements—haunted landscapes, obsessional personalities, and sexual tensions—in other novels, notably *My Cousin Rachel* (1951), whose narrator struggles to determine his cousin's guilt or innocence in her husband's poisoning. Du Maurier's short stories are marked by a sense of menace and bizarre psychological twists. Among the best known, both published in *The Apple Tree: A Short Novel, and Some Stories* (1952; *Kiss Me Again, Stranger: A Collection of Eight Stories, Long and Short; The Birds and Other Stories*), are "The Birds," in which birds turn on humans, and "Kiss Me Again Stranger," in which a cemetery is the scene of a sinister sexual encounter. *Not After Midnight and Other Stories* (1971; *Don't Look Now*) includes "Don't Look Now," a story of mistaken identities involving psychic twins and a dwarf. Like many of du Maurier's works, it was made into a popular film. Du Maurier, who became Lady Browning in 1946 and Dame Daphne in 1969, was in 1977 awarded the title of Grand Master by the Mystery Writers of America.

[*See also* Females and Feminists.]

—Mary Rose Sullivan

DUNLAP, SUSAN (b.1943), American mystery writer known for authentic depiction of police procedure and social work, and founding member of the Sisters in Crime organization. Born Susan Sullivan in Kew Gardens, New York, she was educated at Bucknell University and the University of North Carolina. She became a social worker in Baltimore, Maryland, in New York City and in California. She married Newell Dunlap, an editor, in 1970.

After writing some unpublished novels about a social worker, Dunlap transformed the character into a policewoman. Introduced in the author's first published book, *Karma* (1981), Jill Smith is a strong woman who works her way up to the rank of homicide detective as the series progresses. Each book follows the tried-and-true formula for police procedurals, with detectives working on more than one case and much attention to the interactions among members of the police force. The Berkeley, California scene adds much interest to the series.

Dunlap introduced meter reader Veejay Haskell in *An Equal Opportunity Death* (1984), a novel in which Haskell hurries to solve a crime that she is suspected of perpetrating. The *amateur detective appears in two more books. *The Bohemian Connection* (1985) and *The Last Annual Slugfest* (1986). In 1989, Dunlap launched third series with *Pious Deception*. Here Kieran O'Shaughnessy, who has been fired from her job as a medical examiner, sets herself up as a *private eye in San Diego, California. Dunlap digs deeply in these books, not only into the crimes but into the effect on the sleuth of dealing with violence.

Dunlap co-edited, with Robert *Randisi, *Deadly Al-*

lies II (1994). Her own short story anthology is *The Celestial Buffet and Other Morsels of Murder* (2001).

[*See also* Police Detective.]

—Rosemary Herbert

Dupin, The Chevalier C. Auguste, French detective created by Edgar Allan *Poe. Usually regarded as the first significant fictional detective, Dupin appeared in three stories: "The Murders in the Rue Morgue" (*Graham's Lady's and Gentleman's Magazine*, Apr. 1841), "The Mystery of Marie Roget" (*Snowden's Lady's Companion*, 2 Nov. 1842), based on the murder of Mary Rogers in New Jersey, and "The Purloined Letter" (*The Gift*, 1844). In these hugely influential stories Poe created the fictional detective so familiar thereafter. Dupin is an isolated figure, a *private detective who takes only those cases which stimulate his imagination. Well aware of his intellectual superiority, Dupin is particularly contemptuous of the painstakingly unimaginative methods of the police. He is accompanied on his cases by an unnamed friend, the narrator of the stories.

Dupin's friend provides few facts about the detective's personal life, undoubtedly because Poe wished to base Dupin's characterization exclusively upon his intellect. According to the narrator, apparently an American residing in Paris, Dupin, though from an "illustrious" family, has been reduced by a series of misfortunes to poverty and lives on a small inherited income. The two men meet in an obscure library where they are both in search of the same rare volume. Finding that they are kindred spirits, they move into a "time-eaten and grotesque mansion" in a "retired and desolate portion of the Fauberg St. Germain." A year later, after Dupin has solved the mystery in the rue Morgue, they are still together in the Fauberg St. Germain, though their residence is no longer described as a mansion, but as "chambers" at 33, rue Dunot.

The narrator never describes Dupin physically, confining himself to his friend's "mental character." Perhaps Dupin's most noteworthy idiosyncrasy, shared by his friend, is his fondness for darkness. At dawn he shutters all his windows, preferring the feeble rays of a couple of perfumed tapers for light. Indeed, when meditating, he prefers total darkness. Only at night does he venture out, "seeking . . . that infinity of mental excitement which quiet observation can afford."

Dupin's cases are built upon this contrast between physical darkness and intellectual illumination. In "The Purloined Letter," for example, Dupin is sitting in the dark when he is visited by Monsieur G, the "contemptible" prefect of the Parisian police, who scoffs at Dupin's "off idea" that physical darkness aids reflection. Monsieur G needs Dupin's help in finding a politically damaging letter, which has been stolen and hidden by the despicable Minister D. Characteristically, the prefect's method has been to tear up the Minister D's apartment in a vain attempt to bring to light what is hidden. Dupin, by contrast, takes no action at all until he deduces where the letter *must* be. Believing that the intellect creates its own light, Dupin places himself in the criminal's mind and concludes that the letter is not hidden at all.

In the first two Dupin stories, Poe seems to be groping toward a fiction to represent this idea. "The Murders in the Rue Morgue" seems at first to qualify. Dupin does correctly deduce that the murderer must be "of an agility astounding, a strength superhuman . . . and a voice foreign in tone to the ears of men of many nations." However, instead of following his train of thought to its logical conclusion (that the murderer must be an animal), he shows his friend a tuft of hair, apparently ignored by the Parisian police, which he found clutched in the murder victim's hand. His friend immediately comments that "this is no *human* hair," thus rendering Dupin's deductions utterly unnecessary. In the painstaking "Mystery of Marie Roget," Dupin's deductions are inconclusive at best. Only in "The Purloined Letter" does Poe provide his detective with a case truly worthy of his deductive powers. With this one brilliant solution, Dupin takes his place beside the greatest of fictional detectives.

[*See also* Eccentrics; Great Detective, The.]

—Richard Steiger

DÜRRENMATT, FRIEDRICH (1921–1990), Swiss dramatist and fiction writer. Dürrenmatt received his secondary education in Bern, studied literature and philosophy in Zurich, and returned to his home city to attend the University of Bern. His first published narrative titled "*Der Alte*" ("The Old Man") appeared in 1945 in a Bern newspaper. After marrying Lotti Geissler, he pursued a career as playwright and novelist. His first dramatic success on the German-speaking stage was an account of community corruption, *Der Besuch der alten Dame* (1956; *The Visit*).

The first of his detective novels, *Der Richter und sein Henker* (1950; *The Judge and His Hangman*) introduces Kommissar Bärlach of Berne. A famous detective who faces death from inoperable cancer, Bärlach echoes the character of the loner detective established in American hard-boiled writing. The Bärlach debut novel and its sequel, *Der Verdacht* (1951; *The Quarry*) originally appeared as serials in the Bernese *Beobachter* before being published as books. In *The Quarry*, Dürrenmatt gives his interest in philosophy broad scope through analysis of the character of the nihilistic villain Emmenberger, a sadistic physician who it seems was once, under another name, a doctor in a concentration camp who operated on patients without the use of anesthesia. *Das Versprechen* (1958; *The Pledge*), Dürrenmatt's third detective narrative, commits a parodic critique of the genre that the author evidently believed falsified reality by forcing it into literary formulas. Dürrenmatt's final work that critics assign to the mystery genre was *Die Panne* both a radio play and a short novel, translated as *Traps* (1956). In addition to the influence of hard-boiled detective fiction, critics also descry similarities in Dürrenmatt's work to the fiction of Franz Kafka and Fyodor Dostoyevsky.

[*See also* Police Detective.]

—John Michielsen

E

EBERHART, MIGNON G(OOD) (1899–1996), American mystery writer, originally associated with the Had-I-But-Known school of writing. Born in Lincoln, Nebraska, she was educated at Nebraska Wesleyan University, and after marriage her worldwide travels provided background for many of her novels.

The Patient in Room 18 (1929) and other early novels had medical settings in which her series character nurse Sarah Keate was rescued from the perils of inquisitiveness by detective Lance O'Leary. Similarly, the short stories in *The Cases of Susan Dare* (1934) show the eponymous protagonist enmeshed in murder in menacing circumstances.

Eberhart later began to fuse mystery, romance, and neo-Gothic suspense, showing perceptive exploration of psychology and motivation. In more than fifty novels, from early titles like *The White Cockatoo* (1933) to *R.S.V.P. Murder* (1965) and *Alpine Condo Cross Fire* (1984), she also conveyed the feel and color of her settings and exploited their potential for evil.

[*See also* Menacing Characters.]

—Melvyn Barnes

ECCENTRICS. Eccentric characters fit into detective and mystery fiction much as the Gravedigger fits into *Hamlet* or the Porter into *Macbeth*, with this difference: that the comic form and structure of mystery fiction assimilates them more easily, and rather than being commentators on the action—still less, comic relief—they become kinsmen to the main characters. It is significant that in hard-boiled fiction, which moves closer to tragedy than does the classic form, eccentric characters are much less in evidence.

In Wilkie *Collins's *The Woman in White* and *The Moonstone*, eccentrics abound. In the former novel, the villain, Count Fosco, is comically eccentric, though no less formidable for that, and the ineffectual but malign Mr. Fairlie, comic in his obsessive avoidance of stress, is one of fiction's most convincing hypochondriacs. In the latter novel, both detectives, Sergeant *Cuff and Ezra Jennings, are eccentric outsiders, much of whose effectiveness derives from their being so. Two others, Mr. Candy and Miss Drusilla Clack, one of the supreme creations of the genre, add to the comedy of the novel as well as providing clues to the final solution. This is the double function of the eccentric character.

In the Sherlock *Holmes Canon, aside from the spectacular example of the *Great Detective himself, there are relatively few eccentrics. What eccentricity there is is suggested through characters' names, from Enoch J. Drebber in the first story to Josiah Amberley in the last.

Both are villains, and it is in those who live on the other side of the law that Doyle gives freest rein to eccentricity, from Grimesby Roylott and Professor James *Moriarty to Baron Gruner and Charles Augustus Milverton. But the run of Holmes's clients are commonplace enough, as witness Jabez Wilson, who "bore every mark of being an average commonplace British tradesman, obese, pompous and slow. There was nothing remarkable about the man save his blazing red head"—which may be eccentricity enough.

While Dorothy L. *Sayers peoples her novels with eccentrics, as Edmund Wilson noted, some of these both advance the plot and are interesting in themselves. Miss Alexandra Katherine Climpson's spinsterhood, turned to account in her auxiliary detection, is a more striking metaphor for the aftermath of the Great War than Lord Peter *Wimsey's shellshock. And in the same conventional between-the-wars world of Agatha *Christie, there is an overplus of eccentrics: The dotty old ladies who live in St. Mary Mead fall easily into the category. Sometimes the eccentric brings murder upon himself, like Mr. Shaitana in *Cards on the Table* (1936), or the detestable Mrs. Boynton in *Appointment with Death* (1938); sometimes the eccentric uses her eccentricity either to conceal her involvement in the crime, as Evelyn Howard does in *The Mysterious Affair at Styles* (1920), or simply to cover up another's crime, as Lady Angkatell, one of Christie's most convincing eccentrics, does in *The Hollow* (1946; *Murder After Hours*).

Christie often deals with a stage milieu, rich in eccentrics. Sayers's world is wider, from club types to academics, as well as the ducal family itself, and her range of the dithering and the vaguely confused is correspondingly wider as well. And in the successors to Christie and Sayers—mostly English, like Ruth *Rendell and P. D. *James, and occasionally American, like Martha Grimes—eccentricity, if not the norm, at least comes as little surprise.

One place besides the English village where eccentrics are in their element is the little world of the school or university. The prototype may be Sayers's *Gaudy Night* (1935), followed closely by Michael *Innes's *Death at the President's Lodging* (1936; *Seven Suspects*), and pursued more recently by Colin *Dexter and Robert *Barnard (*Death of an Old Goat*, 1974) on one side of the Atlantic, and on the other by Thomas Kyd, Amanda *Cross, and, in his first novel, *The Godwulf Manuscript* (1973), Robert B. *Parker. Robert Bernard's two novels, *Death Takes a Sabbatical* (1967; *Death Takes the Last Train*) and *Deadly Meeting* (1970), among the best in this subgenre, introduce the reader to a variety of academic eccentrics. Though most of these novels deal with the murderous side of college politics and with the clash between earthly policemen and idiosyncratic dons, much of the emphasis is on the idiosyncrasies. And other closed circles—libraries (as in Jane *Langton's The Transcendental Murder, 1964), monasteries (as in Umberto *Eco's The Name of the Rose 1983), and even the army (as in Richard Brooks's The Brick Foxhole, 1945)—provide characters who diverge from the behavioral norm.

A writer rich in eccentrics, in part because he is one of the most Dickensian of contemporary authors, is John *Mortimer. The judges before whom Horace *Rumpole appears, at the Old Bailey and elsewhere; his colleagues in chambers, especially the most recent head, the relentlessly pious "Soapy Sam" Ballard, and the gaga Uncle Tom, blithely putting golf balls into the wastepaper basket; and not least his clients, beginning with the hereditary criminals the Timsons—all these are of the first order of eccentrics, though recognizably kin to the main character himself. And Jonathan *Gash's *Lovejoy, the antique dealer à la A. J. *Raffles, has gathered around himself, both as auxiliaries and adversaries, a remarkable array of originals: Tinker and Lady Jane, and the egregious Charley Gimble.

If eccentrics seem to predominate in British fiction, the reason lies in its farceur quality and in its broad commitment to the classic form. In hard-boiled fiction, Dashiell *Hammett's Joel Cairo and Gutman in The Maltese Falcon (1930), even Raymond *Chandler's Moose Malloy in Farewell, My Lovely (1940) are arguable examples, but the incidental character whose sole raison d'être is his eccentricity barely exists; even such as the old man who claims to have seen something of the mass killing across the road twenty years before in Loren D. *Estleman's Sugartown (1984) is essential to the plot, as are the numerous oddballs Philip *Marlowe meets in the prosecution of his cases, on which characters such as Estleman's are based.

[See also Villains and Villainy.]

—Barrie Hayne

ECO, UMBERTO (b. 1932), Italian semiotician, literary critic, journalist, and author best known to readers of crime fiction as author of Il nome della rosa (1983; The Name of the Rose). Born in Alessandria, a town 60 miles south of Milan in the mountainous province of Piedmont, Italy, Eco is the son of an accountant. His father pressured him to become a lawyer but Eco soon gave up his law studies at the University of Turin in favor of focusing on medieval philosophy. After earning a doctorate in the subject, he worked as an editor for cultural programs for RAI television network, a job he held until 1959. Following that, he held a variety of jobs—some simultaneously—as editor, professor, journalist, and writer of academic texts, and of experimental fiction. His writings reflect a vast variety of interests and expertise, treating subjects as diverse as comic book characters, James Joyce, and fine points in the highly intellectual field of semiotics.

In 1978, he began to write Il nome della rosa, a book that succeeds as a detective story set in medieval Italy, as well as a gold mine for academics interested in symbolism, textual studies, and layers of meaning. An international phenomenon soon after it was published in 1983, by 2002 it had sold more than nine million copies around the world, funding a lavish lifestyle for Eco and his wife, Renata Ramge, a German-born artist. The couple, who have two children, maintain a home in a former Jesuit school in Rimini, as well as an apartment in Milan that contains the author's 30,000-book library.

Il nome della rosa is celebrated for its allusions to the work of Sir Arthur Conan *Doyle, Jorge Luis Borges and many others. In Eco's medieval whodunit, William Baskerville solves puzzling murders while monks opine on religious theory and heresy and much more. The book was made into a 1986 film of the same title by director Jean-Jacques Annaud.

[See also Singletons.]

—Rosemary Herbert

EDWARDS, (KENNETH) MARTIN (b. 1955), English crime writer, editor, and solicitor. Born in Knutsford, England, Edwards grew up in nearby Northwich. The son of a steel worker and a teacher, he attended local schools and realized by the age of six that he wanted to become a writer. By age nine, when he discovered the works of Agatha *Christie, he'd found his genre. Admitted to Oxford, he decided to take a course of study that he thought would support his writing habit. He graduated from Balliol College with a First Class Honors law degree, and qualified as a solicitor in 1980. Following that, he joined the Liverpool law firm Mace & Jones Grundy Kershaw, where he specializes in labor law. He has published several books and countless articles on legal subjects.

During the 1990s, Edwards rapidly made a name for himself as a writer whose law expertise informs fiction set in a well-drawn Liverpool. Titled after popular songs, his series of novels feature Liverpool solicitor Harry Devlin, who is introduced in All the Lonely People (1991). Devlin also appears in short stories, some of which are collected in Where Do You Find Your Ideas? (2001). Edwards's work as an anthologist is highly regarded. He edited the CWA annual anthologies as well as several books of regional fiction, including Northern Blood (1992) and Northern Blood 2 (1995). After the death of Bill Knox, Edwards completed Knox's novel, The Lazarus Widow (1999).

[See also Lawyer.]

—Rosemary Herbert

ELDERLY SLEUTH. Because popular literature reflects popular culture, detective fiction has produced a growing number of writers whose protagonists are energetic senior citizens. The earlier tendency to present elderly sleuths as figures of ridicule or amusement has diminished, and far fewer caricatures occur. Mild eccentricity or idiosyncrasy does survive, but on the whole mature adults are represented as more integrated into society and are depicted more realistically than they were previously in the twentieth century.

The inquisitive elderly spinster sleuth flourished during the Golden Age and prevailed through World War II. Free of conventional family duties, the spinster had time to observe human behavior and analyze its motives and consequences. The American Anna Katharine *Green contributed the prototype for the middle-aged spinster sleuth in the character of Miss Amelia Butterworth in *That Affair Next Door* (1897). She was succeeded by such figures as Mary Roberts *Rinehart's Rachel Innes and Nurse Hilda Adams (a.k.a. Miss Pinkerton), Stuart Palmer's Miss Hildegarde *Withers, Charlotte Murray Russell's Jane Amanda Edwards, D. B. Olsen's Rachel and Jennifer Murdock, and Phyllis Bentley's Miss Marian Phipps. Not the first in Great Britain but perhaps the best known, Agatha *Christie's Miss Jane *Marple belongs to this group of redoubtable spinster sleuths which also includes Dorothy L. *Sayers's Miss Alexandra Katherine Climpson, Patricia *Wentworth's Miss Maud *Silver, and Josephine *Tey's Miss Lucy Pym.

A small group of widow sleuths contains professional police detectives. Also socially marginal figures, these characters are eccentric to the point of being grotesque. The blatant caricature leads one to infer that only unattractive female misfits would elect to become detectives or that social mores of the time would not countenance married women engaged in criminal investigation. The first to appear, Edgar *Wallace's Mrs. Jane (also Emily) Ollorby, is ugly but cheerful, stout but quick, sentimental but indefatigable. Inspired by Mrs. Ollorby, Nigel Morland's Mrs. Palmyra Pym is also a Scotland Yard professional. Equally eccentric but less physically tough, Gladys *Mitchell's Dame Beatrice Adela Lestrange *Bradley is probably best remembered among the Golden Age widows; she is a psychiatrist who acts as a consultant to the Home Office. G. D. H. and Margaret Cole's Mrs. Elizabeth Warrender, the most conventional of the four, is an amateur who creates a cozy home in Hampstead for her son James, a professional investigator. Subsequently in the U.S., Erle Stanley *Gardner writing as A. A. Fair introduced Mrs. Bertha Cool, whose gray hair and sturdy figure, forceful speech, rough manners, and driving ambition owe a great deal to her doughty predecessors.

The spinster's counterpart, the eccentric but sagacious middle-aged or elderly man, is embodied in the armchair detective, Bill Owen, created by Baroness *Orczy in a series of short stories published in the *Royal Magazine* (1901–04). He would sit in the corner of a London tea shop knotting and unknotting a piece of string while discussing the details of intricate cases with Polly Burton, a young woman journalist. As a priest, G. K. *Chesterton's Father *Brown is socially separated yet enabled by his calling to expose unobtrusively the peccadillos of his fellow man. Christie's Hercule *Poirot was already retired from the Belgian police force when

he first surfaced in England in 1920. In terms of physical image, larger-than-life personality, and unorthodox methods, John Dickson *Carr's rumbustious amateur detectives, Dr. Gideon *Fell and Sir Henry *Merrivale, are the counterparts of the Golden Age widows. In America the single male sleuth can be found in Melville Davisson *Post's short stories featuring Uncle *Abner. Like Carr, Phoebe Atwood *Taylor created two detectives "of a certain age": Asey *Mayo, called the "Codfish Sherlock"; and writing as Alice Tilton, retired Professor Leonidas Xenophon Witherall, a.k.a. "Bill Shakespeare."

In the last quarter of the twentieth century, almost fifty mature detectives emerged. Significant shifts in marital status are apparent. Spinsters and bachelors have been replaced by widows and widowers as the most common type of unmarried sleuth. Mixed sex partnerships occur much more frequently than before World War II.

At least one old-fashioned spinster sleuth survives in Hamilton Crane's new series (1991) extending the career of Heron Carvic's retired drawing mistress and yoga adept, Miss Emily Seeton, a. k. a. "the Battling Brolly." But on the whole, the conventional English maiden ladies of the past have given way to more contemporary characters. In two novels by J. S. Borthwick, Sarah Deane's Aunt Julia Clancy is owner and operator of a riding stable. Mary Bowen Hall's crusty Emma Chizzit, a California salvage company owner who does both the bidding for jobs as well as the physical work of salvaging, breaks conventional "feminine" stereotypes concerning woman as the weaker sex without being unattractively "masculine."

Two divorcées joined the lists of amateur detectives in the 1990s. Stefanie Matteson's Charlotte Graham, an actress of some repute, becomes involved in uncovering foul play against exotic settings such as the Buddhist treasure caves at Dunhuang, China. In England, M. C. Beaton's Agatha Raisin, a public relations executive who sold her prosperous London firm and took early retirement at fifty-three, discovers that a knack for investigation staves off boredom in her too quiet country village.

Modern widows, who are numerous, can be divided into types: homemakers and professional women. While all are independent and resourceful, and a few are zany, none exhibit the bizarre behavior of earlier gender models. Among the homemakers first in the field was Dorothy Gilman's madcap Mrs. Emily Pollifax, who becomes a CIA courier. In Virginia Rich's series, continued by Nancy J. *Pickard, Mrs. Eugenia Potter shares her culinary lore with the reader while she stews over clues to mysterious deaths. Other examples are Serita Stevens and Rayanne Moore's Fanny Zindel, Eleanor Boylan's Mrs. Clara Gamadge, D. B. Borton's Catherine "Cat" Caliban, and Robert Nordan's Mavis Lashley.

Among the professional women, Kate Morgan's Dewey James, a retired librarian and widow of the former police chief in a small town, solves cases for her husband's incompetent successor. James McCahery's Lavina London is a former radio actress; more examples include Carolyn G. *Hart's Henrietta O'Dwyer Collins ("Henrie O"), a retired reporter in her mid-sixties, and Simon *Brett's Mrs. Melita Pargeter, who lives on her husband's generous legacy.

Among the contemporary single men, only one bachelor works on his own. Joan Hadley's Theo Bloomer, retired from the florist business at sixty-one to devote himself to private horticultural pursuits, usually discovers foul play after being conscripted to chaperone or rescue his namesake niece in exotic environs such as Israel or Jamaica. A small group of widowers includes David Laing Dawson's Henry Thornton, a Canadian ex-car agency owner who uncovers murder in his nursing home. E. X. *Ferrars's Andrew Basnett, formerly a professor of botany at London University, applies scientific precepts to contemporary conundrums.

Married and unmarried couples also form a conspicuous group among elderly sleuths. Ann Cleeves's George Palmer-Jones, a former civil servant turned ornithologist in his mid-sixties, is often helped by his wife, Mollie, to explain illegal activities connected with bird-watching and wildlife conservation. In Suffolk, Anthony Oliver's retired police inspector John Webber is joined by the incorrigible Mrs. Lizzie Thomas in an informal partnership to expose skulduggery connected with the world of art and antiques. Another widower, Nancy Livingston's retired British tax inspector, G. D. H. Pringle, takes up detecting in order to support his passion for collecting paintings of the Manchester School. Pringle enjoys the company, cooking, and bed of a lady friend, Mavis Bignell, a red-haired barmaid of Rubenesque proportions and earthy common sense.

[See also Eccentrics.]

—B. J. Rahn

ELKINS, AARON J. (b. 1935), American writer of four mystery series, the best known of which follows the investigations of forensic anthropologist Gideon Oliver. Born in Brooklyn, New York, Elkins was educated at several universities including Hunter College in New York, California State University in Los Angeles, and the University of California at Berkeley. He has worked as a management analyst and consultant and as a professor. Since 1985, he has been a full-time writer. Twice married, he is the father of two children. His second wife and sometime collaborator is Charlotte Elkins.

Elkins introduced Oliver in Fellowship of Fear (1982) and followed that with several more novels that take the character to well-drawn international locations. The novels are enriched by Elkins's impeccable research, flair for descriptive writing, and especially by his anthropological expertise, which inspires original clues and solutions to crimes. Whether the crimes are relatively contemporary, as in Murder in the Queens' Armes (1985), or literally long-buried, as in Curses! (1989)—Oliver has the ability to solve them satisfyingly.

Art expert Chris Norgen makes his first appearance in A Deceptive Clarity (1987), beginning a three-book series that follows a similar formula to that employed in the Oliver books: The *sleuth's expertise is essential to solutions of crimes encountered in atmospheric settings. Another art expert, Ben Revere of Boston, appears in an edgier series that begins with Loot (1999). Elkins collaborates with his wife on the light and lively Lee Ofsted series, which features a woman professional golfer who keeps encountering crime, which she solves in the company of her police detective friend, Graham Sheldon. This series begins with the 1989 novel, A Wicked Slice.

—Rosemary Herbert

ELLIN, STANLEY (1916–1986), American master of the short story. The Brooklyn-born writer emerged in 1948 both as novelist, with Dreadful Summit, and as short story writer with the appearance in the May issue of Ellery Queen's Mystery Magazine of his best-known single work, the subtly chilling classic "The Specialty of the House." Ellin's short stories are marked by a variety of backgrounds, themes, and moods, as well as by unwavering craft, probing explorations of personal and ethical dilemmas, and a keen sense of irony. While the earliest tales, gathered in Mystery Stories (1956), may be the best, with "The House Party" and "The Moment of Decision" especially memorable, the Ellin touch rarely faltered. The quality of his equally varied novels, of which The Eighth Circle (1958) and Mirror, Mirror on the Wall (1972) are most frequently cited, has not eclipsed his primary niche as one of the two or three finest short story writers of this century in the crime field.

—Jon L. Breen

ELLROY, JAMES (b. 1948), American author, practitioner of hard-boiled fiction, or fiction noir, and a self-educated ex-convict, employed at various jobs, including caddying. An active novelist since 1981, Ellroy centers all of his works on a quasi-historical vision of midcentury Los Angeles governed by institutional and individual corruption and brutality. His dense, dark crime novels feature police who are only marginally better than his stomach-churning *villains. His first novel is the semi-autobiographical Brown's Requiem (1984). Investigation into the true-crime mutilation murder of Elizabeth Short in 1947 provides the basis for the plot of The Black Dahlia (1987) and becomes a recurring motif through most of his novels. In his works, including the Los Angeles Quarter (The Black Dahlia 1987; The Big Nowhere, 1988; L.A. Confidential, 1990; and White Jazz, 1992), Ellroy chronicles the often futile attempts of damaged individuals to navigate in a world ruled by violence and duplicity.

—Catherine E. Hoyser

ENGEL, HOWARD (b. 1931), Canadian radio producer, writer of the Benny Cooperman series of *private eye novels, and a founder of the Crime Writers of Canada organization. Born in Toronto, he was educated at St. Catherine's, McMaster University and the Ontario

College of Education. Married twice, he is the father of two sons and one daughter.

When Engel introduced Cooperman in *The Suicide Murders* (1980; *The Suicide Notice*), he also created Grantham, a fictional Ontario town located near Niagara Falls. Cooperman possesses little flair, but that may be his strength. Engel makes him memorable for his commonsense consistency and dogged perserverence. No loner, he has frequent contact with his family. Not concerned with machismo, he is squeamish about violent crime. No gourmet, his meal of choice is an egg-salad sandwich and a glass of milk. Cooperman's Jewish faith is part of his identity, but it is not harped upon in the series. He does cover a sensitive case in the Jewish community in *A City Called July* (1986), when he is asked to investigate the disappearance of a congregant with 2.6 million dollars belonging to the community. Cooperman also takes on cases involving blackmail, Satanism, and protection of celebrities.

Engel also wrote some non-series novels. His *Murder in Montparnasse* (1992) is an historical mystery set in the world of expatriot artists and writers including Gertrude Stein. *Mr. Doyle and Dr. Bell* (1997) has a young Arthur Conan *Doyle wowed by his mentor Dr. Joseph Bell of Edinburgh University. With his wife Janet Hamilton, Engel wrote *Murder in Space* (1985) under the joint pseudonym F.X. Woolf. Engel's two non-fiction works are *Behold the Lord High Executioner: An Unashamed Look at Hangmen, Headsmen and Their Kind* (1996) and *Crimes of Passion: An Unblinking Look at Murderous Love* (2002). He co-edited, with Eric *Wright, the 1992 anthology, *Criminal Shorts*.

—Rosemary Herbert

ESTLEMAN, LOREN D. (b. 1952), prolific American writer of westerns and *private eye fiction. Estleman was born in Ann Arbor, Michigan, and educated at local schools and at Eastern Michigan University. He married and worked as a reporter for several newspapers in the Ann Arbor area before writing fiction full-time beginning in 1980—the same year his character Amos *Walker made his first appearance in *Motor City Blue*. Currently, Estleman lives in Michigan with his second wife, the writer Deborah Morgan.

Estleman may be best known to mystery readers for his series about the hard-drinking, tough guy Detroit private eye, Walker, but his novels about Peter Macklin, Ralph Poteet, and series of short stories about Valentino are memorable additions to the crime genre, too. Macklin is a hit man who keeps getting into fixes. For instance, in *Kill Zone* (1984) he deals with terrorism on a passenger boat. After suffering marital woes in *Roses are Dead* (1985), he remarries, and vows to change his career, in *Something Borrowed, Something Black* (2002). Introduced in *Peeper* (1989), Poteet is the ultimate sleazy gumshoe. Valentino, a film archivist who becomes an *accidental sleuth, first appears in "Dark Lady Down" (*EQMM*, March, 1998). Some of Estleman's many westerns share with his crime writing a preoccupation with law and lawbreakers. His books about Page Murdock, a lawman who has no qualms about breaking the law, are cases in point. Estleman's fame rests on his thoroughly American voice and outlook but his earliest work includes three Sherlock *Holmes pastiches. They include two novels—*Sherlock Holmes Versus Dracula: Or, The Adventure of the Sanguinary Count* (1978) and *Dr. Jeckyll and Mr. Holmes* (1979)—and one play, "Dr. and Mrs. Watson at Home" (in *The New Adventures of Sherlock Holmes*, edited by Martin H. Greenberg and Carol-Lynn Rossel-Waugh, 1987). Estleman has also penned a series of novels about historical crimes in Detroit. His penchant for using fiction to bring alive historical fact was evident from the first. His debut novel, *The Oklahoma Punk* (1976; *Red Highway*, 1994) has its antihero a bank robber based on an actual criminal who perpetrated his crimes in dustbowl Oklahoma.

—Rosemary Herbert

ETHNIC SLEUTH. The ethnic sleuth entered crime and mystery fiction at the very outset. The Chevalier C. Auguste *Dupin, the "ratiocinative" Paris metaphysician in Edgar Allan *Poe's "The Murders in the Rue Morgue" (*Godey's Lady's and Gentleman's Magazine*, Apr. 1841), "The Mystery of Marie Roget" (*Snowden's Lady's Companion*, Nov. 1842), and "The Purloined Letter" (*The Gift*, 1845), serves as a founding ethnic sleuth—along with, in England, the figure of Count Fosco in *The Woman in White* (1860) by Wilkie *Collins.

For modern purposes, however, the key figure is Charlie *Chan, Earl Derr *Bigger's mandarin Hawaiian detective who makes his entrance in *The House Without a Key* (1925). Chan's amiable good manners, sing-song pidgin, and "Confucian" unraveling of each foible, theft, and murder immediately charmed audiences. Here lay the perfect rebuke to the "Yellow Menace" villainy of *Fu Manchu, first introduced by Sax *Rohmer in "The Zaya Kiss" (*The Story-Teller*, 1912) and typically sinister in *President Fu Manchu* (1936).

Chan and other stereotypes of inscrutability have not fared well in a latter-day multicultural age any more than has Fu Manchu or any other fantasy "oriental" villain possessed of a will to global domination and a dark, hardly concealed sexuality, like Shiwan Khan (one of Lamont Cranston's prime antagonists in the *Shadow* series) or Emperor Ming of the Flash Gordon stories and films. For as in film, cartoons, and every other kind of literature, ethnicity in mystery writing has never been less than an ambiguous element. If Chan, or another notably accented puzzle solver like Agatha *Christie's Hercule *Poirot, can bring an outsider's vantage-point to the "plots" of mainstream society, classic detectives like Dashiell *Hammett's eponymous sleuth in *The Continental Op* (1945) can use "ethnicity" (whether Asian or not) to suggest an especially alien or sinister criminality.

The writer who chooses to use an ethnic sleuth has some advantages in particularizing the hero's identity.

Further, the ethnic cop, gumshoe, or *private eye can not only investigate "mainstream" society but also enter and decode a Chinatown, ghetto, *barrio*, tribal homeland, or particular religious community. For the most part, these communities remain closed to most non-ethnic investigators. Ethnicity, used well, thus calls up not just the difference of a name or appearance or setting but of a whole psychology, an interior and understanding derived from "other" roots and mores.

In this respect American fiction offers a panorama—Japanese sleuths in the mold of John P. Marquand's Mr. *Moto introduced in *Ming Yellow* (1935) and of Howard Fast/E. V. Cunningham's Masao Masuto in *The Case of the One-Penny Orange* (1977); Elizabeth *Linington/Dell Shannon's Mexican Luis Mendoza of the San Diego force in *Case Pending* (1968) and its successors; Marcia *Muller's Santa Barbara chicana heroine, Elena Oliverez, in *The Tree of Death* (1983) and *Legend of the Slain Soldiers* (1985); John *Ball's Virgil *Tibbs, the black Pasadena cop whom Sidney Poitier portrayed in the film version of *In the Heat of the Night* (1965); Harry *Kemelman's Rabbi David *Small of bestsellers like *Friday the Rabbi Slept Late* (1964); the mestizo Denver cop, Gabe Wager, whom Rex Burns first introduced in *The Alvarez Journal* (1975); and Barbara *Neely's Blanche White in *Blanche on the Lam* (1992).

Inevitably, the issue of authenticity has arisen. For better or worse, there is debate over whose mysteries offer the more legitimate ethnicity: those written from an outside or an inside perspective? Some would argue that in the case of Afro-America, and of Harlem especially, Ernest Tidyman's John Shaft thrillers simply by dint of being white-written fall short of Chester *Himes's work featuring Coffin Ed *Johnson and Grave Digger Jones. In the case of a chicano milieu, some ask if Margaret *Millar's San Diego mystery *Beyond This Point Are Monsters* (1970) ranks below Rolando Hinojosa's Tex-Mex "Belken County" mystery *Partners in Crime* (1985). Has the acclaimed Navajo-Pueblo series of Tony *Hillerman featuring Sergeant Jim *Chee and Lieutenant Joe Leaphorn—especially a "historical" novel like *A Thief of Time* (1988), which involves the "detection" of the lost Anasazi tribe—eclipsed all others? Or should not Hillerman's cycle coexist with Indian-written mysteries like those of the Oklahoma and Choctaw-born Todd Downing? Certainly the question is accentuated in the multicultural portrait in Ed *McBain's Eighty-seventh Precinct series, where the local police squad includes the Italian Steve Carella, the Jewish Meyer Meyer, the African American Arthur Brown, the Puerto Rican Frankie Hernandez, and the Irish Peter Byrnes.

In the European tradition, similar controversies arise. The ingenious Judge Dee stories by the Dutch-born Robert H. *van Gulik, especially the two he chose to write in English, *The Chinese Bell Murders* (1958) and *The Chinese Maze Murders* (1962), may be open to the charge of ethnic-historical fantasia, but they nevertheless offer a shrewd lens through which to measure contemporary society. If Inspector *Van der Valk, first introduced by Nicolas *Freeling in *Love in Amsterdam* (1962), gives an English-eye view of Amsterdam, there is still a larger story in play—that of the modern city as maze and bureaucracy (a nice comparison could be drawn with the Rio de Janeiro patrolled by Robert L. Fish's Captain Jose da Silva of Brazil's federal police). H. R. F. *Keating's Inspector Ganesh Ninayak *Ghote of the Bombay CID can be read as an assiduous, genuinely nuanced attempt to decipher Indian culture as, notably, in *The Perfect Murder* (1964).

The major shift in ethnic mysteries has been the rise in the number of ethnic authors. In this Chester *Himes holds a special place for the labyrinthine, gallows-humor, and often surreally violent Harlem of the *romans policiers* he began with *For Love of Imabelle* (1957). In his wake have come Ishmael Reed with his Vodoun, "Neo-Hoodoo," and postmodern Papa LaBas in *Mumbo-Jumbo* (1972); Walter *Mosley with his Ezekiel "Easy" *Rawlins series set in postwar black and white *Los Angeles and inaugurated with *Devil in a Blue Dress* (1990); and the black Guyanese British Mike Phillips, whose *Blood Rights* (1989) and *The Late Candidate* (1990), with journalist gumshoe Sam Dean, unravel not only murder but a fast-emerging multicultural England. In *Point of Darkness* (1994) Phillips transfers Dean to a multicultural Bronx and Queens in a plot that extends to California and Arizona. In like manner, the Cuban American Alex Abella writes a chicano East L.A. mystery (*The Killing of the Saints*, 1991) and Martin Cruz Smith explores Hopi culture in *Nightwing* (1977). Smith, in addition, can lay claim to Roman Grey, the Romany investigator of *Gypsy in Amber* (1971) and *Canto for a Gypsy* (1972).

The development of the ethnic sleuth and continuing popularity reflect the broadening of themes and audience of crime fiction, and its maturity as literature.

[*See also* African American Sleuth; Native American Sleuth.]

—A. Robert Lee

EVANOVICH, JANET (b. 1943), American creator of the wisecracking bounty hunter Stephanie Plum. Raised in a working class family in South River, New Jersey, Evanovich married a mathematics professor and stayed home to raise the couple's two children. At age forty-seven, she wrote the first of twelve paperback romance novels. At age fifty-two, Evanovich switched genres and introduced Plum as a failed lingerie buyer-turned-bounty hunter in *One for the Money* (1994). The multi-book Plum series is easily identified by its title pattern with a number word in each *One for the Money* is followed by *Two for the Dough* (1996). The series succeeds by blending elements of hardboiled *private eye writing with romantic comedy. Plum's actions and dialogue can be bawdy, even raunchy, and she is not afraid to drive too fast and engage in violent action, but Evanovich shows her as vulnerable, too, in comically tender moments when she returns to her pet hamster, Rex. Plum lives in "the burg," an ethnic Italian neighborhood in Trenton, New Jersey, where, not unlike Sue *Grafton's Kinsey *Millhone and Sara *Paretsky's V. I. *Warshawski, Plum interacts with a "family" of characters, including memorable elderly people. Ongoing male characters include Joe Morelli, a policeman whom she plans to marry in *Seven Up* (2001), and Ricardo Carlos Mafioso, who is known as Ranger, a darker, more enigmatic character who gets in the way of those wedding plans.

—Rosemary Herbert

F

Fansler, Kate, feminist professor of English literature with a sleuthing sideline, Fansler is the creation of the former Columbia University professor Carolyn Gold Heilbrun, whose nom de plume is Amanda *Cross. Introduced in 1964 in *In the Last Analysis*, Fansler uses the methods of academic research to solve mysteries, not all of which are murders. Described by her creator as a fantasy self, Fansler is middle-aged, independently wealthy, elegantly slim, and sophisticated. Her most striking characteristics are quick intelligence, acerbic wit, and a gift for brilliant conversation, replete with literary allusions and quotations. In the early novels Fansler expresses love for the academy, but beginning with *Death in a Tenured Position* (1981; *A Death in the Faculty*) her view of academe becomes more critical. Fansler's most important relationships are with her niece and nephew and with her husband, attorney Reed Amherst. She investigates the abduction of the latter in *The Puzzled Heart* (1998).

[*See also* Academic Sleuth.]

—Maureen T. Reddy

FARCEURS. The farceurs were identified by Julian *Symons in *Bloody Murder: From the Detective Story to the Crime Novel: A History* (1972; *Mortal Consequences*) as "those writers for whom the business of fictional murder was endlessly amusing." Symons said that the early farceurs functioned in inter-war Britain, a place he felt was more conducive to lightheartedness about crime than the streets of cities like Chicago or Paris. But more recently writers of other nationalities have enjoyed playing with the conventions of the genre in a high-spirited manner, too.

The authors specifically identified as farceurs by Symons are Philip *MacDonald, Ronald A. *Knox, A. A. Milne, Michael *Innes, and Edmund *Crispin. Although there is a vast difference between the sophisticated and skilful writing of Innes and Crispin and what Symons calls the "desperate facetiousness" of Knox, these five writers have much in common in their approach to the rules of the game and the spirit in which they play with them. The subgenre of farceur writing grew out of the conventions of detective writing generally followed in England during the 1920s and 1930s, when the construction of mysteries was perceived by authors as a civilized game played according to rules, ten of which were outlined by Knox himself in his famous Decalogue (reproduced in his introduction to *The Best Detective Stories of the Year 1928*).

In their introductions to their books, the farceurs themselves made frequent references to the importance of the joke or puzzle elements in their writings. In his introduction to *The Maze* (1932), MacDonald refers to his work as "an exercise in detection." Milne, introducing his only mystery novel, *The Red House Mystery* (1922), sets out his intentions in a typically facetious fashion, making it clear that he is not taking matters seriously, nor does he expect the reader to do so. Years later, Innes—writing under his real name, J. I. M. Stewart, in his autobiography *Myself and Michael Innes: A Memoir* (1987)—revealed that his *Appleby on Ararat* (1941) and *The Daffodil Affair* (1942) were "two extravagances" intended to "bring a little fantasy and fun into the detective story. But the impulse has always been present with me, and has justly earned for me Mr. Julian Symons's label as a *farceur* in the kind. Detective stories are purely recreational reading, after all, and needn't scorn the ambition to amuse as well as to puzzle."

Crispin believed that detective stories should be "essentially imaginative and artificial in order to make their best effect." On occasion the reader is actually admitted into the farce: In *The Moving Toyshop* (1946), the character Gervase *Fen refers to Crispin as well as to the book's publisher. (Innes had already made a similar joke: In *The Daffodil Affair*, Inspector Appleby facetiously refers to Innes by name.)

Farceurs commonly use the upper-class society and the country house milieu characteristic of Golden Age detective fiction. Crispin and Innes continued to feature such settings right into the 1970s and 1980s. Elements that immediately mark out these novels as farces include the use of puns in the naming of characters. For example, the family name of Lord Mullion in Innes's *Lord Mullion's Secret* (1981) is Wyndowe. Exaggerated or ludicrous naming occurs when the insurance company employing Ronald Knox's series detective, Miles Bredon, is called the Indescribable Insurance Company.

The detectives created by farceurs are usually amateurs, and are nearly always urbane, sophisticated, and intellectual. Even Innes's John *Appleby, although a professional policeman, bears these hallmarks of the gifted amateur. Other characters are frequently caricatures, often marked out as such by comic nomenclature: A rather backward jobbing gardener is called Solo Hoobin in Innes's *An Awkward Lie* (1971), while a college butler is endowed with the name Slotwiner in Innes's *Death at the President's Lodgings* (1936; *Seven Suspects*).

More recent authors who engage in the spirit of fun echoing that of the farceurs include Charlotte Macleod, Donald *Westlake, Alfred Alcorn, and Lawrence *Block with his Bernie Rhodenbarr series. The works of present-day farceurs rely on lively pace, puzzling situations, and often witty dialogue to keep the reader relentlessly entertained.

Melvyn Barnes's categorizing in his *Murder in Print: A Guide to Two Centuries of Crime Fiction* (1986) is typical of the critical response to this farceur fiction: He refers to it as "the 'Here's a murder, what fun!' school."

—Judith Rhodes

FAULKNER, WILLIAM (1897–1962), American novelist whose work, set in fictional Yoknapatawpha County, Mississippi, won him a Nobel Prize in literature and made him one of the foremost writers of his generation. He also wrote six short stories and a novel featuring the amateur detective Uncle Gavin Stevens.

Born William Falkner (he changed the spelling of his name as a young man), he grew up in Oxford, Mississippi, where he did not complete high school. Faulkner served in the British Royal Air Force in Canada, and worked at a number of jobs including postmaster at the University of Mississippi, where he studied for two years. He lived briefly in New Orleans, writing sketches for newspapers there, traveled to Europe, and returned to his hometown, where he married and had one daughter. He launched his literary career in 1924 with a book of poetry, *The Marble Faun*. He followed that with unforgettable novels revealing the decadence and corruption he saw in the American south, and in southern families.

When Faulkner turned his hand to writing detective fiction, he hoped to win the First Short-Story contest run by *Ellery Queen's Mystery Magazine* in 1946. He tied with six others for second place. The story, "An Error in Chemistry" introduces Stevens, a character who, like Melville Davisson *Post's Uncle *Abner, is an elder with long life experience and a strong moral sense. Written at a time when ratiocination was at the heart of detective fiction, the story begins with a puzzle, focuses on it throughout, and relies on a clue that many readers may recognize early. The story is superlative nonetheless, because it demonstrates qualities Faulkner was famed for: the dark and twisted pride that motivates the criminal, the local color and authentic sound of the dialog, and true pathos delivered in a provincial setting. Faulkner used Stevens in five more stories—which are collected in the anthology *Knight's Gambit* (1949)—and in the novel, *Intruder in the Dust* (1948).

[*See also* Elderly Sleuth; Incidental Crime Writers.]

—Rosemary Herbert

Fell, Dr. Gideon. John Dickson *Carr based his character Dr. Gideon Fell on G. K. *Chesterton, a writer he greatly admired. Fell resembles Chesterton physically, with his great weight and enormous mustache, and in dress, using two walking sticks and wearing a shovel hat and tent-like cape. Fell also wears pince-nez and smokes a pipe. Meeting him, his creator says, is like meeting Old King Cole or Father Christmas.

Introduced in *Hag's Nook* (1933), Fell appears in twenty-three novels. He has a B.A. and Ph.D. from Harvard, as well as an M.A. from Oxford and a law degree from Edinburgh, but he never practiced. He is a lexicographer and historian who writes books on such pseudo-learned subjects as the mistresses of the British kings and English drinking customs, the latter topic quite appropriate for the eccentric, beer-loving Fell.

It is to Fell that Scotland Yard turns when faced with seemingly impossible crimes. He is at his best in the locked room mystery, a subgenre of which Carr was the recognized master. In *The Three Coffins* (1935; *The Hollow Man*) Fell delivers the now-famous lecture on locked rooms. Fell deals with apparent criminal impossibility also in novels such as *The Problem of the Wire Cage* (1939), in which the *victim is murdered on a muddy clay tennis court by a killer who leaves no footprints.

Many Fell novels and short stories involve bizarre settings and unusual murder weapons, such as the crossbow. Because of his love of the *outré*, Fell is especially happy when dealing with witchcraft, ghosts, magic, and satanism. Although his creator was known for his use of logic and fair play, typical features of the Golden Age form, Fell is less orderly in his thinking and often reaches the solution by pursuing the bizarre questions that come to his mind but no one else's.

Fell reflects the British and U.S. influences in the life of Carr; Fell's assistants or American-born Watsons are often thinly disguised versions of Carr. When the detective expresses disgust with Britain's postwar socialist government, he is speaking for Carr; after 1948, when Carr first returned to the United States, Fell solved most of his cases there.

[*See also* Eccentrics.]

—Marvin Lachman

FEMALES AND FEMINISTS. Women writers have been a mainstay of crime and mystery writing. Nineteenth-century British sensationalist writers like Mrs. Henry *Wood and Mary Elizabeth *Braddon contributed to the "mystery" even as Americans Seeley *Regester and Anna Katharine *Green (known as the mother of the detective novel) created early detectives and crime-solving methodology. Although Green's first detective was a policeman, Ebenezer Gryce, she later created both the *spinster sleuth Amelia Butterworth and an early paid woman detective, Violet Strange. In the Golden Age of detective fiction from 1921 to 1930, five women took top honors: British writers Agatha *Christie, Dorothy L. *Sayers, and Margery *Allingham were joined by Josephine *Tey (pseudonym of Elizabeth Mackintosh) from Scotland and New Zealander Ngaio *Marsh. They developed and polished the classic detective formula with its heroic protagonist, intrusive criminal, and eventual restoration of order. In similar fashion, American women writers of the 1980s and 1990s have redefined the hard-boiled private eye novel, with Marcia *Muller, Sue *Grafton, and Sara *Paretsky, among others, capturing the mean streets for women *private eyes.

Between these two notable events, talented women writers extended and reconfigured the conventions of the genre. Suspenseful psychological *thrillers from Patricia *Highsmith, Margaret *Millar, and Ruth *Rendell (also writing under the pseudonym Barbara Vine) unnerved readers with their careful dissection of the evil done by ordinary women and men. While Elizabeth *Linington (also writing as Dell Shannon) and the husband and wife team of Per Wahlöö and Maj *Sjöwall gave new dimensions to conventional police procedurals, Dorothy Uhnak and Lillian O'Donnell went further by introducing the first credible women police officers in procedurally organized novels. In the "Great Detective" model of the Golden Age—but always with a twist—P. D. *James and Elizabeth *George continued the tradition of the erudite police inspector—a "gentleman" of at least comfortable means, highly placed in his professional world, and eccentric. James's Adam *Dalgliesh is a published poet, and George's Thomas Lynley is a titled aristocrat. But George and James broke the mold with their introduction of two working-class women police officers—Sergeant Barbara Havers and Detective Inspector Kate Miskin—whose lives and ideas contrast sharply with those of their superiors. The feminist reevaluation of the male detective model is found consistently from the 1970s on in the works of Antonia *Fraser, Amanda *Cross, Anne *Perry, Barbara Wilson, Barbara *Neely, and numerous others.

Despite their important presence, women writers have consistently received less space in review columns and fewer nominations or awards for their work. In 1986 Sisters in Crime was founded in the U.S. as an advocacy group for women writers, in particular, but also readers, editors, and booksellers.

Female characters play many roles in mystery and detective fiction. They have been *victims, suspects, murderers, accomplices, narrators, *detectives, and onlookers—everything except the orangutan. Although sensation novels focused on the restrictiveness of women's domestic lives, Braddon's Lady Lucy Audley provides an early example of misdirection as an innocent-looking woman who plots and executes crime; her better known "sister in crime" in the nineteenth century is Irene *Adler, Sherlock *Holmes's nemesis, who not only blackmails his client but successfully evades the *Great Detective.

With the rise of hard-boiled detectives in *Black Mask* magazine and subsequent novels by Dashiell *Hammett and Raymond *Chandler, the tempting *femme fatale moved to center stage to charm and deceive the wary detective. In *The Maltese Falcon* (1930), Sam *Spade successfully unmasks the guilty woman before the reader has begun to suspect her; despite their intimacy, he has no reservations about turning her over to the police. Mickey *Spillane's Mike *Hammer takes an even harder line with Charlotte Manning in *I, the Jury* (1947) when he eliminates this threatening woman by killing her. In the hardboiled novels, female sexuality becomes a metaphor for

wickedness which the detective had to root out; like Eve in the Garden of Eden, these women are temptations to be resisted even by a tarnished hero.

As detectives, women first came to the genre as police officers in the 1860s novels by Andrew Forrester, Jr. and William Stephens Hayward as well as in the American dime novels published by Beadle and Adams. Amateur sleuths spanned the continuum from Green's astute Butterworth or Christie's indomitable Miss Jane *Marple to Mary Roberts *Rinehart's more naive heroines, captured in their repeated excuse, "Had-I-but-known."

The greatest impact on women as writers, characters, and readers has been the feminist movement from the 1960s to the present in both Britain and the U.S. Independent characters, often as first-person narrators of their lives, their investigations, and their novels have displaced passive stereotypes. *Forensic pathologists, private eyes, college professors, bookstore owners, lawyers, business owners, caterers, and reporters have solved crimes; from teenagers to senior citizens, women as detectives have taken the heroic role in cozy mysteries, novels of manners, police procedurals, and hard-boiled fiction, matching women's changing roles in society.

[*See also* Lesbian Characters and Perspectives.]

—Kathleen Gregory Klein

FEMME FATALE. The femme fatale is any woman whose presence reveals the vulnerability of a man to sexual charm and thereby threatens the stability of his world. The beguiling sirens of ancient myth luring male mariners to their doom founded the perdurable image of the fatal female, leaving it to generation after generation of males to inscribe her a place in all the genres of art and literature, not excepting popular crime and mystery writing.

Writing that is reflective of a normally populated social environment where the sexes are equal in number makes scant use of the femme fatale; thus, the Golden Age tradition, despite its artifice, has no significant place for characters who are ominous because they are female. On the other hand, the memoirs of early detectives written in the manner of fiction, works such as Edward Crapsey's *The Nether Side of New York; or, The Vice, Crime and Poverty of the Great Metropolis* (1872) and John H. Warren, Jr.'s *Thirty Years' Battle with Crime; or, The Crying Shame of New York* (1874) relate accounts of urban enclaves of prostitution where women's sexuality accords them the power to be active agents of crime. Critical analysis of the memoirs and the successive forms of pulp writing, hard-boiled fiction, and the paperback original novels of the 1950s that bear them close relationship, indicates that the trope of the femme fatale becomes more likely to occur when the social milieu of fiction segregates rich from poor, men from women, established ethnic groups from "others."

The critically acknowledged parents of hard-boiled writing, Dashiell *Hammett and Raymond *Chandler, also both make extensive use of the femme fatale. In *The*

Maltese Falcon (1930), Brigid O'Shaughnessy deploys her wiles to lure Sam *Spade's partner to his death. Her amoral use of sexual power justifies for Spade his own duplicitous treatment of her, but despite his efforts to overcome her force, at novel's end he remains emotionally in thrall, as he says, perhaps in love with her. Nearly all of Chandler's novels include a female character who toys with Philip *Marlowe, enticing him with promises of sex that would compromise his work on a case, and, if not that, then destablize his ethical system.

Other hard-boiled writers share an intuitive sense of the utility of female sexuality as a snare for men. James M. *Cain's best-known novels, *The Postman Always Rings Twice* (1934) and *Double Indemnity* (in *Three of a Kind*, 1944), concern the passionate entanglements of men who lose control of reason and masculine detachment in the arms of women.

The femme fatale was more than a literary convenience for hard-boiled writers: She was a staple of their worldview, literally giving body to anxieties resulting from the sharp demarcation of male and female realms. When the provenance of adventure and real business is dominantly men's, and there is neither language nor protocol available to naturalize sexually generated feeling and to manage it in the interests of the heterosexual companionship that would be possible if the genders were deemed equal, then the unsettling intrusion of women requires a reductive description that can serve both to limit the role of women in the plot of adventure and to justify the habitual segregation of men and women into separate spheres. The trope of the siren or the femme fatale originated for such utility and remains current through all sorts of social change.

The worldview insinuated into hard-boiled fiction at its inception continues to set contested boundaries between male and female. The phenomenon of paperback original publishing in the 1950s kept the image of the femme fatale before audiences by a typical use of cover art picturing near-nude female sex objects and by commonly presenting women in language suggesting ultimately inexplicable character traits. Novels by Jim *Thompson such as *The Getaway* (1959) and *The Grifters* (1963) capture some resonances of the femme fatale, showing that the image has become a staple, while in the fiction of Mickey *Spillane's Mike *Hammer, introduced in *I, the Jury* (1947), the woman, in body and mind, is the vengeful negative force whose sexual difference from men usurps the place usually played in the hard-boiled plot by inequities of wealth. Taking the femme fatale to an historic apex, Spillane practically redrafts the story of crime fighting as a battle of the sexes.

More recent authors of detective fiction, however, are working a reversal of the fatal female trope. Walter *Mosley's *White Butterfly* (1992), for example, opens with echoes of the image but dispels expectations of it as the plot continues. Robert B. *Parker's multivolume project of revision of the hard-boiled *private eye novel includes a redefinition of female character along hu-

manly realistic lines. Most important of all in this respect, the women private eyes in the fiction of Marcia *Muller, Sara *Paretsky, Sue *Grafton, Linda *Barnes, Julie Smith, and others their jobs as the full equals of their male counterparts, reconfiguring the world of adventure, making it sexually integregated, more natural, and no longer hospitable to femmes fatale.

[*See also* Archetypal Characters.]

—John M. Reilly

Fen, Gervase, series detective created by the British composer and anthologist Robert Bruce Montgomery writing as Edmund *Crispin. Fen appeared in five novels and several short stories. A late example of a Golden Age detective, and an *academic sleuth, Fen is an eccentric Oxford don who is both erudite and comic. Although there was a lapse of twenty-six years between the last two novels in which he appeared, *The Long Divorce* (1951; *A Noose for Her Neck*) and *The Glimpses of the Moon* (1977), Fen's portrayal is remarkably consistent. His obliviousness to much that occurs around him contrasts comically with his intuitive and logical methods of solving crimes. Arrogant, learned, paradoxically both cynical and naive, he is an effective central character of novels that are broadly farcical in tone and sharply satiric in social commentary. His spiky hair and his use of literary allusions such as the exclamation, "Oh, my paws and whiskers," borrowed from the White Rabbit in *Alice's Adventures in Wonderland* (1865), make Fen a memorable character.

—Mary Jean DeMarr

FERRARS, E. X., pseudonym of Morna Doris MacTaggart Brown (1907–1995), British writer of detective novels in the malice domestic or cozy tradition who also wrote as Elizabeth Ferrars. Born in Burma, she was educated at the Bedales School in Petersfield, Hampshire, and at University College, London, receiving a diploma in journalism in 1928.

A founding member of the Crime Writers Association, she authored more than seventy books in five and a half decades, working within the Golden Age conventions of the 1920s and 1930s long after that era had passed. Witty and highly literate, her novels are peopled with educated upper-middle-class characters. Her books do not have a constant series detective, although a few characters appear in more than one novel. Toby Dyke, a Bertie Wooster/Lord Peter *Wimsey type who follows in the tradition of the *gentleman sleuth, is featured in novels written in a genteel voice in the early 1940s. Retired professor of botany Andrew Basnett, an *elderly sleuth with endearing habits and methodical detection techniques, appeared in the 1980s, and the unusual detective team of an estranged wife and husband, Virginia and Felix Freer, are central to Ferrars's last novels. She also wrote short stories about a crusty old *amateur detective called Jonas P. Jonas. Publishing more than a book a year throughout her writing career, Ferrars explored many milieus, including the theatrical milieu, the country house milieu, and other settings on both British and foreign shores. Her flair for titles is evident in *Frog in the Throat* (1980), *Skeleton in Search of a Cupboard* (1982; *Skeleton in Search of a Closet*), and *Skeleton Staff* (1969).

—Barbara Sloan-Hendershott

FORENSIC PATHOLOGIST. In the real world of homicide, it is not uncommon that the identity of the assailant quickly becomes known, the assailant having informed the police of the occurrence and details of the killing. The role of the forensic pathologist in such cases may be mere confirmation of the alleged cause of death, although it is not impossible that the pathological findings may complicate what otherwise appears to be a straightforward case. Where a body is found in apparent suspicious circumstances and the details of the events leading to death are unknown, then, again, the role of the forensic pathologist is to determine the cause of death. Moreover, the forensic pathologist will endeavor to gather from the postmortem examination information that may be of assistance in testing the truth of any account of events leading to the death given by an alleged assailant, when—and if—an assailant is found. The forensic pathologist is only one among the representatives of many disciplines and professions that make up the investigating team: As the first person to examine the body in detail, another important function is to recognize and preserve appropriately any evidence upon or within the body which may be analyzed by other members of the team.

It should not be surprising, therefore, that the forensic pathologist as protagonist looms small in detective novels and detective stories. Given the geographical and historical differences between the medical examiner in America and the *coroner in England and Wales, it is equally unsurprising that a single medical examiner figures frequently in a "supporting role" to an American "series detective"—Dr. Emanuel Doremus to Philo *Vance, or Dr. Multooler to Thatcher Colt, for example. In Great Britain, where a coroner still retains the legal right to direct a deceased's general practitioner to perform a postmortem examination—even though that practitioner may have no experience of pathology—and where pathology as a separate discipline is relatively young, it is again unsurprising that postmortem examinations in the detective novels and stories of the Golden Age were carried out largely by frequently anonymous police surgeons. The conclusions given by these characters furnish the basis for the investigation by the protagonists whom they support; but, as befits their supporting role, details of the examinations that yield those conclusions are generally absent.

A similar absence of detail exists in the exploits of the earliest protagonist with a specific forensic bent, Surgeon-Colonel John Hedford, whose exploits were chronicled with sardonic melodrama by Robert Cromie,

in collaboration with T. S. Wilson. Appearing first in the periodical *Black and White*, these twelve exploits were collected in *The Romance of Poisons* (1903). Despite the title—and his soubriquet, "The Specialist in Poisons"—about half of these crimes involve microbiology—typhoid, cholera, an "obscure fungus"—rather than toxicology.

For many, the preeminent practitioners in the field—although for different reasons—are Dr. John *Thorndyke, introduced by R. Austin *Freeman in *The Red Thumb Mark* (1907), although the biography prepared by the author for *Sleuths*, 1931, cites his work for the defense in *Regina* versus *Gummer*, 1897, as his first case; and Reggie *Fortune, introduced by H. C. *Bailey in *Call Mr. Fortune* (1920). In the Thorndyke novels and stories, everything is subordinate to the detail of the pathological and scientific evidence by which Thorndyke brings home the crime to its perpetrator or, as in real life, demonstrates the absence of a crime. That Thorndyke can be both forensic pathologist and forensic scientist reflects the field of knowledge available in the early years of the twentieth century. Where knowledge has advanced to make a comment by Thorndyke unacceptable to the modern reader, as in his remarks concerning the lack of a method allowing identification of an individual from blood in "The Pathologist to the Rescue" in *The Magic Casket* (1927), this serves only to enhance the period flavor. This is particularly so where the advance does not detract from the method used within that story which, although not giving individual identity, yields sufficient information to allow comparison between three disputed blood samples and deductions as to the characteristics of the person who has shed the blood from which one sample is derived. This effect of the "evolution of knowledge" is by no means confined to the early years of the century: The author of *The Expert* (1976), the eminent forensic pathologist Bernard Knight, writing under the pseudonym Bernard Picton, would place far less reliance, less than twenty years later, on the "signs of asphyxia" than does his forensic pathologist, Dr. John Hardy—otherwise the forensic pathologist's fictional forensic pathologist.

What is less acceptable to today's forensic pathologist is the overinterpretation by Thorndyke—however necessary for the plot—of his findings at a postmortem examination in *Mr. Polton Explains* (1940). In this novel a body that has "been exposed to such intense heat that not only was most of its flesh reduced to mere animal charcoal, but the very bones, in places, were incinerated to chalky whiteness" is found in the cellars of a house which has been "burned out from the ground upwards" without "even part of a floor left." The deceased had a room on the first floor. "Looking at that odontoid process" (a part of the second bone of the neck which articulates with the first), Thorndyke is of the opinion that "it was broken before death; that, in fact, the dislocation of the neck was the immediate cause of death." This opinion cannot be supported from the evidence, given those circumstances: If the dislocation of the neck were the cause of death then that dislocation must have occurred during life, evidence for which would be the presence of bleeding, visible to the naked eye, or inflammation, visible under the microscope. Given the description of the remains, it appears difficult to accept that such evidence may still be visible; even if it were, how can Thorndyke exclude the dislocation having occurred as a result of the movement of the body from the first floor to the cellar during the collapse of the house?

The outstanding characteristics of Fortune are his emphasis upon the importance of evidence and his outrage at the failure of the police to appreciate that importance or, worse still, to ignore or resist its thrust where it does not accord with the preconceptions of "the official mind." In these days of "miscarriages of justice," it is remarkable that critics of the genre fail to appreciate this crusading quality in Bailey's writing—save for Erik Routley in his masterly exegesis in *The Puritan Pleasures of the Detective Story* (1972). The paradox of Fortune, given the scarcity in real life of objective pathological evidence that indicates the guilt of a named individual, is his manipulation of events to bring about what he regards as justice, a particularly chilling example being the means he uses to "finish off the case" in "The Dead Leaves" in *Clue for Mr. Fortune* (1936; *A Clue for Mr. Fortune*). Such behavior requires that the conclusions Mr. Fortune draws from the pathological evidence must be unobjectionable but, sadly, this is not always the case. In a cameo appearance in *Clunk's Claimant* (1937; *The Twittering Bird Mystery*), he examines two skeletons found in a garden grave and gives the opinion at the graveside: "time of burial, say twenty years ago. . . . Don't expect to revise that or add." There is even today no method that would allow the dating of skeletal remains within a period of more than five years and less than one hundred years.

Thorndyke and Fortune have sufficient veracity to make credible their extended careers: Given the statements of other fictional forensic pathologists, their sporadic appearances are wholly comprehensible. In *Fatality in Fleet Street* (1933) C. St. John Sprigg's Sir Colin Vansteen, consultant pathologist to His Majesty's Home Office, merely from his examination of a brain can say that the victim was stabbed while asleep!

Equally comprehensible is the subsidiary role of the police surgeon Dr. Jaynes, the narrator of two series of stories by Douglas Newton for *Pearson's Magazine* in 1932 and 1935, whose hero is Paul Toft, a detective with a clairvoyant faculty. In "The Mystery of the Firework Man" (July 1932), his examination of a dead body at the scene of its discovery is so perfunctory that he does not remove the boots, only doing so at Toft's suggestion to discover that a red hot iron had been applied to the soles of the feet. Such a lack of attention to detail might explain the ability of the general practitioner in "Murder on the Fen" in *Physicians' Fare* (1939) by C. G. Learoyd to perform a postmortem on a body, recovered from a river after having been missing for four months so that the condition of the body is "that jellified you could have sucked her through a straw," in three minutes and forty seconds.

In America, the earliest appearance of the medical examiner as protagonist of a series of stories appears to be in 1926 in the pages of *Detective Story Magazine*: Dr. Aloysius Moran, the creation of Ernest M. Poate, appears to Robert Sampson, "afflicted in the head" (*Yesterday's Faces, Volume 4: The Solvers*).

Although not himself a medical examiner, a knowledge of forensic medicine assists Dr. Colin Starr in the cases chronicled by Rufus King in *Redbook*, seven of which were collected in *Diagnosis: Murder* (1941). George Harmon *Coxe's uncollected stories about Dr. Paul Standish, medical examiner of Union City, Connecticut, published in *Liberty* and *Cosmopolitan* from the middle to late 1940s, are quietly absorbing, although there is little overt pathology. The same may be said of the Standish novel *The Ring of Truth* (1966).

Pathology returns to the fore in *Diagnosis: Homicide* (1950), the first collection of stories featuring Dr. Daniel Webster Coffee, pathologist at Pasteur Hospital, Northbank, the creation of Lawrence G. Blochman. This volume and its successor, *Clues for Dr. Coffee* (1964), have introductions by distinguished medical examiners—Thomas Gonzalves in the former and Milton Helpern in the latter. Despite the competence of the pathology, Dr. Coffee lacks the personality of Thorndyke or Fortune.

Not lacking personality—only credibility—is the glamorous Dr. Tina May, heroine of three novels written in the 1980s by Sarah Kemp (pseudonym of the late Michael Butterworth). In *No Escape* (1985), a dismembered torso is found in an advanced state of decomposition; May gives evidence that this victim had taken an amount of whisky before death, in apparent ignorance of the possibility of production of alcohol in the process of decomposition of the body and, even could such postmortem artifact be excluded, the impossibility of determining from what liquor the alcohol found in the body was derived. Such ignorance—together with her deductions as to the state of mind of an assailant from the wounds to the body of a victim (the wise pathologist refrains from forays into forensic psychiatry)—makes one doubt the claim in her newspaper biography that she "wrote, at 23, a book on Forensic Medicine which has become a standard textbook. . . ."

The suspension of disbelief necessary to the detective story becomes strained when the performance of the protagonist is not in accord with the recorded reputation. In *Old Bones* (1987), Aaron J. *Elkins's "Skeleton Detective," Professor of Anthropology Gideon P. Oliver, fails to realize for some sixty hours the significance of "beadlike nodules on the ends of the ribs" of a skeletal torso found in a French manoir. When one learns that the motive for a murder committed during that period of forgetfulness was to prevent recognition of the significance of the nodules by the victim—who had been a medical student for one or two years several decades previously—suspension of disbelief is difficult to maintain.

There is no difficulty in believing the paranoia engendered by a political background to a system of medicolegal investigation of death, a state of mind readily apparent in the fictional chief medical examiner for the Commonwealth of Virginia, Dr. Kay *Scarpetta, protagonist of Patricia D. *Cornwell's *Postmortem* (1990) and later novels. Surrounded by the latest technology of forensic science—from physical evidence recovery kit (PERK) to laser—and supported by experts in criminalistics and forensic psychiatry, forensic pathology, as in real life, does not by itself crack the problems in the Cornwell books. It is curious that this renaissance of the forensic pathologist in crime fiction boasts only female protagonists, May and Scarpetta being followed by Clare Rayner's Dr. George Barnabas and Nigel McCrery's Dr. Samantha Ryan while Gideon Oliver's distaff is Kathy Reich's Dr. Temperance Brennan. John Knox might have had some comment upon this phenomenon.

This historical perspective of fictional forensic pathologists reveals an apparent lack of accuracy on the part of their creators, raising the questions, "What part does forensic pathology play in the mechanics of the genre?" and, "Is inaccuracy inevitable?"

The evidence of the fictional forensic pathologist may define critical parameters of the puzzle, most obviously those necessary to the apparently unbreakable alibi. Where none of the methods of determination of time of death—body temperature, development of rigor mortis, the concentration of potassium in the vitreous humor (a fluid in the eyeball), the rate of digestion or emptying of the stomach—in real life can give a margin of error of less than several (if not many) hours, it appears desirable that, in fiction, these temporal niceties be ignored. Christopher Bush was particularly dependent upon the state of the stomach contents of the deceased—in *The Case of the Running Man* (1958), for example—despite Perry *Mason's destruction of the autopsy surgeon's evidence on this point in *The Case of the Rolling Bones* (1939).

An alternative but equally invalid approach to determining time of death is an opinion as to how long the victim would have lived after having sustained an injury. L. T. Meade and Robert Eustace in "The Luck of Pitsey Hall" (*The Brotherhood of the Seven Kings*, 1899) have it that death must be instantaneous when a man is stabbed through the heart. The interval before death and the victim's capability of movement during that interval are unpredictable and may be astonishing, as is acknowledged by S. S. *Van Dine in *The Kennel Murder Case* (1933). It is a sad irony that the victim of a method of murder which probably would cause almost instantaneous collapse, if not death, walks, hails a taxi and dies five hours later in the Savoy Hotel in *One, Two, Buckle My Shoe* (1940; *The Patriotic Murders*) by Agatha *Christie.

It may be that a knowledge of forensic pathology affords a novel method of murder, but that method impresses more if the knowledge is applied correctly. That is not the case in Dorothy L. *Sayers's *Unnatural Death* (1927; *The Dawson Pedigree*), where air is introduced into an artery rather than a vein to cause death by air embolism. Sayers redeems herself by the novel change rung on the theme of identification from dental evidence in her story "In the Teeth of the Evidence" (*Help Yourself Annual*, 1934). This theme was introduced into fiction by Joseph Sheridan le Fanu in "The Room in the Dragon Volant" (*In a Glass Darkly*, 1872) and elaborated by Rodrigues Ottolengui in "The Phoenix of Crime" in *Final Proof* (1898). It is of interest that the birth of forensic dentistry is considered to be the identification of the victims of the fire at the *Bazar de la Charité* in Paris in May 1897.

The reasons for these forensic fallacies in fiction may be lack of research by the authors or, as already hinted, the evolution of factual forensic knowledge; the references consulted by the authors of the Golden Age might now be considered themselves erroneous. Consider the "real" cause of death of Chloe Pye in Margery *Allingham's *Dancers in Mourning* (1937; *Who Killed Chloe?*). An acknowledged, if poorly defined, entity in pathology until two or three decades ago, *status lymphaticus* is now regarded as nonexistent, a form of words used by the pathologist where the postmortem examination failed to reveal the cause of death. It has been replaced by the accurate, if less abstruse, term "unascertained." An author is well advised to consult the textbooks contemporary with the period of his fiction; contemporary accuracy cannot guarantee freedom from criticism by the forensic pathologist of the future.

Detective fiction is not devoid of instances of curious prescience. Roy Vickers's "The Three-Foot Grave" (*Pearson's Magazine*, Nov. 1934; "The Impromptu Murder") foreshadows by almost fifty years events that followed the discovery of human remains in a peat bog at Lindow Moss in Cheshire (*Regina v. Reyn-Bardt*, 1983). The means of reconstruction of facial features from the skull, pioneered in real life by the Russian palaeontologist Gerasimov and employed by the crime-sculptor Imro Acheson Fitch in Anthony Abbot's *About the Murder of a Startled Lady* (1935; *Murder of a Startled Lady*), caught the public imagination when used by Richard Neave, a medical illustrator at Manchester University, in the case of a skeleton found buried in a carpet in Cardiff in 1989. The method used to murder Sir Raymond Ramillies in Allingham's *The Fashion in Shrouds* (1938) was not brought home to a perpetrator in real life until *Regina v. Barlow*, 1957.

The concern of the factual forensic pathologist with the accuracy of the opinions expressed by fictional counterparts is natural. Potential jurors may be expected to have read more detective fiction than textbooks of forensic pathology; their expectations of the limitations of forensic evidence are more likely to be guided by the former.

—Stephen Leadbeatter

Fortune, Reggie. Highly popular in his day, Reggie Fortune, medical consultant and gadfly to Scotland Yard, appears in ninety-five detective stories and novels written by H. C. *Bailey between 1920 and 1948. These works are notable for the terse wit of the main character and a recurring urgency to protect future victims. The well-fed Reggie moves from his couch to the *corpse on the dissecting table, never surprised by villainy, never restrained in his comment on human folly, and seldom hesitating to act as the agent of Providence. He characteristically appears in long stories published six to those volume; they are variously humorous puzzles, slices of career crime, tales of elaborate revenge, or accounts of twisted love. Fortune concentrates on facts: "You never know what you're looking for, so you have to look for everything," he remarks in "The Greek Play" (in *Delineator,* Mar. 1930).

—Nancy Ellen Talburt

FRANCIS, DICK (b. 1920), British author of mysteries set in the horse racing milieu. The son of a horse trainer, Francis grew up in Wales, aspiring to be a jockey. After serving as an airframe fitter and pilot in the Royal Air Force during World War II, he pursued his racing dreams despite being a little old for a novice and too large to be a flat-racing jockey. As a steeplechase rider, he won his first competitive race in 1947. By 1954, he was champion jockey of Britain. After near victories at the Grand National (the pinnacle of steeplechasing competition), in 1956 Francis was out in front just fifty yards from the finish line when his horse, Devon Loch (owned by Queen Elizabeth the Queen Mother), suddenly and inexplicably stopped. The event was such a sensation that a publisher contracted for Francis's autobiography, *The Sport of Queens: The Autobiography of Dick Francis* (1957). Though he had no previous writing background, Francis's book became a best-seller in Britain. Encouraged by this success, and by his wife's suggestion that he write a thriller, he then produced *Dead Cert* (1962). Each year until 1998 he published at least one new novel, all of them proving so popular that since 1980 his American publisher has promoted him as a "mainstream" bestseller.

There are many affinities between the usual Francis hero and the kind of hard-boiled protagonist described in Raymond *Chandler's "The Simple Art of Murder" (1944). The typical Francis hero is a vulnerable yet stoical loner struggling to do the best he can against corruption but with few illusions about changing the world. Although he always connects his hero (frequently a jockey or former jockey) to the world of racing, Francis rarely repeats a main character. The individual's struggle to retain his honor, professionally and morally, against the forces of evil is Francis's primary interest. His ability to describe pain is one of his most powerful skills as an author, but he never glamorizes brutality.

[*See also* Animals.]

—J. Madison Davis

FRASER, ANTHEA (b. 1930), English author of romance novels, police procedurals, and non-series mysteries. Some of her work is written under the pseudonyms Lorna Cameron and Vanessa Graham. Fraser has also served as secretary of the British Crime Writers Association. Born in Blundellsands, Lancashire, she was educated at Cheltenham Ladies' College in Gloucestershire. She married in 1956 and had two daughters.

Fraser began by writing romance novels followed by books that contained suspense and some supernatural elements. After a decade of this, she launched her mystery writing career with *A Shroud for Delilah* (1984), a novel that introduces Detective Chief Inspector David Webb and Detective Sergeant Ken Jackson. The duo carefully investigates crimes in the fictional town of Shillingham, where the comforting scene and traditional routines of English life are shattered time and again by crime. Fraser follows the sleuths' step-by-step process of crime solving, but allows Webb to act on hunches and insight into the behavior of suspects, often emphasizing the latter as essential to drawing the correct conclusion about a crime. Some of Fraser's books are titled after lines from rhymes. Titles such as *Pretty Maids All in a Row* (1986), *One is One and All Alone* (1996) underline Fraser's skill at showing the dark side of the familiar. Beginning with *The Macbeth Prophecy* in 1995, Fraser returned to writing some non-series novels, while also continuing to turn out Webb books.

[*See also* Police Detective.]

—Rosemary Herbert

FRASER, ANTONIA (PAKENHAM) (b. 1932), English biographer and historian, and author of mystery novels and short stories featuring the television presenter Jemima Shore. The daughter of writer Lord Longford and biographer Elizabeth Longford, she was born in London and educated at the Dragon School Oxford; the Godolphin School, Salisbury; St. Mary's Convent, Ascot; and Lady Margaret Hall, Oxford. Married twice, she has six children by her first husband. Her second husband is the playwright Harold Pinter. Fraser has served as president of English PEN and as chair of the organization's Prison Committee, which works for freedom of speech for incarcerated writers. She also served as president of the Crime Writers Association, in 1986.

Fraser is best-recognized for her scrupulously-researched works of history and biography, some of which treat royal figures. Her most notable works include *Mary, Queen of Scots* (1969), *Cromwell, Our Chief of Men* (1973; *Cromwell The Lord Protector*), *The Weaker Vessel: Woman's Lot in Seventeenth-Century England* (1984), *The Six Wives of Henry VIII* (1992) and *Marie Antoinette: The Journey* (2001). Her 1996 book, *The Gunpowder Plot*, garnered a Gold Dagger award from the CWA for best non-fiction of the year. She also served as editor of the *Lives of the Kings and Queens of England* (1975), compiled anthologies of love letters and Scottish love poems, and translated books about

Chinese martyrs and the fashion designer Christian Dior.

Articulate and well-informed, she is a darling of the media. On occasion, she also joined their ranks, serving as a television commentator for royal weddings, including the marriage of Britain's Prince Charles and Lady Diana Spencer. Prior to that, Fraser had already created Shore, a strong feminist character whose work as the television host of "Jemima Shore Investigates" takes her to places where crimes occur. The first mystery, *Quiet as a Nun* (1977) takes Shore to a convent school, an atmospheric milieu Fraser knows well, since she gained part of her education in such an establishment. The same school figures in the short story, "Jemima Shore's First Case" (in *Jemima Shore's First Case and Other Stories*, 1986). Another academic venue that Fraser knows well is Oxford University, which forms the setting for one of the author's most memorable novels, *Oxford Blood* (1985). Fraser reveals the hoopla that surrounds the lead-up to a royal wedding in *Your Royal Hostage* (1987), a novel in which a princess's wedding is threatened when the bride-to-be is kidnapped by animal rights activists.

—Rosemary Herbert

FREELING, NICOLAS (b. 1927), author of crime fiction. Born in London, reared in France, and residing near Strasbourg, France, Nicolas Freeling, by his life and writing, belongs to that still unusual population better termed European than known by allegiance to a singular culture. In his youth Freeling followed an apprenticeship in French hotel restaurants, which he eventually memorialized in *Kitchen Book* (1970); *The Kitchen: A Delicious Account of the Author's Years as a Grand Hotel Cook*. With the family he started with his Dutch wife in 1955, he lived and worked for hotels in England, Holland, and France—a pattern of relocation that Freeling has described as a continuation of the vagabond existence of his youth.

That life, however, yielded the material Freeling used for release from itinerant employment. When he published his first novel, *Love in Amsterdam* (1962; *Death in Amsterdam*), featuring the cosmopolitan couple, Amsterdam police officer Inspector Piet *van der Valk and his French wife, the talented cook Arlette, Freeling launched a successful career as a crime writer. As the detective protagonist of twelve police procedural novels, van der Valk is often likened to George *Simenon's Inspector Jules *Maigret because of his disregard for the conventions of bureaucracy and his subjective entry into the lives of the criminals and *victims he meets; van der Valk is also considerably more political than his purported model.

Despite the popular following Freeling developed for van der Valk, he concluded the series with the assassination of the inspector in *A Long Silence* (1972; *Aupres de ma Blonde*). Because Arlette has been Piet's partner in detection throughout the series, Freeling can comfortably shift to her narrative perspective in the final section of the novel. He also has given Arlette encore volumes of her own: *The Widow* (1979), *One Damn Thing After Another* (1981; *Arlette*).

Freeling's third detective series bears similarity to the van der Valk books. Henri *Castang is also a police officer, this time in France, and his wife Vera, a Czech, serves as a partner whose cultural distance from her husband's home equips her with lenses that improve the vision of crime.

[*See also* Police Detective.]

—John M. Reilly

FREEMAN, R(ICHARD) AUSTIN (1862–1943), creator of Dr. John *Thorndyke, detective fiction's foremost medico-legal expert. Born and raised in London, Freeman, with exactitude and respect, used London as the setting for thirty of his sixty-five tales.

In 1887 Freeman qualified for membership in the Royal College of Surgeons, then went on to serve with the British colonial administration in Africa. Upon his return to England, four years hence, his health gone, he looked to his pen for income. While making shift as interim medical officer at Holloway Prison, he wrote (as Clifford Ashdown), with J. J. Pitcairn, *Adventures of Romney Pringle* (1902), tales about an engaging miscreant not unlike E. W. *Hornung's A. J. *Raffles. In 1904 the pair wrought tales about a fledgling surgeon-sleuth, Dr. Wilkinson. Striking out on his own, Freeman introduced Thorndyke in a move, he said later, that "determined not only the general character of my future work but of the hero." When Freeman was forty-five Thorndyke made his first full-fledged appearance in *The Red Thumb Mark* (1907), the book extolled by Howard Haycraft as "one of the undisputed milestones of the genre." Over the next thirty-seven years, Thorndyke presided in twenty-two novels and forty short stories. Though he knew the man only through his epoch-making text *The Principles and Practice of Medical Jurisprudence* (1865), Freeman identified Thorndyke's prototype as Alfred Swaine Taylor, the father of medical jurisprudence.

Not only was Freeman the first writer to introduce genuine science into detective fiction, at Gravesend in Kent, his home from 1903 onward, he maintained a laboratory in which he conducted experiments essential to Thorndyke's investigations, contriving there solutions sound enough to stand up in a court of law. Years ahead of the official police in applied criminology, for example, analyzing blood, hair, or fiber, utilizing X-rays, Thorndyke set standards later emulated by law enforcement agencies. His omnipresent tote kit, for example, became regulation issue for the French Sûreté. In law schools Thorndyke became required reading.

Though he created more than 600 characters, Freeman's best were Thorndyke himself and Thorndyke's humble factotum, Nathaniel Polton, lauded by P. M. Stone as "one of the most fascinating, finely portrayed, convincing characters in the entire gallery of detective fiction." Thorndyke's digs, at 5A Kings Bench Walk, in

London's Inner Temple, of themselves a presence in the stories, have a mood of snugness and replenishment rivaling Sherlock *Holmes's 221B Baker Street habitat. In *The Singing Bone* (1912) Freeman achieved another major breakthrough for the genre with the creation of the inverted detective story. The final Thorndyke tale, *The Jacob Street Mystery* (1942), was written (while German bombers soared overhead) in a bomb shelter that the unthwartable Thorndykean octogenarian built in his garden. In September 1979, with the mayoress of Gravesend and fellow novelists H. R. F. *Keating and Catherine *Aird looking on, American admirers set a tombstone in place on Freeman's hitherto unmarked grave. The R. Austin Freeman Society and its journal, the *Thorndyke File*, founded in 1976, continue to provide a forum for a readership unwavering in its loyalty to the man whose two sons, with quiet awe, identified as "the Emperor."

[*See also* Medical Sleuth.]

—John McAleer

French, Inspector Joseph, Scotland Yard detective created by Freeman Wills *Crofts, appeared in some thirty detective novels and many short stories from 1924 to 1957, latterly as chief inspector and superintendent. Sometimes ploddingly pedantic, sometimes ruthlessly insistent and brilliantly intuitive, his success rate is impeccable.

French is happily married and ordinary, from his clean-shaven look to his almost medium height and roughly medium build. His geniality is evidenced by twinkling dark blue eyes, and his nationality proclaimed by tweeds and bowler hat. He takes regular meal breaks, irrespective of his location or the pressing nature of his enquiries. Yet he is no home bird, for he enjoys his holidays and relishes every opportunity to pursue his investigations well away from London.

From his first appearance in *Inspector French's Greatest Case* (1924), involving robbery and murder in London's Hatton Garden diamond district, French quickly established a reputation for demolishing the supposedly unbreakable alibi. While he is consistently meticulous, with his cases as neatly dovetailed as the railway timetables which were his creator's stock-in-trade, this does not mean that his exploits are less readable than those of the more extrovert or omniscient detectives (usually amateurs) created by other writers of the Golden Age. There is an excitement in accompanying French every step of the way, sharing his thoughts, his disappointing leads and lucky breaks, and being presented with every clue at the same moment as the detective.

Although most of the French novels are straightforward narratives with the criminal's identity ultimately exposed, *The 12.30 from Croydon* (1934; *Wilful and Premeditated*) shows the murderer executing his plan and then gives French's explanation of how he closed the case. This inverted technique is used also in many of the

short stories included in *Murderers Make Mistakes* (1947) and *Many a Slip* (1955).

—Melvyn Barnes

Fu Manchu. The repeated appearance in book after book over nearly fifty years of the Chinese criminal genius Fu Manchu illustrates the capacity of popular literature to create and reinforce stereotypes. Reportedly the journalist Sax *Rohmer found the model for his character in London, but the inspiration for the portrayal of a "sinister Oriental" who embodies the alleged mysteries of Asia in combination with mastery of Western learning arose from the bigotry and xenophobia that trumpeted the fearful threat to Western civilization from what was sensationally termed the "Yellow Peril." Rohmer introduced his character in a single short story, "The Zayat Kiss," published in 1912. Within a year the crafty figure began to appear in novel-length works: *The Mystery of Dr. Fu Manchu* (1913; *The Insidious Dr. Fu Manchu*), *The Devil Doctor* (1916; *The Return of Fu Manchu*), and *The Si-Fan Mysteries* (1917; *The Hand of Fu Manchu*). After a hiatus while Rohmer wrote of other criminal doings, the wily doctor reappeared in *Daughter of Fu Manchu* (1931), beginning a series of eight more novels running to 1949. Following another break in publication, Rohmer brought him back in *Re-enter Dr. Fu Manchu* (1957) and *Emperor Fu Manchu* (1959), by which time he had taken the role of an anti-Communist seeking to cleanse his homeland. In his heyday, however, Dr. Fu Manchu moved through vividly atmospheric settings suggesting the ominous purposes he pursued, while eluding his nemeses, the putative heroes of the West—Sir Denis Nayland Smith and his sidekick Dr. Petrie. Racial prejudice has its own appeal, but Rohmer's undoubted narrative skill enhanced its ugly face with the features of a cultural archetype.

[*See also* Ethnic Sleuth.]

—John M. Reilly

FUTRELLE, JACQUES (1875–1912), American author, known for his "Thinking Machine" detective who solves impossible crimes. Born in Pike County, Georgia, Futrelle worked as a newspaperman in Richmond, Virginia, and in Boston, Massachusetts, while publishing short stories featuring a variety of detectives. In 1905 the *Boston American* serialized as part of a contest for readers Futrelle's "The Problem of Cell 13," in which Professor Augustus S. F. X. *Van Dusen, known as the Thinking Machine, proves he can escape from an impregnable prison. The character caught the public's imagination and Futrelle used him in *The Chase of the Golden Plate* (1906), in two collections of stories, *The Thinking Machine* (1907; *The Problem of Cell Thirteen*) and *The Thinking Machine on the Case* (1908; *The Professor on the Case*), and in a novelette, *The Haunted Bell* (1909). Other novels, without the Van Dusen character, combine elements of mystery with romance, such as *The Diamond*

Master (1909) and *My Lady's Garter* (1912). Futrelle was aboard the *Titanic* on its fateful maiden voyage, and died when the ship sank. His wife, L. May Futrelle, also a mystery writer, later expanded his *The Simple Case of Susan* (1908) into *Lieutenant What's-His-Name* (1915). Some uncollected stories published in the *Ellery Queen Mystery Magazine* in 1949–50 brought the total of Thinking Machine stories to almost fifty.

The Thinking Machine is in the tradition of the eccentric genius of Edgar Allan *Poe; the Chevalier C. Auguste *Dupin's name may be detected in Augustus Van Dusen's. A caricature of the cerebral scientist, he has many titles (from Ph.D. to M.D.) and an "almost grotesque" appearance: He is thin and colorless, with eyes "squinting" behind thick spectacles, and a huge head. Arrogant and cantankerous, he emerges from his laboratory only to take on an intellectual challenge, such as the claim, in "The Problem of Cell 13," that "no man can *think* himself out of a cell." He escapes in a week's time, with some help from a reporter friend, but mainly by applying his engineering skills and keen eye for the habits of rodents and jailers.

The solving of an impossible crime by a surprising but rational explanation is the hallmark of the Thinking Machine: He discovers jewels cunningly concealed, in "The Missing Necklace" (*Cassell's*, 1908), and a car vanished from a closely guarded road, in "The Phantom Motor" (*Cassells*, 1908). The device, a variation of the *locked room mystery, was used not only by Poe and Arthur Conan *Doyle but by such contemporaries of Futrelle as Israel *Zangwill, in *The Big Bow Mystery* (1892), and Gaston Leroux, in *The Mystery of the Yellow Room* (1908; *Murder in the Bedroom*). It was particularly popular in the 1930s among such writers of the puzzle plot as Agatha *Christie and Ellery *Queen, and John Dickson *Carr devoted a chapter of *The Three Coffins* (1935; *The Hollow Man*) to various locked room scenarios. Futrelle's contribution to the impossible-crime tradition lay in leavening his *sleuth's implausible analytical skills with humor and irony while playing fair with the reader by providing clear clues. "The Problem of Cell 13" remains one of the most frequently anthologized mystery stories and, along with other original and ingenious tales of Futrelle's, assures the author—despite the brevity of his career—an important place in the history of the genre.

—Mary Rose Sullivan

FYFIELD, FRANCES, pseudonym of Frances Hegarty (b. 1948), English solicitor and author of crime novels under her pseudonym and psychological thrillers under her given name. Born Frances Hegarty, in Derbyshire, England, she earned a bachelor's degree from the University of Newcastle-Upon-Tyne, qualified as a solicitor and worked for the Crown Prosecution Service in London. Her experience in criminal law informs her crime novels, which feature, in one series, the red-headed *lawyer Sarah Fortune and in another, Crown Prosecutor Helen West and Detective Superintendent Geoffrey Bailey, two independent-minded characters who nevertheless work in tandem. All three characters strive to bring to justice criminals who are typically loners with difficult—even traumatic—backgrounds. For instance, the villain in *Deep Sleep* (1991) was a *victim of child abuse, while the twin brothers in *Staring at the Light* (1999) struggle to deal with the aftermath of their incestuous relationship. Interpersonal relationships are important to Fyfield's characterization of her *sleuths in both series. She is particularly adept at portraying the tension West and Bailey experience as they try to balance their attraction to one another with their urgently-felt needs for independence and solitude. In her 2001 novel, *Undercurrents*, Fyfield leaves behind her series characters to write about Henry Evans, a man who refuses to believe a woman he once loved is capable of killing her five-year-old son. The book seems closely akin to the page-turners she wrote as Hegarty, in which suspense is the keynote.

—Rosemary Herbert

G

GABORIAU, ÉMILE (1832–1873), French author of sensational novels of crime. Born in the small town of Saujon, Charente-Maritime, he was apprenticed to a notary but enlisted in the army. Leaving as a sergeant major after four years' service, he settled in Paris in 1856, and worked as a writer and journalist, becoming secretary to Paul Féval, a newspaper editor, dramatist, and popular novelist.

After composing much ephemeral fiction, Gaboriau became famous after the 1865 serialization of his novel *L'affaire Lerouge* (1866; *The Widow Lerouge; The Lerouge Case*) in the newspaper *Le Pays*. This was followed by *Le crime d'Orcival* (1867; *The Mystery of Orcival*), which appeared simultaneously in two newspapers; *Le dossier no. 113* (1867; *File No. 113; Dossier No. 113*); and *Monsieur Lecoq* (1868; *Monsieur Lecoq; Lecoq the Detective*). Although Gaboriau believed that all his novels belonged to one type, which he termed *le roman judiciaire*, only these four have a substantial detective element; others, such as *La clique dorée* (1871; *The Clique of Gold, The Gilded Clique*) and *La dégringolade* (1872; *The Downward Path, The Catastrophe*), deal with crime but do not present a mystery. The four that involve detection feature a police detective, Lecoq (who plays only a minor role in *L'affaire Lerouge*). However, Gaboriau is careless in his use of names and the four Lecoqs, though sharing a name and a profession, otherwise have little in common. An *amateur detective, Père Tabaret (or Tirauclair), formerly a pawnbroker's clerk, has the main role in *L'affaire Lerouge*, and is consulted by Lecoq in *Monsieur Lecoq*. Gaboriau took from Edgar Allan *Poe the detective's ratiocinative method. He was also influenced by earlier French sensational literature, and by his study of past criminal cases: His facts are accurate, and his description of the French legal system exact. His plots, which usually turn on some sexual scandal, are, however, repetitious; the novels lapse into melodrama and are overly dependent on coincidence. Nevertheless, Gaboriau's influence on later authors is considerable. The admirable opening scenes of *Monsieur Lecoq* (in which the detective deduces, from a detailed examination of the scene of the crime, what has occurred and arrives at a description of the participants) were imitated by Arthur Conan *Doyle in the first chapters of *A Study in Scarlet* (*Beeton's Christmas Annual*, 1887). Gaboriau's method of describing the crime in the first part of a novel and the events that engendered it in the second (in *Monsieur Lecoq* the two parts are so tenuously connected that the second is usually omitted in translations) was also imitated by Doyle, who writes in *Memories and Adventures* (1924), "Gaboriau had rather attracted me by the neat dovetailing of his plots." With Lecoq, Gaboriau gave detective fiction its first *police detective, and with Père Tabaret he carried on the tradition of Poe's Chevalier C. Auguste *Dupin. Though now most of Gaboriau's work can only interest the literary historian, the first volume of *Monsieur Lecoq* is still eminently readable.

—T. J. Binyon

GANGSTERS. *See* Menacing Characters; Underworld Figure.

GARDNER, ERLE STANLEY (1889–1970), American author who started by writing for pulp magazines and went on to achieve great success with his books. Despite a busy law practice, between 1921 and 1932, in his spare time, he wrote about 400 stories and created twenty-five series featuring such colorful characters as Speed Dash "The Human Fly," Fishmouth McGinnis, the Patent Leather Kid, and Lester Leith, confidence man. After he wrote *The Case of the Velvet Claws* (1933), introducing lawyer-detective Perry *Mason, Gardner was able to become a full-time writer. Although there had been legal procedurals before Gardner, his books quickly achieved enormous popularity as the first series to combine the inherent drama of the courtroom with action and complex detective puzzles.

As a California lawyer, Gardner had defended the downtrodden—for example, illegal Chinese immigrants. He made Mason the advocate of defendants whose rights were put in jeopardy by questionable police tactics. Mason was especially adroit at juggling physical evidence, usually guns or bullets, but sometimes items as exotic as birds. In having Mason discredit police procedure, Gardner employed tactics he had successfully used in his own law career.

In 1948, Gardner co-founded with the magazine *Argosy*, an unofficial board of investigators, the Court of Last Resort, lending his time and money to investigate cases of people he considered falsely convicted of murder and other serious crimes. He wrote many articles about this organization and a book (*The Court of Last Resort*, 1952) which won him a Mystery Writers of America Edgar for real crime writing in 1952.

After 1932, Gardner remained prolific, publishing almost 500 more stories and articles, as well as about 150 books, including two or three a year featuring Mason. He wrote a series of nine books about Doug Selby, a small-town California district attorney who, in an interesting twist, has to contend with a wily defense attorney, A. B. Carr. In 1939, Gardner adopted a pseudonym,

A. A. Fair, so that he could write more books for his publisher, William Morrow. The result was another successful series—twenty-nine books about Bertha Cool and Donald Lam. Gardner's method of writing became well publicized. He dictated his work to a battery of secretaries in one of his many isolated rural retreats, where he could also pursue his love of nature, including his hobbies of archery and horseback riding.

As one who learned his trade in the pulps, Gardner was primarily a storyteller, relying on almost nonstop action and lively courtroom climaxes. His characters were essentially one dimensional, yet they proved popular with the public, especially Mason and his supporting cast: Della Street, Mason's loyal secretary; Paul Drake, the private detective he employs; and District Attorney Hamilton Burger, his hapless opponent. Mason's clients usually appear to be guilty, and many make his job more difficult by lying to him. However, despite the concerns of Street and Drake, Mason risks disbarment for these clients, sometimes using illegal means to get evidence, which he then produces as a surprise in court.

The setting for most Gardner books is Los Angeles, but the city seldom comes alive, since there is little regional description. Occasional books, like *The Case of the Drowsy Mosquito* (1943) are set in such rural areas as the California desert, and their settings are better realized, reflecting Gardner's interests.

The Gardner Canon is generally consistent, though the Mason books of the 1930s are considered best due to their vigorous writing, intricate plots, and Great Depression atmosphere. By the 1940s, Gardner's books had begun to appear in the slicks (slick magazines) before publication, and though his plotting and courtroom scenes continued to be strong, he made Mason a bit smoother than the pulp-based Mason, who often functions like a tough *private eye. In two of his first three cases, Mason never even enters a courtroom. The books produced during the last decade of Gardner's career are not as well plotted or imaginative, and they even suggest that Gardner was a victim of the success of the Perry Mason television show, which ran for nine seasons (1957–66). A frequent television device, due to time constraints, was a scene in which the killer, illogically, suddenly confesses in court. That never occurred in the earlier Mason books, but did beginning with *The Case of the Long-Legged Models* (1958).

After the Miranda ruling and other U.S. Supreme Court decisions in the 1960s, Mason's unconventional, zealous advocacy of defendants' rights seemed dated and unnecessary. Although the television Mason remains in syndication, there has been a general falling off of interest in Gardner's books. Despite his once being the most popular American mystery writer, with paperback reprints of his work in the millions, Gardner has seldom been reprinted in the 1990s.

[See also Judge; Jury; Sidekicks and Sleuthing Teams.]

—Marvin Lachman

GASH, JONATHAN, pseudonym for John Grant (b. 1933), English author, pathologist and expert in infectious and tropical diseases. The son of mill workers, Gash was raised in his birthplace, the industrial town of Bolton, Lancashire, an area that was economically depressed and bleak in appearance during his World War II boyhood. He was drawn to the beauty of the seminary there, where he received most of his education. He took his first vows toward the Catholic priesthood before he was lured by a medical scholarship and his admitted interest in the opposite sex to move to London. While working toward a medical degree at the University of London, Gash supported himself in part by working on the Petticoat Lane antiques market barrows.

After medical school, Gash served in the British Army Medical Corps. He has practiced medicine in London, Essex, Hanover, and Berlin. He has also taught medicine, serving as Lecturer and Head of the Division of Clinical Pathology at the University of Hong Kong and as a member of the faculty of the University of London. More recently, he has worked as a private consultant in infectious diseases. Before becoming a full-time writer, Gash did a great deal of writing during train commutes to London from the home he shares with his wife, Pamela, in West Bergholt, Essex. The couple has three daughters.

Gash has written several series but none is more memorable than his first series of capers featuring Lovejoy, a "divvie" who can intuitively recognize a genuine antique. Beginning with *The Judas Pair* (1977), the Lovejoy books are remarkable for pairing simultaneous revelations about the truth of human character with the integrity—or lack of it—of apparent antiques. The Lovejoy books focus on scams in the antiques world, and are notable for Gash's tips on "antiques" that aren't what they seem to be. Gash's knowledge in this area is extensive, as readers discover when reading about everything from fine furniture to nipple jewels. They also reveal the author's eye for attractive women and ear for dialects and slang. He also uses the Lancashire dialect of his boyhood in a massive corpus of poems written as John Grant.

Gash prefers a spontaneous writing method that sometimes causes him to write chapters out of sequence. He does not plot his books in advance of writing them and often discovers characters' motivations as he writes the scenes that reveal the truth about them.

In 1997, he introduced a new series character, Dr. Clare Burtonall, in *Different Women Dancing*. He also wrote a non-series suspense novel, the *Incomer* (1981), under the penname Graham Gaunt. As Jonathan Grant, he wrote a trilogy of family saga novels beginning with *The Shores of Sealandings* (1991).

[See also Con Artist; Eccentrics.]

—Rosemary Herbert

GAULT, WILLIAM CAMPBELL (1910–1995), American author of mystery and private eye novels and sports fiction for the juvenile audience. Gault, who also wrote as Bill Gault, Will Duke, and Roney Scott, emerged from the pulp magazine field to win an Edgar for his first novel, *Don't Cry for Me* (1952). He went on to write a number of excellent non-series mysteries, but he is perhaps best known to mystery readers for his two series featuring private eyes Joe Puma and Brock (the Rock) Callahan. While both men are solidly in the hard-boiled tradition of tough heroes, Gault's treatment makes each man unique. Their ethics are their own, but they are men of principle in a world that does not necessarily share their values. Such solidly plotted books as *The Convertible Hearse* (1957) and *Sweet Wild Wench* (1959) demonstrate Gault's feel for character and the telling detail. Gault's short story "See No Evil," published in *New Detective* in 1950, is both an early example of pulp fiction treating the social issue of young Mexican American males attracted to violent recreation and of Gault's skill in endowing male characters with both strength and sensitivity.

[*See also* Hard-Boiled Sleuth.]

—Bill Crider

Gay Characters and Perspectives. For decades, gay and lesbian characters in detective fiction were not overtly identified as such, and the way in which they were depicted tended to reinforce negative stereotypes about homosexuals. For example, in Dashiell *Hammett's *The Maltese Falcon* (1930) and Ross *MacDonald's *The Barbarous Coast* (1956), the gay characters are thieves, murderers, and gangsters. In Raymond *Chandler's *Farewell, My Lovely* (1940), Lindsay Marriott is a weak, effeminate man who is involved in *theft and blackmail. The killer in one of Agatha *Christie's Miss Jane *Marple Mysteries is a lesbian whose attraction to a young heterosexual girl leads to *murder when the girl becomes involved with a man.

Perhaps the works of Mickey *Spillane offer the most offensive portrayal of gay characters. In *I, the Jury* (1947), Spillane includes a group of loud, flamboyant homosexuals at a tennis weekend on a country estate apparently for no other reason than to allow Mike *Hammer to make derogatory comments about them. Spillane's *Vengeance Is Mine!* (1950) chronicles Hammer's attraction to Juno Reeves (the head of a modeling agency), ending with the outrageous revelation that Juno, like her namesake, is in fact a "real queen"—a man in drag.

The first crime novel featuring a gay detective is George *Baxt's *A Queer Kind of Death* (1966), which introduces Pharoah Love, a black New York City homicide detective. However, this book and the two subsequent novels in the series provide little insight into the realities of the gay subculture (or of black society, for that matter). Instead, the novels are more reminiscent of the Philo *Vance mysteries by S. S. *Van Dine that portray wealthy New York society, use a limited number of *suspects, and employ witty dialogue.

Joseph *Hansen's *Fadeout* (1970) marks the true development of the gay detective novel. From *Fadeout* through *A Country of Old Men: The Last Dave Brandstetter Mystery* (1991), the twelfth and final novel in the series, the reader follows the life of Dave *Brandstetter, an insurance investigator. His intelligence, courage, honesty, and concern for others make him a touchstone for later gay detectives.

Since 1980 a fairly large number of novels featuring gay detectives have appeared, and the image of gay males has become increasingly positive in them. Several common characteristics are found in these gay detectives. The modern gay detective is open about his sexual orientation. Donald Strachey, an Albany *private eye in a series by Richard Stevenson, and Henry Rios, a California lawyer in a series by Michael Nava, are good examples of men who do not "shout out" the fact that they are gay—but neither do they attempt to conceal the fact.

Second, the modern gay detective contrasts with the effeminate or weak stereotypes of the past in several ways. Today, he is traditionally masculine in speech and appearance. Both Brandstetter and Strachey, for example, have to turn down amorous advances from women who are attracted to them and who are surprised to discover that the men are gay. Moreover, the contemporary gay detective is connected to traditionally masculine occupations and interests. For example, Dave Brandstetter and Donald Strachey both served in the army; Tom Mason and Scott Carpenter (the two amateur detectives in a series by Mark Richard Zubro) are respectively a Vietnam veteran and a professional baseball player; Doug Orlando, in a series by Steve Johnson, is a New York City homicide detective. Finally, the present-day gay detective is able to handle himself physically when the need arises and is not cowardly or fearful.

Third, in contrast to the stereotype of the promiscuous homosexual, the modern gay detective is usually in a monogamous relationship. At the start of the Brandstetter series, Brandstetter is mourning the loss of his lover of twenty-five years to cancer. In the course of the series, Brandstetter develops another long-term relationship (with Cecil Harris, a young black television reporter). As almost half of the Brandstetter series was written in the 1970s, Dave's monogamous relationships are clearly a matter of choice, not a reaction to fear of contracting AIDS.

With the advent of the AIDS crisis in the 1980s, however, monogamy becomes less a choice than a requirement for survival. This change is mirrored in novels from this period. For example, in the first two Donald Strachey mysteries, from the early 1980s, both Strachey and his lover Timothy Callahan have sex with other people. In the later novels, however, both have accepted the need for sexual fidelity. Donald, while still at times attracted to other men, tries to envision a skull and crossbones on their foreheads.

After years of stereotypical presentations, gays in detective fiction are now likely to be depicted as competent professionals, caring individuals, concerned citizens, and productive members of society. The novels show men who are people first, with their sexual orientation being only a part of their lives.

—David C. Wallace

GENTEEL WOMAN SLEUTH. The *sleuth as a woman of genteel background and breeding is as old as the mystery genre itself. Valeria Woodville in Wilkie *Collins's *The Law and the Lady* (1875) is a twenty-three-year-old woman determined to invalidate the Scotch verdict against her husband; well bred, sensible, and intrepid, she sets a standard of investigation for years to come.

Anna Katharine *Green turned Collins's heroine into two character types. In *That Affair Next Door* (1897), Miss Amelia Butterworth is an amiable spinster in her fifties who enjoys solving crimes while worrying about the proprieties. In *The Golden Slipper and Other Problems for Violet Strange* (1915), Violet Strange is a debutante who becomes a detective to make money on the sly; she moves gracefully through the upper layers of society, never doubting her place among the highest social classes. The former led to the elderly, unmarried woman sleuth whose grandmotherly looks conceal her sharp mind, epitomized by Agatha *Christie's Miss Jane *Marple in *The Murder at the Vicarage* (1930). The latter led to the professional woman detective, such as Patricia *Wentworth's Miss Maud *Silver, introduced in *Grey Mask* (1928).

In the 1920s and 1930s, the sleuth is a professional woman, which facilitates her involvement in criminal investigations. Mignon G. *Eberhart's Nurse Sarah Keate and Mary Roberts *Rinehart's Nurse Hilda Adams take on medical cases connected to police matters; both are respectable spinsters who brook no nonsense. In the 1960s and later, the genteel woman sleuth sought her place in almost every corner of the professional world; she was also younger, smarter, livelier. Amanda *Cross's Kate *Fansler is a university professor engaged in the issues of her time; Anne Morice's Tessa Crichton is an actress; Antonia *Fraser's Jemima Shore is a TV journalist.

The earliest sleuths rely on standard techniques of investigation: reason, deduction, physical pursuit of evidence, and interrogation. By the 1920s, however, praise for the sleuth's intellectual abilities is offered in place of demonstration. Always ready to follow a suspect late at night, Eberhart's Keate has a gaze "like an X ray" and the knack of "being around when things are happening"; Rinehart's Adams looks like a "baby-faced owl" and has a gun. Wentworth's Silver listens closely to gossip and Christie's Marple studies character. Much is made of clues and detecting, but in fact the genteel woman sleuth comes to rely more on intuition, social observation, and coincidence than on evidence and logic.

There are comparable changes in her relations with the authorities. Whereas Woodville persuades others by uncovering evidence, and Butterworth gradually wins the intellectual admiration of a skeptical *police detective, Keate receives amused respect from the police and Adams receives a marriage proposal. In turn, Silver and Marple may treat the police detective as a bright young nephew. In every instance, the genteel woman sleuth is deemed to be different from other women because of her crime-solving abilities.

The question of her involvement in a police matter is solved in a variety of ways. Keate and Adams are introduced as necessary employees, Marple is a harmless old lady nosing about, and Elizabeth *Peters's Dr. Victoria Bliss is a sprightly young woman following her curiosity. Beginning in the 1960s, though the genteel woman sleuth continues to investigate crimes involving people related or known to her, she may gain legitimacy by marrying a policeman, as did Crichton, Shore, and Anne *Perry's Charlotte Pitt, or an assistant district attorney, as did Fansler.

The type is easy to parody. In Rinehart's *The Circular Staircase* (1908), Miss Rachel Innes is forever rushing from one suspicious noise to another; in Gladys *Mitchell's *Speedy Death* (1929), Mrs. Beatrice Adela Lestrange *Bradley treats superstitions as seriously as psychoanalysis, and gives both more credence than reason.

Throughout her history, the genteel woman sleuth challenged the definition and role of women in society. Butterworth is a superb reasoner at a time when men assume women lack intellectual capacity, Keate exudes competence and fearlessness in facing physical danger, and Adams demonstrates imaginative resourcefulness. Fansler legitimates an intellectual life for women, even after marriage, and Pitt is not hampered by raising children. As an elderly woman this sleuth undermines assumptions about physical and mental decline; age is never a bar to her investigative activities. Butterworth may have eye trouble, Keate may have neuralgia, and Adams a weak heart, but Marple's mind typically remains as sharp as any police officer's.

[*See also* Bluestocking Sleuth; Gentleman Sleuth.]

—Susan Oleksiw

GENTLEMAN SLEUTH. The term "gentleman," when used to modify "sleuth," may denote the character's position in the upper class or connote that the detective is a true amateur. The two attributes—being of the monied class and investigating crimes for no payment other than the satisfaction of seeing justice done—work well together, since they allow the character leisure to pursue investigations unhindered by the demands of an ordinary work life.

The most memorable exemplars of gentlemen sleuths are Dorothy L. *Sayers's Lord Peter *Wimsey and Margery *Allingham's Albert *Campion. The second son of the fifteenth duke of Denver, Wimsey attended Eton and is a graduate of Oxford University. He sports such upper-class mannerisms as dropping his final *gs in conversation and is a connoisseur of wine, a collector of incunabula, and an accomplished pianist. His sidekick,

Bunter, who is also his valet, looks after him at their London address at 110A Piccadilly.

Campion's pedigree is more mysterious and exalted. His exact position in the British aristocracy is never pinpointed, but Allingham is said to have told a colleague that her *sleuth was in line to inherit the throne. Created six years after Wimsey was introduced, Campion was conceived as a *silly ass sleuth, who cultivated an appearance of foolishness to mask his intense scrutiny of suspects. His sidekick is a manservant, Magersfonteyn *Lugg, whose resume includes burglary and imprisonment.

Philip *MacDonald's Colonel Anthony Ruthven *Gethryn is introduced as the son of an English squire and a Spanish actress in The Rasp (1924). Gethryn is the publisher of an investigative journal, The Owl, whose mission is to anticipate crimes before they occur. Another character possessing an independent income is Alan Grant. Originally created by Josephine *Tey under the pseudonym Gordon Daviot, Grant was introduced in The Man in the Queue (1929) and makes his most famous appearances in The Franchise Affair (1948) and The Daughter of Time (1951). In the latter, the bedridden sleuth engages in bibliographic detective work in an effort to prove that England's King Richard III did not kill his nephews.

A British policeman who possesses a pedigree is Ngaio *Marsh's Roderick *Alleyn. Named by the author after the actor Edward Alleyn, this sleuth's social position as the second son of a baronet provides him with entrée into the homes and confidence of the upper crust. His diplomatic experience also helps when it comes to their discovery that he is there to invade their privacy. Alleyn's sidekick is Inspector Fox, whose first name is never revealed, although he is sometimes referred to as "Br'er Fox" by his superior.

Another English policeman, Inspector (later Superintendent) John Appleby, proves the point that gentlemanliness in detectives need not be strictly confined to those who sport pedigrees. This creation of Michael *Innes, himself an Oxford don, Appleby uses erudition to insinuate himself into the company of the educated classes and the landed gentry. His appreciation of art and his eye for literary allusion help him to discover many abstruse clues in a series of novels sometimes cited as prime examples of the farceur school of writing.

Another character whose intellectual erudition enhances his gentlemanly qualities is Nicholas *Blake's Nigel *Strangeways. This character, who seems not to need to earn a living, is identified as an Oxford graduate who always seems ready to help out Scotland Yard's Inspector Blount or any number of well-heeled friends in a pinch.

Although the gentleman sleuth is most likely to be a British creation, this character type appeared on the other side of the Atlantic as well. The best remembered example is S. S. *Van Dine's Philo *Vance, whose snobbishness outdoes his gentlemanliness. He lives in luxury in his New York penthouse where his narrator S. S. Van

Dine is kept at his beck and call. He speaks with an affected British upper-crust accent, dropping his g's as does Wimsey. He uses a cigarette holder for his Regie cigarettes and possesses an encyclopedic knowledge of obscure facts, some of which are expounded upon in footnotes in the novels.

[See also Sidekicks and Sleuthing Teams.]

—Rosemary Herbert

GENTLEMAN THIEF. The gentleman thief is a man of good breeding who makes his living by dishonest means. A literary descendant of the gallant highwayman found in such early fiction as "The Squire's Story" by Elizabeth Gaskell (1853; reprinted in Lizzie Leigh and Other Tales, 1855), the gentleman thief was a popular contrast to the *Great Detective epitomized by Arthur Conan *Doyle's Sherlock *Holmes. Most notable among such characters and the prototype of the gentleman thief is E. W. *Hornung's A. J. *Raffles: cricketer, burglar, and gentleman (The Amateur Cracksman, 1899; Raffles, the Amateur Cracksman). A criminal who is willing to contemplate murder (though he does not commit it) to avoid arrest, Raffles has at the same time, as George Orwell points out ("Raffles and Miss Blandish," Horizon, Oct. 1944), a strict code of honor: He will not steal from his host, though a fellow guest is fair game; he is intensely patriotic, returning a stolen antique gold cup to Queen Victoria, and enlisting in the army during the Boer War to die a hero's death in South Africa. Raffles is not only the first, but perhaps also the only pure example of the type: The criminal element is not underplayed, as it is elsewhere, but is the raison d'etre of his character; the stories in which he appears are, from a literary point of view, undoubtedly the best in this genre. A French equivalent is Maurice *Leblanc's Arsène *Lupin (Arsène Lupin: Gentleman-Cambrioleur, 1907; The Exploits of Arsène Lupin); here, however, comic exaggeration leads to parody.

Few followed the Raffles model in every detail. Frank L. Packard's New York club man, Jimmie Dale, the "most puzzling, bewildering, delightful crook in the annals of crime," remains close to the model of Raffles (The Adventures of Jimmie Dale, 1917), as does Bruce Graeme's mystery writer and thief Richard Verrell (Blackshirt, 1925) in a series continued by the author's son Roderic Graeme.

Contemporary with the development of the Raffles character were two variations; the first of these, the crooked *lawyer or investigator, was perhaps more typical of early crime fiction, in which the protagonist was almost as often a criminal as a detective. Examples include Melville Davisson *Post's short stories featuring lawyer Randolph Mason (The Strange Schemes of Randolph Mason, 1896), Arthur *Morrison's detective Horace Dorrington (The Dorrington Deed-Box, 1897), and Clifford Ashdown's (pseudonym of R. Austin *Freeman and J. J. Pitcairn) literary agent Romney Pringle (The Adventures of Romney Pringle, 1902). Pringle, a professional who uses his standing to act the role of Robin Hood, links the two variations. In the second, the protagonist is an honest professional who engages in illegal activity only to right a wrong. Arnold Bennett's Cecil Thorold (*The Loot of Cities*, 1904) and William Le Queux's Italian aristocrat, Bindo di Ferraris (*The Count's Chauffeur*, 1907) follow this pattern.

The gentleman thief evolved into the gentleman adventurer, epitomized by Leslie *Charteris's Simon Templar, known as The *Saint, whose career spans almost sixty years from his introduction in *Meet the Tiger* (1928). Though living beyond the law, Templar has little or nothing of the criminal about him. A modern Robin Hood, pursued by the police in Britain and America, he rights wrongs, succours the poor, and brings criminals to justice through unlawful means. Despite his long career, Templar belongs to the interwar years, just as Raffles belongs to the Victorian era. An updated version is offered by John *Creasey's the Honourable Richard Rollison, known as the Toff (*Introducing the Toff*, 1938).

Later attempts to make the criminal (whether active or reformed), a central character focus on the criminal element rather than on the breeding and code of honor, a sign that this character is perhaps bound more by time and culture than others in crime fiction.

[*See also* Robin Hood Criminal.]

—T. J. Binyon

GEORGE, (SUSAN) ELIZABETH (b. 1949), American writer and teacher known for mystery novels set in English scenes. Born in Warren, Ohio, George was raised in the small town of Mountain View, California. She was educated at Catholic schools before she attended Foothill Community College, the University of California in Berkeley and graduated from the University of California in Riverside, where she later earned a lifetime degree in teaching. She also earned a master's degree at California State University at Fullerton. George began her professional life as a high school teacher, went on to teach writing on the college level, and still teaches writing seminars and workshops.

In her first novel, *A Great Deliverance* (1988), George uses superstition and a fog-enshrouded abbey in Yorkshire, England, to good effect as her sleuths, New Scotland Yard Inspector Thomas Lynley and Detective Sergeant Barbara Havers investigate murder by means of decapitation. The book garnered the Agatha and Anthony awards and the French Grand Prix de Litterature Policiere. The novels that followed take Lynley and Havers to similarly atmospheric destinations in a variety of English settings—the abbey, the country cottage, a prehistoric ring of stones, which the author researched in remarkably quick visits. In her early books, her detectives look at questions of appearances versus reality and determine that individuals are not what they seem. Later, as George's career progressed, she began to use mysterious characters and colorful settings to comment on social ills. Such is the case in her 1997 novel, *Deception on*

His Mind. Set in a depressed town on the coast of Essex, this novel looks at tensions between English and Pakistani residents of Balford-le-Nez.

The contrast between George's aristocratic Lynley, who is she eighth earl of Asherton, and the working-class Havers reliably enlivens the series. The detectives' dealings with their relatives and some other regularly appearing colleagues add depth to the sleuths' characterization, too. George, who is divorced and childless, divides her time between California and South Kensington, London.

[*See also* Police Detective.]

—Rosemary Herbert

Gethryn, Colonel Anthony Ruthven, an *amateur detective created by the British author Philip *MacDonald, was a product of the genre's Golden Age. Born around 1885, the son of an English country gentleman and a Spanish actress who also danced and painted, Gethryn was educated at Oxford, saw army service in World War I, was subsequently in the Secret Service, and ultimately solved crimes in the country house milieu and the English village milieu.

The first of Gethryn's dozen appearances, in *The Rasp* (1924), finds the sleuth in rural retirement with his wife Lucia disturbed by the murder of a cabinet minister. Later, in *The Noose* (1930), Gethryn has just five days to clear a condemned man. His exploits are characterized by sound detection, conducted in an atmosphere reminiscent of that created by Alfred Hitchcock, and featuring wraith-like criminals. Plots in the Gethryn stories hinge upon small clues, and are presented with whimsical humor combined with touches of the bizarre. *The Nursemaid Who Disappeared* (1938; *Warrant for X*) and *The List of Adrian Messenger* (1959) exemplify Gethryn at his best.

[*See also* Gentleman Sleuth.]

—Melvyn Barnes

Ghote, Inspector Ganesh Vinayak. Created by H. R. F. *Keating, Inspector Ghote of the Bombay Criminal Investigation Department (CID) appears in some twenty novels and numerous short stories. Beginning with *The Perfect Murder* (1964), Ghote, with his bony shoulders weighed down by life, seems easily intimidated by the rich and mighty. Dominated by his superiors, nagged by his wife Protima and cajoled by his beloved son Ved Ghote appears diffident, overwhelmed, and error-prone. Yet in pursuit of a criminal, he is shrewd and intelligent. Beneath the humorous figure of a downtrodden policeman lies a formidable adversary.

A man of honor, Ghote struggles to do what is right. In *Under a Monsoon Cloud* (1986), he protects a long-time hero from prosecution and faces an inquiry; in *The Iciest Sin* (1990) he witnesses a venerated scientist commit a murder. In *Inspector Ghote Trusts the Heart* (1972), he draws on his deep compassion when the son of a poor man is kidnapped. An admirer of Hans Gross, early criminologist and author of *Criminal Investigations*, Ghote combines basic principles of detection with intuition and common sense.

[*See also* Ethnic Sleuth.]

—Melvyn Barnes

GILBERT, MICHAEL (b. 1912), English author, a Grand master of the MWA, recipient of the 1994 Diamond Dagger Award. Gilbert was a fledgling lawyer when he began his first novel, but World War II intervened and he did not become either solicitor or novelist until his return to civilian life in 1946. He joined a leading law firm in Lincoln's Inn and set about completing and revising the unfinished novel, published in 1947 as *Close Quarters*. Until his retirement from the law, he sustained two careers, writing his novels and stories in the trains that carried him to and from his legal work. From the start he showed his versatility, determined never to write the same book twice. *Close Quarters* is a classical closed-circle mystery set in the cathedral close milieu. *They Never Looked Inside (1948; He Didn't Mind Danger)*, which followed, is a taut and lively thriller exploiting the tensions of postwar London. Since then, diversity has been a hallmark of Gilbert's work; as Eric Forbes-Boyd remarked, he has shown himself equally adept "with wig and gown or cloak and dagger."

This means that it is not possible to characterize the typical Gilbert novel. *Smallbone Deceased* (1950) is a legal whodunit long assured of classic status; *Death Has Deep Roots* (1951) takes us into an Old Bailey trial; *Death in Captivity* (1952; *The Danger Within*, 1952) draws on the author's experience as a prisoner of war, combining detection with a war story; and *Blood and Judgement* (1959) is a rare full-length case for Patrick Petrella, the protagonist of numerous police stories. *The Etruscan Net* (1969; *The Family Tomb*, 1970) investigates art frauds in postdiluvian Florence; *The Body of a Girl* (1972) and *Death of Favourite Girl* (1980; *The Killing of Katie Steelstock*) are complex police procedurals with less predictable policemen than the decent Petrella; *The Night of the Twelfth* (1976) gives a chilling account of sadism and murder at a prep school; and *Trouble* (1987) is an ambitious thriller dealing in terrorism and racial tensions.

The story collections are equally varied. Two featuring Petrella present a traditional, reassuring image of the police force; two involve Messrs. Calder and Behrens, senior spies who play a grim game without rules; while another, with Jonas Pickett, a semiretired solicitor, shows a world still secure despite the weakening of its "bastions"—"religion, family life, the rule of the law."

Gilbert's respect for established authority is everywhere apparent, and his attitudes do not waver. Criminals are outlaws demanding society's vengeance. Brutes should expect brutality in return, and a righteous end may justify equivocal means. Throughout, Gilbert writes with confidence, ease, and humor. As a narrator he is masterly, able to assemble from diverse encounters and events a tense, absorbing pattern that gains in coherence until the denouement completes the design.

—B. A. Pike

GILL, BARTHOLOMEW, pseudonym of Mark McGarrity (b. 1943), American author of Irish ancestry best-known for a long-running series about Chief Superintendent Peter McGarr of Ireland's Special Crimes Unit. Gill was born in Holyoke, Massachusetts, and educated at Brown University in Providence, Rhode Island, and at Trinity College in Dublin, Ireland. He married and worked as a speechwriter, insurance investigator and other jobs before becoming a full-time writer in 1971.

McGarr first appears in *McGarr and the Politician's Wife* (1977; *The Death of an Irish Politician*), where he is described as a dull-looking but determined sleuth with lower-class Dublin roots, married rather surprisingly to a much younger, and quite beautiful wife named Noreen. Much of the interest in the series comes from the setting in the Irish Republic where McGarr treads carefully in tense political territory. Additional interest comes from McGarr's interactions with his subordinate policemen and the suspects he meets. Often McGarr's insight into character is as useful as physical evidence in getting to the truth of the matter. Gill also wrote books that are strong on suspense under his own name. They include *A Passing Advantage* (1980), *Neon Caesar* (1989) and *White Rush, Green Fire* (1991).

[*See also* Police Detective.]

—Rosemary Herbert

GODWIN, WILLIAM (1756–1836), author of *Things as They Are; or, The Adventures of Caleb Williams* (1794), a novel considered to be a precursor of the novel of mystery and detection, William Godwin became a student of philosophy at the Hoxton Presbyterian Academy. From 1778 to 1783 he served several dissenting congregations as minister. Following his doubts about organized religion, he become an atheist and left the Church for work as writer and political activist. He was connected with the extreme Whigs, worked as a writer for *New Annual Register*, and started a publishing firm, which failed despite its issue of the famous *Tales from Shakespeare* (1807) by Charles Lamb.

Godwin was an associate of the English Romantic writers—it was Samuel Taylor Coleridge who drew him back from atheism to theism—and became their de facto social theorist. His notable work of political theory was *Enquiry Concerning Political Justice* (1793), published during a decade of great activity by Godwin. In 1794 he published the narrative of Caleb Williams, in 1797 he married Mary Wollstonecraft, and in 1803–1804 he issued a two-volume study of Chaucer.

Caleb Williams focuses at its opening on Falkland, a wealthy squire whom critics regard as a fore-runner of Dr. Jekyll and Mr. Hyde because he is both affable and a murderer. The eponymous hero of the story is Falkland's secretary, who finds evidence of his employer's guilt and flees when Falkland threatens to lay the guilt on Williams. Eventually Falkland confesses his crime and Caleb Williams suffers remorse for having contributed to Falkland's disgrace. Politically the work concerns the corruptions of power. In terms of its place in the literary history of crime and mystery it represents a union of the tale of pursuit with an investigation of motive and evidence.

—John M. Reilly

GOODIS, DAVID (1917–1967), American screenwriter and author of pulp fiction and noir novels. Born in Philadelphia, Pennsylvania, Goodis attended Indiana University and earned a journalism degree at Temple University in Philadelphia. He worked as an advertising copywriter and freelance writer. A master of many formulae, he turned out much material, under many pseudonyms, for pulp magazines including *Terror Tales, Western Tales, Fighting Aces* and *Manhunt*. As a crime writer, his vision is dark, uneasy and filled with violence. In books likened to the work of Jim *Thompson and Cornell *Woolrich, Goodis follows the fates of defeated characters whose hopelessness does little to brighten the world of tenements and gutters where they live. The titles evoke the themes and situations in Goodis's oeuvre. *Retreat from Oblivion* (1939), *Street of the Lost* (1952), *The Wounded and the Slain* (1955) are telling examples.

[*See also* Hard-boiled Sleuth; Outcasts and Outsiders.]

—Rosemary Herbert

Goodwin, Archie, the first-person narrator of Rex *Stout's Nero *Wolfe series. Through thirty-three novels and thirty-eight novelettes, Goodwin serves not only as Wolfe's active investigator, but also as his amanuensis and conversational foil. Because Wolfe is almost neurotically opposed to leaving his brownstone on New York's West Thirty-fifth Street, Goodwin does the legwork in the cases they accept.

Goodwin is a sharp-tongued wit and cynic, realistic enough to know that he cannot keep up with Wolfe's superior powers of ratiocination, but confident enough to maintain his self-esteem in their tense, but mutually respectful, relationship. Stout gives Goodwin a private life, including his frequently mentioned but seldom-seen romance with Lily Rowan and his weekly poker games with Saul Panzer. Wolfe's gruff acknowledgment of Goodwin's indispensable place in his life is particularly spelled out in the short story "Christmas Party" (*And Four to Go*, 1958), in which Wolfe leaves his brownstone and disguises himself as a bartending Santa Claus in order to assure himself of Goodwin's well-being.

[*See also* Sidekicks and Sleuthing Teams.]

—Landon Burns

GORES, JOE (b. 1931), American author of *private eye short stories and novels informed by the author's twelve-year career as a private investigator. Born in Minnesota, he was educated at the University of California at Stamford and at Notre Dame. In addition to writing everything from men's adventure short stories to military biographies, television episodes, and the 1975 book *Hammett*, Gores tried his hand at several lines of work in international settings. His job experience includes teaching in Kenya, logging in Alaska, spear fishing in Tahiti, and private eye work in San Francisco. Gores successfully battled discouragement over many early rejections before his first short story, "Chain Gang," was published in *Manhunt* in 1957. His first novel, *Time of Predators*, was published in 1969. Meanwhile, in a short story titled "The Mayfield Case" (*EQMM*, 1967), Gores created Dan Kearny Associates (DKA), a car repossession company that figures in the author's second novel, *Dead Skip* (1972) and a series of later novels. Headed by Dan Kearny, DKA employs a mix of people—including a boxer, a black investigator and an alluring blonde—who become series characters in several books. The memorably-titled *32 Cadillacs* (1992) won the author a larger audience. It is based on a true crime. Gores also produced-non-series novels that are strong on violence. His prison escape story "Goodbye Pops" (*EQMM*, 1969) won an Edgar Award.

[See also Hard-boiled Sleuth.]

—Rosemary Herbert

GORMAN, ED(WARD JOSEPH) (b. 1941), American writer of crime and western fiction, and founding editor of *Mystery Scene* magazine. Born in Cedar Rapids, Iowa, he was educated at Coe College in that state. He then worked for more than two decades in the advertising world before turning to writing and editing full time in 1989. Gorman has created several series characters, three of them introduced in 1987 alone. They are Jack Dwyer, an ex-policeman who appears in the author's first novel, *Rough Cut*; bounty hunter Leo Guild, introduced in *Guild*; and the movie-critic hero Tobin, who enters the scene in *Murder on the Aisle*. Gorman's new characters for the 1990's include Robert Payne, a forensic profiler who first appears in *Blood Moon* (1994) and Sam McCain, a *lawyer introduced in *The Day the Music Died* (1999). As editor of *Mystery Scene*, Gorman has had considerable influence on disseminating fiction and critical evaluations of the crime-writing genre.

—Rosemary Herbert

GOULART, RON(ALD JOSEPH) (b. 1933), versatile American writer of science fiction, mysteries, comic strips, and non-fiction works about genre fiction and comics. Born in Berkeley, California, Goulart attended the University of California and worked in advertising and screenwriting in addition to turning out books. Riding the wave of renewed interest in popular literature, he made a mark with *Cheap Thrills: An Informal History of the Pulp Magazines* in 1972. His 1988 book, *Dime Detectives*, was another nonfiction success. His best-known of a few series characters was the *private eye John Easy, introduced in *If Dying Was All* (1971), until that series was eclipsed by another beginning with *Groucho Marx, Master Detective* (1998), in which a fictionalized Groucho Marx solves crimes. Goulart also contributed to the Hardy Boys series of juvenile mysteries under two pseudonyms—as Franklin W. Dixon and (collaborating with Otto Penzler) as R. T. Edwards.

—Rosemary Herbert

GOURMET DETECTIVES. *See* Culinary Sleuth.

GRAFTON, SUE (b. 1940), American creator of the sassy California *private eye Kinsey *Millhone, who appears in books entitled after letters in the alphabet. The daughter of lawyer and sometime detective novelist C. W. Grafton and chemistry teacher Vivian Harnsberger, Grafton grew up in a household that revered the written word. She has termed her home "classically dysfunctional," since both of her parents were alcoholics. Making an advantage from a liability, Grafton has said that her parents' alcoholism built in her a sensitivity to subtle cues in behavior, and her relatively unsupervised childhood in Louisville, Kentucky, allowed her generous time for outdoor play centered upon the construction of imaginary adventure stories. Often playing the role of the heroine, Grafton said she never depended upon others for rescue but was determined to save herself. These qualities are carried over into the creation of her *sleuth, Millhone.

Grafton married at eighteen and earned a degree in English from Western Kentucky State Teachers College. She became the mother of three, hoping to create an ideal family life that had eluded her when she was a child, but was married three times before she found real happiness. Grafton tried homemaking and work as a consciousness-raising group leader before turning her hand to writing two mainstream novels and numerous screenplays and teleplays. Then, inspired by a sense of helplessness during a custody battle over her children, Grafton created the independent, capable Millhone, a champion of the helpless, and also found her true calling as a detective novelist. Milhone is introduced in *"A" is for Alibi* (1982). Alcoholism is a theme in *"D" is for Deadbeat* (1987).

[*See also* Hard-Boiled Sleuth.]

—Rosemary Herbert

Gray, Cordelia, resourceful fictional private investigator created by P. D. *James and introduced in the 1972 novel *An Unsuitable Job for a Woman*. Upon the suicide death of her mentor and business partner, Bernard "Bernie" G. Pryde of Pryde's Detective Agency, Gray, who "had brought no qualifications or relevant past experience to the partnership and indeed no capital except her slight but tough twenty-two-year-old body, [and] a considerable intelligence," picks up the pieces. Using the limited resources of the detective agency she proves that detective work is a perfectly fitting career for a woman

possessed of intelligence, determination, and courage when she pursues the case of Mark Callender, whose father, a famous scientist, hires Gray to discover why Mark committed suicide.

Gray is remarkably self-possessed for her age, a result of her unusual and unsupportive upbringing. Her mother died when Gray was just one hour old, leaving Gray's father, an "itinerant Marxist poet and amateur revolutionary" either to drag their child around with his "comrades" from lodging to lodging or to farm her out to a succession of foster mothers. Gray's irregular education included convent schooling that offered her incompetent instruction in the sciences but an excellent acquaintance with literature. She puts the latter to good use in interpreting clues in *An Unsuitable Job for a Woman*. Gray is also the protagonist in *The Skull Beneath the Skin* (1982), and she is mentioned in *The Black Tower* (1975) when she sends a hand-picked bouquet of flowers to Commander Adam *Dalgliesh, who is recuperating from atypical mononucleosis at the novel's start.

James has said that she identifies with Cordelia and enjoyed working with "a youngish woman: vulnerable, but I think courageous in setting out regardless." James added, "I suppose I *approve* of Cordelia very much."

—Rosemary Herbert

GREAT DETECTIVE, THE. As the literature of ancient Greece and Rome employed the figure of apotheosis, or elevation of a heroic personage to the rank of a god, so the popular genre of crime and mystery writing uses a secularized version of the device to raise the character of the detective to a position of extraordinary distinction. In both cases, the technique expresses cultural values. The ascription of divinity to a champion of war or statecraft becomes possible when it is believed that the realm of gods interrelates with the world of human beings in such an intimate way as to make moral power personal, the sacred and the mundane interchangeable. The creation of a detective possessing singular powers of discernment and the dauntless ability to restore civil order signifies the modern belief that moral ends, at least so far as they pertain to social order, may be achieved through the resources of individual genius and the techniques of disciplined reasoning.

Given the historical circumstances that form the source of crime and mystery writing, it was inevitable that the detective would take a central narrative role. The complexity and confusion of modern urban society raise a popular desire for an agency that will explain and control events when the older systems of religious and social order seem no longer to do so. For problems of property the agency of explanation became the system of law, and for the problem of crime there had to be an independent force, perhaps a government bureau in the real world, but in the world of imagination, where the profound needs and wishes of a culture take dramatically tangible appearance, disorder was countered by the aggressive mind and engaging personality of the lone detective.

From their beginnings in early detective and police memoirs, narratives of thief catching and crime solving placed an aura of superiority around the detective. The varied adventures of Eugène François *Vidocq gain what unity and coherence they have from portrayal of Vidocq himself. The tales related by Allan Pinkerton from the archives of his detective agency are distinguished by the consistently superior guile and nerve of his agents and by the background presence of Pinkerton presiding over his agency's exploits like King Arthur at the Round Table.

When detection narratives became deliberately and frankly fictitious, as they did in the inventive short stories of Edgar Allan *Poe, their authors crafted nearly all of their technique for the purpose of enhancing the figure of the detective. For example, readers hear of the cases of the Chevalier C. Auguste *Dupin from the distance of a secondary character's memories. The effect is to engender awe, wonder, and no little mystery about Dupin, since the narrative distance prevents him from becoming commonplace. Moreover, Dupin has no family, no evident occupation, no involvement in pedestrian daytime reality. He is free from any responsibility, except that which he chooses to assume, he is independent in his opinions, stellar in his reasoning. The stories are designed to progress intellectually, complete with brief lectures on reasoning from Dupin, so that there is little to detract from the presentation of his mental superiority— no actions occurring within the story, no competing characters, no background material beyond what is required to set the scene and the circumstances of the crime. Dupin is the only figure of consequence in the world Poe makes, and he is inevitably its greatest inhabitant.

The techniques Poe pioneered for stories of detection became the template and convention for his successors. Arthur Conan *Doyle's Sherlock *Holmes is also a man without domestic connection or responsibility, and his cases, too, are the tales told by a sidekick. What Doyle adds to the formula of the Great Detective is detailed eccentricity: pensiveness, the habit of escaping into music, a possible drug habit, and a disarming way of dominating conversations with axioms about observation and reasoning. Some of these assigned behaviors are not particularly functional to the progress of the narratives, but they are decidedly important to the job of distancing Holmes from the ordinary person and making him, thereby, extraordinary.

Once the literary success of the convention of the Great Detective became evident, it spawned great ingenuity. There was the blind detective Max *Carrados created by Ernest *Bramah whose extraordinary abilities include super elevation of his remaining senses, the *Thinking Machine whose feats related by Jacques *Futrelle outdid Dupin's. There were the *gentlemen sleuths of the Golden Age, characters such as Lord Peter *Wimsey and Hercule *Poirot whose mannered eccentricities were designed to reinforce the grand accomplishments of their detection and to assure their inclusion in the list of great, because unusual, detectives. Even as the original models receded into the past, the convention retained vitality. Rex *Stout's Nero *Wolfe, assisted by Archie *Goodwin, a character somewhat hard-boiled, displayed the unusual ability to solve crimes throughout the city from the comfort of his armchair where he settled his hugely obese body, all the while conducting the opinionated conversation that by now has become requisite for any Great Detective.

The advent of hard-boiled detectives such as Dashiell *Hammett's Sam *Spade and Continental *Op or Raymond *Chandler's Philip *Marlowe altered but did not erase the Great Detective. Kinship with predecessors from the Golden Age and earlier can be seen in the isolated status of hard-boiled sleuths. They, too, are sleuths as loners; consequently, their narratives can center entirely on their practice of detection. They are not thinking machines or even especially men of reason, needing instead to use more active means of solving crimes. Still, their authors assign them traits suggesting singularity— sometimes a mood of disappointment, at other times unusual knowledge of seamy life, and always a peculiarly personal tone in their worldly wise voices. The world the hard-boiled detective inhabits seems to show little possibility for any sort of greatness, but, as Chandler argued in his famous essay "The Simple Art of Murder" (*Atlantic Monthly*, Dec. 1944), the detective in a city of mean streets "is not himself mean.... He is the hero, he is everything." In other words, the detective embodies an improvisational morality uncharacteristic of most other people. He is great. Although the hard-boiled mannerisms seem to be spent, and authors increasingly normalize their protagonists as women and men beset by fear and loneliness that earlier writers never would have assigned their characters, the archetype of the Great Detective continues to resonate. The detectives in the fiction of Tony *Hillerman, Sue *Grafton, or Robert B. *Parker are drawn with traits more common than extraordinary, except for the mystique that inspires their careers. They are detectives, after all, trying to put the world right.

[*See also* Eccentrics; Gentleman Sleuth; Superman Sleuth.]

—John M. Reilly

GREEN, ANNA KATHARINE (1846–1935), American author, frequently denominated as the "mother of the detective novel." Green was born in Brooklyn Heights, New York, to a family that traced colonial New England forebears on both sides. She lived in Brooklyn and Manhattan in her early years, married Charles Rohlfs in 1884, and moved to Buffalo, New York, in 1887. Having lost her mother at age two, Green was highly influenced by her father, James Wilson Green, a lawyer prominent in Republican party politics in New York City. She was the only one of his four children sent to college, gaining a B. A. at Ripley Female Seminary in Vermont in 1866 or 1867. Hoping for recognition as a poet, she submitted work to Ralph Waldo Emerson for his criti-

cism; in a carefully worded response dated 30 June 1868, he advised her to write if she felt the desire, but not to try to make a profession of poetry. She put poetry aside and worked for five years on a "criminal romance," producing her landmark novel, *The Leavenworth Case: A Lawyer's Story* (1878), which remained a bestseller for decades and established the type.

Green's novel emphasized rational detection, and developed the early series detective New York City police officer Ebenezer Gryce, nine years before Sherlock *Holmes's appearance in fiction. Such now familiar conventions as the body in the library, the wealthy man about to change his will, the locked room, the use of ballistics evidence, a coroner's inquest, a sketch of the scene of the crime, and a partially burned letter all appeared in this novel. A. E. Murch, in her groundbreaking study *The Development of the Detective Novel* (1958), describes Green as virtually the creator of the detective novel. Green was influenced by Émile *Gaboriau's *roman policier*, with its typically French social and legal procedures, but her novels are distinctively American, many of them set in New York City in the elegant mansions of lower Fifth Avenue. *The Leavenworth Case* attracted the attention of Wilkie *Collins, who wrote commenting on her fertility of invention and depiction of strong women.

Nineteen years and eighteen books later, Green created a *spinster sleuth, a forerunner of Agatha *Christie's Miss Jane *Marple, in Miss Amelia Butterworth (*That Affair Next Door*, 1897). (Christie credits her influence, mentioning Green specifically in her *Autobiography*.) Green also created a young debutante sleuth, Violet Strange. Although Green wrote fiction in order to gain recognition for her poetry, she was spurred by the success of her first novel to go on writing detective fiction: Widely anthologized, her works ran in serial form in newspapers and magazines such as *The Century, Lippincott's, Frank Leslie's Illustrated Newspaper, The New York Ledger*, and later, *The Ladies' Home Journal*. Her last book, *The Step on the Stair* (1924), completed a life's work of thirty-six detective novels, four collections of short stories, one volume of poetry (*The Defense of the Bride*, 1882), and one verse drama (*Risifi's Daughter*, 1887). None of her later works equalled the success of her first book, which continued to sell in many different versions for forty years; still she reigned as a grande dame of detective fiction. Contemporary reviewers praised her ingenious and intricate plotting as surprising from a female writer; some suggested the author might be a male using a pseudonym. Green's melodramatic style won some scornful reviews, but British prime minister Stanley Baldwin, speaking in London in 1928, praised *The Leavenworth Case* as "one of the best detective stories ever written," and the book was used at Yale Law School to demonstrate the weaknesses of circumstantial evidence.

[*See also* Poets as Crime Writers.]

—Joan Warthling Roberts

GREENE, GRAHAM (1904–91), British author, a major figure of twentieth-century letters of biography, plays and screenplays, essays, and criticism, as well as thrillers. Greene was often named as a Nobel Prize candidate, though he never won the award. As for his forays into crime writing and spy fiction, he himself dismissed these most popular of his works as "entertainments." These thrillers include *Stamboul Train* (1932; *Orient Express*) *Brighton Rock* (1938), *The Confidential Agent* (1939), and *The Ministry of Fear* (1943), among others. He also wrote or co-wrote the film adaptations of these books.

The author of twenty-four novels over a sixty-year career, Greene created memorable male characters possessed of wavering morals, trying to make a stand in an equally unsteady world. This is true of the teen killer in *Brighton Rock* (1938). In addition, the unnamed Mexican priest in *The Power and the Glory* (1940; *The Labyrinthine Ways*) is an alcoholic, or "whiskey priest," and has fathered a child. He is on the run from the dogged pursuit of an army lieutenant because, in a society where the church is persecuted by a military government, priests are being executed. This priest is no righteous Jean Valjean, though: He is an immoral man who must live by his wits, placing others in mortal danger by his actions. If he makes a moral stand, it will be at the expense of his own life. In *The Third Man* (1950), Rollo Martins named Holly in the 1949 film must tiptoe through the political and moral debris of post–World War II Vienna as well as its physical rubble. At each step, Martins's beliefs about his closest boyhood friend, Harry Lime, increasingly crack like one of the city's war-ravaged buildings.

The Catholic Church condemned *The Power and the Glory* for its portrayal of the unorthodox priest. Other Greene novels received official condemnation from national governments. In the United States, *The Quiet American* (1955) and *The Comedians* (1966) were read as attacks on America's foreign policy in Vietnam and Haiti, respectively. Yet, while Greene may have had strong liberal opinions about church and government, his topic was really the human soul.

Greene was born in Berkhamsted, Hertfordshire, England. His father was headmaster of Berkhamsted School, which Greene attended preparatory to Balliol College, Oxford. His childhood was unhappy: He suffered a nervous breakdown at Berkhamsted and was treated by a psychiatrist. At Oxford, Greene joined the Communist Party. In 1927, at age twenty-two and just out of Oxford, he converted to Catholicism in order to marry the Catholic Vivien Dayrell-Browning. Years later, he would resist the term "Catholic writer," but religion was central to many of his books, as well as those of his contemporaries. Following Oxford, he worked at the *Times* of London as a copy editor, eventually leaving to become a film critic for several newspapers and journals, including *The Spectator*. He supported his family in that role while writing his earlier novels.

During World War II, he was an intelligence officer

with the Foreign Office. He was sent to West Africa in 1942. He traveled widely during and after the war, his globetrotting lasting as long as he was physically able. Many of his destinations became locales for his stories.

Greene wrote two autobiographies: *A Sort of Life* (1971) and *Ways of Escape* (1980). Divorced, he died in Vevey, Switzerland, at the age of eighty-six.

[*See also* Antihero.]

—Dana Bisbee

GRIMES, MARTHA (b. 1931), American professor, and author of mysteries set in England featuring the series detectives Richard Jury and Melrose Plant. Born in Pittsburgh, Pennsylvania, Grimes was raised in Maryland by her widowed mother. Grimes earned bachelor's and master's degrees from the University of Maryland. She also attended the University of Iowa Writers' Workshop, where she studied poetry. The divorced mother of one son, she taught courses and seminars at various universities. She introduced Jury and Plant in *The Man with a Load of Mischief* (1981), the first of her novels to be titled after a memorably-named English pub. A detective in the classic mold, Scotland Yard detective Jury is tall, attractive and fond of quoting Latin words of wisdom. Plant, too, is a throwback: the eldest son in an aristocratic family, he has the time and resources to pursue amateur detective work. Writing an average of a novel a year, Grimes divides her time between Washington, D.C. and England, where she does research for her books.

—Rosemary Herbert

GRISHAM, JOHN (b. 1955), American *lawyer and author of legal thrillers. Born of working-class parents in Arkansas, he went on to the University of Mississippi Law School and worked as a trial lawyer for more than a decade. He also served on the Mississippi House of Representatives. His first thriller, *A Time to Kill* (1989), was inspired by a rape case upon which he worked. It caused him to imagine consequences that might ensue if a parent perpetrated a revenge killing after a child was molested. His next novel, too, has a central problem at its heart, which the protagonist is horrified to recognize as the action progresses: In *The Firm* (1991), a brilliant young law school graduate is courted and then threatened by a law firm that has underworld connections. *The Pelican Brief* (1992) follows a similar pattern, with an earnest young law student working in the United States Supreme Court lets on that she has figured out some key facts in the murders of two judges. Grisham turned out several more thrillers along these lines, and most were made into blockbuster movies. In 2001, he made a departure with *A Painted House*. Narrated by a young boy, this novel does have murders in it, but the characterization is subtler and the action is therefore more shocking.

[*See also* Judge; Menacing Characters.]

—Rosemary Herbert

H

HAMMETT, DASHIELL (1894–1961), American author whose writing career lasted no more than a decade, but who in that short span of time created a specifically American kind of crime story, loosely called the tough-guy or hard-boiled tale, and made it respectable. Hammett had the hard and varied youth endured by many American writers, working on the railroad, then as a Pinkerton operative whose duties included occasional strikebreaking, then enlisting in the Army during World War I. He was discharged as tubercular and given a small pension, married his hospital nurse, had two children, and suffered poverty before making some money by writing short stories for the pulp magazines that became immensely popular in the U.S. during the 1920s.

As a writer, Hammett began by using and romanticizing his Pinkerton experience. The stories were told in the first person by a short, fat detective called the *Continental Op. The Op had few opinions about anything except his work, which he carried out with ruthless efficiency. Many of the stories were extremely violent, and they were written in a style deliberately bare, stripped of adjectival color. The action is colorful, the writing plain. The style resembles that of early Ernest Hemingway, although any direct influence of either writer on the other is very unlikely.

Hammett wrote mostly for *Black Mask*, the best of the pulps, and quickly became their most popular writer. He also learned his craft. His first novel, *Red Harvest* (1929), is sophisticated and stylized in a way that would have been beyond Hammett's capacities a year or two earlier. There are two dozen deaths in the book, yet among the gunplay and gang warfare are characters vividly realized, including Hammett's first convincing woman. This is Dinah Brand, called a deluxe hustler and a soiled dove, who has "the face of a girl of twenty-five already showing signs of wear," is a tremendous drinker—and one of the most sexually attractive women in crime literature.

Hammett called *The Dain Curse*, published in the same year, a silly book, and it is easy to agree with him. In it he moved away from things he knew about—gunmen, shysters, and local politicos—to deal with family curses and religious cults. But *The Maltese Falcon* (1930) made Hammett famous, and *The Glass Key* (1931) consolidated the fame. In them the Continental Op has been replaced by the dubiously honest but physically attractive Sam *Spade and Ned Beaumont, respectively. Violence is greatly reduced, and almost all of it takes place offstage. The distinctive Hammett style has now been perfected. Characterization is achieved in part through a scrupulous, often detailed account of physical appearance (as of Gutman in the *Falcon*), in part through the revelations of dialogue. *The Maltese Falcon* is a thriller, *The Glass Key* offers the *puzzle of who killed Taylor Henry, but both transcend their plot origins. The first poses particular questions about a detective's ethics and, by extension, about morality in general; the second is about the power and limits of loyalty. Both were recognized as remarkable novels, especially by American critics. Hammett was a prophet honored in his own country.

His last novel, *The Thin Man* (1934), gave a sanitized view of his relationship with Lillian Hellman, and may also be seen as an account of a decadent society viewed from the inside. Hammett had been taken up by Hollywood, and was living in the way which his friend Nunnally Johnson said made sense only if "he had no expectation of being alive much beyond Thursday."

He had also become actively involved with left-wing political causes. In World War II he enlisted in the army (with difficulty because of his health); spent three years mostly in Alaska, where he founded and edited a camp newspaper; and was known to the youngsters as "Pop." In 1951, called to give evidence in a case involving Communists who had jumped bail, he refused to answer questions by pleading the Fifth Amendment, and was sentenced to six months in prison. When he came out it was to find the three radio shows based on his characters taken off the air, his books proscribed and removed from libraries, and all his sources of income removed. He survived for another ten years, but wrote only a Hemingwayesque fragment of a novel called *Tulip*.

The life may be seen as tragic, although Hammett would have deprecated such sentiment. Nor did he think highly of his writing, conceding only in an interview that *The Glass Key* was "not so bad." His standards were high, and often he did not live up to them: but he set his stamp permanently on American crime fiction, and his two finest books provide a benchmark few have reached.
[*See also* Hard-boiled Sleuth; Private Eye.]
—Julian Symons

Hanaud, Inspector. A. E. W. *Mason's Inspector Hanaud of the Paris Sûreté appeared in five novels and three short stories between 1910 and 1946, without showing much development. Writing twenty years after introducing his creation, Mason stated the four specifications he had laid down for his detective: He should be a professional; he should be as physically unlike Sherlock *Holmes as possible; he should be a friendly soul; and he should be willing to act on his intuition. Accordingly, Hanaud is the first important professional policeman after Charles *Dickens's Inspector Bucket, Wilkie *Collins's

Sergeant *Cuff, and Émile Gaboriau's Monsieur Lecoq. He is a big bear of a man, rumpled and jowly, looking like a prosperous comedian. His geniality is disarming, and he uses it to entrap his adversaries. Moreover, his insistence that the facts be viewed with "imagination on a leash" puts him solidly in the line of descent from the Chevalier C. Auguste *Dupin's Bi-Part Soul. Mason's own values are distinctly British and Edwardian, and Hanaud is clearly the projection of these; his main Gallic attribute is his demotic English, more witticism than malapropism, as when he calls Paris one's "spirituous home," or refers to the CID as the QED. With his finicky, wine-fancying widower friend Julius Ricardo, he is one-half of one of the more pleasing Holmes-Watson combinations in the genre.

[*See also* Police Detective.]

—Barrie Hayne

HANDICAPPED SLEUTH. *See* Disability, Sleuth with a.

HANSEN, JOSEPH (b. 1923), American crime writer, self-consciously concerned with gay issues. Born in Aberdeen, South Dakota, and educated there and in Minneapolis, Minnesota, and Pasadena, California, Hansen settled in California. Like the feminist novelists Barbara Wilson, Eve Zaremba, and Mary Wings, Hansen belongs to that group of contemporary writers eager to exploit the crime novel to investigate pressing social issues, reappraising questions of gender and sexuality arising from more traditional detective fiction. Just as the female writers challenge the belittling representations of women in hard-boiled crime writing, so Hansen takes issue with what he sees as the implicit homophobia of Raymond *Chandler. His recurrent central figure is the middle-aged *private eye and insurance investigator Dave *Brandstetter, unapologetically homosexual. From the excellent first novel, *Fadeout* (1970), onward, the interaction of the investigator's troubled private life and the mysteries in which he becomes embroiled is compellingly and sensitively handled. In that novel, Brandstetter's lover dies; as the central character mourns his loss, he becomes involved in a murder case. *Fadeout* was well-received, and started Hansen on his extensive series of Brandsetter adventures, principally set in southern California.

In the tradition of Ross *Macdonald and Armistead Maupin, Hansen is a witty and shrewd chronicler of the fads and eccentricities of that life. Indeed at times his eagerness to indulge in social commentary distracts from the momentum of the plot, and the narratives of some later books, such as *Gravedigger* (1982) and *Nightwork* (1984), seem implausible. However, when Hansen is fully engaged with challenging issues, he is a vivid and distinctive writer within the Chandler tradition. *Death Claims* (1973) and *Early Graves* (1987) are adjudged to be the best novels in the Brandsetter series. The latter proves that crime writing can deal effectively with the issue of AIDS. Hansen also writes fiction outside the private eye genre, under his own name and as James Colton and as Rose Brock, but this work has not yet attracted the attention accorded his Brandstetter mysteries.

—Ian Bell

HARD-BOILED SLEUTH. Narrative elements surrounding the detective are normally brought forward to characterize hard-boiled writing: a tinsel-town milieu, scenes of repeated violence, a tone of cynicism about wealth and authority, and a general sense of disorder. Detective fiction, however, above all concerns detectives doing their jobs. In that, hard-boiled fiction differs not at all from the classic tales of the Golden Age. A case can be made that the hard-boiled detective inhabits a world vastly different from that of the sleuth who is at home in the cozy mystery. Still, when the matter of a detective's work is considered as an issue of narrative construction, rather than a means to document the reality existing outside the text of a fiction, the detectives of literature have an inevitable uniformity in their narrative function.

In both cases, the reader encounters crimes that present a mystery. The criminals are unknown; or perhaps they are known, but retribution for the crime seems impossible. A client seeks the assistance of the detective, forming at least a tacit contract requiring the detective to solve the mystery. To fulfill the contract, the detective by whatever means must construct a cogent explanation of the criminal events. In other words, the detective is employed to produce a hypothesis that will withstand scrutiny. Another way of putting it is to say the detective must discover the true story behind the mystery, but even that is not the whole of it. The detective of fiction also must craft the findings about cause and motive, crime and its intended consequences, into a statement of explanation. That statement becomes a second narrative, a narrative within the framework of the inclusive story which the client sets in motion by seeking the detective's assistance.

This way of looking at detective fiction yields the idea of a double structure. First is the overall story that relates the crime and the detective's method of seeking its explanation. This first story comes to readers in the voice of the story or novel. Second, there is the discourse of explanation created by the detective. This second discourse originates in the detective's mind and may be expressed in a fragmentary way, as the detective's thoughts are shared with readers, or it may be related in a burst of final exposition, as in the characteristic wrap-up scenes where Charlie *Chan, Lord Peter *Wimsey, Hercule *Poirot, or a similar figure—the detective—assembles all the suspects to audit his explanation of whodunit.

Using the idea of the dual narrative, the sleuths of hard-boiled writing can be distinguished by their rare use of the wrap-up scene. They cannot summon the confidence in their intellectual powers to prepare such a performance. For example, while Dashiell *Hammett's Sam

*Spade finds himself among all of the suspects at the ending of *The Maltese Falcon* (1930), they have not congregated to hear him but to keep a watch on him. When Spade undertakes his explanation, it is at best fragmentary, and, in any case, his mind becomes concerned with emotional control of himself, as he tells Brigid O'Shaughnessey why he will turn her over to the police. Having lost intellectual command of events, Spade is relieved when the timely arrival of the police brings his case to its conclusion.

This drama in *The Maltese Falcon* of the detective's mind struggling for control of the novel's second narrative illustrates the circumstances of the hard-boiled sleuth. Preceding detective fiction had valorized the power of reason to explain reality. As a result, detectives such as Sherlock *Holmes and the revised versions of the *Great Detective who populate Golden Age stories treated crimes as intellectual problems, so that they could render their solutions in the form of well-structured demonstrations of mental acuity. For the hard-boiled sleuth, mysteries become existential. Chester *Himes's detective partners, the very tough Coffin Ed *Johnson and Grave Digger Jones, confront the most absurd sorts of crimes, and they are never in doubt, nor are readers, about the inadequacy of reason alone to manage their causes or consequences. The nine books about their adventures form a saga that explores the conditions created by systemic racial prejudice and exploitation that are so corrupt no single mind can fully explain them, let alone institute reasonable order in the world made by racism.

Of course, the speech of hard-boiled sleuths also illustrates their view of the mysteries they meet. Terse, rarely abstract but instead direct and vascular, the sleuths are Huckleberry Finn's cousins in the American vernacular. Perhaps more often than any other type of detective fiction, hard-boiled narratives are written from the first-person detective's point of view. That technical choice, then, simplifies narration, because it eliminates the separation between the voice of the novel and the voice of the sleuth; all of the story's discourse originates in the consciousness of the detective. Ross *Macdonald has described the process of centering the story in the detective's mind as making "the mind of the novel . . . a consciousness in which the meanings of other lives emerge." The economy of narration does not establish a control of mystery. On the contrary, in Raymond *Chandler's stories told by Philip *Marlowe, for instance, the dominance of a weary, disillusioned detective voice affirms the limitations of the mind, while Paul Cain's fictional voice in *Fast One* (1933) and in a short story such as "Trouble-Chaser" (*Black Mask*, Apr. 1934) can seem to be entirely devoted to a record of action.

Under more technical analysis, too, the use of American vernacular in the dialogue and narration of hard-boiled writing illustrates the character of the sleuth and the nature of his world. Complex sentence structures that employ syntactical subordination for purposes of intellectual analysis are considerably rarer in the sleuth's hard-boiled speech than are compound or simple sentences that simply juxtapose thoughts. The stories by Carroll John *Daly, who is considered to have begun the whole mode of hard-boiled writing with "The False Burton Combs" (*Black Mask*, Dec. 1922) and to have set its early patterns in the stories for *Black Mask* about Race *Williams, serve to illustrate the point, as do Hammett's stories about the *Continental Op, who was introduced in *Black Mask* in 1923, or the language used by Raoul Whitfield when he wrote under his own name or as Ramon Decolta.

The weaknesses or afflictions of hard-boiled sleuths sometimes contribute the limitation on their ability to dominate reality through reason. Frederick Nebel's Kennedy, who appeared in *Black Mask* stories in the 1930s, is a drunk. So is Jonathan Latimer's screwball detective Bill Crane, featured in a series of novels beginning with *Murder in the Madhouse* (1935), and Lawrence *Block's Matt *Scudder, who debuted in *The Sins of the Father* (1977). In other instances, the sleuths are world-weary loners. Yet others, we are told by their stories, have just seen too much sleaze.

Still and all, the hard-boiled sleuth who gradually developed in the pages of *Black Mask, Dime Detective, Detective Story*, and other pulp magazines, and then in paperback and hardcover novels, does not express nihilism. A hard-boiled detective can place no faith in conventional verities, but he (and, more recently, female characters too, such as Marcia *Muller's Sharon McCone and Sara *Paretsky's V. I. *Warshawski) does have a code of behavior. Like the philosophical existentialists they resemble, the hard-boiled private eyes practice situational ethics. Relentlessly honest and consistently devoted to the victims in society, the hard-boiled sleuth resists blandishment and bribery and sets his or her own high standards without regard for the conventions of a fictional world in which their style of morality seems unique, although Robert B. *Parker's *Spenser, for one, indicates that the code of tough guy behavior derives from the philosophy to be found, of all places, in the pulp magazine stories of hard-boiled detection.

The argument has been made that the hard-boiled private eye is an American hero descended from James Fenimore Cooper's archetypal Leatherstocking; thus, George Grella has stated that the private detective chooses an instinctive code of justice over "the often tarnished justice of civilization" and "replaces the subtleties of the deductive method with a sure knowledge of his world and a keen moral sense." For Grella, therefore, the hard-boiled story must be classed with the American romance, which the critic Richard Chase suggested was preoccupied by an "interest in alienation and disorder." Regardless of that argument, though, the hard-boiled sleuth also works as a putative philosopher, just as every detective undertaking the fictional genre's requirement to construct the story's second narrative of explanation must be. The traditional detective was a philosopher of order and reason. The hard-boiled sleuth thinks those neoclassical values are inauthentic for the world he or she knows, and that is what makes all the difference.

—John M. Reilly

HARE, CYRIL, pseudonym of Alfred Alexander Gordon Clark (1900–1958), British author of cozy detective novels. He derived his pseudonym from his London residence, Cyril Mansions, in Battersea, and his Temple chambers, Hare Court. A barrister who became a county court judge, Hare made excellent use of his legal knowledge in his fiction. His early books featured Inspector John Mallett of Scotland Yard. *Tragedy at Law* (1942), considered his finest book, introduced Francis Pettigrew, an aging and unsuccessful barrister. Pettigrew reappeared in *With a Bare Bodkin* (1946) and other books, but he remained a reluctant detective; in *That Yew Tree's Shade* (1954; *Death Walks the Woods*), he remarks how much he loathes "this business of detection." *An English Murder* (1951; *The Christmas Murder*) is a spoof of the cozy mystery set in a snowbound castle. The crime is solved by a Czech refugee, Dr. Wenceslaus Bottwink, a character employed by the author to comment on English eccentricities. *He Should Have Died Hereafter* (1958; *Untimely Death*) reunited Pettigrew and Mallett. The posthumously published *Best Detective Stories of Cyril Hare* (1959; *Death Among Friends and Other Detective Stories*), edited by his friend Michael *Gilbert, shows Hare's mastery of the short as well as the long form. Gilbert remembered Hare as having a striking physical resemblance to Sherlock *Holmes and as possessing superb skills as a public speaker.

[*See also* Farceurs.]

—Martin Edwards

HART, CAROLYN G(IMPEL) (b. 1936) American journalist, journalism professor and writer of mysteries for adults and young adults. Born in Oklahoma City, Oklahoma, Hart is the daughter of a pipe organ installer and a housewife. She earned a degree in journalism from the University of Oklahoma where she later edited an alumni newsletter and served as a professor. She also worked as a reporter on the *Norman Transcript* and as a freelance writer.

Hart turned out nine books, including works of romantic suspense and a children's book, before she created bookstore owner Annie Laurance and the man Laurance eventually marries, Max Darling, two characters who appeal to readers of puzzle-centered, cozy mysteries. The first book's title, *Death on Demand* (1987), is taken from the name of Laurance's book shop. It also gave the name to Hart's first series of books. Set on Broward's Rock Island, South Carolina, the "Death on Demand" mysteries are strong on humor. Another hallmark of this series is Hart's placement of literary and visual puzzles within the text of the whodunits.

In 1993, Hart drew on her reporting experience to create a new series sleuth, the Oklahoma journalist Henrietta O'Dwyer Collins—known to fans as Henrie O—

who first appeared in *Dead Man's Island*. Personable and popular, Hart has a large and loyal group of fans who see her as an exemplar of the writer who plays fair with the reader and as one of the best-known living practitioners of the "malice domestic" school of writing. Hart is married and the mother of two children.

[*See also* Journalist Sleuth.]

—Rosemary Herbert

HARVEY, JOHN (BARTON) (b. 1938), British writer of radio, television and film scripts, and author of poetry, books for teens, westerns (many written pseudonymously), and crime novels featuring the Nottingham police Detective Inspector Charlie Resnick. Born in London, Harvey was educated at the University of London, Hatfield Polytechnic, and the University of Nottingham, where he earned a Master's degree in American Studies. Harvey taught courses in literature and film on the secondary and college levels, and served as an instructor in writing workshops. He also headed Slow Dancer Press and edited *Slow Dancer Magazine* during the 1990s. In addition, he performs with a jazz band.

He began his writing career turning out paperback novels for the young adult and adult audiences before writing award-winning dramatizations of novels and short stories for television and radio. Harvey introduced Resnick in the 1989 police procedural *Lonelyhearts*. Resnick is a divorced loner, jazz buff, and cat owner. His superior officer is Superintendent Jack Skelton, a man who does not look eager to promote Resnick. The series is notable for depicting the underside of Nottingham life in books in which the author uses language inventively. In *Still Waters* (1997), an art forger named Sloane has a minor role before he becomes the protagonist of *In A True Light* (2002), a non-Resnick book set in the bohemian art scene of 1950s New York, and in London and Tuscany. Here Sloane pursues a missing person's case with very personal ramifications when the famous painter Jane Graham asks him to search for the adult daughter he conceived with her decades earlier. Harvey's depictions of jazz clubs, ruminations on personal responsibility, and brutally violent scenes make this book memorable. Harvey also authored a number of short stories featuring Jack Kiley, a private eye.

[*See also* Hard-boiled Sleuth.]

—Rosemary Herbert

HEALY (III), JEREMIAH (b. 1948), American law professor and writer of *private eye novels and, under the pseudonym Terry Devane, legal procedurals. Born in Teaneck, New Jersey, Healy was educated in a public high school that offered an intensive writing program to talented students. As a teen, he worked summers in the Bergen County, New Jersey, Sheriff's Office where his duties included everything from filing and fingerprinting to helping to quell a riot. He went on to earn a B.A. from Rutgers University and a law degree from Harvard University. While in law school, he participated in the

Harvard Volunteer Defender Program, a student-run organization that provided legal representation to indigent defendants. After serving in the United States Army Military Police, he worked as a civil litigator with a Boston, Massachusetts, law firm and served on the faculty of the New England School of Law, also in Boston.

Healy introduced his series detective, the Boston private eye John Francis Cuddy, in *Blunt Darts* (1984), a novel that won the Best First Novel award from the Private Eye Writers of America. Cuddy is modeled on the author's father, who was a military police captain during World War II, and on Healy's uncle, an insurance investigator. Cuddy's toughness is tempered, especially in the early books, by the fact that he is in mourning for his wife, Beth, who died young, of cancer. Healy's first legal procedural, written as Devane, is *The Stalking of Sheilah Quinn* (1998), in which the eponymous protagonist tangles with a corrupt *judge. Here, and in the Cuddy series, Healy is at his best when looking at troubling cases where citizens cannot count on the authorities to insure that crimes are properly investigated or that justice is done. For instance, in the Cuddy book *Yesterday's News* (1989), Healy has a reporter investigate allegations of police brutality. When a confidential source is killed, the reporter turns to the private eye rather than to the official authorities for help, since it appears the police may be involved in the killing.

[*See also* Lawyer; Private Investigator.]
—Rosemary Herbert

HEGARTY, FRANCES. *See* Fyfield, Frances.

HESS, JOAN (b. 1949), American author known for regional mysteries written with broad humor. Hess was born in Fayetteville, Arkansas, where she continues to reside. She received a bachelor's degree in art from the University of Arkansas and earned a master's in education from Long Island University. She worked as a preschool art teacher before becoming a full-time writer. Before turning to mystery writing, Hess wrote ten unpublished romance novels. Her first mystery, *Strangled Prose* (1984) introduces Claire Malloy, an amateur sleuth who is also a single mother and bookstore owner living in Farberville, Arkansas. Malloy's next appearance is in *Murder at the Murder at the Mimosa Inn* (1986). The title refers to a killing that takes place during a "mystery weekend," before the eyes of fans who expect to see a murder mystery enacted. Hess' most colorful and quirky work may be a series of humorous mysteries set in the fictional town of Maggody, Arkansas, where Arly Hanks is the female chief of police. Hanks's relatives and friends add considerable interest to this series, which begins with *Murder in Maggody* (1987). Using the pen name Joan Hadley, the author also writes another series about the retired floral designer, Theo Bloomer.

[*See also* Amateur Detective; Police Detective.]
—Rosemary Herbert

HEYER, GEORGETTE (1902–1974), British author of mysteries and historical novels, best known for her Regency romances. In *The Talisman Ring* (1936) and *The Corinthian* (1940) she successfully combined history and mystery. A lifelong best-selling author, Heyer (who also wrote as Stella Martin) remained an intensely private person. She received little critical acclaim for the wit and craftsmanship of her comedies of manners, written, according to Heyer, as a mix of Dr. Johnson and Jane Austen.

Born in Wimbledon, England, Heyer was privately educated. Her first book, *The Black Moth* (1921), was published when she was nineteen. She was a thorough researcher: *An Infamous Army* (1937) retells the Battle of Waterloo. Altogether Heyer published fifty-six novels and a book of short stories.

Beginning in 1932, Heyer wrote twelve thrillers. Howard Haycraft in *Murder for Pleasure* (1941) said that Heyer's lively style showed a new and harder veneer, while in *Bloody Murder: From the Detective Story to the Crime Novel: A History* (1972) Julian *Symons called her one of the last *farceurs of the Golden Age, whose ethical standards were implicit in their social values.

Footsteps in the Dark (1932) appeared the year her son was born, but she regarded the third, *Death in the Stocks* (1935; *Merely Murder*) as her first "real" crime story, featuring the CID's Sergeant Stanley Hemmingway and Superintendent Hannasyde. Her barrister husband, George Ronald Rougier, worked out the plots, while Heyer brought the characters to life; but biographer Hodge suggests that working with her husband inhibited Heyer's genius. Rouget's legal background informs *Duplicate Death* (1951), but most of the mysteries, like *They Found Him Dead* (1937), are set in the English village milieu. Many critics consider *The Blunt Instrument* (1938) and *Envious Casca* (1941) her best books, but Heyer remains best known to readers for her depictions of stately homes and what Dilys Winn, in *Murderess Ink: The Better Half of the Mystery* (1979), termed "that ultra-dry British humor."

—Alzina Stone Dale

HIAASEN, CARL (b. 1953), American journalist and writer of crime novels strong on black humor and social commentary. Born in Fort Lauderdale, Florida, Hiaasen attended Emory University before becoming a journalist. After writing for the city newspaper of Cocoa, Florida, he began to write for the *Miami Herald* in 1976, and has remained with that paper as a reporter and columnist even as his fiction-writing career took off and flourished. His columns are collected in two volumes, *Kick Ass* (1999) and *Paradise Screwed* (2001).

Hiaasen co-wrote his first three novels, *Powder Burn* (1981), *Trap Line* (1982) and *A Death in China* (1984), with William D. Montalbano, a fellow *Miami Herald* reporter. The 1986 novel, *Tourist Season*, is the first novel Hiaasen wrote on his own. Written at a time when car jacking and other assaults on tourists were in the news, the novel takes on this topic. His next book, *Double Whammy* (1987), looks at a rigged deep sea fishing contest while *Native Tongue* (1991) critiques the destruction of natural areas by developers. Both *Skin Tight* (1989), which has not one but several *villains, and *Stormy Weather* (1995), which follows the fates of hurricane victims, showcase Hiaasen's talent for working with numerous important characters at the same time. Among his more recent work, *Basket Case* (2001) is remarkable for being Hiaasen's first book to feature a first-person narrator, in this case a middle-aged obituary writer who has intimations of his own mortality every time he writes up a deceased person who is his age. The book also succeeds as a high-spirited romp-cum-critique of the music industry.

—Rosemary Herbert

HIGGINS, GEORGE V(INCENT) (b. 1939), popular American crime novelist. Educated at Boston College and Stanford University, Higgins was admitted to the Massachusetts bar in 1967. He has been both a federal prosecutor in the Massachusetts office of the U.S. attorney general and a defense attorney, as well as a reporter, columnist, and critic. The main elements of his style were evident in his first novel, *The Friends of Eddie Coyle* (1972): characters drawn from sleazy individuals from both sides of the law, a plot depicting, often with considerable sympathy, the everyday struggles of these characters, and, above all, extraordinarily realistic dialogue that makes few concessions to the conventions of grammar and punctuation that undermine the verisimilitude of most fictional dialogue. Later works of note include *The Digger's Game* (1973), *Cogan's Trade* (1974), *Kennedy for the Defense*, which introduced recurring character Jerry Kennedy (1980), and *A Choice of Enemies* (1983).

—Richard Steiger

HIGHSMITH, PATRICIA (1921–1995), American author who for many years made her home in Europe. Born in Fort Worth, Texas, as Mary Patricia Plaughman, she later took the name of her stepfather. In Europe, particularly in Britain, France, Germany, and Spain, Highsmith is regarded as one of the greatest modern crime novelists. In her native country her reputation is less high but has been growing.

Her first novel, *Strangers on a Train* (1950), later a very successful film directed by Alfred Hitchcock, the wholly individual pattern of her writing. As Graham *Greene said when introducing a collection of her short stories, her *The Snail-Watcher and Other Stories* (1970; *Eleven*), her world is claustrophobic, irrational, and dangerous. Her protagonists are not ruled by the standards and limits of behavior regarded as normal. In that first novel and in several later ones, strangers are emotionally bound to each other through acts of violence in relationships that waver between love and hatred. Characters are obsessed by fantasies that turn into disconcerting reality. In *This Sweet Sickness* (1960), a young chemist buys

and furnishes a house for a woman who has never seen it and has no interest in him. *The Story-Teller* (1965; *A Suspension of Mercy*) finds a young writer pretending he has killed his wife and making a mock burial of her body; he subsequently gets in deep trouble when she actually disappears. Highsmith's books contain no puzzles, and justice is rarely done in them. Emotional problems turn into violent actions, and our concern is to see how they will come out.

This is especially true of her most popular books, the novels about the pleasant, totally amoral young American Tom *Ripley, who gets away with crimes including forgery and murder. *The Talented Mr. Ripley* (1955) is the first and perhaps the best of them, although *Ripley Under Ground* (1970), in which he impersonates a dead artist and is drawn into murder when the deception is about to be discovered, is also chillingly memorable. The later Ripley stories, including *Ripley Under Water* (1991) are less successful.

Highsmith always resisted being typecast as a crime novelist, and as well as crime fiction also wrote "straight" novels, including the powerful *People Who Knock on the Door* (1983), in which fundamentalist religion wrecks an apparently ordinary and secure family in midwest America. An early novel about a lesbian relationship, originally published under the pseudonym Claire Morgan in 1952 as *The Price of Salt*, was reissued in 1990 as *Carol* under Highsmith's own name.

It may be the variety of her work, and the fact that it cannot be categorized—if she is basically a crime novelist she is emphatically not a writer of detective stories—that has delayed American appreciation of her extraordinary talent. Almost every one of the dozen books she wrote between her first novel and *Ripley Under Ground* is unique in the different ways they make irrational behavior seem inevitable. She has also been, without intending it, a prophet: The terrors and delusions driving her psychopaths to violent action are the ones we see enacted now in the apparently motiveless crimes recorded in our daily newspapers.

—Julian Symons

HILL, REGINALD (b. 1936), the British author best known as the creator of the Yorkshire policemen Andrew Dalziel and Peter Pascoe. More recently, he has introduced the black private investigator, Joe Sixsmith, a character Hill bases in Luton, near London. Hill has also produced work under pseudonyms. Under the name Patrick Ruell, derived from his wife's maiden name, Patricia Ruell, he has penned several thrillers that combine international intrigue with mystery elements. As Dick Morland and Charles Underhill, he has examined futuristic problems in works that might be classified as science fiction. He also took Dalziel and Pascoe into the future in *One Small Step* (1990), a slim novel, set in the year 2010, when the pair investigate a murder on the moon.

The son of a professional football (i.e., soccer) player and a factory worker, Hill won a scholarship to Oxford

University. Upon graduation, he became a schoolmaster and the a lecturer in a teachers' college before he took up writing full time. He resides in a Victorian vicarage in England's Lake District.

A subtle writer, he has won many awards, including Gold and Diamond Daggers from the Crime Writers Association. His plots are complex, his characterization sharp, and his dialogue liberally laced with humor. The Dalziel and Pascoe series began conventionally enough with *A Clubbable Woman* (1970) and *An Advancement of Learning* (1971), the latter drawing upon Hill's experience as a college lecturer. *Deadheads* (1983) centers on whether an apparently amiable rose grower is a killer, while in *Exit Lines* (1984) the focus is upon older poeple and the inevitability of death. The grim theme is complemented with much dark humor, including famous last words that head each chapter. Dalziel, fat and coarse, and Pascoe, intelligent and sensitive, contrast superbly; they respect each other but have irreconcilably different outlooks. Increasingly, Hill has sought to explore aspects of British life including a mining community ravaged by the aftereffects of a disastrous industrial dispute in *Underworld* (1988) and the country house milieu in *Recalled to Life* (1992).

[See also Police Detective; Sidekicks and Sleuthing Teams.]

—Martin Edwards

HILLERMAN TONY, (b. 1925), American author, best known as the creator of the *Native American sleuths Joe *Leaphorn and Jim *Chee, tribal police officers whose territory is the Four Corners area of the American Southwest where New Mexico, Arizona, Utah, and Colorado meet. On a philosophical level, these police detectives pursue their work in another intersection, the area where Anglo- and Native American cultures meet.

Hillerman's acquaintance with Native American peoples dates from his boyhood. He was born in the dustbowl village of Sacred Heart, Oklahoma, where he found it easier to identify with his Potawatomie and Seminole Indian friends than with the town boys. The son of a farmer and jack-of-all-trades and a homemaker who had worked as a registered nurse, Hillerman was raised until the age of twelve in a household without a telephone, running water, or electricity, where storytellers were valued and books were luxuries. Nonetheless, Hillerman discovered the work of Arthur *Upfield, whose stories set in the Australian outback featured *sleuths of mixed racial heritage.

Hillerman began to work his way through Oklahoma State University, but his academic career was cut short by World War II. Serving in the U.S. Army, he was wounded in action in France, and while home on convalescent leave, Hillerman experienced two serendipitous occurrences. He met a reporter who had read his letters sent home from the front, who encouraged him to try his hand at writing. Then, while driving a truck on the

Navajo reservation, he witnessed a curing ceremony that was to become the inspiration for his first novel *The Blessing Way* (1970).

Hillerman's long experience as a journalist is reflected in his second novel, *The Fly on the Wall* (1971), and in his 1996 novel, *Finding Moon*. Despite his clean style, Hillerman is remembered by readers for his vivid visual depictions of the Southwest scene, which he establishes through the use of telling details that also illustrate the uneasy meeting of Native American traditions and contemporary American culture.

In addition to authoring novels for adults, Hillerman wrote one children's book, several nonfiction works about the Southwest, including an account of *The Great Taos Bank Robbery and Other Indian Country Affairs* (1973). He edited *The Mysterious West* (1994), an anthology of crime and mystery stories, and coedited *The Oxford Book of American Detective Stories* (1996). The Navajo people found Hillerman's writing so convincing that they declared him a Special Friend of the Dineh, or tribe.

—Rosemary Herbert

HIMES, CHESTER (BOMAR) (1909–1984), African American novelist best known for his darkly comic tales of criminal life in Harlem, and for the creation of *African American sleuths Coffin Ed *Johnson and Grave Digger Jones. Himes came to the writing of crime fiction with firsthand knowledge of the life of the petty criminal, convict, and street hustler living on the edge. Although born into a middle-class family, by 1929 he was in prison for armed robbery. He began writing in prison, first publishing in small-circulation African American magazines. In 1932, his work came to the attention of Arnold Gingrich and began to appear in *Esquire*.

His early novels, beginning with *If He Hollers Let Him Go* (1945), reflected his preoccupations with the destructive power of racism and interracial sexuality. Although marginally successful critically, his failure to gain financial security, combined with the breakup of his marriage, provided the impetus for his emigration to France in 1953.

After several very lean years in Europe, Himes was offered the chance to write for Editions Gallimard's *Série noire*, an acclaimed series of translated American crime fiction. The resulting novel, published in French in 1958 as *La reine des pommes* (*For Love of Imabelle*, 1957; *A Rage in Harlem*), was an instant hit, winning for Himes the prestigious *Grand prix de la littérature policière*, the first such award to a non-French writer. *The Real Cool Killers* (1959), *The Crazy Kill* (1959), *The Big Gold Dream* (1960), and *All Shot Up* (1960) quickly followed. In each, he juxtaposed absurdly comic characters with dark, sinister situations and set them against the grimly realistic backdrop of a teeming, degraded ghetto.

In many of his works, a good-hearted black male, often just trying to get along, finds himself caught up in a desperate struggle for life itself. A morally ambiguous, light-skinned woman is often at the heart of his trouble. Flamboyant religious charlatans, hard-edged gamblers, and drug-crazed killers are also regular members of Himes's "domestic" cast.

As the series grew, Johnson and Jones developed from minor characters into spokesman through which Himes articulated his rage at the cruelty and injustice of American racism. As the series drew to a close with *Cotton Comes to Harlem* (1965), it began to mirror his hopelessness at the race problem. In *Blind Man with a Pistol* (1969) Himes saw such corruption and chaos that even his indomitable heroes could not prevail against it. In *Plan B* (unfinished but published in the United States in 1993), he envisioned a racial apocalypse that would kill his detectives and eventually destroy America.

Himes is best remembered for his remarkable fusion of the sociological protest novel with the hard-boiled detective tale. Like Raymond *Chandler, Himes used the detective story to mirror his times and to articulate his social concerns. Johnson and Jones were the models for Shaft and other black heroes of the sixties and seventies, and Himes's influence can be seen in the work of such diverse writers as Donald Goines, Walter *Mosley, and James *Sallis.

—Robert E. Skinner

HISTORICAL FIGURES. *This entry points out figures from history who are used as characters in crime and mystery writing. The piece is divided into two parts, the first focusing upon royalty, politicians, and statesmen used as figures of fiction, and the second looking at celebrities who become characters in this genre.*

Royals, Politicians, and Statesmen
Celebrities

For further information, please refer to Historical Mystery.

ROYALS, POLITICIANS, AND STATESMEN

Because period mystery novels, like their ancestors' and cousins' historical novels, reach into the past for their plots and characters, it is not surprising that actual people from the past appear in such books. And, as in historical novels, the roles of these historical figures vary greatly.

One of the first to use historical figures in his detective novels, John Dickson *Carr, employed them in a variety of ways. Joseph Fouché, Napoleon's director of the secret police, was the antagonist in *Captain Cut-Throat* (1955); the first two commissioners of the London Metropolitan Police, Charles Rowan and Edward Mayne, were authority figures in *Fire, Burn!* (1957), as was Sir John Fielding, founder of the Bow Street Runners, in *The Demoniacs* (1962); and Wilkie *Collins served as the investigator in *The Hungry Goblin* (1972).

Our earliest example (in real time), however, may be the fourth-century B.C. philosopher Aristotle, in Mar-

garet Doody's *Aristotle Detective* (1978); he appears not as the clues and questions. The first-century A.D. Roman emperor Vespasian serves, in the novels of Lindsey Davis, both as an initiator and rewarder (as in *Silver Pigs*, 1989). Many of the players in the fall of the Roman republic in the last century B.C., men and women like Cicero, Sulla, Caesar, Clodius, Clodia, and Milo, appear at the edges, and seduce or attempt to murder, or befriend Decius Caecilius Metellus, the hero of John Maddox Roberts's novels (e.g., *SPQR*, 1990). This subsidiary role for historical figures is true as well in the novels of Steven Saylor (*Roman Blood*, 1991; *Arms of Nemesis*, 1992), in which Gordianus the Finder, like Roberts's Decius, moves among the great of late-republican Rome.

Beyond the classical period, other prominent figures provide a general background against which the story is set. In Ellis *Peters's chronicles of Brother *Cadfael, beginning with *A Morbid Taste for Bones* (1977), the monk-detective must work out the tangles of his mysteries while, beyond his home in Shrewsbury—and even within the town in *One Corpse Too Many* (1979)—King Stephen and the Empress Matilda (also called Maud) fight out their bloody and seemingly endless civil war. In Leonard Tourney's series featuring Matthew Stock, the constable of Chelmsford, Elizabeth I and her chief minister, Sir Robert Cecil, occasionally appear. Cecil himself may set Stock on the course of an investigation in *Old Saxon Blood* (1988), and Elizabeth's minor roles range from provider of rewards to the target of an attempted assassination in *The Bartholomew Fair Murders* (1986).

In more modern settings, Lillian de la Torre, inspired by the relationship between Sherlock *Holmes and Dr. John H. *Watson, produced a series of books in which Samuel Johnson and his biographer, James Boswell, fill the roles of the two Victorians (e.g., *Dr. Sam: Johnson, Detector: being a light-hearted collection of recently reveal'd episodes in the career of the great lexicographer narrated as from the pen of James Boswell . . .*, (1946). Here, we can observe historical figures playing the role of the protagonist. Cast as protagonists elsewhere are such figures as Albert Edward, the Prince of Wales, in works by Peter *Lovesey (e.g., *Bertie and the Tinman*, 1987); Teddy Roosevelt, as the commissioner of the New York City police in Lawrence Alexander's *The Big Stick* (1986); and Eleanor Roosevelt, who features in a series by Elliot Roosevelt, of which (*Murder in the West Wing*, 1993) is a typical title. (According to Allen J. Hubin some or all of Roosevelt's works were "apparently ghost-written" by William Harrington.) Somewhat different is Josephine *Tey's *The Daughter of Time* (1951), in which the bedridden Inspector Alan Grant investigates (through the printed word) the allegation that King Richard III was responsible for the deaths of the two princes in the Tower in the 1480s.

The advantages of employing an actual historical figure as a detective are several. First, as in the case of Lovesey's "Bertie," the historical character can provide his readers with an entree into a world difficult for the ordinary investigator to penetrate. One has only to observe the constant snubs and sometimes complete rejections that Anne *Perry's imaginary Inspector (later Superintendent) Thomas Pitt and Inspector Monk receive in middle-class Victorian homes to understand what Bertie—and Lovesey—have given us. Second, there is the sheer fun for the writer of recreating a famous (or infamous) person and employing that person in a way more natural to our age than earlier periods. Third, there is the delight for the reader in seeing such a figure come to life in an unexpected way, creating new biographical material, as it were, to add to our actual historical knowledge. This pleasure can even be combined with in-jokes about the figure or period—"Bertie" is an absolute blunderer as an investigator—to turn the form inside out, allowing for a sort of subliminal commentary in which the historical person can be employed to solve the mystery even while being laughed at as an improbable figure for the job.

—Carolyn Higbie *and* Timothy W. Boyd

CELEBRITIES

Numerous crime and mystery writers have woven stories around real-life celebrities. An early example is S. S. *Van Dine's *The Gracie Allen Murder Case*, (1938; *The Smell of Murder*), in which the author captures the essence of the title comedienne—her zany wit, non sequiturs, impulsiveness, and use of a running gag about her missing brother. Three years later, the versatile Craig *Rice, in her capacity as ghostwriter for Gypsy Rose Lee, created *The G-String Murders* (*The Strip-Tease Murders*, 1941) a novel featuring the stripper. Ghostwriting for George Sanders a few years later, Rice introduced the actor as a character in *Crime on My Hands* (1944).

During the 1930s and 1940s, Clayton Rawson, a magician known professionally as "The Great Merlini," published a series of detective novels and short stories under his stage name. The author himself appears as the magician *sleuth in these works, which draw heavily on his professional experience and which established him as one who could perform sleights of hand on the page as well as on stage.

Celebrityhood is put to another use in Peter *Lovesey's *Keystone* (1983), a work of fiction built around such historical figures as Mack Sennett, Mabel Normand, Fatty Arbuckle, and the Keystone Kops. This well-researched novel incorporates numerous factual details including references to the Kops as former tumblers and acrobats, the assignment of the most dangerous stunts to the newest member of the group, and the portrayal of the tumultuous love affair between Sennett Mark and Normand.

Celebrity-based fiction may be closely allied with the true crime narrative in which speculations upon unsolved actual cases serve as plot vehicles. James *Ellroy's *The Black Dahlia* (1987) was inspired by the murder of his own mother as well as the torso killing in 1947 of Elizabeth Short, a bit player in the movies. The 1976 murder of Sal Mineo, which baffled Los Angeles police until 1979, was the basis for Susan Braudy's *Who Killed Sal Mineo?* (1982). The author takes liberties with certain facts but tells an engaging tale of a young New York female reporter turned *amateur detective in the hard-boiled tradition.

Stuart Kaminsky, Andrew Bergman, and George *Baxt have written celebrity-based mysteries laced with elements of parody and satire. Kaminsky and Bergman create plots in which unknown *private eyes handle awkward situations for famous clients. Kaminsky's Toby Peters conducts quiet, secret investigations to avoid scandal for Judy Garland in *Murder on the Yellow Brick Road* (1978), to stop the blackmailing of Errol Flynn in *Bullet for a Star* (1977), and to locate Bette Davis's missing husband in *The Devil Met a Lady* (1993). Bergman enjoys pairing entertainers and politicians in his work—for example, Humphery Bogart and Richard Nixon work together convincingly in *Hollywood and LeVine* (1975). Baxt vividly blends the worlds of politics and entertainment in *The Tallulah Bankhead Murder Case* (1987). He brings other celebrities to life in *The Dorothy Parker Murder Case* (1984) and *The Alfred Hitchcock Murder Case* (1986).

A celebrity himself, Steve Allen drew on his many years in show business and his cerebral humor to write *The Talk Show Murders* (1982), *Murder on the Glitter Box* (1989), *Murder in Vegas* (1991), *The Murder Game* (1993), and *Wake Up to Murder* (1997). Allen and his wife, Jayne Meadows, play various heroes, suspects, and patsies.

—Katherine M. Restaino

HOCH, EDWARD D(ENTINGER) (b. 1930), American author who exemplifies the working writer practicing his craft in a dedicated, reliable fashion. Hoch has written five novels and is the respected editor of anthologies, but his great achievement lies in writing more than 800 short stories and earning his living for more than three decades largely through the writing of short fiction. For more than two and a half decades, beginning in May 1973, he contributed at least one short story per issue to *Ellery Queen's Mystery Magazine*. A native of Rochester, New York, Hoch began to write detective stories when he was in his teens. He continued to write while he was a student at the University of Rochester, during two years in the U.S. Army, while he was employed by Rochester Public Library, during a short stint with Pocket Books in New York City, and while working in advertising and public relations in Rochester. His first story, "Village of the Dead," was published in *Famous Detective Stories* in December 1955 when he was twenty-five. Hoch turned to writing full time in 1968, after he won the Edgar Allan Poe Award for the Best Short Story of 1967 with "The Oblong Room" (in *The Saint*, July 1967). Writing under his own name and seven pseudonyms, he created twenty-six series characters and was one of several writers who wrote as Ellery *Queen, turning out one novel and one short story under that pseudonym. He edited individual theme anthologies and two long-running annual series: *Best Detective Stories of the Year* (from 1976 to 1981) and *The Year's Best Mystery and Suspense Stories* (from 1982 to 1995). He served as president of the Mystery Writers of America in 1982–83.

—Clark Howard

Holmes, Sherlock. Created early in 1886 by the young English doctor Arthur Conan *Doyle, Sherlock Holmes was destined, with Edgar Allan *Poe's Chevalier C. Auguste *Dupin, to become one of the two most important characters in the history of detective fiction. Known for his talent for observation, powers of reasoning, eccentric personality, habits of living, and memorable turns of phrase, this *Great Detective so captured the imaginations of readers that he has often been regarded as a living person rather than as a fictional character. The adventures of the consulting detective are narrated by his friend Dr. John H. *Watson in the form of four novels and fifty-six short stories, known to Sherlockians and literary historians as the Canon.

Holmes came to life when Doyle sketched out notes for a piece of fiction in order to while away idle hours in a rather unsuccessful medical practice in Southsea, Hampshire. Headed "A Study in Scarlet," these notes marked a solid basis for the Holmes series, revealing that the author was initially more concerned with character than *plot and that Doyle prized dialogue in the creation of character. The importance of the narrator, too, is obvious from the fact that he is mentioned first: "Ormond Sacker—from Afghanistan. . . . Lived at 221B Upper Baker Street with Sherrinford Holmes." Doyle changed the characters' names to Watson and Holmes before he penned the work, which was first published in *Beeton's Christmas Annual* in 1887.

Undoubtedly best known for his powers of reasoning, Holmes possessed a flair for drawing conclusions from keenly observed details that is modeled in part on the talents of Doyle's own medical mentor, Dr. Joseph Bell, whom Doyle met at Edinburgh University and to whom he dedicated the first collection of his short stories, *The Adventures of Sherlock Holmes* (1892). A lecturer and surgeon, Bell amazed students with his ability not only to diagnose illnesses but to infer life circumstances based on observations of complexion and other physical characteristics along with wardrobe and behavior. While the popular view holds that Holmes used deductive reasoning, in fact, Holmes generally reasoned abductively, as did Bell, working from the observation of out of the ordinary particulars to form a hypothesis, on the basis of which the observations would be expected. One of the most memorable aspects of the Holmes character is his ability to deliver surprising conclusions based on his recognition of the significance of details that others see as trifles. Holmes's talents in this regard are underlined for the reader by exclamations of astonishment and awe from the narrator, Watson.

Watson is not unmindful, however, of Holmes's dark side, which is detailed in the opening pages of *The Sign of the Four* (1890; *The Sign of Four*). Here Holmes is shown as having been taking three injections of cocaine per day for a period of months. Depressed when he is not engaged in work, Holmes can lie on his sofa "for days on end" in a lethargy hardly broken by his "scraping away" on his violin. Later, his cocaine habit is explained away as "a protest against the monotony of existence."

Otherwise, Holmes is portrayed as a man immune to human weaknesses. With the exception of Irene *Adler, the diva who dupes him in "A Scandal in Bohemia" (*Strand*, July 1891), no woman arouses Holmes's ardor—and although Holmes refers to Adler as "the woman" and requests her photograph in payment for his services, it may be argued that his admiration is more inspired by her cleverness, boldness, and singing ability than by her sexual appeal.

If Holmes "never spoke of the gentler passions, save with a gibe and a sneer," he also found it difficult to express himself as a friend. He is an inconsiderate roommate, smoking up the place with dangerous chemical experiments; shooting bullet holes in the wall on a whim; storing things—like tobacco in a Persian slipper—in bizarre locations; and rousing his sidekick at all hours to accompany him on cases. A master of disguise, Holmes also enjoys startling Watson by appearing in their digs or elsewhere in convincing costume. In "The Adventure of the Speckled Band" (*Strand*, Feb. 1892), a story that demonstrates Holmes's physical courage and emotional nerve, he fails to inform Watson of the mortal danger in which he puts him when the two await the arrival of a poisonous snake in confined quarters. His profound attachment to Watson is, however, revealed in "The Adventure of the Devil's Foot" (*Strand*, Dec. 1910) when, after Holmes and Watson are nearly killed while exposing themselves to a deadly poison, Holmes directly apologizes for putting his friend at risk, causing Watson to reflect, "I had never seen so much of Holmes's heart before." In "The Adventure of the Three Garridebs" (*Colliers*, 25 Oct. 1924), Holmes is even more demonstrative regarding his concern for Watson. When Watson receives a gunshot wound, Holmes exclaims, "You're not hurt, Watson? For God's sake, say that you are not hurt!" Watson observes, "It was worth a wound—it was worth many wounds—to know the depth of loyalty and love which lay behind that cold mask." Otherwise, Holmes is a more devoted adversary than friend, as is demonstrated by his perseverance in eliminating "the Napoleon of crime," Professor James *Moriarty.

Not only does Holmes generally hold himself above the niceties of friendship, but he often places himself above the law, describing himself in *The Sign of the Four* as "the last and highest court of appeal in detection." Holmes allows culprits to escape in "The Adventure of the Blue Carbuncle" (*Strand*, Jan. 1892), "The Adventure of the Abbey Grange" (*Strand*, Sept. 1904), "The Adventure of the Devil's Foot" (*Strand*, Dec. 1910), and other stories. Holmes also occasionally lets accomplices to go unpunished, as in "Silver Blaze" (*Strand*, Dec. 1892).

"Silver Blaze" also contains one of the most memorable exchanges of dialogue in the Canon:

"Is there any other point to which you would wish to draw my attention?"
"To the curious incident of the dog in the night-time."
"The dog did nothing in the night-time."
"That was the curious incident."

This passage at once illustrates Doyle's gift for writing original and fluid prose and Holmes's application of imagination to aid in his reasoning process. Because Holmes can imagine the scene in the night time so fully as to picture and hear it, he recognizes the silence of the dog as a vital clue to the solution of the case.

Doyle was concerned to relate stories or adventures centered around his *sleuth rather than to detail the particulars of Holmes's antecedents or education. Because Holmes took on a life of his own in readers' imaginations, much "biographical" information has been drawn by others from the Canon itself and from other research. The name Sherlock may have come to Doyle's mind since the Sherlocks were landowners in County Wicklow, Ireland, where the Doyle family once held estates. This Irish name is a Gaelic version of the Anglo-Saxon word for short locks or one with short hair: *scortlog*. Doyle borrowed his sleuth's last name from the American jurist Oliver Wendell Holmes, whom Doyle admired.

The only family member who is portrayed in the Holmes stories is the sleuth's elder brother, Mycroft *Holmes, a "corpulent" man who may possess greater talents for observation than his brother but who is too sedentary to pursue a career in crime solving. Evidence in the Canon suggests that one of Holmes's grandmothers was a sister to the French artist Vernet. Otherwise, family background for Holmes is speculative, as is the place of his schooling.

There is no question, however, about Holmes's enduring influence upon the crime and mystery genre and his place in the popular imagination. From Doyle's day to the present, imitators and those who would spoof Holmes have been legion, while Doyle and Holmes have been the subject of numerous biographical and countless academic studies. Television, film, and stage and radio dramas have also featured Holmes and Watson. Virtually all writers of crime and mystery fiction, especially stories of true detection, acknowledge the influence of Holmes on their own work. Holmes carved out the niche of consulting detective and made it his own. In applying the scientific method to the understanding of human affairs, Holmes is an original hero who rights wrongs through the application of the intellect.

[*See also* Eccentrics; Sidekicks and Sleuthing Teams; Superman Sleuth.]

—Rosemary Herbert

HORNUNG, E(RNEST) W(ILLIAM) (1866–1921), British author of fifteen crime novels and ten volumes of short crime stories. There can be little doubt that the fame of Hornung rests upon his twenty-five stories and one novel about A. J. *Raffles, cricketer and gentleman thief, appearing in three volumes including the *Amateur Cracksman* (1899; *Raffles, the Amateur Cracksman*), *The Black Mask* (1901), and *A Thief in the Night* (1905), and later collected editions. The Raffles stories were, in the words of Hornung's brother-in-law, Arthur Conan *Doyle, "a kind of inversion of Sherlock Holmes." Hornung also wrote a novel and two plays in which Raffles appears, but much of his other fiction dealt with crime and convicts in nineteenth-century Australia, where the author lived for three years because of the poor health that plagued him all his life. Hornung was a fine craftsman, creating in Raffles one of the great characters of crime fiction whose name has entered our language.

—Edward D. Hoch

HUNTER, EVAN. *See* McBain, Ed.

I

ILES, FRANCIS. *See* Berkeley, Anthony.

INCIDENTAL CRIME WRITERS. Throughout the history of the mystery genre, writers best known for work in other areas have occasionally added mystery fiction to their lists of works.

In its earliest years, crime fiction was regarded as one genre among several available to the writer. Wilkie *Collins, Elizabeth Cleghorn Gaskell, and Robert Louis Stevenson moved freely from one form of the novel to another. By the time Arthur Conan *Doyle began writing his historical novels, the lines between genres were becoming stricter, at least in the eyes of the reading public. Nevertheless, many writers have continued to move among the genres, choosing the form most appropriate to the story. Their crime novels sometimes become more well known than the rest of their work; mainstream novelist C. H. B. Kitchin, for example, is chiefly remembered for *Death of My Aunt* (1929), the first of four sober, understated whodunits narrated by a prim stockbroker, Malcom Warren. But it was equally likely that the crime fiction was subsumed by the writer's larger body of work. A. A. Milne, celebrated author of *Winnie the Pooh* (1927), turned his hand to many forms of writing, including essays and drama. His talents in mystery writing are well exhibited in *The Red House Mystery* (1922); his crime stories appear in two mixed collections, *Birthday Party and Other Stories* (1948) and *A Table Near the Band* (1950). William *Faulkner, the quintessential novelist of the American South, used the techniques of detective fiction in some of his major works: *Absalom, Absalom!* (1936) and *Intruder in the Dust* (1948). His story collection *Knight's Gambit* (1949), featuring an astute rural attorney, is authentic detective fiction. Mainstream novelist C. P. Snow's first and last novels are detective stories: *Death Under Sail* (1932), a meticulous formal exercise, and *A Coat of Varnish* (1979), more somber and serious of purpose.

The appeal of the genre may be its formal structure or its ability to accommodate variation through a series of books. Winifred Ashton (writing as Clemence Dane) and Helen Simpson together wrote three graceful detective novels featuring the actor-manager Sir John Saumarez, a walk-on in *Printer's Devil* (1930; *Author Unknown*), but otherwise the lead. Several of the novelist, dramatist, and critic J. B. Priestley's works qualify as criminous: two apocalyptic thrillers, *The Doomsday Men* (1938) and *Saturn over the Water* (1961); two diverse spy novels, *Black-Out in Gretley* (1942) and *The Shapes of Sleep* (1962); and a lively whodunit, *Salt Is Leaving* (1966), with a dogged provincial doctor as detective. F.

Tennyson Jesse introduced Solange Fontaine, who employs a "delicate extra sense" that warns her of evil in *The Solange Stories* (1931), and offers a harrowing version of the infamous Thompson-Bywaters murder case in *A Pin to See the Peep-Show* (1934).

The genre has appealed also to writers in nonfiction. The Shakespearean scholar Alfred Harbage wrote four detective novels under the pseudonym Thomas Kyd; a determined policeman, Sam Phelan, figures in these, notably *Blood of Vintage* (1947). Ralph Arnold, a social historian, published a small body of detective novels beginning in the 1930s. Robert Bernard, the literary biographer, follows an eccentric scholar, Millicent Hetherege, in *Deadly Meeting* (1970) and *Illegal Entry* (1972). The critic and historian Audrey Williamson published two stylish whodunits late in her life, both with Superintendant Richard York as the detective. *Funeral March for Siegfried* (1979) draws effectively on her Wagnerian expertise. The critic and commentator William F. Buckley, Jr. has written more than half a dozen spy novels about Blackford Oakes, an American secret agent. The first, *Saving the Queen* (1976), is typical in its political astuteness.

Among contemporary novelists also working in detective fiction, perhaps the best known is Jorge Luis Borges, whose best work includes "The Garden of Forking Paths" in *Ficciones* (1962) and "Death and the Compass" in *Labyrinths* (1962). Paco Ignacio *Taibo II has also turned to detective fiction; his *Life Itself* (1994) comments on political life in Mexico.

—Susan Oleksiw

INDEPENDENT SLEUTH. Largely associated with American hard-boiled private eye fiction, the depiction of the *sleuth as an independent character without personal entanglements is an important tradition in the literary history of the broader genre. Early in the development of the genre, writers realized that it was advantageous to keep the hero's personal attachments limited so that the character could believably pursue clues and suspects at all hours and in dangerous circumstances. A detective without a family might be inclined to take greater personal risks than would one with a spouse or family. A sleuth who is not romantically attached is also useful to the writer who is interested in creating new relationships in the course of a narrative.

Intellectual prowess turned some sleuths into loners. The first private detective, Edgar Allan *Poe's Chevalier C. Auguste *Dupin, had powers of observation and analysis far superior to those of the people around him. Arthur Conan *Doyle's Sherlock *Holmes, too, remained an essentially solitary figure who was more befriended by than connected to his devoted sidekick and narrator, Dr. John H. *Watson. In fact, most of fiction's *Great Detectives essentially stood apart from others—including the professional police—who held them in awe and were not their intellectual equals.

The sleuth as loner came of age in distinctly American fiction published in the 1920s in *Black Mask* magazine. It may be no coincidence that this magazine, initially created by H. L. Mencken to showcase westerns and horror fiction along with crime stories, welcomed stories featuring individualist heroes drawn from the loner hero traditions of America's Old West. Significantly, these heroes did not rely on sidekicks to narrate their work, but instead poured them out in their own vernacular.

The prototypical *private eye was Carroll John *Daly's Race *Williams, who first appeared in *Black Mask* in 1923. He set out the hard-boiled hero's philosophy when he said: "Right and wrong are not written on the statutes for me, nor do I find my code of morals in the essays of long-winded professors. My ethics are my own. I'm not saying they're good and I'm not admitting they're bad, and what's more I'm not interested in the opinions of others on that subject." This attitude is a direct descendent of the mythic codes of honor spelled out in westerns: When the agents of law and order have been bought and corrupted, honorable individuals are bound to take the law into their own hands to preserve fundamental, immutable justice. Of course, some westerns portray official lawmen as honorable, but they are often seen to stand alone against a corrupt crowd. Earlier stories emphasized sparring, both physical and verbal, while more recent stories are stronger on internal monologues, resulting in more profound character development.

Raymond *Chandler's Philip *Marlowe further defined private investigation as the preserve of the lone male hero when he wrote, in his essay "The Simple Art of Murder" (in *Atlantic Monthly*, Dec. 1944): "Down these mean streets a man must go who is not himself mean, who is neither tarnished nor afraid." Chandler identified his private eye prototype as "a lonely man" with a chivalric approach to his work. Many writers after Chandler relied upon his conventions, creating characters who champion the underdog or the poor, are good in a fight, and are introspective to the point of brooding. Ross *Macdonald perfected the brooding sleuth in Lew *Archer, who first appeared in *The Moving Target* in 1949. Late twentieth-century women feminists have proven that the mean streets are not the exclusive preserve of male private eyes, and that the lonely search for the truth can be achieved by a woman.

—Sara Paretsky

INDUSTRY WRITERS. All genres of formula fiction naturally lend themselves to mass production. The formulas exist because they appeal to a reliable market, and they also provide the writer with a replicable product.

The special nature of the detective story formula invites replication to a unique degree. The defining character of the genre—the detective—is, like the catalyst of chemical processes, unaltered by the actions and reactions of any given case. Unlike the usual fictional hero, the detective concludes each case possessing essentially the same status as at the beginning, ready and intact for the next case.

Ever since Edgar Allan *Poe created the Chevalier C. Auguste *Dupin and used him in three mysteries, the possibility of future adventures has probably been a factor in the conception of nearly all fictional detectives. The author knows that if the audience buys the prototype, it will buy a succession of reproductions. Few writers compose models intended to be unique to their first tale; sometimes, when they do, as E. C. *Bentley did in *Trent's Last Case* (1913), they are later tempted to repetition anyway. In this sense a large proportion of detective fiction can claim an industrial premise. But the term "industry writer" is reserved for those whose prolificity has led to their names (and often the names of their *sleuths) becoming household words.

In some cases the fame of the character and presumed author has been the work of a changing cast of industrial workers; thus, the house names Nick *Carter (in the United States; first novel 1886) and Sexton Blake (in England; first novel 1893) have been the bylines for literally thousands of similar products (an estimated 4,000 for Blake) created by an interchangeable battery of writers.

A step up from the laborers who assembled episodes for Carter and Blake are the one-man fiction factories whose output can claim the integrity of a single engineer. The phenomenal exemplars are Erle Stanley *Gardner and John *Creasey. In the fifty years of his writing career (1921–1970) Gardner published more than a thousand titles. Creasey's production was even greater: Between 1932 and 1979 he published more than 500 novels. After his death in 1973 the backlog resulted in the appearance of some twenty posthumous titles. In a single year, 1939, Gardner published at least four novels, eighteen novelettes, two short stories, and five articles. In the same year Creasey published at least thirty-eight novels.

Though they share an almost superhuman capacity for production, Gardner and Creasey pursued different industrial strategies. Gardner invented a character who has become an icon. Although he made efforts to develop subsidiary series, he eventually subsided into producing even more mechanical copies of the archetypal Perry *Mason scheme: a narrow class of characters with a limited menu of motives working at cross-purposes until lawyer Mason extracts the truth. Despite their popularity, none of Creasey's prominent detectives—Richard Rollison "The Toff"; Roger West; Dr. Palfrey; or Commander George Gideon—approached Mason's eminence. On the other hand, Creasey took his writing seriously enough to revise his work with care and to create a three-dimensional fictional world. The Gideon books, for example, written under the J. J. Marric pseudonym, have received special critical praise for their realism.

A number of writers not as prolific as Gardner or Creasey may also be placed in the industrial class. Edgar *Wallace, who between 1906 and 1932 published more than 170 books, more than half of them mysteries or thrillers, belongs in the category; so does Phillips *Oppenheim, with more than 150 novels and short story collections issued between 1887 and 1944.

Georges *Simenon represents the acme of industrial writing: an extremely prolific author who produced 220 novels, eighty-four of them Inspector Jules *Maigret mysteries. In the eleven months between May 1932 and April 1933, he wrote ten novels; at the height of his career he averaged more than five novels a year. Although Simenon accepted the essential structural formula of the genre—murder, investigation, discovery—and relied upon recurring figures, the formulas are subordinated to exploration of character and environment, an exploration which seems to be new in each case, an effect demonstrating that an industry writer can create a quality product.

—J. K. Van Dover

INNES, MICHAEL, pseudonym of J(ohn) I(nnes) M(ackintosh) Stewart (1906–1994), British author, literary critic, and Oxford don. He produced detective novels under his pseudonym, and mainstream novels, including the *Staircase in Sturry* quintet, and literary criticism under his own name. He also used the Stewart name for his works of literary biography, including a study of English novelist and poet Thomas Hardy, and for his contribution to the *Oxford History of English Literature* series.

He took to writing crime fiction in 1936 to pass the time during a sea voyage from Liverpool, England to Adelaide, Australia, where he was a professor of English at the University of Adelaide for ten years, and he continued to write clever, cultivated mysteries for a further fifty years. He is a master of the high, polite tradition of detective fiction and one of the best known of the *farceurs, variously characterized as donnish, civilized, and literate. His detective novels are distinguished by mischievous wit, exuberant fancy and adroit contrivance, with literary allusion a sine qua non. At times his work achieves a bizarre, almost manic brilliance, pushing the form well beyond conventional limits. *Appleby on Ararat* (1941) maroons a picturesque company on a Pacific island; *The Daffodil Affair* (1942) concerns a vanished horse with extrasensory perception; *A Night of Errors*

(1947) features identical triplets; and *Operation Pax* (1951) combines the novel of threat and tension with a full-scale intellectual puzzle.

Many of Innes's books have country-house settings, with priceless assets as the focus for criminal complications. Precious paintings and manuscripts recur as objects of devious desire; equivocal butlers hover and dubious scholars take their chances. The style throughout is immaculate mandarin, irresistible in its poised precision and self-mocking pedantry. Educated jokes abound and abstruse vocabulary enhances the effect of intellectual bravura. Thus, a resounding boom is "latrant, mugent, reboatory"; and a company plays a parlor game requiring them to quote in turn from William *Shakespeare on the theme of bells. The sequence from *Death at the President's Lodging* (1936) to *Christmas at Candleshoe* (1953) is especially memorable and includes some perfect masterpieces: *Lament for a Maker* (1938), a tortuous, protean narrative shared among five narrators, set in a snowbound Scottish mansion, remote, and rat-infested; *Stop Press* (1939; *The Spider Strikes*), an ambitious tour-de-force, dense and elaborate, yet light and subtle, with a fictional master criminal who rises from the page to haunt his creator; *Appleby's End* (1945), an intricate farce, antic and exhilarating, involving a resourceful family in a hectic sequence of fantastic events, in which life appears to imitate art; and *Christmas at Candleshoe* (1953), an entrancing tale with its own magic, lyrical, formal, oblique, and unpredictable.

The later works are less substantial, less closely wrought and teasing to the wits; but even the least of them is deft, intriguing and amusing. Several feature Charles Honeybath, a distinguished painter, much in demand for portraits.

For most of the time John Appleby is in charge, the least procedural of policemen, worldly and self-possessed, with a natural authority. A man of infinite resource and acute practical intelligence, he is at ease in any company and wholly unfazed by eccentric persons or odd events. He is also supremely well-informed, with a formidable range of cultural reference and an infallible gift for apt quotation. His recorded career covers fifty years, from the murder of Dr. Umpleby in 1936 to that of Lord Osprey in 1986. Few fictional detectives have served so long and few crime writers have given such intense pleasure over so many years.

[*See also* Gentleman Sleuth.]

—B. A. Pike

IRISH, WILLIAM. *See* Woolrich, Cornell.

J

JAMES, P(HYLLIS) D(OROTHY) (b. 1920), British writer, considered one of the finest authors of crime fiction and the first author in the genre in modern times to have triumphantly passed over the barriers into mainstream fiction. P. D. James, the Baroness James of Holland Park, has been compared to Jane Austen who, it is said, would be as interested today in murder and death as she was in her time in pride and prejudice. James cites Austen, as well as Evelyn Waugh, Graham *Greene, and Anthony Trollope, as deep influences on her work.

Born in Oxford and educated at Cambridge Girls' High School, James worked as a Red Cross nurse during World War II. She married Connor Bantry White in 1941; he returned from the war mentally ill and she helped nurse him until his death in 1964. From 1949 to 1968 she administrated several psychiatric units for the National Health Service, from which she took background for portions of her novels. Most of her books deal with the failure of one of the institutions by which society hopes to hold back death: concern for unwed mothers in *Cover Her Face* (1962); a psychiatric outpatient clinic in *A Mind to Murder* (1963); a nurses' training school in *Shroud for a Nightingale* (1971); a home for the disabled and dying in *The Black Tower* (1975); a forensic laboratory in *Death of an Expert Witness* (1977); the Anglican Church in *A Taste for Death* (1986); a nuclear power station in *Devices and Desires* (1989); the world of publishing in *Original Sin* (1994); and the courts and barristers' chambers in *A Certain Justice* (1997). Each book reveals a bit more about James's series figure Adam *Dalgliesh, who rises at Scotland Yard from inspector to commander. Each demonstrates a growing command over plot and character: James insists that plot must never twist character out of authenticity. After 1968 James worked as an administrator for the Home Office, in the police department, and in the criminal policy department. From 1979 to 1984 she also was a magistrate, and in recent years she has been much involved with service for the Church of England, especially on the Liturgical Commission—all capacities in which she has occasion to think deeply about death, guilt, and punishment. Indeed, her elevation to the House of Lords in 1991 was as much for her public service, which has included acting as a governor of the BBC. She is a member of the Society of Authors, Fellow of the Royal Society of Literature, and Fellow of the Royal Society of Authors.

James has had the courage to grow, not allowing her increasing and very substantial sales to prevent experimentation. She does not consider the genre limiting, as some commentators do, but liberating. Perhaps twice she has written conscious parodies of the genre, though not all critics recognized them as such; arguably in *Unnatural Causes* (1967), and clearly in *The Skull Beneath the Skin* (1982). In the latter, she dared to use the oldest chestnut there is—a small group of individuals trapped for a weekend on an island off the Dorset coast, surely an obeisance to Agatha Christie's *Ten Little Indians* (1939)—and drew affectionately upon many other plot devices while nonetheless writing a novel enjoyable at more than one level. *Innocent Blood* (1980) moved away from formal mystery to moral fiction, demonstrating how the truth could work to evil purposes. Each subsequent book was a major financial success, and those featuring Dalgliesh spawned an admirable television series with Roy Marsden in the role of the pensive detective. In *The Children of Men* (1992), a morality tale set in 2021, James shows a derelict English society incapable of procreation or community though not, in the end, of love.

James created a second series figure, Cordelia *Gray, in *An Unsuitable Job for a Woman* (1972). Only twenty-two, Gray takes over a ramshackle detective agency from her partner after he commits suicide. James uses Gray as Dorothy L. *Sayers used Harriet *Vane, particularly in *Gaudy Night* (1935), to explore aspects of feminism, though the novel remains a well-crafted mystery and, to some critics, James's finest book. James's own favorites are *The Black Tower, A Taste for Death,* and *Original Sin.* Gray returns in *The Skull Beneath the Skin.*

James's work is notable for the strength of its plots, for the precision of its settings, and for the way in which the narrative grows out of revealed character. She is an elegant stylist, a stern moralist, and a person of alert and orderly mind: Her descriptions show a concern for architectural exactitude, for the rich particularity of place, and for a most subtle laying down of clues.

—Robin W. Winks

JANCE, J(UDITH) A(NN) (b. 1944), American writer of regional mysteries set in two distinctly different parts of the United States, both of which the author has called home: Seattle, Washington and Bisbee, Arizona. Born in Arizona, Jance knew, at seven years old, that she wanted to become a writer but she met almost unbelievable roadblocks on the path to that career. At the University of Arizona in 1964, a professor excluded her from his creative writing class on the basis of her gender. Then Jance endured an eighteen-year marriage to an alcoholic husband who forbade her to write. Jance nonetheless turned out poetry about her plight that was later published in a chapbook she titled *After the Fire* (1984). While raising a family, she also worked as a teacher on an Indian reservation and as a librarian during those unhappy years.

When the marriage ended, she moved with her children to Seattle, got a job selling life insurance and, in limited free time, promptly wrote a 1200-page tome concerning a true crime that had touched her life. Although the manuscript was never published, her next effort, the crime novel *Until Proven Guilty*, was published as a paperback original in 1985. It introduces detective J.P. Beaumont, a middle-aged homicide detective who investigates crime everywhere from the streets of Seattle (in the 2000 novel *Birds of Prey*) the deck on a cruise ship traveling to Alaska. Jance's second series sleuth is Joanna Brady, who fill her husband's shoes as sherriff of cochise county, Arizona, after he is killed. Jance also wrote two books based on stories and legends she listened to on the reservation: *Hour of the Hunter* (1991) and *Kiss of the Bees* (2000). Jance's second marriage, to an engineer, has been a success. The couple resides in Seattle.

[*See also* Police Detective.]

—Rosemary Herbert

JANES, J. ROBERT (b. 1935), Canadian author of police procedurals set during World War II in occupied Paris. Born in Toronto, Janes was educated in Canada and worked as a mining engineer, geologist and educator. In his first crime novel, *Mayhem* (1992; *Mirage*), and following books he imagines how crimes might have been solved during the German occupation of France by pairing a member of the Nazi Gestapo, Hermann Kohler, with a subordinate detective from the French Sûreté, Louis St. Cyr. Cooperation between two such men may at first seem unlikely, but Janes gives them compelling crimes to solve, and the message here is that some crimes, such as the murders of young girls, arouse compassion in each of the adversaries, who are shown as complex characters. Jane's eye for detail brings the wartime scene, with its rationing, worn-out people and clothes, into high relief. In one book, a young female *victim's rather new coat is seen as significant, raising questions of connections with the Black Market. Janes uses the atmosphere of deprivation and unease about individuals' alliances to excellent advantage in this series. The question of French collaboration with the Nazis is at the center of *Kaleidoscope* (1993), a book that takes Kohler and St. Cyr out of Paris into the Provençal countryside.

[*See also* Police Detective.]

—Rosemary Herbert

JAPRISOT, SEBASTIEN, pseudonym for Jean Baptiste Rossi (b. 1931), French screenwriter, film director, and novelist. Born in Marseilles, he got a start in writing early, publishing his first novel at age seventeen. Japrisot first made his mark in crime writing with *Compartiment tueurs* (1962; *The Sleeping Car Murder; The 10:30 From Marseilles*), in which a murder is recounted from several points of view. Following that, he experimented with differing perspectives within the minds of individual characters who are tormented by uncertainty. In *Piège pour Cendrillon* (1965; *Trap for Cinderella*), a woman worries that she may be the murderer or a substitute for the *victim in a crime with lesbian undertones. In *La dame dans l'auto avec des lunettes et un fusil* (1966; *The Lady in the Car with Glasses and a Gun*), the protagonist loses grip on reality after her hand is injured in a random act of violence perpetrated by a stranger. *Adieu l'ami* (1968; *Goodbye Friend*) has a doctor drawn into an embezzlement scheme that goes from bad to worse, and *Un longue dimanche de fiancailles* (1991; *A Very Long Engagement*) concerns a search for the truth about five soldiers in World War I, whose apparent cowardice leads to their deaths.

[*See also* Lesbian Characters and Perspectives.]

—Rosemary Herbert

Johnson, Coffin Ed, and **Grave Digger Jones,** two Harlem police detectives created by Chester *Himes. Carrying identical .38-caliber revolvers, clad in dark suits, and driving a battered Plymouth sedan, Coffin Ed Johnson and Grave Digger Jones inspire fear, respect, and awe as do the "bad men" of African American folklore. Like Chandler's "lonely knight," they are the best men in their world.

Grotesquely scarred by acid flung by a con man in *For Love of Imabelle* (1957; *A Rage in Harlem*), Johnson is subject to lethal rages. Although more contemplative, Jones also finds it difficult to maintain his balance amid death, betrayal, and the ever present racism that challenges black lives.

In *Blind Man with a Pistol* (1969), the two detectives lose their struggle against chaos and corruption. But before Himes makes this last bitter statement, readers journey in eight previous novels with his heroes through a world both terrible and comic, sharing jazz, soul food, and their comradeship.

[*See also* African American Sleuth; Police Detective; Sidekicks and Sleuthing Teams.]

—Frankie Y. Bailey

JOURNALIST SLEUTH. Journalists rank high among those who legitimately go about asking questions and, so, are plausibly involved in criminal investigation. The modern investigative journalist deliberately seeks out crime, as the source of the next story. The press are usually early on a murder scene and sometimes get there first. Fictional crime reporters have friends at court or, at least, a sparring partner within the official ranks.

An early journalist sleuth is Joseph Rouletabille, a reporter for the Parisian newspaper *L'Epoque*. He is featured in novels by Gaston Leroux, preeminently *The Mystery of the Yellow Room* (1908; *Murder in the Bedroom*), which he brings to a successful and startling conclusion while still in his teens. Philip Trent works as "special investigator" for the *Record*, most notably in

Trent's Last Case (1913; *The Woman in Black*). On occasion his dispatch, which travels by train, forms part of the narrative, and in "The Old-Fashioned Apache" (1938; *Trent Intervenes*) it serves as exposition. Roger Sheringham is a popular novelist, employed as "unofficial special correspondent" by the *Daily Courier*, to which he contributes "chattily written articles on murder." His journalism is essentially a sideline and hardly affects his hit-or-miss detective activities. Nigel Bathgate alternates as Boswell and Watson for Superintendent Roderick *Alleyn before the war. A gossip columnist for an unnamed "perverted rag," he is unaccountably absent from the high-society murder of *Death in a White Tie* (1938). In 1939, in *Overture to Death*, he represents the *Evening Mirror* as crime reporter.

Among the various detectives of George Harmon *Coxe are two newspaper photographers, both based in Boston: Flash (sometimes "Flashgun") Casey on the *Globe* and, later, the *Express*, and Kent *Murdock on the *Courier-Herald*. Casey is rougher and tougher than Murdock but both are highly paid and expert at their jobs. Both tend also to be at odds with the official investigators. Barney Gantt appears in novels by John Stephen Strange as a staff photographer on the *New York Globe*, where his shots of murders invariably make the first edition and his future wife writes the "problem page." He wins a Pulitzer Prize and produces special postwar features for *Blue Book*. Reynold Frame, who after eight years with the *New York Herald-Tribune* becomes a freelance writer and photographer, figures in four of Herbert Brean's novels, with a notably odd assignment in *Wilders Walk Away* (1948) and an immensely dangerous one in *The Clock Strikes Thirteen* (1952).

Quinn, contributor of a daily crime column to the *Morning Post*, appears in novels by Harry Carmichael, solo on occasion but more usually with John Piper, an insurance assessor. An abrasive antihero, unkempt and insecure, Quinn employs direct, aggressive methods that perfectly complement those of his subtler collaborator. In four novels by Kenneth Hopkins, Gerry Lee acts as feature writer for the *Post*, running into murder whatever his assignment, the paper's crime reporter coming a poor second. In 1963 he lectures on English journalism in Texas and encounters a *Campus Corpse*. Kate Theobold, the journalist wife of a barrister, is featured in six novels by Lionel Black. She works for the *Daily Post*, initially on the cookery column, later as roving reporter, resourceful but headstrong. Her subjects of investigation include a health farm and, in "the silly season," a seaside hoaxer.

Lillian Jackson *Braun's Jim Qwilleran is a veteran newsman with a distinguished past and two Siamese cats who participate in his investigations. After a stint in the Midwest as art editor of the *Daily Fluxion*, he comes into money and moves north to Pickax, where he writes a column for the local paper. Barbara Ninde Byfield's novels feature Helen Bullock, a photojournalist with an international reputation who made her name on the *Globe*

and, like Barney Gantt, has a Pulitzer Prize among her credits. Known as "Holocaust Helen," she has a reputation for fearlessness and raw candor: Both her writing and photographs have an "unedited 'here-it is' quality." In Lucille Kallen's novels C. B. Greenfield edits and owns the *Sloan's Ford Reporter*, a small-town weekly out to "vanquish corruption, greed, injustice, disease and inferior English teachers in the school system." His cases are narrated by Maggie Rome, his quizzical chief reporter and long-suffering legman.

Rain Morgan is a gossip columnist, sufficiently eminent to have her picture appear in her *Morning Post* column and to be recognized in pubs. She figures in several novels by Lesley Grant-Adamson, of which one, *Wild Justice* (1987), draws heavily on the *Post* for its setting and personnel. The victim is the paper's proprietor.

Amanda Roberts and Samantha Adams are investigative journalists in Atlanta in novels by, respectively, Sherryl Woods and Alice Storey (who also write together as Sarah Shankman). The former joins *Inside Atlanta* as a feature writer after a murder investigation releases her from humdrum assignments; the latter, on the staff of the *Atlanta Constitution*, chooses her own stories and thereby runs repeatedly into danger. In novels by Barbara *D'Amato, Cat Marsala works freelance in Chicago, seeking whomever she may righteously and profitably devour.

—B. A. Pike

JUDGE. While judges rarely, if ever, function as protagonists in crime novels, they must nevertheless preside over climactic scenes of courtroom trials in which the issues are settled and the culprit identified. In his or her courtroom, the judge controls the flow of permissible testimony and constrains opposing counsel from exceeding the bounds of legitimate advocacy.

An established convention of the genre requires the judge to mediate between a zealous defense attorney and a relentless prosecutor avid for career advancement or political office. With both sides mobilizing their legal stratagems and cunning subtleties, frequent objections are inevitable. The judge must sustain or reject, and his rulings provide an author with the opportunity to engage the reader's emotions. Thus, if a reader identifies with the accused whose fate hangs in the balance, an unfavorable ruling will evoke in the reader a sense of misgiving, anxiety, or apprehension.

The stereotype that commonly appears in crime and mystery writing is the judge as generally a political animal, an irritable man who threatens contempt proceedings and is concerned about being reversed in a higher court. Judges lacking in moral compass are less stereotypical and may produce far more engrossing complications. And judges lacking in intelligence but rich with eccentricities can provide both tension and humor as exemplified in stories by John *Mortimer.

In formulaic novels the judge's role is usually marginal. Fans of Erle Stanley *Gardner, anticipating a courtroom confrontation, are often rewarded with a last-minute confession extracted by Perry *Mason's adroit cross-examination. The judge in these cases exists largely to sustain or dismiss objections and to bang the gavel when Mason has satisfactorily wrapped up the case.

In more recent novels, authors have been mining a richer vein for the man with the gavel. In *Death Penalty* (1993), William J. Coughlin (himself a senior United States administrative law judge) introduces several jurists, two of whom—the chief justice of an appellate court and his former colleague on the bench—are egregiously corruptible. The second acts as bagman for the first, who offers to sell his critical vote upholding a lower court's multimillion dollar award in exchange for half the winning lawyer's fee. The parts played by these venal characters—and by a third judge, a man of unimpeachable rectitude and decency, who helps to bring them down—are integral to the main story line, which indeed could not exist without them.

A judge's flagrantly prejudicial conduct is on display in Barry Reed's *The Verdict* (1980). Because of his relationship to a high-ranking prelate, the judge favors a church-affiliated hospital while presiding over a malpractice suit involving the death of a patient. His blatantly biased rulings and cavalier treatment of the plaintiff's lawyer infuriate the reader.

Scott *Turow's *Presumed Innocent* (1987) is arguably a pivotal performance in this particular category. Here the judge is a presence of considerable import, both at pretrial conferences and in the courtroom, a take-charge figure, testy, assertive, and quick to censure any deviation from accepted protocol. These traits contribute color and urgency to a novel that demonstrates how solid characterization and atmosphere can enhance a genre that is viewed primarily as escape literature.

[*See also* Eccentrics.]

—Harold Q. Masur

JURY. Though most big-trial novels and courtroom mysteries include a jury, relatively few have focused on the jurors themselves, and those few rarely put the system in a favorable light. Fictional jurors ignore admonitions not to discuss the case or absorb media accounts, stubbornly apply their own prejudices to considerations of the evidence, and even bring to the jury room extraneous evidence from their own independent investigations. In Dorothy L. *Sayers's *Strong Poison* (1930), Miss Climpson's account to Lord Peter *Wimsey of jury deliberations in the trial of Harriet *Vane shows the arbitrariness with which a juror's charge is sometimes carried out.

Eden Phillpotts's satirical *The Jury* (1927), the first novel to concentrate its action in the jury room, presents a typically jaundiced view. The jurors in George Goodchild and C. E. Bechhofer Roberts's similarly structured *The Jury Disagree* (1934) at least concentrate on the evidence. The best-known and most successful attempt to dramatize jury deliberations, Reginald Rose's 1955 television play *Twelve Angry Men*, includes the quirks and prejudices, but ultimately presents a somewhat more optimistic view of the process's validity. Showing how the one juror voting for acquittal of a Puerto Rican youth gradually brings the other eleven around, Rose's play was subsequently adapted for film and stage versions.

Two of the best British novels focusing on jurors and their deliberations, though not confining their action to the jury room, are Raymond W. Postgate's *Verdict of Twelve* (1940) and Gerald Bullett's *The Jury* (1935). More recent examples include Michael Underwood's *Hand of Fate* (1981), B. M. Gill's *The Twelfth Juror* (1984), and John Wainwright's *The Jury People* (1978). Michael *Gilbert's *The Queen Against Karl Mullen* (1991) provides a rare description of British jury selection, while Donald MacKenzie's *The Juryman* (1957) centers on efforts to fix a juror.

Many American trial novels, including such classics as Robert Traver's *Anatomy of a Murder* (1958) and Al Dewlen's *Twilight of Honor* (1961), devote considerable space to the jury selection process. William Harrington's undervalued debut *Which the Justice, Which the Thief* (1963) may be the most extensive fictional treatment ever of how jurors are chosen. Steve Martini's *Compelling Evidence* (1992) has another of the best sequences on jury selection, while Vincent S. Green's *The Price of Victory* (1992) is unusual in offering details of military jury selection. Warwick Downing's *The Water Cure* (1992) has an unusual angle on the process, with the prosecution's and defense's usual priorities reversed by the nature of the case. Ellery *Queen's *The Glass Village* (1954) shows a small-town court intentionally selecting a bad jury to avoid lynch law and guarantee any conviction will be reversed on appeal. John *Grisham's first novel, *A Time to Kill* (1989), provides details of a Mississippi lawyer's jury research prior to trial, the actual process of selecting a jury, and finally their deliberations, including one juror's inventive and brave measure to bring the deadlocked group to a verdict. Two American novels, Harvey Jacobs's somewhat absurdist *The Juror* (1980) and Parnell Hall's *Juror* (1990), emphasize the jury-duty experience more than specific cases.

—Jon L. Breen

K

KEATING, H(ENRY) R(EYMOND) F(ITZWAL-TER) (b. 1926), novelist and critic, has been a central figure in British crime writing for at least four decades. He was for fifteen years crime critic of the *Times*, and since 1985 has been president of the famous Detection Club. He has edited several books about crime fiction, including *Whodunit? A Guide to Crime, Suspense, and Crime Fiction* (1982) and a collection of essays about Agatha *Christie, written a biography of Sherlock *Holmes, and played the game of choosing his hundred best crime stories in *Crime and Mystery: The One Hundred Best Books* (1987). All his critical writing is marked by a conspicuous generosity of mind, scholarship lightly borne, and perceptions both sharp and subtle.

But creation is more important than criticism, and the tone and manner of Keating's crime stories are wholly original in modern crime fiction. They spring from a mind attracted by philosophical and metaphysical speculation, with a liking for fantasy held in check by the crime story's requirements of plot. Early books like *Zen There Was Murder* (1960) and *A Rush on the Ultimate* (1961) gave readers the pleasure of seeing a writer kick up his heels in defiance of any critical perception of what a crime story *ought* to be like. It is typical of Keating's intense imaginative powers that when Inspector Ganesh Vinayak *Ghote of the Bombay Police first appeared in *The Perfect Murder* (1964), his creator had not visited India, and did not do so for another decade. That first Ghote novel won the Crime Writers Association's Golden Dagger Award and launched its author on the series of books in which Ghote is the central character.

The ambience of the little Indian detective allowed full play to Keating's offbeat humor, and Indian habits and attitudes held an evident attraction to a mind unsatisfied by Western rationalism. Preferences among the Ghote books vary from reader to reader. *Inspector Ghote Hunts the Peacock* (1968), which finds the detective astonished by English ways, and *Under a Monsoon Cloud* (1986), where he is confronted by a moral problem, suggest the range of comedy and seriousness the series can comprehend. *The Murder of the Maharajah* (1980) is a brilliant variation on the classical crime formula, perhaps underrated by its creator.

Keating likes to experiment. Using the name Evelyn Harvey, he wrote in the 1980s three crime stories with a period setting in which the central character was the governess Harriet Unwin. After 1986, however, he abandoned the Harvey pseudonym and Victorian crime and returned to Ghote.

Yet the Ghote stories have not stretched Keating's talent to its limits. That he recognizes this himself is suggested by two of his four excursions into the "straight" novel, *The Underside* (1974) and *A Long Walk to Wimbledon* (1978). The first offered a view of the Victorian sexual underside that was realistic yet infused with fantasy, the second an after-the-bomb vision, a journey through chaos the more powerful because confined to a single viewpoint. If Keating can fuse such themes into a crime story's framework, the result might be his masterpiece.

[*See also* Ethnic Sleuth.]

—Julian Symons

KELLERMAN, FAYE (MARDER) (b. 1952), American author best-known for police procedurals that offer puzzling plots, chronicle the development of a romantic relationship, and examine the role of religious faith in modern living. Kellerman was born in St. Louis, Missouri. She studied mathematics and oral surgery at the University of California at Los Angeles and she has worked in real estate and investment. She is married to mystery writer Jonathan *Kellerman and has two children. In her first novel, *The Ritual Bath* (1985), Los Angeles Police Department Sergeant Pete Decker, a Vietnam veteran, is hardened to his job when he meets Rina Lazarus. She is an orthodox Jew, widow, and mother of two, and she lives on a yeshiva where her sheltered life centers around religious ritual. The couple falls in love and eventually marries. Along the way, Decker, who was born Jewish but raised in a Christian family, takes religious instruction in Judaism from Rabbi Rav Schulman, who is a continuing character in the series. Kellerman's work, especially *Milk and Honey* (1990), reveals that she shares her husband's concerns about the victimization of children. But while Jonathan Kellerman's books look at crimes and the trauma they provoke, her books go beyond his to look at thoughtfully presented themes. For instance, in *Sacred and Profane* (1987), she looks the tension between the religious and secular worlds. Kellerman has also written an historical mystery with romantic overtones: *The Quality of Mercy* (1989) looks at a true crime in Elizabethan England.

[*See also* Police Detective.]

—Rosemary Herbert

KELLERMAN, JONATHAN (b. 1949), American psychologist and author of a series of mysteries that feature the clinical psychologist Alex Delaware. Born in New York City, Kellerman was educated at the University of California. A father of two, he is married to the writer Faye *Kellerman. He has worked as a professor of pediatric psychology, as a director of the Psychosocial Program in the Children's Hospitals of Los Angeles and as a practicing clinical psychologist. His nonfiction work, *Helping the Fearful Child: A Parent's Guide to Everyday and Problem Anxieties* (1981) draws on the same professional expertise that informs his crime fiction. Introduced in *When the Bough Breaks* (1985; *Shrunken Heads*), Delaware is drawn into crime-solving in connection with children he sees in his practice, many of whom have been sent to him for evaluation by the legal system. Frequently, Delaware discovers that his patients have been the victims of sexual abuse. Additional psychological problems, such as agoraphobia in *Private Eyes* (1992), figure in the books. Continuing characters in the series include Delaware's lover, Robin Castagna, and a homosexual pair, Milo Sturgis and Rick Silverman. Set in Jerusalem, his non-series novel, *The Butcher's Theatre* (1988), focuses on psychopathic killer.

—Rosemary Herbert

KEMELMAN, HARRY (1908–1996), American professor, businessman, and mystery writer best known for his series detective Rabbi David *Small. Born in Boston, Massachusetts, he was educated at the Boston Latin School, Boston University, and Harvard University, He taught in secondary schools, evening schools and on the college campuses and also held jobs in wage administration for the United States Army.

Kemelman introduced Small in *Friday the Rabbi Slept Late* (1964), launching a series that was an immediate popular success. At the time, the use of a Jewish sleuth was groundbreaking although Kemelman's portrayal of the Rabbi as a man of intellect, excellent judge of character, and person in the habit of questioning everything was not. It echoed G.K. *Chesterton's winning formula for the *clerical sleuth exemplified in *Father Brown. Small is drawn into some cases by Hugh Lanigan, police chief of fictional Barnard's Crossing, Massachusetts, a well-drawn small town. Kemelman enriches most of his novels by elucidating some aspect of twentieth-century American Jewish life.

—Rosemary Herbert

KIJEWSKI, KAREN (b. 1943), American high school teacher-turned- private eye novelist. Kijewski was born in Berkeley, California, where she attended the University of California. After teaching English for a decade in Massachusetts, she settled in Sacramento, California, where she did bartending to support her writing habit. Her first novel, *Katwalk* (1989), puts that experience to use, since the *private eye protagonist, Kat Colorado, has bartending experience, too. Colorado's background also includes

an unhappy childhood, which some critics say drives her to go to great lengths to help individuals who are in trouble. For examples, in *Katapult* (1990), her heart goes out to an adolescent prostitute; in *Copy Kat* (1992), she forms a bond with the child of a murdered woman; and in *Stray Kat Waltz* (1998), she risks her life to help the battered wife of a policeman. Her past may also account for some insecurity about herself, which is sometimes expressed by means of self-deprecating humor. Despite some vulnerability, Colorado can be brave in the face of *menacing characters, and appealingly sassy, too.

—Rosemary Herbert

KNOX, RONALD A(RBUTHNOTT) (1888–1957), British priest, scholar, satirist, author, and one of the foremost pontificators on the subject of detective fiction, regarded the detective novel as an intellectual test. In his six classic novels he demonstrated his skill at using distinctive British settings, such as the River Thames near Oxford in *The Footsteps at the Lock* (1928) or the Scottish highlands *Still Dead* (1934); however, he has been criticized for constructing implausible plots. Believing that the mystery writer should always play fair with the reader, he provided page numbers for his clues, in case the reader had missed them. He is perhaps best remembered for constructing a set of ten rules for crime writers, known as the Decalogue. These were published as part of his introduction to *Best Detective Stories of the Year 1928* (1929). Knox was one of the first to publish scholarship on Sherlock *Holmes. His "Studies in the Literature of Sherlock Holmes," on which Conan Doyle congratulated him in some amazement, appeared in *The Blue Book 1912*.

—Penelope Fitzgerald

Kramer, Lieutenant, and **Sergeant Zondi**, creations of James *McClure, a native South African now resident in England. The pair are introduced in *The Steam Pig* (1971), the first in McClure's series of police procedurals. Trekkersburg, modeled on McClure's hometown of Pietermaritzburg, is a solid Afrikaner laager in which blacks are "kaffirs" and Englishmen are reviled. Lieutenant Tromp Kramer, a member of the city's murder and robbery squad, is a hard-boiled Boer detective whose belief in Afrikaner supremacy is only slightly mollified by his friendship with his Zulu sergeant, Mickey Zondi, who provides a counterweight to the dominant, white view of society. Both men are committed police officers who daily confront the injustices of apartheid as well as crime.

[*See also* Ethnic Sleuth; Sidekicks and Sleuthing Teams.]

—Chris Gausden

L

LANGTON, JANE (GILLSON) (b. 1922), American writer of children's fiction and of cozy detective novels for adults featuring the *academic sleuth Homer Kelly and his wife Mary. Born in Boston, Massachusetts, Langton moved with her family to Delaware where she enjoyed a carefree childhood despite growing up during the Great Depression. She became interested in science, particularly astronomy, long before she pursued a writing career. She earned a B.S. at Wellesley College and an M.S. at the University of Michigan before

She married and raised two sons not far from historic Walden Pond in Lincoln, Massachusetts. Her most famous children's book, *The Fledgling* (1980) is set in the area, as are several of her mysteries including *The Transcendental Murder* (1964; the *Minuteman Murder*, 1976), *Good and Dead* (1986), and *God in Concord* (1992). Particularly in these books, Kelly, who is enamored of the works of the naturalist Henry David Thoreau, alludes to that author's writings. In *God in Concord,* a student from India makes a pilgrimage to Walden Pond where he is horrified to learn that development of the area into a shopping mall looks likely. Another kind of development—from the past—is central to *Emily Dickinson is Dead* (1984), in a novel that takes the centenary of the American poet's birth as the occasion for a look into the history of a valley that was flooded to form a reservoir. The author's expertise in astronomy is evident in *Dark Nantucket Noon* (1975), which is set during an eclipse on Nantucket Island, off the coast of Massachusetts. Langton has also taken the Kellys abroad to Oxford, England, in *Dead as a Dodo* (1996) and to Florence, Italy in *The Dante Game* (1991). Her interest in art is obvious in the latter and in *The Escher Twist* (2002). Langton has illustrated her mysteries, but not her children's books, with her own line drawings.

[*See also* Eccentrics.]

—Rosemary Herbert

LATHEN, EMMA, joint pseudonym of the late economist Mary Jane Latsis (1927–1997) and Martha B. Henissart (b. 1929), a *lawyer. The American writing pair, who collaborated on novels of amateur detection set against the backgrounds of New York's Wall Street and the Washington, D.C., political milieu, put together the Lathen name by combining the first three letters of each of their last names. Initially they used the pseudonym to hide from their colleagues their identities as mystery writers; later they cultivated a mystique about their identities and an elusiveness that meant they were rarely seen in public together.

The pair introduced their most famous character,

John Putnam *Thatcher, executive vice president of Sloan Guaranty Trust, in *Banking on Death* (1961). During a thirty-six-year collaboration, they portrayed Thatcher as using business savvy and urbane wit to investigate mysteries in a variety of business settings. In *Murder Sunny Side Up* (1968), under the joint pseudonym R. B. Dominic, they introduced another popular series character, Congressman Ben Safford. Safford solves crimes mostly set in Washington, D.C. The success of both series had much to do with the authors' ability to make readers feel like insiders in the worlds they depicted. This is achieved in part by Lathen's insertion of sager pronouncements about the states of affairs in these two realms, expressed in the characteristically debonair and witty dialogue that became the Lathen hallmark.

The characters themselves are powerful and intelligent. Thatcher is rich, handsome, unattached, and endowed with keen intelligence and a huge store of common sense. Safford is a government insider. Both men, in the Golden Age tradition, solve crimes by noticing and remembering details that are more or less furnished to the reader but whose significance is lost to everyone else.

—Rosemary Herbert

LAWYER. *Lawyers are important characters in crime and mystery writing, sometimes playing the role of sleuth as well as legal advisor or advocate, and in other cases appearing simply as secondary characters whose legal expertise or access to privileged information is essential to the development of the plot.*

This entry is divided into three parts, the first two surveying outstanding examples of fictional American and British lawyers who become lead characters performing detective work and the third examining the role of the lawyer as a secondary character.

*It is important to note that some lawyers who are seen as hero-sleuths actually engage in very little hands-on detective work themselves. Despite the fact that they use private detectives to do their footwork, they are seen as sleuths, since their cases are solved by the application of their intellectual powers and legal expertise. Erle Stanley Gardner's Perry *Mason is an example of such a lawyer sleuth.*

American Lawyer-Sleuth
British Lawyer-Sleuth
Lawyers as Secondary Characters

THE AMERICAN LAWYER-SLEUTH

The fictional American lawyer-sleuth has had a long and varied history. Melville Davisson *Post's Randolph Mason, more rogue than detective in *The Strange Schemes of Randolph Mason* (1896; *Randolph Mason: The Strange Schemes*) and *The Man of Last Resort or, The Clients of Randolph Mason* (1897), finds loopholes to help his clients cheat the law. In the later adventures, collected in *The Corrector of Destinies* (1908; *Randolph Mason, Corrector of Destinies*), he reforms somewhat and performs more like a traditional detective. Post's other continuing lawyer-sleuth, Colonel Braxton, whose cases were gathered in *The Silent Witness* (1930), operates in rural Virginia like the more famous Uncle *Abner. Arthur Train's *Saturday Evening Post* character Ephraim Tutt, who appeared in a long series of collections beginning with *Tutt and Mr. Tutt* (1920) and one short novel, *The Hermit of Turkey Hollow* (1921), only occasionally functions as a detective.

By far the most famous lawyer-detective, Erle Stanley *Gardner's Perry *Mason, first appeared in *The Case of the Velvet Claws* (1933), a novel that did not employ courtroom drama. Most of the more than eighty subsequent Mason books, through the posthumous *The Case of the Postponed Murder* (1973), included the patented courtroom climax that later writers have tried, usually not as successfully, to emulate. C. W. Grafton's Gil Henry, a promising lawyer-sleuth in the Mason tradition, appeared in only two books, *The Rat Began to Gnaw the Rope* (1943) and *The Rope Began to Hang the Butcher* (1944). Another successful novel in the Mason tradition was *A Handy Death* (1973), by Robert L. Fish with attorney Henry Rothblatt, but advocate Hank Ross never appeared again. Television lawyer Sam Benedict, based on J. W. Ehrlich, appeared in several somewhat Masonesque novels, most successfully a pair by Brad Williams and Ehrlich, *A Conflict of Interest* (1971) and *A Matter of Confidence* (1973). Jack Donahue's Harlan Cole and D. R. Meredith's John Lloyd Branson are other less successful attempts to create a new Perry Mason. Most competent in capturing the writing and plotting style of Gardner's series has been Parnell Hall writing as J. P. Hailey in the series about Steve Winslow, beginning with *The Baxter Trust* (1988). Thomas Chastain has continued the Mason series proper with a couple of pastiches, beginning with *The Case of Too Many Murders* (1989).

Some of the best-known American lawyer detectives eschew the courtroom and operate more in the tradition of *private eyes: Craig *Rice's John J. Malone, Harold Q. Masur's Scott Jordan, William G. *Tapply's Brady Coyne, and Ed *McBain's Matthew Hope, who finally argues a case in *Mary, Mary* (1993).

Since the accused person is usually innocent in detective stories, defense lawyers have predominated among fictional sleuths. Gardner gave the prosecution not-quite-equal time with small-city district attorney Doug Selby, hero of *The D.A. Calls It Murder* (1937) and subsequent novels. *The Corpse in the Corner Saloon* (1948) launched a series by Hampton Stone (pseudonym of Aaron Marc Stein) whose protagonist, Jeremiah X. "Gibby" Gibson, is an assistant district attorney in *New

York but never gets near the courtroom. Changing social attitudes have made prosecutor heroes more frequent in recent years. Robert K. Tanenbaum's Roger "Butch" Karp, who first appeared in *No Lesser Plea* (1987), is a New York assistant district attorney in a more realistic mode.

Lawyer-sleuths, like fictional sleuths generally, were predominately male for many years. Barbara Frost's defense attorney Marka de Lancey, who appeared in three novels beginning with *The Corpse Said No* (1949), was ahead of her time as an independent female professional. A pioneer on the prosecutorial side was Barbara Driscoll, who appeared in only one novel, *Criminal Court* (1966), by William Woolfolk writing as Winston Lyon. The 1990s saw a plethora of female lawyer-sleuths, including Margaret *Maron's Judge Deborah Knott, who first appeared in the Edgar-winning *Bootlegger's Daughter* (1992), Julie Smith's Rebecca Schwartz, Lia Matera's Willa Jansson and Laura di Palma, and Carolyn Wheat's Cass Jameson.

Many lawyer-sleuths have been the creations of lawyer-writers. Among the characters introduced in the seventies by real-life lawyers were Francis M. Nevins Jr.'s law professor Loren Mensing and Joe L. Hensley's small-town defender Donald Robak. With the best-selling success of Scott *Turow's *Presumed Innocent* (1987), law-trained novelists became a hot commodity. Warwick Downing made an organization rather than a single lawyer the hero in his National Association of Special Prosecutors series, beginning with *A Clear Case of Murder* (1990). Other distinguished attorney-created sleuths are William Bernhardt's Ben Kincaid, who first appeared in *Primary Justice* (1992), and Steve Martini's Paul Madriani, who appears in *Compelling Evidence* (1992) and *Prime Witness* (1993). The novels of John *Grisham, beginning with *A Time to Kill* (1989), feature lawyer-sleuths but, to date, no continuing characters.

Though American legal fiction tends to contain less humor than the works of British writers like Henry Cecil and John *Mortimer, an exception exists in the comic trial scenes of Paul Levine's Jake Lassiter novels, beginning with *To Speak for the Dead* (1990). Challenging the rule that lawyer fiction is usually contemporary are Raymond Paul's Lon Quinncannon series, beginning with *The Thomas Street Horror* (1982), which is set in the nineteenth century, and Richard Parrish's novels featuring Joshua Rabb, who first appeared in *The Dividing Line* (1993), and who operates in the period just following World War II.

—Jon L. Breen

THE BRITISH LAWYER-SLEUTH

The enduring popularity of legal mysteries in Britain is due largely to the skill with which succeeding generations of writers have developed the lawyer-sleuth. That so many lawyers should turn detective is plausible: The work of many solicitors and barristers brings them into contact with crime and criminals, police officers and suspects. The lawyer-sleuth is usually a maverick, prepared to bend or even flout the law in the hope of avoiding ordeals for the innocent and the risk that the guilty will walk free. The danger is that for a professional man or woman regularly to behave in such a way may destroy credibility—a weakness, for example, of Anthony Gilbert's novels about the rumbustious solicitor Arthur Crook and those by H. C. *Bailey about the hymn-singing hypocrite Joshua Clunk.

A sea change in the portrayal of the lawyer-sleuth occurred with the publication of Cyril *Hare's *Tragedy at Law* (1942). In real life, Hare was a barrister and he captured the insular nature of circuit life as well as creating in Francis Pettigrew a barrister-detective all the more credible because he did not win every case and was apt to lapse into melancholy. Later writers built on the foundations laid by Hare; many, like him, have been lawyers and have taken pains to combine a believable picture of the legal world with strong plots which frequently turn on a quirk of law. Hare's most notable disciple has been Michael *Gilbert, a London solicitor whose clients included Raymond *Chandler. In *Smallbone Deceased* (1950), a *corpse of a trustee is found in a deed box; the legal knowledge of a young solicitor, Henry Bohun, helps Inspector Hazlerigg to solve the mystery. Nap Rumbold, another London solicitor, appeared in a number of books and short stories; in *Death Has Deep Roots* (1951), Gilbert intersperses courtroom scenes with Nap's exploits in France, as he tries to establish the innocence of his client. Gilbert's preferred method is to confront a likable young solicitor with a legal mystery which can only be resolved by heroic actions, as in *The Crack in the Teacup* (1966). In *Flash Point* (1974), narrated in part by an employee of the solicitors' professional body, the Law Society, Gilbert combines a lively tale about secret service dirty tricks with a series of skilfully contrasted court scenes. *The Case Against Karl Mullen* (1991), a late and undervalued work, introduces Roger Sherman, who makes good use of his army training after taking on as a client a member of the South African security forces with powerful enemies. In contrast, the elderly sleuth Jonas Pickett has an ex-circus strongman to help with the rough stuff in the ironically titled story collection *Anything for a Quiet Life* (1990).

The legal profession in England and Wales is divided between barristers and solicitors; lawyers who turn, in fictional terms, to crime, almost invariably write about the branch of the profession to which they personally belong. John *Mortimer, a Queen's Counsel, is the creator of Horace *Rumpole, scourge of the Establishment and firmly within the tradition of idiosyncratic amateur detectives. Less radical, but equally entertaining, are Sarah *Caudwell's books about the tax barrister Julia Larwood and her colleagues; they show that even tax law and high finance can supply the raw material for mysteries in the classic tradition. Historically, solicitors have been regarded as leading less glamorous lives than barristers, who perform more regularly in the theatrical

atmosphere of the courts. Yet solicitors' work brings them more directly into contact with the outside world— and in particular with clients who are suspects, culprits, and, occasionally, *victims. M. R. D. Meek's Lennox Kemp has had a checkered career; having at one time been struck off the roll of solicitors, he spent several years working as a *private eye before being allowed to reenter the profession. Roy Lewis seeks to get the best of two worlds: His solicitor-detective, Eric Ward, combines criminal and corporate work and often finds that the two spheres of his practice overlap. Legal series have kept up-to-date with the changing face of the profession in Britain, and lawyers are no longer stereotyped as middle-aged, middle-class, and male. Michael Underwood's Rosa Epton, who first appeared in *The Unprofessional Spy* (1964) is notable as the first British female lawyer-sleuth. Martin *Edwards's Harry Devlin, based in Liverpool, is one of the few provincial solicitor-detectives, while Helen West works, like her creator Frances *Fyfield, in the Crown Prosecution Service.

Today, the lawyer-sleuth is as likely to have a working-class background and to have a clientele composed of the underprivileged (as well as the all too often guilty) as to be a member of a social elite based in elegant chambers in Lincoln's Inn. The books in which such characters appear range from the grimly realistic to the avowedly cerebral and demonstrate that no profession offers so many possibilities for the amateur detective as the law.

—Martin Edwards

LAWYERS AS SECONDARY CHARACTERS

Lawyers have appeared as supporting characters in any number of crime fiction works, whether serving as the Watson figure, adversary, *victim, suspect, murderer, reader of the will to the assembled heirs of the murder victim, or handy legal consultant for the detective. Lawyers play every kind of role, from family adviser to ambulance-chasing shyster to flamboyant courtroom performer. Even in today's lawyer-baiting climate, their roles range from the heroic to the venal.

S. S. *Van Dine's gentleman *amateur detective Philo *Vance is brought into his cases by his friend John F.-X. Markham, district attorney of New York County, who acts as Greek chorus and slightly smarter equivalent of dumb cop sergeant Heath. Arthur Train's long-running attorney Ephraim Tutt, whose partner is a younger lawyer also named Tutt but unrelated (thus the title of the 1920 collection *Tutt and Mr. Tutt*), has recurring villainous adversaries in small-town lawyer Squire Hezekiah Mason and New York assistant district attorney William Francis O'Brion. Similarly, Erle Stanley *Gardner's Perry *Mason invariably opposes a district attorney, in early books Claude Drumm and later the better-known Hamilton Burger, whose primary function is to put the wrong suspect on trial. To liven up the series about prosecutor hero Doug Selby, Gardner introduced a character he seemed to have greater fondness for, sneaky defender

A. B. Carr, in *The D.A. Draws a Circle* (1939)—while Carr is invariably vanquished, he proves a much more interesting character than Drumm, Burger, or (most ironically) Selby.

Some British legal series characters have whole casts of continuing associates. John *Mortimer's Horace Rumpole of the Bailey shares chambers with a variety of fellow advocates—Claude Erskine-Brown, Phillida Trant ("the Portia of our chambers"), Uncle Tom, the outspokenly evangelical Soapy Sam Bullard, the left-leaning Fiona Allways, and most notably the trouble-prone Guthrie Featherstone, QC, M.P., who somehow rises from head of chambers to the High Court bench. Rumpole also appears repeatedly before the dreaded Judge Bullingham. Sara Woods's Antony Maitland is supported by his uncle and housemate, Sir Nicholas Harding, QC, and frequently has the same junior counsel (Derek Stringer), prosecution opponent (Bruce Halloran), and presiding judge (Carruthers).

Several secondary lawyer characters recur in Henry Cecil's comic fiction, most notably Mr. Tewkesbury, the drunken solicitor who first appears in *The Painswick Line* (1951). The brilliant advocate Sir Impey Biggs recurs in Dorothy L. *Sayers's Lord Peter *Wimsey novels, most memorably in *Clouds of Witness* (1926). Michael Underwood's solicitor Rosa Epton has a partner, Robin Snaith, and a romantic interest, Peter Chen, who reappear from book to book. Oliver Rathbone, QC, became a more and more important secondary figure in Anne *Perry's series about amnesiac Victorian detective William Monk and Crimean War nurse Hester Latterly.

Most of the better big-trial novels have vivid and interesting lawyer characters in supporting roles. The secondary characters in Robert Traver's *Anatomy of a Murder* (1958), prosecutor Claude Dancer and Judge Harlan Weaver, are especially effectively drawn. The old lawyer, sometimes a drunk, who is drawn in to help the younger hero has become something of a stock character in such books. A recent example is disbarred alcoholic Lucien Wilbanks, who helps out Jake Brigance in John *Grisham's *A Time to Kill* (1989). Among the most interesting secondary characters in the 1990s flood of legal procedurals are those in Steve Martini's novels *Compelling Evidence* (1992) and *Prime Witness* (1993): Quite a few of them are (if only to the naive nonlawyer, perhaps) incompetent beyond belief, particularly the laggardly assistant district attorney Roland Overroy. Both books also feature money-hungry defenders with more interest in book and film contracts than justice.

[*See also* Sidekicks and Sleuthing Teams.]

—Jon L. Breen

LeBLANC, MAURICE (MARIE ÉMILE) (1869–1941), French writer who created the gentleman burglar Arsène *Lupin. Leblanc is, with Gaston Leroux, the leading figure in early French detective fiction.

Leblanc was born in Rouen. Early novels (*Une femme*, 1893; *L'oeuvre de mort*, 1896) and short stories (*Des couples*, 1890) reveal the influence of Flaubert and Maupassant.

In 1905 he was solicited to contribute a short story, to be written in the manner of the Sherlock *Holmes tales, to a new French magazine that was modeled on the *Strand*. "*L'arrestation d'Arsène Lupin*" was published in July of that year. (It was translated as "The Arrest of Arsène Lupin" in *The Exploits of Arsène Lupin*, 1909.) Leblanc subsequently detailed the adventures of the exceptional thief, treasure hunter, Don Juan, and shrewd detective in a series of novels including *L'Aiguille creuse* (1909; *The Hollow Needle*, 1910) *813* (1910), and *La demeure mystérieuse* (1929; *The Melamare Mystery*) and collections of short stories such as *Arsène Lupin contre Herlock Sholmes* (1908; *Arsène Lupin versus Holmlock Shears*, 1909). Novels in addition to the Lupin series include *Dorothée, danseuse de corde* (1923; *Dorothy the Rope Dancer*) and the science fiction work *Les trois yeux* (1920; *The Three Eyes*, 1921).

[*See also* Gentleman Thief.]

—Jacques Baudou

LE CARRÉ, JOHN, pseudonym of David John Moore Cornwell (b. 1931). British author of spy fiction, considered the most outstanding political novelist of the Cold War period. Le Carré began to write while working for British intelligence, so he knew the secret world from the inside. At the time, Ian Fleming's James Bond novels were immensely popular, but in published interviews le Carré made it clear that he did not share the current enthusiasm. An important stimulus for his writing was his desire to create an alternative form of thriller, replacing glamorizing fantasy and facile heroics with a more authentic portrait of the intelligence world and of Cold War realities.

George Smiley, the series character le Carré launched in his first two novels, *Call for the Dead* (1961) and *A Murder of Quality* (1962), is Bond's antitype, a short, fat, middle-aged, bespectacled, and inconspicuous cuckold. With his much more original third novel, *The Spy Who Came in from the Cold* (1963), le Carré achieved a huge international success and transformed the spy novel. This terse, chilling, and powerful story of multiple deception and betrayal explores the rhetoric and ethics of the Cold War in order to subvert standard pieties, especially those of the supposedly morally superior West concerning freedom, justice, and democracy. For the Circus, le Carré's fictional equivalent of MI5, the end justifies the means, as it does for its Marxist counterparts, and the lovers central to the novel are exploited and sacrificed in the name of expediency. The vulnerability and fragility of human love in a world of power politics is an important theme in le Carré's novels. In *The Looking Glass War* (1965), le Carré's bleak, pessimistic narrative of a British intelligence operation that goes terribly wrong focuses on the department responsible, which lives nostalgically in its glory days. Out of touch with reality, this organization is a microcosm of British society, like the public school in *A Murder of Quality*, so that both books are "condition of England" as well as genre novels.

By the mid-1960s le Carré was a full-time writer and his style subsequently became more expansive and detailed than it was in his spare, compact early novels. In *A Small Town in Germany* (1968), an intelligence probe into the disappearance of a supposed defector is a way of dealing with the shadow cast on contemporary German politics by the Nazi past. Le Carré then abandoned mystery and spy conventions for the first and only time, but his most self-consciously literary novel, *The Naive and Sentimental Lover* (1971), was not well received. Le Carré immediately returned to Smiley, the Circus, and Cold War espionage with the widely praised *Quest for Karla* trilogy he wrote during the 1970s: *Tinker, Tailor, Soldier, Spy* (1974), *The Honourable Schoolboy* (1977), and *Smiley's People* (1980). These books established his reputation as one of the most important of postwar English novelists. The scope of this realistic yet mythic trilogy is vast, geographically, politically, and humanly. It encompasses such themes as loyalty and betrayal, memory, time, innocence, love, and the conflict between public and private values, and contains brilliant analyses of postimperial Britain, bureaucratic institutions, and the corporate mind. The trilogy was not exactly le Carré's farewell to Smiley, who is the unifying figure in *The Secret Pilgrim* (1991), something of a literary throwback, but all his other novels since 1980 have broken new ground. *The Little Drummer Girl* (1983) explores the Israeli-Palestinian conflict in considerable depth. *A Perfect Spy* (1986), his most autobiographical novel as well as one of his best, relates the extraordinary English childhood of a spy to his later success as a "perfect" double agent. *The Russia House* (1989) was le Carré's response to the Gorbachev phase of glasnost and perestroika, when the Cold War was ending but the organizations that fought it were still intact, and *The Night Manager* (1993), about the vast business of drug smuggling, was his first reply to the question, Where does the spy novel go after the Cold War? Succeeding novels have provided a variety of answers. In *Our Game* (1995) the complex relationship between two Englishmen formerly engaged in Cold War intelligence leads both of them, hunter and hunted, into the dangerous world of Caucasian religion and politics in the 1990s. Very different is his much-lauded Central American novel, *The Tailor of Panama* (1996), in which machinations and intrigue arise from concern about the future of the Panama Canal. A British Customs intelligence investigation into financial corruption on a vast international scale is central to the fast-moving and action-packed *Single & Single* (1999), which resembles *A Perfect Spy* in being an English father-and-son story while also featuring a prominent Russian mafia family.

—Peter Lewis

LEHANE, DENNIS, (b. 1965), American crime writer known for depicting the gritty underside of urban life—

and the true grit exhibited by characters who live in tightly-knit ethnic neighborhoods. Lehane was raised in Dorchester, Massachusetts, a then Irish Catholic, blue-collar enclave that is part of the city of Boston. The son of a Sears & Roebuck truck driver and a mother who processed foods for the Dorchester schools, he attended St. Margaret's parochial school. By the time he was eight years old, he knew he wanted to become a writer. He graduated from Boston College High School and attended two colleges before settling down in a creative writing program at Eckard College in St. Petersburg, Florida. He also pursued a master's degree at Florida International University in Miami. He returned to Boston in 1993, where he supported his writing by working as a valet and then as a chauffeur for the Ritz hotel. He wrote sections of his first novel, *A Drink Before the War* (1994), behind the wheel of a limosine, while waiting to drive clients to their destinations. The book features Patrick Kenzie and Angela Gennaro, a pair of *private eyes who appeared in four more books before Lehane turned out his "break-out novel," *Mystic River* (2001). Set in the working-class neighborhood of Buckingham—a fictional mix of four Boston neighborhoods—the poignant and powerful novel tells the tale of three boyhood buddies whose lives are linked again in middle age, when the daughter of one is brutally murdered.

—Rosemary Herbert

LEONARD, ELMORE, (b. 1925) leading contemporary American author of realistic crime fiction. He was born on 11 October in New Orleans and raised in Detroit. After service in the navy during World War II, he enrolled at the University of Detroit. Following graduation in 1950, he worked for the next decade as an advertising copywriter. His earliest publications (written in the early mornings before he left for work) were short stories aimed at the western pulp magazines which were still flourishing in the early 1950s. His first five novels were also westerns (as were several original screenplays he wrote). But when the western market began to disappear in the early 1960s, he shifted his attention to contemporary crime fiction, beginning with *The Big Bounce* (1969).

In 1972, after reading George V. *Higgins's *The Friends of Eddie Coyle*, a comic novel about small-time Boston hoodlums narrated largely through dialogue, Leonard began experimenting with new ways of telling his stories. He began relying more heavily on realistic dialogue while limiting the narrative perspective to his increasingly colorful characters. The result of this experiment was *Fifty-Two Pickup* (1974), his first major success as a crime novelist.

In 1978, Leonard was commissioned by the *Detroit News* to write a nonfiction article about the local police. Originally planned as a brief assignment, Leonard's visit with the police eventually lasted for over two months as he found himself fascinated by the colorful parade of characters, criminals and police alike, who passed through the squad room. This experience led to *City Primeval* (1980), his first novel to feature a policeman as protagonist. Four novels quickly followed over the next three years—*Split Images* (1981), *Cat Chaser* (1982), *Stick*, and *LaBrava* (both 1983)—earning him a reputation as a fresh new voice in contemporary crime fiction.

To further enhance the realism of his work, Leonard also began drawing upon the efforts of a part-time researcher. Whether the subject is Atlantic City gambling casinos or the federal witness security program, Leonard's novels provide an authentic behind-the-scenes view along with a richness of detail that heightens their believability.

With the publication of *Glitz* (1985), Leonard's popularity finally caught up with his growing critical reception. Since then, his novels have routinely shot to the best-seller lists while his critical reputation continues to soar.

Rather than employing a single recurring hero, Leonard's novels instead feature a changing cast of memorable characters set against a variety of vividly portrayed urban backgrounds (Detroit, Atlantic City, New Orleans, Miami Beach). His characters range from cops and *judges to thieves, drug dealers, bookies, loan sharks, and assorted killers. However, by intentionally blurring the distinction between the "good guys" and "bad guys," Leonard creates the kind of unpredictable interaction between his characters that produces fast-moving plots filled with unexpected twists. Despite their importance, setting and plot never overshadow character development, which is the hallmark of a Leonard novel. Leonard is particularly skilled at humanizing his villains. He possesses an uncanny ability to mimic the distinctive voices and to get inside the heads of his characters, allowing their quirky thoughts and pungent language to carry the story. The result is an impressive body of fiction (over twenty crime novels to date) that is notable for its richness of detail, comic dialogue, and fascinating variety.

[*See also* Police Detective.]

—David Geherin

LESBIAN CHARACTERS AND PERSPECTIVES.
With a history of being considered a marginal genre and with its emphasis on secrets, detective fiction is particularly suited as a forum for the concerns of lesbian writers. Women writers of traditional detective fiction have presented lesbian characters as part of their densely peopled lists of *victims and suspects. In *Unnatural Death* (1927; *The Dawson Pedigree*), Dorothy L. *Sayers presented Vera Findlater, a nasty villain who hates men and has decided to live with another woman, despite Miss Climpson's hope that eventually a nice man will come along for each of them. Harriet *Vane in *Strong Poison* (1930) has a lesbian friend. Agatha *Christie's Miss Jane *Marple offers Miss Murgatroyd and her companion, Miss Hinchliffe, in *A Murder Is Announced* (1950).

The 1980s saw an explosion of lesbian detectives, as members of the police, private investigators, or inquisi-

tive women were in the right place when crime occurred. Often these detectives are involved with crime directed toward the lesbian and gay communities. In Katherine V. Forrest's *Murder by Tradition* (1991), Kate Delafield recognizes a murder as part of a pattern of gay bashing, and in investigating the murder she is threatened with being revealed as gay, or "outed," in her department.

Claire McNab's Carol Ashton books, set in Sydney, also feature a police inspector whose colleagues support her when she is threatened with being outed. While readers of detective fiction are never surprised when the detective becomes romantically involved with a suspect, Ashton's lack of restraint in *Lessons in Murder* (1988) is shocking. Among the most interesting aspects of the Ashton stories are the dilemmas she sometimes faces, whether in pursuing a straight woman or, in *Dead Certain* (1992), telling her son about her lesbianism.

Penny Sumner's Victoria Cross, introduced in *The End of April* (1992), is a document analyst and *private eye who won't carry a gun or do divorces; this rich, well-written debut includes coming out, pornography, drugs, and gay-bashing issues as well as homophobic college administrators. A strong political message is conveyed in Lauren Wright Douglas's *The Daughters of Artemis* (1991), featuring Caitlin Reece as a lesbian private eye addressing vigilantism and rape. *Keeping Secrets*, Penny Mickelbury's 1994 debut, presents a conflict between police lieutenant Gianna Maglion, head of the Hate Crimes unit in Washington, D.C., and Mimi Patterson, a reporter, over issues of public information involving multiple murders of gays. In the insightful *Long Goodbyes* (1993), Nikki Baker's Virginia Kelly, a lesbian financial analyst in Chicago, confronts the problem of coming out in her middle-class African American family.

In *Murder in the Collective* (1984), Barbara Wilson, cofounder of Seal Press, introduced Pam Nilsen as an amateur sleuth recognizing herself as a lesbian. *The Dog Collar Murders* (1989) is intriguing for its discussion of the pornography debate in the feminist community, especially as it affects lesbians; the rescue of an elderly woman accused of murder is the backdrop for discussions of language theory, European history, and goddess worship in *Trouble in Transylvania* (1993), part of the Cassandra Reilly series.

Probably the most popular lesbian detective in mainstream detective fiction, Lauren Laurano from Sandra Scoppettone's *Everything You Have Is Mine* (1991), enjoys wordplay and wit and is embroiled in familiar detective concerns: helping out a friend with her professional services and looking for *missing persons. Her identity as a lesbian rarely is a strong factor in her work, but her marriage, her partner's gay brother, AIDS, and the gay and lesbian community they live in are important plot elements. Ellen Hart's series featuring Jane Lawless, a Minneapolis restaurateur, is also winning a mainstream audience, although it doesn't dodge issues and even depicts homophobic characters confronting Jane about her lifestyle in *Stage Fright* (1992) and in *Hallowed Murder*

(1989). These novels' lightness of tone often makes the mayhem seem less threatening.

With Lindsay Gordon in *Report for Murder* (1987), Val *McDermid explores the life of a lesbian journalist from Scotland; in *Union Jack* (1993) she writes about homophobia in the media while showing how the passage of ten years has changed it. Laurie R. King's *A Grave Talent* (1993) features Kate Martinelli, an inspector for the San Francisco Police Department who is investigating a series of child murders while facing the problem of a closeted lesbian whose partner wants her to come out.

Other lesbian detectives have various reasons for becoming involved in crime: *Final Session* (1993) by Mary Morell features Lucia Ramos, a lesbian police officer who addresses issues of sexual abuse; Joanna Michaels's *Nun in the Closet* (1994) presents Callie Sinclair, an alcoholic, and the effects of abuse on adult survivors as well as the issue of lesbian nuns; Maria-Antonia Oliver's Lonia Guiu in *Antipodes* (1987), Claudia McKay's Lynn Evans in *The Kali Connection* (1994), and Diana McRae's Eliza Pirex in *All the Muscle You Need* (1988) investigate missing persons while pursuing love interests; Carole Spearin McCauley's bisexual Pauli Golden talks of being a "litmus test" for her lovers as she investigates the murder of one of them in *Cold Steal* (1991). Other writers presenting lesbian heroes or strong lesbian characters, some in international settings, include Elizabeth Bowers, Stella Duffy, Lisa Haddock, Randye London, Mary Logue, Elizabeth Peterzen, Rosie Scott, Carol Schmidt, Jean Taylor, and Pat Welch.

Several mainstream straight women detectives recognize lesbians in their communities, notably in Sara *Paretsky's *Killing Orders* (1985), Martina Navratilova and Liz Nickles's *The Total Zone* (1994), McDermid's Kate Brannigan series, and Patricia D. *Cornwell's *All That Remains* (1992) and *The Body Farm* (1994). In *Final Option* (1994), Gini Hartzmark depicts a character's lesbianism negatively, as evidence of her instability.

Lesbian detective fiction enables writers to engage in open and sympathetic political discussion of lesbian concerns and to depict lesbian romance as much as detection plots. Moreover, in this fiction, readers explore the implicit boundaries of mainstream life and the deceptions that keep them in place. In *The Case of the Not-So-Nice Nurse* (1991), for example, Mabel Maney reminds us just how compulsory the heterosexuality of the 1950s was, offering a vivid contrast to the sensitive exploration of self and sexuality possible today.

[*See also* Gay Characters and Perspectives.]

—Georgia Rhoades

LININGTON, ELIZABETH (1921–1988), American author of some eighty novels, most written in the police procedural, multi-storyline tradition. Born in Aurora, Illinois, she settled in California where, in addition to achieving her prolific output as a novelist under her own name and the pseudonyms Anne Blaisdell, Lesley Egan,

Egan O'Neill, and Dell Shannon, she was a right-wing political activist, principally for the John Birch Society.

She is the author of three series. Her first, written as Dell Shannon, is her most long-running and successful, incorporating thirty-eight books published over twenty-seven years. It features Luis Mendoza of the Los Angeles Police Department. When he was first introduced in *Case Pending* (1960), Mendoza was a relatively rare example of a Mexican American protagonist in this genre. His relationships with his fellow police officers and his personal life are developed throughout the series.

Under her own name, Linington created Sergeant Ivor Maddox and other members of the Hollywood Police Department in a thirteen-book series that also features the capable policewoman Sue Carstairs (later Maddox). Beginning with *Greenmask!* (1964) this series uses domestic detail and the details of the characters' romantic lives as a counterpoint to crime-solving. As Lesley Egan she created two occasionally overlapping series focusing on Jesse Falkenstein, a lawyer, and Vic Verallo, a policeman, and the crimes that each encounters.

Overall the moral imperative in this author's work is strong. There is a clear opposition of good and evil and a marked sensitivity to the suffering endured by the *victims of crime. While she makes a deliberate effort to deglamorize police work and to deal with the realities of urban life, Linington's style is not a bluesy vernacular. In fact, even when dealing with the grimmest details, she exercises a kind of constraint (not to be confused with prudishness) that makes hers a memorable delivery of the details of police procedure.

[*See also* Police Detective.]

—Frankie Y. Bailey

Lovejoy, forger and "divvy"—one who can divine the authenticity of antiques. Created by Jonathan *Gash, Lovejoy first appears in *The Judas Pair* (1977), where he becomes memorable for use of colorful slang, tips about the identification and care of antiques, and eye for nubile women. These characteristics remain constants in a series of books that show Lovejoy exposing—and often participating in—scams and heists centered around different types of antique items ranging from oil paintings and fine furniture to nipple jewels. Narrated in the first person by the scruffy and frequently penniless Lovejoy, the action is fast-paced and often humorous. The opening lines of *Firefly Gadroon* (1982) are typical: "This story begins where I did something illegal, had two rows with women, and got a police warning, all before midafternoon. After that it got worse, but that's the antiques game for you. Trouble."

[*See also* Con Artist, Eccentrics.]

—Rosemary Herbert

LOVESEY, PETER (HARMER) (b. 1936), English author of witty historical mysteries, contemporary crime novels, mystery short stories, sports history, television plays and, under the pseudonym Peter Lear, three non-

mystery novels. Born in Whitton, Middlesex, he was educated at Hampton Grammar School and the University of Reading, before he served as education officer in the Royal Air Force. He taught English literature and worked as an educational administrator before becoming a full-time writer in 1975.

Lovesey penned his first novel, *Wobble to Death* (1970) as writing contest entry. Introducing series characters Sergeant Cribb and Constable Thackeray, the novel is centered on the quirky Victorian endurance walk known as a wobble. The success of this book led Lovesey to explore additional Victorian passions in seven more novels featuring Cribb and Thackeray, including the highly humorous *Swing, Swing Together* (1976), in which the author has three suspicious characters imitate the trio in Jerome K. Jerome's *Three Men in a Boat* (1889).

Lovesey looked at twentieth-century crime and high jinks in *The False Inspector Dew: A Murder Mystery Set Aboard the S.S. Mauretania, 1921* (1982). Keystone (1983), *Rough Cider* (1986), and *On the Edge* (1989) are also set in the twentieth century. Then, beginning with *Bertie and the Tinman: From the Memoirs of King Edward VII* (1987), Lovesey launched another series, in which a fictionalized Albert Edward "Bertie," Prince of Wales solves mysteries set in Victorian high society. In 1993, Lovesey introduced yet another series *sleuth, murder squad detective Peter Diamond of Bath, England, in *The Last Detective*. Diamond's character is deepened in *Diamond Dust* (2002), a novel in which he investigates the murder of his wife. Lovesey is also known as a writer of short stories memorable for the depiction of human foibles that lead individuals to perpetrate crimes.

—Rosemary Herbert

Lugg, Magersfontein. Created by Margery *Allingham, Magersfontein Lugg is Albert *Campion's unorthodox manservant and assistant in detection. Lugg's first name commemorates a British victory in the Boer War; his surname defines his work and hints at his lugubrious nature. Though a former cat burglar once sentenced to Borstal (a reform institution for youth), he now moves like a circus elephant and has a large white face. A Cockney with a rich, eccentric utterance, he is by turns a valet, heavy, underworld expert, and nanny. He has served as a bohemian butler and pig-keeping air-raid warden, faced near-death at the hands of the Kepesake murderer, and survived a pretentious spate of self-improvement when a peerage loomed for his employer. He is Campion's sense of humor.

[*See also* Sidekicks and Sleuthing Teams.]

—Susan Oleksiw

Lupin, Arsène. A *gentleman thief created by French writer Maurice *Leblanc in the short story *L'Arrestation d'Arsène Lupin* (in the magazine *Je sais tout*, 1905), Arsène Lupin is the hero of fourteen novels and five collections of short stories as well as several plays and radio dramas by Maurice Leblanc (some of them in collaboration with other writers).

Born in 1874, Arsène Lupin is the son of Mademoiselle d'Andrésy and of Théophraste Lupin, a boxing teacher and crook who was jailed and who died in the United States. His vocation as a burglar begins early: At the age of six, he steals the famous Queen Marie-Antoinette necklace in order to avenge his mother for the humiliations inflicted by her family. In him the thief is always partly a dispenser of justice.

Grown up, he practices burglary as an art, with gallantry. He attacks the rich, stealing their purses, their jewelry, their works of art, and sometimes their secrets, too, with inventive and virtuoso plans; he is also very keen to amuse the public, and never wastes an opportunity to have his feats celebrated in the press, or to duel with his adversaries: Herlock Sholmès, Isidore Beautrelet, l'Inspecteur Ganimard.

Lupin is also a consummate actor, able to juggle his many identities: Horace Velmont, Don Luis Perenna, Prince Paul Sernine, Jim Barnett, or, more paradoxically, Victor Hautin, Inspecteur de la Brigade Mondaine, or Monsieur Lenormand, Chef de la Sûreté. Last, but not least, he is a great seducer and a great lover, terribly sentimental. Many of his adventures deal with historic secrets, such as the secret of the kings of France exposed in *L'Aiguille creuse* (1909; The Hollow Needle).

In the 1970s, Pierre Boileau and Thomas Narcejac imagined a continuation of Arsène Lupin's adventures in *Le secret d'Eunerville* and other works.

—Jacques Baudou

M

MacDONALD, JOHN D(ANN) (1916–1986), American writer, born in Sharon, Pennsylvania. His seventy-plus novels and over five hundred short stories range from "straight" novels, science fiction, and fantasy to his preferred subject, crime.

MacDonald's career tracks one of the major developments in mid-twentieth-century American crime and mystery fiction. Beginning in the 1920s, when publications such as *Black Mask* began to present the innovative treatments of crime written by the hard-boiled school, pulp magazines served as a venue of choice for authors of the naturalistic tales of private investigators in a tough world. Although the most successful among these writers often drew upon their pulp stories to craft full-length novels, the pages of the pulp magazines continued through the 1930s and 1940s to provide writers the space for experimentation and the opportunity for speedy publication. The growing popularity of paperback books changed that. In the 1950s, Fawcett Gold Medal and other imprints entered the market, peddling books written for original paperback publication, priced at a cost only slightly higher than the older pulps.

MacDonald became an established writer at that historic moment. Educated at Syracuse University, where he completed a B.S. in 1938, and Harvard University (M.B.A., 1939), he served with the Office of Strategic Services during World War II. Following the war, he wrote pseudonymously and under his own name for pulp magazines, but ended his apprenticeship with the publication of his first paperback original novel for Fawcett, *The Brass Cupcake* (1950).

His work culminated in the enormously popular Travis *McGee series, in which earlier themes, attitudes, concerns, and ideals find memorable expression. MacDonald excels at characterization, and much of the series's popularity stems from McGee's complexity: an unofficial *private eye, an honest *con artist who swindles the swindlers. Leading a sybaritic existence aboard his houseboat *The Busted Flush* in Fort Lauderdale, Florida, he serves as a court of last resort for those who have been cheated by the wealthy and powerful, who seem beyond the reach of legality. Calling himself a "Salvage Consultant," McGee takes fifty percent of what he recovers.

MacDonald showed McGee's relationship to the rough hard-boiled detective tradition by depicting him as a man of great size, quickness, and strength who is a formidable opponent in a fight. His active sex life is viewed by author and character as therapeutic for McGee's female partners. It also involves considerable soul-searching, expressions of affection, and honest self-

doubt. With his introspection and his preference for using his wits rather than his brawn whenever possible, McGee displays qualities similar to Ross *Macdonald's sleuth Lew *Archer and Robert B. *Parker's *Spenser.

McGee's economist friend Meyer, who lives on a nearby houseboat, occasionally becomes co-protagonist of the novels. Meyer's engaging personality, expertise in business and finance (reflecting MacDonald's M.B.A.), professional contacts, and perceptive insights make him an ideal sidekick.

The McGee novels are serious, penetrating exposés and analyses (with sermonic asides by McGee) of important social issues. The abuses that lust for money and power may engender underlie all the plots, which explore subjects such as corruption in business and government, environmental depredation, the dissolution of purpose and meaning in modern life, and the vagaries of personal relationships.

Thematically and technically MacDonald did not discover new ground for detective fiction, but he did explore the established territory with a skill that helped to bring some matters to the forefront of popular consciousness. Starting with Junior Allen in the first McGee book, *The Deep Blue Goodbye* (1964), MacDonald portrayed the now chillingly familiar type, the sadistic psychopath. An even greater service is MacDonald's early and repeated commentary on environmental destruction. The nonseries book *A Flash of Green* (1962) describes efforts to save a bay from developers, while the McGee series extends environmental concern in passages such as the two-page, scientifically accurate lecture on the ways we have ravaged the Everglades (*Bright Orange for the Shroud*, 1965) and the account of harbor pollution in Pago Pago (*The Turquoise Lament*, 1973).

After two decades of producing paperback originals which, despite their great popularity, seldom were promoted or reviewed like mysteries in hardcover, MacDonald became a crossover author. The phenomenon of paperback originals had passed, but this stalwart author survived the loss and began to publish steadily with firms who issued his books as part of their preferred list of A-line mysteries, thus completing a career that epitomizes the fortunes of hard-boiled writing both in terms of the art of fiction and the currents of publishing history.

[*See also* Serial Killers and Mass Murderers; Sidekicks and Sleuthing Teams.]

—Donald C. Wall

MacDONALD PHILIP (1899–1981), British author of detective novels, who also wrote as Martin Porlock,

Oliver Fleming, and Anthony Lawless. After collaborating on two books with his father Ronald, Philip MacDonald created Colonel Anthony Ruthven *Gethryn in *The Rasp* (1924). Gethryn was a conventional upperclass Englishman, but several novels in which he appeared, such as *The Choice* (1931; *The Polferry Riddle*, *The Polferry Mystery*), had plots which were ingenious and extraordinary even by Golden Age standards. *Murder Gone Mad* (1931) and *X v. Rex* (1933; *Mystery of the Dead Police*, *The Mystery of Mr. X*, published under the name Martin Porlock in the United Kingdom) were fascinating nonseries novels. MacDonald moved to Hollywood in 1931 and he collaborated on the screenplay of *Rebecca* (1940). He also wrote short stories, three of which featured the seer-detective Dr. Alcazar. After a long absence, Gethryn returned in MacDonald's last novel, *The List of Adrian Messenger* (1959), an unorthodox mystery which became a gimmicky but entertaining film.

—Martin Edwards

MacDONALD, ROSS, is the pseudonym of Kenneth Millar (1915–1983), who is the Canadian-American author widely credited, along with Dashiell *Hammett and Raymond *Chandler, with elevating hard-boiled fiction to the status of literature.

"We never forgive our childhood. What makes a novelist is the inability to forget his childhood," Macdonald said in 1974. Poised uneasily between these imperatives, Macdonald's considerable body of work ponders at length the possibility and necessity of escaping an often terrifying past. So thoroughly do his fiction and life intertwine that consideration of Macdonald's writing properly begins with his origin.

Born in Los Gatos, California, Kenneth Millar spent his childhood scuttling across Canada, living on the charity of relatives with his impoverished mother. His father had abandoned them when the boy was three, in quest of a series of wild fantasies that he pursued until his death in 1932. Millar later recalled that he had lived in fifty different rooms by the age of sixteen. At six he was nearly placed in an orphanage, a narrow escape he would remember all his life. Yet the pain of these years fired his imagination: *Oliver Twist* was an early favorite of his, and Charles *Dickens's own difficult childhood furnished constant inspiration. He also took Dickens as his model of the democratic artist whom the critics respected but the masses could read. As an adult Millar reread F. Scott Fitzgerald's *The Great Gatsby* (1925) annually and repeatedly introduced Gatsbyesque figures into his novels, usually depicting them with a pained understanding that honors the quality of their dreaming but attends to the devastation they wreak.

He attended college on the proceeds from his father's dying bequest, then married and began graduate school at the University of Michigan, where he studied European literature under W. H. Auden. Encouraged by Auden's love of mysteries and by the quick success of his wife, Margaret *Millar, in the field, he turned out his first novel in only one month. Discharged from the navy in 1946, he settled in Santa Barbara, California, with his wife and began to write in earnest. His next three novels did not so much develop a voice as pay homage to Hammett and Graham *Greene, but flashes of incisive characterization and sociological acuity hinted at what was to come.

With *The Moving Target* (1949) he began to explore his major themes. Published under the name "John Macdonald"—in memory of his father, John Macdonald Millar—it was the first novel to feature the *private eye Lew *Archer. After protest from John D. MacDonald, Millar wrote as John Ross Macdonald and, after 1956, Ross Macdonald, though his identity was revealed on the cover of *Find a Victim* (1954). For Macdonald nothing was clear-cut. As Archer explains in his first appearance, "Evil isn't so simple. Everybody has it in him, and whether it comes out in his actions depends on a number of things. Environment, opportunity, economic pressure, a piece of bad luck, a wrong friend."

Family tragedy stimulated Macdonald's art; further pain forced its maturity. Shattered by his daughter Linda's arrest for vehicular homicide as well as "seismic disturbances" rising from his past, in 1956 Macdonald suffered a breakdown and spent a year in psychoanalysis. Both of his succeeding novels, *The Doomsters* (1958) and *The Galton Case* (1959), probe tormented families to discover roots of present trauma in the betrayal of children by parents and suggest that the worst violence is that which individuals inflict on themselves. Archer becomes less interested in meting out justice than in simply listening to and understanding others.

In *The Galton Case* Macdonald rewrote his own youth along Oedipal lines: A young man who is stolen from his parents' estate and raised in poverty eventually regains his true birthright. Over the next decade he turned out a succession of classic novels that worked repeated variations on the theme of troubled children fleeing and coming to terms with damaging pasts. His plots, generally of Byzantine complexity, drive down the mean streets of every subdivision in suburban southern California, sympathizing with both puzzled adults and angry children poisoned by "a kind of moral DDT" bequeathed by parents whose dreams have gone irrevocably sour. Concurrently, ecology and the ruin of the environment, which he had touched on as early as *The Drowning Pool* (1950), became a major theme in *The Underground Man* (1971) and *Sleeping Beauty* (1973).

From the first, Macdonald won the admiration of critics in the mystery field, particularly his longtime friend and supporter Anthony *Boucher. In the early sixties he began to attract academic attention. Paul Newman's *Harper* (1967), the film version of *The Moving Target* (which was released in England under the book title), made him wealthy, but the real break came in

1969, when the front page of the *New York Times Book Review,* carrying a review by Eudora Welty, proclaimed his work "the finest series of detective novels ever written by an American."

—Jesse Berrett

MACLEOD, CHARLOTTE (MATILDA HUGHES)

(b. 1922), Canadian-born writer of cozy mysteries under the Macleod name and pseudonyms. Born in Bath, New Brunswick, Canada, she was educated at public schools in Weymouth, Massachusetts and at the Art Institute of Boston before beginning a career in the Boston advertising firm, N.H. Miller. She became a full-time writer in 1982. Macleod is a naturalized American citizen.

Macleod has written books for teens and children, but she is much better known for four series of light comic mysteries that depend upon interactions of memorable pairs and other continuing characters for humor, which is often brought out in witty dialogue. Under the Macleod name, she introduced Sarah Kelling and the extended Kelling family in *The Family Vault* (1979). It quickly becomes clear that the Kellings are a clan of *eccentrics, most of whom who are denizens of Boston's posh Beacon Hill neighborhood. In books that succeed as romantic comedies as well as mysteries, Kelling's love life is recounted as she is courted by married to Max Bittersohn, an art expert with a penchant for nabbing thieves. Also as Macleod, the author created agriculture Professor Peter Shandy, of Balaclava Agricultural College. Shandy first appears in *Rest You Merry* (1979), a Christmas mystery in which the professor meets his future wife, Helen. In this series crime and highly humorous high jinks always occur hand-in-hand, as is the case when a prize hog is held hostage in *The Luck Runs Out* (1979).

Writing as Alisa Craig, the author created two more series. Beginning with *A Pint of Murder* (1980), one series is centered around the work of *Royal Canadian Mounted Police detective Madoc Rhys, who solves cases in New Brunswick, Canada. In 1981, she launched another high-spirited series with *The Grub and Stakers Move a Mountain,* in which a gardening club called The Grub and Stakers cultivates a passion for solving crime. As Craig, she also wrote a non-series mystery, *The Terrible Tide* (1983). Macleod also wrote *Had She But Known: A Biography of Mary Roberts Rinehart* (1994) and edited two anthologies of holiday-related detective stories, *Mistletoe Mysteries* (1989) and *Christmas Stalkings* (1991).

[*See also* Amateur Detective.]

—Rosemary Herbert

Maigret, Inspector Jules, the creation of Georges *Simenon, quiet, plodding "mender of destinies" and *commissaire* of the Paris police. He appeared in more than

seventy novels and over two dozen short stories. Maigret does not solve crimes by making logical deductions based on shrewd observation, but rather by his patience and ability to understand human nature. He is described as tall and bulky, but otherwise no details of his facial features are given.

Jules-Amédée-François Maigret was born in central France, near Moulins, his grandfather a tenant farmer. His mother died when he was eight years old. A few years later Maigret became a medical student at the Collège de Nantes but quit school on the death of his father. He joined the police force and rose in the ranks from bicycle patrolman to homicide detective. Such details are found in *La première enquête de Maigret* (1949; Maigret's First Case) and *Les mémoires de Maigret* (1951; Maigret's Memoirs).

Throughout the original French series Maigret is promoted in his profession, but the books were translated out of sequence and a reading in English in the original published sequence can be confusing. Different 1963 English translations of three 1931 titles render his title as inspector, chief inspector, and superintendent. In *Une confidence de Maigret* (1959; Maigret Has Doubts) he is a *commissaire,* or superintendent, while in *Maigret aux Assises* (1961; Maigret in Court) he has been promoted to *commissaire divisionnaire,* translated as divisional chief inspector.

His wife, Madame Louise Maigret, is introduced in the final chapter of the first book written, *Pietr-le-Letton* (1931; The Strange Case of Peter the Lett; Maigret and the Enigmatic Lett), and shares an apartment with him in the Boulevard Richard-Lenoir. It is to Madame Maigret that her husband imparts his thoughts on difficult cases; in later years their social group includes Dr. and Mrs. Pardon. That apartment and the office in the Quai des Orfèvres, with the office stove valiantly keeping off the chill, have become as familiar to readers as Baker Street. Maigret is seldom without his pipe and on his desk in his office he keeps a selection of several pipes. The pipe, his bowler hat, and his overcoat are recognizable to every follower of the series. Maigret's colleagues Coméliau, the examining magistrate, and his assistants Lucas, Janvier, and Lapointe comprise his official family. Another one of these assistants, Torrence, was killed in *Pietr-le-Letton* in 1931, but later resurrected because Simenon forgot the details of the earlier story.

The Maigret stories fall into two distinct groups: those published between 1931 and 1934, when he retires, and the remainder, in which he returns without reference to retirement, published between 1942 and 1972. For many readers, the earlier books filled with atmosphere and character are superior to the rambling later ones. Others prefer the dark complex vision of the world in the later novels to the relatively simple, uncomplicated early period. By the final novel, *Maigret et Monsieur Charles* (1972; Maigret and Monsieur Charles) the *commissaire* is offered the position of head of the Police Judiciaire, but he is more interested in contemplating his real retirement.

—J. Randolph Cox

Marlowe, Philip. Raymond *Chandler's Philip Marlowe is one of the most persistently interesting detectives in the history of mystery literature. Arguably the most famous hard-boiled *private eye, Marlowe is thirty-three years old in *The Big Sleep* (1939), the first of his seven appearances, and forty-two nineteen years later in his last (*Playback*, 1958); in between he appears in *Farewell, My Lovely* (1940), *The High Window* (1942), *The Lady in the Lake* (1943), *The Little Sister* (1949), and *The Long Goodbye* (1954).

He is ruggedly attractive at just under 6'1" and 190 pounds, with brown hair and eyes; he has no siblings, his parents are dead, and he has no close living relatives. Born in 1906 in Santa Clara, California, he attended a state university in Oregon before drifting to southern California where he became an investigator, first for an insurance agency and then for the district attorney of Los Angeles County, a position he lost for being insubordinate. At this point he went into business on his own.

In the hard-boiled private eye tradition that he helped to shape, Marlowe is single, talks tough, and delivers memorable wisecracks. He is celebrated for his deftness with figurative language, especially similes, as when he says in *The Big Sleep* (1939) of an enfeebled old man that "a few locks of dry hair clung to his scalp, like wild flowers fighting for life on a bare rock." If Marlowe too often overindulges his appetite for metaphor, this is consistent with his character: He smokes and drinks excessively too. His cigarette of choice is a Camel, which he fires up with kitchen matches snicked to life with his thumbnail, and he also smokes pipes in his more contemplative moods. Although he dislikes sweet drinks, he will eagerly—and frequently—imbibe almost any other alcoholic beverage. He has the private eye's obligatory bottle in the office drawer and drinks from it alone or with clients; at home he is often a solitary drinker.

Marlowe's primary points of reference—his office and apartment—are predictably anonymous. His place of business occupies a room and a half on the sixth floor of an office building, and is furnished institutionally: a few chairs, a commercial calendar on the wall, a squeaky swivel chair behind a glass-top desk, and five green metal filing cabinets, "three of them full of California climate." He has no partner, secretary, or referral service, underscoring his independence, his professional marginality, and his rejection of middle-class values.

If Marlowe's office provides him with a link to the workaday world, such is seldom the case with his apartment. A sixth-floor efficiency, Marlowe's apartment complements his office and reflects the spareness of his existence; he has a radio, a few books and pictures, a chess set, and some old letters containing his memories. It may not be much, but it is a refuge from the tawdry, threatening world outside.

Although he has a network of professional associates, Marlowe has no friends; nor, until the end of his career, does he have a love interest. He entertains himself by listening to classical music, going to movies, and pondering chess problems. He is, in the tradition of American heroes, a loner.

Marlowe's modus operandi is pragmatic—he follows his nose, often bruising it and other parts of his anatomy in the process. He doesn't use snitches or hobnob with *underworld figures. He would never be mistaken for a ratiocinator like Sherlock *Holmes or Hercule *Poirot: although he moves about energetically, he observes, questions, listens, and waits for the truth to find him.

Marlowe's name is an amalgam of literary reference to Sir Philip Sidney, Christopher Marlowe, and the Marlow who occupies the moral center of several of Joseph Conrad's tales. Chandler originally intended to name his detective Mallory, alluding to Sir Thomas Malory whose chivalric romance, *Le morte d'Arthur* (1485), simultaneously dramatizes the heroic deeds of the Arthurian knights and portrays the less glamorous side of knighthood. Indeed, Marlowe is often a knightly hero. He places himself in the service of others; he is honest, brave, self-effacing, stoic, and witty in the face of danger; he resists temptations (except alcohol use) and constantly risks his life in pursuit of justice and truth. His code is his character.

Marlowe is not perfect, to be sure. He harbors many of the prejudices of his age, notably racism and homophobia. Because he decries homosexuality yet is reluctant to sleep with women, it has been suggested that Marlowe is himself a homosexual. Perhaps in response, Chandler involved Marlowe in two casual sexual encounters in *Playback* and planned to marry him off in *Poodle Springs*, an unfinished novel.

It could be argued that Marlowe's character changed over time. Surely he developed a greater tolerance for evil by the end of the series and became wearier and more disillusioned. Still, he is the best man in Chandler's world—"and a good enough man for any world," as Chandler puts it in "The Simple Art of Murder" (*Atlantic Monthly*, Dec. 1944).

[*See also* Hard-Boiled Sleuth; Independent Sleuth; Private Detective.]

—David Rife

MARON, MARGARET (b. 19??) American writer of two mystery series, one featuring the Manhattan policewoman Lieutenant Sigrid Harald and the other centered on cases investigated by the North Carolina attorney Deborah Knott. Born in Greensboro, North Carolina, Maron was raised on her family's farm near Raleigh, where she lives today. She has also lived in Brooklyn, New York, and taught at Hunter College in Manhattan. Maron was educated at the University of North Carolina, on the Greensboro and Charlotte campuses.

Introduced in *One Coffee With* (1981), Harald is a self-consciously feminist police lieutenant keen on living up to the promotion she has been granted. When she finds herself attracted to art Professor Oscar Naumann, she is not at first comfortable with revealing the femininity that she believes she must conceal to succeed in a man's world. As the series progresses, Harald learns to take more risks emotionally. Not coincidentally, at the same time, she slowly uncovers information about her late father, a policeman who was killed before she got to know him. While the books featuring Harald have devoted fans, critics agree that Maron's second series, which features Knott, is superior. The series begins with the 1992 novel, *Bootlegger's Daughter*. Here, first-person narration, a southern rhythm to the words and the powerfully-drawn setting in the author's native rural North Carolina lend a sense that the author is profoundly at home in this series. Knott, who faces challenges as she solves cases and strives to become a *judge, is more comfortable with herself than Harald, making her a more appealing character.

[*See also* Lawyer; Police Detective.]

—Rosemary Herbert

Marple, Miss Jane an *amateur detective and *genteel woman sleuth created by Agatha *Christie, first appeared in short stories in the late 1920s. Christie did not perceive her as a rival to Hercule *Poirot, but in the end Miss Marple was featured in twelve novels and twenty stories. She became the quintessential detective of the cozy mystery.

Introduced at sixty-five to seventy years old, Miss Marple could only live to a great age. In *At Bertram's Hotel* (1965) she looks a hundred and throughout the Canon her great age is stressed. Her hair is white, her face sweet, placid, pink, and crinkled; her china blue eyes appear innocent. She flutters and twitters, and her hands are often occupied with knitting. In her old-fashioned clothes she is every inch a lady. Indeed her childhood, apart from some education in Italy, was spent in a cathedral close. She has high-ranking and aristocratic relatives, and her circle of acquaintances is large. Gardening is among her chief interests. She helps with Girl Guides and serves on an orphanage committee. Cultural pursuits are not important to her: In London she prefers shopping to visiting galleries or museums, although she likes the outdated artists Charles-Blair Leighton and Sir Lawrence Alma-Tadema. Other than a preference for devotional books for late-night reading in bed and film magazines for research, she exhibits little interest in literature; she has a good literary background, however— she understands the significance of the John Webster quotation in *Sleeping Murder* (1976).

All in all, Miss Marple seems a very unlikely investigator of crime, but her background, appearance, and age are no handicap; instead, they camouflage her detective abilities and agile mind. Police officers who encounter her are amazed at her shrewd mind, adjectives used by Inspector Curry in *They Do It with Mirrors* (1952; *Murder with Mirrors*) and Inspector Neele in *A Pocketful of Rye* (1953), among others. Mr. Rafiel describes her as conscientious and as having a logical mind in *A Caribbean Mystery* (1964). Her friend Sir Henry Clithering, formerly of Scotland Yard, marvels that her mind can plumb the depths of human iniquity, and do it merely as part of a day's work, in *The Body in the Library* (1942).

The secret of her success lies in her English village background, with its network of gossiping ladies and servants. St. Mary Mead seems to be a tranquil, conservative place—Marple's nephew Raymond West calls it a stagnant pool. His aunt, however, observes that nothing is so full of life under a microscope as a drop of water from a stagnant pool. Her years of observing village life, sometimes with binoculars, have thus given her an understanding of human nature and behavior on which to base deductions in her crime cases. She always believes the worst because she has seen so much evil in villages. Her own hobbies, usually gardening, sometimes provide clues.

St. Mary Mead itself is the setting for crimes in three novels and many of the stories, but thanks to her network of friends and her nephew's generosity, Marple is able to travel and thus use her skills elsewhere. Strange locations do not intimidate her; she merely draws comparisons with people and situations she has previously encountered. In two cases she is forced to rely on information fed to her by associates, in *4:50 from Paddington* (1957; *What Mrs. McGillicuddy Saw!*) and *The Mirror Crack'd from Side to Side* (1962; *The Mirror Crack'd*). In the latter book she is confined to her house because of old age and illness, and bitterly regrets her inability to tend her garden. When the book was published Christie herself was seventy-two and beginning to chafe against the constraints imposed by age. Yet despite her frailness, Marple went on to solve three more cases, even facing physical danger in *Nemesis* (1971).

[*See also* Elderly Sleuth; Spinster Sleuth.]

—Christine R. Simpson

MARRIC, J. J. *See* Creasey, John.

MARSH, (EDITH) NGAIO (1895–1982), New Zealand author and theater director; one of the "Queens of Crime" in the British Golden Age. She established herself firmly in the classical tradition of the English detective novel with her first book, *A Man Lay Dead* (1934), written during her first visit to England. Trained as a painter at Canterbury College School of Art in Christchurch, where she was born, she continued to paint and sketch all her life, but by the 1930s she had begun to realize that her greatest talent lay with words, not in paint.

Her background was not wealthy (her English-born father was a bank clerk), but her parents valued education and the arts and as an only child her talents were cherished. From her mother came a great love of the theater, and the whole family were enthusiastic amateur actors. Marsh went on to become a formative influence on the development of theater in New Zealand, and it is for this work, not for her writing, that she is best remembered in New Zealand today.

Marsh claimed that her first novel was swiftly written in imitation of existing popular styles, but she soon began to develop an individual approach which was very much character-led: "I invariably start with people. . . . I must involve one of them in a crime of violence. . . . I have to ask myself which of these persons is capable to such a crime, what form it would take and under what circumstances would he or she commit it." By carefully building and defining her characters, she attained high praise in the United States in the 1940s for the psychological depth of her fiction. As with all crime writers who focus on characterization rather than relying on intricate turns of the plot to hold the reader, Marsh was sometimes in danger of conflicting with the accepted restrictions of the genre, and of reluctantly introducing tidy solutions which jar with the complexity of her created world.

She increasingly found her life divided between two very different spheres of operation. At home in New Zealand she would lock herself away to write her novels, then work with huge energy to produce plays by William *Shakespeare with young actors from Canterbury University College. On her regular visits to England, always traveling by ocean liner, she would stay with her aristocratic English friends who lived in country houses in the Home Counties or in fashionable flats in London. Somewhat to her surprise Marsh found herself feted in the United States (she made one visit in 1962) and in England as a detective novelist. She had been awarded the OBE in 1948, and in 1966 was created Dame Commander of the British Empire (in her words, "her damery").

The services of Inspector Roderick *Alleyn, Marsh's series detective, are retained throughout all thirty-two novels—"I've never got tired of the old boy," she said—and the author passes on to him her love of theater and an ability to quote Shakespeare. Whether there is wish fulfillment in creating his wife Agatha Troy as a painter is hard to say, but Marsh herself retained her independence and never married, remaining a private person all her life who seldom revealed her feelings to any but her very close friends.

The novels of Marsh fall naturally into four thematic categories, but even these overlap slightly. Many are set in comfortable country houses in small English villages not far from London: *Death and the Dancing Footman* (1941), one of her most popular books, is an example. Some deal with the world of the theater; Marsh had a particularly acute ear for the repartee of actors, revealing both their pretensions and their insecurities, as in *Killer Dolphin* (1966; *Death at the Dolphin*). The role of Troy dictates the plot in several novels, where commissions to paint famous people such as the African politician in *Black as He's Painted* (1974) can unexpectedly lead to the involvement of Alleyn in solving a violent crime. Finally,

Marsh's love for the landscape of New Zealand emerges strongly in the four novels set in her native country, but undoubtedly the most ingenious is *Colour Scheme*, written in 1943, which uses a boiling mud pool as a murder weapon.

The achievement of Marsh will always be associated with the elegance of her writing, her wit, and her painterly ability to evoke a scene. Admired during her lifetime for her skill at extending the confines of the classical form without losing its definition, she is appreciated by a new generation who respond to her sharp observation of social structures and the freshness of her invention.

—Margaret Lewis

MASON, A(LFRED) E(DWARD) W(OODLEY)

(1865–1948), British author of detective, historical, and adventure novels, short mystery and espionage fiction, crime and courtroom drama. London-born, Oxford-educated, Mason began his career as an actor and playwright. His experiences as a Liberal Party member of Parliament for Coventry (1906–10) and an operative in British naval intelligence during World War I resulted in a political novel, *The Turnstile* (1912), and short stories of espionage. His best-selling work was a nonmystery, *The Four Feathers* (1902), and he also wrote a biography of Francis Drake and a stage history. His best-known character, Sûreté Inspector *Hanaud, debuted in *At the Villa Rose* (1910). In the tradition of Wilkie *Collins, Mason employs varying points of view, especially those of the innocent and threatened, to inspire fear. He deromanticizes the detective, draws characters from his experience, and never repeats his ingenious plots.

[*See also* Police Detective.]

—Michael Cohen

Mason, Perry lawyer-detective hero in extremely popular novels by Erle Stanley *Gardner. He first appeared in *The Case of the Velvet Claws* (1933), which was followed by eighty-five other novels (five of them published posthumously), a number of short stories, and two authorized novels by Thomas Chastain published in 1989 and 1990. The continued popularity of his exploits was doubtless enhanced by eight films in the 1930s, a radio program in the 1940s, and especially the popular television series, starring Raymond Burr, which played for nine seasons (1957–66) and lives on in reruns. The series was reprised in twenty-six television movies that appeared at irregular intervals from 1985 until Burr's death in 1993.

The novels are simply written (most of them dictated) and contain a good deal of dialogue. While they all adhere to the same formula, they are fast-moving, often with extremely complicated plots and a number of surprises along the way. Mason practices law in Los Angeles, where he is assisted by his able and attractive secretary, Della Street, and Paul Drake, the head of a detective agency. Perry typically uses a number of quasi-legal tricks to protect his clients or establish their innocence, often moving them around from one address to another to escape the police, to the constant annoyance of Lieutenant Tragg of the Los Angeles Police Department. Drake and Street are constantly warning Perry Mason that he is "skating on thin ice," but he is not deterred. He maintains that his tactics are within the letter if not the spirit of the law, and they change as the law of the land changes. It is in the courtroom, however, when his client stands trial, that Perry proves his or her innocence after a display of legal pyrotechnics that exasperates the district attorney, Hamilton Burger, and trips up the killer on the witness stand.

[See also Judge; Jury; Sidekicks and Sleuthing Teams.]

—Henry Kratz

MASTER CRIMINAL. The threatening figure of the master criminal, or the criminal mastermind, has been prominent in crime writing since the late nineteenth century, often embodying the motiveless principle of evil which the virtuous protagonist has to combat and to overcome. In more simple allegoric forms, the master criminal is evil incarnate. His confrontation with the hero represents a stylized form of the constant fight between the forces of good and evil in the world—witness the conflict between Superman and Lex Luthor, or between Batman and the Joker, the Penguin, and Catwoman, or between James Bond and Ernst Stavro Blofeld. These quasi-allegoric forms retain a residual presence in a great deal of crime and spy writing—the evil in the Erskine Childers's The Riddle of the Sands (1903) or in John Buchan's stories may be conspiratorial rather than individualized, but there is always the sense of some unidentified and invisible hand orchestrating the mayhem. However, in the more strictly generic forms of crime writing, the master criminal may share similarities with the hero, whatever his differences with the readership, as he so clearly does in Fantômas (1911) by Pierre Souvestre and Marcel Allain.

In the Sherlock *Holmes stories, the *Great Detective faces a number of powerful adversaries, including Irene *Adler and Charles Augustus Milverton, but his archenemy is the evil Professor James *Moriarty, "the Napoleon of crime." Author of a brilliant treatise on the binomial theorem at the age of twenty-one, and renowned throughout Europe as a mathematician, the ex-Professor Moriarty has devilish cunning. He also posesses an insatiable appetite for evil, but it is suggested that he is at least a worthy opponent for the equally gifted detective, and at the moment of Holmes's death at the Reichenbach Falls, described in "The Final Problem" (Strand, Dec. 1893), he is symbolically entangled with his greatest adversary. No less brilliant than Moriarty, Holmes's intelligence is at the service of justice where his opposite number's does tremendous harm by stealth, and the conflict between the two extravagantly gifted figures greatly intensifies the drama of the tales.

Holmes and Moriarty may be equals in their gifts, but later versions of the master criminal do not put him alongside a commensurate adversary. In the highly melodramatic *Fu Manchu tales by Sax *Rohmer (pseudonym of Arthur Sarsfield Ward), written between 1913 and 1959, the evil mastermind has diabolical plans to rule the world, and his opponents are at first no more (and no less) than fairly ordinary citizens, personified by the dogged Nayland Smith, the Burmese commissioner. In his earliest appearances, Fu Manchu represents the "yellow peril," the xenophobically constructed Oriental plot to conquer the West. In later appearances, he changes sides, if not colors, and takes on the fight against the "red menace" of Communist China, proving himself even wilier than before, as well as versatile in his capacity to create or allay anxieties. The Fu Manchu stories are extremely lurid and sadistic, as well as shoddily written, and it is hard to take them seriously now.

Two other variants on the theme of the master criminal need to be mentioned. In Ed *McBain's Eighty-seventh Precinct series of police procedurals, the carefully crafted urban realism is suspended in some stories by the appearance of an arch-villain called "the Deaf Man." This character haunts the life of Steve Carella and his fellow cops by committing the most awful crimes and disappearing without a trace. He makes his first appearance in The Heckler (1960), and reappears in Fuzz (1968) and in Let's Hear it for the Deaf Man (1973). His longevity and continuing vitality are on display in Mischief (1993), in which he orchestrates a particularly violent caper. The use of this master criminal seems incongruous in McBain's otherwise scrupulously realistic technique, but the enigmatic nature of the central character makes it surprisingly successful.

The final version of the master criminal comes from the notion of organized crime. In many stories about the Mafia, or Cosa Nostra, individual figures are brought to the fore as the principal custodians of evil in contemporary society. The best example of this is the patriarchal Don Corleone in Mario Puzo's The Godfather (1969), who presides over his own criminal empire. Puzo's novel is profoundly ironic, in that it paints Corleone as both the master criminal and the most responsible of citizens, representing a belief in family and in loyalty which lie at the heart of American ideology. Corleone does not exhibit the diabolic ingenuity of Moriarty, the grotesqueness of Fu Manchu, or the motiveless malignity of the Deaf Man, but in his stealthy organization of society around his criminal aims, he stands for the most modern and plausible version of the master criminal.

[See also Underworld Figure; Villains and Villainy.]

—Ian Bell

MATSUMOTO SEICHŌ, pseudonym of Matsumoto Kiyoharu (1909–1992), Japanese novelist. Born to working-class parents in Kokura city on the island of Kyūshū, Seichō worked odd jobs after finishing middle school; during and after World War II, he designed advertisements for the *Asahi* newspaper. His literary career blossomed only in 1952, when his *"Aru Kokura nikki den"* (1952; A Story of the Kokura Diary) won the prestigious Akutagawa Prize. By the mid-1950s he had turned to crime literature, rejecting what he called the "haunted-house" contrivances of prewar Japanese mysteries in favor of the painstaking study of motive and, above all, the critical portrayal of contemporary society. In his typical 1957 best-seller *Ten to sen* (*Points and Lines*, 1970), detectives break the alibis of a businessman and a powerful bureaucrat whose scheme to conceal a bribery scandal involves killing an ordinary waitress. Seichō's injection of anti-establishment consciousness into the crime novel won it unprecedented popularity with the general reader in Japan. Besides his dozens of mysteries, he wrote historical fiction, science fiction, history, and criticism. *Suna no utsuwa* (1960-61) has been translated as *Inspector Imanishi Investigates* (1989). *The Voice and Other Stories* (1989) contains some of his shorter fiction.

—Mark Silver

Mayo, Asey, protagonist in a series of twenty-four books published between 1931 and 1951, and an archetypal American *amateur detective. A scion of Mayflower stock, Mayo lives on Cape Cod in Wellfleet, Massachusetts, where his creator Phoebe Atwood *Taylor maintained a summer cottage. A jack of all trades—mechanic, carpenter, and seafaring man of the world—he relies on common sense and Yankee ingenuity to solve cases that are masterpieces of comic mystery. His personal history is ambiguous, since he seems to have engaged in secret work during World War I but once claimed to have spent the war years peeling potatoes. It is known, however, that he went to sea at age eight; sailed on the last of the clipper ships; drove a Porter automobile coast to coast in 1899; and tested racing cars at Daytona Beach in 1904. During a brief stint as police constable in Wellfleet he solved two murders, but decided to quit while he was ahead—a typical Taylor irony, given his subsequent career as a famous *sleuth, frequently pictured in rotogravures and labeled the "Codfish Sherlock." Of indeterminate age, he is described as tall, thin, tough, tanned, and rugged, with twinkling blue eyes. Dressed in corduroys, a flannel shirt, and either a Stetson or a yachting cap, he is comfortable in any company.

—Mary Helen Becker

MAYOR, ARCHER (HUNTINGTON) (b. 1950), American author who brings to his crime writing direct experience as town constable of Newfane, Vermont, as his state's assistant medical examiner, and as volunteer fireman and emergency medical technician. Born in Mt. Kisco, New York, he was the son of a businessman who moved the family frequently due to job requirements. He lived in so many international venues that his parents feared he would lose his English language skills and sent him to a boarding Suffield Academy in Suffield, Con-

necticut, before he went on to earn a Bachelor's degree in United States history at Yale University. Before taking on the above-mentioned jobs, he worked as an editor of scholarly books, stage photographer, lab technician and photo editor for the French magazine *Paris-Match,* and as a journalist and author of two history books. Like his father, Mayor let his employment take him to many places before he settled in Newfane, Vermont, at age 30.

In 1988, Mayor introduced his series sleuth, Lieutenant Joe Gunther of the Brattleboro, Vermont, police department, in *Open Season.* Working with a plot that looks at the troubles that ensue after a jury with provincial attitudes convicts a black man and outsider of a sex-murder, the book establishes the author's flair for description of the New England scene and for advancing the plot through dialogue. The police procedure here is well anchored in the details of daily life in Brattleboro, a small city that is a large place by Vermont standards. At times it is a place with big-city problems, such as the home invasion by Asian gang members that is at the heart of *The Dark Root* (1995). Gunther leaves his Brattleboro turf for an even smaller place in *Borderlines* (1990), when he looks at a cult group that has bought up much of the real estate in the town of Gannett near the United States/Canada border. In *The Skeleton's Knee* (1993) he visits Chicago to follow-up on a case of a skeleton with a metal knee found buried on Vermont land owned by a hermit with a mysterious past.

As is typical of mysteries written in the 1980s and onward, Mayor's work depicts the protagonist's personal relationships. The ups and downs of Gunther's interactions with his lover, Gail Zigman, sometimes form subplots to the policeman's activities. For examples, in *Borderlines,* he his eager to take on the North Country investigation, since he has had a falling-out with Zigman, and in *Fruits of the Poisonous Tree* (1994) he deals with his emotional reaction to her rape while seeking to bring her attacker to justice. The series is narrated in the first person by Gunther until Mayor employs a third-person voice in *The Sniper's Wife* (2002). Although Gunther plays a role in this book, the novel focuses on Gunther's subordinate, Willy Kunkle, a one-armed, troubled police officer whose life becomes even darker when his wife is killed in new York City.

[*See also* Police Detective.]

—Rosemary Herbert

McBAIN, ED (b. 1926), pseudonym of Evan Hunter, American author of police procedurals and other crime fiction. Although he maintains "The city in these pages is imaginary," he has used New York City, where he was born, raised, and educated, as a model setting for the forty-plus novels in his Eighty-seventh Precinct series another Series featuring *lawyer Matthew Hope is set in Florida. After writing for pulp magazines he achieved success with *The Blackboard Jungle* (1954), based in part upon his experiences teaching in a Bronx high school. Under his legal name of Evan Hunter he has written sixteen more novels and screenplays. He has been named a Grand Master by the Mystery Writers of America.

Cop Hater (1956) was his first police procedural. Although he was determined to have as his hero the entire detective squad, Steve Carella quickly emerged as the chief player in McBain's ensemble approach to character and action. Other mainstays include Lieutenant Peter Byrnes, Meyer Meyer, Cotton Hawes, Bert Kling, Arthur Brown, Andy Parker, Hal Willis, and Eileen Burke.

Carella confronts many villains but has one nemesis as sinister and as indestructible as Sherlock *Holmes's Professor James *Moriarty: the Deaf Man, who appears in several books.

McBain says he conceives of each Eighty-seventh Precinct novel as a chapter in one long book. He plans for these chapters to appear even after his own death.

Despite detours into political satire in *Hail to the Chief* (1973) and the supernatural in *Ghosts* (1980), McBain concentrates on the day-to-day operation of the justice system. A stickler about the details of police work, he often lightens descriptions of routine with touches of humor. He learned the routine by visiting station houses, jails, and labs and continues to keep current on procedures and forensic science. For example, his detectives no longer attend lineups. Sam Grossman, head of the police lab, usually explains scientific advances during telephone conversations with Carella.

About half the novels have a single dominant plot, but others are built on multiple story lines, which may or may not be related. Only the coincidence in timing ties them together. In *'Til Death* (1959) the apparent single plot bifurcates at the end. In *Hail, Hail, the Gang's All Here!* (1971) each detective pursues his own case.

Lean prose and crackling dialogue propel the Precinct and Hope books, although in the Hunter novels the style varies with the subject. One of McBain's trademarks is the insertion into the text of visuals, such as police forms or handwritten notes.

[*See also* Police Detective.]

—John D. Stevens

McCLURE, JAMES (b. 1939), British writer born in Johannesburg, South Africa, and educated in Pietermaritzburg. McClure worked as a photographer, teacher, and reporter before emigrating with his family to England. He has worked for newspapers in Scotland and England. Inspired by Ed *McBain and Chester *Himes, McClure turned to the police procedural to explore the world of and relationship between Afrikaner lieutenant Tromp *Kramer and his Zulu sergeant Mickey Zondi. With his first book, *Steam Pig* (1971), McClure began a painful but honest depiction of life in South Africa. Kramer and Zondi trust and respect each other, but under the crippling rule of apartheid they must hide their friendship and alter their public behavior. The crimes they investigate arise out of the distortions of South African society: A white family is reclassified as Cape Coloured in *The Steam Pig;* the racist activities of a young boy lead

to his murder in *The Caterpillar Cop* (1972); and a government spy is murdered in *The Gooseberry Fool* (1974). The ugly experience of life under apartheid is tempered with humor and compassion. McClure has also written a thriller and two nonfiction studies of police in Liverpool and San Diego.

[*See also* Ethnic Sleuth; Police Detective; Sidekicks and Sleuthing Teams.]

—Susan Oleksiw

McCRUMB, SHARYN (ARWOOD) (b. 1948), American writer known for comic mysteries, science fictional capers, and the more contemplative "Ballad" series of crime novels set in Appalachia. McCrumb was born in Wilmington, North Carolina, and educated at the University of North Carolina, Chapel Hill and at Virginia Tech. She is married and has three children.

Beginning with *Sick of Shadows* (1984), McCrumb's first mystery series centers on Elizabeth MacPherson and her many relatives. As the series progresses, McCrumb humourously chronicles the progress of MacPherson's education, career as a forensic anthropologist and marriage. McCrumb launched her science fictional mysteries with *Bimbos of the Death Sun* (1988), a parody set in a fan convention called the Rubicon, where two professors fret over securing tenure at their universities, fall in love, and solve a crime. They appear again in *Zombies of the Gene Pool* (1992), to solve a crime and find a time capsule put together by science fiction writers of the 1950s. McCrumb's critically-acclaimed "Ballad series is so called because the titles of the books are drawn from traditional music. The first book, *If Ever I Return Pretty Peggy-O* (1990), introduces Sheriff Spenser Arrowood and sets the underlying pattern of linking current conundrums with personal and social history for the series. McCrumb's work has deepened over the years as she has worked with increasingly complex plots, themes, and characters.

—Rosemary Herbert

McDERMID, VAL (b. 1955), journalist, playwright and crime writer, best-known to mystery readers as creator of the lesbian *journalist sleuth Lindsay Gordon, the Manchester, England-based private eye Kate Brannigan, and policewoman Carol Jordan. Born in Kircaldy, Scotland, McDermid was raised in a working-class household until she left for St. Hilda's College, Oxford, where she earned a bachelor's degree in English language and literature. After graduating in 1975, she became a journalist, writing over the years for a number of publications including a tabloid newspaper called *The People*, the *Scottish Daily Record*, the *Tatler* and the *Sunday Independent*. She also did work for the National Union of Journalists. McDermid's dramatic works include *Like a Happy Ending* and a childrens' play, *Beyond the Black Hole*.

In her first mystery novel, *Report for Murder* (1987), Gordon's feature assignment turns into a murder investigation when a famous cellist is strangled. It established

McDermid's reputation for writing openly about the gay subculture by portraying her characters' professional and personal lives. In fact, personal connections drive Gordon to solve crimes in a few of the books. In *Common Murder* (1989), for instance, Gordon is assigned to cover a demonstration by protestors at the Brownlow Common missile base only to find that her former lover has been arrested there. A former lover has been convicted of murder in *Final Edition* (1991; *Open and Shut*, 1991) while in *Union Jack* (1993), Gordon herself is the chief suspect in a murder investigation. In the 1992 novel, *Dead Beat*, McDermid introduced Brannigan as a partner in Mortensen and Brannigan, a private investigation firm in Manchester. In that book, a missing person's case becomes a murder investigation. In *Kick Back* (1993: *Kickback*, 1993) Brannigan investigates real estate fraud. In these and other books featuring Brannigan, the lifestyles portrayed and cases solved are more conventional than those shown in the novels featuring Gordon.

In 1995, McDermid broke into new territory again, this time into the world of the psychological thriller, with *The Mermaid Singing*. In this novel, McDermid introduces policewoman Jordan, and Tony Hill, an expert in criminal profiling. The duo appears in *The Wire in the Blood* (1998) and in the *Last Temptation* (2002). McDermid's *A Place of Execution* (1999), is a thriller introducing George Bennett, a police inspector in the English dales who recounts his investigation of a decades-old murder to a journalist, until new information plunges him into profound doubts.

[*See also* Lesbian Characters and Perspectives.]

—Rosemary Herbert

McGARRITY, MARK. *See* Gill, Bartholomew.

McGee, Travis, hero in a series of twenty-one mystery novels written by John D. *MacDonald. A self-described beach bum, McGee lives aboard *The Busted Flush*, a fifty-two-foot houseboat moored at Slip F-18, Bahia Mar, Fort Lauderdale, Florida. McGee is not a professional detective but what he terms a "salvage expert": He retrieves valuable lost items for friends and keeps half of what he recovers.

What ordinarily prompts McGee to abandon his pleasurable retirement aboard his boat is not the promise of reward but a quixotic sense of knight-errantry. McGee rushes to the defense of the defenseless (especially if they are beautiful women) and risks his life for his clients, all while struggling to adhere to a personal code of moral behavior.

McGee is also a knowledgeable man who (along with economist buddy Meyer) imparts fascinating tidbits of information on a wide array of subjects. MacDonald routinely employs McGee as a vehicle for expounding his views on social issues, especially those related to the destruction of the environment of his beloved Florida.

McGee's comfortable lifestyle excites escapist fantasies while his courage and bravery earn admiration. Add

to this his insistence upon proper moral behavior, and he exemplifies the virtues of both living well and doing right.

—David Geherin

McNEILE, H(ERMAN) C(YRIL) (1888–1937), short story writer and novelist; he used the pseudonym Sapper in his native Britain. He served in the Royal Engineers during the First World War and was awarded the Military Cross. His pseudonym was suggested by Lord Northcliffe, proprietor of the *Daily Mail*, in which the author's war stories appeared. Described by a reviewer as "far more terrible than anything Kipling or Stephen Crane or Tolstoy or Zola ever imagined," these stories were collected as *The Lieutenant and Others* (1915) and *Sergeant Michael Cassidy, R. E.* (1915; *Michael Cassidy, Sergeant*). Each collection sold over 200,000 copies in a year. Equally successful were Sapper's postwar works. The series of novels, for which he is best known, in which the hero is Captain Hugh "Bulldog" *Drummond (the first of which is *Bull-Dog Drummond: The Adventures of a Demobilized Officer Who Found Peace Dull*, 1920); and the novels and short stories with Ronald Standish—sometimes a detective, sometimes a secret service agent—or the adventurer Jim Maitland as hero. Gerard Fairlie (1899–1983), an officer in the Scots Guards and noted amateur boxer, on whom Drummond was modeled, and who continued the series after McNeile's death, quotes (in *With Prejudice: Almost an Autobiography*, 1952) the latter, a fanatical golfer, as likening the perfect short story to "the perfect iron shot." Certainly the best short stories ("The Man in Ratcatcher," for example, in *The Man in Ratcatcher and Other Stories*, 1921) are technically excellent—McNeile's favorite authors were Guy de Maupassant, Ambrose Bierce, and O. Henry (whose stories he edited)—and superior to the novels, which suffer from repetitious plot elements. Though, as a popular writer, Sapper has few equals for exciting narration, his work, with its reactionary political views, anti-Semitism, and curious blend of chivalry and brutality, belongs to the interwar years and is scarcely acceptable to the modern reader.

—T. J. Binyon

Medical Sleuth. The popularity of the medical *sleuth dates from the opening of the twentieth century, a time, not incidentally, of growing fascination with science and the scientific view of life. In many ways the medical detective seems an ideal choice for a sleuth, given his or her precise knowledge of the physical world. The medical sleuth has grown and changed since then, but writers have returned to this template time and again.

R. Austin *Freeman created the definitive medical sleuth in Dr. John Evelyn *Thorndyke, who first appears in *The Red Thumb Mark* (1907). Thorndyke, qualified in both medicine and law, lectures on medical jurisprudence at a London teaching hospital. He is an expert in the examination of cadavers and fragmentary human remains, demonstrating in *The Eye of Osiris* (1911; *The Vanishing Man*) that a supposed Egyptian mummy is the *corpse of a recent murder *victim, and identifying the traces of cumulative arsenic poisoning in a lock of hair from a dead girl in *As a Thief in the Night* (1928). Unlike many contemporary sleuths, Thorndyke is on good terms with the police and respects the work of his assistants. He is entirely professional, even distant, with clients. Although this can make for dry characterization, the best stories are absorbing cases of material clues.

Among later writers who continued the pattern established by Freeman is Lawrence G. Blochman. His detective, Dr. Daniel Webster Coffee, a pathologist at a hospital in a fictional midwestern city, uses recondite knowledge and skilled laboratory work to solve crimes in numerous short stories and one novel, *Recipe for Homicide* (1952). Another rigorous approach to criminal pathology is found in Patricia D. *Cornwell's Dr. Kay *Scarpetta, chief medical examiner for the Commonwealth of Virginia. In her first appearance (*Postmortem*, 1990), Scarpetta battles institutional sexism while assembling the forensic evidence necessary to find a serial killer.

Not all scientific detectives demonstrate or rely on true scientific reasoning. H. C. *Bailey's Reggie *Fortune, a London physician and surgeon and a special adviser to the CID, demonstrates little medical knowledge. In *The Shadow on the Wall* (1934), Fortune attends a Buckingham Palace garden party and then proceeds to Lady Rosnay's ball, where he encounters attempted murder. Throughout these mannered writings Fortune is more of a socialite and talented *amateur detective than a doctor. Margaret Scherf's Dr. Grace Severance is a retired pathologist who relies more on intuition than on expert knowledge; in *To Cache a Millionaire* (1972), she investigates the disappearance in Las Vegas of a fictional counterpart of Howard Hughes. Jonathan Stagge's Dr. Hugh Westlake is a general practitioner in a small Pennsylvania town who correctly suspects murder behind inexplicable or apparently supernatural occurrences. *Turn of the Table* (1940; *Funeral for Five*) includes a seance in which a murder is accurately predicted as well as a killer who may be a vampire.

Many writers turned to the psychologist as sleuth and found here greater scope for character development within the range of scientific worlds. Gladys *Mitchell's Mrs. Beatrice Adela Lestrange *Bradley is a psychiatric consultant to the British Home Office in a long series beginning with *Speedy Death* (1929) and reaching a peak in the author's favorite, *The Rising of the Moon* (1945), a vivid, atmospheric work in which the narrator is a thirteen-year-old boy with knowledge of a serial killer. The psyche of the child becomes central in the unflinching, sometimes harrowing novels of Jonathan *Kellerman. His series investigator is Dr. Alex Delaware, a child psychologist in Los Angeles, who usually works with police detective Milo Sturgis. In *Private Eyes* (1991), Delaware is drawn back into the traumatic life of a teenage

girl who had been his patient nine years before. In some cases the professional title can be little more than costuming. Professor Henry Poggioli appears in stories by T. S. Stribling, some of which are collected as *Clues of the Caribees* (1929). Although he has a degree in medicine and teaches psychology at Ohio State University, the whimsical Poggioli generally solves crimes by applying skepticism to the deceptively exotic.

A major advantage of the medical sleuth is that the doctor remains a respected figure whose dispassionate view commands the trust of the reader. The doctor can go anywhere and ask almost anything without raising suspicion; he or she has almost as much freedom as a police officer. J. B. Priestley used this figure to advantage in *Salt Is Leaving* (1966). Dr. Salt, an unconventional, restless widower who has been working in general practice in a grim English Midlands town, delays his departure in order to investigate the disappearance of a young woman patient. Ignoring obscure threats and the indifference of the local police, he uncovers a domineering industrialist's family secrets, including a bizarre murder, and finds a new wife for himself. C. F. Roe's Dr. Jean Montrose seems fully occupied by her general practice in Perth, Scotland, and by the demands of her family, but is sometimes consulted on questionable and suspicious deaths by Detective Inspector Douglas Niven. *Death by Fire* (1990) finds her investigating an apparently authentic case of spontaneous human combustion complicated by the possibility of supernatural intervention. Roe's novels, with their regional flavor and realistic portrayal of a physician integrated into the daily life of a small community, suggest the continuing viability of the medical sleuth.

[*See also* Coroner.]

—Christopher Bentley

MENACING CHARACTERS. The long-standing practice whereby detective fiction puzzles distance the crime from its solution leaves little room for representing characters with an evil mien, since one of the intended effects of closed circle stories is to present crime as an unusual intrusion into stable or commonplace life. When writers take a contrary view of society, however, seeing it as disorderly and unfortunately hospitable to crime, characters with an aura of menace about them become highly functional.

The memorable radio drama of the 1940s "Sorry, Wrong Number" features the harassment of a bedridden woman by the repeated ringing of her telephone by an anonymous caller preying on her condition of solitude. Although the caller is faceless, genderless, and voiceless, his or her messageless signals are sufficient to suggest that beyond the *victim's bedroom lies not a mundane world but one that poses threatening violence. In this case the villain is nothing more than menace adumbrated. By contrast, menace takes on the particulars and traits of the antagonist who challenges the detective protagonist in such stories of serial killers as Lawrence Sanders's *The Second Deadly Sin* (1977), with the result that the two figures assume roles as champions of the light and darkness of the world.

The works of Robert Bloch and Jim *Thompson extend the use of menacing characters to the point that they create the diametrically opposite world to that of classic puzzle stories. Bloch's *The Scarf* (1947), *The Kidnapper* (1954), and the renowned *Psycho* (1959) all produce fictional realms where peril and danger are the norm, because the narrative leads are taken by psychopaths. Thompson elevates the sense of menace even further by using disturbed, deeply sick narrators to relate the stories in *The Killer Inside Me* (1952), *Savage Night* (1953), *After Dark, My Sweet* (1955), and *Pop. 1280* (1964). The deceptively ordinary but actually dysfunctional narrators of Thompson's books include such characters as a police officer and a hit man whose occupations have something to do directly with crime, but who are also megalomaniacs, alcoholics, and certifiably distressed souls. Collectively they populate an environment beyond reason and predictability.

While the entrance of a menacing character into crime fiction generally signals that an uncommon side to pedestrian reality is to be revealed, the character does not necessarily remake the fictional world of the short story or novel in his or her image. Sherlock *Holmes's nemesis Professor James *Moriarty and Dr. Grimesby Roylott, the *villain in "The Adventure of the Speckled Band" (*Strand* Feb. 1892), challenge the Great Detective without destroying the optimistic expectation that the narratives will show order restored by application of the eccentric detective's brilliant method. Menace is contained in another fashion in such thrillers as Eric Ambler's *The Mask of Dimitrios* (1939; *A Coffin for Dimitrios*) where the eponymous character is found by the detective writer Charles Latimer to typify the sordid reality of Europe on the eve of war without the revelation's obliterating the humanistic values that form the source of Latimer's, and the reader's, shock.

Even writers of hard-boiled fiction will make use of characters who serve to signify the presence of base motives yet whose menacing aspects are softened by a mannered veneer. Caspar Gutman, his armed bodyguard Joel Cairo, and Brigid O'Shaughnessy in Dashiell *Hammett's *The Maltese Falcon* (1930) typify this sort of balanced use of menacing characters.

[*See also* Master Criminal; Underworld Figure.]
—John M. Reilly

Merrivale, Sir Henry, series character created John Dickson *Carr Writing as Carter Dickson. Better known as "H. M." or "the Old Man," from 1934 to 1955 he appeared in twenty-two detective novels and one novelette, all of them requiring him to solve locked room mysteries or other impossible crimes. He is in his sixties, and his features—big belly, bald head, wrinkled face, small eyes behind tortoise-shell glasses—are those of a bespectacled Buddha. He expresses his opposition to af-

fectation and artificiality in many ways, including favoring a rather shabby mode of dress, displaying a predilection for risqué books and movies, and communicating in phrases of his own coinage. A composite of several people, including Winston Churchill and Carr himself, H. M. is variously described as barrister and physician, as Britain's chief of intelligence and the former head of espionage, even as a lifelong, energetic socialist, a connection that Carr drops in the late 1930s. Through this character, Carr attacks pretense, provides humor, and connects H. M.'s love for games with his abilities as a detective who solves the case by determining the murderer's motive.

[*See also* Eccentrics.]
—Dale Salwak

MERTZ, BARBARA. *See* Peters, Elizabeth.

MICHAELS, BARBARA, *See* Peters, Elizabeth.

Millhone, Kinsey. Introduced in the 1982 novel *"A" Is for Alibi* by American author Sue *Grafton, Kinsey Millhone is one of the earliest female private investigators in the hard-boiled tradition. In Millhone's first nine appearances in the alphabetically titled series, Grafton's *private eye operates in the tradition of the *sleuth as loner. Orphaned at age five, Millhone is twice divorced and lives simply and on her own. Millhone is slow to establish intimate connections despite genuine affection for her elderly landlord, Henry Pitts, and the owner of her favorite bar. However, in *"J" Is for Judgment* (1993), Grafton introduces Millhone's previously unknown relatives, inevitably changing both the future course of the novels and the construction of her detective.

Grafton sets up her character plausibly. A former police officer, Millhone has experienced sex discrimination firsthand. An independent private investigator, she often questions her motives, methods, and successes. She typically wisecracks her way through confrontations, usually winning the verbal battles. She is also physically tough: she runs, engages in target practice, and continually tests herself; but she also gets attacked, shot at, and beaten. Still, she describes her job as methodical and routine, comparing it to women's typical work. In *"B" Is for Burglar* (1985), she notes that "there's no place in a p.i.'s life for impatience, faintheartedness, or sloppiness. I understand the same qualifications apply for housewives" (even though Millhone eschews housework).

The cases which Grafton details through Millhone's first-person narration, like those of Ross *Macdonald's Lew *Archer, tend to focus upon the past. In *"A" Is for Alibi*, Millhone reopens a murder case when a convicted killer, newly released from prison, hires her. A seventeen-year-old murder draws her into *"F" Is for Fugitive* (1989); in *"I" Is for Innocent* (1992), she takes over a murdered colleague's reinvestigation of the Isabelle Barney case. In *"G" Is for Gumshoe*, Millhone finds herself threatened by a killer she had fingered. Despite significant evidence of the shortcomings of the traditional legal/police system, Millhone persists in believing in its efficacy. Although many of her cases arise from errors perpetrated by the legal system, she typically hands over the criminals she has uncovered to the legal establishment.

The novels in which Millhone appears are told in a straightforward manner. Grafton uses an opening prologue in which her *sleuth reintroduces herself to the reader as though in a report to a client. As of *"F" Is for Fugitive*, Grafton occasionally drops the epilogue that she had used in the earlier novels, with its formal closing, "Respectfully submitted, Kinsey Millhone."

[See also Hard-Boiled Sleuth.]

—Kathleen Gregory Klein

MILLAR, MARGARET (ELLIS STURM) (1915–1994) was born in Ontario, Canada, and educated in Canada before she met and married Kenneth Millar, who later gained fame writing as Ross Macdonald. She wrote her first mystery novel while convalescing from a heart ailment and soon became known for her psychological development of characters and talent for evoking uneasiness, exemplified in her novel *A Stranger in My Grave* (1960).

Millar's first three novels—*The Invisible Worm* (1941), *The Weak-Eyed Bat* (1942), and *The Devil Loves Me* (1942)—were novels of manners. They featured a *sleuth, lightly patterned after such Golden Age characters as Philo *Vance, to whom Millar assigned the profession of psychiatrist and amusingly named Dr. Paul Prye. She continued the practice of using a dominant sleuth to preside over the narrative in two subsequent novels presenting Inspector Sands of the Toronto Police Department—*Wall of Eyes* (1943) and *The Iron Gates* (1945). The more significant change represented by the Inspector Sands stories, however, was Millar's modernization of conventions of the Gothic novel for the serious purpose of investigating human psychology. Description of the workings of the mind—illusions and deceptions, latent influences on behavior, and apparent deviance—became such a compelling interest to Millar that she replaced the sleuth at the center of her narratives with strongly plotted accounts of eruptions from the depths of the unconscious: a stunning example of dual personality in *Beast in View* (1955); the story of a woman who first dreams about, and then sees her own grave in *A Stranger in My Grave* (1960); the distortions of personality created by the stress of past associations in a present setting of a religious cult in *How Like an Angel* (1962); and the indeterminacy of mental illness in *The Fiend* (1964).

In her later work Millar revived the use of a dominant sleuth for a series of novels about Tom Aragon, who searches for a missing husband in *Ask for Me Tomorrow* (1976), a young retarded woman in *Mermaid* (1982), and the solution to the mystery surrounding a wealthy widow in *The Murder of Miranda* (1979).

The observation that Margaret Millar was married to Kenneth Millar (i.e., Ross *Macdonald) is included in most critical comment on her work, as is the remark that both writers probed the complexity of family relationships in a Freudian manner. More to the point, however, is the fact that Margaret Millar placed her own personal signature upon the mystery genre with a skillful handling of narrative atmosphere that conveys a profound sense that the ultimate mysteries are mental.

—John M. Reilly

MISSING PERSONS. A missing person is one who has disappeared for a specified period of time, and is not presumed to have died by murder or accident. The causes for the disappearance are various, and the incident may shade into a number of crimes: murder, kidnapping, espionage, blackmail, and so on. The theme of the missing person is prominent in detective fiction, perhaps because the fear of being lost, never to see family or home again, is one of childhood's worst. Reports of missing persons, ships, or aircraft are extensively covered in newspapers, and often serve as the basis for crime fiction.

The missing person theme appears in one of the earliest detective stories, Edgar Allan *Poe's "The Mystery of Marie Roget" (*Snowden's Lady's Companion*, Nov. 2, 1842), which is based on the real-life disappearance of the beautiful cigar-store clerk Mary Rogers. In Poe's story, the young Marie Roget disappears for a week, returns amid much speculation about what might have happened to her, then disappears a second time, about five months later; she is finally found drowned in the Seine. The suspense created by the disappearance and reappearance makes the theme attractive to all subgenres of crime fiction. In William Irish's haunting work *Phantom Lady* (1942), a man searches for a mysterious woman in an orange hat, whose testimony alone can save his friend from the electric chair; she is a woman whom witnesses say does not exist. In the police procedural *So Long as You Both Shall Live* (1976) by Ed *McBain, a policeman's bride becomes a missing person on her wedding night. There is a military police background in *The Third Man, and The Fallen Idol* (1950; *The Third Man*) by Graham *Greene; Rollo Martins, a second-rate writer, goes to visit his friend Harry Lime in post–World War II Vienna, but Lime dies in a car accident before Martins arrives. Soon Martins begins to question what he knows about his dead friend, and to search for the third man at the accident scene, who disappeared immediately afterward. In Robert Bloch's thriller *Psycho* (1959), a woman looks for a girl last seen heading out of town with someone else's money. Lawrence *Block's private eye Matt *Scudder hunts for a missing New York actress in *Out on the Cutting Edge* (1989). F. R. Buckley uses the theme in a historical adventure, "Of a Vanishment" (*Adventure*, Mar. 1930), in which a Renaissance duke disappears from the midst of his troops at the moment of victory.

The missing person plot may encourage a greater emphasis on surprise endings. The killer in Jonathan Latimer's rowdy novel *The Lady in the Morgue* (1936), for example, steals a *corpse to prevent its identification and the inevitable revelation of the killer. Writers also often use the theme to explore contemporary social problems: lonely hearts columns and the people they attract in *Loves Music, Loves to Dance* (1991) by Mary Higgins *Clark; child sex rings in *Bump in the Night* (1988) by Isabelle Holland; drug rings in *The Bohemian Connection* (1985) by Susan Dunlap; antiques rackets in *Pearlhanger* (1985) by Jonathan *Gash.

The missing person device may be one element in a bizarre or fantastic crime. In Herbert Brean's *Wilders Walk Away* (1948) an entire family disappears, and in Edmund *Crispin's *The Moving Toyshop* (1946) a poet steps into an open toyshop, discovers the body of an elderly woman, gets hit on the head, and awakes in a closet; he escapes and returns with the police, but the toyshop is gone.

The missing person plot has produced a subgenre of its own: stories based on real people and ships, for example, that disappear without a trace. Arthur Conan *Doyle's short story "J. Habakuk Jephson's Statement" (in the *Cornhill Magazine*, Jan. 1884) offered a solution to the mystery of the brig *Mary Celeste*, which was found drifting off the Azores in 1872 with no trace of captain or crew. Mary Roberts *Rinehart's novella "The Buckled Bag," in *Mary Roberts Rinehart's Crime Book* (1933) was based on two cases, the disappearance of Elizabeth Canning in London in 1753 and that of heiress Dorothy Arnold on a wintry day in New York in 1910. Josephine *Tey's *The Franchise Affair* (1948) is a modern retelling of the Canning case. Karen Campbell, a former stewardess, based her novel *Suddenly in the Air* (1969; *The Brocken Spectre*) on the real losses of two Tudor IV airliners, in 1948 and 1949. In the novel, a plane loaded with gold is flying the South Atlantic route over which another gold-carrying plane had disappeared only a year earlier.

—Frank D. McSherry, Jr.

MITCHELL, GLADYS (MAUDE WINIFRED)

(1901–1983) was a British author in the classical school. Born in Oxfordshire, Mitchell attended the University of London and University College, London, receiving a degree in history in 1926; she enjoyed a long career as a secondary school teacher. Mitchell's novels are more striking and idiosyncratic than the term "classical" would suggest; they often contain an element of spoof or satire as well as accommodating the untoward, ambiguous, or unaccountable, giving them a unique flavor. Indeed, some are constructed on the thicket principle in detective writing with complications abounding, leading the odd commentator to take the playful author to task.

In her first novel, *Speedy Death* (1929), Mitchell introduces her sleuth, Mrs. (later Dame) Beatrice Adela

Lestrange *Bradley, an elderly psychologist who consults for the Home Office. Unlike the typical sleuth, Bradley is not physically attractive, often holds questionable moral positions, and is not above committing murder. Fascinated by myth, folklore, and the occult, Mitchell often packs her stories with supernatural monsters as in *Winking at the Brim* (1974) or witchcraft as *Tom Brown's Body* (1949). Several novels including *The Saltmarsh Murders* (1932), feature vivid descriptions of place. Others describe corners of working life, such as pig farming in *Spotted Hemlock* (1958).

[*See also* Elderly Sleuth.]

—Patricia Craig

MOODY, SUSAN (ELIZABETH HORWOOD) (b.

1940), English mystery writer best-known as the creator of two series characters, Penny Wanawake and Cassie Swann. Born Susan Elizabeth Horwood in Oxford, England, she is the daughter of an Oxford don and the sister of the writer Michael Horwood. She was educated at Oxford High School for Girls and at the Open University. Married twice, she is the mother of three sons. With her first husband, she lived in Tennessee for ten years. She has worked as an assistant to an orchid grower in France, taught creative writing at H.M. Prison, Bedford, England, and served as vice chair of the Crime Writers Association.

She introduced her first series character, Penny Wanawake, in *Penny Black* (1984). The six-foot-tall, 126-pound black woman is a larger—and slimmer—than life figure with an aristocratic background that gives her entrée into upper crust mileus. The daughter of Senegaland's ambassador to the United Nations and a titled English lady, Wanawake possesses impeccable breeding, and excellent education, a lavish all-white wardrobe, strings of pearls—and a sassy, superior attitude. She is also a skilled photographer. Lovers are hers for the taking, although she sometimes lives with Barnaby Midas, who gained his "education" at Eton, and in Parkhurst Prison, where he was briefly incarcerated as a thief.

With the *Takeout Double* (1993; *Death Takes a Hand*), Moody introduced the expert bridge player, Cassie Swann. She appears in a series of novels titled after plays, hands or individual cards known to bridge players. On the whole, Swann, who is overweight and struggles to earn her living, is a much more believable character than Wanawake. Moody recounts Swann's ups and downs with a sense of humor that gives the series a light and amusing reputation, even though Swann investigates the death of her father in one book and is the victim of a hit-and-run driver in another.

Moody also writes non-series novels that are strong on suspense, and short stories. As Susanna James, she wrote *Love Over Gold* (1993), a playful book based on the romance between two coffee lovers who appeared in the Gold Blend coffee commercials on television. Her 1995 novel, *Misselthwaite,* is s sequel to Frances Hodgson

Burnett's *The Secret Garden* (1911). In it she maps out lives of the characters in adulthood.

—Rosemary Herbert

Moriarty, Professor James. Created by Sir Arthur Conan *Doyle to serve as an arch-enemy and intellectual equal to Sherlock *Holmes, Professor James Moriarty is portrayed as possessing the greatest criminal mind in England. As "The Napoleon of crime," Moriarty is said to be responsible for half of the evil and most of the undetected crime in London.

Moriarty's genius is chronicled in seven stories also featuring Holmes, who respects the professor's brilliant organizational powers, which permit Moriarty to do little himself other than plan. By delegating authority to his subordinates, he is able to "sit motionless like a spider in the center of his web" while his agents carry out their sinister tasks.

Moriarty is also revealed to be a man of great academic scholarship. His treatise on the binomial expansion earned him a university chair in mathematics prior to his taking control of London's underworld. His book, *The Dynamics of an Asteroid*, was found by Holmes to have "ascended to such rarefied heights" that no one was capable of criticizing it.

Doyle captured the public's imagination by depicting Moriarty as a figure of mythical proportions. The professor's protruding forehead and peering eyes staring out of an oscillating head suggest the appearance of a terrifying human reptile.

The dramatic confrontation between the two contrasting masterminds, Moriarty and Holmes, in the latter's lodgings, ranks as a great moment in English storytelling. The dynamics of their dialogue set the stage for their later inevitable duel to the death at Reichenbach Falls, where the two personify nothing less than the struggle between evil and good.

The exploits of Moriarty may not be true crime. Nonetheless, in literature, his acts are truly criminal.

[*See also* Master Criminal; Villains and Villainy.]

—Joe Fink

MORRISON, ARTHUR (1863–1945), British writer of realistic accounts of life in London's East End slums, short detective fiction, lighthearted short stories, and a significant study of Japanese painting. Born to working-class parents, he was employed as a clerk for a charity institution before doing editorial work for the London *Globe*. His realistic fiction (*Tales of Mean Streets*, 1894; *A Child of the Jago*, 1896; and *The Hole in the Wall*, 1902) are minor classics, while his chief contributions to detective fiction remain his creation of the solicitor's clerk-cum-sleuth, Martin Hewitt, a "cheerful" average man who used ordinary talents to solve crimes, in the Sherlock *Holmes tradition, and his stories about the unscrupulous Horace Dorrington. The Hewitt stories were collected into three volumes, *Martin Hewitt, Investigator*

(1894), *Chronicles of Martin Hewitt* (1895), and *Adventures of Martin Hewitt* (1896), with a fourth volume of connected episodes, *The Red Triangle: Being Some Further Chronicles of Martin Hewitt* (1903). Dorrington appears in only one collection, *The Dorrington Deed-Box* (1897). Morrison conformed to the status quo, working smoothly within established tradition without breaking new ground. Hewitt does not claim to employ a special system in his detective work, merely common sense and good eyesight. His ability as a detective is equal to that of Holmes, but he lacks the ego of his contemporary.

[*See also* Plainman Sleuth.]

—J. Randolph Cox

Morse, Chief Inspector Endeavor, is a fictional police detective featured in the works of British author Colin *Dexter. A middle-aged bachelor, Morse (whose Christian name is not divulged until his appearance in *Death is Now My Neighbor*, 1997), is a chief inspector in the Thames Valley Police CID whose cases frequently bring him into contact with Oxford's academic community. Unorthodox, restless, and headstrong, he works largely by a process of free association, trial and error, and sheer inspiration rather than by following strict police procedure. While his reasoning is often flawed and his conclusions premature, Morse is tenacious. A loner by nature, he is both tender and tetchy. His sympathy for the *victims of crime and his wistful longing for unattainable women match his disgust with criminal behavior, his disdain for abusive authority figures, and his impatience with the pretentious and superficial; he understands that life is far more complex than sociology or the law would have us believe. Morse brings a passion for real ale, the operas of Mozart and Wagner, crossword puzzles, and poetry to bear in his investigations. He is assisted by the ordinary but able Sergeant Lewis, who regards Morse with both awe and annoyance. Actor John Thaw portrayed Morse vividly in a British television series in the 1980s and 1990s. Like author Dexter, Morse suffers from diabetes, which leads inevitably to the chief inspector's death in *The Remorseful Day* (1999).

[*See also* Police Detective; Sidekicks and Sleuthing Teams.]

—John Drexel

MORTIMER, JOHN (CLIFFORD) (b. 1923), British novelist, playwright, screenwriter, journalist, critic, and translator, is best-known to readers of crime and mystery fiction as the creator of the rumpled, eccentric, poetry-spouting barrister Horace *Rumpole. Known to many as "Rumpole of the Bailey," after the title of one of the several volumes of short stories and the television series that Mortimer also penned, Rumpole was modeled on Mortimer's father, an eccentric barrister who specialized in divorce cases. Other regular characters and some incidents depicted in the series were inspired by people and events that Mortimer encountered or witnessed during his own career in the law.

Mortimer is the only child of a highly literate and eccentric barrister and his wife. He was raised in his parent's flat in London's Inner Temple and later in a house and garden designed by his father, situated in England's Chiltern Hills. He spent a rather solitary childhood during which he enjoyed acting out scenes by William *Shakespeare on his own and taking long walks in the company of his father, who recited Sherlock *Holmes stories to him from memory. His father, who was blinded in an accident in his garden, was a great influence on Mortimer, convincing him to practice law and serving as a model not only for Rumpole but for the father figure in Mortimer's autobiographical play, *A Voyage Round My Father* (1971). Mortimer rewrote that play as the memoir *Clinging to the Wreckage* (1982) and followed it with two more autobiographical volumes, *Murderers and Other Friends* (1994) and *The Summer of a Dormouse* (2000).

Mortimer attended the Dragon School in Oxford, then Harrow, and Brasenose College at Oxford University. During World War II, Mortimer served as an assistant director and scriptwriter in the Crown Film Unit, making documentary films. He then studied law and was called to the bar in 1948. He worked as a divorce barrister before practicing criminal law as a Queen's Counsel. During the latter part of his law career, he defended in celebrated cases concerned with questions of freedom of expression and censorship.

Mortimer's first courtroom drama was *The Dock Brief*, penned for radio in 1958. In it an old barrister and an unsuccessful criminal converse in a jail cell. In the 1970s Mortimer decided to create another barrister character, and penned the first of many Rumpole stories and screenplays, sometimes writing the latter first for television. Two of Mortimer's novels that do not feature Rumpole have strong crime elements. *Summer's Lease* (1988) is plotted around mysterious circumstances investigated by an English housewife holidaying with her family in Italy. *Felix in the Underworld* (1997) examines a paternity suit that turns out to be a murder case. Another novel, *Dunster* (1992), features a key courtroom scene. Mortimer is also editor of *Great Law and Order Stories* (1990), and two non-fiction compendia, *Famous Trials* (1984) and *The Oxford Book of Villains* (1992),

—Rosemary Herbert

MOSLEY, WALTER (b. 1952), son of a schoolteacher mother and a reputedly footloose father who worked as a school custodian, born in South Central Los Angeles, an African American neighborhood famous for its dramatically resistant attitude to the city's predominantly white police force. Educated in the public schools of Los Angeles and at Johnson State College, Vermont, Mosley worked in a variety of occupations, including potter and computer programmer, before beginning a serious study of writing at the City University of New York. His first

novel, *Gone Fishin'*, was completed in the 1980s but did not see print until 1996. By that time he had built an enviable reputation with a series of novels that chronicle the adventures of Ezekiel "Easy" *Rawlins, an unlicensed investigator, and his sociopathic sidekick Raymond "Mouse" Alexander.

Taking the American hard-boiled, first-person style of narration and combining it with African American oral and protest traditions, Mosley has crafted a series that has been critically hailed for its affinity to the foundational works of hard-boiled writing. This affinity is found in the serious use to which Mosley puts the popular genre—examination of racism's constraints of liberty—and in his use of a Southern California setting of the 1940s and 1950s that was contemporary for Dashiell *Hammett and Raymond *Chandler but reconstructed history for Mosley.

Although African American crime writing has included the notable series about Harlem cops written by Chester *Himes in the 1960s, and instances of criminal plots and detection in popular writing appearing in African American magazines throughout the century, Mosley's novels about Rawlins are the first major works in the crime genre to induce a large biracial audience to cross over the line that typically separates the black and white mainstreams of popular literature.

The stories in which Rawlins is the reluctant detective and *Gone Fishin'*, in which he is the narrator, are but one way Mosley explores the reality of American multicultural life. In *R. L.'s Dream* (1995) he recaptures the career of Robert Johnson in a genre he terms the blues novel, and in 1997 he introduced a new protagonist, Socrates Fortlow, a philosophically minded ex-convict, in *Always Outnumbered, Always Outgunned*. Fortlow appears again in *Walkin' The Dog* (1999). The author introduced another pair of African American characters in *Fearless Jones* (2001), a novel set in 1950's Los Angeles.

[*See also* African American Sleuth.]

—Robert E. Skinner *and* John M. Reilly

Moto, Mr. A fictional character created by the American author John P. Marquand, Mr. Moto is portrayed as Japan's top secret agent. Moto appears in six novels, beginning with *No Hero* (1935; *Mr. Moto Takes A Hand*). All are set in exotic locales including Hawaii, Singapore, and Peking and are worked around a formula featuring young European or American couples who become involved either professionally or inadvertently in international espionage.

The stories are told from the perspectives of these Western protagonists who encounter Moto as they struggle to deal with the threatening situations they are facing. In fact, Moto sometimes seems peripheral to the action, but when he is on stage, the delicately made, self-effacing secret agent steals the scene.

Educated at two American universities, Moto is a skilled linguist who speaks perfect English. He is a dapper dresser, sometimes tending toward flamboyant European outfits. Moto is a master of disguise who at various times masquerades as manservant, bartender, or tourist. His talents include a proficiency in judo.

The American agent in *Stopover: Tokyo* (1957; *The Last of Mr. Moto, Right You Are, Mr. Moto*) suspects that Moto is a member of the Japanese aristocracy. Whatever his background, Moto has enough influence with an "august personage" to be able to circumvent the military's actions. Although this is a touchy diplomatic matter, as always Moto is cool in a tight spot, and efficient in dealing with his foes. In this last book in the series, however, Moto reveals his fallibility by making two serious errors of judgment.

Moto, like his contemporary Charlie *Chan, is the antithesis of the "yellow peril" characters symbolized by Sax *Rohmer's Dr. *Fu Manchu, generally emerging as an ally of the Western hero. And yet, much about Mr. Moto remains a mystery.

[*See also* Ethnic Sleuth.]

—Frankie Y. Bailey

MOYES, PATRICIA (1923–2000), Irish-born writer of cozy mysteries that feature Scotland Yard detective Henry Tibbett and his wife, Emmy. Moyes brought to her writing a variety of career experiences and familiarity with a number of international settings where she lived. Her World War II work in the radar section of the Women's Auxiliary Air Force (WAAF) during World War II shows up in *Johnny Under Ground* (1965), in which she looks at Emmy's past work for the WAAF. Her work as a secretary for Peter Ustinov Productions, Ltd., informs *Falling Star* (1964). Her highly-regarded *Murder a la Mode* (1963) draws upon Moyes' first-hand knowledge of the fashion magazine industry, acquired while she served as an assistant editor on *Vogue*. Married twice, Moyes lived in England, Switzerland, the Netherlands, Washington, D.C., and the British Seward Islands. *To Kill a Coconut* (1977; *The Coconut Killings*) and *Angel Death* (1980) are enhanced by their island

setting. Using amusing banter among characters and carefully-constructed puzzles, Moyes excelled at playing variations on classic plot situations. In *Who Saw Her Die?* (1970; *Many Deadly Returns*) an elderly eccentric is murdered on her birthday. The problem of doppelganger heirs is at the heart of *Who is Simon Warwick?* (1978), and the simultaneous solution of a challenging crossword puzzle and a house party murder are central to *A Six-Letter Word for Death* (1983).

—Rosemary Herbert

MULLER, MARCIA (b. 1944), American author of private eye novels, anthologist, and critic of crime fiction. Muller was born in Detroit, Michigan, and earned a bachelor's degree in English and a master's degree in journalism from the University of Michigan in Ann Arbor. After holding several jobs, she became a full-time writer in 1983. Credited with creating the first contemporary American female private eye, Sharon McCone, in *Edwin of the Iron Shoes* (1977), Muller has written three series centered on women detectives. These heroines are McCone, a professional detective who eventually opens her own agency; Joanna Stark, co-owner of an art security firm, introduced in *The Cavalier in White* (1986); and Elena Oliverez, art museum director and *amateur detective, introduced in *The Tree of Death* (1983). In collaboration with her husband, Bill *Pronzini, Muller wrote *Beyond the Grave* (1986); with Oliverez investigating a century-old mystery. All three series are set in California, where Muller has lived for more than three decades.

Personal and professional relationships between the sexes form a significant theme in the McCone books, as the detective struggles to balance work and love, often learning that men find her job troubling. In the McCone and Oliverez series, race and ethnicity are also recurring themes, as both detectives are minority group members—McCone is part Native American and Oliverez is Latina—who sometimes confront prejudice.

—Maureen T. Reddy

N

NABB, MAGDALEN (b. 1947), English writer known for a series of police procedurals set in Italy, featuring Sicilian Marshal Salvatore Guarnaccia. Born in a village called Church, Lancashire, Nabb trained and worked as a potter in England before moving to Florence, Italy, in 1975. In addition to writing mysteries, she has turned out children's books, a play, and newspaper articles.

Her first mystery, *Death of an Englishman* (1981), won the British Crime Writers Association award for best first novel. It introduced Guarnaccia, a corpulent officer of the law who often wears dark glasses due to a condition that causes his eyes to water. The first book depends upon the author's experience of expatriate living. Dead or missing foreigners are also central to the *Death of a Dutchman* (1982), *Death in Springtime* (1983), *Death in Autumn* (1985), and *Marshall and the Murderer* (1987). In the latter, Nabb demonstrates her understanding of the painful past including secrets from World War II that haunt some Italians. The past is important, too in *The Marshal and the Madwoman* (1988), which is enriched by flashbacks to the 1966 flood in Florence.

All of Nabb's work is carefully researched and plotted, and the characters are memorable. More unforgettable by far is her flair for describing the beauty—and the sinister underside—of the city of Florence and environs. It is fair to liken Nabb's depiction of Florence to Arthur Conan *Doyle's description of London or George *Simenon's portrait of Paris: In all three writers' hands character of the cities takes on a similar importance. Nabb also co-authored one non-series novel with Paolo Vagheggi: *The Prosecutor* (1986) is based on the kidnapping and murder of Italian premier Aldo Moro.

[*See also* Missing Persons; Police Detective.]

—Rosemary Herbert

Nameless Detective, The. Introduced by Bill *Pronzini in *The Snatch* (1971), The Nameless Detective is a former military intelligence officer and policeman turned *private eye. Based in San Francisco, the middle-aged *sleuth also solves crimes elsewhere, as Pronzini uses him in traditional investigations such as missing persons cases and then in increasingly inventive and issue-oriented plots. For example, unwelcome development of a Gold Rush town is at the center of *Nightshades* (1984). Nameless is memorable for his refusal to carry a gun, his taste for beer, and his passion for collecting pulp magazines. The latter takes Nameless to a pulp magazine collector's convention in *Hoodwink* (1981). He attends another convention, this time one that brings together private investigators, in *Double* (1984). Co-authored by Marcia Muller, the latter book follows separate cases under in-

vestigation by Nameless and by Sharon McCone. Nameless is romantically involved with a woman called Kerry, whom he marries in *Hardcase* (1995). The Nameless Detective is referred to as Bill, in *Twospot* (1978), a novel co-authored by Collin Wilcox.

—Rosemary Herbert

NATIVE AMERICAN SLEUTH. The introduction of the Native American sleuth into detective fiction has added new dimensions to the genre. These include cultural materials that, when organically connected to the plot, expand the methods of detection to incorporate different value systems and processes of thought; the invocation of spaces, such as the harsh and inhospitable landscapes of the southwestern reservations, previously unexplored in detective fiction; and the opening of the genre into political processes such as the rights of indigenous peoples and the ecological impact of the commercial exploitation of resources on cultures closely tied to the land. Native American detectives first appeared in the popular dime novels of the 1880s. Judson R. Taylor's *Phil Scott, the Indian Detective: A Tale of Startling Mysteries* (*Phil Scott, the Detective*), published in 1882, marks one of their earliest appearances in book form. Popular interest in the conquest of the American West and in Native American cultures then perceived as exotic led to numerous reprints of titles like T. C. Harbaugh's *Velvet Foot, the Indian Detective, or, The Taos Tiger* (1884). Even Buffalo Bill, best known for his Wild West Show, penned a mystery with a Native American detective, *Red Renard, the Indian Detective, or, The Gold Buzzards of Colorado: a romance of the mines and dead trails*, published in 1886. *Pawnee Tom, or, Adrift in New York: A Story of an Indian Boy Detective* by Old Sleuth appeared in 1896. The "Indian detective" of these titles had skills in tracking, an intimate knowledge of the landscape, spoke several languages, and could negotiate several cultures with ease. In "A Star for a Warrior" (*EQMM*, Apr. 1946), Manly Wade Wellman introduced tribal policeman David Return, a member of the Tsichah, an imaginary tribe for the creation of which Wellman borrowed Cheyenne and Pawnee elements. Return's methods of deduction arise out of deep knowledge of traditional mythology and ceremonials.

In the 1970s, Brian Garfield published *Relentless* (1972) and *The Threepersons Hunt* (1974) featuring a Navajo protagonist, Arizona state trooper Sam Watchman, who investigates crimes closely linked to the landscape, such as battles over water rights and the complex relations between state and federal agencies and the reservations. In 1971 Richard Martin Stern published the first in his series about Johnny Ortiz, a part-Apache, part-Spanish officer in the Santa Cristo Police. In *Murder in the Walls* (1971), *Death in the Snow* (1973), and *Missing Man* (1990), Ortiz and his African American cultural anthropologist friend, Cassie Enright, investigate crimes stemming from clashes between traditional Pueblo cultures and progressive urbanization.

The best-known series of Native American mysteries are Tony *Hillerman's novels featuring Sergeant Jim *Chee and Lieutenant Joe Leaphorn. Alongside his convincing puzzles, Hillerman offers in-depth studies of Navajo and Zuni culture and folklore and considerable insight into the idiosyncrasies of the Native American character. Their popularity inspired three more recent series. Jean Hager has developed two interconnected series featuring Oklahoma Cherokee detectives Mitchell Busyhead, a police chief introduced in *The Grandfather Medicine* (1989), and Molly Bearpaw, a young female officer who is featured in *Seven Black Stones* (1995) and *The Spirit Caller* (1997). Jake Page introduced his blind Santa Fe sculptor detective Mo Bowdre and his Anglo-Hopi girlfriend Connie Barnes in *The Knotted Strings* (1995). Here, and in its 1996 sequel, *The Lethal Partner*, Page writes with authority and feeling about Hopi tribal life, offering glimpses into kachina ritual dances and writing movingly of a tribal elder's grief over the loss of his gods. More recently, Aimee Thurlo has introduced a series centered on Pueblo Indians featuring half-Navajo botanist Belara Fuller, beginning with *Second Shadow* (1993).

In the wake of multiculturalism, the Native American detective has emerged as a popular figure in juvenile literature, where the mystery genre is put to the task of educating children about Native American cultures, religions, and oral traditions. Examples are Anna Hale's *Mystery on Mackinac Island* (1989), Kate Abbott's *Mystery at Echo Cliffs* (1994), Rob MacGregor's *Prophecy Rock* (1995), and Nat Reed's *Thunderbird Gold* (1997).

[*See also* Ethnic Sleuth.]

—Lizabeth Paravisini-Gebert

NEELY, BARBARA (b. 1941), American writer, radio commentator and creator of the *African-American sleuth, Blanche White. Born in Lebanon, Pennsylvania, Neely was raised by a poor but loving family of independent women and natural storytellers. When, in 1992, she wrote her first mystery, *Blanche on the Lam,* she worked in the tradition of the *accidental sleuth—the character who is not a professional detective but who applies pluck and other skills to solving a mystery. In this case, the protagonist is a domestic worker who uses her entrée into private worlds and her invisibility as a person her employers hardly heed as assets in crime solving. In the first novel and in *Blanche Cleans Up* (1998), White works for Boston Brahmin families. In *Blanche Among the Talented Tenth* (1994) Neely examines questions of color and class at an exclusive all-black resort in Maine. In *Blanche Passes Go* (2000), White travels to Fairleigh, North Carolina, where she confronts a man who raped her in the past.

Although Neely has never been the victim of sexual abuse, she worked for 30 years with victims of this and other crimes. Before she could afford to write full-time, she served as a coordinator of the ABCD Head Start Program, as a designer and director of Pennsylvania's first community-based correctional facility for women, and as a director of the YMCA in Pittsburgh, Pennsylvania. She has also worked as an executive director of Women for Economic Justice, as a radio producer for the Africa News Service, and as the host of the radio program, *Commonwealth Journal.* She lives in Jamaica Plain, near Boston, Massachusetts.

—Rosemary Herbert

NEWSPAPER REPORTERS AS DETECTIVES. *See* Journalist Sleuth.

North, Mr. and Mrs. Though they were not the first, much of the popularity of husband-wife detective teams derives from the success of Pamela and Jerry North, creations of Frances and Richard Lockridge. They appeared in twenty-six novels and one short story.

They are suspects in their first case, *The Norths Meet Murder* (1940; *Mr. and Mrs. North Meet Murder*), when Pamela rents a Greenwich Village apartment for a party but discovers a *corpse in its bathtub. Lieutenant Bill Weigand, who investigates, becomes their friend. Though exasperated by the frequency with which Pamela discovers corpses, he is usually glad for the Norths' assistance. In *Death of a Tall Man* (1946), Pamela sees Weigand driving to a murder scene and follows him. She barges in, but he lets her stay.

Jerry, busy earning a living in publishing, plays a smaller role, though he occasionally provides important clues. The detective work is done by Weigand and, unofficially, by Pamela, who frequently is stalked by the killer. Often, Bill and Pamela arrive at the solution simultaneously, albeit by different methods. Though she has a reputation for dizziness (perhaps because played in the movies by Gracie Allen), Pamela is bright; she just speaks in a way that seems strange to those who don't understand her mental shorthand.

The background of many North books reflects the Lockridges' experience. Richard was a drama critic, and Frances held important positions with charities. They were known for their love of Siamese cats, and those owned by Pamela and Jerry were based on the cats who shared the Lockridge household.

Frances Lockridge died in 1963. Though Richard wrote mysteries for another twenty years, he abandoned the Norths, saying Pamela had been based too closely on his wife.

—Marvin Lachman

Norton, Irene. *See* Adler, Irene

NOSY PARKER SLEUTH. Nosy parker sleuths, or amateur detectives who invite themselves to explore the private lives of people who are strangers to them or with whom they have only slight acquaintance, are frequently found within the pages of mysteries. Self-appointed and driven by their own curiousity or a perceived sense of justice, these often zany sleuths confuse the issues, discard obvious clues, jump to unwarranted conclusions, and interfere with the official investigators. They frequently promote a romance between two characters who are most affected by a crime, one of whom is apt to be a suspect. Authors use these characters as farcical figures who provide contrast to dogged but nonetheless unsuccessful official sleuths. Given their muddled approach to crime solving, it is entertaining and surprising to find that, in the end, nosy parkers manage to identify the culprit and explain the motive.

Unlike *amateur sleuths, who are invited by police or neighbors to get to the truth of a situation, or *surrogate detectives, such as journalists and medical personnel, who use professional credentials in fields other than detection to gain entrée to crime scenes and who employ specialized skills to interpret clues found there, nosy parker sleuths have no legitimate reason for involving themselves in a case. They may be *accidental sleuths, who happen to be on the scene when a crime occurs. More likely, they have barged their way into such scenes, inspired by irresistible curiosity.

A prime example of the self-appointed snooper is Jane Amanda Edwards, identified as "Pauline Pry" by her author, Charlotte Murray Russell. This nosy neighbor prides herself on knowing all there is to know about the private lives, incomes, and social standing of the denizens of Rockport, Illinois, where she intrudes and interferes with great aplomb in adventures written during the 1930s and 1940s, including the aptly titled novel *The Bad Neighbor Murder* (1946).

—Ellen Nehr

O

OATES, JOYCE CAROL (b. 1938), American novelist, playwright, literary critic, professor, and founder of *The Ontario Review*. A prolific writer of extraordinarily consistent quality, Oates was nominated twice for the Nobel Prize in Literature. While crimes of the heart are central to much of her fiction, she has written several novels under the pseudonym Rosamund Smith, and short stories under her own name, that fall directly into the crime writing genre.

The daughter of working-class parents, Oates was born and raised in Lockport, New York. She received her elementary education in a one-room schoolhouse, and began writing in earnest when, at age fourteen, she received a typewriter as a gift. She wrote unpublished novels before graduating high school, and while still in college, at Syracuse University in upstate New York, she won her first major writing contest and publication in *Mademoiselle* magazine. She went on to the University of Wisconsin, where she earned a master's degree in English, and met the man she would marry, Raymond J. Smith. She spent the first ten years of her marriage in Detroit, and taught across the Canadian border at the University of Windsor, while establishing herself as one of the most important writers of her generation.

In 1978, she and her husband moved to Princeton, New Jersey, where she became a professor of creative writing. Using a small press, she and her husband also founded *The Ontario Review*, a literary magazine. In Princeton, Oates continued to turn out fiction and other writings, including a series of novels containing gothic elements, beginning with *Bellefleur* (1980). The third volume in this series, *The Mysteries of Winterthurn* (1984) is constructed around a mystery and detection.

Although Oates' versatility was already welcomed by legions of readers, in 1987 Oates decided to use a pseudonym to write a crime novel. *Lives of the Twins* (1987; *Kindred Passions*) was published under the name Rosamund Smith. Oates was eager to cast off the expectations that came along with her own name, and to see how she would be treated by publishers who thought "Smith" was a new voice. Her secret was short-lived, however. After a friend leaked the information, her longtime agent and publisher—both of whom were not involved in the "Smith" book deal, were offended. *Lives of the Twins* and following crime novels written under the pseudonym were nonetheless reviewed very favorably.

Under her own name, Oates has penned many short stories with crime elements. Some are collected in two anthologies: *Haunted: Tales of the Grotesque* (1994) and *Faithless: Tales of Transgression* (2001).

—Rosemary Herbert

OBTUSE SLEUTH. *See* Plainman Sleuth.

ODDBALLS. *See* Eccentrics.

Old Man in the Corner. The creation of Baroness Emmuska *Orczy, the Old Man in the Corner is the prototype of the *armchair detective, an *amateur detective for whom crime solving is an intellectual exercise conducted at a distance from the scene of the crime. Snuggled up in a London tearoom, he works out his solutions to puzzling crimes recounted to him by journalist Polly Burton. Stories featuring him were first published between 1901 and 1904 in the *Royal Magazine*. A total of thirty-eight tales are collected in *The Case of Miss Elliott* (1905), *The Old Man in the Corner* (1909; *The Man in the Corner*), and *Unravelled Knots* (1925).

While drinking glasses of milk and untying knots in a piece of string, the Old Man works the case backward, noting details that the police overlook and making deductions based on ratiocination and intuition. Although he bases most of his solutions upon newspaper reports, he does attend inquests and trials and makes visits to crime scenes after the fact in some cases. Therefore, he is not wholly sedentary.

Orczy never names the Old Man, but in "The Mysterious Death in Percy Street" (*The Old Man in the Corner*), she suggests that he is Bill Owen, who likely murdered his aunt. In his narrative, however, the Old Man tells Burton only that the uncaptured killer was "one of the most ingenious men of the age" and his crime "one of the cleverest bits of work accomplished outside Russian diplomacy."

[*See also* Great Detective.]

—Gerald H. Strauss

OMNISCIENT SLEUTH. *See* Great Detective, The; Superman Sleuth.

OPPENHEIM, E(DWARD) PHILLIPS (1866–1946), British thriller writer of the Golden Age who also wrote as Anthony Partridge. Oppenheim left England for France and Guernsey in 1922 and served in the Ministry of Information during World War I. His prolific output of 115 novels and 44 collections of short stories made him enormously wealthy, and he lived like many of his heroes.

In his thrillers, a fabulously rich man uses his wealth to gain power over business or government and bring an end to evil; pacifism, the virtues of wealth and the aristocracy, and redemption through philanthropy are recurring themes. For example, in *Up the Ladder of Gold*

(1931), the hero seeks to end war for forty years. Oppenheim's detectives are usually amateurs with a modest public persona, such as Louis, the crippled maître d' of the Milan Hotel, or the wealthy layabout who redeems himself through meeting unexpected challenges in *The Great Impersonation* (1920).

[*See also* Amateur Detective.]

—Chris Gausden

"Op, The." *See* Continental Op, The.

ORCZY, BARONESS EMMUSKA (Emma Magdalena Rosalia Maria Josefa Barbara), (1865–1947), British author, known for creating the *armchair detective and for her early portrayals of the capable female sleuth. Hungarian-born daughter of musician Baron Felix Orczy, she was educated abroad and in London, where she studied art and married illustrator Montagu Barstow in 1894. She is best known for *The Scarlet Pimpernel* (1905), and her main contribution to detective fiction is the development of detection based entirely on reported information, foreshadowed in Edgar Allan Poe's "The Mystery of Marie Roget" (*Snowden's Lady's Companion,* Nov. 1845). In a series of stories collected in *The Case of Miss Elliott* (1905), *The Old Man in the Corner* (1909; *The Man in the Corner*), and *Unravelled Knots* (1925), the Old Man sits in a café, playing with string and working out, in conversation with a newspaperwoman, solutions to baffling crimes. Armchair detection, as this came to be known, was adapted by Ernest *Bramah, for his blind Max *Carrados, and by Agatha *Christie, for her amateur crime solvers in *The Tuesday Club Murders.* Orczy also created a woman detective in *Lady Molly of Scotland Yard* (1910), in which the aristocratic heroine, heading the "Female Department of the Yard" while working to clear her husband's name, is assisted by her maid, who also narrates their adventures. Lady Molly deMazareen is a forerunner to the contemporary feminist detective who breaks cases by wit and daring rather than intuition.

[*See also* Aristocratic Sleuth; Females and Feminists.]

—Mary Rose Sullivan

ORDINARY PERSON AS DETECTIVE. *See* Accidental Sleuth; Plainman Sleuth.

OUTCASTS AND OUTSIDERS. The universe of crime and mystery fiction abounds in closed worlds that serve as microcosms for demonstrating the consequences and possible remedies for social violations. Whether the closed worlds comprise an enclave of wealthy residents, academics, hardened criminals, professionals, or residents of a set locality, they have indigenous manners, tastes, and, of course, a common background and value system.

The task for the writer plotting a tale of attack upon a particular social order is to enact the eruption of crime. An excellent means of doing so is through interlopers who may be, or appear to be, catalysts for criminal disorder. Associated with outbreaks of crime, the conventional character type of the alien outsider or its allied type, the deviant, appears to deserve to be cast out of the community.

In fiction that shows closed worlds as positive ideals for human society, such as Golden Age writing, the outsider may be described in terms resonant of comedies of manners; thus, the *villain eventually revealed in Dorothy L. *Sayers's *Gaudy Night* (1935) is a woman who sides with the cause of men in what she presumes is the battle against them initiated by the female academics of the Oxford college. Besides despising the inherently feminist outlook of the women in the community, her background, education, and social class differ entirely. In essence, therefore, she is totally alien, the complete outsider. A similar rendition of the outsider figure appears in the stories by Agatha *Christie about Miss Jane *Marple, doyenne of a timeless village, whose adventures are littered with hints that the newcomer is a person who must be watched carefully.

A curious modification in the use of the outsider as the likely criminal in upper-class society can be discovered in stories of *gentleman thieves like the adventures of A. J. *Raffles related by E. W. *Hornung. Raffles possesses sufficient accomplishments of learning and style to be the consummate insider, yet his actions put him in the role of the invasive outsider, violating the expectations of mannered behavior. The witty effect of this play with stereotypes is further heightened by observable similarities between Raffles, the violator, and Sherlock *Holmes, the idealized defender of the social order.

Away from the environs of social privilege, in the gritty cities where hard-boiled writers place their stories, social milieus take other forms, but they can be just as closed as the habitats of the wealthy and just as protective against outsiders. The police officers in Joseph Wambaugh's *The Onion Field* (1973) become tragic outcasts when they give up their guns to criminals, thereby violating the decorum of police behavior. In a variation on this formula, E. Richard Johnson's *Case Load—Maximum* (1971) tells of a parole officer who faces ostracism from his occupation because he has lowered the defensive shield of wariness and trusted a parolee when he should not have.

Law enforcement, as a matter of fact, provides especially rich opportunities for authors to develop themes about closed environments through the use of outsider characters. Dorothy Uhnak's *Law and Order* (1973), in telling of generations of Irish American police officers, plays on the insider-outsider theme by demonstrating that insiders within a corrupt department are a better hope for reform, because of their knowledge, than high-minded outsiders. Uhnak's other significant treatment of an outsider is her story of Christie Opara, a woman officer in the male-oriented police force. Characters who are inevitably outsiders, although they are official cops, also appear in Chester *Himes's series about the Harlem detectives Grave Digger Jones and Coffin Ed *Johnson.

Effective enforcers of law, but also sympathetic protectors of the little people of Harlem, Jones and Johnson can never be anything but outsiders, because in a society and city run by a predominantly white power structure, blacks are always the "other."

In confirmation of the utility of outsiders or outcast characters the authors of underworld stories use them to convey the sense of Mafia exclusivity, as in the Godfather film and stories of Mario Puzo. The adopted Irish boy grows up to be the organization's lawyer, but without the all-important blood ties he can never be a fully fledged member of the crime family.

Other examples of outsiders who can never integrate into the tight crime family are to be found in the classic puzzle stories deriving from the patterns of the Golden Age, which show that most often this character type is used to best advantage in secondary roles. This only stands to reason, for despite the intrinsic interest an author may have in such characters, their greatest usefulness lies in the way they mark the boundaries of the many closed worlds in crime and mystery literature.

[See also Prodigal Son/Daughter.]

—John M. Reilly

P

PARETSKY, SARA (b. 1947), American writer of detective novels and short stories. Born in Ames, Iowa, Sara Paretsky was educated at the University of Kansas (B.A., 1967) and the University of Chicago (M.B.A. and Ph.D., 1977). From 1971 to 1985, she worked as a writer for several Chicago-area businesses.

Paretsky chose the mystery genre for her first attempt at fiction writing because she was a mystery fan and wanted to try a form she knew well. *Indemnity Only* (1982), with a complicated plot informed by Paretsky's extensive knowledge of the insurance industry, introduced private investigator Victoria Iphigenia "V. I." *Warshawski. As signaled by the title's echo of James M. *Cain's *Double Indemnity,* Paretsky's novel both enters and begins to revise the hard-boiled detective genre. Paretsky has continued this revision with the next six Warshawski books: *Deadlock* (1984), *Killing Orders* (1985), *Bitter Medicine* (1987), *Blood Shot* (1988; *Toxic Shock,* 1988), which won the Silver Dagger Award from the Crime Writers Association, *Burn Marks* (1990), and *Guardian Angel* (1992).

In the tradition of hard-boiled detectives, Warshawski narrates the novels, but with results very different from the "bare style" of Paretsky's male predecessors. Paretsky's novels share other features with conventional hard-boiled fiction. For example, both give readers exhaustive catalogs of the flotsam and jetsam of daily life—meals cooked and eaten, clothing (Warshawski is partial to Bruno Magli pumps and silk blouses), baths, finances—along with intricate details about specific locales the detective knows well (in Warshawski's case, Chicago). Paretsky, however, introduces far more intimate explorations of her character's psychology than is usual in the genre. One staple of hard-boiled fiction is the tough, loner hero. Paretsky's detective often questions the value of toughness and worries that her job diminishes human connection. Two of the most interesting continuing characters in the series—Lotty Herschel, a physician who is Warshawski's closest friend, and her neighbor Mr. Contreras, an elderly character who finds Warshawski's work exciting and wants to be part of it—often figure in the sleuth's ongoing struggle to balance independence and interconnection.

The plots of Paretsky's novels link specific crimes—usually murders committed in order to preserve or consolidate power—with wider social problems. In *Bitter Medicine* Warshawski uncovers corruption in the medical profession, for instance, while in *Blood Shot* her investigation leads her to both a child abuser and an environmental polluter. The other novels' plots turn on corruption in such areas as banking, shipping, and or-

ganized religion. The position of women in society and the possible meanings of social justice are important themes in all the novels, as is the question of violence.

Paretsky has received more critical accolades and attracted more readers with each new book. She is one of the most popular contemporary feminist writers of detective fiction, and one of the most important figures in the current proliferation of female crime writing. A film based on her fiction, *V. I. Warshawski,* starring Kathleen Turner as the detective, was released in 1992; critics agree that Hollywood did not do justice to Paretsky's work. Her novels are intricately plotted but intensely character-driven, elegantly written, and thematically rich. Named a Woman of the Year by *Ms.* magazine in 1987, Paretsky is a founder and former president of the Sisters in Crime organization.

[*See also* Hard-Boiled Sleuth.]

—Maureen T. Reddy

PARKER, ROBERT B(ROWN), (b. 1932), American author, widely regarded as a leading contemporary writer of private eye fiction. Parker was born 17 September 1932, in Springfield, Massachusetts, and educated at Colby College in Maine. Following graduation in 1954 and a two-year stint with the army in Korea, he worked at a variety of jobs (technical writer, co-owner of an advertising agency), earning his Ph.D. in English from Boston University in 1971. In 1968 he joined the faculty as an English professor at Boston's Northeastern University.

Parker's interest in detective fiction began at the age of fourteen when he first read Raymond *Chandler. Later, he wrote his Ph.D. dissertation on the novels of Chandler, Dashiell *Hammett, and Ross *Macdonald. At the age of thirty-nine, he decided to try his hand at a private-eye novel in the knight-errant tradition of Chandler. *The Godwulf Manuscript* (1973) introduced the character of *Spenser ("with an s, like the poet"), a Boston *private eye with the build of a prizefighter and the soul of a poet. Parker's admiration for Chandler eventually prompted him to write two "new" Philip *Marlowe novels: *Poodle Springs* (1989), a completion of Chandler's unfinished novel, and *Perchance to Dream* (1991), a sequel to *The Big Sleep* (1939).

Though originally modeled on Marlowe, Spenser differs from him in several respects. Most significantly, Parker abandoned the traditional model of the lone-wolf private eye. Spenser's long-term relationship with psychologist Susan Silverman comprises an eloquent celebration of enduring love that counters the uglier elements of his chosen profession. His African American sidekick, Hawk, a former adversary, is now a trusted ally, especially in dangerous situations. Unhampered by conscience, Hawk is also used to accentuate Spenser's efforts to develop a personal code of ethical behavior. Among the more compelling books in the series are *Mortal Stakes* (1975) and *Paper Doll* (1993), in which Spenser struggles to resolve the conflicting demands of his profession and his conscience and to balance his Arthurian fantasies of heroism with the implacable demands of the real world.

Parker's novels are noted for their humor (Spenser is master of the wisecrack and flippant one-liner) and polished style, with literary allusions from the well-read Spenser liberally sprinkled throughout the series. Though he addresses a variety of topical issues, from feminist politics in *Looking for Rachel Wallace* (1980) to urban youth gangs in *Double Deuce* (1992), Parker's main theme is family relationships, especially the damaging effects on children of parental failures at love. In *Early Autumn* (1981), Spenser even finds himself playing mentor and counselor to the emotionally damaged Paul Glacomin, who subsequently assumes the role of surrogate son in Spenser's extended family.

Parker introduced two new series characters during the 1990s: Jessie Stone first appears in *Night Passage* (1997) and the female sleuth Sunny Randall debuts in *Family Honor* (1999).

Critics agree that Parker's plots are occasionally thin and the exchanges between Spenser and Susan can become coy, but they also point out that Parker is consistently entertaining. And Spenser, a two-fisted hero with a tender heart, a man who can throw his weight around as deftly as he whips up gourmet meals or quotes poetry, has become the very model of the private eye for our time.

[*See also* Hard-Boiled Sleuth; Sidekicks and Sleuthing Teams.]

—David Geherin

PARTNERSHIPS, LITERARY. Collaborations between crime writers range from those absorbing both partners' creative energies over the long term to those occurring once in an author's lifetime. Some pairs share a joint pseudonym; others identify each partner. Some literary collaborators are also married couples. The ultimate collaborator was perhaps Richard Wilson Webb, whose thirty novels over twenty years include two written with one coauthor, two with another, and twenty-five with a third. (L. T. Meade also had three collaborators, but she was more prolific without one.) Webb was the lynchpin of a complicated operation serving three pseudonyms: Q. Patrick with each coauthor in turn and Patrick Quentin and Jonathan Stagge with Hugh Wheeler. Though Wheeler kept the Quentin byline alive after breaking with his partner, Webb wrote nothing more. Evidently he was a natural collaborator. So, too, were Frederic Dannay and Manfred B. Lee, whose remarkable contribution to mystery fiction was made jointly, primarily as Ellery *Queen. They wrote only in collaboration, Dannay with other writers for some of the later titles in the Canon. Francis M. Nevine Jr. states that Dannay was largely responsible for "the conceptual work" of the books and Lee for "the detailed execution," including "the precise choice of words." Another commentator remarked on "the interlocking of their mental processes," making conversation with them "like talking to one man."

Francis Beeding also was the pseudonym of two men: Hilary St. George Saunders and John Palmer, friends with complementary literary gifts. Saunders is reported to have said: "Palmer can't be troubled with description and narrative and I'm no good at creating characters or dialogue." Manning Coles combined the talents of a man and a woman: Adelaide Manning and Cyril Coles, the latter with direct experience of British intelligence doubtless invaluable in the composition of spy fiction. Emma *Lathen and R. B. Dominic were pseudonyms used together by Mary J. Latsis and Martha Henissart. They discussed each book before starting to write, "to get a fix on the characters." Then each wrote separate chapters, which were jointly checked for errors and omissions and dovetailed into the final narrative. Collaboration spared them "the hardest part of the author's lot, the loneliness": Each had "the knowledge that someone else is going to get a crack at it."

Barrie Hayne suggests the likely division of labor in the collaboration of Clemence Dane and Helen Simpson: Their actor detective, "one guesses, along with his theatrical background, is more Clemence Dane's creation, the plotting of the mystery more Helen Simpson's." Bo Lundin confirms that Maj *Sjöwall and Per Wahlöö "wrote together, each writing alternate chapters after long research and detailed synopses."

G. D. H. Cole wrote one detective novel solo and a further twenty-seven with his wife Margaret. In *Meet the Detective* (1935) she describes their taking turns to do "the main bit of the work" on each novel: "We settle on a plot ... then one of us does a first draft and shows it to the other for criticism. Then the fun begins ... And so it's altered and eventually turns up as a book, all in proper form." The Lockridges proceeded differently, Richard doing the writing from plot outlines by Frances. Interestingly, after his wife's death, Richard Lockridge continued to produce crime novels for many years. The roles of planner and writer were reversed for John and Emery Bonett, whose Penguin biography records that "John, besides having imagination and plot-sense, has also grammar, spelling and a sense of humor and from the time they met he has done most of the spadework" on his wife's stories. The methods of Darwin and Hildegarde Teilhet were described by Douglas G. Greene in *The Armchair Detective*. Darwin invented characters and "devised the plots," which he and his wife then "vigorously" discussed. Since he was "less interested in plot details and development," Hildegarde often contributed "such points during discussion." Darwin then wrote the first draft and Hildegarde "rewrote and edited the manuscript." Even later novels signed individually are to some extent collaborations.

Some famous writers collaborated on occasion. John *Rhode wrote *Drop to His Death* (1939; *Fatal Descent*) with Carter Dickson, who, as John Dickson *Carr, co-wrote certain *Exploits of Sherlock Holmes* (1954) and wholly wrote others. Dorothy L. *Sayers and Ngaio *Marsh both collaborated with doctors for medical accuracy. Stuart Palmer records that Craig *Rice's "real contribution" to *People vs. Withers and Malone* (1963), "apart from the unique character of Malone," was "in the gimmicks, the gadgets, the slant—a beginning or an ending or a line or two of dialogue."

—B. A. Pike

PEARSON, RIDLEY (b. 1953), American musician and writer of thrillers with espionage elements and crime fiction well grounded in forensic science. Raised near Greenwich, Connecticut, Pearson was educated at the Pomfret School in Connecticut, the University of Kansas, and Brown University in Providence, Rhode Island. After leaving Brown, he spent many years as a musician and songwriter, touring New England with group called Big Lost. More recently, he played with bands called Rock Bottom Remainders and the Toast Points. Pearson got his start in writing fiction while still performing music at night. In his prose writing as in his songwriting, he has said that his aim is always to entertain. Pearson and his wife are the parents of one biological daughter and an adopted Chinese daughter. The family has settled in St. Louis, Missouri.

He wrote several screenplays that were never produced before turning his hand to writing thrillers, including *Never Look Back* (1985), *Blood of the Albatross* (1986), and *The Seizing of Yankee Green Mall* (1987; *Hidden Charges*). The first is an espionage novel involving a train journey in Canada. The next involves FBI work in Seattle. The third book entails hostage taking at a mall.

With *Undercurrents* (1988), Pearson introduced his first series characters, Sergeant Lou Boldt, a member of the Special Forensic Task Force of the Seattle, Washington, police department, and Daphne Matthews, a police psychologist. The two utilize their complementary professional skills to reveal the mind of the murderer as shown through physical evidence discovered at the scenes of crimes and interviews with suspects. In his emphasis on the forensic science as essential to crime solving, Pearson broke ground that was later well-tilled by Patricia D. *Cornwell. Over the course of the series, Pearson takes on social issues and Boldt and Matthews develop as characters. In *The Angel Maker* (1993), he looks at the selling of human organs and in *Pied Piper* (1998), he reveals Boldt's softer side as the sleuth reflects upon his relationship with his daughter. He is not afraid to take on controversial subjects. In *Chain of Evidence* (1995), he looks at castration as treatment for sex offenders, and writes about the brave new world of manipulating genes for social control. Using the penname

Wendell McCall, Pearson has also written a series of novels featuring Chris Klick. The first one is *Dead Aim* (1988).

[*See also* Forensic Pathologist.]

—Rosemary Herbert

PELECANOS, GEORGE (b. 1957), American writer of *private eye novels set in the underclass world of his native city, Washington, D.C. The son of a fruit vendor who later owned a take-out restaurant, Pelecanos worked in the latter to put himself through the University of Maryland. He later worked as a shoe salesman, electronic appliance store clerk, dishwasher, bartender, and in the film industry before beginning to make a name for himself as a crime writer during the 1990s.

His first novel, *A Firing Offense* (1992) introduced Nick Stefanos, a man struggling with alcoholism whose day work draws on the author's resume. In the first book, Stefanos is PR man for a chain of electronics stores who moonlights as a private eye. In *Nick's Trip* (1998), he combines bartending with detective work. The 1996 novel, *The Big Blowdown*, set during the 1940s and 1950s, established Pelecanos's penchant for setting his work in the recent past while raising his reputation, too. Its well-researched 20-year span and hard look at the dark side of Washington, D.C., won critical acclaim. *King Suckerman* (1997) is set two decades later, in 1976. It focuses on two friends—Greek-American Dimitri Karras and Marcus Clay, a black Vietnam veteran—who live in a capital city where violence is endemic. The pair appears in *The Sweet Forever* (1998) set in the 1980s, and in *Shame the Devil* (2000), which takes place during the 1990's. In the latter, Karras's family life is shattered when his young son is killed. Throughout the series, Karras can't quite kick his drug habit.

In *Right as Rain* (2001), Pelecanos introduced another pair of series sleuths, Derek Strange, a black ex-cop turned private eye and Terry Quinn, another ex-policeman who was forced off the force after he accidentally shot another officer. The pair returns in *Hell to Pay* (2002), a novel that won a wider audience for the author and cemented his reputation as a writer with an ear for the voices and other sounds, especially popular music, that define his characters. Pelecanos lives with his wife and three adopted children in Maryland.

[*See also* Outcasts and Outsiders.]

—Rosemary Herbert

PENTECOST, HUGH, pseudonym of Judson P(entecost) Philips (1930–1989), American writer of mystery novels, short fiction, screenplays, radio and television scripts, and 1973 Mystery Writers of America Grand Master. Although he was first published while still in college, he took his pseudonym on winning the Dodd Mead "Red Badge" Prize Competition in 1939 with *Cancelled in Red*. He graduated from Columbia University in 1925, the same year he sold his first short stories to the pulp magazines. In the 1930s and 1940s, he contributed short stories and novels to publications such as *Argosy*, *Flynn's*, and *Detective Fiction Weekly*, for which he created the Park Avenue Hunt Club series. He wrote stories with varied settings for the slicks, especially *American Magazine*. Pentecost enjoyed telling stories, and his own observations of people, his interests, and his research provided a rich background for his fiction. Critics praise his skillful plots, well-defined settings, and believable characters. His work as Pentecost is in the tradition of classic detection, while that written as Judson Philips offers increased thrills and suspense. Though Pentecost considered series characters restricting, most of his fiction involves continuing characters. His own favorites were written under the Pentecost pseudonym. They include John Jericho, a red-bearded Greenwich Village artist, and Uncle George Crowder, a former county attorney. Favorites with the public have been Pierre *Chambrun, who strives to keep things running smoothly even in the face of terrorism at New York's Hotel Beaumont; Julian Quist, a public relations man; and Peter Styles, a one-legged magazine columnist with a definite vendetta against the underworld.

—J. Randolph Cox

PEREZ-REVERTE, ARTURO (b. 1951), Spanish writer of thrillers that are strong on mystery, romance and detailed information about the author's passions for chess, book-collecting, antique maps and the like. A bestselling author in Spain, Perez-Reverte leads a life not unlike some of his wealthy characters do, residing in a mountain retreat complete with a 10,000-volume library in El Escorial, a mountainous area outside Madrid. He also enjoys getaways on a sailboat he helped to design, which contains a 300-volume library.

Before launching his career as a novelist, Perez-Reverte spent 20 years as a journalist covering major conflicts around the world, including events in the Middle East, the Falklands, El Salvador and Sarajevo. The wartime horrors he witnessed led him to look at the world as an uncivilized place where betrayal is rampant and honorable individuals are rare. This attitude lends excitement to his books in which no reliable character is pitted against a world where nothing is what it seems to be, betrayal is likely to be fatal, and intimacy offers no promise of trust.

Several of the author's books are translated into English. *La table da Flandes* (1990; *The Flanders Panel*, 1994), looks at the world of chess. Rare books are central to *El Club Dumas* (1993; *The Club Dumas*, 1996). The Vatican is at the heart of *La piel del tambor* (1995; *The Seville Communion*). Fencing runs through *The Fencing Master* (1999), first published as *El maestro del esgrima* (1988; The Fencing Master, 1999), and rare maps inspire a treasure hunt in *La carta esferica* (2000; *The Nautical Chart* 2001)

—Rosemary Herbert

PERRY, ANNE pseudonym of Juliet Marion Hulme (b. 1938). English author of two series of historical mysteries

set in Victorian London. Perry is distinguished from most of her colleagues in the crime writing genre in that she served time in prison for murder. Born Juliet Marion Hulme in London, she was traumatized by the London blitz During World War II, suffered ill health as a child, and moved with her family to New Zealand. There she formed an intense friendship with another girl, Nora Parker. When the two faced separation because Perry's family planned to leave New Zealand, the pair killed Parker's mother. After being convicted of murder at the age of fifteen in 1954 and serving five years in prison, Perry changed her name and lived in England and in California, where she worked in a variety of jobs. Eventually, she settled in the village of Portmahamock, Scotland.

Perry wrote two historical novels before launching her first mystery series with *The Cater Street Hangman* (1979). Like the following volumes in this series, the book is titled after a London location, set in the Victorian era, and it features the policeman Thomas Pitt and his higher-born wife Charlotte. In this book as well as others in the series, Pitt's official investigations are aided by information and gossip to which his wife is privy, thanks to her entrée into higher society. After Perry turned out eight mysteries in this series, she introduced another series character, Inspector William Monk, in *The Face of a Stranger* (1990). In that novel, Monk is a Victorian chief inspector who struggles to solve a case while he also strives to overcome amnesia regarding key facts of his own identity. The more he remembers, the less he likes himself. In both of her series, Perry is often preoccupied with moral dilemmas and questions of reputation.

Perry wrote a non-series novel, *One Thing More* (2000). She also edited two anthologies of detective stories. The story of her murder case was filmed as *Heavenly Creatures* (1994).

[*See also* Police Detective.]

—Rosemary Herbert

PETERS, ELIZABETH, pseudonym of Barbara Louise Gross Mertz (b. 1927). Egyptologist and non-fiction writer (as Barbara Mertz), author of romantic thrillers (as Barbara Michaels) and author of romantic suspense novels (as Elizabeth Peters). Born Barbara Louise Gross in Canton, Illinois, she earned three degrees, including a doctorate in Egyptology, from the Oriental Institute of the University of Chicago. This expertise provides background to her series of mysteries—strong on humor and feminist overtones—featuring the Victorian archaeologist Amelia Peabody, written under the Peters pseudonym. Peabody often works on archaeological sites in the company of her husband Radcliff Emerson and the couple's pesky son Ramses. Using the Peters pseudonym, this author also penned a series about the art historian Vicky Bliss; another series about Jacqueline Kirby, a librarian who is memorable for toting tools of detection in a large handbag; and a number of non-series mysteries. Particularly when the author is writing as Peters, her work is enlivened by playful—even witty—dialogue, and she is not afraid to spoof the conventions of the genres within which she works. Lively, outgoing and witty, she is a favorite author at mystery fan conventions.

—Rosemary Herbert

PETERS, ELLIS, pseudonym of Edith Mary Pargeter (1913–1995), British author who is best known for her chronicles of Brother *Cadfael, mysteries set in Shrewsbury's Benedictine Abbey of Saint Peter and Saint Paul in the twelfth century. Born in Shropshire, England, on the Welsh border, Peters was educated at local schools and worked as a pharmacist's assistant before publishing her first novel at the age of twenty. She also translated Czechoslovakian literature. During World War II she served in the Women's Royal Naval Service and earned the British Empire medal. She returned to writing after the war and became known for historical novels written under her own name including *The Heaven Tree* trilogy (1960–63) and *A Bloody Field by Shrewsbury* (1972, *The Bloody Field*).

In 1959 she published her first historical mystery under the Ellis Peters name about Shropshire Police Inspector George Felse. In 1977 she introduced the herbalist monk Cadfael in *A Morbid Taste for Bones*. He appears in some twenty novels. Peters has also produced *A Rare Benedictine* (1988) and *Shropshire,* (1992) which she wrote with Roy Morgan. Peters also produced two mysteries as Jolyon Carr and one as John Redfern early in her career. The popularity of Peter's Cadfael mysteries has inspired fans to contribute to the Abbey Restoration Project. Derek Jacobi appeared as Cadfael in a television series.

[*See also* Clerical Sleuth.]

—Alzina Stone Dale

PICKARD, NANCY (b. 1945), American writer best known for the Jenny Cain series of mysteries, in which small-town matters, personal and family relationships, and sleuthing take equal importance. Born in Kansas City, Missouri, Pickard earned a bachelor's degree in journalism from the Missouri School of Journalism, and worked as a reporter and freelance writer before turning to fiction writing full time. She is married with one son.

In *Generous Death* (1984), Pickard introduces Cain, an *accidental sleuth who works for a charitable organization in the fictional town of Port Frederick, Massachusetts. Although the series sets off with the less-than-promising notion that benefactors are an endangered species—in the fist book, the more you give, the more likely you are to be murdered—Pickard soon developed the tightly-linked connection between Cain's family and the small town, which makes this series work. It appears Cain's father's mismanagement of his company, once a big employer in town, caused the business to fail and resentments to be harbored in Port Frederick. Jenny's mother, a psychiatric patient, seems to have been particularly vulnerable to the situation. As one of the leaders of the 1980s trend to portray women as individuals who

gain strength through experience, Pickard shows Cain as a woman determined to understand her family history, find a mate who respects her, and stand up for underdogs and social causes. Two of the most important books in the Cain series are *I.O.U.* (1991) and *But I Wouldn't Want to Die There* (1993).

During the 1990's, Pickard also turned out three titles continuing a series of culinary mysteries created by Virginia Rich. Pickard's first solo effort on this series is *The Blue Corn Murders* (1998). It followed *The 27-Ingredient Chili Con Carne Murders* (1993), a novel she completed for Rich. In 2000, Pickard put her journalism experience to work with the creation of Marie Lightfoot, a true crime writer. In her first outing, *The Whole Truth* (2000), Lightfoot looks into the case of an escaped child-killer. Children are *victims, too, in *Ring of Truth* (2001), in which Lightfoot focuses on a case involving a minister's affair with a beautiful parishioner. Pickard is the author of award-winning short stories and editor of well-received mystery anthologies that are strong on women's fiction. She served as president of the writers' organization Sisters in Crime.

—Rosemary Herbert

PLAINMAN SLEUTH. The portrayal of the *sleuth as a noticeably ordinary man or woman may have been done in reaction to the proliferation of *Great Detectives in fiction published around the turn of the nineteenth century. In contrast to the *superman sleuth endowed with an extraordinary intellect or professional access to the scene of the crime as official investigator, the plainman sleuth surprises readers by solving crimes via the application of ordinary powers of observation and commonsense reasoning.

As early as 1894, Arthur *Morrison introduced his "cheerful"-looking, average man, Martin Hewitt, in the pages of the *Strand,* the same magazine in which Arthur Conan *Doyle's omniscient Sherlock *Holmes was often featured. Hewitt insisted that he had "no system beyond the judicious use of ordinary faculties."

Samuel Hopkins Adams introduced a sleuth so average-looking that "he was, so to speak, a composite photograph of any thousand well-conditioned, clean-living Americans between the ages of twenty-five and thirty." It turns out that Jones is commonplace in appearance only. His nickname is him, Average Jones, drawn from his initials, A. V. R. E., followed by the J. In fact, Adrian Van Reypen Egerton Jones is a man of grand financial expectations and strong deductive powers who pursues the "hobby" of setting himself up as the "Ad-visor" who helps clients who have been cheated by false advertising. The 1911 volume *Average Jones* features eleven stories about the Ad-visor.

Irish author M. McDonnell Bodkin created a more genuinely average man as sleuth in Paul Beck, who anticipated Margery *Allingham's *silly-ass sleuth Albert *Campion by sporting an expression of mild surprise that masked his intelligence. Beck is described as looking as innocuous as a milkman and giving the impression of being less than brilliant. Beck says, "I just go by the rule of thumb, and muddle and puzzle out my cases as best I can." Bodkin's anthology *Paul Beck, the Rule of Thumb Detective* was published in 1898. This was followed by the publication of *Dora Myrl, the Lady Detective* in 1900. While Myrl is too eccentrically genteel to qualify as a plainwoman sleuth, she marries Beck in *The Capture of Paul Beck* (1909). Plain attributes dominate in their off-spring, who is introduced in *Young Beck, a Chip off the Old Block* (1911).

Closely related to the plainman sleuth is the obtuse sleuth, personified in the title character in *Philo Gubb: Correspondence School Detective* (1919). This comic creation of Ellis Parker Butler solves crimes despite his talent for interpreting clues incorrectly and his flair for sporting mail-order disguises that inevitably fail to mask his purposes.

On a more serious note, a plain approach to the interpretation and even the discovery of clues provides the truth about guilt in Susan Glaspell's poignant story, "A Jury of Her Peers," first penned as a play and later published as a short story in 1917. Based on a case of spousal abuse that Glaspell had covered as a journalist, the perfectly titled story demonstrates how two housewives from the American heartland are able to discover the motive for murder in their neighbor's sewing box, while the police blunder about upstairs, looking for more obvious clues.

These sleuths prove that ordinariness can be an asset in winning readers who may find it easier to identify with ordinary people than with super intellects, and who may enjoy feeling superior to the more comic of the plain sleuths. Average people as sleuths can demonstrate an advantage over professional or intellectually gifted detectives in possessing insight into the details of everyday existence. Similarly, the best *amateur detectives, *accidental sleuths, *nosy parker sleuths, and even inexperienced *private eyes, such as P. D. *James's Cordelia *Gray in *An Unsuitable Job for a Woman* (1972), find that it takes a commonsense approach and everyday experience to get to the truth of their cases.

—Rosemary Herbert

POE, EDGAR ALLAN (1809–1849), American short story writer, poet, and critic, widely considered as founding the genre of detective fiction. His seminal story, "The Murders in the Rue Morgue" (*Graham's Lady's and Gentleman's Magazine*, Apr. 1841), introduces the ratiocinative *sleuth The Chevalier C. Auguste *Dupin. Poe is also an early author of crime stories, for example "The Cask of Amontillado" (*Godey's Lady's Book*, Nov. 1846), in which he probes the psychology of crime.

Edgar Poe was born in Boston, Massachusetts, 19 January 1809, to Elizabeth Arnold Poe, a popular actress, and David Poe, a failed actor and alcoholic who soon deserted his wife and three children. Edgar's older brother and sister were placed with relatives in Baltimore, but Elizabeth kept Edgar with her as she toured

with a theatrical company. Stranded in Richmond and ill with tuberculosis, she died a lingering death when Edgar was two. The boy was taken in by Frances Allan, the childless wife of a merchant who raised but never formally adopted him. They took Edgar with them when John Allan went on business to England from 1815 to 1820.

Edgar took Allan as his middle name. He was sent to the University of Virginia on a scant allowance. There, among sons of wealthy planters, he ran up tailor's and gambling debts Allan refused to pay. Allan, who fully expected Poe to join his business, had no sympathy with his charge's literary ambitions. They parted with acrimony, and thereafter Poe signed his work "Edgar A. Poe," suppressing "Allan." Poe enlisted in the army, then enrolled at, and dropped out from, West Point. He went to live with his aunt, Maria Clemm, and her young daughter, Virginia. When the girl reached thirteen, Poe married her.

Poe's first work, *Tamerlane and Other Poems*, was published anonymously ("by a Bostonian") in 1827. He made a meager living as a magazine contributor and editor, writing scores of stories and sketches, some fifty poems, and more than three hundred book reviews. His "The Raven" (*The Raven and Other Poems*, 1845) was an immense success. He was a brilliant author and editor, but his occasional binge drinking led to his brief tenures at *The Southern Literary Messenger* (1835–36), *Burton's Gentleman's Magazine* (1839–40), *Graham's Lady's and Gentleman's Magazine* (1841–42), the *New York Evening Mirror* (1844–45), and the *Broadway Journal* (1845). Despite his literary successes, Poe had no regular income, and his wife, his aunt, and he himself were often near starvation. In the winter of 1847, his wife died of tuberculosis, as had his mother and Mrs. Allan before her.

After Virginia's death, Poe conducted agitated courtships of several literary ladies. Returning from a visit to one in Richmond, he stopped in Baltimore and was found insensible in the gutter. Taken to a hospital, he died on 7 October 1849. The circumstances of his death have never been satisfactorily explained.

Poe's preeminence as deviser of the modern detective story rests on four tales, "The Murders in the Rue Morgue," "The Mystery of Marie Roget" (*Snowden's Lady's Companion*, Nov. 1842), "The Gold Bug" (*Philadelphia Dollar Newspaper*, 21 June 1843), and "The Purloined Letter" (*The Gift*, 1845). Poe's depictions of detective work are remarkable, especially considering that he wrote at a time when few American cities had police departments and even Scotland Yard had not yet established its Detective Department. According to *The Oxford English Dictionary*, the word "detective" first appeared in a British legal journal in 1843, two years after Poe wrote "The Murders in the Rue Morgue."

Poe is more concerned with detection than with crime. In "The Gold Bug," the crime occurred many years prior to the action, which centers on recovery of the pirate's treasure through decoding a set of directions written in a cipher. The proof of William Legrand's genius is his ability to read this code. The crime, or crimes—theft of the treasure, murder of accomplices—are not solved at all. The tale concentrates on several of Poe's obsessive motifs: cracking the code as a metaphor for discovering hidden truths; embodiment of the ratiocinative principle, separated from the emotions by Poe's facultative psychology; and the contrivance of a tale in which every detail contributes to the desired effect.

Poe originated an astonishing number of conventions in detective fiction. The brilliant detective, the locked room mystery, and the bungling of inept police are among the more obvious. The use of sleight of hand—placing all clues in sight while leading the reader to regard them from a point of view that will not reveal the truth—is another of Poe's inventions. His construction of the detective story has become classic. The most salient feature of Poe's detective tales is the introduction, as narrator, of an unnamed voice, the contrast with whose bland and obtuse normality dramatizes the genius of the detective. This unperceptive narrator is of course a surrogate for the reader, who shares his astonishment at the ingenious and intuitive processes by which the hero's mind leaps from the available facts to the hidden truths of the case.

Dupin and Legrand are reclusive heroes of mind and imagination, set apart from ordinary men by their erudite pursuits, arcane hobbies, special knowledge. Poe's unique achievement is to have recast as detective the Romantic hero of sensibility.

Poe's innovations have influenced many later writers, including Arthur Conan *Doyle, P. D. *James, and Colin *Dexter. Most later writers resemble Poe in having their detectives work outside the police bureaucracy. From this tension derive the private eye fictions of Raymond *Chandler, Dashiell *Hammett, and a host of others, in whose tales the elegance of Poe's milieus and characters are replaced by postnaturalistic tough guys and mean streets. Yet their descent from Poe's conceptions is nonetheless plain. Poe's genius is evident, too, in the psychological depths his tales reveal to the reader prepared to probe them. Preeminent among the few authors whose philosophical detective fictions extend Poe's influence are G. K. *Chesterton (The Man Who Was Thursday, 1908) and Jorge Luis Borges. Most crime and detective writers, however, have been more concerned with plot than with character. By their skillful manipulations of the conventions of these genres, many invented by Poe, the best of them have given us an ever growing literature of popular entertainment.

—Daniel Hoffman

POETS AS CRIME WRITERS.

From the time Edgar Allan *Poe wrote "The Murders in the Rue Morgue" (Graham's Lady's and Gentleman's Magazine, Apr. 1841), poets have also turned their hand to writing tales of mystery and imagination. Presumably, they are attracted to a literature that shares with much poetry the importance of form and structure. In Ellery Queen's Poetic Justice, 23 Stories of Crime, Mystery, and Detection by World-Famous Poets from Geoffrey Chaucer to Dylan Thomas, (1967) Ellery *Queen argues that poets, like detectives, seek to make order from chaos. Support for this thesis may be found in poet W. H. Auden's important essay, "The Guilty Vicarage" (Harper's Magazine, May 1948). Although Auden did not himself write crime fiction, he was an enthusiast of the genre who contended that the most satisfying detective stories introduce crime into the "great good place" and then portray the restoration of order by the detective. Queen also points out that some poetry can be considered to fall within the crime and mystery genre, citing as examples Robert Frost's "The Witch of Coos" (Poetry: A Magazine of Verse, 22 Jan. 1922) and T. S. Eliot's "Macavity: The Mystery Cat" (Old Possum's Book of Practical Cats, 1939).

The mysteries written by poets do not fall into a single category. E. C. *Bentley, inventor of the clerihew (a verse form comprising two rhymed couplets) wrote the prototype for the Golden Age detective story, Trent's Last Case (1913; The Woman in Black). His contemporary Hilaire Belloc also wrote lighthearted detective fiction, but this has failed to stand the test of time. The Big Clock (1946; No Way Out) by Kenneth Fearing, a talented poet of the Depression era, is a masterpiece of suspense. In the 1980s and 1990s, Stephen *Dobyns wrote a series of novels featuring the Saratoga private investigator Charlie Bradshaw, as well as several volumes of verse.

As a generalization, it seems that poets become crime writers rather than vice versa. Julian *Symons founded and edited the influential magazine Twentieth-Century Verse and published collections of his own poetry before achieving distinction as an author and critic of mystery novels, while two of his friends and fellow poets, Ruthven Todd and Roy Fuller, flirted with the genre before abandoning it. Symons has related that Todd, writing as R. T. Campbell, wrote twelve detective novels in six months shortly after the Second World War, although only eight appear to have been published. Fuller's three mysteries appeared between 1948 and 1954; they include The Second Curtain (1953), which gives a bleak account of a writer's brush with violent crime. Agatha *Christie was one of many mystery novelists who dabbled with poetry before concentrating on prose. Reginald *Hill said he realized he was destined to write a crime novel after penning one poem that featured Death as a hitman and another taking the form of an interrogation of suspects in a country house murder mystery. Others, like Dobyns, have continued to write both mysteries and poems. John *Harvey, creator of the Nottingham policeman Charlie Resnick, not only writes poetry but also runs the small press that publishes it. No one, however, has worn the two hats of poet and crime writer more successfully than Cecil Day-Lewis. Under the pseudonym Nicholas *Blake, he created the detective Nigel Strangeways, a character based on W. H. Auden. Blake's finest novel is probably The Beast Must Die (1938), but he continued to write mystery novels until shortly before his death in 1972, despite his continuing commitment to poetry, which culminated in his appointment as Poet Laureate.

—Martin Edwards

Poirot, Hercule. Agatha *Christie's Belgian *sleuth was conceived as little more than a collection of foibles, yet today Hercule Poirot is acknowledged as second only to Sherlock *Holmes in the pantheon of *Great Detectives. His distinctive appearance, habits, and techniques established in Christie's first book, *The Mysterious Affair at Styles* (1920).

Short and dignified with an egg-shaped head and waxed mustache, Poirot has an obsession for neatness, order, and method. Formerly with the Belgian police, he retired and was smuggled out of France and into England during 1916 and soon renewed his acquaintance with Captain Arthur Hastings, whom he had previously met in his home country. Poirot's English is fractured and his use of idiom particularly eccentric, but the sharpness of his mind is undeniable. Comically immodest, he refers to his gift for detection as little more than the use of "the little grey cells" of his brain. After he solves a complex poisoning mystery at Styles court, he, though already into his sixties, embarks on a second career as a private inquiry agent in England.

In *The Mysterious Affair at Styles* and thirty-three later novels and five collections of short stories, Poirot is seen through the eyes of his friend Hastings. The relationship between the men resembles that of Holmes and Dr. John H. *Watson, and many other of Christie's touches in the early cases—including the pair's shared rooms at 14 Farraway Street in London as well as several of the puzzles themselves—echo the work of Arthur Conan *Doyle. As her skill and confidence developed, Christie recognized that Hastings was hardly capable of plausible growth and banished him, following marriage, to Argentina. Poirot moves to a large luxury flat, where he is assisted by an efficient secretary, Miss Felicity Lemon, and his manservant, George, whom Poirot addresses as Georges; his friends and acquaintances include police officers and the detective novelist Ariadne Oliver.

Christie came in time to tire of Poirot, but she did not make Doyle's mistake and seek to discard her most popular character; indeed, his flair for penetrating to the heart of a mystery continued to spark his creator's imagination, and he is the central figure in many of her best books, including *The Murder of Roger Ackroyd* (1926), *The ABC Murders* (1936; *The Alphabet Murders*), and *Cards on the Table* (1936), in which there are only four suspects, yet the revelation of the truth still comes as a surprise. Because a conceited elderly bachelor such as Poirot had limited scope for development, Christie abandoned the Holmesian ambience and turned her detective's traits cleverly to advantage. In *Three Act Tragedy* (1935; *Murder in Three Acts*), Poirot acknowledges that speaking broken English is an enormous asset, since it tempts suspects to underestimate him and thus let their

guard slip. Christie was not afraid to poke fun at him, but in his "bourgeois" disapproval of murder he reflects her attitudes. In *Hallow'en Party* (1969), Christie emphasizes that Poirot always thinks first of justice and is suspicious of an excess of mercy. In *One, Two Buckle My Shoe* (1940; *The Patriotic Murders, An Overdose of Death*), he is prepared to see the downfall of a pillar of the establishment rather than allow the deaths of insignificant, and in some cases odious, individuals to go unavenged. He often speaks of the need to understand psychology, but his principal gift is for relentless logic. An acute observer of people, Poirot has a particular interest in the nature of murder *victims, explaining that without an understanding of the individual who has been killed, it is impossible to see the circumstances of a crime clearly. He develops a taste for fictional crime, and in *The Clocks* (1963) he treats his friend Colin Lamb to an entertaining discourse on the subject. He takes his last bow in *Curtain* (1975), a book written more than thirty years prior to its publication, when Christie's powers were at their peak. The plot follows to its ultimate conclusion the belief that, in order to bring about justice, a Great Detective may need to act outside the law. "Murder is a drama," Poirot notes in one of his subtlest investigations, *Five Little Pigs* (1943; *Murder in Retrospect*), and no *sleuth ever left the stage with a more dramatic flourish.

—Martin Edwards

POLICE DETECTIVE. A private detective may reject cases. An amateur detective might also, but the police detective must take every case presented. That fact underlies the police procedural in its attempt to capture the daily routine of police professionals in which teamwork is all-important, even though it may be frustrated by political interference or the incessant demands of the official agency's caseload.

In fiction there are, of course, detectives who are police officers in name only. Seen more often with civilian sidekicks than at police headquarters, they address unusual and dramatic crimes. Anomalous cases, however, are the exception for the detective pictured as an integral part of the force charged with the public safety and security.

There seems to be no singular personality type on the force. Joyce *Porter's Inspector Wilfred *Dover stands out because he is childish, selfish, and physically disgusting. He backs into solutions others reach through painstaking footwork or agonizing thought. Others, like Martha *Grimes's Inspector Richard Jury or P. D.*James's Commander Adam *Dalgliesh have uniquely distinctive personalities that develop from novel to novel, so that the reader will sympathetically follow their progress in earning professional approval or weathering personal disappointments. The most capable police detectives would not necessarily make sparkling dinner guests. While Michael *Innes's Sir John *Appleby and Josephine *Tey's Inspector Alan Grant may move comfortably in all circles, many other police detectives are socially inept. Some, such as Joseph Wambaugh's uniformed officers, feel an isolation from the civilian world. What they best share is dedication to the job that helps them survive low pay, redundant paperwork, danger, and long hours.

The police detectives handle their career pressures differently. Some internalize their tensions until they develop stomach problems, like Maj *Sjöwall and Per Wahlöö's Martin *Beck, or depression, like his friend Lennart Kollberg. Some become workaholics, eschewing vacations, like Rex Burns's Gabriel Wager, or a social life, like Margaret *Maron's Lieutenant Sigrid Harald. Many are shown by their authors losing out in personal relationships.

There are exceptions, for John *Creasey's Roger West is happily wed, as is Michael *Gilbert's Patrick Patrella. Dorothy Simpson's Detective Inspector Luke Thanet leaves stress behind when he goes home to his family. Ruth *Rendell's Chief Inspector Reginald *Wexford or Bartholomew *Gill's inspector, later chief-superintendent, Peter McGarr may be helped on cases by their spouses, while Ngaio *Marsh's inspector (later superintendent) Roderick *Alleyn carries on a courtship while sleuthing.

Police detectives in fiction come from assorted backgrounds. K. C. *Constantine's Mario Balzic is a product of the American immigrant working class, and Robert *Barnard's Inspector Perry Trethowan comes from an advantaged but quirky family, which Trethowan, in one novel, must investigate. Sheila Radley's Inspector Douglas Quantrill dropped out of school at age fourteen, a fact about which he is very self-conscious, while Henry *Wade's Detective Inspector, later Chief Inspector, John Poole passed his bar exams and spent a year in chambers before joining the CID. Although Leo *Bruce's Sergeant William *Beef is anything but a gentleman, Marsh's Alleyn is definitely to the manner born.

Often a better-educated officer will explain things to his subordinate, as Colin *Dexter's Inspector Endeavour *Morse explains Wagnerian opera to Sergeant Lewis, but some authors develop generational tension by reversing that order. Inspector Douglas Quantrill must contend with Sergeant Martin Tait, fresh from both college and the police academy, and Reginald *Hill's balding Andrew Dalziel may hold the rank of superintendent, but it is Sergeant Peter Pascoe who holds the degree.

Police detectives' methods of solving crimes range from the ratiocination similar to that exhibited by Golden Age detectives to the techniques from which the police procedural takes its name. The latter include using informants, tailing suspects, staking out suspicious locations, interviewing *witnesses, combing the scene of the crime, and poring over forensic evidence. In addition, Alan Hunter's Inspector, later Superintendent, George Gently has long philosophical discussions with suspects; Freeman Wills *Crofts's Inspector Joseph *French breaks alibis by concentrating on timetables; Arthur W. *Upfield's Inspector Napoleon *Bonaparte goes undercover to get the information he needs.

Edgar Allan *Poe's "Murders in the Rue Morgue" (in Graham's Lady's and Gentleman's Magazine, Apr. 1841), generally credited as the earliest detective story, presents a prefect of police, but he takes a backseat to the independent detective the Chevalier C. Auguste *Dupin. Charles *Dickens's Inspector Bucket was followed in the nineteenth century by Wilkie *Collins's Sergeant Richard *Cuff and Émile Gaboriau's Monsieur Lecoq, but the detective as a member of a police force continued to be a minor figure until the twentieth century. Then, in 1910, A. E. W. *Mason's Inspector *Hanaud of the Paris Sûreté, took center stage. Although Hanaud's striking powers of perception and observation are employed on behalf of the official order, they are applied like those of private *sleuths who flourish between the world wars in the country houses and watering holes of Europe. Inspector Jules *Maigret, creation of the prolific Georges *Simenon, comes on the scene in 1933 as an officer who works in many milieus. Indeed, the bourgeois investigator solves his cases through gifted intuition and methodical immersion in the ambience of assorted crime scenes high and low.

For all the popularity of Maigret in France or of Alleyn or Appleby in England, American writers tended to avoid official detectives in favor of hard-boiled private investigators until after World War II. Then in 1945, Lawrence *Treat's V as in Victim (1945) gave the world an American police procedural. Hillary *Waugh's Last Seen Wearing followed in 1952. Meanwhile, John *Creasey had introduced Roger West to England, following him up with Commander George Gideon in works written as J. J. Marric. Since then, the realistic depiction of police work has remained a strength of crime and mystery writing.

Despite attempts to wax poetic about Isola, a.k.a. New York, Ed *McBain typifies the procedural approach in language of clipped speech and concentration on "just the facts," a concept already proved popular by the television show Dragnet. To reinforce the cooperation necessary for police success, McBain presents his Eighty-seventh Precinct characters as a collective protagonist; once McBain even attempted to kill off Steve Carella when he became more popular than others in his cohort. McBain's example is reflected today in the work of the British author John *Harvey. His jazz-loving Charlie Resnick is more fully developed than the rest of his squad, but the focus is on the group, and each member takes a turn in the spotlight.

Inevitably readers will see social themes in fiction devoted to detectives enrolled as professional agents of society. An early author to capitalize on this disposition was Earl Derr *Biggers, who deliberately created detective sergeant and inspector Charlie *Chan as an affirmative contrast to the Chinese villains of popular twenties fiction. The Martin Beck novels by Sjöwall and Wahlöö are highly critical of Sweden's welfare state. The pre-independence South African setting of James *Mc-Clure's novels featuring Lieutenant Tromp *Kramer and Sergeant Mickey Zondi automatically demands social comments. Although this team of an Afrikaner and a Zulu works together well, the novels clearly reveal the injustices of apartheid. John *Ball's Virgil *Tibbs novels are written with a multicultural message, not only about the relationship between African Americans and Caucasians, but also about the Eastern cultures in which Ball is well versed.

For many years police detectives have been stalking international terrain. One can find Nicolas *Freeling's Inspector *Van der Valk in Amsterdam, H. R. F. *Keating's Inspector Ganesh Vinayak *Ghote in India, Bartholomew *Gill's Inspector McGarr in the Irish Republic, and James Melville's Superintendent Tetsuo Otani in Japan. As might be expected, American tradition has begun to exhibit cultural and ethnic variety of police detectives. Chester *Himes's Coffin Ed *Johnson and Grave Digger Jones began working in Harlem in 1959, while Dell Shannon's Lieutenant Luis Mendoza hit the West Coast in 1960. Today Tony *Hillerman's Jim *Chee and Joe Leaphorn, Navajo detectives, bring details of Native American culture into police plots.

Gender diversity is newer. Joan *Hess's Police Chief Arly Hanks is just assuming her job while she gets over a divorce. As the number of real women choosing police work as a profession is increasing, they are more frequent in fiction. Barbara Paul's Marian Larch seems to fit into her New York department with little difficulty. Susan *Dunlap's Sergeant Jill Smith, like Margaret *Maron's Lieutenant Sigrid Harald, takes advantage of equal employment opportunities to move ahead despite resentment from older, male officers.

Some see the fictional detective as one who brings order to a disorderly world. In police detection, however, return to order is as elusive in the fictional plot as in the society it models. The most police detectives can do is affect temporary closure, one story at a time. For many readers, that is enough.

—Marcia J. Songer

PORTER, JOYCE (1924–1990), British author of satiric detective novels and spy fiction. Born in Cheshire and educated at King's College, London, she served in the Women's Royal Air Force. Her British police procedural series introduced the sixteen-stone antihero Detective Chief Inspector Wilfred *Dover (in *Dover One,* 1964), who manages to solve unsavory cases, some concerned with cannibalism and castrations in *Dover and the Unkindest Cut of All* (1967), while satisfying his considerable desire for comfort. In the Honourable Constance Morrison-Burke series, beginning with *Rather a Common Sort of Crime* (1970), the insensitive Hon Con, an amateur, is warned off every crime scene by the police, but remains convinced of her importance to the investigation. With satiric jabs at sexism, elitism, and codes of honor, and with repulsive and unsavory char-

acters, Porter creates an earthy world whose bleakness is tempered by humor.

[*See also* Police Detective.]

—Georgia Rhoades

POST, MELVILLE DAVISSON (1869–1930), American author, *lawyer, and political figure. Born and raised in West Virginia, Post obtained a law degree and practiced there for a dozen years, while emerging as a prominent figure in the state's Democratic Party politics. In 1896 he published *The Strange Schemes of Randolph Mason,* a collection of stories about an unscrupulous lawyer who exploits legal loopholes to the benefit of his clients. Another similar volume, *The Man of Last Resort; or, The Clients of Randolph Mason* appeared in 1897, followed by *The Corrector of Destinies* (1908), in which Mason does a turnabout and labors now on the side of justice.

Although he wrote scores of crime stories, his greatest success came with *Uncle Abner, Master of Mysteries* (1918), a collection in which Post drew on the rugged rural mountain setting he knew so well and created the righteous, Bible-quoting Uncle Abner, a country squire who roams the lawless Virginia backlands of the 1850s, a scourge of evil, avenging crimes against God and man. The Uncle Abner tale in that volume, "The Doomdorf Mystery," is a classic regaded by critics as one of the most extraordinary locked room mysteries ever written.

—Donald A. Yates

Priestley, Dr. Lancelot, an *amateur detective sometimes called "the sage of Westbourne Terrace." Created by British author John *Rhode, he appears in more than seventy novels and some short stories. Except for his early cases, Priestley works in the tradition of the *armchair detective, solving problems in cerebral splendor with a minimum of physical activity; relying largely on others to do the legwork and collect information.

Grim and virtually humorless, although a good host when discussing murder, he is a mathematician of formidable intellect. His declining years (hardly an appropriate term) are spent in applying logic to crime puzzles brought to him by friends from Scotland Yard.

Following *The Paddington Mystery* (1925), which introduced Priestley and other recurring characters, the series extending to 1961 is known for its variety of ingenious murder methods. Perhaps the best is *The House on Tollard Ridge* (1929), concerning the death of a rich eccentric.

[*See also* Eccentrics.]

—Melvyn Barnes

PRIVATE DETECTIVE. The private detective is one of the three main types of fictional detective, the others being the *amateur detective and the *police detective. Although characters who may be described as private detectives are occasionally to be met with in Victorian mystery fiction, they almost invariably play a peripheral role in the works in which they appear. An exception is

The Notting Hill Mystery (1863), by Charles Felix, an author of whom little is known. This consists of reports and letters compiled by an insurance investigator, Ralph Henderson, to mount a case against a certain Baron R who is suspected of his wife's murder. As an insurance investigator Henderson is not, strictly speaking, a private detective; in addition, he remains throughout the story a shadowy, disembodied figure. The first real private detective in fiction is therefore also the greatest and the best-known, Arthur Conan *Doyle's Sherlock *Holmes, who made his first appearance in *A Study in Scarlet* (1887). To create Holmes, Doyle borrowed characteristics from Edgar Allan *Poe's Chevalier C. Auguste *Dupin and Émile *Gaboriau's Monsieur Lecoq, giving him superhuman powers of ratiocination and making him a master of disguise. From Poe he also took the relationship between the brilliant detective and the imperceptive, but admiring friend and narrator, humanizing both participants in the process: the Holmes-Watson paradigm was to be much imitated by later authors, commending itself chiefly as the fairest way of laying the clues of a detective puzzle before the reader.

The success of Holmes led to the appearance in the years preceding the First World War of a number of private detectives most of whom are now—perhaps deservedly—forgotten. Unlike Holmes, however, they are for the most part decidedly ordinary characters, lacking their predecessor's seemingly miraculous powers of deduction. As with Doyle, the format almost universally adopted was that of the magazine short story, collections of which were later published in book form. Among the first to follow Doyle was Arthur *Morrison, whose character Martin Hewitt, a former solicitor's clerk, runs a private detective agency near the Strand (*Martin Hewitt, Investigator*, 1894). More interesting, as one of the first female detectives, is George Sims's Dorcas Dene, "a professional lady detective," forced into the profession when her husband goes blind (*Dorcas Dene, Detective*, 1897). Victor L. Whitechurch's Thorpe Hazell, a vegetarian, takes only cases concerned with the railways (*Thrilling Stories of the Railway*, 1912), while William Hope Hodgson's Carnacki occupies himself solely with the allegedly supernatural (*Carnacki the Ghost Finder*, 1913). An American example is the scholarly Fleming Stone, who appears in novels by Carolyn Wells (*The Clue*, 1909).

The inter-war years, the Golden Age of the detective story and in which the novel regained its dominance, were ushered in by the appearance of the private detective who was almost to rival Holmes in popularity, Agatha *Christie's Hercule *Poirot (*The Mysterious Affair at Styles*, 1920). A. E. W. *Mason's Inspector *Hanaud has been suggested as a model for Poirot; it seems also that Christie might have deliberately constructed her detective as an antipode to Holmes, since his characteristics are diametrically opposed to those of his predecessor. But she remains true to the original in making Poirot, like Holmes, a *superman sleuth, and in imitating the Holmes-Watson pattern of narration, using for this purpose Captain Arthur Hastings, Poirot's almost too obtuse friend. However, the majority of those writers—again, for the most part, now forgotten—who produced private detectives in the following decade favored a third-person over a first-person narrative, and broke further with the Holmes-Poirot tradition by abandoning the concept of the *sleuth with superhuman powers of ratiocination. Among the characters of this period are, in England, Lynn Brock's Colonel Wyckham Gore (*The Deductions of Colonel Gore*, 1924), Edgar *Wallace's Mr J. G. *Reeder (*The Mind of Mr J. G. Reeder*, 1925), J. S. Fletcher's Ronald Camberwell of the Chaney and Camberwell Detective Agency (*Murder at Wrides Park*, 1931) and R. A. J. Walling's Philip Tolefree (*The Fatal Five Minutes*, 1932); and, in America, Octavus Roy Cohen's Jim Hanvey of New York (*Jim Hanvey, Detective*, 1923) and Anthony *Boucher's Fergus O'Breen of Los Angeles (*The Case of the Crumpled Knave*, 1939). Two authors of this period, however, stand out above the rest: the English Nicholas *Blake and the American Rex *Stout. For his novels about the private detective Nigel Strangeways, which begin with *A Question of Proof* (1935), Blake chooses a third-person, occasionally omniscient narrator, and although he gives Strangeways, like Holmes, a number of eccentricities, he follows the contemporary trend by making him fallible and much less than superhuman. In creating Nero *Wolfe, who first appeared in *Fer-de-Lance* (1934), Stout takes the opposite path, returning to Poe and Doyle to produce another in the line of superman sleuths, and employing Archie *Goodwin, Wolfe's assistant, as a first-person narrator to continue the Holmes-Watson tradition.

Although Holmes and Poirot probably still form the popular image of the fictional detective, few other examples of this type—fewer, certainly, than in the case of the amateur or *police detective—can be placed by their side. In addition, Strangeways and Wolfe appear to mark the end of the tradition that began with Holmes. Although an occasional example can be found—P. D. *James's Cordelia *Gray (*An Unsuitable Job for a Woman*, 1972), for instance—in general the place of the private detective in fiction has been usurped by the *private eye: a process which began with the emergence of the private eye novel in America in the early 1920s. The typical private detective novel is thus a product of the classical period of detective fiction, and hence usually conforms strictly with the conventions then in force. That is, it presents a puzzle—most often the identification of a murderer among a closed group of suspects—scrupulously makes available all the clues to which the detective has access, and challenges the reader to arrive at the solution before the detective.

[*See also* Great Detective, The; Private Eye.]

—T. J. Binyon

PRIVATE EYE. The private eye, or private investigator (from whose initials the sobriquet derives), is the detective hero of a peculiarly American type of crime fiction that had its beginnings in the early 1920s. The gangster-ism and violence engendered by Prohibition provided the subject, the popular pulp magazines of the time—*Detective Story, Dime Detective*, and *Black Mask*, for ex-amples—constantly demanded new and exciting mate-rial, while the hero himself owes something to the hero—the lone individual—of the American Western. The first private eye story is generally taken to be Carroll John *Daly's "The False Burton Combs," published in *Black Mask* in 1922. Daly's hero in a long series of short stories and novels is the tough, fearless, and violent Race *Wil-liams, who is capable of firing his two revolvers simul-taneously yet making only one hole between the eyes of his *victims. There is an element of sadism in this hero's violence that, while in general foreign to the type and indeed unthinkable in most cases, was to resurface in the behavior of Mike *Hammer, Mickey *Spillane's private eye.

In 1923 Dashiell *Hammett produced the first of a number of stories about a short, tubby, forty-year-old known only as the *Continental Op, who works for the Continental Detective Agency in San Francisco. In 1930 Hammett published *The Maltese Falcon*, believed by many to be the finest private eye novel of all, whose central character, Sam *Spade, provides an exemplar of the type. In 1939 Raymond *Chandler, who had written a number of short stories with a variety of heroes for pulp magazines, added a new dimension to the type with the creation, in *The Big Sleep*, of his private eye, Philip *Marlowe. In contrast to characters such as Spade, who have an eye for the main chance and pursue their own interests as ruthlessly as those of their client, Marlowe is a man of high moral principle, altruistic, always ready to sacrifice himself for his client, a blend of knight and father confessor, with touches of sainthood. Chandler made his intentions clear in "The Simple Art of Murder" (*Atlantic Monthly*, Dec. 1944), writing: "Down these mean streets a man must go who is not himself mean, who is neither tarnished nor afraid. . . . He must be . . . a man of honor . . . He must be the best man in his world and a good enough man for any world." This can be compared with Hammett's remark, in the introduction to a 1934 edition of *The Maltese Falcon*, that Spade is "a hard and shifty fellow, able to take care of himself in any situation, able to get the best of anybody he comes in contact with, whether criminal, innocent bystander or client."

The canonical formula had become firmly estab-lished by the 1940s: Occasionally working for an agency, sometimes with a partner, but more often alone, the pri-vate eye, who usually tells the story in the first person, is entrusted with a case that brings him into conflict with criminals or organized crime and frequently with the—usually corrupt—police; in the latter respect the narra-tive as a whole may often be read as an implicit or ex-plicit commentary on American society and politics. Cynical and witty, with a keen and sometimes even po-etic eye for his surroundings, he usually conceals a soft

heart beneath a hard-boiled exterior. Regularly beaten up or shot at, and regularly replying in kind, he may also become sexually involved with his client or his secretary: characteristics that distinguish him from his more gen-teel counterpart, the English private detective.

The genre also introduced a new form, as well as a new character, into crime fiction. The detective story is closed and circular: It begins with a crime, most often murder, that is succeeded by the detective's investigation of a small group of subjects, and ends with a recapitu-lation of the opening event. The private eye story, by contrast, is open and linear. The initial impetus is a cli-ent's problem; in investigating this the private eye moves from place to place, encountering a succession of new characters and uncovering a deeper intrigue. The reso-lution of this, rather than the original problem, provides the ending, and a murder or murders may occur at any point and are often ancillary to the main plot. Ten years after Marlowe's first appearance, Ross *Macdonald pub-lished *The Moving Target* (1949), his first Lew *Archer novel written as John Macdonald. Though Archer shares many of Marlowe's characteristics, Macdonald's concern for the problems of the dysfunctional family—the dom-inant theme in his novels—led him to give the character a psychotherapeutic bent: he becomes a surrogate father to the abandoned and lost children he encounters. Chan-dler's work and hero, however, were to provide the model for future authors; his influence on style and char-acter creation has been immense, leading, at times, to almost parodic imitation, as in Robert B. *Parker's early novels about a Boston private eye, *Spenser.

Though the traditional setting—used by Hammett, Chandler, and Macdonald—for the private eye story is California, other real and fictional cities throughout the United States have been employed as the locale. Authors who have contributed to the genre include Jonathan Lat-imer, whose hero, Bill Crane, works in Chicago; Henry Kane, whose Peter Chambers works in New York; Wil-liam Campbell *Gault with Brock "The Rock" Callahan in Los Angeles; Michael Z. Lewin, whose Albert Samson works in Indianapolis; Michael Allegretto, whose Jacob Lomax works in Denver; Jonathan Valin with Harry Stoner in Cincinnati; Loren D. *Estleman with Amos *Walker in Detroit; Walter *Mosley's Ezekiel "Easy" *Rawlins in Los Angeles; and James *Crumley, although his characters Milo Milodragovitch and C. W. Sughrue, both of Montana, are not, strictly speaking, private eyes.

A now well-established development is the emer-gence of the female private eye: Marcia *Muller's Sharon McCone, one-eighth Shoshone Indian, who works in San Francisco and appeared in *Edwin of the Iron Shoes* (1977), was the first, succeeded by Sue *Grafton's Kinsey *Milhone, also a Californian, Sara *Paretsky's V. I. *War-shawski of Chicago, and Linda *Barnes's Boston detec-tive, Carlotta Carlyle. To these can be added two British examples: Liza *Cody's Anna Lee (*Dupe*, 1980) and Sarah Dunant's Hannah Wolfe (*Birth Marks*, 1991). Attempts to domicile the male private eye in Britain have been without success, however. While the traditional detective story, with a private or *amateur detective as its central character, now seems almost moribund, the private eye formula, by contrast, is full of life. The evidence for this lies not only in the continual emergence of new private eye novels, but also in the fact that the hallmarks of the genre—its style, its dialogue, its narrative method, and its central character—have been adapted to serve a wide variety of genres, from the adventure story to the espionage novel.

[See also Hard-boiled Sleuth.]

—T. J. Binyon

PRODIGAL SON/DAUGHTER. It is easy to understand why the story of the prodigal's return has inspired succeeding generations of mystery writers. The arrival of a stranger in a small community often brings out into the open deep-rooted tensions. If that stranger happens to be a son or daughter who has come back to the heart of a family following a lengthy estrangement, old grudges are apt to be rekindled and long-concealed truths about ancient misdeeds may finally be brought to light. A prodigal is apt to disturb the comfortable certainties of those who stayed at home, particularly if he or she now lays unexpected and unwelcome claim to a handsome inheritance.

Elements of the Biblical tale appear in the work of many mystery writers, but few have made such effective use of it as Agatha *Christie. Harry Lee, the returning black sheep in Hercule Poirot's Christmas (1938; Murder for Christmas, A Holiday for Murder), makes repeated references to the parable. On first arriving at the family home for Christmas, he points out that in the original story, "the good brother" resented the prodigal's return and draws a direct analogy with the hostility of his own brother, Alfred. Later, explaining why he has come back after an absence of twenty years, he claims that he too had tired of the "husks that the swine do eat—or don't eat, I forget which." In A Pocket Full of Rye (1953), Inspector Neele is quick to characterize Lance Fortescue as the prodigal son and Lance readily accepts that description after returning home from Paris following the death of his tycoon father. Again, the stay-at-home elder brother Percival is dismayed by Lance's plan to rejoin the family business and another murder occurs. Christie's use of the parable here is as explicit and ingenious as in the earlier novel. In contrast, in Dead Man's Folly (1956), her plot hinges upon the scheme of a returning prodigal, yet that is not apparent until the solution to a triple murder is revealed.

Josephine *Tey's celebrated novel of impersonation Brat Farrar (1949; Come and Kill Me) draws in a different way upon the Biblical precedent. The eponymous Brat is persuaded to masquerade as Patrick Ashby, a presumed suicide who had disappeared eight years earlier and who would now have been about to come into his inheritance. When the family solicitor first meets Brat, he talks about the fatted calf while making it clear that this is more than just a simple matter of a prodigal's homecoming, since the ultimate destination of a fortune is at stake. Patrick's twin brother Simon also refers amiably to the parable, but his hostility toward Brat soon becomes apparent. In a final twist, it emerges that the prodigal in this case is not a son, but a nephew. The fraud in Brat Farrar is discussed and emulated by the conspirators in Mary Stewart's The Ivy Tree (1961), a novel of romantic suspense and Martha *Grimes's The Old Fox Deceiv'd (1982) also has echoes of Tey's book, although the atmosphere is macabre and the mystery more elaborately contrived. Grimes's prodigal is a woman called Gemma Temple who claims to be Dillys March, the long-lost ward of Colonel Titus Crael.

The prodigal theme is found often in the books of writers working within the tradition of the classic whodunit. In recent years they have included Unruly Son (1978; Death of a Mystery Writer) by Robert *Barnard, Death of a God (1987) by S. T. Haymon, Peter Robinson's The Hanging Valley (1989), and most notably Ruth *Rendell's Put on by Cunning (1981; Death Notes), which concerns a female prodigal whose claim to an inheritance raises questions about her true identity. Yet books with a harder edge may also derive some elements from the old story. Blue City (1947) by Kenneth Millar (who became better known by the pseudonym Ross *Macdonald) is an example in which an angry young man returns to his hometown and becomes involved in an attempt not only to solve the mystery of his father's murder but also to understand how his father contributed to the town's ethos of corruption. For any writer fascinated, like Millar, by complex family relationships, the tale of the returning prodigal provides many thought-provoking plot possibilities.

[See also Missing Persons.]

—Martin Edwards

PROFESSOR SLEUTH. See Academic Sleuth; Bluestocking Sleuth.

PROFILER. See Forensic Pathologist.

PROLIFIC WRITERS. See Industry Writers.

PRONZINI, BILL (WILLIAM JOHN PRONZINI) (b. 1943), versatile and prolific American writer of mystery, suspense, science fiction and westerns. Best-recognized as the creator of a *private eye known as The *Nameless Detective, Pronzini has also produced a considerable output of novels and short stories written under his own name, under pseudonyms, and in collaboration with his wife Marcia *Muller, Barry N. Malzberg, John Lutz, Collin Wilcox, and others. He has also written extensively about pulp fiction, edited numerous short story anthologies, and ghost-written some stories about Mike *Shayne.

Born in Petaluma, California, Pronzini held a variety

of jobs, including sports reporter and civilian guard with the U.S. Marshall's Office, before turned to writing full time in 1969. He married his third wife, Muller, in 1992.

Pronzini's first book, *The Stalker* (1971), is a suspense novel concerning six men, linked by a crime they perpetrated together in the past, who find themselves targeted by a killer. Pronzini followed that page-turner with *The Snatch* (1971), in which he introduces Nameless, a middle-aged former military intelligence officer and San Francisco policeman turned private eye who, like Pronzini, collects pulp fiction. Pronzini also wrote period mysteries set in the nineteenth century featuring John Quincannon, a whisky-drinking secret service agent whose work takes him to Nevada in *Quincannon* (1985), and to Idaho in *Beyond the Grave* (1985), a work co-authored by Muller. As Jack Foxx, Pronzini wrote numerous short stories and a series of novels about Dan Connell. He also turned out suspense fiction as Alex Saxon and short fiction as William Jeffrey. Pronzini's editorial skills and sense of humor are evident in *Gun in Cheek: A Study in "Alternative" Crime* (1982) and *Son of Gun in Cheek* (1987), books that bring together pulp fiction of a quality that may be likened to that of "B" movies.

—Rosemary Herbert

PSYCHIC SLEUTH. With the rise of modern Spiritualism after 1848, a new breed of *sleuths appeared in public life. They were not *police detectives empowered to uphold civil law and order; but scientists, philosophers, and professional magicians dedicated to proving or disproving psychic phenomena and the activities of mediums and occultists of the day. Moreover, these figures—as diverse as Sir William Crookes, William James, and Harry Houdini—became the models for a detective unique in literature, the psychic sleuth. Like the classical ratiocinators, the psychic sleuths sought to separate fraud from fact and employed the traditional methods of observation and deduction; unlike them, they possessed special psi powers and a knowledge of occult practices. They embodied a new spirit of inquiry and speculation, functioning by turns as detectives, physicians, scientists, inventors, healers, and priests.

Although major novelists like Nathaniel Hawthorne, William Dean Howells, George Eliot, Edward Bulwer-Lytton, and Henry James had occasionally tackled occult subjects in their works, it was left to minor masters in the field to create the first full-fledged psychic sleuths. The prototype was Joseph Sheridan Le Fanu's Martin Hesselius, a self-styled "medical philosopher" who first appeared in 1864 in a classic ghost story, "Green Tea" (*All the Year Round*, 23 Oct. 1869). "I believe that the essential man is a spirit," Hesselius declared, "that the spirit is an organized substance, but as different in point of material from what we ordinarily understand by matter, as light or electricity is." Le Fanu may have molded him after two famous German ghost-hunters of the day, Justinius Kerner and Heinrich Jung-Stilling.

Subsequent works by other authors extend and develop Hesselius's example, including Algernon Blackwood's five John Silence stories, beginning in 1903; William Hope Hodgson's eight Carnacki the Ghost Finder tales, collected in 1913; Dion Fortune's eleven Dr. Taverner stories in *The Secrets of Dr. Taverner* (1926); Seabury Quinn's ninety-three Jules de Grandin stories, which began appearing in the pulp magazine *Weird Tales* in 1925; Sax *Rohmer's Dream Detective stories (1920); Jack Mann's Gregory George Gordon "Gees" Green novels, including *Gees's First Case* (1936), *Grey Shapes* (1937), and *The Glass Too Many* (1940); Manley Wade Wellman's Silver John stories, collected in *Who Fears the Devil?* (1963); Randall Garrett's Lord Darcy stories, a science fantasy series collected in *Too Many Magicians* (1967); and Joseph Payne Brennan's twenty-five Lucius Leffing tales, collected in *The Casebook of Lucius Leffing* (1973), *The Chronicles of Lucius Leffing* (1977), and in *The Adventures of Lucius Leffing* (1990).

These unusual detectives demonstrate affinities with their more traditional brethren. Some, like Leffing and Carnacki, have no special psychic gifts of their own but employ, respectively, the dogged investigative methods characteristic of Ellery *Queen and a scientific technology like that used by Craig Kennedy. Among those sleuths with psychic gifts, the Dream Detective's aesthetic musings prefigure Philo *Vance's talky connoisseurship; Jules De Grandin's eccentric French mannerisms recall Hercule *Poirot's idiosyncrasies; Lord Darcy's bizarre cases are reminiscent of Gideon *Fell's more exotic investigations; and Silver John's backwoods milieu belongs to the world of Uncle *Abner.

Silver John also reminds us of another classic investigator, Father *Brown, in that his central concern is not the apprehension of a wrongdoer but the saving of a soul. This is no mere cops-and-robbers formula, but a cosmic struggle against hostile forces. In Le Fanu's words, "There does exist beyond this a spiritual world—a system whose workings are generally in mercy hidden from us—a system which may be, and which sometimes is, partially and terrible revealed. I am sure—I *know* . . . that there is a God—a dreadful God—and that retribution follows guilt, in ways the most mysterious and stupendous—by agencies the most inexplicable and terrific."

—John C. Tibbetts

Q

Queen, Ellery. Because Frederic Dannay and Manfred B. Lee wisely used the same name, Ellery Queen, for their joint pseudonym and their detective, they created a name recognition that made Queen the best-known American detective during the 1930s and much of the 1940s. He appeared in a long series of novels and short stories, beginning in 1929 and continuing through 1971. Even radio scripts of the successful *The Adventures of Ellery Queen* (1939–48) program found their way into print.

Ellery Queen is introduced in *The Roman Hat Mystery* (1929), in which he is depicted as a handsome, aloof young man in the mold of Philo *Vance, then one of American fiction's most popular *sleuths. Queen is a dilettante who carries a walking stick, wears pince-nez, and drives a Duesenberg. In the character's first appearance, he is called away from a rare book buying expedition to a Broadway theater in which a murder has taken place. He is a writer, but during his first decade as a fictional character he is also a willing unofficial consultant on difficult cases for his father, Inspector Richard Queen of the New York Police Department, with whom he shares a Manhattan brownstone.

Queen's most notable trait is his intelligence; and he is described as Sherlock *Holmes's logical successor. Using unassailable logic, he sifts through complex clues, motives, and alibis to arrive at solutions. His forte is solving bizarre murders, as in *The Egyptian Cross Mystery* (1932), with its crucifixions. Later in his career, he becomes a highly proficient interpreter of dying messages, obscure notes or objects left by murder *victims which, only if interpreted correctly, point to the killer.

By *The Devil to Pay* (1938), the Queen character is more serious about his writing, having been hired by a Hollywood studio as a screenwriter. However, he is not given assignments, and so relieves his frustration by solving murders. After a one-book stint (*The Dragon's Teeth*, 1939) as a paid *private detective, Ellery enters the most serious period of his career as writer and *amateur detective.

In *Calamity Town* (1942), to gain privacy to write a book, he goes to Wrightsville, a fictional New England village. While there, he becomes so deeply involved with Wrightsville's residents that he returns to the village throughout his career to help solve local crimes. He becomes more down to earth and less inclined to show off his mental prowess when explaining a solution. In *The Murderer Is a Fox* (1945) he helps a war veteran who has been accused of murder. In *Ten Days' Wonder* (1948) and *Double, Double* (1950; *The Case of the Seven Murders*), he relies less on physical clues, now applying his wide reading of psychology and religion.

In New York City, he discovers a greater, if occasionally reluctant, involvement in social problems. In *Cat of Many Tails* (1949), the randomness with which a serial killer picks his victims brings the city to the brink of hysteria and class warfare. Only at the request of the mayor does Ellery agree to find the killer. At about this time, Ellery solves a series of short cases dealing with current New York City problems, including juvenile delinquency.

His later cases refer to prior exploits. *The Finishing Stroke* (1958) is a flashback to 1929 when, as a newly published author, he attends a Christmas party and faces a case of murder among guests isolated by a snowstorm. *And on the Eighth Day* (1964) is set in 1944 when Queen, returning from Hollywood where he wrote war films for the government, is stranded in the desert community of a religious sect, which treats him as its possible messiah.

It is not only a name that Queen shares with his creator. Parallels, especially to Dannay, are many. Queen, the character, and Dannay were both bibliophiles, each amassing a valuable library of first editions. Dannay and Lee also both spent time in Hollywood, years of frustration in which they never received script credit. Following Dannay's near fatal automobile accident in 1940, the writers showed greater awareness of social issues, as did Ellery Queen, the detective.

—Marvin Lachman

QUEEN, ELLERY. Joint pseudonym of Frederic Dannay (Daniel Nathan; 1905–1982) and Manfred B. Lee (Manford Lepofsky; 1905–1971), a team of American detective writers, magazine editors, anthologists, bibliographers, and chroniclers of the history of detective fiction. Dannay and Lee also employed the pseudonym "Barnaby Ross" for four detective novels in 1932–33 featuring Drury Lane, a deaf, ex-Shakespearean actor. (The true identity of Ross was not revealed until 1936.) To further complicate matters, the Queen name was used by other writers to fill out plots created by Dannay, and the name Ellery Queen, Jr. was appropriated by James Holding for a series of eleven juvenile novels featuring the Queens' orphan-boy-of-all work, Djuna, written between 1941 and 1966.

Nathan and Lepofsky were first cousins, born nine months and five blocks apart, of immigrant Jewish stock in Brooklyn, New York. By the late 1920s Dannay was working as an advertising copywriter and Lee as a movie company publicist. Attracted by a $7,500 prize contest sponsored by *McClure's Magazine*, they submitted *The Roman Hat Mystery*, which employed the then-novel idea of giving both author and detective the same name,

Ellery Queen. The magazine changed hands but the novel was published by Frederick A. Stokes in 1929. Success came quickly, and after the publication of the third "Queen" novel in 1931, *The Dutch Shoe Mystery*, the two collaborators gave up their jobs to write full time. Individually and together they toured on cross-country promotions, wearing masks while they autographed books and lectured on college campuses. When appearing together, they developed a platform routine impersonating "Ellery Queen" and "Barnaby Ross," challenging each other's skill as detectives. In Hollywood in the late 1930s they worked as scriptwriters for Columbia, Paramount, and M-G-M. Their frustrations as scenarists (they never received a screen credit) were reflected in their character's struggles in the movie industry in *The Devil to Pay* (1938; *The Perfect Crime*) and *The Four of Hearts* (1938). Back in New York by 1939, working out of a tiny office in the Fisk Building near Columbus Circle, they spent the next decade writing weekly scripts for *The Adventures of Ellery Queen* radio show on CBS (the first hour-long dramatic show in the history of radio), building up one of the world's finest private libraries of crime fiction, co-founding Mystery Writers of America in 1945, and beginning a new magazine, *Ellery Queen's Mystery Magazine* (*EQMM*).

The pair's work as editors, anthologists, scholars, and bibliographers was more prolific than their output of fiction. Their first venture in editing was the legendary magazine *Mystery League*, which folded after only four issues, October 1933 through January 1934. Dannay and Lee assumed the entire work load. *EQMM* began in 1941 and, despite Dannay's death in 1982, continues to this day. Among the more than 100 outstanding anthologies also edited under the Queen byline were the annual *The Queen's Awards* (1946–59; continued as *Mystery Annuals*, 1958–62) and the seminal *101 Years' Entertainment: The Great Detective Stories of 1841–1941* (1941) and *The Female of the Species: The Great Women Detectives and Criminals* (1943; *Ladies in Crime; A Collection of Detective Stories by English and American Writers*). Nonfiction works about the mystery genre included *The Detective Short Story: A Bibliography* (1942) and *Queen's Quorum:*

A History of the Detective-Crime Short Story as Revealed by the 106 Most Important Books Published in This Field Since 1845 (1951). "Much though we may admire Queen the writer," said Anthony *Boucher, "it is Queen the editor who is unquestionably immortal."

In contrast to the lively activities of Queen the detective and Queen the man of letters, Dannay and Lee led relatively quiet lives. Lee lived in suburban Connecticut with his wife and eight children. When not working on his authorial duties, he pursued his various stamp, record, and medal collections. Dannay and his family settled in Larchmont, New York. Dannay's autobiography, *The Golden Summer* (1953), is a loving tribute to his childhood in Elmira, New York during the summer of 1915. The pair's last Ellery Queen novel, *A Fine and Private Place*, was published in 1971, shortly before Lee's death. For the remaining eleven years of his life, Dannay continued alone to edit *EQMM* and several crime fiction anthologies, including a multivolume series collectively entitled *Masterpieces of Mystery*.

Queen was voted a Grand Master of the mystery story in 1960 by Mystery Writers of America. Other awards included five Edgars from the MWA and a TV Guide Award in 1950 for Best Mystery Show on Television.

The working relationship between Dannay and Lee was complex. Near the end of his life, Dannay described the process: "One of us does the plotting, the other does the writing, it doesn't matter which. We kind of try to top each other. It's a collaboration, but also a competition."

The diversity and quality of Queen the detective's activities reflect the entire range of modern crime fiction. No matter how varied the scholarly pursuits and the writing styles of the fiction—from the classic tradition of ratiocination to the more modern hard-boiled and psychological schools—the Queen standard was always marked by wit, a literature style, dazzling ingenuity, erudition, and respect for the reader (vide, the famous "Challenge to the Reader").

—John C. Tibbetts

R

Raffles, A. J. is the upper class *gentleman thief and safecracker who appears in E. W. *Hornung's short stories first published between 1895 and 1923. Raffles appears to be the complete English gentleman of his day: public schoolboy turned into urbane bachelor of private means. In fact, Raffles cannot claim aristocratic birth. His social elevation derives from his celebrity as a cricketer and from his personal charm. These gain him entrée into the homes of the wealthy from whom he steals to support his posh lifestyle, including highly respectable London digs in The Albany.

Raffles rationalizes some of his crime by redistributing wealth that he believes has fallen into the wrong hands. There are occasions when he acts with great aplomb, as when he celebrates the Diamond Jubilee of Queen Victoria by sending her a gold cup that he has stolen from the British Museum.

Pitted against the indefatigable Inspector Mackenzie, Raffles proves to be a master of disguise and a trickster of great ingenuity, but his social graces and amateur love of the game for its own sake make him more akin to the gentleman adventurer than the loathsome *master criminal. As George Orwell described the stories in "Raffles and Miss Blandish" (in *Horizon*, Oct. 1944), "the main impression they leave behind is of boyishness." As his criminal career becomes increasingly fraught with danger, Raffles does the decent thing and goes off to fight in the Boer War. After a particularly heroic exploit during which he unmasks an enemy spy, he is killed at the front, an appropriately redemptive ending for such a morally ambiguous figure.

[*See also* Robin Hood Criminal.]

—Ian Bell

Ramotswe, Mma Precious, *private detective created by Alexander McCall *Smith. Introduced in *The No. 1 Ladies' Detective Agency* (1998), she is described as a "traditional-sized" woman of abundant intuition and intelligence, who sets up the only female-operated private detective agency in Botswana, Africa. Funded by the sale of cattle inherited from her father, a miner-turned-cattle farmer, Ramotswe's modest agency is furnished with two desks, two chairs, a telephone, and an old typewriter. She shares the office with a talented typist, Mma Makutsi. The office is recognized by it's colorful, hand-painted sign, which reads, "The No. 1 Ladies' Detective Agency. For All Confidential Matters and Enquiries. Satisfaction Guaranteed For All Parties. Under Personal Management."

Ramotswe also counts as assets a small white van and a house on Zebra Drive. In addition, she has a dear friend, garage owner Mr. J.L.B. Maketoni, and a housemaid, Rose, who are steady sources of companionship in her daily life. Readers understand why she hesitates to marry Maketoni, since Smith reveals a great deal about her past, including the fact that she married an abusive jazz musician and lost her only child in a miscarriage induced by her husband's violence.

Ramotswe's childhood, too, was touched by tragedy. She was a much-loved infant, but lost her mother in a railroad accident. After that, she was raised by a childless aunt who doted on her, and instilled in her charge powers of observation and math skills built through gameplaying. Ramotswe was also influenced by Mma Rothibi, a Sunday School teacher who taught her the difference between good and evil, but failed to make her believe in the miracles described in the Bible. While still a student, Ramotswe worked in the Upright Small General Dealer, taking inventory of the stock. After her marriage ended, she returned to her father's house and cared for him until his death, after which she founded her detective agency.

The circumstances of Ramotswe's life and investigations are fascinating in themselves, but the charm in the characterization comes from Smith's ability to quietly convey her attitudes toward people she encounters. There is much humor, too, when the sleuth follows—usually with disastrous consequences—the advice she reads in *The Principles of Private Investigation* by Clovis Anderson, a book she acquired via mail order. His tips do not measure up to her natural instincts for investigation, which stem from a profound understanding of human nature and a practical, step-by-step approach to following up clues.

—Rosemary Herbert

RANDISI, ROBERT J(OSEPH) (b. 1951), prolific American author of private eye fiction, police procedurals, thrillers and westerns, written under his own name and several pseudonyms. Born in Brooklyn, New York, he graduated from Canarsie High School before working in several jobs, including as a mailroom manager and as an administrative aid for the New York City Police Department. He was a founder of the Private Eye Writers of America and co-founder of *Mystery Scene* magazine.

Randisi's first mystery is *The Disappearance of Penny* (1980), which features gumshoe Henry Po. The author is better known among mystery fans as the creator of three series *sleuths: Miles Jacoby, a *private eye who is a former boxer; Brooklyn-based hard-boiled private investigator Nick Delvecchio; and New York Police Department Detective Joe Keogh. Jacoby makes his first appearance in *Eye in the Ring* (1982), Delvecchio debuts in *No Exit From Brooklyn* (1987), a novel which represents Randisi's crime writing at its best. Here the urban scene is more than a backdrop to the problems Delvecchio must wrestle with and conquer. The city is essential to the Keogh series, too, which begins with Keogh investigating serial killings in *Alone With the Dead* (1995). Randisi also contributed to the Nick Carter series, writing under the Nick Carter name. He has worked as a ghostwriter, and as a collaborator, with Christine Matthews, on a series about amateur sleuths Gil and Claire Hunt. He wrote a non-fiction guide, *Writing the Private Eye Novel* (1997), and served as editor on many well-regarded anthologies. His own crime short stories are collected in *Delvecchio's Brooklyn* (2001) and *Black and White Memories* (2002).

Randisi's crime-writing output may be substantial, but he has turned out even more westerns. His better-known western series include the Gunsmith books, written under the penname J.R. Roberts, and the Tracker series, written as Tom Cutter. In many of his westerns, the quest for justice is often at the heart of the stories, just as it is in his crime fiction.

[*See also* Amateur Detective; Police Detective.]

—Rosemary Herbert

RANKIN, IAN (b. 1960), Scottish crime writer and creator of the Edinburgh police inspector, John *Rebus. The son of a grocer, Rankin grew up in a working-class Presbyterian family in the former mining town of Carnenden, Fife, at a time when the coal industry that fueled the area's economy was depressed. By turns bookish and one of the lads, Rankin was both a dreamer and realist. While a student at Edinburgh University, he wrote a thesis about Muriel Spark, the Scottish author of *The Prime of Miss Jean Brodie* (1961) while also turning out award-winning poetry and three novels. Along the way, he received encouragement from writer-in-residence Allan Massie, a novelist. He also sang with a band called The Dancing Pigs and worked as a swineherd, too. His first novel, *Summer Rites*, remains unpublished. It is a black comedy set in a hotel in the Scottish highlands. His second, *The Flood* (1986) is a coming of age story.

His 1987 novel, *Knots and Crosses*, was the first to feature Rebus of the Edinburgh CID. Intending to write a new interpretation of the Jeckyl and Hyde figure, Rankin was taken by surprise when the book chiefly garnered the attention of mystery fans. It's no secret why it did. Named for a picture puzzle, the dour and introspective protagonist investigates the underside of Edinburgh and environs, an area that is not overworked by other crime novelists. Rankin's reputation grew steadily so that ten years after he published *Knots and Crosses*, his 1997 novel *Black and Blue*, based on a true case, gained him international attention.

American mystery writer James *Ellroy called Rankin the "King of tartan noir." Rankin has also written a spy novel, *The Watchman* (1990); *Westwind* (1990), a novel

set in the United States; and three thrillers under the pen name Jack Harvey. Married with two children, Rankin maintains homes in Edinburgh and France.

[*See also* Police Detective.]

—Rosemary Herbert

Rawlins, Ezekiel "Easy." The African American protagonist of Walter *Mosley's mysteries, Ezekiel "Easy" Rawlins narrates his own peripatetic adventures in a wisecracking voice that evokes the time and place as surely as does the first-person narration of Raymond *Chandler's Philip *Marlowe. Mosley's post–World War II Los Angeles, as described by Rawlins, is a place where racism runs rampant and is mostly confronted sub rosa.

Rawlins engages in unlicensed private snooping that inevitably brings him into conflict with gangsters of both races, and with racist police officials. He enters each adventure reluctantly, and then only for self-preservation or in order to maintain for his children a tenuous grasp on security. Through the use of his native wit and courage, Rawlins achieves the stature of a folk hero who must face down brutal adversaries, despite his aversion to violence. He is aided by Raymond "Mouse" Alexander, a childhood friend whom Rawlins both loves and fears. Like Hawk in Robert B. *Parker's Spenser series, Alexander is an amoral and conscienceless killer who commits acts of violence that would be impossible for Rawlins to execute.

[*See also* African American Sleuth.]

—Robert E. Skinner

Rebus, Detective Inspector John, introspective Edinburgh policeman created by Ian *Rankin. Introduced in the 1987 novel *Knots and Crosses*, his surname comes from the term for a picture puzzle. His first name, John, was taken from the black private eye John Shaft, created by the white American author Ernest Tidyman. Although Tidyman's work has been criticized as exemplary of "blaxploitation," his books and the films based on them won the attention of young Rankin, who has a keen interest American literature. In *Knots and Crosses*, Rebus is introduced as at 38-year-old former member of the army. Divorced and often cynical, he is sometimes shown making mistakes in his investigations of crimes, which he usually solves through a combination of perseverance and understanding of the dark sides of others.

[*See also* Police Detective]

—Rosemary Herbert

Reeder, Mr. J(ohn) G., a character created by Edgar *Wallace, works for the Public Prosecutor's office, Scotland Yard, and Banker's Trust. This Golden Age figure appears in short stories collected as *The Mind of Mr. J. G. Reeder* (1925; *The Murder Book of Mr. J. G. Reeder*), together with two other volumes of stories and the novels *Room 13* (1924) and *Terror Keep* (1927).

Middle-aged, outwardly meek, emotionless, and unassuming he is Victorian in appearance and manners. He wears side-whiskers, pince-nez, and an old-fashioned derby hat and carries an unfurled umbrella irrespective of weather or time of day. Such apparent eccentricities are deceptive, since the umbrella handle conceals a knife and he also carries a revolver. His apparently mild outward personality belies his ability to be fierce when the occasion demands.

Reeder is no weakling, despite his penchant for meditation, playing patience, and philosophizing. These attributes belie his tenacity and the danger he poses to wrongdoers. His skills at solving robberies, his expert eye for forgery, and his ability to identify with the "criminal mind" are used to great effect in solving both locked room mysteries and other crimes.

[See also Eccentrics.]

—Melvyn Barnes

REEVE, ARTHUR B(ENJAMIN)

REEVE, ARTHUR B(ENJAMIN) (1880–1936), American writer of mystery novels, short stories, and screenplays, principally about Craig Kennedy, a character often referred to as "the American Sherlock *Holmes," a professor of chemistry at a New York university. Reeve graduated from Princeton in 1903 and attended New York Law School before choosing journalism as a career. His articles on science, politics, crime, and social conditions led him to write short stories about scientific crime detection. Reeve's success depended less on his characters than on the way he employed the latest scientific discoveries in a series of short stories and novels for the Hearst publications. From the first short stories anthologized in The Silent Bullet (1912) to the final novel, The Stars Scream Murder (1936), the detective depends more on lie detectors, ballistics, voiceprints, and wiretapping to solve crimes than observation and deduction. Most of the stories are narrated by his reporter friend, Walter Jameson, a Dr. John H. *Watson figure, in an appropriately journalistic style. Like Holmes, Kennedy kept files of information regarding paper types, inks, and other materials that he had studied. His creator's reputation for such fictional scientific sleuthing was noted by the U.S. government, which asked Reeve to create a scientific crime lab for anti-espionage purposes during World War I.

[See also Scientific Sleuth.]

—J. Randolph Cox

REGESTER, SEELEY

REGESTER, SEELEY, pseudonym of Metta Victoria Fuller Victor (1831–1885), American author who wrote the first detective novel in English. Born in Erie, Pennsylvania, she published her first book, The Last Days of Tul: A Romance of the Lost Cities of Yucatan (1846), while still in her teens. She also collaborated with her older sister, Frances Barritt Fuller, to produce a collection of poetry, Poems of Sentiment and Imagination, with Dramatic and Descriptive Pieces (1851). She married the publisher Orville James Victor, head of Beadle and Adams, who invented the dime novel. Metta Victor was a versatile writer whose titles represent a wide variety of pop-

ular genres from sentimental, sensation, and adventure fiction to cookery and humor. She also contributed to a great many periodicals such as the Saturday Evening Post and Godey's Ladies Book. In addition to her writing, she served as hostess at her husband's literary gatherings and was the mother of nine children.

The Dead Letter, the first American detective novel, was serialized in Beadle's Monthly in 1866 and published as a complete work by Beadle and Company in 1867. When Metta Victor wrote The Dead Letter using the nom de plume of Seeley Regester, the only models of detective fiction in English were Edgar Allan *Poe's short stories, Charles *Dickens's detective subplot in Bleak House (1852–53), and Wilkie *Collins's suspense novel, The Woman in White (1860). While revealing suggestive similarities to the work of Poe and Dickens, Regester's novel is original enough to dispel any charge that she merely imitated the work of widely admired male predecessors.

Regester's primary accomplishment lies in extending the puzzle plot of the detective short story to the longer narrative form of the novel. She contributed further to the development of the detective novel by enhancing the personality and the methods of the detective. She rejected the misanthropic bent of Poe's *sleuth in creating her investigator, Mr. Burton, whose character eschews the bizarre excesses of the reclusive, aristocratic Chevalier C. Auguste *Dupin as well as the working class vulgarity of Dickens's Inspector Bucket. Mr. Burton is portrayed as an attractive, well-adjusted, and sociable person. A gentleman of private means, he leads a normal family life and takes great delight in his children. Although Mr. Burton works with the police on a regular basis, he refuses to accept financial payment. Thus, he becomes the prototype for the gifted *amateur detective so popular in the early decades of the twentieth century.

Without sacrificing any of the rational skills of Dupin, Regester also augmented the talents of her sleuth. For example, Mr. Burton has an amazing ability to intuit character from samples of handwriting. His astonishing physical description of and insight into the character of the dead letter writer, expressed with arrogant egotism, are confirmed later in the narrative. This passage, now so reminiscent of the spectacular deductions of Sherlock *Holmes from a bit of cigar ash or a frayed coat sleeve, appeared twenty years before Arthur Conan *Doyle introduced his famous sleuth. It may be the first time this kind of inference appeared in print. Burton is also hypersensitive to atmosphere and realizes when he is in the presence of evil. His daughter is also clairvoyant.

Seeley Regester also enlarged the role of the assistant beyond that of Poe's anonymous "I." Richard Redfield contributes to the solution instead of merely recording events.

In meting out punishment to villains, Regester set a precedent that satisfied the demands of morality and literary decorum, without marring the happy ending by leaving the culprit to face capital punishment. To spare the feelings of his family, the villain of *The Dead Letter* is banished rather than turned over to the police, but his life in exile presents a bleak prospect.

It is quite possible that Regester's innovations influenced other contemporary authors, notably Anna Katharine *Green, whose *The Leavenworth Case* (1878) was cited as the first American detective novel before Regester's work was discovered by modern literary historians. Regester also wrote *Figure Eight; or, The Mystery of Meredith Place* (1869), which critics consider to be inferior in plot construction to *The Dead Letter*.

—B. J. Rahn

RENDELL, RUTH (b. 1930), also writes as Barbara Vine. British author of detective novels and psychological crime fiction. Born in London on 17 February, the daughter of Arthur and Ebba (Kruse) Grasemann, Rendell attended Loughton High School in Essex, and worked on Essex newspapers from 1948 to 1952. In 1950 she married Donald Rendell, whom she divorced in 1975 and remarried two years later; they have one son and live in Polstead and London. Her first book, *From Doon with Death* (1964), introduced police Inspector Reginald *Wexford of Kingsmarkham in Sussex, the protagonist of what has become a popular series of detective novels and stories. Wexford, a kindly father-figure, solves crimes by persistent examination of witnesses and talking through the cases with his assistant Mike Burden. Rendell emphasizes development of the detectives' characters as much as their crime solving: readers see the straitlaced Burden grow, particularly through the loss of his wife and near-loss of his career in *No More Dying Then* (1971), into a person more tolerant of human frailty; they follow the sturdy but aging Wexford through bouts of ill health and self-doubt to where, in *Kissing the Gunner's Daughter* (1992), estrangement from a favorite daughter distracts him from obvious clues to a killer's identity. In *Simisola* (1994), quiet Kingsmarkham is besieged by contemporary urban problems, from racism to domestic enslavement; the depiction of a community rent by social ills from which no class or family is immune has caused this novel to be compared with George Eliot's *Middlemarch: A Study of Provincial Life* (1871–72). Between Wexford novels Rendell writes crime novels without detectives, in which the absence of reason and moral order makes the plots both more suspenseful and more disturbing: in *A Demon in My View* (1976), a psychology student organizing a children's game inadvertently sets off a neighborhood psychotic killer; *A Judgement in Stone* (1977) features a mentally disturbed housekeeper, *Heartstones* (1987), an anorexic teenager and a bloody suicide. Many of Rendell's non-Wexford stories, in volumes such as *The Fallen Curtain and Other Stories* (1976) and *The Fever Tree and Other Stories of Suspense* (1982; reprinted in *Collected Stories*, 1988) also depict bizarre behavior, which Rendell makes both fascinating and repellent.

In the 1980s Rendell added to her other two categories of fiction a new kind of novel, for which she uses the pen name Barbara Vine. Feeling the need, she said, for "a softer voice speaking at a slower pace, more sensitive perhaps, and more intuitive," she has, in *A Dark-Adapted Eye* (1986), a woman recount her unnerving investigation into the family's role in the crime for which her aunt was executed thirty years earlier. In *The Brimstone Wedding* (1995), a young woman reveals her own guilty love affair to an elderly patient and learns, in turn, of the older woman's more appalling secret. The Vine novels show that even offenses deemed non-punishable by law may in fact be unpardonable. Rendell is not only prolific, with more than fifty books published, but also among the most highly acclaimed of mystery writers for her skill at plotting and psychological insight. She has received major British and American mystery awards, including Edgar Allan *Poe and Silver and Gold Dagger awards.

[*See also* Police Detective.]

—Mary Rose Sullivan

REPORTERS AS DETECTIVES. *See* Journalist Sleuth.

RHODE, JOHN, the punning pseudonym of Major Cecil John Charles Street (1884–1965), a prolific British detective novelist who also wrote as Miles Burton, the author of 144 mystery novels. He served in France during the First World War, and afterwards in Ireland, and was awarded the Military Cross. Under his own name he wrote widely on contemporary European history and politics.

As Rhode he produced sixty-nine novels, beginning with *The Paddington Mystery* (1925), with the mathematician Dr. Lancelot *Priestley as detective. At first an active investigator of crime, Priestley later confines himself to offering enigmatic advice to the police. Endowed with superior powers of reasoning, he follows the tradition of the *Great Detectives Sherlock *Holmes and Dr. John *Thorndyke, being especially close to the latter in his use of scientific evidence. Among Rhode's best novels are *The Davidson Case* (1929: *Murder at Bretton Grange*), *The Claverton Mystery* (1933; *The Claverton Affair*), and *Death in Harley Street* (1946).

As Miles Burton he wrote of the *amateur detective Desmond Merrion, who during the war becomes involved in counter-espionage in *The Secret of High Eldersham* (1930) and *Dead Stop* (1943).

Street's work sits squarely in the tradition of the British detective story of the interwar years; its merits are a constant ingenuity and inventiveness in the devising of situations and details.

—T. J. Binyon

RICE, CRAIG, the most favored pseudonym of Georgiana Ann Randolph Craig (1908–1957). Her other pen names included Daphne Sanders, Ruth Malone, and Michael Venning, but it was Craig Rice, that identified her authorship of *8 Faces at 3* (1939), the first of her twenty-two published novels and the one introducing her series characters the lawyer John J. Malone and his friends Jake and Helene Justus. Today's readers are likely to be startled at the quantities of alcohol the characters consume while they joke their serendipitous way through bars, versions of high and low society, and criminal cases. The alcohol, though, is a literary sign indicating to readers that they are in the stylized world of sophistication exploited by many writers during the 1930s and 1940s, while the mixed milieu and the cast of reappearing supporting characters of police officers, *underworld figures, and saloon keepers place the Malone series in the American hard-boiled tradition, except that the mordancy of the *sleuth and the instability of the social order characteristic of hard-boiled writing is so exaggerated that the narratives take on the atmosphere of the cinematic screwball comedy.

Rice also created a comic series featuring the accidental detectives Bingo Riggs and Handsome Kusak, who dream of making it big in movies. The subject was something Rice knew well from working in Hollywood as a screenwriter for films about The Falcon and as a publicist. Her skills in publicity may well have led her to the jobs she undertook as a ghostwriter, first for the burlesque personality Gypsy Rose Lee and then, with Cleve Cartmill, for the film star George Sanders. The Lee novels appeared as *The G-String Murders* (1941) and *Mother Finds a Body* (1942); the Sanders novel appeared as *Crime on My Hands* (1944).

Randolph also created under her favored pseudonym three collections of short stories, two of them in collaboration with Stuart Palmer and the last published after her death. Several Rice titles have returned to print in paperback, and for curators of some of the most distinctive writing of the 1940s and 1950s at least sixty-five uncollected short stories by Craig Rice and her alter ego Ruth Malone remain in archives of popular mystery magazines.

—John M. Reilly

RINEHART, MARY ROBERTS (1876–1958), American mystery and romance writer. She was born in Allegheny, Pennsylvania, in 1876. She trained as a nurse and married Dr. Stanley Rinehart in 1896. Although her health was poor and she had three small children at home, she began to write short stories in the first decade of the twentieth century and published her first full-length novel, *The Circular Staircase*, in 1908. It was a bestseller, and she remained a highly popular author for more than forty years. Although Rinehart is best remembered for her mysteries, she also wrote comic stories, romances, and plays, as well as editorials and feature articles.

Rinehart had a strong aversion to the realism of the 1920s; she found it offensive. However, she did not have an aversion to making her novels realistic, and she made

a point of setting them in American places and using American *amateur detectives. She did create a quasi-professional detective in Hilda Adams, a nurse who is hired by the police department to go undercover in some of their more difficult investigations. Most of her mysteries take place in upper-class surroundings, although she occasionally and, not particularly successful, attempted to portray the working classes. Her mystery work bears most resemblance to some of the more cozy British writing of the period, but has no references to an aristocracy and contains a good deal more violence, although Rinehart would never be mistaken for a hard-boiled novelist.

As befitted the wife of a physician, Rinehart often incorporated interesting medical problems into her work. She was also somewhat interested in spiritualism, although never fully convinced of its validity and the possibility of spirit communication is raised in *The Red Lamp* (1925). Rinehart was also interested in incorporating "true" situations into her novels: *The Case of Jennie Brice* (1913) takes place during flooding in Pittsburgh, and *The Confession*, published with *Sight Unseen* in one volume in 1921, is based on the discovery of a written confession to an old murder.

Rinehart is probably best known as the writer of Had-I-But-Known fiction, which typically includes a young woman narrator commenting on the story from a position of increased wisdom. However, Rinehart often used older women for her narrators, as well as men of all ages. For the most part, these narrators have had no previous experience with crime (even her lawyers have most of their experience in noncriminal law), and are sharing their stories because they are so unusual. Rinehart's best-known mystery novels include *The Circular Staircase* (1908) and *The Man in Lower Ten* (1909), her first two, but her popularity as a mystery writer continued unabated until the late 1940s. At this time, her sales began to decline, as the reading public was now more interested in a harsher realism than Rinehart was willing to produce. Her novels are still being reissued, attesting to her popular appeal more than forty years after her death.

Her work has been marketed differently in different periods. During the first half of the century, much of Rinehart's appeal lay in her humor, and her primary marketing tool was the short stories that appeared in magazines such as the *Saturday Evening Post*. Later, her work was reissued with covers more appropriate for Gothic novels, and currently the blood in the cover designs has been emphasized. While her humor has certainly survived the test of time, critical judgment has tended to categorize her as a writer of romantic mysteries. Her mysteries have survived in part because of the comic bafflement of her narrator, however, who always seems to feel that he or she should have known better at the time.

[*See also* Menacing Characters.]

—Mary P. Freier

Ripley, Tom, remorseless *con artist created by Patricia *Highsmith. Introduced in *The Talented Mr. Ripley* (1955), the character shocked by killing with both legal and emotional impunity. Film versions of the book— *Plein soliel* in 1960 and *The Talented Mr. Ripley* in 1999 – paint Ripley as an attractive charmer. In book and film versions alike, a good deal of the shock value derives from audiences' horror at themselves when they realize they wish Ripley would get away with murder. In *The Talented Mr. Ripley* and the following four books, suspense derives from the reader's recognition that danger to others lurks in Ripley's feelingless detachment, which characters he encounters fail to see. Others are so taken in by his exterior air of normalcy that he even acquires a wife. As in Highsmith's *Strangers on a Train* (1950), chance meetings start wheels turning in the villain's mind. In *Ripley's Game* (1974), a frame maker who rubs Ripley the wrong way at a party ends up a party to murders Ripley engineers. In *Ripley Under Water* (1991), an inquisitive English couple gets quagmired in Ripley's forgery scheme.

[*See also* Villains and Villainy.]

—Rosemary Herbert

Robicheaux, Dave, Cajun *police detective turned *private eye created by American writer James Lee *Burke. Introduced in *The Neon Rain* (1986), Robicheaux is a police detective battling alcoholism and a Vietnam veteran who cannot conquer haunting memories of his war experiences. By the end of that novel, he has left the police force to open a fishing bait shop, but he takes on additional cases in later books. Burke develops Robicheaux's personal life as the series progresses. In *The Neon Rain* Robicheaux meets and falls in love with Annie Ballard, who is a social worker and cellist. In *Heaven's Prisoners* (1988), he and Ballard, now married, take on the care of a young girl Robicheaux has rescued from a plane wreck. In a horrific development, the hit men who are after Robicheaux end up murdering Ballard. In *Black Cherry Blues* (1989), Robicheaux is haunted by dreams of his deceased wife and father, while he gets involved in dangerous doings on an oil field. In *A Morning for Flamingos* (1990) he marries a woman called Bootsie, who suffers from lupus. In *Purple Cane Road* (2000), Robicheaux discovers that his own mother was a prostitute and a murder victim, as he investigates a parallel case. Along the way he comes to grips with a few of his own emotional demons.

—Rosemary Herbert

ROBIN HOOD CRIMINAL is a phrase that provides a broad umbrella for a variety of criminal or semi-criminal types; it includes the lovable rogue, committing crimes for his own personal benefit, and those who prey on criminals or do crime for ultimate good. the latter perhaps derives as much from Don Quixote as from Robin Hood. What all have in common is a morality which in some way does not cohere with that of authority.

Around the true Robin Hood type there exists a distinct aura of romance, although his (and it is almost invariably a he) morality is generally questionable and his code of conduct frequently bizarre. He is depicted as being more sophisticated than a mere criminal-as-hero; the morality of the latter (e.g. Richard Stark's Parker, *The Hunter*, 1962; *Point Blank*) is generally uncompromisingly straightforward and usually the reader is not asked to find him romantic or even particularly sympathetic.

The modern trend of the heroic criminal as opposed to the criminal-as-hero was begun by E. W. *Hornung's A. J. *Raffles, continued by Maurice *Leblanc's Arsène *Lupin, Leslie *Charteris's The *Saint, and John *Creasey's The Toff and brought up to date by, among others, John D. *MacDonald's "salvage operator," Travis *McGee. Of all these it is Raffles, the acknowledged archetype, whose conduct is the most irredeemably unsavory. Whereas Lupin cooperates with the police and solves crimes, The Saint and The Toff work outside but alongside the law and McGee is acknowledged by his author to be a knight-errant, Raffles steals almost exclusively for personal gain (although he does occasionally right wrongs) and is always pitted against the law. In the century since Raffles, cricketer and "amateur cracksman" (i.e. thief), first appeared, social attitudes have undergone an immense change and the then noble sentiments of Raffles and his sidekick Bunny Manders now seem strange indeed. For example, Raffles will not steal from a house in which he is a guest, but makes an exception when he has been invited there solely on account of his cricket, as is the case in "Gentlemen and Players" (in *Cassell's*, Aug. 1898); in "The Gift of the Emperor" (in *Cassell's*, Nov. 1898), Bunny speculates that as stealing enables him not to run up bad debts, "the more downright dishonesty seemed to me less the ignoble." Far more acceptable in the light of current morality are The Toff and The Saint, who operate outside the law for no discernable reason other than love of adventure (The Toff), or to find a way of helping people when authority fails to do so (The Saint).

Other Robin Hood criminals and crooked characters include Frank Parrish's likable poacher, Dan Mallett in *Fire in the Barley* (1977), Bruce Graeme's Blackshirt, Gregory Mcdonald's investigative reporter Fletch, Arnold Bennett's millionaire thief Cecil Thorold in *The Loot of Cities* (1904), and Philip St. Ives, the character created by Ross Thomas writing as Oliver Bleeck (*The Highbinders*, 1974, etc.), who recovers stolen property by fair means or foul. A more minor character whose behavior is closer to the original Robin Hood is Susan *Moody's Barnaby Midas, the lover of investigator Penny Wanawake; he is a professional jewel thief but much, if not all, of the proceeds of his thefts are used to help Third World countries. Of these individuals, some reveal characteristics that serve as metaphors for the whole genre:

for example, Parrish's Mallett. The poacher is frequently a sympathetic character in fiction, skillfully stealing from those who can well afford it in order to supply his own basic physical needs—and thus the Robin Hood criminal, although here the needs are as often moral. Raffles's prowess as a cricketer is equally significant, not only symbolizing the sporting element in many of the Robin Hood criminal activities but also pointing a contrast between the most honorable of pastimes and a most dishonorable activity.

[*See also* Gentleman Thief.]

—Judith Rhodes

ROBINSON, PETER (b. 1950), English-born author of police procedurals that feature Yorkshire Inspector Alan Banks. Born in Castleford, Yorkshire, Robinson earned a Bachelor's degree in English Literature from the University of Leeds. Following that, he moved to Canada, where he earned a Master's degree at the University of Windsor, where he studied under Joyce Carol *Oates. He married a Canadian and settled in Canada, teaching at various colleges in Toronto and at the University of Windsor.

Robinson aspired to be a poet, but it is his crime writing that has gained him fame. Set in the fictional town of Swainsdale in the atmospheric Yorkshire dales, the novels are located in a milieu that offers the author opportunities to play with descriptive language. His work also demonstrates his talent for constructing edgy plots and exploring the psychological motivation that drives characters to commit crime. Introduced in the 1987 novel, *Gallows View*, Banks is a character typical of many that entered the pages of detective fiction during the 1980s: He is a professional who takes his job seriously, and he is also an individual who faces up and downs in his private life.

In Robinson's best work, Banks solves crimes while gaining insight into his personal troubles and relationships. A strong example is *Aftermath* (2001), in which Banks investigates heinous crimes perpetrated by a serial torturer and murderer of adolescent girls, while he also deals with the fallout from his own divorce. Even more outstanding is *Close to Home* (2002), in which Bank's idyllic vacation on a Greek isle comes to an abrupt end when the inspector reads, in an English newspaper, of the discovery of a child's skeleton that might be that of his missing boyhood friend. As Banks returns to his hometown to investigate, he also revisits the world of his 1960s boyhood, a place where both memories and secrets surface.

[*See also* Missing Persons; Police Detective.]

—Rosemary Herbert

ROHMER, SAX (1883–1959), British writer of mystery, fantasy, and supernatural novels, short fiction, plays, comic verse and music for the English music hall, and student of the occult. Born Arthur Henry (later Sars-

field) Ward in the Ladywood district of Birmingham, England, of Irish parents, he is best remembered as the creator of Dr. *Fu Manchu, would-be world conqueror protagonist of thirteen novels and four short stories.

Married to Rose Elizabeth Knox, Rohmer made his home in a succession of urban houses and country estates in England, as well as in White Plains, New York. He counted illusionist Harry Houdini among his friends. He created his own image of a legendary, romantic figure to the outside world, but seldom revealed the real man behind the image. His appearance as a successful writer was part of the facade, because the money was spent almost as fast as he earned it. No business man, Rohmer was also defrauded by his literary agent. Besides writing prose fiction he wrote or edited many of the radio scripts based on his work.

Rohmer's lifelong interest in ancient Egypt and his travels to the Middle East gave him a supply of material for stories for magazines and books. He wrote mostly of places he had visited. His favorite setting was Egypt and *Brood of the Witch-Queen* (1918) is considered by many to be his best work. Having adapted his journalist's knowledge of London's Chinatown to his Fu Manchu stories, Rohmer continued the series when publishers offered him more money for it than for his other work.

Rohmer was an uneven writer. The best of his more than fifty books rely upon atmospheric suspense or fantasy told in carefully crafted prose, while others are written to a formula. He balanced descriptions of the everyday world with references to unknown horrors, based upon his extensive reading and travels and tempered with a sardonic sense of humor. Included among his best works are *The Dream-Detective* (1920), *Tales of China-town* (1922), and *White Velvet* (1936).

[*See also* Ethnic Sleuth.]

—J. Randolph Cox

ROYAL CANADIAN MOUNTED POLICE. The Royal Canadian Mounted Police may have the greatest reputation of any in the world for benevolence, handsome uniforms, and an ability to catch criminals. Founded in 1873 by Canada's first prime minister, Sir John A. Macdonald, the force, consisting of 300 men, was originally called the North West Mounted Rifles and was soon renamed the North West Mounted Police. Its headquarters were at Fort MacLeod in Alberta, from which the men set out to deal with traders from the United States who were stirring up unrest among the natives of the area by trading whiskey for buffalo hides. The "Mounties," as they were popularly known, used determination and tact to drive the traders home and to calm the natives. In addition, their assistance to waves of new settlers in the Canadian wilderness during the nineteenth century earned them more praise. Their scarlet jackets and broad-brimmed hats also made them among the world's most recognizable lawmen.

In 1904 the word "Royal" was added to the name and in 1920, when it became a federal force, the name was changed to the Royal Canadian Mounted Police. Today the acronym RCMP is almost as recognizable as the term "Mounties." After a newspaper account described the force as a group that "fetched their man every time," the phrase was reshaped by later writers to read, "they always get their man."

As early as 1893, in Gilbert Parker's *Pierre and His People*, the Mounties appeared in fiction. The first series of novels featuring a Mountie was by the Canadian author Luke Allan, who created Blue Pete, a reformed cattle rustler who became a North West Mounted Police agent. True exploits undertaken by the Mounties inspired many Westerns and adventure stories. The Mountie hero Sargeant Major Samuel B. Steele, who arrested moonshiners, skirmished with rebellious metis (people who are mixed White and Indian), pacified Canadian Pacific Railway workers, and stomped out lawlessness among gold rushers in the Yukon, is fictionalized in Harwood Steele's *The Marching Call* (1955) and Bill *Pronzini's *Starvation Camp* (1984), to name only two novels.

Some generalizations hold true about Mountie characters as created by Canadians and other nationals. To Canadian authors, the Mountie is an arbitor, instituting civilized order and values for their own sake. British writers often depicted their Mountie heroes as men of the upper class who ventured to Canada for adventure, and brought justice to the settlers along with attitudes stemming from social standing. American writers often permitted logic and individual decisions about justice to override legal considerations in their Mounties, who often seem like transplanted Texas Rangers.

By the middle of the twentieth century, a steady stream of RCMP adventure stories and motion pictures made the force world famous. A television series, *Sergeant Preston of the Yukon*, won a huge juvenile audience; it depicted a strong and earnestly kind hero whose every case closed satisfactorily, usually after a dog-sled chase led by a huskie called King. The Mountie story became so over-popularized that it was not until the late 1970s that the Mountie hero was again treated seriously. Today these characters flourish in cozy mysteries, police procedurals, spy fiction, and even horror fiction, largely written by Canadians. Examples include cozy mysteries by Alisa Craig featuring Inspector Madoc Rhys; Scott Young's depiction of an Inuk hero, Inspector Matthew "Mateesie" Kitologitak, who investigates the disappearance of a bush airplane in *Murder in a Cold Climate* (1988); and American L. R. Wright's suspense-crime novels about Staff Sargeant Karl Alberg of British Co-

lumbia, noteworthy for their intense psychological depictions.

[*See also* Police Detective.]

—Bernard A. Drew

Rumpole, Horace, is the hero and first-person narrator of thirteen collections of stories by John *Mortimer Q. C., amiably satirizing the follies of the Bar, the judiciary, and the British Establishment in general. All have been made into successful television series.

Since his first appearance in *Rumpole of the Bailey* in 1978, Rumpole himself has changed little. While other members of his Chambers have aged and progressed, he has obstinately remained in his late sixties. Overweight, badly dressed, soup-stained, smoking the smallest cigars and drinking the cheapest claret, he does not look like a successful barrister, nor indeed is he: he is an "Old Bailey hack"—a barrister who has never attained the rank of Queen's Counsel, and whose practice deals almost entirely with crime rather than the more lucrative commercial cases. Defending perpetrators of petty crime is his forte. Although he encounters the occasional murderer, he is far more often to be found speaking out for a shoplifter or unsuccessful burglar.

At first sight, the stories and the central character seem mutually contradictory. Rumpole is represented as an effective advocate and skillful cross-examiner, and as quick as Sherlock *Holmes or Hercule *Poirot to observe the clue that turns the case upside down and reveals the truth: usually, though not always, he wins his case. And yet, by most worldly standards—certainly by those of his wife Hilda, "She Who Must be Obeyed," and of the other members of his Chambers, who regularly conspire to persuade him into retirement—he is a failure.

The audience gradually see, however, that his virtues, rather than his shortcomings, preclude success. As a lover of the language of William Shakespeare and William Wordsworth, he cannot become fluent in the latest fashionable jargon; as a lawyer who puts his duty to his client first, he cannot be expediently polite to prejudiced or overbearing *judges; as a man of humanity and imagination, who understands what life is like in prison, he cannot summon up the ambition to appear for the prosecution, still less to pass sentence. He attains heroic stature not despite failure, but because of it: success, for Mortimer, is always a trifle suspect.

[*See also* Lawyer: The British Lawyer-Sleuth; Lawyer: Lawyers as Secondary Characters.]

—Sarah Caudwell

S

Saint, The. Created by Leslie *Charteris, Simon Templar, or the Saint, is a rambunctious adventurer who believes in old-fashioned romantic ideals and is prepared to lay down his life for them. Using considerable wit and intelligence, the Saint often avenges innocent *victims.

The Saint became a British pop culture sensation in the early 1930s, his notoriety cutting across class lines. When Charteris adopted American citizenship in the 1940s, so did Simon Templar. During World War II, the Saint was an undercover agent for the U.S. government; after the war, Templar resumed his globetrotting escapades of benevolent outlawry.

Charteris introduced the Saint in *Meet the Tiger* (1928) and his character appeared in numerous novels, novelettes, and short stories, some published in the magazines named for him, including *The Saint Detective Magazine*, *The Saint Mystery Magazine*, and *The New Saint Magazine*. He also appeared in comic books, newspaper cartoon strips, motion pictures, and radio and television programs.

—Burl Barer

SALLIS, JAMES (b. 1944), American translator, poet, biographer, music and literary critic, and author of science fiction, an espionage novel, and noir fiction. Raised in Helena, Arkansas, Sallis was a scholar and fellow of Tulane University in New Orleans, Louisiana. He has lived in several cities including London, Paris, New York City, Boston and Phoenix. When he was in his twenties, he came under the influence of Michael Moorcock, then a leading-edge writer of science fiction so thought provoking that it was often termed "speculative fiction." Like Moorcock and Brian W. Aldiss, who was also influential at the time, Sallis was interested not only in creating new worlds but in using language inventively while doing so. A similarly creative preoccupation with word choice is noticeable in his poetry, collected in *Sorrow's Kitchen* (2000).

Sallis's crime writing demonstrates the author's fascination with the work of Chester *Himes in style, conventions employed, and in characterization. Sallis even uses Himes as a character, but Lew Griffin—a black professor and recovered alcoholic who pens poetry and fiction and escapes the pressures of life by listening to blues music—is the series character here. While pursuing *missing persons, he is also on a quest to discovery his own identity. *The Long-Legged Fly* (1992) is the first Griffin novel. Here Sallis brings to life a steamy, cockroach-infested slum known as the Channel, where characters speak in "emphysematous" whispers. And the new they have is not happy. Griffin's last outing is in *Ghost of a*

Flea (2001), a tour de force that makes a fitting climax to the series.

Sallis's contribution to the study of crime writing is significant. His *Chester Himes: A Life* (2000) is notable not just for being well-researched, but for being written by a sytlist who understands Himes' approach to writing. His book reviews, and his essays on noir writers collected in *Difficult Lives: Jim Thompson, David Goodis, Chester Himes* (1993), are influential, too. In addition, Sallis produced three anthologies of his own short fiction, edited books on science fiction and the jazz guitar, and translated work by Raymond Queneau.

—Rosemary Herbert

SAPPER. See McNeile, H. C.

SAYERS, DOROTHY L[EIGH] (1893–1957), English author of detective fiction, the greatest and most widely read of the British Golden Age. Her aristocratic detective, Lord Peter *Wimsey, like Sherlock *Holmes, has become a household name.

The only child of the Reverend Henry and Helen Sayers, she was born in Oxford, where her father was headmaster of Christ Church Cathedral Choir School. When she was four years old, her father accepted a living in the fen country of East Anglia, a region she used as the setting of one of her best-loved novels, *The Nine Tailors: Changes Rung on an Old Theme in Two Short Touches and Two Full Peals* (1934). Educated by governesses until she was fifteen and then at the Godolphin School, Salisbury, she won a scholarship to Somerville College, Oxford, where she achieved a first-class degree in French.

Her early love was poetry, which she continued writing most of her life. She was also a playwright, and her twelve radio plays on the life of Christ, *The Man Born to Be King: A Play-Cycle on the life of Our Lord and Savior, Jesus Christ* (broadcast 1941–42) made broadcast history. She was at work on a verse translation of Dante's *Divine Comedy* at the time of her death.

An admirer of Wilkie *Collins (of whom she began a biography) and of Arthur Conan *Doyle, she aimed at restoring detective fiction to the literary level from which it had lapsed since their time. She attached importance to the "fair play" rule (every clue to be as perceptible to the reader as to the detective), to the creation of character, and to the integration of theme and plot. Her criteria are set out in her introduction to the first volume of *Great Short Stories of Detection, Mystery and Horror* (1928–34; *The Omnibus of Crime*) an authoritative selection of detective fiction, which was definitive in its day and remains a cornerstone anthology.

Among her contemporaries, those who influenced her most were G. K. *Chesterton and E. C. *Bentley. She regarded Chesterton's article "How to Write a Detective Story" (*G. K.'s Weekly*, 17 Oct. 1925) as the soundest advice on the subject. E. C. Bentley's detective, Philip Trent, was a forerunner of Wimsey, and her first novel, *Whose Body?* (1923), contains echoes of *Trent's Last Case*. Wimsey was also drawn from life. In appearance he was based on Maurice Roy Ridley, an Oxford graduate she had seen in 1913. For his sartorial elegance she drew on an old Etonian, Charles Crichton, whose manservant was the origin of Bunter. For his sophistication she drew also on a personal friend, Eric Whelpton. She admitted a resemblance to Bertie Wooster, although P. G. Wodehouse's character was scarcely known in 1923. Both Wooster and Wimsey reflect an actual lifestyle of the time: A well-known example was the writer Michael Arlen.

Wimsey's enduring vitality is mainly due, however, to his creator's own wit, exuberance, and intellectual energy. The same is true also of Sayers's character Harriet *Vane, a detective novelist with whom Lord Peter falls in love and whom he eventually marries. Sayers's achievement was not only the creation of a modern, independent woman—still a role model for many young women readers—but the perilous introduction of a love situation into detective fiction that becomes not only credible and moving but also an integral part of the plot. The relationship begins in *Strong Poison* (1930), continues in *Have His Carcase* (1932), and reaches betrothal in *Gaudy Night* (1935) and marriage in *Busman's Honeymoon* (1937, first written as a play).

Sayers's detective fiction (with the exception of some of the short stories) is drawn from the author's own life. She used settings that were familiar to her—a fishing and painting community in Scotland in *The Five Red Herrings* (1931), an advertising agency in *Murder Must Advertise* (1933), the fen country in *The Nine Tailors*, and Oxford in *Gaudy Night*. Her characters read the books she read, quote the poets she knew, play and sing the music she herself enjoyed. They speak as she and her contemporaries spoke and comment similarly on current affairs. This provides what she (agreeing in this with Collins) considered an essential ingredient in detective fiction, namely "a vivid conviction of fact," on the basis of which the reader can be induced to accept the imaginary. Another consequence is that her novels are a vivid reflection of the social, economic, and cultural life of her time.

As a practicing Christian, Sayers was in no doubt as to the distinction between right and wrong, between free will and individual responsibility. In her day, the penalty for murder was death by hanging. There is no sign that she was opposed to capital punishment, but she endows Wimsey with grave misgivings as to his right to bring about a criminal's undoing. Beneath his external frivolousness, a self-defensive disguise, he is vulnerable. To

readers who respond positively to him, this adds to his credibility as a human being. Others dislike him for his mannerisms, his aristocratic birth, and his wealth. The charge of snobbery has often been brought against his creator. Yet the society she depicts is mobile: Wimsey marries a commoner; his sister marries a chief inspector; his friend, the Honorable Freddy Arbuthnot, marries the daughter of a self-made Jewish financier, who is himself married to a Gentile.

The legacy of Sayers to present-day detective novelists has been acknowledged by P. D. *James, who sees her as an innovator of style rather than of form. Her murder methods are thought to have been too ingenious, and it is asserted that one or two of them would not work. Some critics consider her novels overwritten and too literary. In her day she was widely acclaimed, and her novels were translated into most European languages. Of all detective novelists, she is perhaps the most reread. This suggests that the murder method and the solving of the mystery are the least important elements in her work. The quality of her writing is the factor that ensures her continued importance.

—Barbara Reynolds

Scarpetta, Dr. Kay, series character created by Patricia D. *Cornwell. Introduced in the 1990 novel *Postmortem*, Scarpetta is the chief medical examiner for the city of Richmond, Virginia. In the course of her work, she encounters and interprets grisly—and often bizarre—evidence left by serial killers, most of whom target her, too, before they are brought to justice. The competent ash-blonde doctor is rarely unnerved as she employs the latest in forensic methods to examine cadavers, but she is moved by the victims' plights to risk her own life, if necessary, to make sure their murderers are identified. Often, Scarpetta works in concert with Richmond homicide detective Pete Marino and FBI agent Benton Wesley. Scarpetta's niece Lucy, who first appears as a child and matures as the series progresses, helps to humanize Cornwell's sleuth, who is seen to feel protective of the girl.

[*See also* Forensic Pathologist.]

—Rosemary Herbert

SCIASCIA, LEONARDO (1921–1989), Italian playwright and mystery and true crime writer known for realistic depiction of Mafia corruption in the author's native Sicily. Born in Racalmuto, Sicily, he has served on the Palermo city council and in the Italian and European parliaments. He launched his writing career with short nonfiction treating the pervasive influence of the Mafia on the lives of ordinary Sicilians. In 1961, he used the same theme to drive the action in *Il giorno della civetta* (1963; *Mafia Vendetta; The Day of the Owl*). Here, an investigator looking into a bricklayer's murder is stonewalled by *omerta*, or silence inspired by fear, as he seeks information in a crime that was witnessed by a crowd. In an ending that rings true, justice is not done in this case. Justice is elusive, too, in *Il contesto* (1971; *Equal Danger*), even though the investigator here seeks to nab a murderer of judges. Here Inspector Rogas, who doggedly pursues his quarry despite the recognition that he is up against great odds, makes a refreshing contrast with a self-satisfied judge. The versatile Sciascia has turned his talents to historical true crime writing and even humor. Past crimes are recounted in *La scomparasa di majorana* (1975; *The Disappearance of Majorana*) and *I pugnalatori* (1976; *The Knifers*) and in *1912 + 1*(1986). In contrast, the aptly-titled *Una storia simplice* (1989; *A Straightforward Puzzle*) demonstrates the author's flair for humor in a classic puzzle plot centered around a murder made to look like suicide.

—Rosemary Herbert

SCIENTIFIC SLEUTH. For its informing principle the genre of detective and mystery fiction owes an incalculable debt to science. Amid the disruptive changes in Europe and the Americas during the nineteenth century—the insecurity evoked by the shift of populations to the city where the miserable conditions of the poor starkly contrasted with the unprecedented personal wealth in the possession of people who were neither princes nor bishops, the alterations in modes of work that gave the machine precedence over its human operators, the anonymity consequent to migrations that eroded the foundations of traditional institutional and social relationships—amid the confusion of the journey to a new way of living impelled by vast economic and technological changes, intellectuals and others among the literate public found comfort in scientific optimism. The techniques of disciplined inquiry promised the means of comprehending a new order. The mind, it seemed, had power to give the world rationally apprehensible form, and, with the application of reason, the minds of men and women could address the mysteries of the physical world and thereby ameliorate the problems of the social world. Realism would single out such problems as crime; with the example of science before everyone, though, there was optimism to spur the will.

Such optimism readily entered popular literature. When the scientifically trained Dr. John H. *Watson meets the research scientist Sherlock *Holmes and bears witness to the inimitable series of inferences characterizing Holmes's way of greeting clients and the world at large, the consulting detective character emerges as the reader's Virgil, a guide through the latter-day inferno of modern life. The method of Holmes is innocent of theory. His studies of cigar ashes and soil samples are empirical and taxonomic, but they are sufficient to confirm Holmes as a champion of investigative reasoning.

Among the creators of rival *sleuths who sought to tap the popularity Holmes generated for the emergent genre of detective fiction, few tried to imitate the portrayal of a practicing scientist. Instead they took the optimism inspired by science as a given element of narration upon which to work their own variations. In the next generation of detective writers, however, R. Austin *Freeman selected the scientific vocation as the substance of investigation. As Ian Ousby has written in *Guilty Parties: A Mystery Lover's Companion* (1997), Doyle dealt with the principles of science "to convey its glamorous aura," but Freeman pursued the details of science, replacing the lodgings in Baker Street with the laboratory bench as the locale of criminal study. Freeman's sleuth, Dr. John *Thorndyke, is a forensic scientist who explains the intricacies of fingerprinting in *The Red Thumb Mark* (1907), zoology and marine science in other works. Edgar Allan *Poe had provided his detective, the Chevalier C. Auguste *Dupin, with full opportunity to discourse upon method, but where Dupin's disquisitions derived from *a priori* principles of logic, Thorndyke's scientific method was founded on contemporary research in physical science.

The character of the practical scientist reappeared in the United States in the works of Arthur B. *Reeve, whose detective, Professor Craig Kennedy, was once known as the American Sherlock Holmes. A professor of chemistry at Columbia University in New York City, Kennedy typically exhibited his method by the use of a new device or technique—blood sampling, the Dictaphone, the X ray, typewriter analysis, and so on—that he demonstrated before the assembly of suspects and officials gathered for denouement in his laboratory. From 1911 when he issued his first collection of Kennedy short stories, *The Poisoned Pen*, until the appearance of *The Clutching Hand* (1934) and the novelettes about Kennedy adapted by Ashley Locke as *Enter Craig Kennedy* (1935), Reeve held a place in the top rank of genre writers, although his dependence upon apparatus that came to seem gimmicky makes his work dated in a way that the stories of Holmes have never become.

Doyle, Freeman, and Reeve had in common a conception of character that made science a wholly defining feature of character. Their sleuths were not just heroes, but scientific heroes. In the process of introducing greater complexity into characterization, later writers have reduced the emphasis upon their characters' scientific profession; thus, Elizabeth Peters embeds Amelia Peabody's archaeological expertise among a range of engaging character traits, and Aaron *Elkins's physical anthropologist, Gideon Oliver, employs his learning in the solution of crime, but engages as well in adventure requiring other attributes of strength and character besides. In that regard the inspiration of science that was once featured by some writers as the defining element of the detective hero has become a settled convention. All detectives, whether or not they display scientific method or learning, are now heirs to the imaging of mental powers once associated specifically with scientific learning.

Still, there are fashions and development in the representation of science. When John R. Feegel published *Autopsy* (1975), he suggested the possibilities for renewing interest in forensic science. Today Patricia D. *Cornwell's series about Dr. Kay *Scarpetta, medical examiner and resolute investigator, shows in its great popularity the continuing satisfaction that a scientist sleuth offers to readers who appreciate disciplined scientific technique as a source of entertainment and satisfaction.

[See also Forensic Pathologist; Medical Sleuth.]

—John M. Reilly

Scudder, Matthew, *private detective created by Lawrence *Block. First appearing in three paperback originals—*In the Midst of Death* (1976), The *Sins of the Fathers* (1976) and *Time to Murder and Create* (1977)—Scudder is a former New York city cop burdened with a drinking problem and tremendous guilt over his accidental killing of a young girl in a barroom shootout. Block chronicles the sleuth's slide into despair in *Eight Million Ways to Die* (1983). As the series progresses, the author chronicles Scudder's efforts to get control of his alcoholism and personal life, which he does with increasing success while he has the *sleuth solve challenging cases . The Scudder books are as memorable for the *private eye's battles with his inner demons as they are for an exceptionally well-drawn New York City scene.

—Rosemary Herbert

SERIAL KILLERS AND MASS MURDERERS. Those who take the lives of multiple *victims are referred to as either "mass murderers" or "serial killers." Serial killers are those who kill multiple victims over an extended period, usually one victim at a time; Peter Sutcliffe, the "Yorkshire Ripper," murdered at least thirteen women over about six years in England. "Mass murderer" is a term generally applied to those who kill several people at once; in 1984 James Huberty shot twenty-one people at a McDonald's restaurant in San Ysidro, California.

Much that has been written on the subject of killers of multiple victims is to be found in works by journalists and authors of nonfiction books in the true crime genre. Newspaper and magazine articles tend to focus on the horrific nature of the crimes or the innocence of the victims rather than the pathology of the killer and rely on mostly secondary sources. True crime books may involve more direct interview techniques. Psychiatric theories have been based on small and biased samples and have been limited by the high incidence of suicide among the perpetrators, particularly mass murderers, resulting in a lack of availability of subjects for clinical study.

The characteristics of mass murder do not lend themselves readily to crime and mystery writing and are usually developed by those writers concentrating on the "thriller/horror" genre. The act is short-lived, explosive, and violent, and it is these aspects of it and the buildup to them that are available for development rather than mystery or intrigue.

Serial killings, on the other hand, are a staple of much crime and mystery writing. While the conventional whodunit formula, as employed in the Golden Age, tended to feature additional killings only as necessary to protect a murderer who was motivated to perpetrate one central killing, the formula is used successfully to accommodate serial killings today by such authors as John *Harvey and Patricia D. *Cornwell. While these contemporary exemplars possess medical or forensic knowledge, it may be that limited scientific knowledge of this subject has facilitated the fantasy exploration by writers who have felt little restraint from realism in a field that is shadowy and unknown even to many experienced mental health and police professionals. The subject allows for full development of many aspects of the craft of crime, presenting unusual challenges to the skills and abilities of the detectives, the systematic seeding of clues leading to denouement, and exotic, unlikely methods of perpetration. The psychopathology of the killer is often explored only by inference and is secondary to the development of an atmosphere of horror and evil.

A notable treatment of the topic is to be found in *Devices and Desires* (1989) by P. D. *James. Here the serial killings are perpetrated in the environment of a nuclear reactor plant, allowing the author to explore current social and moral themes alongside the treatment of serial killing.

Authors vary in their depictions of serial killers. Cornwell consciously refrains from portraying the killers' sick pleasure, while Dean Koontz and others focus both on the victims' plight and the perpetrators' lust for murder.

—Marion Swan

SHAKESPEARE, WILLIAM. The works of the Elizabethan poet and dramatist William Shakespeare (1564–1616) have long been sources of inspiration for crime and mystery writers who have turned to his plots, methods of murder, titles, and famous lines to enrich their own work. While Shakespeare is often viewed as the icon of high culture, it is also true that he epitomized the popular writer. As both master and transcender of formulas, he was able to see in the stylized conventions of Plautine comedy and Senecan tragedy the material to move and grip an audience. A master, too, of the bloody and sensational—*Hamlet*, for example, contains six corpses and a ghost—his plots are full of violent passions: revenge, jealousy, bigotry, lust, and ambition. Shakespeare himself used what he believed to be true crime sources, particularly in his tragedies and histories.

Most crime and mystery writers who use Shakespeare as a source are Shakespeare aficionados rather than scholars, although one noted Shakespearean, Alfred Harbage, wrote mystery fiction using the name of the bard's contemporary, Thomas Kyd, for a pseudonym. Ngaio *Marsh knew Shakespeare's plays intimately, since she had acted and directed many productions of them. Oxford don J. I. M. Stewart possessed scholarly expertise about Shakespeare and was adept at using Shakespearean literary allusions in his detective novels written as Michael *Innes.

Shakespeare's most obvious influence upon mystery and crime writing is evident in titles borrowed from his texts. Scores of writers have used quotes from the plays to title their books, borrowing from comedies, as in P. M. Hubbard's *Kill Claudio* (1979) and Elizabeth Powers's *All That Glitters* (1981; *The Case of the Ice-Cold Diamond*), and tragedies, as in Agatha *Christie's *Sad Cypress* (1940) and Margaret *Millar's *How Like an Angel* (1962). Because titles are not protected by copyright, a Shakespearean phrase may be used as the title of more than one mystery: *A Dying Fall* was used by both Henry *Wade (1955) and Hildegarde Dolson (1973). Some writers make a play on the bard's words to produce titles like Craig *Rice's *My Kingdom for a Hearse* (1957) or Emma *Lathen's *Double, Double, Oil and Trouble* (1978). Since her 1962 *Bloody Instructions,* Sara Woods has used Shakespearean quotations to title all of her books.

Writers also turn to Shakespeare when inventing detectives. Ellery *Queen, writing as Barnaby Ross, created a detective who had been a Shakespearean actor, named Drury Lane after the London theater. Forced to retire from the stage because of his deafness, Lane solves cases in four mystery novels published in 1932 and 1933. In *Drury Lane's Last Case* (1933), the crime is the theft of Shakespearean manuscripts. Phoebe Atwood *Taylor writing as Alice Tilton has eight comic novels featuring Leonidas Witherall, who is called Bill Shakespeare because he looks like the bust based on the Droeshout portrait of the bard. Shakespeare himself is the detective in Faye *Kellerman's *The Quality of Mercy* (1989), in which Shakespeare finds the murderer of a friend while becoming involved in a doomed romance with a *conversa*, a Jewish woman posing as a Christian.

Ellery Queen's plot idea concerning missing or spurious Shakespeare manuscripts shows up in several other stories. In the Sherlock *Holmes pastiche *The Unique Hamlet* (1920) by Vincent *Starrett, a client announces himself as "the greatest Shakespearean commentator in the world." A fellow collector has entrusted to him a unique copy of a 1602 *Hamlet* quarto, with additions in Shakespeare's own hand. Holmes solves the disappearance of this book and proves it a forgery. Chris Steinbrunner and Otto Penzler say this is "generally conceded to be the best Holmes pastiche ever written" in their *Encyclopedia of Mystery and Detection* (1976). In one of Lillian de la Torre's historical mysteries featuring Dr. Johnson and narrated by Boswell, *The Detections of Dr. Sam* (1960), Johnson detects the spuriousness of a "new" Shakespeare manuscript during the play's production by David Garrick.

Writers use Shakespearean plot situations to enliven their mysteries. The villain in *Foul Deeds* (1989) by Susan James admits to borrowing his modus operandi from the Vincent Price movie *Theatre of Blood* (1973). The Price character used Shakespearean methods to kill off the critics of his hammy performances, and in *Foul Deeds* one victim is hanged like Cordelia, another strangled like Desdemona, and so on.

Some mystery tales set out to correct or improve on the bard. In James Thurber's comic story "The Macbeth Murder Mystery" (*New Yorker,* 2 Oct. 1937), a woman who devours a mystery every night before going to sleep gets a paperback *Macbeth* by mistake. She explains to the narrator how neither Macbeth nor his wife did it, but Macduff, and that Macduff is the Third Murderer as well. These revelations unnerve the narrator, who "solves" the *Macbeth* murder mystery in a different way and then determines to solve *Hamlet* also.

Josephine *Tey's *The Daughter of Time* (1951) is a more ambitious and serious attempt to rewrite Shakespeare's idea of whodunit in a historical murder. Tey's detective, Inspector Alan Grant, bedridden after an injury, becomes interested in the historical case of the princes in the Tower when a portrait of Richard III convinces him that Shakespeare's "Crookback Dick" could not have been the murderer. Helped by an American researcher, Grant decides that the real culprit was the person who ultimately gained most by the crimes.

The most ambitious uses of Shakespeare in mysteries occur in books that describe productions of his plays. Invariably, such stories build toward a murder, either in rehearsal or in performance. Innes wrote one of the most famous of these books in *Hamlet, Revenge!* (1937), in which the lord chancellor of England, playing Polonius, is killed at an amateur production of *Hamlet,* performed by the duke of Horton's houseguests. Innes's Sir John Appleby gets the case because he isn't intimidated by the suspects but also presumably because he can cap their frequent quotations. Thickening the plot are disturbing notes using lines from Shakespeare, a gardener familiar with arcane Shakespearean criticism, and a mystery writer who—like Innes—is also an Oxford don. The book ties mystery and play together: The production is a reading of *Hamlet* as a play of statecraft and the lord chancellor is engaged in international intrigue. The conclusion contains a witty allusion to *The Winter's Tale.* Innes turned his attention to *Othello, the Moor of Venice* a few years later in his short story "Tragedy of a Handkerchief" (*Appleby Talking,* 1954; *Dead Man's Shoes*). Appleby watches a touring company perform *Othello* in a provincial theater. When Desdemona is actually killed in the smothering scene, Appleby investigates, declaiming apt lines from the play as he does.

In Marvin Kaye's *Bullets for Macbeth* (1976), rehearsals for *Macbeth* in the Felt Forum at Madison Square Garden lead to murder. Publicity agent Hilary Quayle and her assistant Gene are present when Banquo is killed in dress rehearsal by the Third Murderer, a cloaked figure who then escapes from the theater. The director has kept secret the identity of the Third Murderer, and since the director is also playing Banquo, the secret dies with him. To solve the murder, Quayle and Gene must also solve the Shakespearean mystery about the identity of the Third Murderer, who shows up unexpectedly to help

Macbeth's two henchmen kill Banquo and his son Fleance.

As the Innes and Kaye examples show, mysteries about Shakespearean productions often give interpretive readings of the plays, address problems of performance, and make use of theatrical traditions such as the bad luck attendant upon productions of *Macbeth*. In Ngaio Marsh's *Light Thickens* (1982), the recurrent subject is the superstition about *Macbeth*, whose title and lead characters are not to be named but called instead "the Scots play," "the Thane," and "the Lady." Marsh takes us through the rehearsals, opening nights, and beginning run of a production of *Macbeth* at the "Dolphin" theater in London. She has strong ideas, expressed through the director, about what is *not* Shakespeare's in the printed play, discusses other relevant matters about production such as how the convention of the soliloquy can be gracefully handled in modern productions, and provides much incidental appreciation. "Nobody else could write about the small empty hours as this man did," thinks the actor who plays Banquo.

John Dickson *Carr's Dr. Gideon *Fell solves a murder that occurs during a dress rehearsal of *Romeo and Juliet* in *Panic in Box C* (1966). More recent books using productions of Shakespeare include P. M. Carlson's 1985 *Audition for Murder*, about *Hamlet*, and James Yaffe's 1991 *Mom Doth Murder Sleep*, about *Macbeth*.

—Michael Cohen

Shayne, Mike (also Shane) was created in 1939 by Davis Dresser (1904–77) writing as Brett Halliday. Purportedly based on an acquaintance, Dresser's *private eye works out of Miami and sometimes New Orleans. His cases, however, take him to a variety of settings. One of the longest-lived of series characters, Shayne has appeared in more than seventy novels so far, as well as hundreds of shorter tales. Since around 1958, his adventures have been ghostwritten, and ghostwriters continued the Mike Shayne stories until the demise of the *Mike Shayne Mystery Magazine* around 1986.

In the tradition of Dashiell *Hammett's and Raymond *Chandler's characterization, Shayne is a loner whose pride and sense of justice are paramount, though he's always interested in his fee. Described as "semi-hardboiled," he tends to use his wits more than his fists to solve convoluted cases. Red-headed, big, and lanky, with an appetite for Martell's cognac and a ready appreciation for women, Shayne has remained essentially the same: a "hard-drinking, tough-minded guy on the wrong side of thirty."

[*See also* Loner, Sleuth as.]

—Rex Burns

SIDEKICKS AND SLEUTHING TEAMS. There are advantages for both detective and author when a "sidekick" or closely associated, subordinate partner is added to the cast of characters in a mystery. In those books where a trusted sidekick is utilized, he or she may become so crucial to the development of the detective as a character that the detective becomes paired in readers' minds with the helper.

Arthur Conan *Doyle let Sherlock *Holmes share a flat with Dr. John H. *Watson. Dorothy L. *Sayers gave Lord Peter *Wimsey the services of Bunter. Agatha *Christie's Hercule *Poirot and Rex *Stout's Nero *Wolfe could send Captain Arthur Hastings and Archie *Goodwin, respectively, to do the legwork on their cases. Even Ian Fleming let James Bond have a sidekick, Felix Leiter, to share the bullets, if not the girls and martinis.

A competent and trusted associate can expand the area of a detective's search. For example, Wimsey's upper-class status limits him in hunting for leads and gossip among working-class people, but a servant, Bunter, is able to investigate areas barred to the gentry, mingling with servants in the kitchen and locals in the pubs. An associate can also help provide balance for a detective's quirks. Because of his physical girth and the demands of tending his orchids, Wolfe seldom strays far from his overstuffed chair. This *armchair detective could not solve cases without Goodwin's legwork.

For the audience, these assistant detectives can provide comic relief or increase the tension. Thy may also direct attention toward or away from the truth, serving up all manner of red herrings to confuse the reader. Sidekicks are also sounding boards, intimate friends with whom detectives can discuss cases in the presence of the reader, who is especially likely to identify with the sidekicks who serve as narrators. They stand in for the reader, asking the obvious questions and worrying after the fate of the usually eccentric, always cerebral hero.

While sidekicks are sometimes less brilliant than the Great Detectives they aid, their common sense can be necessary to solving crimes. This is often the case with Colin *Dexter's Inspector Endeavor *Morse and his Sergeant Lewis. The classic sidekick should also be in awe of the detective, demonstrating the esteem the writer hopes will transfer to the reader when the final twist is explained.

Watson is the classic sidekick: brave, capable, observant, and faithful. His very name is now generic: A detective's associate is universally known as his "Watson." But Watson was not the first of these very important characters. Like so many other aspects of mystery writing, the idea of an observing assistant came from Edgar Allan *Poe.

In Poe's "The Murders in the Rue Morgue" (*Graham's Lady's and Gentleman's Magazine*. Apr. 1841), the Chevalier C. Auguste *Dupin is introduced by his sidekick, an unnamed narrator so far from omniscient that his very thoughts are an open book to the detective. Poe's narrator serves three basic functions of the able assistant: He is first and foremost a friend, therefore also a confidant, to the detective; he is able to stand in for the reader, asking the questions or listening to the facts that move the story along; and, he admires Dupin.

In 1887, Doyle created Holmes, a detective so piercingly brilliant; that no reader could ever identify with him. Watson serves to tone down Holmes, to balance out the coldness with warmth. It is Watson with whom the reader identifies in the Holmes Canon. Watson is the narrator and the one who tries, like the reader, to solve the mystery with Holmes. The reader sees only what Watson sees, after all. When Watson expresses care and concern for Holmes, he helps the reader to see the human side of the Great Detective.

Holmes is introduced in terms of his work in *A Study in Scarlet* (*Beeton's Christmas Annual*, 1887) as a "consulting detective" to the police, who bring their problems to him. Watson's presence increases Holmes's mobility, since Watson can remain at 221B Baker Street while Holmes disguises himself and stalks the darker recesses of London. Watson can even face the horrific hound of the Baskervilles virtually on his own, while the absent Holmes sets himself up comfortably in the moor to spy on the suspects.

The Holmes-Watson relationship suffers in motion picture versions, where Watson is usually treated as a character supplying only comic relief. When the late actor Jeremy Brett was offered the role of Holmes for a British television series, he accepted because he wanted to put the literature right, particularly the character of Watson. Brett referred to Watson as "—not a buffoon, but the *bestest* [*sic*] friend any man ever had," in a *Boston Herald* interview (14 Nov. 1991).

In the wake of Doyle's success, detective duos were rife in the early twentieth century. An exemplary pair are Margery *Allingham's Albert *Campion and his henchman Magersfontein *Lugg.

Later, during the hard-boiled era of crime writing, detectives were cast as outsiders, virtually friendless loners. In *The Maltese Falcon* (1930), author Dashiell *Hammett gives Sam *Spade a partner, Miles Archer, whose only function in the plot is to get himself killed immediately. Although Spade does have the help of a secretary, Effie Perrine, her role is minor. She does however exhibit all the strengths of a good sidekick: she is tough and reliable, and she loves the detective she serves.

From one associate to no associate, the historic trend eventually had to swing to multiple associates. The post–World War II police procedurals pitted squads of detectives against the big city's killers. When Ed *McBain created his Eighty-Seventh Precinct detectives in *Cop Hater* (1956), Detective Steve Carella did not stand out as the group's leader. Carella became the luminary of the series, but importance is still given to Bert Kling, Meyer Meyer, and the rest of the squad.

The same is true in the police procedurals by the Swedish duo of Maj *Sjöwall and Per Wahlöö. Martin *Beck is the team leader, but the books are as much about the interaction among the other cops as they are about finding a criminal.

The police forces in contemporary British mysteries are less apt to indulge in squadroom camaraderie, however. Rank still matters and there is much still separating the poor sergeant from his or her higher-ranked inspector. In Dexter's Inspector Morse series, for example, Lewis is the classic beleaguered underling but plays a subordinate role by definition of his rank, not because the inspector does not trust him.

American writer Elizabeth *George has created a British pair that functions despite being polar opposites of each other. Inspector Thomas Lynley comes from a higher station than does his sergeant, Barbara Havers, an inelegant commoner. While Havers does not like Lynley, and even admits it publicly, the two respect each other's abilities and so form a tentative, professional friendship.

More than a century after Holmes and Watson, the sidekick became a full partner in the case. Teamwork became the hallmark of detecting duos of the 1990s.

Robert B. *Parker's poetry-quoting *Spenser originally began as loner, in the tradition of his immediate literary predecessor, Philip *Marlowe. Hawk was just a hired thug in *Promised Land* (1976), but his role grew over the course of the series and he became Spenser's virtual partner in a relationship based on unwavering trust. The clients may hire Spenser, but he and Hawk work for each other.

Across the ocean, Dutch writer Janwillem *van de Wettering's Adjutant Grijpstra and Sergeant DeGier also work as a team. Grijpstra is the senior officer, but they solve their cases as equal partners and are equally in awe of their Zen-master-like *Comissaris*.

Tony *Hillerman's Navajo detectives Joe Leaphorn and Jim *Chee began by working alone, each with his own series of books. Hillerman brought them together in *Skinwalkers* (1987) and created a new interpretation of detecting duos. Each detective works independently, sometimes not aware that the other is on the case. When they meet, having taken different routes to the same spot, it is a confirmation to both that the crime has been solved.

—Dana Bisbee

SILLY-ASS SLEUTH. The silly-ass *sleuth is primarily a creation of the British Golden Age mystery novelists. These *private detectives or amateur sleuths are distinguished by foppish demeanor and appearance. The most notable examples of the silly ass are Dorothy L. *Sayers's Lord Peter *Wimsey and Margery *Allingham's Albert *Campion. The closest American counterparts are S. S. *Van Dine's Philo *Vance, who affects British mannerisms, and the early Ellery *Queen with his various mannerisms and pince-nez. Upper-class detectives who are in fact police, such as Ngaio *Marsh's Roderick *Alleyn and Elizabeth George's Inspector Thomas Lynley, do not fit this character type.

The English silly-ass sleuths come from the British upper class, adopting behavior that serves to disguise their sleuthing. They rely on deception, covering up their real abilities and serious nature with silliness both of action and language. Their actions are designed to make others regard them as of no consequence, for being underestimated keeps their quarry off guard. The reader, who realizes the truth behind the misleading behavior, is both amused and at an advantage over characters who are confused by their casual, even flippant air.

Usually their relationships with the upper echelons of police are friendly because these elites recognize the abilities of the talent behind the fractious facades and tolerate the behavior of the silly-ass sleuth, usually welcoming his or her entry into the investigation, while sometimes the ordinary constables are skeptical of the sleuth's abilities but respectful of his or her class.

The silly-ass sleuths themselves are upper-class, even members of the nobility, who can afford to act the part of the overbred, perhaps effete, Oxbridge-educated dilettante. Their language often borders on the ridiculous, and they frequently act the part of the complete fool. For instance, in the opening scene of *Mystery Mile* (1930), Campion's almost childish insistence on sacrificing his mouse establishes his disguise as an absurdly juvenile figure, a pose reinforced by his business card, which declares "Coups neatly executed/ Nothing sordid, vulgar or plebeian." Likewise, Wimsey performs flamboyant acts, such as diving into the fountain in *Murder Must Advertise* (1933), all the while speaking in affected Oxbridge slang. These sleuths, however, are taken seriously by some, for both Campion and Wimsey are entrusted with cases of great importance requiring not only their investigative skills but also their utmost discretion and loyalty to the Crown. It is interesting to note that both Campion and Wimsey outgrow their silliness as their series progress. The type virtually disappears from English mysteries with World War II, about the time that Wimsey and Campion discard their affectations.

The American silly-ass type shares the mannerisms and mannered language, but in a nominally classless society such qualities do not have the same impact. Philo Vance, educated at Harvard and Oxford, is an aesthete who can be intellectually insufferable, while the scholarly Queen, who spouts quotations from the classics, is an investigative aristocrat as the son of a police inspector. Queen, like Campion and Wimsey, develops over the course of a long series and does not remain the youthful silly ass of the early novels, while Vance remains essentially static in a much shorter series. Neither Vance nor Queen is, however, the comic equivalent of Campion or Wimsey, although those around them frequently regard them in much the same way that the British detectives are regarded by those surrounding them.

Silly-ass sleuths invariably have sidekicks who provide balance in their adventures by taking care of practicalities, behaving predictably, and having the ability to mingle among servants and villagers.

—Paula M. Woods

Silver, Miss Maud, is the principal series character in the detective novels of Patricia *Wentworth. Although the mousy, nondescript former governess turned *spinster sleuth has a predilection for knitting, helping young lovers in distress, and underscoring her investigations with moral lectures complete with quotations from the poetry of Lord Tennyson, Miss Silver is a determinedly professional *private detective who relies on logic rather than mere intuition in her work. She uses her unthreatening outward appearance to considerable advantage in order to mislead suspects, who frequently do not take her seriously while she employs acute powers of observation and thorough investigative techniques to solve her cases, usually set in the English village milieu or country house milieu or in London, where she keeps a home office in her drawing room. With the support of Scotland Yard's Detective Inspector Frank Abbott and Chief Detective Inspector Lamb, as well as her former pupil, Chief Constable Randal March, Silver uses her skills in the interests of truth and *innocence over the course of twenty-three cozy novels, making her debut in *Grey Mask* (1928) and her final appearance in *The Girl in the Cellar* (1961).

—Barbara Sloan-Hendershott

SIMENON, GEORGES (1903–1989), Belgian novelist and short story writer, born in Liège of Flemish Catholic parents Désiré and Henriette Simenon. Georges Simenon was close to his father, but estranged from his mother for most of his life. Early accounts of his life contain inconsistencies because he told different versions of the same events to different interviewers. Even his twenty-seven volumes of autobiographical writings, including two novels, a diary, and a series of "intimate" memoirs, are unreliable sources.

Simenon left school at age fifteen, the same year his father suffered a heart attack. Eventually he became a crime reporter with the *Gazette de Liège*. He published his first novel, *Au Pont des Arches*, in 1921, the year his father died, and he became engaged to Régine Renchon. In 1923 he married and had one of his short stories accepted by Colette for *Le Matin*. He began writing pulp novels under the pen name "Georges Sim" and eventually published more than 100 pulp novels under several pen names.

In 1930, Simenon began to take his work more seriously and signed a contract with the publisher Fayard for a series of detective novels about a Parisian policeman, Jules *Maigret. Most of the first nineteen books were written over the next three years, largely on board his boat, the *Ostrogoth*, moored near Delfzijl in the Netherlands. In later years, Simenon claimed never to have done any research on police procedure, and never to have set foot inside the Quai des Orfèvres, the main police station in Paris. In point of fact, he attended a series of lectures on forensics at the University of Liège in connection with some articles he wrote as a young reporter.

The Maigret books received good reviews, although some critics had reservations about the speed with which they had been written. Simenon and his publisher staged an elaborate party in 1931 to celebrate the publication of the first two titles, *M. Gallet, décéde* (1931; The Death of Monsieur Gallet) and *Le pendu de St. Pholien* (1931; The Crime of Inspector Maigret). Author and publisher had reason to celebrate, as it had not been easy for the former to convince the latter that these unorthodox detective novels were worth publishing.

Three years later Simenon told Fayard he wanted to quit writing about Maigret to concentrate on serious fiction. To prove his point the nineteenth Maigret novel, *Maigret* (1934; *Maigret Returns*, 1941) depicts the detective in retirement. By the time it appeared, Simenon had broken with Fayard and signed a contract with Gallimard to write six novels a year.

Comfortably off, Simenon made a visit to Tahiti and returned to France to live in a succession of luxurious homes. When Germany invaded Belgium, Simenon was appointed commissioner for Belgian refugees at La Rochelle. He began work on a series of autobiographical writings and wrote his first Maigret novel in six years, *Cécile est morte* (1942; *Maigret and the Spinster*, 1977). There is no reference in it to the commissaire's retirement in 1934.

During the 1940s, Simenon wrote more than twenty novels, alternating the Maigrets with the dark, psychological novels, which he referred to as *romans durs, romans romans*, or *romans-tout-court*, Alication is the theme that predominates in his non-Maigret works. He left France with his family to settle in St. Luc Masson, Canada. It was there that he hired a French-Canadian, Denyse Ouimet, as his secretary. He renamed her Denise and she became his mistress.

Simenon and his family moved to the United States in 1946. In 1950 he divorced his wife, married Denise, and settled at Shadow Rock Farm, Lakeville, Connecticut where he lived for five years. He continued to write at a rapid rate and his sales reached 3 million a year. During this period he made a triumphant visit to Paris as a celebrity and was elected a member of the Belgian Académie Royale.

In 1955 Simenon moved back to France where he lived first at Cannes and later in a castle outside Lausanne in Switzerland. In 1963 he and his wife had a large house built to their own design at Epalinges. At about this time, Denise suffered a series of mental breakdowns and entered a psychiatric clinic. They separated a few years later.

In 1966, forty of Simenon's publishers staged a celebration of the creation of Maigret in the Netherlands, where a statue of the commissaire was unveiled at Delfzijl. In 1971 Simenon wrote his last psychological novel, *Les innocents* (1972; *The Innocents*, 1973), a few months later he finished the last Maigret, *Maigret et M. Charles* (1972; *Maigret and Monsieur Charles*, 1973). The rest of his writing life he devoted to his memoirs.

—J. Randolph Cox

SINGLETONS. Crime and mystery readers sometimes refer to authors who have written only one book in the genre as singletons. Whether such authors also have writing careers outside of the genre or are known for other careers and have simply written one book, they usually win the term "singleton" because their work in the crime and mystery field is singular in both number and memorability. Their books, too, may be called singleton mysteries. Some such novels arise out of the occupations of their writers, who use their expertise or experience to enrich a single detective novel.

Between her terms in Parliament, Ellen Wilkinson wrote *The Division Bell Mystery* (1932), an impossible crime story dependent on a point of ritual at the House of Commons. Eric Blom became "Sebastian Farr" for *Death on the Down Beat* (1941), drawing heavily on his musical learning for an epistolary tour de force much admired by Edmund *Crispin. *Exit Charlie* (1955), set in and around a provincial repertory theater, is the richer for Alex Atkinson's years of experience as an actor. Xantippe's familiarity with radio is everywhere apparent in *Death Catches Up with Mr. Kluck* (1935), in which a wireless engineer investigates the murder of a program sponsor.

The singleton novel may be an offshoot of an academic career. In *The Ariadne Clue* (1982), Carol Clemeau made her detective a classics professor like herself. Philip Spencer set *Full Term* (1961) at Oxford, where he himself was a teacher. Cecil Jenkins's *Message from Sirius* (1961) was joint winner of the Crime Club's competition for dons in 1961. Margaret Doody's *Aristotle Detective* (1978) arose from amateur enthusiasm for the classics rather from than her professional discipline, which is literary criticism.

Certain mainstream writers have a single crime novel to their credit, such as James Hilton, who used the name "Glen Trever" for *Murder at School* (1931; *Was It Murder?*); Somerset Maugham, whose *Ashenden; or, The British Agent* (1928) retains its reputation as a classic of spy fiction; H. F. M. Prescott, whose *Dead and Not Buried* (1938) stands apart from the biographies and historical novels with which she made her name; Charlotte Hough, a prolific children's writer, whose attractive detective novel, *The Bassington Murder* (1980), has had, regrettably, no sequel; and Forbes Bramble, who entered the field in 1985 with the admirable *Dead of Winter* but has not set foot in it since.

Sometimes the singleton is the launching pad to a different career. Penelope Fitzgerald won the Booker Prize in 1979 with her third novel, having begun as a fiction writer in 1977 with a distinctive crime story, *The Golden Child*. Timothy Robinson's *When Scholars Fall* (1961) was the only detective novel in Hutchinson's New Authors series. A donnish story of great charm and narrative ease, it appeared to herald a distinguished career—and perhaps did so, but not in crime writing. *Landscape with Dead Dons* (1956) is even more fetching, an Oxford novel in the high manic tradition with a notably audacious clue; but the author, Robert Robinson, became famous as a journalist and broadcaster rather than as a rival to Michael *Innes and Edmund Crispin.

The singleton mystery, inevitably, has less chance to establish itself than would a shelf of books from the same author, but a number have come to acquire something like classic status. Godfrey R. Benson's *Tracks in the Snow* (1906) and T. L. Davidson's *The Murder in the Laboratory* (1929) have the Jacques Barzun-Wendell Hertig Taylor seal of approval, as does *The Mummy Case* (1933; *The Mummy Case Mystery*), a diverting Oxford novel by Dermot Morrah, sometime editor of the *Times*. *The Face on the Cutting Room Floor* (1937) by Cameron McCabe is "dazzling" according to Julian *Symons in *Bloody Murder: From the Detective Story to the Crime Novel; A History* (1972; *Mortal Consequences*), but Barzun and Taylor qualify their praise. Whatever its merits, the book is clearly uniquely clever: Symons calls it "unrepeatable." Helen Eustis's *The Horizontal Man* (1947) is an undisputed classic, combining with immense aplomb the literary novel of detection and the psychological novel of suspense and unease. (Her other book, *The Fool Killer*, 1954, is mainstream fiction.) Frank Morley's *Dwelly Lane* (1952; *Death in Dwelly Lane*) appeared in 1952 to a chorus of praise from T. S. Eliot, Walter de la Mare, and Herbert Read, among others. Though deriving from Sherlock *Holmes, it does so obliquely, achieving its own identity with wit, imagination, and choice invention.

Other singletons deserve a wider fame: *She Died Without Light* by Nieves Mathews (1956), an intricate, sinister story set in a pension in Geneva; Clara Stone's *Death in Cranford* (1959), a decorous village mystery made memorable by a shrewd narrator with a waspish narrative manner; E. M. A. Allison's *Through the Valley of Death* (1983), a fourteenth-century mystery akin to Ellis *Peters's Brother *Cadfael chronicles and *Il Name della Rosa* (*The Name of the Rose*; 1983) by Umberto *Eco; and *The Random Factor* by Linda J. LaRosa and Barry Tannenbaum (1978), an intensely exciting novel set in New York, concerning a series of murders without apparent motive.

—B. A. Pike

SJÖWALL, MAJ (b. 1935) and **PER WAHLÖÖ** (1926–1975), Swedish husband and wife team who collaborated for a decade (1965–1975) to produce the remarkable series of ten novels featuring Superintendent Martin *Beck of Sweden's National Homicide Squad. Planned in advance as a 300-chapter (297 in English translation) analytic portrait of Sweden's experiment in social democracy, the Beck novels may be judged as well-wrought entertainments in the police procedural tradition, but also as a coherent ideological (leftist) indictment of social justice in contemporary Sweden.

The immediate inspiration for the series came from Ed *McBain's Eighty-seventh Precinct novels, some of which Sjöwall and Wahlöö translated into Swedish in the 1960s. McBain offered a precedent for the close attention to realistic police procedure, for the exploitation of humor and sex and sexuality as added attractions, and, above all, for the focus upon a central cadre of investigators, each with his or her own personality. Beck is undoubtedly the hero of the series, but his colleagues, such as Lennart Kollberg and Gunvald Larsson, also make important contributions—both as investigators and as commentators upon the investigations.

The first five novels in the series from *Roseanna* (1965) to *Brandbilen som försvann* (1969; The Fire Engine that Disappeared), are fairly straightforward procedurals; signs of social malaise are evident, but not emphasized. The next two novels, *Polis polis Potatismos!* (1970; Murder at the Savoy) and *Den Vedervardige mannen fran Saffle* (1971; The Abominable Man) neatly balance the demands of the detective novel and social criticism: each serves to advance the other. The crime is fixed in a social matrix, and the detective must expose the more general veins of corruption in the body politic as they excise the individual criminal. The final three novels tilt toward social criticism with a strong element of farce competing with the procedural realism.

Both Sjöwall and Wahlöö had worked as journalists and had been active in leftist politics. Wahlöö had published several political thrillers before coming to the collaboration; this background gave the Beck series its distinctive strengths: the careful embedding of Martin Beck's detective adventures in the historical realities of Sweden from 1965 to 1975 and the strong ideological perspective that the novels adopt toward the criminal matters they narrate. In the end, though he still engages in detecting individual murderers and assassins, Martin Beck shares his authors' view that the ultimate villain is the oppressive organization of the collapsing Welfare state.

[*See also* Police Detective.]

—J. K. Van Dover

SLEUTH. A term dating from at least as early as 1194, "sleuth" first denoted a track or trail of a person or animal. By 1470, the word was used to refer to dogs used for tracking, as in sleuth-hound. In the United States the term became interchangeable with bloodhound, and by 1872 the noun form was a word for detective while the verb meant to track, investigate, or ferret out. During the twentieth century, the term has very commonly been used to refer to heroes who investigate and solve crimes in detective novels, stories, dramas, and films. A distinction that might be drawn between the crime novel and the detective novel is that, whereas the former may have no sleuth or may employ one only in a secondary role, in the latter the presence of a sleuth as the central figure is obligatory. Moreover, the detective novel, unlike perhaps any other genre, is, as its name suggests, character-led: Its history is the history of its central character. Though Dorothy L. *Sayers (*Great Short Stories of Detection, Mystery and Horror*, 1928) endeavored with some success to trace the science of deduction back to antiquity, she discovered no real sleuths in the remote past. The history of the character cannot be justifiably traced back beyond April 1841, when Edgar Allan *Poe's "The

Murders in the Rue Morgue" (*Graham's Lady's and Gentleman's Magazine*) appeared, and the type sprang fully formed into existence in the shape of the Chevalier C. Auguste *Dupin.

Dupin provided a paradigm for future sleuths in two respects: first in the manner of operation—the minute examination of evidence, on which the sleuth's powerful ratiocinative abilities are brought to bear—and second in the manner of narration—in the first person by the sleuth's friend and companion, who describes the evidence but cannot interpret it and who constantly marvels at the sleuth's deductions. This method, later used by writers as varied as Arthur Conan *Doyle, R. Austin *Freeman, Agatha *Christie, S. S. *Van Dine, and Rex *Stout, is not only the most traditional but also undoubtedly the fairest way of presenting the mystery to the reader, and was to be characterized in the eighth of Ronald A. *Knox's ten commandments for the detective novelist: "The stupid friend of the detective, the Watson, must not conceal any thoughts which pass through his mind; his intelligence must be slightly, but very slightly, below that of the average reader" (introduction to *The Best Detective Stories of the Year 1928*, 1929; *The Best English Detective Stories: First Series*).

Dupin is not only the first real fictional sleuth but also the first *amateur detective. He is under no obligation to investigate mysteries but is motivated by curiosity, interest, and the desire to exercise his mind. This category, that of amateur sleuth, is one of the three into which, generally speaking, all sleuths may be divided. The others are the sleuth whose duty it is to investigate crime, and who is therefore usually a member of the police, and, lastly, the sleuth who is paid to investigate crime, usually a *private detective, sometimes a lawyer. Though the police sleuth has forerunners in the shape of characters such as Charles *Dickens's Inspector Bucket (*Bleak House*, (1852–3) and Wilkie *Collins's Sergeant *Cuff (*The Moonstone*, 1868), these are not central personages in the novels; the distinction of creating the first police sleuth lies with the French writer Émile *Gaboriau. His character, Monsieur Lecoq, plays only a subordinate role in the author's first novel, *L'Affaire Lerouge* (1866; The Widow Lerouge, 1873), but is the central figure in his best and most influential work, *Monsieur Lecoq* (1868; in English, 1880). The first private detective is, of course, Doyle's Sherlock *Holmes, introduced in *A Study in Scarlet* (*Beeton's Christmas Annual*, 1887), whose conception owed much both to Poe and Gaboriau.

The amateur sleuth may appear in any guise, ranging from the Roman Catholic priest—G. K. *Chesterton's Father *Brown (*The Innocence of Father Brown*, 1911)—to the elderly spinster—Christie's Miss Jane Marple (*The Murder at the Vicarage*, 1930). Academics are frequent—John Rhode's Dr. Lancelot *Priestley (*The Paddington Mystery*, 1925), Edmund *Crispin's Gervase *Fen (*The Case of the Gilded Fly*, 1944; *Obsequies at Oxford*) and Amanda *Cross's Kate *Fansler (*In the Last Analysis*, 1964)—but the character who perhaps most gives the

tone to this category is that of the rich, young man-about-town, sometimes aristocratic, often a connoisseur of the arts, and usually facetious in speech: Sayers's Lord Peter *Wimsey (*Whose Body?*, 1923), *Van Dine's Philo *Vance (*The Benson Murder Case*, 1926), and Margery *Allingham's Albert *Campion (*The Crime at Black Dudley*, 1929; *The Black Dudley Murder*) are the best-known examples. Of the three categories that of amateur sleuth is naturally the least realistic, the most artificial, and the novels in which they feature often embody the same characteristics: settings may be *outré*, as in Allingham or Ellery *Queen (*The Roman Hat Mystery*, 1929), sleuths larger than life—John Dickson *Carr's Dr. Gideon *Fell (*Hag's Nook*, 1933)—and, most of all, plots become intricate logical puzzles with no pretensions to realism, which explicitly invite the reader, to whom all the evidence has been fairly presented, to arrive at the solution to the mystery before it is given by the sleuth: a type exemplified, above all, by Ellery *Queen and John Dickson Carr. The inter-war years were the heyday of the amateur sleuth; since then, though the type has continued, and still continues, to appear, the incidence is less frequent, while the character has lost the dominance in the genre it earlier possessed. The most recent tendency is, perhaps, the attempt to draw this sleuth into a more realistic environment by giving him or her an occupation that is more likely to provide involvement with crime than that of the academic or idle aristocrat. An example is Jonathan *Kellerman's California child psychologist, Alex Delaware (*When the Bough Breaks*, 1985; *Shrunken Heads*).

The history of the private sleuth who is a private detective is marked by the immense influence of Doyle. The detective, like Holmes, is characterized by a complex of eccentricities, and the relationship between detective and assistant echoes that between Holmes and Watson. Christie's Hercule *Poirot (*The Mysterious Affair at Styles*, 1920), whose cases are usually narrated by the imperceptive Captain Arthur Hastings, appears to have been conceived by negating Holmes's obvious characteristics: Holmes is English, tall, lean, clean-shaven, and surrounded by domestic disorder; Poirot is foreign, short, stout, mustached and obsessed by order. Stout's Nero *Wolfe (*Fer-de-Lance*, 1934; *Meet Nero Wolfe*), whose chronicler is his assistant, Archie *Goodwin, seems to be a Montenegrin reincarnation of Mycroft *Holmes, of whom Holmes remarks in "The Greek Interpreter" (*The Memoirs of Sherlock Holmes*, 1894): "If the art of detection began and ended in reasoning from an armchair, my brother would be the greatest criminal agent that ever lived." Nicholas *Blake's Nigel Strangeways (*A Question of Proof*, 1935) is an exception: Though possessing eccentricities, he derives many of these from the poet W. H. Auden, and does not otherwise fit the Holmesian pattern, while the narration is in the third person, not in the first by a Watson figure. In fact, though characters such as Holmes and Poirot provide the popular image of the fictional sleuth, private detectives have always been less numerous than amateur or police sleuths, and the type is now, to all intents and purposes, extinct. Its place has been usurped by the *private eye, a new type of sleuth who emerged in the United States in the early 1920s; the best-known examples are Dashiell *Hammett's Sam *Spade (*The Maltese Falcon*, 1930), Raymond *Chandler's Philip *Marlowe (*The Big Sleep*, 1939), and Ross *Macdonald's Lew *Archer (*The Moving Target*, 1949, as John Macdonald). Unlike the traditional sleuth, the private eye does not rely on the accumulation of evidence, nor is emphasis placed on the character's ratiocinative abilities. Instead the private eye, a far more active character, gains information generally through conversation and may arrive at the solution by chance. Further, whereas the traditional detective story is conservative and upholds the values of society, the private eye novel may be radical, subversive, or promote a cause: From Macdonald onwards ecological concerns are a recurrent theme.

The foremost example of the private sleuth who is a lawyer is Freeman's Dr. John *Thorndyke (*The Red Thumb Mark*, 1907). Though Freeman often adopts the Holmes-Watson pattern of narration in his novels and short stories, he consciously constructed the character as an antipode to Holmes: Thorndyke has no eccentricities, and his reasoning, unlike that of his contemporary, is distinguished by its rigorous logic—considered purely as a detective, he is perhaps the most impressive of all fictional sleuths. Later lawyers—Erle Stanley *Gardner's Perry *Mason (*The Case of the Velvet Claws*, 1933) is the best known—are closer to the private eye model than that of the private detective.

Despite Gaboriau's example, the *police detective took longer to become established than either the amateur or the private sleuth. The reason for this seems to have been twofold. On the one hand, the image of the policeman as incompetent and unimaginative, invariably drawing the wrong conclusions, and hindering or obstructing the sleuth in his investigations, which Doyle canonized in the figures of Lestrade and Holmes's other official rivals, militated against the use of the type as a central character. On the other, the social position of the policeman, inferior to that of the characters who at that time usually made up the dramatis personae of the detective story, presented another obstacle: While the police sleuth might be at no disadvantage when dealing with servants or retainers, he might—as indeed is the case with Lecoq in the conclusion to *Monsieur Lecoq*—be at a loss when confronted with their masters or mistresses. A. E. W. *Mason circumvents the difficulty with Inspector *Hanaud (*At the Villa Rose*, 1910), essentially by turning the character into another Holmes with a Watson in the form of Mr. Ricardo.

The first of the modern police sleuths, however, is Freeman Wills *Crofts's Inspector Burnley (*The Cask*, 1920), the prototype for the author's better-known detective, Joseph *French of Scotland Yard (*Inspector French's Greatest Case*, 1925). In creating the type Crofts

confronted both problems head-on and turned them into advantages. French is plodding and unimaginative, but instead of concealing his thoughts and narrating the story from the standpoint of a Watson, Crofts allows readers to follow every step in the construction of theory after theory until a solution is eventually reached. And in making French solidly bourgeois he conferred a certain degree of realism on the character. French was followed by a number of similar characters—Henry Wade's Chief Inspector Poole (*The Duke of York's Steps*, 1929), J. J. Connington's Superintendent Ross (*The Eye in the Museum*, 1929), Sir Basil Thomson's Scottish policeman Superintendent Richardson (*P. C. Richardson's First Case*, 1933)—and the type and method initiated by Crofts has maintained itself in British detective fiction up to the present. Recently, however, instead of attaching the police inspector to Scotland Yard, authors have preferred to base their characters in the provinces: Examples are Ruth *Rendell's Chief Inspector Wexford (*From Doon with Death*, 1964), who works in Sussex; Dorothy Simpson's Kent Policeman, Inspector Luke Thanet (*The Night She Died*, 1981); and Colin *Dexter's Inspector Endeavor *Morse of Oxford (*Last Bus to Woodstock*, 1975). Georges *Simenon's Jules *Maigret of the Paris Police Judiciaire (*M. Gallet décédé*, 1931; *The Death of Monsieur Gallet; Maigret Stonewalled*) is, like French, quintessentially bourgeois, but this is the only trait he shares with this detective and his successors. Perhaps the best-known, and certainly the best, of all police detectives, his creation owes nothing to any of the progenitors of the genre; it is unique, both in the mode of detection and manner of narration, and those who have sought to imitate him have never succeeded in catching more than the most superficial traits of the character. While Crofts accepted the social status of the police sleuth as natural, other writers sought to solve the problem it posed by adapting the character of the gentlemanly amateur sleuth: Josephine *Tey's Inspector Alan Grant (*The Man in the Queue*, 1929; *Killer in the Crowd*), Ngaio *Marsh's Inspector/Superintendent Roderick *Alleyn (*A Man Lay Dead*, 1934), Michael *Innes's Sir John Appleby (*Death at the President's Lodgings*, 1936; *Seven Suspects*), and even, surprisingly, P. D. *James's Adam *Dalgliesh (*Cover Her Face*, 1962) are all policeman, but are all recognizably descendants, to a greater or less degree, not of Lecoq and French but of Lord Peter *Wimsey. In America, Anna Katharine *Green produced an early example of the police sleuth in Ebenezer Gryce (*The Leavenworth Case: A Lawyer's Story*, 1878), but the character, and the novel itself, look back to Dickens and Collins rather than forward to Gaboriau; and over the next century American crime fiction conspicuously lacks the regular procession of police officers which, from 1920 onwards, is a feature of the British variant. Some isolated examples may be noted: Anthony Abbot's Thatcher Colt, the police commissioner of New York, a blend of Wimsey and Philo *Vance (*About the Murder of Geraldine Foster*, 1930; *The Murder of a Man Afraid of Women*); Coffin Ed *Johnson and Grave Digger Jones, the police detectives in Chester *Himes's surreal, comic, and violent novels of black Harlem, originally published in French (*La reine des pommes*, 1958; *For Love of Imabelle; A Rage in Harlem*); and Tony *Hillerman's Navajo Indians Jim *Chee and Joe Leaphorn (*The Dark Wind*, 1982; *The Blessing Way*, 1970), who are more akin to the heroes of James Fenimore Cooper than to the traditional sleuth. As in Britain, the disinclination to the use the police sleuth is attributable to the conception of the character as incompetent, compared to the brilliance of the amateur or private sleuth, a view perpetuated, for example, both in the work of Van Dine and Stout; but a contributory factor must also have been the image of the police put forward, particularly in the private eye novel, as corrupt, and hence almost as much an enemy to the sleuth as the criminal. The situation changed in the 1950s with the emergence of the police procedural novel. Up to this time the sleuth had always been an individual, sometimes with an assistant, engaged in the investigation of a single crime. In the police procedural the individual is replaced by a collective—a police squad—which is often engaged in the simultaneous investigation of several crimes. Ed *McBain (*Cop Hater*, 1956) is the bestknown in this genre, but its conventions have been adopted, to a greater or lesser extent, by most American writers who have taken the police as their subject.

The choice of sleuth indicates the author's general intention. To employ an amateur sleuth with no connection with crime, a private supersleuth, or a gentlemanly police officer implies that the work is primarily an entertaining puzzle, and that no social comment can be expected. As the short history above makes clear, the general tendency of the detective novel has been to move away from artificiality towards a certain degree of realism, often combined with social criticism, and the character of the sleuth has changed in consequence. The dilettante amateur has been largely replaced by the semiprofessional, the private detective by the private eye, and the individual police officer, gentlemanly or bourgeois, by the police squad. Though the older types may never die out completely, as the detective novel can never aspire to complete seriousness, it seems, however, likely that this tendency will continue, and that the days of the traditional sleuth are numbered.

[*See also* Academic Sleuth; Accidental Sleuth; Armchair Detective; Bluestocking Sleuth; Clerical Sleuth; Couples: Sleuth Couples; Elderly Sleuth; Ethnic Sleuth; Great Detective, The; Hard-Boiled Sleuth; Journalist Sleuth; Juvenile Sleuth; Lawyer: The American Lawyer-Sleuth *and* The British Lawyer-Sleuth; Medical Sleuth; Native American Sleuth; Plainman Sleuth; Psychic Sleuth; Scientific Sleuth; Silly-Ass Sleuth; Spinster Sleuth; Superman Sleuth; Surrogate Detective.]

—T. J. Binyon

Small, Rabbi David. The first rabbi in the line of clerical sleuths that follows from G. K. *Chesterton's Father Brown, Harry Kemelman's Rabbi David Small makes an ideal detective both because of his vocation and his special place in the Yankee town of Barnard's Crossing, Massachusetts.

Unlike other clergymen, the traditional rabbi is not a spiritual leader or examplar of religious zeal but primarily a man of intellect, a lifelong student of the Hebrew book of law, the Talmud. Small relies on the rabbinical art of *pilpul*, the "tracing of fine distinctions." His detection is promoted also by the intellectual openness asserted for Judaism, its "questioning of everything."

Kemelman frankly uses the detective fictions involving Small, his family, and his Conservative congregation to explore the social and religious situation of contemporary American Jewry. The rabbi usually is drawn into cases by his friend, Chief of Police Hugh Lanigan; however, the detection often helps to resolve a problem within his congregation or to defend someone in the Jewish community.

Like Brown, Small understands people through both a sacred book and wide experience. In his investigations of lawbreaking, the rabbi combines firm judgment (necessary to maintain any law, God's or humankind's) with a restraint and tolerance that are promoted as "worldly" Judaism.

[*See also* Clerical Sleuth.]

—T. R. Steiner

SMITH, ALEXANDER McCALL (b. 1948), African-born lawyer and author of mysteries set in Botswana, featuring the series detective Mma Precious *Ramotswe. Born in Rhodesia (now Zimbabwe), he was educated there and at the University of Edinburgh in Scotland, where he became a professor of medical law. He also helped to establish a school of law at the University of Botswana. Presently, he also serves as vice-chairman of the Human Genetics Commission of the United Kingdom, as chairman of the British Medical Journal Ethics Committee and as a member of the International Bioethics Commission of UNESCO. Married to a physician, he is the father of two daughters. For recreation, he plays wind instruments, including the bassoon, in an amateur orchestra he co-founded, called The Really Terrible Orchestra.

Smith has produced more than fifty books, as author or editor, including legal studies such as *Forensic Aspects of Sleep* (1997) and popular children's books. He entered the mystery writing field with the 1998 publication of *The No. 1 Ladies' Detective Agency*. Originally published by Polygon, the fiction imprint of Edinburgh University Press, the book found a wide audience by word of mouth. By the time Anchor Books published it in 2002, Smith had produced three more novels in the series, begun another Ramotswe book, and also completed the first book in a new series set to be launched in 2003, featuring the Scottish American sleuth Isabel Dalhousie, who investigates crimes in Edinburgh.

In *The No. 1 Ladies' Detective Agency*, Ramotswe

solves a number of cases, ranging from finding out what a rich man's daughter gets up to when she goes out of her house to searching for a small boy who may be the *victim of witch doctors. The book establishes the strengths of the series, which have much to do with Smith's descriptions of everyday life in Africa and his affectionate portrait of the "traditionally built" Ramotswe, a woman who is philosophical about the troubles in her own past and about the cases she takes on. A great charm of the series is Smith's ability to convey Ramotswe's attitudes toward the failings and foibles of her clients without making direct comments about them. There is humor, too, in the contrast between Ramostwe's knack for investigation and the advice she reads—and sometimes follows to ill effect—in a book she purchased by mail order, *The Principles of Private Investigation* by Clovis Anderson.

[*See also* Private Detective.]

—Rosemary Herbert

Spade, Sam, is the *private eye and main character in Dashiell *Hammett's novel *The Maltese Falcon* (1930). Although he also appears in three stories included in the volume edited by Ellery *Queen in 1944 as *The Adventures of Sam Spade and Other Stories* and assumed the lead in a series of 1940s radio dramas, Spade earned his place as the literary model of the *hard-boiled sleuth with Hammett's best-selling book and became an archetypal figure in the popular imagination through Humphrey Bogart's portrayal in the film version of *The Maltese Falcon*.

Sam Spade's most notable quality is his absolute adherence to a private code of ethics. Hammett's novel, written in the third person, offers little biographical background for Spade, but readers are apprised of the philosophical outlook he has drawn from his professional experience. In the midst of the novel, Spade tells the story of a missing person he pursued named Flitcraft. The man had left his home and business in Tacoma. When Mrs. Flitcraft employs Spade to find her husband, the detective turns him up in Spokane, living a life identical to the one he left behind, even to the extent of having a second wife similar to the one he abandoned. Flitcraft explains to Spade that a near fatal accident taught him that life is a set of chance events, but according to Spade, Flitcraft does not realize that he has settled back into determinative routine. What Spade likes about the story is that Flitcraft's philosophical inconsistency reveals the real premises of life to lie in immediate material situations.

The importance Spade sees in the Flitcraft tale helps explain Spade's existentialist consciousness. His terse speech shows him refusing the rituals of language he deems empty. His sexual affair with the wife of his partner and his resistance to the claims of affection that follow upon his relationship with Brigid O'Shaughnessy, the *femme fatale of the novel, indicate that Spade is forever seeking to retain control. For the same reason he

mocks the personal relationship of the villain Gutman with his gunsel Wilmer, and refuses to cooperate with the police.

As a hard-boiled sleuth, Spade is a departure from the classical detective. Whereas the detectives of the Golden Age functioned as conservative agents of wealth and its preferred order, Sam Spade expresses Hammett's radical worldview. His mistrust of virtually all those around him; his cynicism about any code other than the one he has crafted—these are the traits necessary if one is to function successfully in a dangerous, threatening, and fundamentally corrupt world.

Hammett completed his effective formula for the hard-boiled sleuth by setting Spade to work in the nighttime streets of San Francisco whose dark intensity limns a crime-ridden city where the thoughtful man could never find a home and might as well, then, become a freelance, if lonely, truth seeker.

—Bonnie C. Plummer

Spenser. The protagonist of Robert B. *Parker's series of private eye novels, Spenser—who always goes by the single name only—is introduced in *The Godwulf Manuscript* (1973). A disenchanted former employee of the Suffolk County, Massachusetts district attorney's office, this existential hero is guided by a self-inscribed code of conduct modeled on that of Raymond *Chandler's Philip *Marlowe. Aided by his strongman sidekick, the enigmatic African American, Hawk, he is known for his wisecracks edged with sarcasm, often delivered as one-liners. While an imposing physical presence establishes him as a tough guy, when he was created he was remarkable for his sensitivity. Comfortable in physical confrontation, he also knows the importance of rapport in relationships. He is as believable jabbing and hooking at a punching bag as he is cooking up a gourmet meal to share with his psychologist-lover Susan Silverman, while drawing upon her professional insights for clues to psychological motivation.

[*See also* Hard-boiled Sleuth; Sidekicks and Sleuthing Teams.]

—John M. Reilly

SPILLANE, MICKEY (Frank Morrison, b. 1918), American author of the hard-boiled *private eye novel. Born in Brooklyn, New York, Spillane grew up in a rough Elizabeth, New Jersey neighborhood where his father was a bartender. Spillane was a born storyteller—particularly of ghost stories—and began to submit stories to the pulp magazines as a teenager. After a brief stint at Kansas State College, he returned to New York and began writing short stories and scripts for comics books. In World War II he enlisted in the army and served as a fighter pilot instructor in Greenwood, Mississippi.

Spillane returned to writing after the war, publishing his first novel in 1947; he interrupted his career in 1952 after a religious conversion, and again in 1973 to become a Miller Lite beer spokesman. These decisions divide his career into three distinct periods: 1947–52; 1961–73; and 1980–89; but the periods do not reflect significant changes in his writing.

In 1946 Spillane created a comic book private eye called Mike Danger who became Mike *Hammer in the bestselling novel *I, the Jury* (1947). Hammer is a World War II veteran who sets out to avenge the death of a man who once saved his life, and vows to let nothing stand in his way, especially not the law. He is assisted by his loyal and sexy secretary, Velda. The novel is typical of Spillane's work, drawing together right-wing politics, unrestrained violence, and strong, sexual women. Hammer executes his friend's killer but struggles thereafter to convince himself of the legitimacy of his act.

Subsequent stories adhere to the formula of vengeance, violence, and sex. The book titles are indicative: *I, the Jury* (1947), *My Gun Is Quick* (1950), *Vengeance Is Mine*: (1950), *The Big Kill* (1951), and *The Girl Hunters* (1962). Throughout the series Hammer ages but does not mellow, from the white-hot vigilante in *I, the Jury* to the older, more world-weary but still deadly Hammer of *The Killing Man* (1989) and *Black Alley* (1996). The series has been extremely popular; the sixth book, *Kiss Me Deadly* (1952), was the first mystery novel to appear on the *New York Times* best-seller list.

In the 1960s Spillane created Tiger Mann, an imitation of James *Bond who appeared in four novels and never achieved the stature of Hammer. Spillane also wrote nonseries books that continued his mix of conservative politics, violence, and sex.

One book stands out for its narrative purpose. In *One Lonely Night* (1951) Spillane offers an especially effective defense of his perspective to those who criticize him rather than analyzing his fiction. In the story Hammer challenges a liberal judge who condemns him and his actions. While Hammer is confronting the judge, Spillane is confronting his liberal critics.

From Hammer's first appearance Spillane captured the psyche of America, from its loss of innocence after World War II to the late 1980s loss of purpose and direction. His books offer a savagely lyrical depiction of the wounded American soul.

[*See also* Hard-boiled Sleuth.]

—James L. Traylor *and* Max Allan Collins

SPINSTER SLEUTH. The term "spinster," originally appended to names to indicate the profession of spinner, has been used since the seventeenth century to denote a woman who is unmarried, especially a woman who is past the usual marrying age. In crime and mystery fiction, the spinster sleuth is usually an elderly woman with time on her hands and an observing eye. She may claim the advantage of detachment, and with scant personal life of her own, she may find the lives of others a consuming interest. Her low social profile, as a person both unmarried and elderly, may afford her natural camouflage. To quote Lord Peter *Wimsey in *Unnatural Death*

(1927; *The Dawson Pedigree*), she can ask freely "questions which a young man could not put without a blush."

The prototype for the meddlesome old maid with time on her hands is Amelia Butterworth, who assists Ebenezer Gryce in two novels by Anna Katharine *Green, *That Affair Next Door* (1897) and *Lost Man's Lane* (1898). It seems agreed Butterworth had no immediate successors. Three decades later, Dorothy L. *Sayers refined the detecting potential of the "superfluous" woman when she introduced Miss Katharine Climpson in *Unnatural Death*. This redoubtable lady runs a typing pool, or secretarial agency, which has the dual purpose of providing occasional sleuthing assistance to Wimsey. Her exclamatory reports to Wimsey enhance the appeal of *Strong Poison* (1930), in which her investigations help to save Harriet *Vane from the gallows.

In 1928, Agatha *Christie introduced Miss Jane *Marple, an apparently unassuming elderly woman whose infallible insight into human affairs is based on her ability to make parallels about the suspects she encounters with villagers whom she knows more intimately. During the same year Patricia *Wentworth created Miss Maud *Silver in *Grey Mask* (1928); a former governess turned *private detective to the gentry, who knits assiduously, inspires instant confidence, and, with thirty-two recorded cases, must be the busiest of all spinster detectives.

In 1931, Stuart Palmer's Miss Hildegarde *Withers took a class to the New York zoo where she became an *accidental sleuth. She is exactly the assertive, prying spinster of caricature, complete with horse face, angular frame, pince-nez, and a "sharp, commanding voice" of "unmistakeable authority." Ethel Thomas who is also a New Yorker, is irresistibly drawn to investigate murder, and figures in four novels by Courtland Fitzsimmons. D. B. Olsen's Rachel Murdock continually shocks her prim sister, Jennifer, with whom she lives in Los Angeles. Her look of "a Dresden-china model with silky white curls" belies her adventurous spirit. Jane Amanda Edwards appears in a series by Charlotte Murray Russell, set in Rockport, Wisconsin. She boasts of her pedigree and confesses that she "sees all, hears some, and tells everything." Matilda Perks is the most disagreeable of spinster detectives. A fearsome old party with a mustache and a harsh, abrasive manner, "Miss Perks cared for nobody . . . and took no trouble to dissemble the fact." She figures in two of R. C. Woodthorpe's novels.

Julia Tyler is a retired Latin teacher in Rossville, Virginia, in Louisa Revell's novels. Her cases occur away from home, as far afield, even, as England and Italy. Despite her disciplined shrewdness, she tends to reach the wrong conclusion. Two British teachers turn professional in retirement. Austin Lee's Flora Hogg sets up in South Green, charging "two guineas a day and expenses" on her first case in 1955. Miss Emily Seeton taught art and has an eerie facility for psychic portraiture, invaluable to Scotland Yard. She features in Heron Carvic's novels, operating more by instinct than judgment. Amanda and Lutie Beagle have professionalism thrust upon them when they inherit their brother's New York detective agency. Torrey Chanslor's two novels record their response to the challenge. Other spinsters encounter murder in the course of their working lives: the brave young governess, Harriet Unwin, in three novels by Evelyn Hervey; the nurses Sarah Keate and Hilda Adams, in books by Mignon G. *Eberhart and Mary Roberts *Rinehart, respectively; and the missionary pair in Matthew Head's African novels, Dr. Mary Finney, large, downright imperturbable, and untouched by fashion, and Emily Collins, small and wispy, "like a bundle of dried twigs tied up with a string."

Grace Severance is featured in four late novels by Margaret Scherf. A Chicago pathologist retired to Montana, she is clever and competent and dryly humorous about her new way of life, in which, predictably, her expertise continues to be called upon. Melinda Pink is Gwen Moffat's detective, well defined by the first title to feature her, *Lady with a Cool Eye* (1973). A seasoned naturalist and climber, she does most of her detecting in the open air.

The Honorable Constance Morrison-Burke is, like Joyce *Porter's male protagonists, a comic grotesque. A tomboy with a hockey stick, forty years on, she is a detective of the do-or-die school, lacking any sense of her own limitations, which are legion.

Some of the current spate of young women detectives are spinsters, though none would thank one for calling her so. They are unmarried by choice, either lesbian or resistant to conjugal ties. Antonia *Fraser's Jemima Shore exemplifies their sexual freedom.

[*See also* Elderly Sleuth; Nosy Parker Sleuth.]

—B. A. Pike

STABENOW, DANA (HELEN) (b. 1952), American writer best known for crime novels set in Alaska and featuring the native Aleut investigator, Kate Shugak. The daughter of a pilot and a mother who held a variety of jobs, the Anchorage, Alaska-born author was partly home-schooled. She graduated from a local high school and earned a B.A in journalism and an MFA from the University of Alaska. Stabenow held several jobs before she launched her writing career. They included work with an air-taxi company that transported outdoorsmen to and from fishing sites, house-sitting, and serving as a public relations person for British Petroleum in the Prudhoe Bay oil fields.

Stabenow began her writing career in 1987, when she wrote a mystery she did not send out for publication. Following that, she wrote and published *Second Star* (1991), a science fiction adventure. On the advice of her publisher, she cleaned up her first mystery manuscript and it was published as *A Cold Day for Murder* in 1992. The book introduces Shugak and Mutt, a canine companion who becomes a memorable character in the series. As Shugak journeys through the Alaskan wilderness by dogsled in search of a missing park ranger, Stabenow establishes her strengths in describing landscape and weather conditions that possess both majesty and ferocity. She also uses her work to support protection of the wilderness, as in *A Fine and Bitter Snow* (2002), in which Shugak's friend Dan O'Brien's park ranger position is threatened by those who would like to replace him with a person less committed to environmental protection. In 1998, Stabenow began another series set in Alaska. *Fire and Ice* (1998) and following books chronicle the emotional problems and work life of Liam Campbell, an Alaska State Trooper who is assigned to the remote fishing village of Newenham. He is reluctant to go there at first, but as the series progresses, he becomes attached to the rugged place and to a woman who lives there.

[*See also* Animals; Police Detective.]

—Rosemary Herbert

STARRETT, (CHARLES) VINCENT (EMERSON), 1886–1974. Vincent Starrett was born in Toronto but moved at an early age to Chicago, where he became a celebrated newspaperman and spent most of his life. He was a prolific essayist and was recognized as an outstanding bookman for his bibliographies and critical studies of a wide range of writers. Starrett was a scholar of crime fiction, as well as a notable writer of mystery novels, and is credited with introducing Western readers to the pleasures of Chinese detective fiction through his seminal essay "Some Chinese Detective Stories" in his *Bookman's Holiday: The Private Satisfactions of an Incurable Collector* (1942). One of the grand old men of Sherlockianism, he was a cofounder of the Baker Street Irregulars. His remarkable *The Private Life of Sherlock Holmes* (1933) is the first biographical study of a fictional detective hero.

—David Skene-Melvin

STEWART, MARY (FLORENCE ELINOR) (b. 1916), British author of romantic suspense and historical novels and former lecturer in English at Durham University. Her novels, especially those set in the Arthurian world, are informed by her training in English literature.

Stewart's first ten novels, written during the 1950s and 1960s, are exemplars of romantic suspense in which the plucky heroine finds herself in an exotic locale where mysterious circumstances become increasingly sinister and an element of romance makes it difficult to separate the hero from the villain as the action develops. These novels bear some hallmarks of the Gothic novel, especially in their maintenance of suspense by keeping the protagonist in constant peril. In *Touch Not the Cat* (1976) Stewart also used elements of the occult, in common with the Gothic tradition. Despite her romantic and perilous circumstances, the typical Stewart protagonist possesses some common sense which, when finally employed, rescues her from danger and causes her to consider the truth of the matter in a clear-headed manner.

The story type that results has come to be known as Had-I-But-Known.

[*See also* Females and Feminists; Menacing Characters.]

—Judith Rhodes

STOUT, REX (TODHUNTER) (1886–1975), creator of Nero *Wolfe and Archie *Goodwin, perhaps the most successful detective team in American mystery fiction, was born in Noblesville, Indiana of parents who moved the family west to Kansas before he was a year old. He received early encouragement in reading from his mother and his teacher father, and had read all 1,126 books in his father's library by the time he was eleven. He went on to become the state's spelling champion at the age of thirteen.

One of nine children, Stout was prevented from entering the University of Kansas due to his family's lack of money. He joined the U.S. Navy at the age of eighteen and served as a yeoman on President Theodore Roosevelt's yacht for nearly two years. Some of his poems were published in *Smart Set* magazine, and he supported himself in a variety of jobs for four years after leaving the navy. For a time he returned to writing, publishing four serialized adventure novels in *All-Story Magazine* from 1913 to 1916, as well as more than thirty short stories in other magazines. Always a rapid calculator and bookkeeper, he achieved early success by founding the Educational Thrift Service with his brother Bob. Earnings from the school banking system enabled him to travel extensively in Europe with his first wife, Fay.

Stout returned to writing full time in 1927, leaving his job as president of Vanguard Press, a company he had helped found. In 1929 Vanguard published the first Stout novel to appear in book form, *How Like a God.* Though not usually listed with his crime and *detective novels, the book contains a fair amount of suspense and culminates in a murder.

Stout's personal life changed in 1932 with his divorce from his first wife and marriage to Pola Hoffman. He was publishing literary and romance novels at this time, but he still remembered the hundreds of detective stories he'd read since his boyhood. In October 1933, the same month his daughter was born, he created Wolfe and Goodwin, and began work on the first Wolfe novel, *Fer-de-Lance.* Nero Wolfe, weighing in at some 270 pounds, was a gourmet who loved orchids and beer. (His first recorded sentence, on the second page of *Fer-de-Lance,* is, "Where's the beer?") Like his creator he held firm, mainly liberal views on a variety of subjects. He rarely left his brownstone on New York's West 35th Street. In short, he was something new in American detective fiction. His relationship with confidential assistant Goodwin, with its interplay of clever conversation and flashes of wit, was the most successful pairing since Sherlock *Holmes and Dr. John H. *Watson, and often compensated for some lapses in the plotting of later books.

There can be little doubt that four of the first six Wolfe novels are among the best of the series. *Fer-de-Lance* (1934; *Meet Nero Wolfe*), with its deadly golf club and titular serpent, set the stage for all that followed. The character of Wolfe had mellowed a bit by the second book, *The League of Frightened Men* (1935), but its plot remains one of the strongest in the series. In the fifth and sixth books, *Too Many Cooks* and *Some Buried Caesar* (both 1938; *The Red Bull*), Wolfe makes two of his rare ventures outside New York City.

After 1941 Stout abandoned most of his other detective characters such as Tecumseh Fox and Alphabet Hicks to concentrate on Wolfe, turning out a total of thirty-three novels and forty-one novellas about the rotund sleuth. Following the early high spots in the saga, Wolfe probably hit his peak with the Zeck trilogy consisting of *And Be a Villain* (1948; *More Deaths Than One*), *The Second Confession* (1949), and *In the Best Families* (1950; *Even in the Best Families*). Each of the novels is complete and clever in itself, and together they tell of Wolfe's duel of wits with *master criminal Arnold Zeck, a man so powerful he finally drives Wolfe out of his home and into hiding.

Late in the series, Stout continued to communicate his social concerns. *A Right to Die* (1964) deals with the civil rights movement, while Wolfe battles the abuses of J. Edgar Hoover's F.B.I. in *The Doorbell Rang* (1965). The final Wolfe novel, *A Family Affair* (1975), was published shortly before Stout's death. Despite some plot weakness it is a fitting conclusion to the saga, dealing as it does with those closest to the master sleuth.

[*See also*: Armchair Detective; Eccentrics; Great Detective, The; Sidekicks and Sleuthing Teams.]

—Edward D. Hoch

STRIBLING, T(HOMAS) S(IGISMUND) (1881–1965) was born in Tennessee and in 1905 graduated from the University of Alabama's law school. He practiced law only briefly before becoming a professional writer. The first five of his thirty-six witty and ironic works appeared in the pulp magazine *Adventure* in 1925 and 1926. They feature the *psychological sleuth Dr. Henry Poggioli, shown traveling through the Caribbean and Latin America. Variously identified as a professor of psychology, psychiatry, and criminology at The Ohio State University, Poggioli relies on his insights into human behavior more than upon the interpretation of physical clues to unravel baffling mysteries. In perhaps his best-known story, "Passage to Benares" (*Adventure*, 20 Feb. 1926) Poggioli is hanged for a murder that he has solved. But Stribling resurrected Poggioli in *Clues of the Caribbees* in 1929 and again in a final series of works published from 1945 to 1957. Stribling's detective fiction is notable for satirical asides that reveal a keen understanding of the paradoxes of human nature and a respect for racial and ethnic minorities. Although Stribling is today remembered best for his detective fiction, he also wrote mainstream novels, winning the Pulitzer Prize for best novel with *The Store* (1932), the middle novel in a trilogy that began with *The Forge* (1931) and concluded with *Unfinished Cathedral* (1934).

—Richard Bleiler

SUPERMAN SLEUTH. Edgar Allan *Poe, who founded modern detective fiction with "The Murders in the Rue Morgue" (*Graham's Lady's and Gentleman's Magazine*, Apr. 1841), in the same story gave the genre its first superman sleuth: the Chevalier C. Auguste *Dupin. Dupin bears the characteristics that were to become the hallmark of the type: He is an *eccentric genius who possesses what Poe describes as "a peculiar analytic ability" that enables him, through observation, to follow another's train of thought or to deduce, after the examination of evidence, the solution to a crime that has baffled the police. Poe also bequeathed to his successors a narrative format: The tales are told by a loyal, admiring, but imperceptive and uncomprehending friend whose astonishment at Dupin's powers gives added refulgence to the latter's brilliant feats of deduction.

Émile *Gaboriau added one more to the characteristics established by Poe: His detective, Lecoq, in *Le Crime d'Orcival* (1867; *The Mystery of Orcival*), is a master of disguise—so much so that his real appearance is known only to a few. Finally, to produce the definitive superman detective—Sherlock *Holmes—Arthur Conan *Doyle merged the qualities of Dupin and Lecoq, supplementing them with traits that became integral to the type. Insensible to normal human emotions, and conscious of his own superiority, indeed conceited, Holmes is impatient with police obtuseness, but aids Inspector Lestrade and others, allowing them to take the credit for success. Yet Holmes is above the law and at times takes justice into his own hands, as in "The Adventure of Charles Augustus Milverton" (*Strand*, Apr. 1904). Holmes also has a store of recondite knowledge that can be brought to bear on the interpretation of evidence; he has written, for example, "a little monograph on the ashes of 140 different varieties of pipe, cigar, and cigarette tobacco," as noted in "The Boscombe Valley Mystery" (*Strand*, Apr. 1891). And in Dr. John H. *Watson Doyle rounded out the figure of Poe's anonymous narrator, creating the archetype of the detective's friend and assistant. Ronald A. *Knox, in the ninth of his ten commandments for the detective novelist (*The Best Detective Stories of the Year 1928*, 1928), codified the type, writing: "the stupid friend of the detective, the Watson, must not conceal any thoughts which pass through his mind; his intelligence must be slightly, but very slightly, below that of the average reader." At the same time, in Mycroft *Holmes, even superior in reasoning power to his brother, Doyle devised another superman, who was in addition the prototype of the *armchair detective. R. Austin *Freeman's Dr. John *Thorndyke in *The Red Thumb Mark* (1907) was obviously conceived as an antipode to Holmes; while possessing some of the charac-

teristics of the superman—intellectual power, depth of knowledge, and a Watson-like narrator—he lacks the type's defining characteristics of inhumanity and eccentricity. However, Jacques *Futrelle's Professor Augustus S. F. X *Van Dusen, a scientist known as the Thinking Machine who first appeared in *The Thinking Machine* (1907), is undoubtedly a superman. So is John *Rhode's mathematician Dr. Lancelot *Priestley, introduced in *The Paddington Mystery* (1925). A. E. W. *Mason varied the formula by making his superman a French policeman, Inspector *Hanaud, whose Watson is Julius Ricardo in *At the Villa Rose* (1910), and was imitated by Agatha *Christie with the Belgian Hercule *Poirot and Captain Arthur Hastings in *The Mysterious Affair at Styles* (1920) and later novels. S. S. Van *Dine returned to Doyle's formula, though replacing conceit with intellectual arrogance, in his Philo *Vance novels beginning with *The Benson Murder Case* (1926). *Stout, taking Mycroft, rather than Sherlock, as his model, but preserving all other characteristics of the type, in *Fer-de-Lance* (1934; *Meet Nero Wolfe*) introduced Nero *Wolfe and Archie *Goodwin, undoubtedly the most successful attempt to replicate the Holmes Watson relationship. Of female detectives, only Gladys *Mitchell's Mrs. Beatrice Adela Lestrange *Bradley, introduced in *Speedy Death* (1929), has claims to belong to the type: She is eccentric and intellectually far above those around her, although she is not accompanied by a Watson figure. The same is true of John Dickson *Carr's Dr. Gideon *Fell, created in *Hag's Nook* (1933), who perhaps just scrapes into this category, rather than that of *Great Detective. The categories are not congruent: that of superman or superwoman is a subset of that of the Great Detective, and the characteristic that distinguishes him or her is inhumanity. E. C. *Bentley, in *Those Days: An Autobiography* (1940), wrote that he wanted to make his detective, Philip Trent who first appears in *Trent's Last Case* (1913; *The Woman in Black*), "recognisable as a human being." Once this aim was generally accepted, the type was doomed: allowed to experience emotion and even to fall in love, the detective could no longer be pure animated reason, a "thinking machine."

[*See also* Scientific Sleuth.]

—T. J. Binyon

SURROGATE DETECTIVE. The term "surrogate detective" is applied to characters who solve crimes yet who are neither amateur nor professional detectives. Like the *accidental sleuth, the surrogate *sleuth may simply have stumbled upon the crime scene, but whereas the accidental sleuth acts out of pluckiness or sometimes self-defense in order to prove who committed the crime, the surrogate sleuth feels compelled to act by applying expertise that he or she brings to the situation. Areas of expertise that surrogate sleuths find useful to crime solving include the scientific, as is the case with R. Austin *Freeman's Dr. John *Thorndyke; the psychological as exemplified in the work of Jonathan *Kellerman's character Alex Delaware; and a professional eye for domestic detail as displayed by Barbara *Neely's domestic worker, Blanche White. The surrogate sleuth's profession often provides entrée to the scene of the crime at the start of the narrative and helps to keep doors open for the sleuth throughout the story. The prime example of the surrogate sleuth is the *journalist sleuth, who is able to gain access to a murder scene and to remain in contact with suspects whom the character interviews with practiced professionalism.

—Rosemary Herbert

SYMONS, JULIAN (GUSTAVE) (1912–1994), established a high reputation in the crime and mystery field resting on his work as a crime novelist and literary historian of the genre and biographer of Edgar Allan *Poe and Arthur Conan *Doyle. Symons also penned poetry, literary criticism, military history, and biographies of other figures. Symons was born in London, the youngest child in a talented, tightly knit, and strangely isolated family. He received no encouragement from a severe Victorian father whose fortunes rose and fell like those of Charles *Dickens's Mr. Micawber. After demonstrating an early ability to recite poetry, Symons developed a stammer so severe that he was sent to a school for backward children. His mother and siblings were supportive, and he soon formed friendships with everyone from neighborhood cricket and snooker players to intellectuals, writers, and poets. As a youth, Symons plunged into self-education with a passion. By his own estimation, he succeeded as a "minor poet," and edited the small but influential journal, *Twentieth-Century Verse*, an enterprise that he supported by means of a tedious job as secretary at the slightly seedy company, Victoria Lighting and Dynamo.

Symons married Kathleen Clark, served in World War II, and worked as an advertising copywriter at the London firm of Humble, Crowther, and Nicholas until 1947, when he became a full-time writer. From the start, he turned his talents in multiple directions. One of his earliest book manuscripts, *The Immaterial Murder Case*, was penned in 1939. Symons's wife discovered this parody of the classic detective novel in the back of a drawer and urged him to publish it, which he finally did in 1945. This novel introduced Inspector Bland and the *amateur detective Teake Wood. Bland appeared again, but Symons soon launched into work that illustrated his belief, expressed in his tract *The Detective Story in Britain* (1962), that post–World War II writers could no longer take the view that human affairs were ruled by reason and that "virtue, generally identified with the order of society, must prevail in the end." Symons felt that modern crime writers were more concerned with character and motive than with puzzle elements, and more inclined to be preoccupied with the question of whydunit than whodunit. In his own work, he did incorporate puzzles and surprises, but was more absorbed with finding psychological explanations for the violence behind

respectable faces than with step-by-step detection leading to identification of perpetrators of crimes.

In 1972 Symons published his study of the crime and mystery writing genre, titled *Bloody Murder: From the Detective Story to the Crime Novel: A History* in the English edition and *Mortal Consequences* in the first American printing. Two later revisions were given the original title in all editions. This seminal work stands as an important literary history of the genre and a persuasive argument for Symons's notion that the psychologically centered crime novel represents a step forward from the classic detective story. Along with outlining developments in the crime and mystery genre, this book did much to win support within academic circles for crime fiction as a literary genre worthy of study. Symons's work as a literary critic for the *London Sunday Times* was as important as Anthony *Boucher's reviewing for the *New York Times Book Review* in winning critical regard for this popular fiction.

—Rosemary Herbert

SYNDICATE AUTHORS. Nineteenth-century publishers of popular fiction quickly adopted the practices of commodity manufacture. Like their counterparts who produced soap or clothing or foodstuffs for a mass market, makers of magazines and books realized that high-volume distribution of uniformly patterned items under a distinctive trade name could lead to commercial success. The repeated use of an author's name for an extended series of tales was a common way to achieve the uniformity that would assure readers of a predictable quality. Prolific authors such as William Adams, who wrote more than twenty serials for *Golden Argosy* and *Golden Days* under the name Oliver Optic from 1853 to 1897, or Horatio Alger, whose approximately 100 didactic tales of luck and pluck starting with *Ragged Dick* (1867) achieved reported sales of over twenty million were especially valuable resources of both labor and raw material to be marketed in this way. When a single writer could not maintain that high level of output, though, publishers had recourse to the use of house names; thus Street & Smith used Nicholas Carter as the author's name on the three serials written by John Russell Coryell, the more than four hundred written by Frederic Van Rennselaer Dey, the twenty-two written by Edward Stratemeyer, and all of the adventures about Carter written by thirty-five or forty staff writers.

While Dey claimed, incorrectly, to have written more than 1,000 Nick Carter stories, it was actually Stratemeyer whose prolific output accelerated production of commodity fiction in the crime and mystery genre. Deirdre Johnson maintains that Stratemeyer employed eighty-three pen names, but more significantly he employed many other writers in a new means of organizing production that he termed a "literary syndicate." Stratemeyer learned the publishing business with Street & Smith, the firm that published his work in a boys' weekly known as *Good News*, Merriam who issued his Richard

Dare stories, and Frank J. Earll's *Young People of America*. His innovation began with his hiring writers to fill in the outlines of plots he devised. He then contracted directly with a publisher to provide the finished products that could be marketed under a common name. These books centered on sleuths such as the Rover Boys, Tom Swift, or Nancy Drew. Effectively Stratemeyer the entrepreneur carried forward the process of dividing the levels of book production. He took on the business of creating intellectual property, leaving to Grosset & Dunlap, his favored publisher, the physical production and distribution of books.

For many years very little about the Stratemeyer Syndicate authors was known to the public. In order to protect the image of Carolyn Keene (the name on the Nancy Drew stories) and others, the identities of the actual writers were concealed and they were not permitted to claim authorship or a share in royalties. Howard Garis, one of the first writers hired by Stratemeyer's Syndicate after its founding in 1904, was paid $75 for the first Tom Swift book.

Syndicate authors, in general, were competent writers, not hacks. Because the income from Syndicate writing was steady, Stratemeyer had little trouble attracting writers to do the piece work of fleshing out plots and casts of characters. There was evidently opportunity for the hired writers to place their stamp on the work. Mildred Wirt Benson's initial interpretation of Nancy Drew's character had much to do with that series' success. Similarly, Leslie McFarlane, who wrote the first eleven Hardy Boys stories, set the tone for those books. Other important employees of the syndicate were Lillian Garis, St. George Rathbone, W. Bert Foster, and James Duncan Lawrence (author of most of the Tom Swift, Jr. books). Several of these authors also wrote and published books under their own names, and these publications have no connection to the syndicate.

Even though the Stratemeyer productions are among the most famous, and most researched, serial publications, they represent a modest percentage of the total product issued by publishers of adventure and mystery stories for young readers. According to Johnson's findings, there were 115 series in circulation by 1909, and between 1910 and 1930 more than 480 series were being published.

In addition to what syndicate writing shows about the development of the mass market for books, the products also illustrate literary changes. Many of the older stories released under house names stressed more or less traditional virtues while changing protagonists from tale to tale. The Horatio Alger stories illustrate this. Syndicate productions, however, stressed the appearance of recurring heroes and, in a very significant development, introduced new milieus such as aviation and the motion pictures that endorsed modern technological progress. Moreover, the syndicated protagonists, detective and other, became increasingly detached from a fixed home community so that their adventures came to provide readers in an increasingly mobile society the added interest of changing settings.

The relationship of these literary developments in the syndicated work for young readers to mainstream detective fiction for adult readers may be seen in the modern offerings of two syndicate-style series. Davis Dresser began his Michael Shayne stories in 1939 under the name Brett Halliday, but all of the novels written after 1958 about Shayne were written by authors employed by Dresser, as were all the short novels signed Brett Halliday that appeared in *Mike Shayne Mystery Magazine* (1956–90). The cousins Frederic Dannay and Manfred B. Lee began their memorable writing as Ellery *Queen in 1929, but between 1961 and 1972 a series of twenty-eight paperback originals signed by Ellery Queen were reportedly written by other writers under contract to Dannay and Lee.

—John T. Dizer

T

TAIBO III, PACO IGNACIO (b. 1949), Spanish-born crime writer, social critic, translator, and a founder of the Asociacion Internacionale de Escritores Policianos (IAEP, or International Association of Crime Writers). In Mexico, where he has resided since 1958, he is in demand as a social and literary commentator on media talk shows. Internationally, he is best-known as a crime writer whose works succeed as heated critiques of corruption in Mexico City and environs. His international reputation extends beyond the Spanish-speaking world to include significant readership in France and the United States. Taibo's series characters are the *private eye Hector Belascoaran Shayne and Jose Daniel Fierro. The latter is a crime writer who gets involved in investigating criminal cases. Taibo uses a good deal of violence in his earnest portrayals of political corruption and social ills, but this is leavened by the author's keen awareness of the absurd, and by his irrepressible sense of humor. His 1993 novel, *Leonardo's Bicycle*, won him critical acclaim and a broader audience.

—Rosemary Herbert

TAPPLY, WILLIAM G(EORGE) (b. 1940), American writer of the Brady Coyne series of myssteries, set in Boston, Massachusetts. Born in Waltham, Massachusetts, Tapply grew up fly-fishing with his father, a *Field & Stream* magazine editor, and eventually followed in his father's footsteps, serving as a contributing editor for the same sportsman's magazine. He was educated at Amherst College, Harvard University, and Tufts University, all in Massachusetts. Before becoming a full-time writer, he worked as a teacher and then as house master at Lexington High School in Lexington, Massachusetts. Three times married, he is the father of three.

Tapply's series character, Coyne, first appears in *Death at Charity's Point* (1984), a book that establishes the author's ability to blend memorable descriptions of the outdoors with a well-plotted puzzle. Coyne is a *lawyer so successful that he may pick and choose his clients with an eye to whether or not they interest him—and are prepared to pay his high fees. Coyne finds himself working for his clients by finding *missing persons, dealing with a blackmailer, and pursuing other matters that require direct action, rather than courtroom machinations or paper-pushing. Many of his clients are elderly, and some are *eccentrics. All count on Coyne to keep their private affairs under cover. Coyne, too, is reticent about his personal affairs. Some of Tapply's best writing is found in his portrayal of the poignant awkwardness Coyne experiences during interactions with his ex-wife.

Tapply also collaborated on two mysteries, writing *Thicker Than Water* (1995) with Linda Carlow, and *First Light* (2001) with Phil Craig. Tapply's books on outdoor pursuits include *Those Hours Spent Outdoors* (1988) and *A fly-fishing Life* (1997). He also wrote a non-fiction guide, *The Elements of Detective Fiction* (1995).

—Rosemary Herbert

TAYLOR, PHOEBE ATWOOD (1909–1976), who also wrote as Alice Tilton, Freeman Dana, American author of detective novels. In *The Cape Cod Mystery* (1931), Taylor introduced Yankee detective Asey *Mayo, the prototype for the shrewd, homespun detective who uses his wits and knowledge of the locale and inhabitants to solve crimes. Writing as Alice Tilton, Taylor also created Leonidas Witherall, a professor in a private boys' school who loses his job during the Depression. Witherall, who cultivates a beard to exploit his resemblance to William *Shakespeare, first appears in "The Murder in Volume Four" (1933) in *Mystery League* magazine, edited by Ellery *Queen. *Murder at the New York World's Fair* (1938) by Freeman Dana, based on an earlier Tilton novel, was commissioned by Bennett Cerf to predate that 1939 event.

All Taylor's books explore the details of contemporary life on Cape Cod or around Boston, such as unmodernized boardinghouses, local legends, and natives profiting from tourists. Her emphasis is on humor and character rather than plot, and her sense of atmosphere and locale is superb. Especially well delineated is the effect of World War II on the civilian population on a sea coast with rationing, threat of sabotage, and possible invasion of German spies.

[*See also* Academic Sleuth.]

—Ellen A. Nehr

Templar, Simon. *See* Saint, The.

TEY, JOSEPHINE, is the better-known pseudonym of Scottish author and playwright Elizabeth Mackintosh (1896–1952). She kept her personal life private, refusing interviews and preferring to be listed as Gordon Daviot (another pseudonym) in *Who's Who* and even in her death notice, which appeared on page one of the *Times* (London), and characteristically specified "no flowers." Born at Inverness, Scotland, she completed her education at Anstey Physical Training College near Birmingham in 1918 and taught in Liverpool, Oban, Eastbourne, and Tunbridge Wells schools until 1926, when she resigned to keep house for her widowed father. A product of the Golden Age of detective fiction, she soon developed a popularity that overshadowed her fame as a playwright, psychological novelist, and biographer.

Tey's prestige as a mystery writer rests on eight novels she dismissed as "her 'yearly knitting,' " according to John Gielgud's foreword to *Plays, by Gordon Daviot* (1953–54). Of these, the best-known and most critically debated is *The Daughter of Time* (1951), in which Inspector Alan Grant investigates, from his hospital bed, the fifteenth-century murders of Richard III's two nephews in the Tower of London, for which the king was vilified by William *Shakespeare and others. While contemporary critic Anthony Boucher praised it as "recreating the intense excitement of scholarly research" (in the *New York Times Book Review*, 24 Feb. 1952), some 1970s historians saw Tey's acquittal of Richard III as a "sophomoric" slap at their profession, according to Guy M. Townsend in the *Armchair Detective* 10 (summer 1977).

Tey began her characteristic defense of the wrongly accused with *The Man in the Queue* (1929; republished posthumously under the Tey pseudonym as *Killer in the Crowd*, 1954), published under the Gordon Daviot name, which she later reserved for what she regarded as more serious works. This classically plotted mystery introduces Inspector Grant and establishes his reputation for "flair," a combination of intelligence, intuition, integrity, and Scottish tenacity. Letting misconceptions cloud his judgment, Grant nearly drowns his innocent suspect before intuition leads him to the murderer, who goes unpunished. Tey repeated this successful formula in *A Shilling for Candles* (1936), revealing her scorn of greedy poseurs and the mass media. In *Miss Pym Disposes* (1946) she examined the consequences of favoritism in a school like Anstey, proving popular psychology no guarantee against fallibility. *The Franchise Affair* (1948), her fourth crime novel, was a murderless locked room mystery based on the Elizabeth Canning case of 1754 and set in a walled English country house inhabited by two uncongenial females whom a mendacious teenager denounces as kidnappers. It was quickly followed by *Brat Farrar* (1949; *Come and Kill Me*), a novel featuring a sympathetic impostor. Here Tey ponders the identification between a charming drifter who strikingly resembles Patrick Ashby, whose murder by his selfish twin Brat uncovers while posing as Patrick. Her sixth, *To Love and Be Wise* (1950), a murderless mystery, asks Grant to solve the disappearance of a charismatic photographer. Tey's eighth and last crime novel, *The Singing Sands* (1952), a work with nuances of Brat Farrar, leads Grant from a cryptic poem to the riddle of Shangri-La. All these novels remain in print, suggesting a loyal following.

The author's fame as Gordon Daviot rests on six plays—*Richard of Bordeaux* (1932), *The Laughing Woman* (1934), *Queen of Scots* (1934), *The Stars Bow Down* (1939), *Leith Sands* (1946), *The Little Dry Thorn* (1947); three novels—*Kif, An Unvarnished History* (1929), *The Expensive Halo* (1931), *The Privateer* (1952); and a biography—*Claverhouse* (1937).

—Jean A. Coakley

Thatcher, John Putnam, the *amateur detective created by Mary Jane Latsis and Martha Henissart, who wrote together under the pseudonym Emma *Lathen, is vice president of the Sloan Guaranty Trust Bank of New York City. He is a silver-haired widower in his sixties. As a detective Thatcher uses his acute powers of observation, but also calls upon long experience in banking, which has left him knowledgeable about the U.S. financial system and properly cynical about human nature. Because of his financial expertise, he is a prime example of the *surrogate detective.

In his first case, *Banking on Death* (1961), Thatcher searches for a missing heir. Thatcher often travels to a Sloan-financed company to investigate its financial soundness and stays to solve a murder that threatens the bank's investment. In *Murder Makes the Wheels Go Round* (1966), Michigan Motors unveils a new luxury car as part of a comeback attempt. When the car door is opened, a body tumbles out. Even on vacation, Thatcher comes upon murder; in *Pick Up Sticks* (1970), he finds a body while hiking. Thatcher's cases reflect the detailed financial knowledge of his creators, an economist and a lawyer.

—Marvin Lachman

"Thinking Machine, The." *See* Van Dusen, Professor Augustus S. F. X.

THOMPSON, JIM (James Myers) (1906–1977). Born in Oklahoma, the recipient of a B.A. from the University of Nebraska, Thompson held jobs as both a blue-collar oil well worker—providing realistic cultural detail for his fiction—and a more-or-less white-collar position in the Federal Writers Project in Oklahoma during the 1930s. After this apprenticeship he became a prolific author of paperback original novels, beginning with *Now and on Earth* (1942).

Thompson shows the darkest side of fiction noir by using unreliable narrators and protagonists whose mental state constantly verges toward and often enters psychosis. *The Killer Inside Me* (1952) is deservedly his most famous dark descent. Deputy Lou Ford, the psychopathic narrator, pretends to be a simpleminded hick but is actually a cunning killer responsible for the murders he is supposedly investigating. Through masterful craft the narration deludes the reader, just as Ford's character fools the townspeople of Central City.

The presentation of madness as the norm is characteristic of Thompson's best works. These include *Pop. 1280* (1964), a humorous reversal of *The Killer Inside Me*; *The Grifters* (1963), which shows the training of a young *con artist by a "loving" mother; and *After Dark, My Sweet* (1955). The cumulative effect of the view of reality

Thompson proffers in these works is portrayal of a world of "sickness."

Nowhere is the overwhelming sickness more prevalent than in *Savage Night* (1953), the story of a diminutive hit man Charlie "Little" Bigger who falls in love with the woman sent to spy on him by the man who hired him. Isolated in a secluded house, the would-be lovers become increasingly mad. Bigger hides in the basement where Ruthie attacks and chops him up with an ax. The dismembered Bigger crawls about the basement and meets Death, who "smelled good."

Thompson's works have undergone varying treatments in the films that have added to his reputation. *The Getaway* (1959) has had its roughness smoothed twice for the screen, while *After Dark, My Sweet, The Grifters,* and *Pop. 1280* have been stylishly handled on film. Thompson himself worked briefly in films, receiving screen credit on Stanley Kubrick's *Paths of Glory.*

—James L. Traylor and Max Allan Collins

Thorndyke, Dr. John, the creation of R. Austin *Freeman, surveys crimes and criminals from his residence at 5A King's Bench Walk in London's Inner Temple, with a detached, analytical eye. A man of many talents—lawyer, forensic scientist, authority in subjects as diverse as Egyptology, archaeology, ophthalmology, criminal jurisprudence, and botany—Thorndyke is commonly acknowledged as the first and greatest medicolegal deective of all time. His intrepid assistants are aide and chronicler Christopher Jervis and butler and jack-of-all-trades Nathaniel Polton.

Of Thorndyke's past and personal life Freeman offers us relatively little, save that he was born on 4 July 1870, educated at the medical school of St. Margaret's Hospital, London, where he later became professor of medical jurisprudence, and remained a bachelor all his life. Freeman noted that the character's professional pursuits had a real-life inspiration, Dr. Alfred Swaine Taylor, considered to be the father of medical jurisprudence. His first case was *The Mystery of 31, New Inn,* depicted in a novel written around 1905 but not published until 1912. His first appearance in print was *The Red Thumb Mark* (1907), a mystery novel whose solution revolved around the possibilities of fingerprint fabrication, a plot device that Freeman used subsequently in "The Old Lag" (*The Singing Bone,* 1912) and the novel *The Cat's Eye* (1923). English stories appeared in rapid succession in *Pearson's* magazine in 1908–9 and were collected in book form in *John Thorndyke's Cases* in 1909.

It was about this time that Thorndyke's "The Case of Oscar Brodski" (*Pearson's,* 1910) introduced an entirely new form of detective story, in which the reader is aware from the start of the secret of the crime. "Here, the usual conditions are reversed," explained author Freeman; "the reader knows everything, and the detective knows nothing, and the interest focuses on the unexpected significance of trivial circumstances." In Freeman's inverted detective story, the first part is typically narrated in the third person and the second is related by Jervis. Additional inverted tales appeared in the seminal collection *The Singing Bone* (1912). The novels *The Shadow of the Wolf* (1925) and *Mr. Pottermack's Oversight* (1930) are also in this form.

Throughout the 1920s Thorndyke stories appeared in, successively, *Dr. Thorndyke's Case Book* (1923; *The Blue Scarab*), *The Puzzle Lock* (1925), and *The Magic Casket* (1927). In 1929 an omnibus volume of thirty-seven stories was published in England, *The Famous Cases of Dr. Thorndyke.* The American edition, entitled *The Dr. Thorndyke Omnibus* (1932), contained one more story. For the remainder of his life Freeman produced no more Thorndyke short stories but featured him in several more novels, including *Mr. Pottermack's Oversight* (1930), *Dr. Thorndyke Intervenes* (1933), *The Penrose Mystery* (1936), *The Stoneware Monkey* (1938), and *The Jacob Street Mystery* (1942; *The Unconscious Witness*), his last case. In all, the good doctor appeared in twenty-one novels and forty short stories.

[*See also* Forensic Pathologist, Medical Sleuth; Scientific Sleuth.]

—John C. Tibbetts

THREATENING CHARACTERS. *See* Menacing Characters.

Tibbs, Virgil. Author John Dudley *Ball created African American detective Virgil Tibbs in 1965's *In the Heat of the Night,* the first of a Tibbs series. The violent-crimes specialist at the Pasadena, California, police department, Tibbs is about thirty years old throughout the series. He is a slender and extremely well dressed, well read, and physically fit, an expert in karate and other martial arts.

The Tibbs novels are whodunits rather than typical police procedurals, since they emphasize the thinking rather than the procedure of the hero. His deductions are based on observation of minute detail and small slips of speech. His approach is therefore Sherlockian, and the *Great Detective is often referred to in the series.

His race can create antagonism in suspects and *witnesses, particularly in his debut book. While he can turn this to his advantage in interrogation, he mostly confronts racism with a prodigious patience. It is his politeness and correctness that win the trust of witnesses.

In 1967, *In the Heat of the Night* was adapted into an Academy Award-winning film starring Sidney Poitier as a Tibbs with an angrier edge. The real film is mentioned in succeeding novels, and the fictional Tibbs is embarrassed by it. In *The Eyes of Buddha* (1976), Tibbs is told that he does not look like Sidney Poitier, the film *In the Heat of the Night* is mentioned as a missing woman's favorite, and, when undercover, Tibbs's identity is compromised because people have seen the film. His formidable patience almost withers at these times.

[*See also* African American Sleuth.]

—Dana Bisbee

TREAT, LAWRENCE, pseudonym of Lawrence Arthur Goldstone (1903–1998). The writer who was to become best known as the author of police procedurals and puzzle books under the pseudonym Lawrence Treat was born in New York City and educated at Dartmouth College and Columbia University. He began his writing career with the novel *Run Far, Run Fast* (1937), penned under the Goldstone name, before using the Treat pseudonym to launch his first four-book series featuring the intuitive criminologist Carl Wayward in 1940. He followed these with a series of police procedurals featuring Lieutenant Bill Decker, Detective Jub Freeman, and Detective (later Lieutenant still later Police Officer) Mitch Taylor. The capable Decker administers the NYPD's Homicide Department, Freeman is a technical wizard, and Taylor is a fallible character whose developing greed and involvement in graft lead to his being demoted and removed from the NYPD in *The Big Shot* (1951). Long before Sue *Grafton used the device to advantage, Treat was known for titling his works after alphabet letters. Many of these were short stories. His "H as in Homicide" (*Ellery Queen's Mystery Magazine*, 1964), for example, won an Edgar Award for best short story of the year. Treat's puzzle books for adults and children include *Crime and Puzzlement: Twenty-Four Solve-Them-Yourself Mysteries* (1981–88) and *You're the Detective!* (1983).
—Richard Bleiler

TRUSTED FIGURES AS CRIMINALS. Most long-established societies have within them figures in whom trust and authority is vested by virtue of the positions these persons hold.

Many of the situations around which crime fiction is centered, particularly in works set in the Golden Age of detective fiction, feature characters who would appear to be utterly reliable. They are often holders of minor public office, the clerically ordained, and members of the judiciary, the police force, and the professions. These are callings once greatly esteemed by the general public. Nearly always male and middle-aged, these incumbents are usually seen to have much to gain by their criminal activities or, conversely, a great deal to lose by being exposed.

Within the framework of both real life and much detective fiction is the unwritten social convention, implicit in the nature of their occupations, that such people are thoroughly trustworthy in every respect. The improbability of having one of these trusted figures as the murderer offers the added advantage to the writer of disarming the early suspicions of the reader. A memorable and utterly unexpected fall from grace by a member of the staff of the British Inland Revenue Service, an occupation notably free from perfidy, takes the reader by surprise in Michael *Gilbert's short story "Mr Portway's Practice" (*EQMM*, May 1958).

It also follows that the more important or improbable the fictional villain, the more profound will be the shock at the unveiling of his or her lapse from the ac-

cepted mores of the society in which the book is set. The murderer in *Whose Body* (1923) by Dorothy L. *Sayers, a man greatly elevated both professionally and socially, is a good example of this, while the perpetrator of the crime in *The Murder of Roger Ackroyd* (1926) by Agatha *Christie is similarly a surprise but in two quite different and separate respects. The identity of the murderer in the medical milieu of *The Attending Physician* (1980) by R. B. Dominic is carefully concealed by the double entrendre of the title.

Few vocations have proved immune in fiction from having murderers within their ranks. Certainly not the Church, which numbers several surprising clerical criminals among the shepherds of its various flocks in *The Vicar's Experiments* by Anthony Rolls (1932; *Clerical Errors*) and Julian Callender's *A Corpse Too Many* (1965).

That of *judge is an even more unexpected role in which to find the culprit but Christie uses this in *Ten Little Niggers* (1939; *Ten Little Indians*; *And Then There Were None*).

Also taking an oath of allegiance and ordinarily not expected to depart from the straight and narrow are policemen. Guilty ones may be found at the high levels of chief constable in *The Noose* (1930), by Philip *MacDonald, and chief of police in G. K. *Chesterton's "The Secret Garden" in *The Innocence of Father Brown* (1911), and in a lowly constable in *A Blunt Instrument* (1938) by Georgette *Heyer. A corrupt policeman appears in *Death of a Favorite Girl* (1980; *The Killing of Katie Steelstock*) by Gilbert.

An unusual and graver extension of this breach of the accepted norm is where there is a failure in fealty and the criminal is found to be tied by bonds of friendship to the *victim. Here, too, natural suspicions are at first disarmed by the sheer unlikelihood of the breaking of this ancient and primitive taboo by the murderer, as in *Slay-Ride* (1970) by Dick *Francis. Emma *Lathen combines something of this with an unlikely candidate for crime who is both in a position of trust and not quite friendship in *Going for GOLD* (1981; *Going for the Gold*).

The use of the trusted figure as criminal in crime fiction not only changed parameters and added to the uncertainties within the genre but also implied a more subtle approach by the writer, manifested in the progressive moving away from the stereotyped allocation of villainy to a stock character with all the assigned traits associated with culpability.

The seeming probity of the professions has also been used in a different and doubly disconcerting way. These are the cases where the device has been extended still further by the use of the respectability of the suspect's occupation to allay suspicion, only for the reader to find later rather than sooner that the murderer is an impostor. Trusted by virtue of their assumed positions and a medical and religious aura have been criminals in *Dr Goodwood's Locum* (1951; *The Affair of the Substitute Doctor*) by John *Rhode and *Hag's Nook* (1933) by John Dickson *Carr.

More recently this "professional indemnity" has become a less useful artifice. The possession of clay feet by some members of most professions has been drawn to the attention of readers in real life, and a more radical view has gathered strength in an altogether less trustful climate.

[See also Villains and Villainy.]

—Catherine Aird

TUROW, SCOTT (b. 1949), American attorney and author known for thrillers set in the world of *lawyers. Born in Chicago, Illinois, Turow was educated at Amherst College in Amherst, Massachusetts, at the Stanford University Creative Writing Center, in Stanford, California, and at the Harvard Law School in Cambridge, Massachusetts. After graduating from the latter in 1978, he serves as Assistant United States Attorney in Chicago until 1986. A partner in the Chicago law firm, Sonnenschein Nath and Rosenthal, he still practices law, sometimes on a pro bono basis. Married since 1971 to the painter Annette Turow, he is the father of three children.

Turow's first book, *One L: An Inside Account of Life in the first Year at Harvard Law School* (1977; *What They Really Teach You at Harvard Law School*), is based on his own experience. Ten years passed before he published his first novel, *Presumed Innocent* (1987), a novel narrated by Rusty Sabich, a chief deputy prosecuting attorney who falls under suspicion when his old flame is murdered. While treating readers to an insider's look at the day-to-day pressures of a life in the law, the author establishes himself as a master manipulator of the truth. The plot teases and tantalizes by presenting incidents that seem to lead toward answers at the same time that they raise new questions. Ultimately, the reader begins to ruminate on the very nature and value of veracity, and about what it means to be innocent.

Turow followed his first book with *Burden of Proof* (1990), *Pleading Guilty* (1993), *The Laws of Our Fathers* (1996), *Personal Injuries* (1999), and *Reversible Errors* (2002). In each case, a firm grounding in legal matters adds substance to a plot enlivened by surprising developments faced by a character in jeopardy. The books rise above the formulaic work of a writer such as John *Grisham by delivering far more thought-provoking conclusions.

[See also Judge; Jury.]

—Rosemary Herbert

U

UNDERWORLD FIGURE. The underworld figure has long provided writers a means of characterizing the environment of crime. The anonymous author of *Richmond; or, Scenes from the Life of a Bow Street Runner* (1827) introduces a sequence of criminal types into the narrative of the picaresque hero's adventures in order to illustrate his aptitude for containing the forces of an evil underworld. The vignettes of gang members, burglars, bunco men, and other criminal types in Benjamin P. Eldridge and William B. Watts's *Our Rival—The Rascal, a Faithful Portrayal of the Conflict Between the Criminals of the Age and the Defenders of Society—the Police* (1897) serve to establish a theme of eternal conflict between forces of evil and agents of domestic protection. As tales of crime control migrated from memoirs into the fictional forms of short story and novel, however, underworld figures lost their prominence because the treatment of detection shifted dramatic focus to the methodology for solving crimes and the character of the *sleuth. Since the point of detection stories, notably in the Golden Age versions, was to introduce the puzzles of crime into the orderly precincts of established society, the image of a vast underworld network was no longer desirable. Underworld figures were eclipsed by criminals of apparently higher repute.

The sea change in crime and mystery writing represented by the appearance of hard-boiled writing provided the opportunity for authors to reinsert underworld figures into their criminal dramas. The radical hard-boiled view of a world fundamentally corrupted by capitalism and its attendant materialistic values naturalized the underworld character as a representative of that world. American pulp magazine stories such as those featured in *Black Mask* and *Dime Detective* during the 1920s and 1930s often came populated with underworld figures demanding tough responses from the detectives. The underworld figures in these works helped to register their claim to realism. Prohibition had alerted the public to the existence of organized criminal syndicates engaged in hijacking, smuggling, extortion, and bloody turf wars; consequently, the appearance of underworld figures in fiction staked its claim to recording the way crime actually took place.

The greater their power, the grander the aura of glamour surrounding the underworld figure becomes. Not surprisingly, then, the gangster became a hero as well as a villain for fiction. W. R. Burnett's *Little Caesar* (1929) made the underworld figure representative of his time. Burnett's invention of the gangster protagonist, extended by countless repetition of the type in films, eventually turned into grounds for a controlling myth in crime and mystery writing, the myth of the omnipotent Mafia. Mario Puzo's treatment in *The Godfather* (1969) of a family of underworld figures who conduct their business in the manner of a corporation took the myth to its acme. Once again the cinema joined in spreading the image until it became a general impression in popular consciousness.

As the underworld organizations once known simply as "the Mob" became particularized in the Mafia, or one of its related names such as Cosa Nostra, and as its agents—soldiers, counselors, and hit men—became familiar to the public, writers found in them a convenient shorthand for introducing into narrative resonances of social disorder and peril. The appearance of an underworld figure requires little elaboration any longer. His entry into a story becomes sufficient to remind an audience that the specific crime they are reading about has larger implications. In addition, the reputation of organized crime lends immediate credibility to the use of an underworld figure as the expediter of crime. There is no need to plumb for his motive. He just makes crime happen.

Recent fiction most commonly places its underworld figures in drug traffic. Robert B. *Parker's *Double Deuce* (1992) effectively exploits the prevailing image of underworld figures in presenting an entire housing project governed by drug lords. Like other contemporary authors of the urban detective story, such as Carl *Hiaasen, James Lee *Burke, and Richard Hoyt, Parker also uses his underworld characters to explore a relationship to "respectable" society and show generalized complicity in crime.

The works of George V. *Higgins illustrate another use for underworld figures in fiction. In Higgins's novels underworld figures are not heroic. More often than not they are only small-time bunco artists and low-level hirelings. Nor are they used by Higgins as symptoms of social illness. Rather he employs them for the color they give to his mannered comedies by their speech and personality quirks. In that regard the underworld figures for Higgins are subjects for latter-day local color writing.

The existence of an underworld of diverse criminal types may have been news for some nineteenth-century readers of detective memoirs, and the audience for Golden Age and cozy detective fiction may rarely meet characters from the underworld, but audiences of the remaining types of crime and mystery writing recognize underworld figures as part of the genre's stock company, so capable of variation and so valuable to plot that they are indispensable.

[*See also* Antihero; Master Criminal.]

—John M. Reilly

UPFIELD, ARTHUR W(ILLIAM) (1888–1964), Australian author of detective novels. Born in Gosport, Hampshire, England, Upfield was the eldest of five sons of a prosperous draper. Apprenticed at sixteen to a firm of estate agents, he failed the qualifying examination and his father shipped him off to Australia.

Upfield was fascinated by the wildness of the country and by the colorful characters he met. During the next ten years, he worked as bullock-wagon driver, boundary rider, and drover; he prospected for opals; but most of all, he roamed Australia's vastness. When war came, he joined the Australian Imperial Force and survived campaigns in Flanders and Gallipoli. His marriage to a nurse, Anne Douglas, produced a son, Arthur James. When the marriage failed he returned to Australia.

All of Upfield's books are set in Australia and draw heavily upon his experience. Although he wrote four serious novels from 1928 to 1932, none sold well. Instead, it was his crime novels that brought success. These feature the half-aboriginal detective Inspector Napoleon *Bonaparte, a character based upon Leon Wood, a tracker employed by the Queensland Police and introduced in *The Barrakee Mystery* (1929). While trying to think out a device for the disposal of the body for his second novel, *The Sands of Windee* (1931; *The Lure of the Bush*), Upfield discussed his problem with a group that included a drifter, "Snowy" Rowles, who promptly used the method in three slayings.

Upfield's mysteries appealed to a considerable public outside Australia and sold well, but they attracted harsh criticism. He was never admitted to the Australian literary establishment, upon which he took an oblique revenge in *An Author Bites the Dust* (1948).

His writings are made especially memorable by their evocations of Australia's natural environment—of bright skies and sunshine, dust storms and sand clouds, bush fires, drought and rabbit plagues, sudden rains and the reflooding of long-dry lakes. The characterization of Napoleon Bonaparte, perpetually torn between the different worlds of his paternal and maternal inheritance and with a perilous vanity that can endure no defeats, is central. The rich array of other characters, formidably diverse but almost always depicted with sympathy, is an important adjunct. Upfield was good at depicting tough females—huge Mary Answerth and her evil sister in *Venom House* (1952) and policewoman Alice McGorr in *Murder Must Wait* (1953) and *The Battling Prophet* (1956)—but much less successful with gentler women, who tend to be idealized and unmemorable. His sympathetic characterization of the aborigines and clear appreciation, both of their abilities and their problems in a white-dominated world, gives his novels a particular appeal at a time when attitudes to indigenous peoples are being so vigorously reassessed.

[*See also* Hillerman, Tony.]

—William A. S. Sarjeant

V

Vance, Philo, created by American author S. S. *Van Dine (pseudonym of Huntington Willard Wright) in 1926, is one of many *gentleman sleuths of mystery writing's Golden Age. He might also be the biggest snob among them. In *The Bedside Companion to Crime* (1989), H. R. F. *Keating writes that Manfred Bennington Lee, cocreator of Ellery *Queen, once called Vance "the biggest prig that ever came down the pike."

Beginning with *The Benson Murder Case* (1926), Vance appears in eleven novels over twelve years, concluding with the self-satirizing *The Gracie Allen Murder Case* (1938; *The Smell of Murder*). As first-person narrator and putative author, Van Dine is more Boswell than Watson. Vance's sidekick is District Attorney John F. X. Markham, who asks Vance to help solve the more perplexing cases that come up in the New York City of the Roaring Twenties.

Working in Prohibition-era New York, Vance, with his aristocratic airs, stands out against workaday cops. His laconic, bemused, and drowsy eyes; imperious demeanor; bored speech patterns; and upper-class pretensions (art collecting, for example) all contribute to his perceived priggishness.

In his second book, the locked room classic *The Canary Murder Case* (1927), Van Dine came to his sleuth's defense: "His manner was cynical and aloof; and those who met him only casually, set him down as a snob.... I knew that his cynicism and aloofness, far from being a pose, sprang instinctively from a nature that was at once sensitive and solitary."

Like Sherlock *Holmes and Hercule *Poirot, Vance has a cerebral technique. Mistrusting the complexity of clues that may lead nowhere or may even be deliberately placed red herrings, Vance observes the scene and characters and gets at the truth through a psychological study of the crime. Often, he sits in on police interrogations of *witnesses and, at the end, tosses off some question in an indolent drawl, usually clipping off syllables and even calling Markham "my dear," perhaps an attempt by Van Dine to give his character a British accent. The whole packaging, though, looks facetious to modern readers and recalls a phrase used by the late U.S. Vice President Spiro Agnew: "effete intellectual snob."

—Dana Bisbee

Van der Valk, Inspector Piet. the Amsterdam police officer who departs from the common convention governing detective and sidekicks by discovering his best professional support lies in his wife Arlette, was the creation of the British writer and cooking specialist Nicolas *Freeling. Piet Van der Valk first appeared in *Love in*

Amsterdam (1962; *Death in Amsterdam*), a novel that critics adjudge to be derived from the author's own experience with false arrest and imprisonment. The successful debut of the Dutch inspector in that tale led to a series of twelve police procedural novels and at least a dozen more short stories published in *Ellery Queen's Mystery Magazine* between 1969 and 1976.

Freeling has averred dislike for the tendency of series stories to become mechanical. Accordingly in *A Long Silence* (1972; *Aupres de Ma Blonde*) he dispatched Van der Valk, leaving Arlette to complete the criminal tale and to undertake yet other adventures on her own in *The Widow* (1979) and *One Damn Thing after Another* (1981; *Arlette*). Devotees of the inspector, who became a commissioner before his death, had one more opportunity to enjoy his work when Freeling "recovered" a story from Van der Valk's career for a reprise entitled *Sand Castles* (1989).

—John M. Reilly

VAN DE WETERING, JANWILLEM (b. 1931) is best known as the author of a police procedural series featuring Adjutant Henk Grijpstra and Sergeant Rinus De Gier of the homicide squad of the Amsterdam Municipal Police.

The Dutch author began his writing career with two autobiographical books. *Der Lege Spiegel* (1971; *The Empty Mirror: Experiences in a Japanese Monastery*) was an account of more than a year he spent as a disciple in a Zen Buddhist monastery in Kyoto, Japan. *A Glimpse of Nothingness: Experiences in an American Zen Community* (1975) detailed his further Zen study in the United States. Van de Wetering has also authored a series of short stories about Inspector Saito, a Japanese cop whose deductions are aided by an ancient Chinese crime manual. He has also written children's books.

The son of a prosperous financier, van de Wetering was born in Rotterdam. When he was a child, his homeland was occupied by the Nazis. He fled Holland at nineteen to live in South Africa, England, and Japan. Returning to Amsterdam, he worked for seven years as a reserve police officer to discharge his military obligation. He moved to South America, where he married. He then worked briefly in Australia before settling on the coast of Maine in the United States.

His police experience and his Zen training are seen in *Outsider in Amsterdam* (1975), the first in a series of police procedurals featuring the overweight Grijpstra, the handsome De Gier, and their wise Commissaris, the elderly commissioner of Amsterdam's "murder brigade."

Different from police procedurals by Ed *McBain or

Maj *Sjöwall and Per Wahlöö, van de Wetering's works show his *sleuths to be as likely to meditate over cups of coffee as to gumshoe around the dikes looking for clues. The Commissaris, very much like van de Wetering's Zen master, encourages politeness, gentleness, and thought over action.

—Dana Bisbee

VAN DINE, S. S., pseudonym of Willard Huntington Wright (1887–1939), American author who created the Philo *Vance series of detective novels. Wright was already well established as an important literary editor and art critic, when he began his first detective novel at the age of thirty-seven. A member of a circle that included H. L. Mencken, Theodore Dreiser, and Alfred Stieglitz, he had seen himself as helping make the world ready for modern art and the new realist fiction. His standards and aspirations were high, and his tolerance for popular success in the arts was limited. Indeed, as book critic for the *Los Angeles Times* in 1908, Wright had dismissed detective novels as a notoriously low order of literature appealing to small minds.

By 1924, however, Wright's time as a well-known member of the avant-garde was over. He was broke, ravaged by a drug addiction that had lasted for several years, and eager to remake himself in a form that would be both dramatic and lucrative. Aware that Americans in the postwar years were paying more attention than ever to British detective fiction, he devoted himself to an exhaustive study of the genre and approached Max Perkins, a renowned editor at Scribner's, with a plan for a series of detective novels that would feature an American *sleuth as memorable as Sherlock *Holmes, a Manhattan flavor, and a style of detection that was more concerned with creating a psychological portrait of the murderer than with any mere deciphering of physical clues.

The result was a publishing phenomenon in the United States. The Philo Vance novels of S. S. Van Dine sold more than a million copies by 1930, demonstrating that there existed a vast market for American detective fiction. In *The Benson Murder Case* (1926), *The Canary Murder Case* (1927), and *The Greene Murder Case* (1928), readers were introduced to a self-consciously sophisticated, cynical, and verbose *amateur detective, a Nietzschean intellectual with a private income and a healthy ego. His presence in the ten novels Scribner's published between 1926 and 1939 is the distinctive feature of all the Van Dine books; plot, dialogue, relationships, plausibility—everything is secondary to Vance's flamboyant persona and the charm of his New York in the last years of the Jazz Age.

The changes in detective fiction that came with the Great Depression had a predictable impact on Van Dine's career. He was unable to adapt to the new interest in hard-boiled detectives, grimy urban settings, and terse dialogue and descriptions. By the mid-1930s Philo Vance seemed more than ever a period figure, a holdover from the day of the speakeasy and the flapper. When Vance does engage in stakeouts and car chases, as in *The Kidnap Murder Case* (1936), the result is a stilted, formulaic novel obviously written with the new market in mind. Van Dine died in 1939, a bitter and angry man, well aware that his audience had abandoned him for the rowdier style of crime fiction he disdained.

[*See also* Gentleman Sleuth.]

—John Loughery

Van Dusen, Professor Augustus S.F.X., Ph.D., LL.D., F.R.S., M.D., MD.S., also known as "the Thinking Machine," detective-protagonist of one novel and forty-six known short stories by Jacques *Futrelle. A professor in an unnamed American university, he first appears as, a small man aged fifty, with a scholar's squint and a disproportionately large skull. He believes the human mind can master any problem. His cases have won him fame; it is newspaper reporters who have given him his nickname. One reporter, Hutchinson Hatch, gathers information for him in a manner later developed further by Rex *Stout in his Nero *Wolfe/Archie *Goodwin stories.

The Thinking Machine first appears in "The Problem of Cell 13," still the best-known story, serialized in the *Boston American* beginning 30 October 1905. On a bet, the Thinking Machine vows to escape from the death cell of a penitentiary, equipped only with polished shoes, tooth powder, and $25. The story appeared in six parts; readers were offered $100 for the best solution. Stories that followed similarly feature a locked room mystery or impossible crime. All cases yield to the detective's logic, emphasized at the expense of character development, plot, or setting; subtle humor ensures readability. About half the stories were collected in *The Thinking Machine* (1907; *The Problem of Cell 13*) and *The Thinking Machine on the Case* (1908; *The Professor on the Case*). The detective also appears in *The Chase of the Golden Plate*, written before "The Problem of Cell 13" but not published until 1906. Other stories remain uncollected.

[*See also* Great Detective.]

—Betty Richardson

Vane, Harriet. A fictional character created by Dorothy L. *Sayers, Harriet Vane is one of the best-known female *amateur detectives in the genre. When Sayers introduced Vane as a person on trial for the murder of her lover in *Strong Poison* (1930), the author's intent was to have Wimsey marry Vane and thereby end the Wimsey series of novels. At the time, the *sleuth as loner predominated in detective fiction, and romance was seen as incompatible with the ratiocincation central to stories of detection. Sayers soon found, however, that it would not be in character for Vane, a feminist and intellectual, to accept Wimsey without further development of the latter's character. Sayers may also have kept the pair in three more novels and two short stories because in Vane she had an alter ego through whom she could write about issues that concerned her, including character, integrity, the academic life, and thwarted love. Vane is, like Sayers, a detective novelist who has suffered an unhappy, illicit love affair.

Sayers delays marrying Wimsey to Vane by having the female sleuth refuse his many proposals in *Have His Carcase* (1932), a novel in which Vane investigates a murder at a seaside resort. In *Gaudy Night* (1937), set in the fictional Shrewsbury College of Oxford University, Vane finally consents to marry Wimsey, but only when he proposes to her in Latin, in a moment of dialogue that has caused countless critics to celebrate Wimsey's meeting Vane as an equal on her own terms. While Wimsey is instrumental in helping the case to come to a conclusion, *Gaudy Night* is remembered for its detailed depiction of the lives of female academics in a world mostly closed to men. Vane is considered to be the ideal detective to investigate a case involving poison pen missives, because she is a woman who has experience of the academic life. Much of Vane's character development occurs in this book, in which she acts largely on her own to understand the pressures experienced by other women who are leading the academic life.

Busman's Honeymoon (1925) shows the married duo solving a case that they come across during their honeymoon. A sequel, called *Thrones, Dominations*, was left uncompleted at Sayers's death. It describes the Wimseys' early married life. The manuscript was finished by Jill Paton Walsh and published to good reviews in 1998. Vane also appears in the short stories "Haunted Policeman" (*Harper's Bazaar*, Feb. 1938) and "Talboys" (written in 1942 and published in *Lord Peter* in 1972), which concerns the Wimsey children, Bredon, Roger, and Paul.

As a viewpoint character whom Wimsey seeks to impress and win as a wife, Vane seems to have served as in inspiration for further development of the Wimsey character. Vane provides a prototype for the female, intellectual, feminist sleuth whose personal life is often as challenging as the detection that she undertakes.

—Rosemary Herbert

VAN GULIK, ROBERT H(ANS) (1910–1967), Dutch diplomat, linguist, and scholar who translated and then authored tales featuring Judge Dee, a character based on the seventh-century Chinese judge Dee Jen-djieh. Born in the Netherlands, van Gulik spent his childhood largely in the then Dutch colony of Java where his father served as a military doctor, and where his own talent for languages was awakened. When he returned to the Netherlands at age twelve, he studied Sanskrit, Chinese, and the language of North America's Blackfeet Indians, later studying additional languages at the University of Leyden. Upon completing his university work, van Gulik entered the Dutch foreign service in 1935. In 1940, he came across an anonymous eighteenth-century manuscript, *Wu tse t'ien ssu ta ch'i an*, which he translated into English as *Dee Goong An: Three Murder Cases Solved by Judge Dee* (1949). He subsequently composed his own stories centered around Dee, working his Asian expertise

into them and illustrating them with his own woodcuts. Van Gulik also wrote nonfiction on a wide variety of subjects, including the Chinese flute, erotic art, and sexual practices in ancient China. In 1956 he published an English translation of a thirteenth-century Chinese casebook, *T'ang-yin pi-shih*.

—Rosemary Herbert

VICTIM. Every murder mystery requires a victim, but until recently writers devoted far more attention to suspects and culprits. During the Golden Age of crime and mystery writing, the victim was usually a cipher and the discovery of a body, whether in a country house library or elsewhere, was simply a signal for a battle of wits to begin between murderer and *sleuth and, often, between author and reader. Even when authors began to explore psychology, their main interest lay in the motivation of killers rather than in the circumstances of the slain. In this, the genre mirrored life: Everyone has heard of Jack the Ripper, but few recall the names of his victims.

The traditional whodunit demanded a closed circle of suspects, each possessing a credible motive for murder. Most victims were odious or very rich, characteristics highlighted by the parodist E. V. Knox in his story "The Murder at the Towers" (*This Other Eden*, 1929), while the second victim in a book tended to be a witness to the first crime or a blackmailer. In a different way, victims in hard-boiled fiction, however well written, were also apt to be two-dimensional; in books like Dashiell *Hammett's *Red Harvest* (1929), it is easy to lose count of the number of bodies. Yet eventually, the most skillful writers began to play games with readers' expectations. In *The Face on the Cutting Room Floor* (1937), Cameron McCabe combines the roles of narrator and murderer with that of victim. More commonly, in multiple murder cases, an unexpected common link might connect victims seemingly chosen at random, as is the case in *The ABC Murders* (1936; *The Alphabet Murders*), *Peril at End House* (1932), *One, Two, Buckle My Shoe* (1940; *The Patriotic Murders; An Overdose Of Death*), and *By the Pricking of My Thumbs* (1968), all by Agatha *Christie. In Richard Hull's *The Murder of My Aunt* (1934), an intended victim turns the tables on her would-be murderer; a killer also gets his comeuppance in *Little Victims* (1983; *School for Murder*) by Robert *Barnard. In *The Disposal of the Living* (1985), Barnard describes the activities of an apparently obvious "murderee," but when death strikes, the victim is someone entirely unforeseen.

Francis *Iles's *Before the Fact* (1932) was ahead of its time in providing a compelling psychological study of a born victim, but from the 1940s on more writers began to draw victims in depth. In *Laura* (1943) by Vera Caspary, the detective falls in love with a portrait of a supposed victim, thus giving a carefully crafted mystery an extra dimension. Patricia McGerr's *Pick Your Victim* (1946) inaugurated the who-was-dun-in, and in *The Widow of Bath* (1952) by Margot Bennett, the character of the victim, a stern and legalistic *judge, is the key to the explanation for his death. Today, the victims of murder are usually rather more than a mere excuse for a mystery; even in comic novels, they are now seldom treated as figures of fun. Sometimes they may be seen as having brought their fate upon themselves, as in Margaret Yorke's *Dangerous to Know* (1993), but they are equally apt to be portrayed as deserving of pity, as in *A Helping Hand* (1966) by Celia Dale and *The Secret House of Death* (1968) by Ruth *Rendell. Such books reflect the genre's move away from fantasy and toward a realistic depiction of those destroyed by crime as well as of those who commit it.

[*See also* Corpse.]

—Martin Edwards

VIDOCQ, EUGÈNE FRANÇOIS (1775–1857), founder of the first official and *private detective agencies and hero of the first police procedurals. Born in Arras, France, and educated by Franciscans, Vidocq fought in the royal army during the 1789 revolution, attaining officer rank but deserting to live as a gambler and vagabond. His frequent arrests and escapes became legend, but, late in 1798, he faced slave labor in the naval yards when convicted of forging release papers for a fellow prisoner. The sentence was lengthened thanks to his repeatedly escaping and being recaptured; then, in 1809, apparently to win a pardon, he volunteered his services to the police, convincing officials that plainclothes agents, especially those who themselves had been criminals, would be more effective than uniformed officers in curbing the high crime rate.

By 1811, Vidocq was training new agents and, in 1812, he was given command of the Brigade de la Sûreté or security police. By 1814, Vidocq was a deputy prefect; by 1824, he was in charge of tens of detectives. He instituted a detailed record system of criminals and criminal activity, held patents on tamperproof paper and ink that reduced counterfeiting and forgery, and may have been the first to recognize the importance of fingerprinting, ballistics, and blood testing in criminal investigation.

After political intrigue forced his resignation in 1827, he published his four-volume—and certainly partly fictional—*Mémoires de Vidocq* (1828–29; *Memoirs of Vidocq; Vidocq, the Police Spy*), 50,000 copies of which were sold within a year. By 1832, after the July Revolution brought Louis-Philippe to the throne, Vidocq had resumed his duties as chief of the Sûreté. He was dismissed in 1833 and established the first-known private detective agency, the Bureau des Renseignements. Problems with the official police led to his final retirement after he was exonerated from criminal charges in 1842. He then wrote, or had ghostwritten, *Les vrais mystères de Paris* (1844), *Quelques mots sur une question à l'ordre du jour* (1844), and *Les chauffeurs du nord* (1845–46). Other works are attributed to him as well.

Edgar Allan *Poe acknowledged his debt to Vidocq, and Honoré de Balzac used him as the basis for the char-

acter Vautrin in the multivolume *La comédie humaine* (1842–48; *Comedy of Human Life*, 1887–96); he appears as well in stories collected as *Crimes célèbres* (1841; *Celebrated Crimes*, 1843) by Alexandre Dumas *père*. Vidocq's theories of criminal reform influenced Victor Hugo in *Les misérables* (1862) and Eugène Sue in *Les mystères de Paris* (1842–43); *Mysteries of Paris*, 1843).

—Betty Richardson

VILLAINS AND VILLAINY. The contest between good and evil is a constant theme of mystery writing, but as the certainties of the Victorian era have given way to the moral ambiguities of modern times, the genre's villains, or wrongdoers, and their ignominious acts, or villainy, have moved from exemplars of evil to relatively sympathetic characters and behavior and back to ignominious again. When Wilkie *Collins was constructing *The Woman in White* (1860), he regarded the ingenuity necessary to the central crime as beyond any Englishman and thus created in Count Fosco an Italian villain who seemed all the more sinister because of his gross physical appearance, his habit of allowing pet mice to frolic over his waistcoat, and his superficial charm. Equally formidable was Joseph Sheridan Le Fanu's Silas Ruthyn, whose plot to murder his heiress niece was abetted by a wicked French governess, Madame de la Rouguierre. The book was originally to be called *Maud Ruthyn*, but Le Fanu soon recognized that the dominating presence was the villain's and changed the title to *Uncle Silas* (1864; *Uncle Silas: A Tale of Bartram-Haugh*).

Less subtle successors also made use of foreign villains, not so much from a desire to make their clever crimes credible but rather from a dislike and distrust of anything un-English. Especially popular in the early years of the twentieth century were Sax *Rohmer's books about *Fu Manchu—the classic Oriental villain—and the series in which H. C. *McNeile, or Sapper, pitted his clean-cut clubland hero Hugh "Bulldog" *Drummond against the archfiend Carl Peterson. English-born villains were often portrayed as members of the upper social class. Professor James *Moriarty, Arthur Conan *Doyle's "Napoleon of crime" was of good birth and excellent education, as was his sometime chief of staff, Colonel Sebastian Moran. Equally cultivated were *gentlemen thieves such as Grant Allen's Colonel Clay and E. W. *Hornung's amateur cracksman, A. J. *Raffles. Doyle expressed disquiet about the way in which his brother-in-law Hornung celebrated Raffles's villainy, but writers from far afield took their cue from the exploits of the man who played cricket at the highest level by day and burgled wealthy families by night. Maurice *Leblanc's Arsène *Lupin was notable as a master of disguise, but more sophisticated were the stories about the unscrupulous American lawyer Randolph Mason created by Melville Davisson *Post. *The Strange Schemes of Randolph Mason* (1896; *Randolph Mason: The Strange Schemes*) was intended to show how knowledge of legal loopholes could enable the thwarting of justice. Yet it is difficult to write a series about any character, however villanous, without endowing him with some virtues: Raffles, Lupin, and Mason, as well as G. K. *Chesterton's daring colossus of crime Flambeau, all eventually decided to put their talents to the cause of justice—although in moving away from the windy side of the law, they sacrificed much of their original appeal.

Supercriminals have never fallen altogether out of fashion. Rex *Stout matched Nero *Wolfe with Arnold Zeck and more recently Ed *McBain's cops of the Eighty-seventh Precinct have been confronted time and again by the Deaf Man. In the postwar era, British writers—notably Ian Fleming, creator of *master criminals Auric Goldfinger and Ernst Stavro Blofeld as well as James Bond—have on occasion succumbed to the temptation to equate foreignness with exotic villainy. In hard-boiled American novels, W. R. Burnett's Cesare Bandello, alias Rico or "Little Caesar," and Caspar Gutman, whom Dashiell *Hammett immortalized in The Maltese Falcon (1930) and whose sinister obesity is reminiscent of Fosco's, were made all the more menacing by their obsessive single-mindedness. In contrast, the tone of books by British-based authors such as Leslie *Charteris and John *Creasey about those "durable desperadoes" Simon Templar (the Saint) and Richard Rollison (The Toff), both characters firmly within the Robin Hood tradition, are much lighter.

Another strand of writing concentrates more upon explanation of the personality traits that give rise to villainous behavior than upon the physical effects of that behavior. Many readers will sympathize with the predicaments of Andrew Taylor's William Dougal even when, as in Odd Man Out (1993) he kills an acquaintance, while in Walter Satterthwait's Miss Lizzie (1989), the supposed ax murderer Lizzie Borden turns detective a gen-eration after the killing of her own parents. Patrick Hamilton's Ernest Ralph Gorse, who first appeared in The West Pier (1951), was an early example of the cold-blooded and amoral charmer. Patricia *Highsmith is widely hailed as a writer who has created distinctive and memorable modern villains, starting with Bruno, who proposes an "exchange of murders" to the respectable Guy Haines in Strangers on a Train (1950). Her most celebrated criminal protagonist is Tom *Ripley, but although he has appeared in five novels over a period of more than thirty years, The Talented Mr. Ripley (1955), in which he made his debut, remains the most successful. Ruth *Rendell's insight into the criminal mind is equally acute and A Fatal Inversion (1987), written under the pseudonym of Barbara Vine, is but one of her compelling novels, which, while never condoning evil deeds, makes them explicable.

Today mystery readers have come to appreciate that villainy is not the prerogative of those who come from other countries or different social classes—any person may, in certain circumstances, be capable of it. As Julian *Symons put it, writers are apt to be concerned and "fascinated by the violence behind respectable faces" and the random nature of crime. While some writers continue to make the psyches of criminals understandable and their crimes sometimes, therefore, pardonable, others portray monstrous villains in the form of serial killers who personify deviance and dementedness. Patricia D. *Cornwell and Thomas Harris are exemplars of authors who have brought a new frisson to readers' views of villainy.

[See also Robin Hood Criminal.]

—Martin Edwards

VINE, BARBARA. See Rendell, Ruth.

W

WADE, HENRY, pseudonym of Sir Henry Lancelot Aubrey-Fletcher (1887–1969), British crime writer active between 1927 and 1954. Wade was an influential figure in his day, chiefly in England, where all of his works were published, in contrast to the United States, where only some of his fiction saw publication. He has been compared with Freeman Wills *Crofts, R. A. J. Walling, J. S. Fletcher, and G. D. H. and Margaret Cole as a member of what Julian *Symons called the "Humdrum" school of comfortable and systematic police mysteries.

Wade was born in Surrey and educated at Eton and at New College, Oxford. A decorated veteran of World War I, he succeeded to the baronetcy in 1937. He served as a justice of the peace and county alderman and high sheriff in Buckinghamshire.

Wade's earliest novels, *The Verdict of You All* (1926) and *The Missing Partners* (1928), deal with possible miscarriages of justice, their plots revolving around precisely handled factual detail. *The Duke of York's Steps* (1929) introduced the series character Chief Inspector Poole, who also appeared in *No Friendly Drop* (1931), *Constable, Guard Thyself!* (1934), *Bury Him Darkly* (1936), and a number of less successful later novels. Wade continued to write into the 1950s, when his work seemed rather old-fashioned and antiquated. Nonetheless, *Too Soon to Die* (1953) and *A Dying Fall* (1955) are highly accomplished and interesting classical tales, and some signs of Wade's influence linger on in the work of P. D. *James.

[*See also* Police Detective.]

—Ian Bell

Walker, Amos, hardboiled Detroit *private eye created by Loren D. *Estleman. Introduced in *Motor City Blues* (1980), Walker is a Vietnam veteran returned to a city that is as down-and-out as he—and considerably more corrupt. Tough in talk and action, Walker is a gun-toting, chain-smoking cynic who drinks to excess. Walker went to college, where he learned to box and picked up a degree in sociology. The former skill may be more useful than the degree in his hard-hitting profession, but Walker's sociological bent is sometimes heard in his internal monologues. An exemplar of the sleuth as loner, he did not make it through the police academy. He may have few attachments but, paradoxically, his work often involves helping clients to reestablish broken connections. Missing person's cases are at the heart of *The Glass Highway* (1983), the Edgar Award-winning *Sugartown* (1984) and *Every Brilliant Eye* (1999). In *Sinister Heights* (2002), Walker helps a wealthy widow locate the illegitimate offspring of her deceased husband. An aficionado of old movies, Walker often speaks like characters in film

noir. His first-person observations are often memorable for metaphors and similes that grab the senses. In *Sinister Heights*, for instance, a character has "black eyes with no more expression in them than nailheads in sheetrock." When Walker greets him, he notes, "It was like shaking hands with a boneless chicken breast." Walker uses similarly original similes to describe vehicles. "The driver's seat of the viper gripped my thighs like a big hand in a soft glove," he says in *Sinister Heights*.

—Rosemary Herbert

WALLACE, (RICHARD HORATIO) EDGAR (1875–1932), British author, dramatist, and journalist who wrote in many genres but is best remembered as the "King of Thrillers." The illegitimate son of an actor, he was born in Greenwich (London) and adopted in infancy by a Deptford fish porter. After leaving school at the age of twelve, he took numerous jobs, and later served with the Royal West Kent Regiment and the Medical Staff Corps in South Africa. A subsequent period with Reuters during the Boer War launched him on a lifelong career in journalism—as reporter, racing editor, and proprietor of newspapers and racing journals.

Wallace's commercial approach to writing was evident from the outset, when he founded the Tallis Press and published *The Four Just Men* (1905), an incomplete locked room mystery containing a tear-out slip offering £500 to readers furnishing the solution. This proved to be financially disastrous, but it was to become his best-known book and was followed by several sequels.

In the crime fiction field alone, Wallace produced some ninety novels and numerous short stories and plays. He often worked simultaneously on several books, and reputedly dictated *The Coat of Arms* (1931; *The Arranways Mystery*) in one weekend and his play *On the Spot* (1930) in just four days. The latter is nevertheless regarded as his best drama, showing his skill in plot construction and gift for writing dialogue. These indeed were the hallmarks of his success, together with his ability to build suspense, to combine comedy and terror, and to cling steadfastly to the triumph of good over evil. He also made excellent use of his humble background when portraying small-time crooks and chirpy cockneys, his knowledge of Africa in the series beginning with *Sanders of the River* (1911), and his luckless love of the turf in tales such as *Educated Evans* (1924).

While his writing could be slapdash, his situations predictable, and his characters wooden, Wallace knew what his public wanted and gave it to them—in novels of gangland such as *When the Gangs Came to London* (1932), in such clever detective puzzles as *The Crimson*

Circle (1922) and *The Clue of the New Pin* (1923), and in a host of pure thrillers. His economy of style made him a master of the short story, most notably those collected in *The Mind of Mr. J. G. Reeder* (1925; *The Murder Book of J. G. Reeder*).

—Melvyn Barnes

WALTERS, MINETTE (CAROLINE MARY JEBB)

(b. 1949), English magazine journalist and romance writer who became, at midlife, an award-winning crime writer. Born in Bishop's Stortford, Hertfordshire, she was nine years old when her father, a military officer, died and her mother, an artist, became a single parent to three children. Minette won a scholarship to and became Head Girl at the Godolphin School for Girls in Salisbury, a boarding school that boasts Dorothy L. *Sayers as an alumna. Next, she did volunteer work before attending Durham University. After university, she worked as a writer and copyeditor for IPC, a company that published magazines and books.

On a dare from a colleague, she produced a romance novel. When it was accepted for publication, she followed it with thirty more, all written under pseudonyms that she is loathe to reveal. When she married, Walters took a temporary break from writing to devote herself to raising two children. At the age of forty-three, she celebrated publication of her first crime novel, *The Ice House*. It was an immediate success, winning that year's Crime Writers Association John Creasey Award for the best first novel. Like her next three novels, *The Ice House* focuses on emotionally wounded women in uneasy or desperate situations. In her fourth novel, *The Echo* (1997), Walters turned her attention to a group of male characters. Walters volunteered for more than five years as a visitor to inmates incarcerated in the prison at Winchester, where she says she has learned that ordinary people are capable of terrible things, particularly if they come from dysfunctional families. Like P.D. *James, Walters describes grisly crime scenes in great detail, with the effect of keeping the horror of murder in the minds of readers and causing them to consider the enormity of the crime as it is solved.

—Rosemary Herbert

Warshawski, V(ictoria) I(phigenia), Sara Paretsky's feminist American hard-boiled *private eye, appearing first in *Indemnity Only* (1982). Warshawski, who insists on using her initials to avoid being patronized, has left behind the Chicago public defender's office, a brief marriage, and her initial naïveté to take on the culturally privileged social institutions whose power and authority are used to protect the guilty. Challenging the insurance industry and labor unions in *Indemnity Only*, the Catholic Church and organized crime in *Killing Orders*, (1985), the medical establishment in *Bitter Medicine* (1987), and even the police department, Warshawski uncovers the corruption which accompanies unchecked power. Unlike Raymond *Chandler's Philip *Marlowe,

who takes on similarly corrupt criminals, Paretsky's feminist detective clearly articulates patriarchal privilege as the site of sanctioned oppression. Warshawski's clients include women and girls, the elderly, the poor, and Hispanics in unequal battles against the wealthy, powerful Chicago establishment.

Warshawski's private life differs as much as her professional one from those of the conventional male *hard-boiled sleuth of Chandler, Dashiell *Hammett, and Ross *Macdonald. Despite being orphaned and divorced, she is no isolated loner. Instead, Paretsky has woven together an improbable "family of choice" for Warshawski; although the most important is Dr. Charlotte "Lotty" Herschel, a Holocaust survivor, Warshawski also values her intrusive neighbor, Mr. Contreras, and his enthusiastic golden retriever, Peppy, as well as her father's old friend, police lieutenant Bobby Mallory. And, in each novel, beginning with *Deadlock* (1984), Paretsky weaves Warshawski's professional and personal lives together so that her friends and family also become her clients.

As a first-person narrator, Warshawski directly engages readers in her life: her messy apartment, her fascination with the Chicago Cubs, and her precious, inherited Venetian wine glasses are as well articulated as her passion for causes like abortion rights or affirmative action and against sexual harassment or racial discrimination. She is intensely self-aware; recognizing her own limitations, motives, and ambivalence, Warshawski follows neither the formula of the hard-boiled private eye nor the polemics of the separatist feminist. In Warshawski, Paretsky has created a "heroic" character, carving out new territory for both women and detectives.

—Kathleen Gregory Klein

WATSON, COLIN (1920–1982), author of thirteen comic mystery novels satirizing the world of the classic village mystery as well as of a scathing study of prejudice and sentimentality in crime fiction (*Snobbery with Violence: Crime Stories and Their Audience*, 1971). He was born and educated in Croydon, Surrey, and worked in advertising and print and television/radio journalism.

The harbor town of Flaxborough and its environs in Lincolnshire is home to a bawdy population forever engaged in erotic behavior, criminal and otherwise. Introduced in *Coffin, Scarcely Used* (1958), Watson's series character Inspector Purbright is patient, astute, and down to earth while he tracks down criminals who run sideways and widows who disappear into unexpected occupations. Watson mocks the middle-class devotion to good works in *Charity Ends at Home* (1968) and the lust hidden beneath apparent intellectual activities in *Broomsticks over Flaxborough* (1972; *Kissing Covens*). His books are invariably funny with ribald humor and vivid secondary characters, such as Lucilla Teatime, a genteel criminal who appears in *Lonelyheart 4122* (1967).

—Susan Oleksiw

Watson, Dr. John H. When Arthur Conan *Doyle created Sherlock *Holmes, he simultaneously created Dr.

John H. Watson, a companion and intellectual foil who is so essential to the optimum deployment of Holmes's art that, to most readers, the two men have become firmly linked. As he recorded the character and a few titillating biographical details of Watson, Doyle could never have anticipated that every scrap of information would be so meticulously analyzed by subsequent Holmes devotees. Doyle remains consistent as to the outlines of Watson's biography, but there are important inconsistencies in details. The bullet wound he suffered while upon military service in Afghanistan wanders from his leg to his shoulder, he has been married at least twice, yet Holmes on occasion refers to Watson's last marriage as his first. Even his name raises problems. He is usually, and often definitively, Dr. John H. Watson, yet his wife calls him James, perhaps the *H* standing for Hamish, the Scottish form of James, as was suggested by Dorothy L. *Sayers.

Although the immediate intimacy of the Holmes/ Watson association varies greatly during their time together, principally depending upon Watson's marital state—one year goes by with Watson being involved in only three cases—the basic terms of the association change little. Except in the final story, "His Last Bow" (*Strand*, Sept. 1917), neither Holmes nor Watson matures or ages significantly during the more than thirty years of their recorded collaboration. Watson marries, becomes a widower, and is remarried. He changes the location of his practice at least three times during the course of his civilian medical career, but he remains his same solid self. Today's public sometimes believes Watson to have been dense, if not positively stupid; but, in fact, Doyle implies this only to the minimal extent that is necessary to show off Holmes's brilliance. As Watson says in "The Adventure of the Creeping Man" (*Strand*, Mar. 1923), "I was a whetstone for his mind; I stimulated him; he liked to think aloud in my presence."

Watson fulfills many distinct functions for Holmes (and Doyle), more, in fact, than most other characters cast in similar roles. As well as being his trusted confidant, Watson is a friend whose commitment is profound. He refers to Holmes as "the man whom above all others I revere" in "The Problem of the Thor Bridge" (*Strand*, Feb. 1922) and "the best and wisest man whom I have ever known" in "The Final Problem" (*Strand*, Dec. 1893). The emotional depths of the association are rarely plumbed. Once only, when Watson is wounded in "The Adventure of the Three Garridebs" (*Collier's*, 25 Oct. 1924), does Holmes's anxiety reveal, if only for an instant, "the great heart within." Watson is the usual narrator of the stories. When he is not—as in "The Adventure of the Blanched Soldier" (*Liberty Magazine*, 16 Oct. 1926)—he is sorely missed.

Watson is the counterbalance to Holmes's misanthropic tendencies, especially with respect to women, Holmes being essentially immune to the "gentler passions," while Watson enjoys a reputation as a ladies' man.

Watson always provides a wondering, astonished, and loyally admiring audience for Holmes's explanations of his deductions, however incompletely convincing the certainty of his reasoning may be. "Elementary, my dear Watson" reflects this aspect of Watson, even though it is not a true canonical quotation.

[*See also* Sidekicks and Sleuthing Teams.]

—John D. Constable

WAUGH, HILLARY (BALDWIN), (b. 1920). A pioneer in the development of the American police procedural, Hillary Waugh had published three promising novels in the late 1940s before producing his best-known book, *Last Seen Wearing—* (1952). Told in a deliberately unsensational style with an uncluttered plot line and a killer who remains just offstage, Waugh's novel was coolly received by some critics. It was not until Raymond *Chandler praised it and Julian *Symons included it on a list of the hundred best crime stories that readers began to recognize it as a true classic.

Chief Frank Ford, the detective in the New England college town that is the setting for *Last Seen Wearing—*, never reappeared in Waugh's work, but Waugh created a similar *sleuth, Chief Fred Fellows, who worked in another New England town. Fellows appeared in eleven novels, notably *The Missing Man* (1964) and *The Con Game* (1968), before Waugh moved on to a big-city detective, Frank Sessions, introduced in *"30" Manhattan East* (1968).

Born in New Haven, Connecticut, Waugh received a bachelor's degree from Yale University in 1942, where he later taught mystery writing. He also worked as a cartoonist, newspaper editor, and high school teacher.

Waugh has written nearly fifty novels, some under the pseudonym Elissa Grandower, and served as president of the Mystery Writers of America. The organization honored him with its Grand Master award in 1989.

—Edward D. Hoch

WENTWORTH, PATRICIA (1878–1961), British author of detective novels. Born Dora Amy Elles in Mussoorie, India, Wentworth was educated privately and at the Blackheath High School for Girls in London. She married twice and had one daughter with her second husband, Lt. Col. George Oliver Turnbull, who assisted her in preparing her manuscripts for publication. After 1920, Wentworth lived in Surrey, and beginning in 1923, produced novels at a steady rate. Thirty-two of Wentworth's seventy-one novels feature governess-turned-detective Miss Maud *Silver, who first appeared in *Grey Mask* (1928). Wentworth excelled in creating the world of the cozy mystery novel in which Silver, with her knowledge of human nature, chatted with suspects and discreetly gossiped until she found the truth. Tidy plots, a conventional world, and an unassuming, genteel detective make Wentworth's novels appealing seven decades after the series began. Among the most highly regarded is *The Benevent Treasure* (1956).

[*See also* Elderly Sleuth; Genteel Woman Sleuth; Spinster Sleuth.]

—Dean James

WESTLAKE, DONALD E(DWIN)

WESTLAKE, DONALD E(DWIN) (b. 1933), American screenwriter and prolific and versatile author of sexy adventure novels, political thrillers, science fiction with crime elements, comic crime capers and, more recently, thoughtful work that has won him new critical acclaim. Born in New York City, he attended the State University of New York at Plattsburgh and at Binghamton. Westlake served in the United States Air Force, worked in a literary agency and wrote novels of sexual adventure before he turned out five novels about the ciminal underworld, beginning with *The Mercenaries* (1960).

In 1965, he changed course, producing his first comic crime novel the *Fugitive Pigeon*. Also beginning in the 1960s, Westlake wrote a series about the ex-cop Mitch Tobin, under the pseudonym Tucker Coe. Westlake is probably best-known for two series. One, written under the pseudonym Richard Stark, centers around the ungentlemanly thief, Parker, who is introduced in *The Hunter* (1962). Much more humorous is the series featuring the hapless John Dortmunder, who is introduced in *Bank Shot* (1972), a caper in which an entire bank is stolen. Westlake said he got the idea for that plot during a commute that took him past a bank that was con ducting business from a trailer while its building was under repair. This inventive and humorous take on the ordinary is typical of him. Additional series characters created by Westlake include the actor-thief Alan Grofield and Samuel Holt, a former policeman who has become a television personality. Westlake's *The Hook* (2000) shows the author at his best using humor to comment on the writer's life and a publishing business that is driven by big names and money rather than a concern for literary quality. Westlake is also the author of numerous short stories. His screenplays include *Cops and Robbers* (1972) and *The Grifters* (1990).

—Rosemary Herbert

Wexford, Chief Insepctor Reginald. Chief Inspector Reginald Wexford is the central character in a series of novels by Ruth *Rendell. He made his initial appearance in Rendell's first novel, *From Doon with Death* (1964), and has featured in over fifteen novels since. (The character also served as the the basis for a popular British television series of the early 1990s.) Throughout the sequence, Wexford remains as a senior police officer in Kingsmarkham, a fictional mid-Sussex town. He is in his fifties, of a pragmatic temperament, but no mere follower of standard procedures, and capable of sudden intuitive insights. He forms a contrast with his subordinate associate, Inspector Mike Burden, an altogether more severe figure, much less sympathetic to the modern world, and much more traditional in his attitudes. The interaction of these characters can be compared to the rela-

tionship of the policemen Andrew Dalziel and Peter Pascoe in the work of Reginald *Hill, and there are many other parallel cases in British crime writing. Although the character of Burden is carefully developed— in *No More Dying Then* (1971) he has to handle a complex case while mourning the death of his wife—it is the senior officer whose personality dominates the books. Alongside the difficulties of policing, Wexford has to deal with domestic problems involving his wife Dora and his daughters, one of whom (Sheila) becomes a successful actress with the Royal Shakespeare Company. He also undergoes a stressful middle age, culminating in his suffering a stroke in *Murder Being Once Done* (1972). The Wexfords have a wide circle of friends and acquaintances in Kingsmarkham, as well as a taste for dinner parties, so that the police work is always situated within a recognizable middle-class social context. The cases investigated by Wexford often deal with extreme psychological conditions and sudden outbreaks of catastrophic violence. While police procedure is important in the Wexford novels, more central is the portrayal of a fundamentally decent and talented man confronting a world in which mayhem may break out at any time. As he investigates cases of internecine strife or sexual frustration or child abuse (Rendell's recurrent themes), Wexford strives to act dispassionately and struggles to maintain the security of his family. Again and again, the central character has to reappraise his own life and that of his wife and daughters in the light of the sordid revelations arising from the cases he investigates. While Wexford is never given a full poetical veneer, he is nonetheless a cultivated man of sensitivity and humanity, and the brutality he encounters in his work often disturbs him. In the best Wexford novels— *Some Lie and Some Die* (1973), *Shake Hands Forever* (1975), and *A Sleeping Life* (1978)—the intricacies of the plot combine with the familiarity of the central figure to produce complex and satisfying tales of the madness of modern life.

[*See also* Police Detective.]

—Ian A. Bell

WHITNEY, PHYLLIS A(YAME)

WHITNEY, PHYLLIS A(YAME) (b. 1903), prolific author of highly popular novels of romantic suspense and of suspenseful mysteries for the juvenile market. An American born in Yokohama, Japan, Whitney has lived in Japan, China, the Philippines, and the United States and has set novels for both of her audiences, adult and juvenile, in these countries and in other exotic settings that she investigated during research trips.

Whitney's work is preoccupied with showing female protagonists in the process of discovering themselves through finding the solutions to old family secrets and crimes. Predictably, there is danger, or the distinct threat of it, along the way, with the villain often turning out to be one of the protagonist's own relatives while the initially frightening suspicious character may be the person to whom the heroine turns for rescue in the end. Usually, romantic tension accompanies danger in Whitney's novels, with the two resolved together at the close.

Whitney has worked as a dance instructor, children's book editor for two newspapers, and instructor in children's book writing. She is also known for writing about the art of writing and sharing her "how-to" tips with aspiring authors.

[See also Menacing Characters.]

—Rosemary Herbert

Williams, Race. Although Carroll John *Daly created the prototype of the *private eye in his short story "The False Burton Combs" (*Black Mask*, Dec. 1922), the protagonist in that story, possibly because he remained unnamed and was not a series character, did not gain the fame of Daly's character Race Williams, who has gone down in the pages of literary history as the prime exemplar of the hard-boiled dick. The tough-talking Williams toted two forty-fives to back up his heroic courage in the face of the *underworld figures and corrupt politicians that he encountered in eight novels and numerous short stories, many of which were published in *Black Mask* and the pulp magazines. A selection of the short stories is collected in *The Adventures of Race Williams* (1987). The Williams character helped to establish the hard-boiled traditions of working according to a personal code of honor and of viewing most women with suspicion or indifference. Williams is pursued by a red-haired siren known as "The Flame."

[See also Hard-Boiled Sleuth.]

—Rosemary Herbert

Wimsey, Lord Peter. Created by Dorothy L. *Sayers as her major series character, Lord Peter Wimsey is surely the best-remembered *aristocratic sleuth. The second son of the fifteenth duke of Denver, Peter Death Bredon Wimsey was introduced in *Whose Body?* (1923) and appeared in ten subsequent novels and twenty-one short stories. Sayers claimed she did not "remember inventing Lord Peter," that he "walked in complete with spats" into her imagination. This may be true, but she toyed with him as a character in an unpublished detective story for children and an unfinished play before he appeared in print. His last appearance in a novel is in *Busman's Honeymoon* (1937), though he figures in two later short stories, some wartime propaganda articles in the *Spectator* (1939–1940), and a 1954 radio feature on Sherlock *Holmes.

Various sources of inspiration have been suggested with more or less justification as influencing Sayers in her creation of Wimsey, but a literary derivation seems most plausible, from Philip Trent, the protagonist of E. C. *Bentley's *Trent's Last Case* (1913; *The Woman in Black*). Wimsey and Trent share many attributes, including their "amateur" attitude toward investigation; in earlier books Wimsey also resembles P. G. Wodehouse's

Bertie Wooster, a likeness heightened by the Jeevesian qualities of his manservant Mervyn Bunter. Sayers's desire to raise the artistic standing of the detective story to that of a novel of manners meant humanizing Wimsey to make him a three-dimensional hero and a plausible marriage partner. The result is a rounder, mellower character, more vulnerable than the majority of fictional detectives, at least those of the Golden Age, and one of the few that matures with the passage of time.

Wimsey is given a varied career. Born in 1890, educated at Eton and Balliol, he took a first-class honors degree in history and was decorated for his service in World War I. His first love affair ended during the war. After the war he resides with Bunter at 110A Piccadilly. In keeping with his education, he is knowledgeable about art, a musician of "some skill and more understanding," and a book collector with a wide literary appreciation. Thanks to his skill with words, he fares nicely as a temporary advertising copywriter in *Murder Must Advertise* (1933). Wimsey is also a gourmet with an encyclopedic knowledge of wine; he is skilled in campanology, espionage, and cracking codes; a renowned cricketer; and adept in the arts of self-defense. These qualities, except perhaps the music, assist him in his cases, as do his wealth, generosity, and way with women. He is a kind of ideal Englishman, like Holmes before him, but only up to a point, for he has his faults. He is not racist by the standards of his time or even, as some commentators have asserted, snobbish, but his arrogance is sometimes resented and his rudeness to an admittedly tiresome houseguest in *Talboys* (1942) is embarrassing. His quick-witted intelligence is not generally in doubt, but one feels he is slow to tumble to the truth in *Have His Carcase* (1932) and *The Nine Tailors* (1934).

Sayers surrounds her *sleuth with a diverse group of relatives and associates, who constitute much of the attraction of her novels. Bunter, who was Wimsey's sergeant during World War I, later serves as photographer, valet, cook, and factotum. Wimsey also is assisted by Alexandra Katherine Climpson, who runs a typing pool. Wimsey's older brother is charged with murder in *Clouds of Witness* (1926), and his sister falls in love with and marries an inspector from Scotland Yard. The defining moment of Wimsey's career and his life, however, comes when he meets Harriet *Vane, with whom he falls in love in *Strong Poison* (1930), when she is on trial for murder. Harriet, because of her experiences, is slow to succumb but Wimsey finds strength and fulfillment in his courtship with her in *Gaudy Night* (1935) and their marriage in *Busman's Honeymoon;* they eventually have three sons. In every story Sayers carefully depicts the English social background of the interwar years in which Wimsey operates. So deeply did she imagine Wimsey that eventually she produced a volume entitled *Papers Relating to the Family of Wimsey*, which was published privately in 1936. It is hardly surprising that his creator said that his affairs were more real to her than her own.

[See also Gentleman Sleuth; Great Detective; Sidekicks and Sleuthing Teams.]

—Philip L. Scowcroft

Withers, Miss, angular of frame and equine of face, is the creation of Stuart Palmer and appears in fourteen novels and more than two dozen short stories published between 1931 and 1969. A spinster schoolteacher (rarely observed at her profession), Hildegarde Withers wears elaborate hats, carries a cotton umbrella and an oversized handbag, and is accompanied by an apricot poodle, Talleyrand. Miss Withers solves crimes with her good friend and cigar-smoking foil, Inspector Oscar Piper of the New York Police Department. She is sometimes referred to as being on leave from her duties at Jefferson Grammar School or P. S. 38, or in the later books recently retired, to explain how she has time to detect. In retirement, she moves to Los Angeles, occasionally returning to New York to bedevil Piper. She is sharp of eye and wit, noticing the small things others overlook and solving mysteries by intuition. In print, she is more a figure of eccentricity than the broad caricature portrayed in films. Miss Withers keeps regular hours and picks a lock with ease, but is no mistress of disguise. On occasion, she has been known to solve criminous puzzles in the company of Craig *Rice's John J. Malone.

[See also Spinster Sleuth.]

—J. Randolph Cox

WITNESS. An essential character in virtually all crime and mystery fiction, the witness may be defined as one who has observed an activity, remark, or other piece of information that is germane to understanding the case in question. Such observations may be accomplished visually, auditorily, or by means of various technologies, including by means of sophisticated surveillance. Even more sophisticated means of witnessing include the application of special knowledge like art or antiques expertise, archaeological skills, or cultural awareness that permits one to see from a special perspective what others see in a less informed and therefore less revealing manner.

Witnessing not only involves being in the right place at the right time to observe an action but also entails giving evidence to a detective or, more formally, doing so in a courtroom. In the first case, the delivery of information may occur in the proverbial library or any one of a variety of isolated settings, or in the police interrogation room. Since such witnesses usually are not overheard by other witnesses, the reader may feel at an advantage in evaluating their accounts of the crime. A courtroom witness, however, must deliver his or her testimony in public or in front of other characters who may then alter their own testimony with the knowledge of what has been said by the earlier witness. Writers, like the lawyers that they portray, often enjoy pitting one witness against another, thereby increasing courtroom drama and manipulating the reader.

Vitally useful to the author, the truthful or reliable witness can substantiate or negate the truth at many stages of a criminal investigation or courtroom drama. The unreliable witness can conveniently confuse the *sleuth—and reader—along the path to a solution to the crime or throughout the courtroom action. Most crime and mystery novels employ a number of witnesses and, because the writer does not identify which are trustworthy and which are not, it is essential for the reader to evaluate the reliability of each. Sorting out the often conflicting accounts or testimonies of witnesses often becomes a central action in crime and mystery fiction, both for the detective and the reader. Doubt about the reliability of each assures that those who play the roles of witnesses must also be viewed as suspects until the case is finally solved.

Witnesses may also be used to advantage by the author to enhance suspense, increase emotional drama, and provide points of view beyond simple observation of criminal activity. Frequently, suspense is sustained when a witness becomes vulnerable to the criminal. If the witness is also a child or in some manner helpless, suspense is further heightened. Examples are the boy in Bert Hall Nicholas *Blake's The Whisper in the Gloom (1954) and the wheelchair-bound Hal Jeffries in Cornell *Woolrich's "Rear Window" (Dime Detective, Feb. 1942), both of whom put themselves in jeopardy when they play at crime solving.

Witnessing need not be limited to observing an action. One of the most memorable witnesses in detective fiction is the dog that failed to bark in the night in Arthur Conan *Doyle's "Silver Blaze" (Strand, Aug. 1908), whose silence testified to the animal's familiarity with a person on the premises. This story also proves that one need not be human to be an effective witness.

[See also Animals.]

—Rosemary Herbert

Wolfe, Nero, perhaps the best-known private investigator in mystery fiction after Sherlock *Holmes and Hercule *Poirot. Weighing approximately "one-seventh of a ton," Rex *Stout's great man changes almost not at all (he remains in his mid-fifties) in the series of 33 novels beginning with Fer-de-Lance (1935) and 38 novelettes. Wolfe is a man of fixed routine and multiple eccentricities. His enormous size is maintained by the superb cuisine provided by his chef, the incomparable Fritz Brenner, by his daily consumption of a good amount of beer, and by his sedentary life; he is memorable for an aversion to leaving his brownstone on New York City's West Thirty-fifth Street and for a horror of riding in mechanized vehicles; his irascibility is well known, as is his insistence on a daily regimen and the "rules" of the house (e.g., no smoking and no business conversation during meals). A voracious reader of intellectually challenging books, Wolfe can remember their content down to the page number, and he spends four hours a day in his fourth-floor plant rooms, where he and his gardener,

Theodore Horstmann, cultivate some 10,000 priceless orchids. His ratiocinative detection is internationally famous, as is his behavior toward his clients, which is condescending at best and often downright rude. His unapologetic misogyny and pedantic attitude toward grammar stand in stark contrast to his sensual delight in dining.

Since Wolfe is immobile and, according to Archie *Goodwin, so lazy, it is imperative that he have an active partner for legwork—and in Goodwin he has found the perfect man. Goodwin also serves as Wolfe's amanuensis and conversational foil, the person who goads him into taking cases when the bank account is low, and, ultimately, as his friend.

Wolfe's *modus operandi* is to ponder the information Goodwin gathers; to interview clients and others involved in the case; to plan strategies for tripping up nervous *suspects; and, while seldom giving even Goodwin a hint about what he is thinking, to narrow the list of suspects while never varying his daily personal routine. His signature device is to summon all those involved to his office in order to announce his conclusion and how he arrived at it. Since it is not Wolfe's job to arrest the criminal, usually Inspector Cramer of the New York Police Homicide Division, with whom Wolfe has a distinctly adversarial relationship, is present at these sessions, which Cramer calls Wolfe's "charades."

Like that of many heroes in literature and myth, Wolfe's personal background is mysterious and ambiguous. At one point he claims to have been born in the United States in the early 1890s; at another, that he is a naturalized citizen, having been born in Montenegro. There is even speculation that Sherlock Holmes was his father (accounting genetically for his deductive powers) and that Irene *Adler, the opera star created by Arthur Conan *Doyle, was his mother. The years 1913–16 are identified as a time when Wolfe served in Austro-Hungarian intelligence and the Montenegrin army; in 1917–18 he walked 600 miles to join the American Expeditionary Force and killed 200 Germans; from 1918 to 1921 he "moved around" and returned to the Balkans, where he adopted a daughter; 1922–28 are his "lost years"; and in 1930 he bought the brownstone, hired Goodwin, and began his career as *private detective. Meanwhile, his purported twin brother, Marko Vukcic, is mentioned frequently and eventually becomes the owner of Rusterman's restaurant in New York—one of the few places at which Wolfe will eat outside his own house.

A unique character, Wolfe remains unchallenged in the field of American deductive investigators. From his yellow pajamas to his folded hands over his immense girth, from his grumpy disposition to his brilliant mind, this notoriously taciturn character stands as one of fiction's most memorable *Great Detectives.

Since Stout's death in 1975, Robert Goldsborough, has continued the Wolfe saga, with the blessing of Stout's heirs and with modest success, starting with *Murder in*

E Minor (1986) and adding a new novel almost every year thereafter.

[*See also* Armchair Detective; Eccentrics; Sidekicks and Sleuthing Teams.]

—Landon Burns

"Woman, The." *See* Adler, Irene.

WOOD, MRS. HENRY, (1814–1887), born Ellen Price, English novelist and short-story writer whose work frequently included an element of crime. She is best known for the novel *East Lynne* (1861), which was successful both in print and as adapted to the Victorian stage. Suspected murder figures in the novel *Trevlyn Hold; or, Squire Trevlyn's Heir* (1864), actual murder in *The Red Court Farm* (1865). It is the twelve volumes of *Johnny Ludlow* short stories (1874–99), however, which most closely resemble detective fiction.

According to E. F. Bleiler (*Twentieth Century Crime and Mystery Writers*, 2nd ed., 1985), Mrs. Wood is interested not so much in crime itself as in its impact on the social fabric and on the personalities of suspects. In this regard she can be counted among those whose explorations of "the problem of crime" contributed to the rise of the modern crime and detective genre.

—John M. Reilly

WOOLRICH, CORNELL (GEORGE HOPLEY), (1903–1968), popular and prolific American author of novels and stories in the noir manner. Woolrich published dozens of stories in the 1930s in such magazines as *Argosy*, *Black Mask*, and *Dime Detective*. The first of his suspense novels was *The Bride Wore Black* (1940; *Beware the Lady*), followed by the rest of his "black" series: *The Black Curtain* (1941), *Black Alibi* (1942), *The Black Angel* (1943), *The Black Path of Fear* (1944), and *Rendezvous in Black* (1948). Under his pseudonym William Irish, he wrote *Phantom Lady* (1942), *Deadline at Dawn* (1944), *I Married a Dead Man* (1948), and *Strangler's Serenade* (1951). Under the name George Hopley, he penned *Night Has a Thousand Eyes* (1945). His fiction has been the basis of many films, radio plays, and television productions. Among the best-known are the films *Phantom Lady* (1944), *Rear Window* (1954, directed by Alfred Hitchcock, based on the story "It Had to Be Murder" in *Dime Detective*, Feb. 1942; "Rear Window"), and *Le mariée etait en noire* (1968, directed by François Truffaut, based on *The Bride Wore Black*).

By all accounts a lonely and tormented man, homosexual in an intolerant era, Woolrich was brought up in Latin America and New York by his ill-matched parents, a civil engineer and a socialite. He studied writing at Columbia University, wrote two romantic novels, and worked in Hollywood as a scriptwriter. His own marriage dissolved in a matter of weeks, after which he lived in a series of New York hotels with his mother until her death and then on his own as a virtual recluse. He found the ideal outlet for the bitterness and isolation of his own life in fiction noir melodrama. The most common themes of his novels are mistaken identity, revenge, and lost love; his most frequently used plot device is the desperate race against time, usually concluding with an improbable victory for the protagonist. Critics in his own day judged Woolrich's plotting often awkward and unconvincing, his style tending to overwrought, and his characters one-dimensional. But against this must be weighed the fertility of Woolrich's imagination and the sheer power of his dark visions. In the "black" series in particular, he is remarkably adept at depicting the anxiety of the hunter and the hunted, usually in a darkly atmospheric urban setting. His stark vision of life, however, is somewhat vitiated by Woolrich's wish to satisfy his audience's presumed desire for romantic idealization and conventional resolution. As recent interest in his work shows, Woolrich's suspenseful novels and stories continue to strike a responsive chord in readers.

—Richard Steiger

WRIGHT, ERIC (b. 1929), English-born professor and mystery writer best known as the creator of Canadian police detective Charlie Salter. Born in London, Wright emigrated to Canada in 1951 and was educated at the University of Manitoba and the University of Toronto. He served in the Royal Air Force before serving as a professor of English at Ryerson College in Toronto until he retired in 1989.

Wright reached age fifty-four before he published his first crime novel, *The Night the Gods Smiled* (1983), in which Salter investigates the death of an English literature professor whose life circumstances mirror some of the sleuth's. Established here, the policeman's preoccupation with family matters remains a hallmark of the series. Salter investigates crimes in several Toronto venues, but he also leaves the city in some books. *In Death in the Old Country* (1985), he solves a crime while on holiday in England, and in *A Body Surrounded by Water* (1987), his family vacation on Prince Edward Island is interrupted when a local historian is killed. It seems Salter cannot take a vacation from murder.

Wright introduced two more series characters during the 1990s. Retired policeman Mel Pickett is a secondary character in *A Sensitive Case* (1990), but he takes the lead in *Buried in Stone* (1996). Lucy Trimble Brenner, a librarian who takes over a detective agency, is introduced in *Death of a Sunday Writer* (1996). In 2000, Wright introduced yet another lead character, English literature lecturer Joe Barley, in *The Kidnapping of Rosie Dawn*. He also co-edited, with Howard *Engel, *Criminal Shorts* (1992), and wrote the well-received memoir, *Always Give a Penny to the Blind Man* (1999).

[*See also* Police Detective.]

—Rosemary Herbert

Y

YATES, DORNFORD, pseudonym of Maj. Cecil William Mercer (1885–1960), British author and barrister who assisted in the prosecution of Hawley Harley Crippen and served in both world wars. As well as humorous light romances, some of which have a detective element—like *Adele and Co.* (1931) and *The House That Berry Built* (1945)—Yates wrote a number of adventure stories, set for the most part in Austria or southern France, in which the hero—usually Richard Chandos—often confronts the same gang of crooks. The standard motifs include booby-trapped treasure—as in *Blind Corner* (1927) and *Safe Custody* (1932)—and mass murder—as in *She Fell Among Thieves* (1935). Though the books were best-sellers during Yates's lifetime, his reactionary political views and anti-Semitism, together with his lush style, now obscure their merits. Along with H. C. *McNeile and John Buchan, Yates is one of three major thriller writers of the 1920s and 1930s.

—T. J. Binyon

YORKE, MARGARET, pseudonym of Beda Larminie Nicholson (b. 1924), English author of numerous non-series mysteries and creator of the *amateur detective Patrick Grant, an Oxford professor. Born in Compton, Surrey, she was educated at Prior's Field, Goldaming, before she served in the Women's Royal Naval Service from 1942–1945. Divorced and the mother of two children, she also worked as a librarian at Oxford University.

Yorke introduced her series detective, Grant, in *Dead in the Morning* (1970) and used him in four more novels. She is better known for her non-series books, which typically depict contemporary English villages where the idyllic is only skin-deep. Juvenile delinquency, voyeurism, adultery, rape and similar misdeeds and crimes frequently figure in Yorke's fiction, which often gains *frisson* from the fact that the miscreants are not necessarily hardened criminals. Instead, they may be ordinary people who are steered off the straight and narrow path by frustration, chance or coincidence. Yorke's uneasy worlds prove Sherlock Holmes's dictum: "It is my belief, Watson, founded upon my experience, that the lowest and vilest alleys in London do not present a more dreadful record of sin than does the smiling and beautiful countryside."

—Rosemary Herbert

Z

ZANGWILL, ISRAEL (1864–1926), British novelist, short story writer, essayist, playwright, poet, and translator. Born to immigrant parents in London's Whitechapel ghetto, Zangwill was best known for his fictional portrayals of Anglo-Jewish life in London's East End and as a spokesperson for Jewish nationalism and other political and social causes. Although Zangwill's only major contribution to crime and mystery writing was *The Big Bow Mystery* (1892), this single novelette, serialized in 1891 in the London *Star*, exemplifies three conventions of the genre—the locked room mystery, the perfect crime, and the least likely suspect. Set in the working-class milieu of London's East End, the novelette interweaves satiric views of detection and detectives and of the aesthetic movement of the 1880s. *The Big Bow Mystery* shares with Zangwill's other fiction not only its witty, ironic tone but also its use of newspaper accounts to build the narrative, the mark of Zangwill's own work as a journalist. Thematically, the novelette shares the concern with multiple identities that recurs throughout the author's fiction, including the short story "Cheating the Gallows" (*The King of Schnorrers: Grotesques and Fantasies*, 1893), the only other of Zangwill's works that approaches *Big Bow's* focus on crime and mystery. Three films have been based on *The Big Bow Mystery: The Perfect Crime* (1928), *Crime Doctor* (1934), and *The Verdict* (1946).

—Martha Stoddard Holmes

Zen, Aurelio, Italian *police detective created by Michael *Dibdin in books that read as *homages* to the Italian scene, as well as satisfying crime novels. Introduced in the 1988 novel *Ratking*, Zen is a *sleuth whose talents, flaws and foibles cause him ups and downs in his career and add interest to a series of books that are most memorable for their portraits of Italian people and places. Zen rises to the rank of Vice Questore with Criminelpol but falls to the lesser position of Naples commander of harbor police in *Cosi Fan Tutti* (1996), after he stumbles through a plot that works as a kind of comedy of errors. Dibdin also uses Zen to solve classic types of cases—kidnapping in *Ratking*, a missing person (or body) in *Dead Lagoon* (1994)—and has him targeted by the Mafia in *Blood Rain* (1999) and in *And Then You Die* (2002). Dibdin, who has lived in Italy, is comfortable working Italian phrases into dialogue that helps bring alive a flawed policeman working in lovingly-described locations such as Venice and Naples.

—Rosemary Herbert

Index